U0035166

專賣在美國的華人

英文萬用短句

5000

高頻度英文慣用表達

English Expressions 5000

全書MP3一次下載

5000all.rar

※ iOS系統請以
非Safari瀏覽器下載

前言

英美母語人士絕對不用會困難的表達方式來說英文！

你知道嗎？英美母語人士絕對不會用困難的表達方式來說英文！為什麼他們只用簡單的詞彙就能說好英文呢？

非母語學習者之所以無法把英語說好，理由不外乎「害怕犯錯」、「太過追求完美」。你是否也因為這些原因，就算在學校、補習班學了超過十年的英語，面對外國人還是像啞巴一樣呢？或者就算覺得犯錯也沒關係，但腦子裡卻連一點可用的句型也沒有？每天學習的內容，真正存進腦海裡的到底有多少？

聰明的英語學習法

要能快速學習英文，並且現學現賣、立即運用，唯一的方法就是把母語人士愛用的簡單表達方式大量存進腦中，這才是最適合現代人的高效率英語學習法。本書經由美國母語人士的幫助，網羅他們使用頻率最高的 5000 個慣用語，依照各種不同的場合與狀況來分類，使讀者能夠快速理解、長久牢記。在閱讀時，請不要只用眼睛看過，也要跟著大聲唸出來，才能加強印象。只要確實記住這些常用的表達方式，在需要用到的時候，就能脫口而出。如此一來，開口說英語也會變得有趣，而不再是件恐怖的事了。

英語會話的終極寶典

雖然能夠知道困難的句型也很好，但就日常生活的會話而言，本書的內容已經相當足夠了。請記住，就算只懂得簡單的表達方式，也能把英語說得很好。對於學習者而言，本書無疑是英語會話的終極寶典。只要能精通本書的內容，征服英語會話的一天也就不遠了。

本書特色

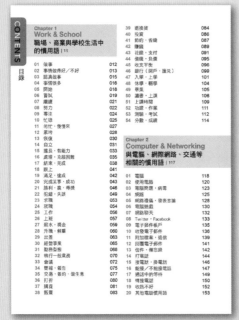

9 大類 365 種場合
5000 個慣用語隨選隨用

全面網羅從職場、網路到行為、情緒等各種生活面向，只要按照分類查詢，隨時隨地都能找到適合的表達方式，心裡想的都能用英文說。

道地用法與典故講解
正確使用不出錯

參考母語人士意見，除了中文解釋以外，更說明每個慣用語的使用情況與使用方式，並且適時解說慣用語的由來，增加學習的趣味性。

一種場合多種說法
相關用語觸類旁通

每一種場合都有 4~5 個主要條目，並且列出各個條目的相關用語和句型，合計至少 10 種說法，讓你舉一反三，輕鬆變換各種表達方式。

一來一往用法示範
培養瞬間反射應答能力

例句以一來一往的簡短對話撰寫，幫助掌握慣用語的使用情境，還能培養如同反射動作般簡短應答的能力。在主要例句之外更追加 2~3 個例句，全書合計約 10000 句，讓你充分練習、確實學會。

馬上去做 表達了「會去做」的心情或念頭，或說明「現在已經在做了」的狀況。

● Have you finished cleaning up?
● I'm on it. I'll be done in an hour.
　●你打掃完了嗎？　●我現在去弄，一小時後就會打掃完畢。
▶ I'm on it. It won't take long.
　我現在去處理，不會花太多時間的。
　I'm on it. You can count on me.
　我現在去處理，你可以相信我。

以中學程度字彙撰寫，英文菜鳥也能輕鬆說

完全貼近日常英語會話大量使用基礎單字的特色，避免不必要的艱澀詞彙，簡簡單單就能說出各種場合需要的英文會話。

copy 的各種意義

隨著電腦的普及，copy 這個已經成為十分常用的單字。但如果把 copy 當成名詞使用呢？這時 copy 代表由原稿複製而成的「副本」，或是書報雜誌等的「一份、一本、一冊」。因此，如果想跟空服員要一份報紙，我們可以說「Can I get a copy of the New York Times?」；如果想要一份今天的會議行程表，則可以說「Can I have a copy of the schedule for today's meeting?」。讓我們再回到 copy 的動詞用法。見到祕書，想要她幫忙影印的時候，我們可以說「I need you to copy these documents.」。如果有某個文件不能影印，否則有觸法之處時，則可以說「Don't copy that. It's against the law.」。

進階英文知識補充突破學習盲點

針對一般學習者容易忽略或誤解的表達方式補充說明，徹底釐清所有困惑，讓你登上英文學習的更高境界。

附慣用語Ａ～Ｚ索引方便複習與查詢

所有主要條目皆以字母順序列出，對於已經學過但還不太清楚意思的慣用語，只要利用索引就能重新複習。對於沒看過的慣用語，也可以使用索引查詢。

Chapter 3
Social Life with Others
和人見面、道別等
社交生活中的慣用語 | 183

Chapter 4
Everyday Life Activities
一天從起床到就寢，
日常生活行為的慣用語 | 267

Chapter 6
Thoughts & Attitude
能夠傳達自己想法和態度
的各種慣用語 | 419

Chapter 5
Information & Understanding
聆聽、觀看、理解等與訊息
相關的各種慣用語 | 361

Chapter 7
Emotions & Situations
開心、生氣、各種狀況的慣用語 | 489

Chapter 8
Various Actions
日常生活中各種行為舉止的慣用語 | 563

Work & School

職場、商業與學校生活中的慣用語

01 做事 work on

1-01.mp3

work on

· work together
　一起工作
· work as usual
　像往常一般工作

做與…相關的事，致力於… work on sb 意為「為了某件事而努力說服某人」。

● I'm so stressed out these days.
● Oh? Do you have to **work on** a big project?
　●我這陣子壓力好大。　●哦？你需要負責一個大案子嗎？

▶ I'm going to work on this stuff at home tonight.
　我今天晚上要在家處理這件事。
　Did you hand in the report you were working on?
　你把之前在做的報告交出去了嗎？

get to work

· get back to work
　回去工作
· get down to business
　（正式地）著手做某事

去工作 與 get down to work 意義相同，依照上下文語意，有時也可以表示「去上班」。

● Hey Nick, how about we get some beer?
● I'd like to, but I have to **get back to work**.
　●嘿，Nick，要不要一起去喝點啤酒？　●我很想，但我得回去工作。

▶ I have got to get to work. So can I call you back later?
　我需要工作，晚點回你電話好嗎？
　How long does it take for you to get to work?
　你要花多少時間通勤？

get right on it

· Get (right) on it.
　現在馬上去做。

現在馬上去做 在 get on 的中間加上「right」，強調「現在馬上去做」。

● This needs to be done quickly.
● Don't worry, I'll **get right on it**.
　●這需要趕快完成。　●別擔心，我馬上會弄。

▶ If it's urgent, I'll get right on it.
　如果這很緊急，我會馬上去處理。
　I understand. I'll get right on it.
　我了解了，我會馬上去處理。

1 職場・學校

2 電腦・網路

3 社交生活

4 日常生活

5 訊息・理解

6 想法・態度

7 情緒・狀況

8 行為舉止

9 時間地點・副詞片語

be on

・I'm on it.
　我現在馬上去做；
　我正在做。

馬上去做 表達了「會去做」的心情或念頭，或說明「現在已經在做了」的狀況。

● Have you finished cleaning up?

● I'm on it. I'll be done in an hour.

　● 你打掃完了嗎？　● 我現在在去弄，一小時後會打掃完畢。

▶ I'm on it. It won't take long.

　我現在去處理，不會花太多時間的。

　I'm on it. You can count on me.

　我現在去處理，你可以相信我。

do one's job

・do this job
　做（處理）這件事

做分內的事 這邊的 job 是指分內的事，不一定是職場上的工作。

● I have to **do my job** at night.

● Does it work for you?

　● 我今天晚上得做事。　● 你沒問題吧？

▶ Don't mention it. I'm just doing my job.

　別客氣，我只是做自己分內的事。

　Please get out of my way so I can do my job.

　麻煩讓開一下，讓我做事。

---

02 事情做得好／不好
do a good job

1-02.mp3

do a good job

・do a good job at / on /
　-ing
　做…做得很好

・You did a good job.
　你做得很好。

事情做得好 依照好的程度，good 還可替換為 great, super 等。

● I thought you always **did a great job** on exams.

● Yeah, but actually I cheated all the time.

　● 我以為你每次考試都考得很好。　● 是啊，但事實上我每次都作弊。

▶ You did a good job! I was very impressed.

　你做得很好！我印象非常深刻。

　You did a great job organizing the fundraiser.

　你的募款活動辦得很好。

do good work

· do good work on...
做…做得很好

事情做得好 將 job 替換為 work，不單指職場上的表現，也可以用來形容在學校活動或其他工作上「表現得很好」。

● I just got a new hairdresser.
● Does she do good work?

●我剛換了一位新的髮型設計師。　●她剪得好嗎？

▶ My mechanic does good work on cars.
我的維修技師修車技術很好。
You should do good work in class.
你應該認真上課。

do a terrible job

· do a really poor job -ing
做…做得很糟

事情做得很糟 如果想追加說明是哪件事做得不好，後面要接動詞的 -ing 形。

● You're doing a terrible job.
● Don't be so hard on me.

●你做得很糟。　●不要對我那麼苛求。

▶ I did a terrible job painting the room.
我把房間的牆壁粉刷得很糟。
You did a terrible job cooking last time.
你上次煮菜煮得很糟。

do sth (so) stupid

· do sth habitually
習慣性地作某事
· do the right thing
做正確的事

做了某件蠢事 something 用形容詞修飾時，形容詞放在後面。

● Oh my gosh, I did something really stupid!
● Are you dating your ex-boyfriend again?

●我的天啊，我做了一件好蠢的事！　●妳又要跟妳前男友約會嗎？

▶ Jane did something stupid at work.
Jane 在工作上做了件很蠢的事。
I think he's going to do something stupid.
我覺得他會做出蠢事。

miss work

曠職，缺勤 沒有上班的缺勤狀態。

● Why are you staying at home?
● I miss a couple of days of work.

●你怎麼還在家裡？　●我好多天沒去上班了。

▶ You may often miss school or work. 你可能經常曠課或曠職。
It's unusual for you to miss work. 你曠職沒上班很不尋常。

03 認真做事
work hard

1
職場・學校

2
電腦・網路

3
社交生活

4
日常生活

5
訊息・理解

6
想法・態度

7
情緒・狀況

8
行為舉止

9
時間地點・副詞片語

1-03.mp3

work hard

- work harder
  更認真工作
- Don't work too hard.
  別工作得太累。
  （告別的寒暄用語）

認真做事 hard 在這邊是副詞，意思是「努力地」。同理，study hard 是指「認真讀書」。

- You have to **work hard**. Don't let me down.
- I'll do my best, boss. Believe me.
  - 你要認真工作，別讓我失望。
  - 我會盡我所能的，老闆，相信我。

▶ We work hard and we deserve to relax.
我們認真工作，放鬆一下也是應該的。
My boss said I need to work harder.
我老闆說我需要更認真工作。

work all night

- work all day
  工作一整天
- work all week
  工作一整個星期
- work all weekend
  工作一整個週末

工作一整晚 惡質雇主的座右銘。all 之後接的名詞還可以替換為 day, week, month 等。

- This wedding cake looks great.
- I **worked all night** baking it.
  - 這個結婚蛋糕看起來很棒。　● 我花了一整晚烤的。

▶ We'll need to work all night to complete this.
我們將需要花上一整晚來完成這件事。
I was working all last night to create a new plan.
我昨天花了整整一個晚上設計了一個新的方案。

work late

- work late tonight
  今晚工作到很晚
- work late every night
  每天晚上都工作到很晚
- work late on Tuesday
  星期二工作到很晚
- work overtime
  加班

工作到很晚 如果想追加說明是「哪一天」工作到很晚的話，可以用「work late on + 星期」的句型。

- I have to **work late** tonight, honey.
- Not again, this is the third time this week.
  - 我今晚得工作到很晚，親愛的。
  - 別又來了，這已經是這禮拜第三次了。

▶ I would rather work late than come in early tomorrow.
我寧可今天工作到晚一點，也不要明天一大早來上班。
I don't want to work overtime every day.
我不想要每天加班。

15

work around the clock

- work too many hours
  工作時數過多
- work one's way to…
  為了…而努力

日以繼夜地工作 24 小時都在工作之意。

- You guys look really tired.
- We **worked around the clock** yesterday.
  ●你們看起來好累。　●我們昨天工作了一整天。

▶ Everyone at the factory works around the clock.
  工廠裡的每個人都日以繼夜地工作。
  I'm working around the clock to get it done.
  我為了完成它,工作了一整天。

keep up the good work

- keep it up
  繼續努力

繼續努力 這個用法用在「已經做了,並且仍然在努力做」的情況。

- You are doing great work. **Keep it up!**
- Gee, thanks a lot for noticing all my hard work.
  ●你做得很棒,繼續加油！　●啊,很謝謝你注意到我的一切努力。

▶ This looks good. Keep up the good work.
  這看起來很棒,繼續保持。
  You did a great job. Keep up the good work.
  你做得很棒,繼續加油。

---

04 | 事情很多
have a lot of work

1-04.mp3

have a lot of work

- have a lot of work
  to do
  有很多事要做
- have much to do
  有很多要做
- have much work to do
  有很多事要做

有很多工作 在這個片語中,我們還可將 a lot of 替換為「much」來使用；work 後面常接上「to do」。

- I came here to see if you were finished.
- No, I still **have a lot of work** to do.
  ●我來看你是否已經完成了。　●還沒,我還有很多工作要做。

▶ If you don't mind, I have a lot of work to do.
  如果你不介意的話,我還有很多事要做。
  Don't waste your time. We've got a lot of work to do.
  別浪費時間,我們有很多事要做。

get held up at work

· be stuck at work
  深陷在工作中
· be up to one's ears
  忙得不可開交
· be up to one's neck in work
  忙得不可開交

被工作淹沒 慣用語 be held up 意為「被困住而不能動彈」。

● You should have been here an hour ago.
● I'm sorry but I **got held up at work**.

　●你應該一小時前就要來了。　●我很抱歉，但我被工作絆住了。

▶ Steve got held up at work last week.
　Steve 上週完全被工作淹沒了。
　Sorry I'm late, I was stuck at work.
　抱歉我遲到了，我被工作絆住了。

be up all night working...

為了做某事而熬夜一整晚 be up 意為「不睡覺」，all night 則是「整晚」，然後再接上 working，意為「為了處理某件事情而整晚沒睡」。

● What's wrong with you? You look tired.
● I **was up all night working** on a report.

　●你怎麼了？你看起來好累。　●我為了做一份報告整晚沒有睡覺。

▶ Students are often up all night working.
　學生們常常熬夜讀書。
　Jim was up all night working on the project.
　Jim 熬夜一整晚處理那個案子。

be swamped at/with

· I'm swamped with work.
  我為工作忙得焦頭爛額。

窮於應付…，為了…備受煎熬 swamp 本意為「沼澤」，因此我們可以把這個片語聯想成「陷入沼澤中，使勁地掙扎、奮鬥」。

● You look like you need some rest.
● We**'ve been swamped at** my job.

　●你們看起來需要休息。　●我們忙著做我的工作。

▶ I'm swamped with work for my classes.
　我為功課忙得焦頭爛額。
　He was swamped with dinner invitations.
　他為了晚宴請帖而忙得不可開交。

have one's hands full

忙得不可開交，分身乏術 兩隻手上滿滿的都是東西，用來形容非常忙碌的樣子

● Can you help me with my homework?
● I'm sorry, but I **have my hands full**.

　●你可以幫我做作業嗎？　●我很抱歉，但我真的分身乏術。

▶ She had her hands full with the children's party.
　她為孩子的派對忙得不可開交。
　I've got my hands full with the project.
　我為這個案子忙得不可開交。

1 職場・學校
2 電腦・網路
3 社交生活
4 日常生活
5 訊息・理解
6 想法・態度
7 情緒・狀況
8 行為舉止
9 時間地點・副詞片語

05 開始
get started on

start to

- start/begin with+N
  從…開始
- begin to do
  開始做…

開始… 也常說 be starting to...，表示「正要開始」。

- Are you working out these days?
- Yeah, I **started to** go to the gym every day after work.

  ●你最近有在運動嗎？　●是啊，我開始每天下班後去健身房了。

▶ Many people have started to save money.
很多人開始儲蓄了。
We need to start with netiquette education for children.
我們該開始對孩子們進行網路禮儀教育了。

get started on

- get moving
  出發，開始
- get sth moving
  使某事開始進行

開始 這個慣用語帶有一種「某件事有點遲了」，所以得加緊腳步，趕快開始的意味。

- I'm in. I'm always on your side.
- Good. Let's **get started on** the plan.

  ●算我一份。我永遠都站在你這邊。
  ●很好，那讓我們快點開始這個計畫吧。

▶ You need to get started on a diet.
你需要開始減肥。
It's time to get moving. We don't want to be late.
該動身了，我們不希望遲到。

get a head start on

- break ground
  動工，開始
- ground-breaking
  破土開工的，開創的

搶先做… head start 意為「比任何人都早一步去做」，也就是「start earlier」。

- Why are you leaving work so early?
- I need to **get a head start on** the heavy traffic.

  ●你為什麼要那麼早下班？　●我需要早點動身以避開大塞車。

▶ The students got a head start on their English lessons.
這些學生早一步上了英語課程。
We can get a head start on this paperwork.
我們可以先開始進行這份書面作業。

set out to

- set off to do
  開始做⋯
- set off on a journey
  動身去旅行

開始做⋯ 這個慣用語帶有「有確實的計畫或目標，而開始去進行」的意味。

- ●Where is Marsha this morning?
- ●She **set out to** buy some food.
  - ●Marsha 今天早上在哪裡？　●她去買些食物。

▶ Barry set out to become a doctor.
　Barry 開始努力成為一位醫生。
　Some church members set out to help poor people.
　有些教會的信徒開始幫助窮人。

hit the road

開始，出發 這個慣用語直譯為「上路」，引申為「開始做某事」或「出發」之意。

- ●Are you ready to start our trip?
- ●I sure am. Let's **hit the road**.
  - ●你準備好要開始我們的旅程了嗎？　●當然，我們出發吧。

▶ I want you to pack up your things and hit the road.
　我希望你去打包你的東西然後出發。
　Let's have some food before we hit the road.
　我們上路前先吃點東西吧。

06 嘗試
give it a try

1-06.mp3

try to

- try writing
  寫寫看
- try on
  試穿（衣物）
- try food
  嘗試食物

試圖做某事 若使用 try -ing 的形態，意為「做某件事試試看」。

- ●I'm serious. She's in a really bad mood.
- ●I'll **try to** avoid her.
  - ●我說真的，她心情真的很糟。　●我會試著避開她。

▶ I'll try to get back as soon as I can.
　我會努力盡速回覆你。
　Why are you trying to get away from me?
　你為什麼試圖疏遠我？

1 職場・學校

2 電腦・網路

3 社交生活

4 日常生活

5 訊息・理解

6 想法・態度

7 情緒・狀況

8 行為舉止

9 時間地點・副詞片語

try again

· worth a try
  值得一試

再試一次 「不要被挫折打敗，再試一次」。幫人打氣或給予建議時可以使用。

● I don't know what I'm going to do.

● Don't worry. You can **try again**!

　●我不知道我該怎麼做。　●別擔心，你可以再試一次！

▶ Even though Carrie failed, she'll try again.

　雖然 Carrie 失敗了，她還是會再試一次。

　Exactly! Get out there and try again.

　沒錯！採取行動，再試一次。

try out

· try out new recipes
  嘗試新的食譜
» cf. try out for
  （為了成為其中一員）
  參加…的選拔

試驗，嘗試看看 意為「試試看某個新的方法、嘗試一條新的路」等。

● Is this the new smart phone?

● Yes it is. You should **try it out**.

　●這是那台新出的智慧型手機？　●是啊，你該試用看看。

▶ Can I try out this laptop computer?

　我可以試用這台筆記型電腦嗎？

　Mom is trying out different chicken salad recipes.

　媽媽正在嘗試不同的雞肉沙拉食譜。

give it a try

· have a shot at sth
  試一次看看
· give it a shot
  試一次看看
· go for it
  試一次看看

試試看 與 have a shot at 或 give it a shot 同義，帶有「不要在意結果，試一次看看」的意味。

● Why don't you **give it a try** right now?

● Okay, let's do it.

　●你為什麼不現在就試試看呢？　●好，來試試看吧。

▶ I've never played baseball, but I'll give it a try.

　我從來沒有打過棒球，但我會試試看。

　Come on, you have the time. Go for it!

　嘿，你有時間的，去試試看！

make an attempt

· make an attempt
  to do
  試圖做…
· in an attempt to do
  為了試著去做…

試圖 可以在後面接上「to do」進一步說明想做的事。

● I'm going to **make an attempt to** date Patty.

● She isn't going to go out with you.

　●我會試著約 Patty 出去。　●她才不會跟你出去。

▶ The team made an attempt to climb Mt. Everest.

　這個隊伍嘗試攀登聖母峰。

　My girlfriend made an attempt to cook dinner.

　我的女朋友試著煮了晚餐。

07 | 繼續 keep -ing

1-07.mp3

1 職場・學校

2 電腦・網路

3 社交生活

4 日常生活

5 訊息・理解

6 想法・態度

7 情緒・狀況

8 行為舉止

9 時間地點・副詞片語

keep (on) -ing

· Keep going!
繼續做下去！

繼續做… keep 後面的「on」也可以省略。

● I don't think I can finish this race.
● Come on! **Keep on running**!
　●我覺得我沒辦法跑完。　●嘿！繼續跑啊！

▶ Do you think the stock market will keep going up?
你覺得股市會繼續上漲嗎？
Never say die. You must keep trying.
別氣餒。你必須繼續嘗試。

continue to

· continue -ing
繼續…

繼續做… continue one's effort 意為「繼續努力」。

● Do you think Cindy will quit this job?
● No, she'll **continue to** work here.
　●你覺得 Cindy 會辭職嗎？　●不，她會繼續在這裡工作。

▶ You should continue to learn for your lifetime.
你應該終生持續學習。
I'd rather continue working until this is finished.
我寧可繼續把這個做完。

go on with sth

· go on -ing
繼續做某事
· go on with my story
繼續說我的故事

繼續… go on with sb 意為「和某人相處」；而 What's going on with you? 則是在詢問對方「發生了什麼事？」。這裡的 go on 與「happen」同義。

● It looks like it will snow today.
● I still want to **go on with** our trip.
　●看來今天會下雪。　●我還是想繼續我們的旅程。

▶ Ted didn't go on with the speech.
Ted 沒有繼續演說下去。
We should go on with our game.
我們應該繼續比賽。

get on with

繼續做⋯ get on with sb 則是 be friends with sb 的意思。
- I'm not feeling well today.
- You've still got to work. **Get on with** it!
  - 我今天不太舒服。 ●你還是得工作。繼續做事！

▶ It was difficult to get on with the gardening.
繼續園藝工作很困難。
She decided to get on with her studies.
她決定繼續她的學業。

carry on

· carry on+N/-ing
  不停止，繼續做某事

繼續 carry on 後面接名詞或動詞 -ing 形，表示繼續做某事而不停歇。
- Andy can't **carry on** with so much stress.
- So, do you think he's going to quit?
  - Andy 沒辦法繼續負擔那麼多壓力。 ●所以你覺得他會辭職嗎？

▶ Please carry on with the presentation.
請繼續發表。
They carried on kissing when there was a knock at the door. 有人敲門的時候，他們還是持續親吻對方。

---

08 | 努力 do one's best

1-08.mp3

do one's best

· try one's best in…
  盡某人所能於…

盡自身所能 將 do 替換為 try 的慣用語 try one's best 也很常用。
- You'll have a good job interview. Cheer up.
- Thanks. I'll **do my best**.
  - 你的面試會很順利的。加油。 ●謝謝，我會盡我所能。

▶ I'll do my best to remember your birthday next year.
明年我會盡我所能記住你的生日。
You just have to be brave and try your best.
你只需要勇敢，然後盡你所能去做。

try hard to...

· try harder to...
　更努力做…

努力做… 可以換成比較級 harder 表示更加努力去做。

● To be frank with you, you have to **try harder**.

● Please let me know what I should do.

　●說實在的，你需要更努力。　　●請告訴我該怎麼做。

▶ I'm trying hard to get a job!

　我正在努力找工作！

　You have to try harder if you want to pass the exam.

　如果你想通過這個測驗，你需要更努力。

make an effort

· put every effort into
　傾注所有努力於…
· make the best of
　充分利用…

努力 可以在 make an effort 後面加上 to do 說明努力做什麼事。

● We have to **make an effort** to keep those receipts.

● I'll ask everyone to submit the ones that they have.

　●我們必須努力保留那些收據。　　●我會請每個人交出自己的收據。

▶ I need to make an effort to exercise.

　我需要努力運動。

　You have to make an effort to make your wife happy.

　你必須努力讓你的妻子開心。

strive to

· be desperate to do
　不顧一切地做某事
· wrestle with+N
　與…努力搏鬥

努力奮鬥 除了接 to do，也可改接 for sth。

● Jack **strives to** eat healthy foods.

● He is in good shape for his age.

　●Jack 努力吃健康食品。　　●以他的年齡而言，他很健康。

▶ They strive to get high grades in class.

　他們努力在課堂上取得好成績。

　I'm striving to get a good job.

　我正在努力找一份好工作。

do everything in one's power

· do (all) the best one
　could
　盡最大的努力

盡其所能做… 可以在後面加上 to do 說明所做的事。

● I can't believe that Levi died.

● We **did everything in our power** to save him.

　●我不敢相信 Levi 死了。　　●我們已經盡我們所能去救他了。

▶ I do everything in my power to be a good person.

　我盡我所能當個好人。

　Dee did everything in her power to stay awake.

　Dee 盡她最大的努力保持清醒。

1 職場・學校

2 電腦・網路

3 社交生活

4 日常生活

5 訊息・理解

6 想法・態度

7 情緒・狀況

8 行為舉止

9 時間地點・副詞片語

09 | 專注
be devoted to

1-09.mp3

be devoted to

- be devoted to sth/-ing
  專心致力於…，對…虔誠
- devote/commit
  oneself to
  投身於…
- keep one's mind on
  常將…放在心上

專心致力於… devoted 常換成 committed。注意 to 後面接名詞。

- My mom attends church every day.
- She must **be devoted to** her religion.
  - ●我媽媽每天都去教會。　●她一定對自己的信仰很虔誠。

▶ Sam was devoted to his new girlfriend.
  Sam 對他的新女友很忠實。
  We're devoted to our favorite teacher.
  我們很專心上我們最愛的老師的課。

be enthusiastic about

- be/get hooked on
  對…著迷
- get hooked on booze
  and women
  沉迷於酒色

對…熱衷 跟「be crazy about」的意思相同。

- Vera **is enthusiastic about** collecting stamps.
- I know. She is always talking about it.
  - ●Vera 對集郵很熱衷。　●我知道，她總是在談集郵。

▶ Many people are enthusiastic about making money.
  有很多人熱衷於賺錢。
  John was enthusiastic about his trip to Europe.
  John 之前非常熱衷於他的歐洲旅行。

be absorbed in

- be absorbed in sth/-ing
  全神貫注於…
- be occupied with/in
  忙於…
- be preoccupied with
  全神貫注於…，入神於…

全神貫注於… in 的後面接名詞或動名詞，可以補充說明專注於什麼事。

- Kathy, why didn't you answer the phone?
- I **was so absorbed in** my book that I didn't hear it!
  - ●Kathy，你為什麼沒有接電話？
  - ●我看書看得太專心，所以沒有聽到！

▶ My girlfriend was absorbed in her favorite TV show.
  我女朋友完全被她最喜歡的電視節目吸引住了。
  The workers were absorbed in constructing the building.
  工人們全神貫注於建設大樓。

apply oneself to

· apply one's mind to
心思專注於…

· give oneself up to sth
沉迷於某事物（主要用來表示沾染了某項惡習）

致力於… to 的後面接名詞或動名詞，說明在做什麼。

● My math class is so difficult.
● You must **apply yourself to** solving the problems.
　●我的數學課好難。　　●你必須盡力去解題。

▶ Tim applied himself to finishing the job.
Tim 致力於完成工作。
The mechanic applied himself to fixing the car.
技師致力於修車。

concentrate (one's efforts) on

· focus (one's attention) on sth
集中（注意力）在某事上

集中精力做… one's efforts 也常換成 one's energies。

● What are your plans for the new year?
● I'm going to **concentrate on** losing some weight.
　●你的新年新計畫是什麼？　　●我要努力減肥。

▶ You need to concentrate on being a better person.
你需要努力當個更好的人。
I'm just trying to focus on this.
我正努力專注在這件事上。

---

10 忙碌
be tied up

1-10.mp3

be very busy

· be (always) busy with
（總是）忙於…

· be busy -ing
忙於…

非常忙碌 如果忙碌的程度比較低，可以說 kind/sort of busy。

● It **has been a very busy** day.
● That's for sure. I haven't had a break.
　●今天真是非常忙碌的一天。　　●真的，我完全沒休息。

▶ They were busy traveling this weekend.
他們這個週末忙於旅行。
I'm busy with a client at the moment.
我現在忙著應付一位客戶。

1 職場・學校
2 電腦・網路
3 社交生活
4 日常生活
5 訊息・理解
6 想法・態度
7 情緒・狀況
8 行為舉止
9 時間地點・副詞片語

keep oneself busy

保持忙碌 意為「讓自己保持忙碌」。

- How do you avoid being bored?
- I like to keep myself busy.
  - 你避免讓自己感到無聊的方法是什麼？　●我喜歡讓自己保持忙碌。

▶ Sam kept himself busy at work.
　Sam 讓自己一直忙於工作。
　You can keep yourself busy using the computer.
　你可以用電腦讓自己一直有事做。

---

be tied up

- be tied up with
  忙著做…
- be tied up all day
  整天都很忙
- be tied up with
  housework all day
  整天忙著做家事

為了…而忙碌 tie 意為「拴住、綑綁住」，因此 be tied up 便是用來形容「被某件事綁住，無法做其他的事」。

- When can I stop by to pick up those books?
- Well, I'm kind of tied up all day. How about next week?
  - 我什麼時候可以順道去拿那些書？
  - 嗯，我整天都會有點忙，下星期好嗎？

▶ I'm tied up with something urgent.
　我忙著處理某件緊急的事。
　I'm tied up all day. How about tomorrow?
　我整天都很忙，明天好嗎？

---

be hectic

- have a pretty hectic
  day
  度過相當忙碌的一天
- hectic/tight schedule
  緊湊的行程

非常忙碌 hectic 的意思是「鬧哄哄、忙得亂七八糟」。

- Can you spare a few minutes to talk?
- I'm sorry, but it's very hectic right now.
  - 你可以抽幾分鐘時間談談嗎？
  - 我很抱歉，但現在真的忙得不像話。

▶ The tour schedule was hectic.
　旅行的行程十分緊湊。
　It was hectic getting to the airport on time.
　為了準時抵達機場，一直忙著趕路。

---

haven't got all day

很忙碌，沒有多餘的時間 意思是「整天都很忙，沒有太多空閒的時間」。

- Just give me ten more minutes.
- No way. I haven't got all day.
  - 只要再多給我十分鐘就好。　●不行，我沒有閒工夫等你。

▶ Work faster. We haven't got all day.
　做快一點，我們沒那麼多時間。
　Haven't you finished? We haven't got all day.
　你還沒完成嗎？我們沒那麼多時間。

11 匆忙，慢慢來
take one's time

1-11.mp3

1 職場・學校
2 電腦・網路
3 社交生活
4 日常生活
5 訊息・理解
6 想法・態度
7 情緒・狀況
8 行為舉止
9 時間地點・副詞片語

be in a hurry

· be hurrying to do
　趕著做…
· hurry as fast as one
　can
　盡其所能的趕著

匆忙 也可以把 hurry 換成 rush，意思一樣。
- Why is everyone rushing around?
- They **are in a hurry** to clean up the place.
  - 為什麼大家都這麼忙？　● 他們急著把這個地方打掃乾淨。
▶ Pam and Tina are in a hurry to finish their homework.
  Pam 跟 Tina 在趕作業。
  I am in a hurry to get to my house. 我正趕著回家。

get a move on sth

· Let's get a move on.
　快點。（= hurry up）

快去做某事 多用在命令句型中，要對方快點去做某事。
- **Get a move on** it!
- I'm going as fast as I can.
  - 快點！　● 我已經盡我最快的速度了。
▶ Get a move on it! We're already late. 快點！我們已經遲到了。
  Let's go! Get a move on it! 走吧！快點！

there's no rush

· there's no rush to do
　不用急著去做（某事）
· be in no rush
　不急
· do without being in a
　rush
　慢慢做

不用急 向對方表示「別急，慢慢來」的意思。
- I'll have this done in a few minutes.
- **There's no rush.** Take your time.
  - 我幾分鐘後就會把這個弄好。　● 不用急，你慢慢來。
▶ There's no rush to complete this project.
  這個案子不用急著完成。
  Take your time. I'm in no rush. 慢慢來，我沒有在趕時間。

take one's time

· take one's time -ing
　從容地做某事
· Hold your horses!
　稍安勿躁！

慢慢來 有「不必趕著完成，要慢慢地、慎重地做好」的意思。
- I'll be back in ten minutes.
- **Take your time.** It's not that busy.
  - 我十分鐘後會回來。　● 你慢慢來，沒有那麼忙。
▶ Hold your horses, honey. I'll be home in 30 minutes.
  冷靜點，親愛的。我三十分鐘後會到家。
  Just hold your horses! We have a lot of time.
  慢慢來！我們有很多時間。

27

take it slow

- slow down
  慢下來

慢慢來，從容地做 表示「不要急，要慢慢把它做好」。

- I've got to get this work done quickly.
- **Slow down.** You're going to make mistakes.

  ●我得趕快把這件事完成。　●慢慢來，你會出錯的。

▶ Take it slow and do a good job. 慢慢來，把它做好。
  I think it's good to take it slow. 我想慢慢來是好的。

---

12 | 累垮
be tired out

1-12.mp3

---

be tired out

- look a bit tired
  看起來有點累
- be dead tired
  累垮

累垮了 be 也可以換成 get 或 become。接在後面的 out 表示強調的意思。

- I don't understand why my wife **is so tired** all the time.
- Put yourself in her shoes and you'll see why.

  ●我不懂為什麼我太太總是這麼累。
  ●設身處地為她著想，你就知道為什麼了。

▶ I'm tired of hanging around this boring town.
  我對於悶在這個無聊的城鎮感到很厭倦。
  It seems that you are really tired because of this homework. 你看來因為這份作業而非常累。

be exhausted

- be completely
  exhausted (from)
  （因為某件事）完全累癱
- exhaust oneself
  精疲力盡

精疲力盡 想更加強調時，可以在 be 後面加上 totally 或 completely。

- Well, it looks like you haven't had much sleep lately.
- Isn't that the truth? I'm **exhausted**.

  ●看來你最近都睡得不多。　●可不是嗎？我累垮了。

▶ You must be exhausted from doing two jobs.
  一次做兩份工作，你一定累死了。
  They were exhausted from driving all afternoon.
  他們因為開了一整個下午的車而精疲力盡。

be fatigued with

· be worn out with fatigue
累到精疲力盡

因為…而疲勞 想要更加強調時，可以在 be 後面加上 entirely 或 utterly。

● How do you find yourself today?

● I **am** totally **fatigued with** my office work.

　●你今天覺得怎麼樣？　　●我因為工作完全累癱了。

▶ I feel pleasantly fatigued with exercise at the health club.
健身俱樂部的運動課程讓我累得很開心。

If you are feeling fatigued, please stop the work and relax. 如果你覺得累了，請停下工作放鬆一下。

be knocked out

· be knocked out from
因為…而累垮了

累垮了 挨了一記拳頭而倒地，引申為被疲倦打倒的意思。

● Why did he lie like a log?

● He **was knocked out** from overwork.

　●他為什麼躺在那裡不省人事（像塊木頭）？
　●他工作過度，累垮了。

▶ He was knocked out in the first round.
他在第一局被擊倒了。

Everybody in the office was knocked out.
每個在辦公室的人都累垮了。

be burned out

· be worn out
精疲力盡

· be wiped out
精疲力盡

完全筋疲力盡 彷彿燃燒殆盡般，十分疲倦，失去所有力氣的狀態。

● Burt always looks so tired.

● He **is burned out** from being here.

　●Burt 看起來總是好累。　　●光是待在這裡就累垮他了。

▶ I am totally burned out from doing this job.
我因為這份工作完全累癱了。

I'm going to have to cancel. I'm totally wiped out.
我必須取消。我精疲力盡了。

1 職場・學校

2 電腦・網路

3 社交生活

4 日常生活

5 訊息・理解

6 想法・態度

7 情緒・狀況

8 行為舉止

9 時間地點・副詞片語

13 恢復
get over

1-13.mp3

get over

恢復，克服 可以表示疾病痊癒，或是脫離某個困境等。
- I'm so angry with my wife for deceiving me!
- You'll **get over** it.
  - ●我真的很氣我太太欺騙我！　●會過去的。
- ▶ He can't get over his father's death.
  他沒辦法脫離他父親死亡的陰霾。
  Don't worry. She'll get over it in a few weeks.
  別擔心，她幾個星期後就會沒事的。

get back on one's feet

- get back on track
  重回正軌
- get back out there
  重新開始
- get back in the game
  回到比賽中

恢復 原意為「重新站起來」，引申為從悲傷或疾病等狀況中恢復。與 get back on track 意義相近。
- I have no job and no money.
- You'll **get back on your feet** soon.
  - ●我沒有工作也沒有錢。　●你很快就會東山再起的。
- ▶ I'm weak, but I'm getting back on my feet.
  我很虛弱，但我正在恢復中。
  I want you to get back on your feet. 我希望你能夠東山再起。

get one's act together

- get one's strength back
  恢復精力
- gather one's strength
  恢復精力

振作精神 與 pull oneself together 同義，督促對方要努力上進。
- These grades are terrible. **Get your act together.**
- I'm doing the best I can.
  - ●這些成績糟透了。打起精神好好努力吧。　●我正在盡我所能。
- ▶ Shelia needs to get her act together. Shelia 需要振作精神。
  Stop lying and get your act together. 別再躺了，快打起精神。

be up and about

- come around
  甦醒，恢復健康

好轉，起床走動 用來形容病患的情況好轉，或是起床後走走，活動一下的樣子。
- Where did mom and dad go?
- They've been **up and about** for a few hours.
  - ●爸媽去哪裡了？　●他們起床後出去晃了幾個小時。
- ▶ Everyone was up and about early this morning.
  所有人今天早上都很早就起床走動了。
  The patient was up and about. 病患的狀況好轉了。

be refreshing to...

· It's refreshing to do
做…讓人感到新鮮／充滿
活力

做…讓人感到新鮮／充滿活力 形容某件事讓人重新得到活力。

● I just love working at Samsung.
● It's **refreshing to** meet someone who likes her job.
   ● 我真的很喜歡在三星工作。
   ● 遇見一個喜歡自己工作的人實在很新鮮。

▶ It's refreshing to see a park in the city.
   在城市中看見公園，有精神一振的感覺。
   It was refreshing to visit such a kind people.
   拜訪了一個如此親切的民族，感覺耳目一新。

---

14 自立
on one's own

1-14.mp3

on one's own

獨自一人；獨立、自立的 就算有困難，但仍然靠自己獨立完成所有的事。

● Does Gina still live with her parents?
● No, she's been **on her own** for a few years.
   ● Gina 還跟她的父母住在一起嗎？ ● 沒有，她一個人住好幾年了。

▶ I live on my own in the center of New York.
   我一個人住在紐約市中心。
   Few students can pay for school on their own.
   很少有學生能夠自己負擔學費。

do sth on one's own

· do sth (by) oneself
獨自做某事
· do sth alone
獨自做某事

靠自己做某件事 用 on one's own 修飾 do sth 的句型。

● Have you asked your father for help?
● No, I want to **do this on my own**.
   ● 你有請你父親幫忙嗎？ ● 沒有，我想要靠自己。

▶ He can fix the car on his own.
   他可以靠自己把車修好。
   I want to do something on my own from now on.
   從現在開始，我想要靠自己做點事情。

1 職場・學校
2 電腦・網路
3 社交生活
4 日常生活
5 訊息・理解
6 想法・態度
7 情緒・狀況
8 行為舉止
9 時間地點・副詞片語

stand on one's own feet

自立 字面上的意思是「靠自己的腳站著」，引申為「自立」或「自給自足」。

- Why won't you give me any more money?
- You need to **stand on your own feet**.
  - ●你為什麼不會再給我更多錢？ ●你需要自立。

▶ Perry stood on his own feet after graduating.
Perry 畢業後就過著自給自足的生活。
I can't stand on my own feet yet.
我還無法自立。

support oneself

· support oneself
  financially
  在經濟上自立

靠自己養活自己 食衣住行等方面要用錢的時候，都能夠自己支付，表示經濟上的自立。

- How do you like your new job?
- It's OK, but I can't **support myself** with the salary.
  - ●新工作怎麼樣？ ●還可以，但我沒辦法靠我的薪水自立。

▶ I can support myself now that I am working.
我現在在工作了，可以自立了。
She used the extra money to support herself.
她用了額外的錢來養活自己。

be independent

· earn one's (own) way
  自行謀生
· live one's own life
  過自己的生活

獨立 independent 不只可以表示國家的獨立，也可以表示個人的獨立／自立。

- You need to get married soon.
- **Live your own life** and leave me alone.

  ●你需要快點結婚。 ●管好你自己就好，別來管我。

▶ You're telling me to be independent?
你現在是告訴我要獨立嗎？
We are strong and independent career women.
我們是堅強且獨立的職業女性。

15 擅長，有能力
be good at

1 職場・學校
2 電腦・網路
3 社交生活
4 日常生活
5 訊息・理解
6 想法・態度
7 情緒・狀況
8 行為舉止
9 時間地點・副詞片語

1-15.mp3

be good at
· be poor/terrible at
  不擅長…

擅長… 與 be great at 同義。at 的後面接名詞或動詞 -ing 形態。
- Your son **is good at** sports.
- He's the best athlete in the family.
  - 你兒子對運動很在行。　● 他是這個家族裡最棒的運動選手。
▶ Actually, I'm not good at using smart phones.
  事實上，我不太會用智慧型手機。
  My boss says I'm good at discussing things with clients.
  我老闆説我很擅長跟客戶討論事情。

be able to
· be unable to do
  沒有能力做…

有能力做… be capable to 也是表示「有能力做某事」。
- How soon will you **be able to** get here?
- That depends on the traffic conditions.
  - 你能多快到這裡？　● 要看交通狀況。
▶ She will be able to do better next time. 她下次能做得更好。
  We hope you'll be able to join us. 我們希望你能加入我們。

have the ability
· lose the ability (to do)
  失去（做某事的）能力
· beyond one's ability
  超出某人的能力

有能力 在後面加上 to do 可以說明是怎樣的能力。
- I just got a visa for the United States.
- Great! Now you **have the ability** to travel there.
  - 我剛拿到美國簽證。　● 真棒！那你就能去那邊旅行了。
▶ Susan has the ability to make me laugh.
  Susan 有能力讓我笑。
  What makes you think that you have the ability to do
  that? 你為什麼覺得自己有能力做那件事？

do well on
· do fine on
  在…表現不錯

在…表現良好 主要用來表示測驗考得很好。
- Did you **do well on** the exam?
- Yes, I think I got a high grade.
  - 你考試考得好嗎？　● 嗯，我想我應該得了高分。
▶ You must do well on the college entrance test.
  你一定要在大學入學測驗拿到好成績。
  We can do well on the interview questions.
  我們回答面試的問題時可以表現得很好。

be capable of

· show A one's capabilities
向 A 展現某人的能力

有能力做… of 後面要接名詞或動詞 -ing 形態。

● What do you think of Linda?
● She **is capable of** doing good work.

●你覺得 Linda 怎樣？　●她有能力能把事情做好。

▶ Mark is capable of winning the race.

Mark 有能力贏得這場比賽。

Are you capable of driving all night?

你能夠開一整晚的車嗎？

get ahead of

· get ahead of sb
凌駕某人
· get ahead of sth
領先，避開…
· be ahead of the times
走在時代的尖端
· be far/way ahead of sb
遠遠領先某人（= leave sb far behind）

領先… 如果後面接的是人，表示「凌駕、壓過某人」。

● People always want to **get ahead of** each other.
● Sure. Everyone wants to be the most successful.

●人總是想要壓過對方。
●那當然，每個人都想要當最成功的那一個。

▶ I got ahead of everyone else in line.

我排在隊伍的第一個。

We got ahead of the big traffic jam.

「我們領先了塞車」→我們因為提早出發而避開了車潮。

be better than

· be worse than
比…差

比…好 最基本的比較句型，表示兩個比較對象的優劣關係。

● This ice cream **is better than** the other one.
● Yeah, this ice cream is delicious.

●這個冰淇淋比另一個好。　●嗯，這個很好吃。

▶ Your apartment is better than mine.

你的公寓比我的好。

Joe's car is better than his neighbor's.

Joe 的車比他鄰居的好。

feel up to

· feel up to+N/-ing
想做…，覺得能夠做…
· be equal to the task
能夠勝任這項任務（比較強調「能力」的表現方式）
· I don't feel up to it
= I'm not up to that yet
我不想做那件事

想做…，覺得能夠做… 相較於「能力」，這個片語更強調「想要做」。to 的後面要接名詞或動名詞。

● Do you **feel up to** going for a walk?
● Oh no, I'm feeling very sick.

●你想去散個步嗎？　●噢不，我覺得很不舒服。

▶ They didn't feel up to celebrating last night.

他們昨晚不想慶祝。

Harry felt up to carrying the heavy bags.

Harry 覺得他能夠搬這些很重的袋子。

know how to

· know the ropes
（對某件事情）知道要領

知道該怎麼做 將常使用的 how to 句型和 know 結合而成的表現方式。

● Do you **know how to** make cheese from milk?
● Not really. But I'm sure it's difficult.
　●你知道怎麼用牛奶做出乳酪嗎？
　●不是很清楚耶，但我想一定很困難。

▶ Do you know how to get there? 你知道怎麼去那邊嗎？
　I know how to play this game. 我知道怎麼玩這個遊戲。

lose one's touch

失去感覺（要領） 原本很拿手的事情，突然不會做了。和「fail at what one used to do well」同義。

● This food tastes pretty bad.
● The cook here has **lost his touch**.
　●這食物很難吃。　　●這裡的廚師手藝變差了。

▶ The music was terrible after the band lost its touch.
　這個樂團自從失去格調之後，音樂也變糟了。
　You're losing your touch these days.
　你最近對事情變得生疏了。

---

1 職場・學校
2 電腦・網路
3 社交生活
4 日常生活
5 訊息・理解
6 想法・態度
7 情緒・狀況
8 行為舉止
9 時間地點・副詞片語

16 ｜ 處理，克服困難
take care of

1-16.mp3

take care of

· take care of the fax
處理傳真
· take care of sth for sb
為了某人處理某事

處理 of 的後面如果接人，一般而言表示「照顧」的意思。但如果是黑道、流氓等人這麼說，則是表示「殺死他」。

● I can't find the time to make a dentist appointment.
● Let me **take care of** it for you. You're too busy.
　●我完全抽不出時間預約牙醫。　　●我來幫你處理吧。你太忙了。

▶ Who's going to take care of your kids while you're away? 當你不在的時候，誰會幫你照顧孩子？
　Can you take care of my work while I'm away?
　當我不在的時候，你可以處理我的工作嗎？

deal with

- deal with a problem/matter
  處理問題
- deal with sth successfully
  成功地解決某事
- deal with sb
  應付某人，和某人交涉

應付，處理 為了解決問題，而去做些努力。with 的後面接要處理的問題。

- I'm having some problems with my girlfriend.
- You should **deal with** them right away.
  - 我跟我女朋友有些問題。 ● 你應該馬上處理這些問題。

▶ Can you deal with those customers?
  你可以應付那些顧客嗎？
  I am going to deal with that noisy dog.
  我要去對付那隻很吵的狗。

handle sth well

- handle the case
  處理事情
- handle difficult clients
  應付難纏的客戶

把某事處理得很好 針對某個困難的狀況，做了圓滿的處理。人事物皆可為其受詞。

- Was Harriet sad about failing?
- Yes, but she **handled it well**.
  - Harriet 因為失敗很難過嗎？ ● 是啊，不過她調適得很好。

▶ You handled the interview well.
  你面試時表現得很好。
  Hillary didn't handle the bad news well.
  Hillary 不太能接受這個壞消息。

manage (with)

- manage with/without
  靠／不靠…去應付
- manage stress
  應付壓力

設法應付 把問題或困難的狀態處理得很好、很成功的樣子。

- I've got so much to do.
- Don't worry. You can **manage** it.
  - 我有好多事要做。 ● 別擔心，你可以應付的。

▶ The shop can manage with a few workers.
  那間商店只靠幾個店員就能經營下去。
  We can manage with a little help.
  就算只有一點點的幫助，我們還是能做得很好。

take it easy on

- take it easy on sth
  輕鬆看待某事
- take it easy on sb
  溫柔和藹地對待某人

輕鬆看待… 在 take it easy 後面接 on…，表示「以輕鬆的心情處理…」。

- Aurora is causing big problems for me.
- **Take it easy on** her. She's still young.
  - Aurora 給我製造了大麻煩。 ● 別對她太嚴格，她還年輕。

▶ Take it easy on the freshmen students.
  放輕鬆看待那些大學新鮮人吧。
  Take it easy on your new car.
  對於你的新車，放輕鬆點吧。

Easy does it

· Easy!
  小心點！

保持著注意力慢慢來 用來提醒正在搬重物的人小心處理，或是要勉強做某事的人慢慢來。

- I could work all night long.
- **Easy does it.** You're going to get tired.

  ●我可以工作一整晚。　●慢慢做，你會累的。

▶ Easy does it. We've got plenty of time.
  慢慢來，我們有很多時間。
  Stop driving so fast. Easy does it.
  不要開那麼快，慢慢來。

go easy on

· go easy on sb
  寬容溫和地對待某人
· go easy on sth
  節約地使用某物

寬容溫和地對待… 和 take it easy on 意義相近。on 可接人事物。

- My new assistant is really stupid.
- **Go easy on** him. He will learn more.

  ●我的新助理很笨。　●對他寬容點吧，他會學到更多的。

▶ Go easy on your little sister.
  對你的妹妹寬容點。
  Go easy on punishing Bill.
  處罰 Bill 時寬容點。

pull through

度過（疾病、難關等） 使用於真的非常困難的狀況。

- I heard your grandmother was in the hospital.
- She was very sick, but she **pulled through**.

  ●我聽說你的祖母在醫院。　●她病得很重，但她撐過來了。

▶ The old man wasn't able to pull through.
  那位老先生沒能撐過去。
  He may not pull through after his car wreck.
  他可能沒辦法撐過車禍帶來的重傷。

make it through

· make it through+N
  度過…，克服…

度過困難 有「克服了某個困難或難關」的含意。

- Jim didn't **make it through** the training period.
- I guess he wasn't tough enough to finish.

  ●Jim 沒能度過訓練期。　●我想是他不夠堅強，才沒辦法完成。

▶ We had to make it through a cold winter.
  我們必須克服寒冷的冬天。
  The family made it through a hard time without money.
  這個家庭撐過貧困的那段時光，走了過來。

1 職場・學校

2 電腦・網路

3 社交生活

4 日常生活

5 訊息・理解

6 想法・態度

7 情緒・狀況

8 行為舉止

9 時間地點・副詞片語

cope with

· overcome trials and tribulations
克服試煉和苦難

克服，妥善處理 和 overcome 同義，代表「成功克服、度過了困難」。

● How has Dina been since her dad died?
● She's trying to **cope with** her situation.

●父親過世後，Dina 過得好嗎？　●她正努力克服現狀。

▶ I can't cope with the noise my neighbor makes.
我無法忍受我鄰居製造的噪音。

You'll have to cope with stress at school.
你必須克服學校的壓力。

17 結束，完成
be finished with

1-17.mp3

finish -ing

做完… finish 後接名詞或動名詞，也就是 -ing 形。

● What time do you think you will show up?
● I'll come after I **finish working**.

●你覺得你幾點會到？　●我工作結束後就會去。

▶ I'll check if he's finished working.
我會確認一下他是否完成工作了。

Have you finished the project you started?
你之前開始做的案子，完成了嗎？

be finished with

· be finished with a book
讀完一本書
· be 90% finished
完成了 90%

結束… with 接人時表示終結與某人的關係，接事物時表示看完、寫完、做完…等意義。

● Bring back that paper when you**'re finished with** it.
● Don't worry, I will.

●你讀完那份報告以後要拿回來。　●別擔心，我會的。

▶ Let me know when you're finished with that.
你完成之後，跟我說一聲。

I'm not finished with the report.
我還沒完成報告。

be done with

- be done with sth
  結束／完成某事
- be done with sb
  終結與某人的關係
- You done?
  你完成了嗎？

結束⋯，完成⋯ done 可以換成 finished，兩者意義相近。

- Why are you working so hard on that project?
- I just want to **be done with** it.
  - 你為什麼那麼拼命做那個案子？ - 我只是想要完成它。

▶ Are you done with cooking for tonight?
  你今晚的晚餐煮好了嗎？
  I'm not sure if he's done with it yet. 我不確定他是否完成了。

get sth done

結束⋯，完成⋯ get it done 是很常見的表達方式，和 finish 同義。這個說法常帶有「硬是完成某件事」的涵義。

- Please **get it done** right away.
- Don't worry, you can count on me.
  - 請立刻完成。 - 別擔心，你可以相信我。

▶ I will get the homework done tonight. 我今晚會把功課完成。
  Don't worry. I'll get it done for you. 別擔心，我會幫你完成。

be through -ing

- be through talking on the phone
  結束通話
- be through with sth
  結束某事
- be (all) through
  （完全）結束⋯

做完⋯ be through with sb 的句型則表示終結與某人的關係。

- Can I use the exercise machine?
- Sure, I'm **through exercising** right now.
  - 我可以使用這個運動器材嗎？ - 當然，我才剛運動完。

▶ Sarah is through showering. Sarah 沖完澡了。
  He is through eating his dinner. 他吃完了晚餐。

get through

完成工作，度過難關，通過 可以不接受詞，也可以接要克服的課題或難關等。

- Should we drive to the party?
- We can't **get through** the traffic jam.
  - 我們該開車去參加派對嗎？ - 我們沒辦法通過車陣的。

▶ Did you get through the DVD yet? 你看完 DVD 了嗎？
  You need to get through this course. 你需要上完這門課程。

get sth over with

做完／處理掉某事 有「把某件一點也不想處理的事情趕緊弄完」的意味。

- I hate swimming in cold water.
- Jump in the pool and **get it over with**.
  - 我討厭游冷水。 - 跳進泳池裡，撐過去就對了。

▶ Clean up your room and get it over with.
  快點把你的房間打掃乾淨。
  Get your studying over with before we go.
  在我們動身之前，快把你的功課做完。

1 職場・學校
2 電腦・網路
3 社交生活
4 日常生活
5 訊息・理解
6 想法・態度
7 情緒・狀況
8 行為舉止
9 時間地點・副詞片語

be over

- be over sb
  完全結束，並且遺忘與某人的關係
- be up
  結束 (= expire)

結束 要結束的事接在 be 動詞前面。

- Am I in time to see the soccer match?
- No, it's over. You missed it.
  - ●我有趕上看足球比賽的時間嗎？ ●沒有，比賽結束了，你錯過了。

▶ The time for our coffee break is over.
  我們的休息時間結束了。
  The dinner was over and people went home.
  晚餐結束，人們也回家了。

come to an end

- put/bring sth to an end
  結束／終止某事
- come to a close/conclusion
  終結，解決

結束 把 come 換成 put 或 bring，可以表示「使…結束」。

- This debate must come to an end.
- Yes, it's a bit ridiculous, isn't it?
  - ●這場辯論該結束了。 ●是啊，這有點可笑，不是嗎？

▶ I guess all good things must come to an end.
  我想，所有好事都有結束的一天。
  Let's bring this matter to a close.
  讓我們為這件事畫下句點吧。

wrap up

- complete
  完成
- wind up in/at/with -ing
  以…告終

完成 口語中很常見的用法，和 finish 同義。

- The conference will wrap up on Saturday.
- It will be very busy until then.
  - ●會議星期六會結束。 ●在那之前都會很忙碌了。

▶ You need to wrap up what you're doing.
  你需要完成你正在做的事。
  Let me wrap up the speech I made.
  讓我總結我的演說。

18 跟上
keep up with

1-18.mp3

1 職場・學校

2 電腦・網路

3 社交生活

4 日常生活

5 訊息・理解

6 想法・態度

7 情緒・狀況

8 行為舉止

9 時間地點・副詞片語

catch up

· catch up on sb/sth
 趕上…

· catch up on some sleep
 補眠

趕上… 趕上前面的人，成為與他們水準相同的人。

● Are you planning to **catch up with** your high school friends?

● Yeah, I'm going to have to run after them.

 ●你打算趕上你高中的朋友們嗎？ ●是啊，我在後面可得追了。

▶ She needed to work hard to catch up with her classmates. 她需要努力跟上她同學的程度。

 You go ahead. I'll catch up with you later.
 你先走，我等一下會跟上。

 I need to catch up on the class lessons.
 我需要追上課程的進度。

keep up with

· keep up with sb
 跟上某人

· keep up with sth
 追上某件事的進度

跟上… with 後面接不想落後、要努力跟上的人事物。

● How's your new job going?

● It didn't work out. I couldn't **keep up with** all the work.

 ●你的新工作怎麼樣？ ●不太成功，我沒辦法跟上工作進度。

▶ Try to keep up with the fastest runner.
 試著跟上跑得最快的人。

 I can't keep up with Tina's studying.
 我跟不上 Tina 的學習速度。

 I couldn't keep up with my parents.
 我跟不上我的父母。

keep track of

· keep a record of
 持續記錄某事

追蹤…，記錄… 反義語為 lose track of，意為「失去（聯繫、線索等）」。

● What are you writing down?

● I'm **keeping track of** the money I spend.

 ●你在寫什麼？ ●我在記錄我花的錢。

▶ David's wife should keep track of him.
 David 的太太應該掌握他的行蹤。

 Some parents don't keep track of their children.
 有些家長不管自己孩子的行蹤。

keep pace with

· be abreast of the times
與時代並駕齊驅

和…並駕齊驅 也可以說 keep abreast of，意思一樣。

- Are you good at running races?
- I can **keep pace with** any runner.

   ●你對於賽跑拿手嗎？　●我能和任何跑者並駕齊驅。

▶ Try to keep pace with the rest of the group.
   試著和團體中的其他人保持相同步調。
   I couldn't keep pace with the other workers.
   我跟不上其他員工。

---

19 滿足，達成
meet the deadline

1-19.mp3

---

meet the needs of

· meet the demands
滿足需求

滿足…的需求 the needs 可以替換為 the demands，意義相同。

- Does Larry like living in this small apartment?
- It **meets the needs of** his lifestyle.

   ●Larry 喜歡住在這間小公寓裡嗎？　●這很符合他的生活方式。

▶ The car was old, but it met my need for transportation.
   這車很舊了，但它能滿足我的交通需求。
   The loan met Jim's needs while he was a student.
   當 Jim 還是學生的時候，那筆貸款滿足了他的需求。
   This computer will meet the demands of my work.
   這台電腦可以滿足我的工作需求。

meet the deadline

· meet the requirements
符合必要條件

趕上期限 meet 除了「遇見、見面」的意思之外，也有「滿足、符合」的意思。

- This has to be ready by tomorrow morning.
- We're never going to **meet the deadline**.

   ●這個必須在明天早上之前準備好。　●我們不可能趕上截止期限的。

▶ If you hurry, you'll meet the deadline.
   如果你快一點，你就能趕上期限。
   Kevin got a bad grade because he didn't meet the deadline. Kevin 沒趕上（作業／報告的）期限，所以他的成績很差。
   All new soldiers must meet the requirements of their training. 所有新兵都必須符合訓練的必要條件。

1 職場・學校

2 電腦・網路

3 社交生活

4 日常生活

5 訊息・理解

6 想法・態度

7 情緒・狀況

8 行為舉止

9 時間地點・副詞片語

live up to

不辜負…；實踐… 後面常常接 sb's expectation。

- Your father wants you to be successful.
- It's difficult to **live up to** his expectations.
  - ●你父親希望你能成功。　●要達到他的期望很困難。

▶ You need to live up to your teacher's expectations.
你要達到你老師的期望。

Ted didn't live up to his expectations.
Ted 辜負了他的期望。

satisfy one's wishes

· satisfy one's curiosity
滿足某人的好奇心

達成／滿足某人的願望

- I can never **satisfy my husband's wishes**.
- What does he want you to do?
  - ●我永遠沒辦法滿足我先生的願望。　●他要你做什麼？

▶ The Christmas gifts satisfied the children's wishes.
耶誕禮物滿足了孩子們的願望。

This money has satisfied my wishes.
這筆錢滿足了我的願望。

20 | 完成某事，成功 make it

1-20.mp3

make it

· I made it!
我辦到了！

· make it on one's own
靠自己完成

完成某事，成功 如果是「make it to 地點」的句型，則表示「及時趕到」的意思。

- I can't do this any more.
- Yes, you can. You can **make it**!
  - ●我沒辦法再做下去了。　●你可以的，你辦得到！

▶ The basketball player wants to make it in the NBA.
這位籃球選手想要在 NBA 嶄露頭角。

I tried to come to the party, but I couldn't make it.
我努力趕上派對，但我還是沒有成功。

I'm sure you'll make it as a businessman.
我相信你能夠成為一位企業家。

make one's way

· make one's way
through
奮力穿越

前往，努力前進，成功 字面意義是「創造路並且往前走」，引申為「雖然一路上有許多困難，但仍努力向前」。

● Can I come over to visit you?
● Sure. **Make your way to** my apartment.

　　● 我可以去拜訪你嗎？　　● 當然，來我的公寓找我吧。

▶ Ray was drunk and couldn't make his way to his home.
Ray 醉得找不到路回家。
We'll have to make our way to the store.
我們得去那間店。
Bill Gates made his own way with computer.
比爾蓋茲藉由電腦事業成功。

go pretty well

· be not going so well
進展得不是很順利

⋯進展得很順利 主詞多為派對、慶典或是約會等活動。

● Did you meet your boyfriend's parents?
● I sure did. It **went pretty well**.

　　● 妳跟妳男朋友的父母見面了嗎？　　● 見了，還蠻順利的。

▶ The festival is going pretty well.
慶典進行得很順利。
My blind date went pretty well.
我的聯誼進展得很順利。

get there

· get somewhere
成功
· get nowhere
失敗

達成目標 表示「達成目標」時，和 attain 或 achieve 同義。

● How do I become a rich person?
● It takes a lot of hard work to **get there**.

　　● 我該怎麼做才能變成有錢人？　　● 要花很多努力才能達成。

▶ They tried to finish, but they didn't get there.
他們試圖完成，但最後還是沒有辦到。
I hope we all get there after we graduate.
我希望我們畢業後，都能達成自己的目標。

come off well

· come off
成功，依計畫進行
· break through
經過一番努力後成功

進展得很好，表現得很好 特別可用在「在競爭中得到好結果」的狀況。

● How did your presentation go?
● I think it **came off well**.

　　● 你的發表進行得怎麼樣？　　● 我覺得進行得不錯。

▶ The date with Natalie came off well.
和 Natalie 的約會進展得不錯。
Everything came off well at school today.
今天在學校每件事都很順利。

work out for sb

對某人而言順利，適合某人　主詞對某人而言很適合，因而進展得很好的狀態。

- I really like my new job.
- It will probably **work out for** you.
  - ●我真的很喜歡我的新工作。　●那可能很適合你。

▶ The schedule worked out for me.
那行程很適合我。
I'm sorry it didn't work out for you.
我很抱歉那對你而言進展得不順利。

get it right

· do all right
　在工作或生活上很成功

把事情做好　以「get + 受詞 + 補語」的形式表現，也就是要將 it 所指的那件事順利完成（right）之意。

- Did you answer her question?
- I did, but I didn't **get it right**.
  - ●你回答她的問題了嗎？　●回答了，但我回答得不好。

▶ If you try to do something, get it right.
如果你試圖做一件事，就把它做好。
He quit because he couldn't get it right.
因為做不好，所以他放棄了。

pull off

· pull it off
　做成某事
· He pulled off the deal.
　他談成了那筆交易。

做成某事，成功　尤其在一件很困難的事成功的時候，可以使用這個表達方式。

- Did someone rob the bank next door?
- Yeah, three crooks **pulled off** a robbery.
  - ●隔壁銀行發生搶案了嗎？　●嗯，有三個搶匪搶了銀行。

▶ You can't pull off a stunt like that.
你沒辦法做出像那樣的特技的。
The baseball team pulled off a big win.
這支棒球隊贏得了很大的勝利。

manage to

· manage to do
　設法做到…

設法做到，勉力完成　很努力地試著完成某件困難的事，最終得到好結果。

- Did you **manage to** lose some weight?
- Yeah, but I have to continue my diet.
  - ●你有設法減肥嗎？　●有，但必須繼續減下去。

▶ I didn't manage to find a dance partner.
我找不到舞伴。（雖然努力過，但找不到。）
You'll have to manage to buy another car.
你必須想辦法買另一輛車。

1 職場・學校
2 電腦・網路
3 社交生活
4 日常生活
5 訊息・理解
6 想法・態度
7 情緒・狀況
8 行為舉止
9 時間地點・副詞片語

21 勝利，贏，得獎
win the game

1-21.mp3

win the contest

· win the math contest
在數學競賽中獲勝

贏得比賽 在 win at a card game 的情況下，win 是不及物動詞，同樣是「贏、勝利」之意。

● How did you get that prize?
● I **won the spelling contest**.
●你怎麼得到那個獎品的？　●我贏了拼字比賽。

▶ Frank won the school's contest.
Frank 在學校的比賽中獲勝。
I want to win the poetry contest.
我想要贏得詩詞比賽。

win the game

· win the marathon
在馬拉松賽跑中獲勝
· win the soccer game
在足球比賽中獲勝
· win the chess game
在西洋棋競賽中獲勝

贏得比賽 除了 game 以外，也可替換為各種運動競賽的名稱。

● Will our team **win the football game**?
● No, I think they're going to lose.
●我們的隊伍會贏得（美式）足球比賽嗎？　●不，我想他們要輸了。

▶ We won the game after playing three hours.
比賽進行了三個小時後，我們贏了。
So tell me who won the game yesterday?
跟我說昨天誰贏了？

win the first prize

· win an award for excellence
得到優秀獎
· get/receive an award
得獎
· get a prize
得獎
· win the first prize at a speech contest
在演講比賽中得到優勝

得到第一名 win 的受詞大多是 award、prize 等贏得比賽後會得到的東西。

● I **won a small prize** in the contest.
● It's better than nothing.
●我在比賽中得了個小獎。　●有總比沒有好。

▶ She won the first prize for being the most beautiful.
她贏得了選美冠軍。
You'll win the first prize in the cooking contest.
你會在烹飪大賽取得優勝的。

win money at casino

- win the bet
  打賭贏了
- win some money from the lottery
  玩樂透贏了點錢
- win all the money
  贏得所有的錢

在賭場贏錢 win money 這種說法大多用在賭博或玩樂透的情況下。

- I **won the bet**; my team won the final game!
- You really hit the jackpot there, didn't you?
  - 我打賭贏了。我支持的隊伍得到優勝！
  - 你真是中大獎了，不是嗎？

▶ Did you hear that I won the lottery? I am a millionaire now! 你有聽說我中樂透了嗎？我現在是百萬富翁了！
  I found it hard to believe that I won the lottery.
  我很難相信自己中樂透了。

win the election

當選 在這個表達方式中，win 的受詞變成 election（選舉）。

- Mr. George wants to **win the election**.
- If he wins, he'll become the President.
  - 喬治先生希望自己能當選。　●如果他贏了，他將會成為總統。

▶ Mrs. Philips won the election after a long campaign.
  在漫長的競選活動之後，菲利浦女士當選了。
  I don't know who will win the election.
  我不知道誰會當選。

beat the other team

擊敗另一支隊伍 beat 是及物動詞，後面接被擊敗的對象。

- Who won the game last night?
- Barcelona FC **beat the Real Madrid** five to one.
  - 昨晚比賽誰贏了？　●巴塞隆納以五比一擊敗了皇家馬德里。

▶ The Celtics beat the other team.
  賽爾提克隊擊敗了敵隊。
  Our school's team couldn't beat the other team.
  我們學校的隊伍無法擊敗敵隊。

defeat

- defeat A by 2 goals to 1
  （足球類）以二比一擊敗了 A
- admit defeat
  承認失敗（defeat 為名詞）
- be defeated
  被擊敗

擊敗… 除了 beat 以外，也可以用 defeat 表示「擊敗」的意思。

- What happened in the soccer match?
- We **defeated Scranton** 3-1.
  - 足球比賽的結果怎麼樣？　●我們以三比一擊敗了 Scranton。

▶ The boxer couldn't defeat his opponent.
  那位拳擊手無法擊敗他的對手。
  They defeated us in the championship.
  他們在錦標賽中擊敗了我們。

1 職場・學校
2 電腦・網路
3 社交生活
4 日常生活
5 訊息・理解
6 想法・態度
7 情緒・狀況
8 行為舉止
9 時間地點・副詞片語

lead by two points

· win by three points
以三分之差獲勝

領先兩分 用來表示在比賽中領先的分數。

- What was the score at halftime?
- The Eagles **led by two points**.

  ●中場的比數怎樣？　●Eagles 領先兩分。

▶ They led by two points, but then they lost.
他們本來領先了兩分，最後卻輸了。
The other team is leading by two points.
另一隊領先兩分。

get the better of

· get the better of sb
贏了某人

勝過，擊敗 形容在比賽或爭論中，佔對方上風，最後獲勝的狀況。of 後面可以接人。

- Did Tim win the computer game?
- No, the other guy **got the better of** him.

  ●Tim 贏了電腦競賽嗎？　●沒有，另一個人贏了他。

▶ I got the better of my new teacher.
我打敗了我的新老師。
You'll never get the better of me.
你永遠贏不了我的。

lose the game

· lose the contest
輸掉比賽

輸掉比賽 輸了的時候，動詞用 lose，受詞大多是比賽或考試等名詞。

- It's too bad you **lost the contest**. Nice try.
- Maybe I'll win next year.

  ●你輸了比賽真是太可惜了，但你很努力了。　●也許我明年會贏。

▶ If you quit, you'll lose the game.
如果你放棄，你就會輸掉這場比賽。
His team lost the game by one point.
他的隊伍以一分之差敗北。

1 職場・學校

2 電腦・網路

3 社交生活

4 日常生活

5 訊息・理解

6 想法・態度

7 情緒・狀況

8 行為舉止

9 時間地點・副詞片語

22 犯錯，失誤 make a mistake

1-22.mp3

make a mistake

· be one's mistake
…是某人的失誤

· by mistake
錯誤地

be one's fault

· be one's fault for -ing
…是某人的錯

· be one's fault that
S+V
…是某人的錯

· That is no one's fault.
那不是任何人的錯。

be wrong

· be dead wrong
完全錯誤

· be wrong about sb/
sth
對某人／某事有所誤解

· be wrong with sb
某人有問題／不正常

· What's wrong with
you?
你怎麼回事？

犯錯 如果是很大的失誤，可以在 mistake 前面加上 awful, terrible, huge 等形容詞修飾。

● You shouldn't have hit your brother.

● Right. I **made a mistake**.

●你不該打你哥哥的。　●是，我犯了錯。

▶ I made a mistake. It's my fault.

我犯了錯，這是我的錯。

I'm sorry. I dialed your number by mistake.

不好意思，我錯撥了你的號碼。

…是某人的錯／責任 率直地承認自己犯了錯時，可以說 It's my fault.。

● You don't have to say you're sorry.

● Sure I do. It **was all my fault**.

●你不用道歉。　●當然要，這都是我的錯。

▶ I kind of feel like it's my fault.

我覺得這似乎是我的錯。

It's not my fault I'm late. The train broke down.

遲到不是我的錯，是因為列車故障了。

不對的，錯的 後面接 with 時，表示 with 後面的人事物「有問題」；接 about 時，表示對 about 後面的人事物「有誤解」。

● What's **wrong with** your throat?

● I'm not sure. I just can't stop coughing.

●你的喉嚨怎麼了？　●我不知道，就一直咳嗽咳不停。

▶ There's something wrong with my wife.

我太太有些古怪。

Sorry, I was dead wrong.

抱歉，我完全錯了。

go wrong

· go wrong with
　…出了問題

出錯 go wrong 常用來表示機器無法正常運作，或是事業、人際關係出了問題。

- Ariel **went wrong with** her new boyfriend.
- I don't like him at all either.
  - Ariel 跟新男友的感情生變了。　●我也完全不喜歡他。

▶ Did something go wrong with the surgery?
　手術出了什麼問題嗎？
　What happened? Obviously something went wrong with him. 發生什麼事了？顯然他出了什麼問題。

get it all wrong

· get sth wrong
　誤會／搞錯某事
· get it all wrong about
　完全誤解…
· do it (all) wrong
　（完全）做錯

完全搞錯 表示誤會某事。也可將 get 替換為 have。

- Is the story in the newspaper true?
- No, they **got it all wrong**.
  - 報紙上說的是真的嗎？　●不是，他們完全弄錯了。

▶ I got it all wrong about your family.
　我完全誤解你的家庭了。
　He got it all wrong when studying.
　他讀書的時候完全弄錯了。

do something stupid

· do the stupidest thing
　做最蠢的事
· say something stupid
　說蠢話

做某件蠢事 口語中很常見的用法，不確切說出到底是什麼事，總之就是「出包」。

- I'll act very nice. I promise.
- I don't believe you. You'll **do something stupid**.
  - 我會表現得很好的，我保證。　●我不相信，你一定會做出蠢事。

▶ I did something stupid at the party.
　我在派對上做了件蠢事。
　Cheryl's husband did something stupid.
　Cheryl 的先生做了件蠢事。

get the wrong idea

· get the wrong idea
　about…
　對…有所誤解
· It's/That's not what
　you think
　事情不是你所想的那樣

想錯了 沒有確認事實，而心中的想法與事實不符。

- Wow, Mindy's dress is sexy.
- Don't **get the wrong idea**. She's a nice girl.
  - 哇，Mindy 的洋裝好性感。　●別亂想，她是個好女孩。

▶ He got the wrong idea about the stranger.
　他誤解那位陌生人了。
　I think you've got the wrong idea about me.
　我想你誤會我了。

be way off base

- be on the wrong track
  走錯方向，想得不對
- drop the ball
  失誤

大錯特錯 源於棒球用語，原本是「跑者離壘包很遠」的意思，後來引申為「與事實不符」。

- Does your family have a lot of money?
- No. You **are way off base**.
  - 你家很有錢嗎？ ● 不，你大錯特錯。

▶ Jill was way off base about her friend.
  Jill 完全誤會她朋友了。
  Your ideas are way off base.
  你的想法大錯特錯。

goof up

- goof up -ing
  做某事時出錯

出錯，失誤 口語中常使用的表達方式，表示因為粗心而出錯。

- Did you spill soda on these papers?
- Yeah, I **goofed up** when I opened the can.
  - 你把汽水弄翻在這些文件上了嗎？
  - 是啊，我打開罐子時不小心灑出來了。

▶ Peter goofed up when he sent the e-mail.
  Peter 寄電子郵件時不小心出了錯。
  I goofed up remembering her birthday.
  我把她的生日記錯了。

fail to

- fail to do
  做不到…
- be a complete failure
  完全失敗

做…失敗，沒能… 就是「失敗」的意思，表示沒有成功或辦不到某件事。

- Why did Eli get in trouble?
- He **failed to** pay for the item he took.
  - Eli 為什麼惹上了麻煩？ ● 他付不起他拿的東西。

▶ Leo failed to get a good job.
  Leo 沒能找到好工作。
  He has failed to close many deals.
  他有許多交易無法成交。

blow it

- screw up
  搞砸

錯失良機，搞砸 因為失誤、不注意而讓機會溜掉。

- I am meeting Wendy for a date today.
- She likes you. Don't **blow it**.
  - 我今天要跟 Wendy 約會。 ● 她喜歡你，別錯失良機了。

▶ We were winning, but we blew it.
  我們原本要贏了，但我們錯失了良機。
  Jeff blew it before he finished.
  Jeff 在他要完成前搞砸了。

1 職場・學校
2 電腦・網路
3 社交生活
4 日常生活
5 訊息・理解
6 想法・態度
7 情緒・狀況
8 行為舉止
9 時間地點・副詞片語

mess up

· make a mess (of)
（把…）弄糟／弄得亂
七八糟

搞砸 有「弄得亂七八糟，幾乎無法收拾」的意思，表示搞砸了一件重要的事。

● It sure is windy out today.
● My hair is going to **get messed up**.

　●今天外面的風真的很大。　●我的頭髮要變得亂七八糟的了。

▶ These new classes will mess up my schedule.
　這些新課程會把我的行程打亂。
　I didn't mess up your room. 我沒有把你的房間弄亂。

fall through

無法實現，（計畫等）失敗 計畫、約會等安排無法照原訂計畫進行。

● Are you still going to the opera tonight?
● No, our plans to go out **fell through**.

　●你們今天還要去看歌劇嗎？　●沒有，我們外出的計畫告吹了。

▶ The deal to buy the house fell through.
　買房子的交易最後失敗了。
　Jason and Heather's wedding fell through.
　Jason 和 Heather 的婚禮告吹了。

get nowhere with

· get nowhere -ing
　…沒有進展
· get nowhere with this
　report
　在這份報告上沒有進展
· go to pieces
　破碎，身／心崩潰

…沒有進展／結果 「哪裡也到不了」，表示沒有任何進展或結果。

● Did you ask the boss for a raise?
● Of course, but I **got nowhere with** him.

　●你有跟老闆要求加薪嗎？　●當然有，但最後沒有結果。

▶ You'll get nowhere with that policeman.
　你跟那個警察打交道不會有進展的。
　He got nowhere asking Kim on a date.
　他約 Kim 去約會，但沒有下文。

---

 mess up vs. mess with

　　mess up 意為「搞砸」、「弄亂」。而 mess with sth 的受詞大多是危險或不太好的事情，如「mess with drugs」（沾上毒品）。如果 mess with 後面接的是人，多半有「和品行不太好的人扯在一起」的感覺。另外也常表示「招惹對方」。

　　Ex. No one here wants to mess with him. 這裡沒有人想跟他扯上關係。
　　　　Don't mess with that big dog. 別去招惹那隻大狗。

23 | 求職
have a job interview

1-23.mp3

1 職場・學校
2 電腦・網路
3 社交生活
4 日常生活
5 訊息・理解
6 想法・態度
7 情緒・狀況
8 行為舉止
9 時間地點・副詞片語

have a job interview

· have a job interview at City Bank
  在 City Bank 有個面試
· go for an interview
  參加面試
· be called for an interview
  獲邀參加面試
· conduct an interview
  主持面試

有面試 和公司約好接受求職面試。後面接「at + 公司名」可以說明是哪間公司，接 tomorrow 等時間副詞可以表示時間。

● You seem to be worried about something.

● I **have a job interview** this afternoon.

  ●你看起來好像在擔心什麼。　●我今天下午有面試。

▶ I've got a job interview next Monday. Wish me luck.
  我下星期一有個面試，祝我好運吧。

  A good cover letter will help you get an interview.
  一封好的求職信，能幫助你得到面試機會。

  Helen was called for an interview at the UN.
  Helen 獲邀在聯合國參加面試。

send one's resume

· send one's resume to…
  把某人的履歷寄到…
· submit one's resume
  提交某人的履歷
· prepare a resume
  準備履歷，寫履歷

寄履歷 請特別注意 resume 的發音為 [`rɛzjume]。

● I'd like to apply for a job here.

● You need to **send us your resume** first.

  ●我想要應徵這裡的工作。　●你需要先把你的履歷寄給我們。

▶ Randy sent his resume to IBM.
  Randy 寄了他的履歷給 IBM。

  I've sent out over one hundred resumes!
  我已經寄超過一百封履歷了！

  You can submit your resume at the office.
  你可以在辦公室提交你的履歷。

apply for a job

· apply for a job at the university
  應徵大學的工作
· look for a new job
  找新工作

應徵工作 可以指在職場上找工作，或是申請同一間公司內的其他職位。

● That's a nice suit you're wearing.

● I'm going to **apply for a job**.

  ●你穿的套裝真好看。　●我要去應徵工作。

▶ I applied for some jobs over the Internet.
  我透過網路應徵了一些工作。

  You need to apply for a job to get hired.
  想被雇用的話，你需要先應徵工作。

be qualified for a job

- be highly qualified
  非常有資格
- be fully qualified
  完全符合資格

符合應徵職位的資格條件 可以在 be 的後面加上 well 或 highly 等副詞，強調「真的很適合」。

- Make sure that all of the applicants **are qualified for the job**.
- When are we going to schedule the interviews?
  - 請確認所有應徵者的資格都符合這份工作。
  - 我們什麼時候要開始安排面試？

▶ Tracy is qualified for a job with the airlines.
  Tracy 有資格應徵航空公司的工作。
  He is not qualified for a job with the police force.
  他沒有資格應徵警察的工作。

---

24 就職
get a job

1-24.mp3

---

get/find a job

- get/find another job
  找到另一份工作
- get/find a better job
  找到更好的工作
- get/find a job with a great salary
  找到高薪的工作

找到工作 這裡的 job 指的是領雇主薪水的工作。

- I'm sure I will **get a job** with a high salary.
- Maybe not. Nothing is as easy as it seems.
  - 我相信我能得到一份高薪的工作。
  - 也許不能。沒有什麼事是像表面上看起來那麼簡單的。

▶ It is getting so hard to find a job right now.
  現在找工作越來越難了。
  You should get a job and make some money.
  你應該找到一份工作然後賺錢。

get/find a job as + 業種

- get/find a job as a nurse
  找到護士的工作
- get a job overseas
  找到海外的工作

找到…的工作 口語用法，說明找到的工作是什麼類型。

- I **got a job as** a car designer.
- That's great! I hope you'll be successful.
  - 我找到汽車設計師的工作了。　● 太棒了！我希望你能成功。

▶ He couldn't get a job as a garbage man.
  他無法獲得垃圾清潔員的工作。
  I want to get a job as an actor in Hollywood.
  我想要在好萊塢找到一份演員的工作。

take a job

· take a job overseas
接下海外的工作
· accept a job at one's company
接受某人公司的工作

接下工作 take 有「經過選擇之後，取得某個東西」的含義。

- Brian is living in England now.
- He **took a job** as a university instructor.
  - ●Brian 現在住在英國。　●他接下了大學講師的工作。

▶ Paula took a job at the factory.
Paula 接下了一份工廠的工作。

Will you take a job with our company?
你會來我們公司工作嗎？

offer sb a job

· offer sb a job (on the stock market)
提供某人一份（股票市場的）工作
· be offered a job (in Japan)
獲得了一份（在日本的）工作

提供某人工作 請某人擔任某職務時使用。如果要表示某人獲得一份工作，改為被動態即可。

- Who **is offering you the job** with such a high salary?
- Guess who? The CEO of the company himself.
  - ●誰開那麼高的薪水雇用你？　●你猜是誰？就是那間公司的 CEO。

▶ We want to offer you a job as a general manager.
我們想提供你一份總經理的工作。

He was offered a job post in Chicago.
他獲得了一份在芝加哥的工作。

be hired as

· be hired as a technician at the new GM factory
被雇用為新的 GM 工廠的技師

被雇用為⋯ as 的後面可以接各種職業名稱，例如 teacher, secretary, new computer technician 等等。

- What kind of work do you do?
- I **was hired as** a lawyer.
  - ●你從事怎樣的工作？　●我是律師。

▶ Cindy was hired as a school teacher.
Cindy 被雇用為老師。

I'm going to be hired as an editor.
我將被雇用為編輯。

1 職場・學校
2 電腦・網路
3 社交生活
4 日常生活
5 訊息・理解
6 想法・態度
7 情緒・狀況
8 行為舉止
9 時間地點・副詞片語

25 | 工作
work for

have a job

- have a job at this company
  在這間公司有工作
- have a part-time job
  有一份兼職工作
- have a full-time job
  有一份全職工作
- moonlight
  做兼職

have been in + 業界 + for

- have been in the insurance industry for 2 years
  在保險業界做了兩年了
- be in the insurance business
  在保險業界

work for

- work for sb
  為某人工作，在某人之下工作
- work for + 業種／業界
  在⋯工作
- work at/in + 公司名稱
  在⋯工作
- work for the government agency
  在政府機構工作

work as + 職業

- work as a computer salesperson
  當電腦銷售員
- work as a lawyer for an insurance company
  在一間保險公司當律師

有工作，在工作 job 後面接動詞 -ing 形可以說明工作內容。

- Neil seems very happy with his work.
- He **has a job** working with children.
  - Neil 看起來工作得很開心。　●他的工作會和孩子們在一起。
- ▶ They have a job in Japan. 他們在日本有工作。
  Each person has a job at the company.
  在這間公司，每個人都有工作。

在某個業界任職了多久 請注意要使用現在完成式。

- What does your husband do?
- He **has been in sales for** 13 years.
  - 你先生的工作是什麼？　●他做業務做了 13 年。
- ▶ I have been in management for a year.
  我在管理部門做了一年了。
  Liz has been in therapy for seven years.
  Liz 擔任治療師已經七年了。

在⋯工作 和中文的慣用說法有點不同。後面除了接公司的名稱，也可以接老闆的名字，表示「為⋯工作」。

- Do you enjoy your job?
- Yes, I **work for** a television station.
  - 你喜歡你的工作嗎？　●是的，我在電視台工作。
- ▶ Jason works for his father.
  Jason 替他爸爸工作。
  I want to work for a university.
  我想在大學工作。

當⋯（職業） as 後面通常接具體的職業或職位名稱。

- Is this office building where you work?
- Yes, I **work as** a lawyer here.
  - 這是你工作的辦公大樓嗎？　●對，我在這裡當律師。
- ▶ My uncle works as a company director. 我叔叔是公司董事。
  Sue wants to work as an airline attendant. Sue 想要當空服員。

work part-time

- work full-time
  全職工作
- work on a part-time basis
  兼職工作
- work overseas
  在海外工作

兼職工作 part-time 的反義詞是 full-time。

- ●I never see your daughter anymore.
- ●She goes to college and also **works part-time**.

  ●我都沒再見到你女兒了。　●她上大學了，而且在打工。

▶ Gary works part-time at the department store.
  Gary 在百貨公司打工。
  I work part-time as a French tutor.
  我兼差當法文家教。

---

26 上班
go to work

1-26.mp3

---

go to work

- go to work at
  去…上班
- drive to work
  開車上班
- on the way to work
  在上班途中
- get back to the office
  回到辦公室（或指上班）

上班 如果說 go to work at the bar，這個人的職業可能是酒保。

- ●Wake up! You have to **go to work**.
- ●Just let me sleep a few more minutes.

  ●快起床！你要去上班。　●再讓我多睡幾分鐘就好。

▶ Howard's father goes to work on the subway.
  Howard 的爸爸坐地鐵上班。
  She went to work at the clothing store.
  她去服飾店上班。

go for the day

- have gone for the day
  已經下班
- get off/out of work
  下班
- get out of the office
  （暫時）離開辦公室

下班 經常使用完成式 have gone for the day。

- ●Excuse me. Is Mr. Jones in his office right now?
- ●I'm sorry, but he's **gone for the day**.

  ●不好意思，Jones 先生現在在他的辦公室嗎？
  ●抱歉，他已經下班了。

▶ I need to get off work early on Friday.
  我星期五需要早點下班。
  You need to get out of the office sometimes for fresh air.
  你需要偶爾離開辦公室，呼吸一下新鮮空氣。

1 職場・學校
2 電腦・網路
3 社交生活
4 日常生活
5 訊息・理解
6 想法・態度
7 情緒・狀況
8 行為舉止
9 時間地點・副詞片語

call it a day

· Let's call it a day.
  我們今天就到此結束吧。
· after work
  下班後

結束一天的工作 也可以把 day 替換成 night。也常說 call it quits。

● I'm so exhausted. Let's **call it a day**.
● Sounds good to me.

  ●我好累，今天就到此結束吧。　●我同意。

▶ Let's call it a day and get some beer.
  我們今天就到這邊，去喝點啤酒吧。
  Would you like to have a drink after work?
  你下班後想去喝點酒嗎？

skip work

· skip lunch
  不吃午餐
· call in sick
  請病假
· take a leave of
  absence
  請假

蹺班 skip 有「逃掉，不去做該做的事」的意思。因此蹺課是 skip school。

● The holiday will start on Monday.
● That's why I'm going to **skip work** Friday.

  ●假期是從星期一開始。　●所以我星期五要蹺班。

▶ Cindy skipped work because she was tired.
  Cindy 因為很累，所以蹺了班。
  Dave was fired for skipping work.
  Dave 因為蹺班而被炒魷魚。

be on/off duty

· duty officer
  值星官
· night duty
  夜班
· off duty hours
  下班時間

值班／沒有值班 on 有正在進行中的意思。off 是停止的意思，表示沒有在做之前做的事。

● Will you have to work a long shift?
● Oh yes. I'll **be on duty** all night.

  ●你接下來的班很長嗎？　●是啊，我要工作一整晚。

▶ The cop was on duty near my house.
  警察在我家附近執勤。
  Kevin will be off duty until 10 pm.
  Kevin 在晚上十點前都沒有班。

27 薪水，獎金
get paid

1-27.mp3

1 職場・學校

2 電腦・網路

3 社交生活

4 日常生活

5 訊息・理解

6 想法・態度

7 情緒・狀況

8 行為舉止

9 時間地點・副詞片語

get a (pay) raise

· get a pay increase
獲得加薪

· have/get one's salary raised
獲得加薪

· ask for a raise
要求加薪

獲得加薪 如果要表示公司為某人加薪，則說 give sb a raise。

● We need to **give** the secretary **a raise**.

● When was the last time we gave her one?

　●我們需要給祕書加薪。　●我們最後一次給她加薪是什麼時候？

▶ I'm curious whether I will get a raise next year.
我很好奇明年我是否會獲得加薪。
I'm hoping to get a raise at work in the spring.
我希望春天能獲得加薪。

cut sb's pay

· accept a 5% pay cut
接受調降 5% 的薪水

· have a delayed payment (of wages)
延遲付款（付薪水）

減薪 pay raise 的反義詞是 pay cut，意為「減薪」。

● What made you quit your job?

● They **cut my pay** and my vacation time by two weeks.

　●你為什麼辭職了？
　●他們減了我的薪水，還把我的休假減少兩週。

▶ The company decided to cut everyone's pay.
公司決定要降低每個人的薪水。
They are either going to cut back staff or give us a pay cut. 他們要嘛裁員，要嘛降低我們的薪水。

get paid

· get paid + 金額 + an hour
時薪為…（一小時可以領多少錢）

· get a + 金額 + advance in one's salary
預支（多少金額的）薪水

· get a paycheck
收到薪資支票

· payday
發薪日

得到報酬 將 pay 改成被動態 get paid，表示得到錢或其他報酬。

● I'm going to **get paid** on Friday.

● You'll have money to buy Christmas presents.

　●我星期五會領到薪水。　●那你就有錢買耶誕禮物了。

▶ Hey, Tom, did you get paid this month's wages?
嘿，Tom，你領到這個月的薪水了嗎？
I don't get paid for working overtime.
我沒有加班費可領。

59

get a bonus

· get overtime pay
得到加班費
· weekly pay
週薪

得到獎金 get a year-end bonus 表示領到年終獎金。

- How can you spend such a lot of money for gifts?
- You know, I **got a bigger bonus** than last year.

  ●你怎麼能花那麼多錢買禮物？　●因為我今年獎金比去年多。

▶ Mary got the biggest bonus for her sales record.
Mary 因為她的銷售業績而得到最高的獎金。
Are you going to get a Christmas bonus this year too?
你今年也會拿到耶誕獎金嗎？

have a travel allowance

· maternity allowance
生產津貼
· housing allowance
房屋津貼

有出差費 allowance 在職場上指「津貼」，在家中則指「零用錢」。

- It's expensive to stay at this hotel.
- No problem. I **have a big travel allowance**.

  ●住在這間旅館好貴。　●沒問題的，我的旅行津貼很優渥。

▶ Most of the salesmen have a travel allowance.
大部分業務員都有旅費津貼。
My new job has a travel allowance.
我的新工作有旅費津貼。

28 升職，解雇 get promoted

1-28.mp3

get promoted

· get the promotion
獲得升職
· get along at one's job
在工作上進展得很好

獲得升職 後面接「to + 職位」，可以具體說明升到什麼職位。

- You know what? I just **got promoted**.
- Good for you! You deserve it.

  ●你知道嗎？我升職了。　●太棒了！你應得的。

▶ You're not going to believe it. I got promoted!
你不會相信的，我升職了！
I didn't get the promotion.
我沒有獲得升職。

get fired

- get sacked
  被解雇

被解雇 後面可以接 from one's job。如果要用主動態表示「解雇…」，這時候的句型是 fire sb from one's job。

- What happened to your co-worker?
- She **got fired** for stealing things.

  ●你的同事怎麼了？　●她因為偷東西，被解雇了。

▶ Brian is going to get fired for being late.
  Brian 因為遲到，要被解雇了。
  I heard you got fired a few weeks ago.
  我聽說你幾個星期前被解雇了。

lose one's job

- between jobs
  待業中
- be out of a job
  失業中

失業 失去現在的工作，還沒確定下一個工作時，可以用 between jobs 表示處於待業中的空檔。

- Cheer up! You look so sad.
- I just **lost my job** and my wife has threatened to leave me!

  ●開心點！你看起來好難過。　●我剛失業，我太太威脅要離開我！

▶ My dad lost his job at the bank. 我父親失去了銀行的工作。
  Farah may lose her job next week.
  Farah 下星期可能會失去工作。

lay sb off

- let sb go
  解雇某人
- let go of…
  解雇…
- get layoff
  被解雇

解雇某人 公司因為財務或其他方面的困難，而終止雇用員工。但其實 lay off 還有另一個意思，就是不要去打擾某人。lay off 的受詞是人，當受詞是代名詞時接在 off 前面，如果不是代名詞則接在 off 後面。

- My company **is laying everyone off**.
- Are they going out of business?

  ●我的公司要把所有人解雇。　●他們要倒閉了嗎？

▶ We're going to have to lay off at least 100 people.
  我們至少要解雇一百個人。
  We're going to be laying off people in every department.
  我們每個部門都要解雇一些人。

quit one's job

- leave one's job
  辭職

辭職 quit 是指主動辭職。當再也無法忍受，真的想要辭職時，便可大聲地吼出「I quit!」

- What would you do if you had a lot of money?
- The first thing I'd do is **quit my job**.

  ●如果你有很多錢，你要做什麼？　●我要做的第一件事就是辭職。

▶ Joan hated her boss and quit her job.
  Joan 討厭她的老闆，於是她辭職了。
  I'm going to quit this job. I mean it. 我要辭職了，我說真的。

1 職場・學校
2 電腦・網路
3 社交生活
4 日常生活
5 訊息・理解
6 想法・態度
7 情緒・狀況
8 行為舉止
9 時間地點・副詞片語

resign from

· step down
（從高位）辭職，卸任
· accept one's resignation
接受某人的辭呈

辭職，卸任 resign 也是用在主動離職的狀況下，是比 quit 更正式的說法。

● So, what brings you here at such a late hour?

● I came by to tell you that I need to **resign**.
　●什麼風在這麼晚的時間把你吹來了？　●我是來跟你說，我要辭職。

▶ Perry resigned from the sales department.
　Perry 從業務部辭職了。
　I handed in my resignation this morning.
　我今天早上遞出了我的辭呈。

retire from

· plan to retire
計畫要退休
· retirement plan
退休計畫
· think of early retirement
考慮提前退休

從⋯退休 retire 用在因為達到退休年齡等因素，而離開公司的狀況。from 的後面接「公司的名稱」或「業界」等。

● Sad to say, but Rick is **retiring**.

● We should organize a retirement party for him.
　●說來難過，但 Rick 要退休了。　●我們應該幫他辦個退休派對。

▶ Bob is really looking forward to his retirement.
　Bob 真的很期待退休。
　I gave it some serious thought and I've decided to retire.
　經過認真的思考後，我決定要退休。

be transferred to

· be transferred from
被調離⋯

被調到⋯ 被調到同一間公司的其他分公司或部門。

● I heard you will be moving.

● My dad **was transferred to** England.
　●我聽說你要搬家了。　●我爸爸被調到英國了。

▶ Kathy wants to be transferred to Florida.
　Kathy 想被調到佛羅里達州。
　Next month, I'm getting transferred to a new office location. 我下個月會被調到一個新的辦公地點。

be posted to an overseas office

· be assigned to...
被調派到⋯
· foreign/overseas assignment
海外調派

被調派到海外分公司 也可以把 be posted to 換成 be assigned to，意思相同。

● Why did you decide to take a job with Sony?

● I hope to **be posted to Sony's overseas branch**.
　● 為什麼你決定去 Sony 工作？　●我希望能被調到 Sony 海外分公司。

▶ Three employees will be posted to an overseas office.
　有三位員工會被調派到海外分公司。
　No one wants to be posted to the overseas branch.
　沒有人想要被調派到海外分公司。

29 出差
go out of town

1-29.mp3

1 職場・學校

2 電腦・網路

3 社交生活

4 日常生活

5 訊息・理解

6 想法・態度

7 情緒・狀況

8 行為舉止

9 時間地點・副詞片語

go on a business trip

· leave on business
出差

· be on a business trip
出差中

· take sb on a business trip
帶某人一起出差

出差 也可以說 go on a trip for business，意思相同。

● Jack is about to **go on a business trip**.
● Where is he going to travel?

●Jack 正要去出差。　●他要去哪裡？

▶ My uncle went on a business trip to Japan.
我叔叔去日本出差了。
Can you take your wife on the business trip?
你可以帶太太一起出差嗎？

be out of town

· go abroad on business
到國外出差

出差 以出差的名義，去其他地方的意思。

● Can I call you on Friday?
● No, I'll **be out of town** all next week.

●我星期五可以打電話給你嗎？　●不行，我下個星期都在出差。

▶ They are out of town until January 1st.
他們要出差到一月一號才會回來。
I'll be out of town all next week.
我下個星期都在出差。

be out on business

· be away on business for a week
出差一週

因公事外出中，出差中 也可以說 be away on business。

● Can I speak to Randy?
● I'm sorry. He's **out on business** for this week.

●我可以跟 Randy 說話？　●抱歉，他這個星期出差。

▶ Bette is out on business until this afternoon.
Bette 要出差到今天下午才回來。
I'm thrilled. I'm going away on business to Paris next month. 我好緊張，我下個月要去巴黎出差。

go to + 地點 + on business

· travel a lot on business
很常出差

去…出差 地點後面加上「for + 期間」，可以說明出差的時間長度。

● How about we get together next Thursday?
● Sorry. I have to **go to Boston on business** on Thursday.

●我們下週四碰面怎麼樣？　●不好意思，我下週四要去波士頓出差。

▶ I'm going to Japan for a week on business.
我要去日本出差一星期。
I have to go to China on business.
我要去中國出差。

send sb on a business trip

派某人出差 表示公司派某位員工出差執行任務。

● Where is Richard this week?
● Mr. Donnelly **sent him on a business trip**.

●Richard 這禮拜去哪裡了？　●Donnelly 先生派他出差了。

▶ Mary was sent on a business trip to China.
Mary 被派到中國出差了。
My company sent me here on a business trip.
我的公司派我來這邊出差。

be in town on business

· be here on business
來出差
· be in NY on business
去紐約出差
· visit (a place) on business
去（某地）出差

因出差而到某地 把 town 換成 New York 就表示到紐約出差。

● What's the purpose of your visit?
● I'm **visiting on business**.

●你的來訪目的是什麼？　●我來出差的。

▶ Is Roy going to move here?
Roy 要搬來這邊嗎？
No, he is just in town on business.
沒有，他只是來出差的。

come to town on business

· come to town on business for + 時間
來出差（多久）

因出差而來 字面上的意思是「因為出差而進城」，但要注意的是，這邊的 town 並不是指鄉下那種小城鎮，而是「市中心」等商業區。

● I'm going to **come to town on business**.
● Let's meet up for lunch when you come.

●我會來出差。　●你來的時候，我們一起吃個午餐吧。

▶ I came to town on business for my company.
我代表我的公司來出差。
She will come to town on business next month.
她下個月會來出差。

1 職場・學校

2 電腦・網路

3 社交生活

4 日常生活

5 訊息・理解

6 想法・態度

7 情緒・狀況

8 行為舉止

9 時間地點・副詞片語

meet sb on a business trip

· buy sth on a business trip
出差時買某物

出差的時候和某人碰面 在出差的期間，見預定要見的客戶，或是順便見見朋友，都可以這麼說。

● How did you meet your girlfriend?

● I **met her** in California **on a business trip**.

●你怎麼見到你女朋友的？　●我去加州出差時見到她的。

▶ The salesman met his clients on the business trip.
這位業務出差時見了他的客戶。

I may meet some old friends on my business trip.
我出差時可能會遇見一些老朋友。

get back from a business trip

· be home from one's business trip
出差結束後回家

· return from one's business trip
出差回來

出差回來 與 return from a business trip 同義。

● Have you been home long?

● I **got back from a business trip** yesterday.

●你回家很久了嗎？　●我昨天剛出差回來。

▶ We'll get back from our business trip next week.
我們出差到下禮拜回來。

Just wait until I get back from my business trip.
就等到我出差回來吧。

30 經營事業 run a business

1-30.mp3

run a business

· run one's own business
經營自己的事業

· run one's business from one's home
在家創業

經營事業 business 不僅有「事業」的意思，也可以代表「企業」。

● Maybe we should start our own company.

● No, I don't know how to **run a business**.

●也許我們應該開自己的公司。　●不，我不知道該怎麼經營事業。

▶ Mike's family ran a small business.
Mike 的家人經營了一門小生意。

She decided to run a business with her partner.
她決定和她的搭檔一起經營事業。

start a new business

· start (up) one's own business
開始自己的事業
· be in the restaurant business
從事餐廳業

開始新的事業，創業 自己開創一門新的生意。

● Are you going to get a job after you graduate?
● No, I'm going to try **starting up my own business**.
●你畢業後要找工作嗎？ ●不，我要嘗試自行創業。

▶ It takes a lot of money to start a new business.
創業要花很多錢。
I think this is a good time to start our own business.
我想現在是我們創業的好時機。

open a business

· open a clothing store
開一間服飾店
· be open for business
營業中
· close a business
結束事業

開業 把 start 換成 open，意為開業。

● What are those workers building?
● Someone is going to **open a business** there.
●那些工人在蓋什麼？ ●有人要在那邊開業。

▶ Let's open a business together.
讓我們一起開業吧。
He wants to open a business when he graduates.
他畢業後想要開業。

own one's own business

· work for oneself
為了自己工作
→自己當老闆
· be self-employed
自雇的→自由業的
· be one's own boss
自己當老闆

有自己的事業 第一個 own 是動詞，表示「擁有」，第二個 own 則是形容詞，意為「自己的」。

● Rick always seems very busy.
● Well, he **owns his own business**.
●Rick 看起來總是很忙。 ●因為他自己開公司。

▶ The businessman owned his own business.
這位企業家擁有自己的事業。
I'd like to own my own business.
我想要擁有自己的事業。

do business with

· do business internationally
從事國際商務
· do business overseas
在海外做生意

和…做生意 with 的後面可以接有合作關係的人或公司名稱。

● Is your company international?
● We **do business with** people in many countries.
●你的公司國際化嗎？ ●我們和很多國家的人做生意。

▶ I can't do business with my friends.
我沒辦法和朋友做生意。
We stopped doing business with that firm.
我們停止了和那間公司的業務往來。

go into business with

· go into business for oneself
開始自己的生意

和…開始事業關係　把 do 改成 go into，更能生動地表達「投入」、「跳進去」的感覺。

● I invented a new kind of computer.
● You should **go into business with** me.
　　●我發明了一種新的電腦。　　●你應該和我一起做生意。

▶ John went into business with his brothers.
　　John 和他的兄弟一起開業。
　　She found a partner to go into business with.
　　她找到了一個可以一起做生意的夥伴。

expand one's business

擴張某人的事業　expand 這個單字同時涵蓋了 increase（量的增加）和 extend（範圍擴張）的概念，也就是向四面八方擴張。

● It looks like you're selling a lot of things.
● Yes, we're about to **expand our business**.
　　●你們看起來有賣好多種東西。　　●是啊，我們要擴張事業了。

▶ McDonald's is always expanding its business.
　　麥當勞總是在擴張它的事業版圖。
　　Heather expanded her design business.
　　Heather 擴展了她的設計事業。

go out of business

· lose one's business
失去某人的事業

歇業　go out 意為「脫離、離開」，因此這個慣用語是指店家或公司倒閉。

● No one ever goes into that store.
● They'll probably **go out of business**.
　　●那家店從來沒有客人走進去過。　　●他們可能要倒店了。

▶ It went out of business because there was no money.
　　由於資金不足，所以它（公司）倒閉了。
　　Many Internet companies went out of business this year.
　　今年有許多網路公司倒閉。

go bankrupt

· file for bankruptcy
申請破產

破產　go 也可以替換成 be，意義相同。

● You and your wife spend a lot of money.
● I'm afraid we'll **go bankrupt**.
　　●你和你太太花很多錢。　　●我擔心我們會破產。

▶ Our store needs business or we'll go bankrupt.
　　我們的店需要一些生意，不然我們就要破產了。
　　The company went bankrupt last September.
　　這間公司去年九月破產了。

1 職場·學校
2 電腦·網路
3 社交生活
4 日常生活
5 訊息·理解
6 想法·態度
7 情緒·狀況
8 行為舉止
9 時間地點·副詞片語

31 勤務型態
be on a night shift

five-day work week

· be off on every other Saturday
隔週六休假

一週工作五天 由 five-day 和 work week 結合而成的名詞片語。

● The schedule here is pretty nice.
● Yeah, I love a **five-day work week**.

●這日程表很不錯。　●是啊，我很喜歡一週工作五天。

▶ Most businesses have a five-day work week.
大部份的公司都是一週工作五天。
Sharon is too lazy for the five-day work week.
Sharon 太懶惰，不適合一週工作五天。

be on a night shift

· on two shifts
採兩班制
· be on three-shift basis
採三班制

上夜班 白天班稱為 day shift。

● Brian, you look really tired.
● I'm on the night shift this week.

●Brian，你看起來好累。　●我這禮拜是上夜班。

▶ You'll earn more if you're on a night shift.
你上夜班的話，就會賺得更多。
I can't sleep when I'm on a night shift.
我上夜班的時候不能睡覺。

work the late shift

· work two shifts
上兩班，值兩個班

上夜班 也可以說 work the later shift。

● I've worked the late shift for nine years.
● Is it difficult to be up all night?

●我連續九年都是上夜班。　●整晚不睡會不會很難？

▶ My father stays up to work the late shift.
我父親為了上夜班而熬夜。
I quit because I couldn't work the late shift.
我無法上夜班，所以辭職了。

cover one's shift

· cover for sb
  幫某人處理工作

幫某人代班 cover 有「掩護」的意思，由此衍生出「為了幫忙某人，而代替他做某事」的意思。

- I need you to drive me to the airport.
- Someone will need to **cover my shift** at work.
  - ●我需要你載我去機場。　●那需要有人幫我代班。
- ▶ None of the employees could cover my shift.
  沒有任何員工可以幫我代班。
  If you cover my shift, I'll pay you.
  如果你幫我代班，我會付錢給你。

be on call

待命中，值勤中 不論何時，只要打電話就一定能找到人。適用於醫生或消防隊員這種需要隨時待命的職業。

- I'd like to become a doctor.
- Doctors **are on call** 24 hours a day.
  - ●我想要當醫生。　●醫生一天 24 小時都要待命。
- ▶ I'm on call. Let me know if there are problems.
  我在值勤中。如果發生問題請告訴我。
  Who is going to be on call tonight?
  今晚由誰值勤？

work as a temp

· be employed on a
  temporary basis
  被臨時雇用

當臨時工 temp 是從 temporary 衍生出來的名詞，代表臨時雇員。

- My cousin **works as a temp**.
- Does she have a good salary?
  - ●我表妹在當臨時工。　●她的薪水好嗎？
- ▶ I'm only employed here on a temporary basis.
  我只是暫時受雇在這邊工作。
  Some people work as temps until they get better jobs.
  在找到更好的工作之前，有些人會當臨時工。

hire contract workers

· hire workers on a
  contract basis
  以約聘方式雇用員工

雇用約聘員工 contract worker 並非正式職員，而是以約聘方式雇用的員工。通常會協議好工作的期間，時間結束合約就會終止。

- How is the company saving money?
- They decided to **hire contract workers**.
  - ●公司要怎麼節省開銷？　●他們決定要雇用約聘員工。
- ▶ The university hires workers on a contract basis.
  這間大學以約聘的方式雇用員工。
  They hired contract workers at the computer factory.
  他們在電腦工廠雇用約聘員工。

1 職場・學校
2 電腦・網路
3 社交生活
4 日常生活
5 訊息・理解
6 想法・態度
7 情緒・狀況
8 行為舉止
9 時間地點・副詞片語

work freelance from home

· work for oneself as a freelance writer
當自由作家

在家當自由工作者 freelance 可以是形容詞或副詞，指不受公司束縛，獨立接案、自由工作的狀態。

● Everyone needs extra money.
● Some housewives **work freelance from home**.

●每個人都需要額外的錢。　●有些家庭主婦在家當自由工作者。

▶ Mr. Johnson works for himself as a freelance writer.
Johnson 先生以自由作家的身分工作。
I'd prefer to work freelance from home.
我偏好在家當自由工作者。

---

32 | 執行一般業務
give a task

1-32.mp3

---

give sb a task

· give sb another difficult assignment
給某人另一份困難的任務／作業

· be assigned to a job/post
被分配某個工作

給某人任務 task 也可以換成 job 或 assignment，意思相同。

● Can someone clean up this room?
● I'll **give** Elaine **that job**.

●可以來個人打掃這間房間嗎？　●我會交代 Elaine 來打掃。

▶ He gave his students a difficult assignment.
他給了他的學生們一份困難的作業。
Let's give her a fun task to complete.
我們給她一份有趣的任務吧。

complete the work

· finish working on…
完成…的工作

· finish one's work
完成某人的工作

完成工作 complete 除了「完成」的意思以外，也可以用在「填好表格」的情況。

● Have you finished your report?
● I worked all night, but I didn't **complete the work**.

●你報告做完了嗎？　●我弄了一整晚，但沒做完。

▶ You can complete the work tomorrow.
你可以明天再把工作完成
Jay completed the work his boss gave him.
Jay 把他老闆交付的工作做完了。

send the proposal

· send the proposal via e-mail
用電子郵件寄送提案

寄送提案 後面接「to...」可以說明寄送的對象或目的地。

● We need to **send the proposal** today.
● We're almost finished with it.

　　●我們得在今天寄出提案。　●我們差不多要完成了。

▶ Can you send the proposal via e-mail?
你可以用電子郵件寄出提案嗎？
Send the proposal to my bank.
把提案送到我的銀行來。

make a copy of

· make copies of...
影印…

· make some copies
影印幾份

影印… 複數形態 make copies of 表示影印很多份。

● What are those papers you're carrying?
● I have to **make copies of** some files.

　　●你拿的那些紙是什麼？　●我要影印一些檔案。

▶ Make some copies of your passport.
把你的護照影印幾份。
Jen made copies of her study sheets.
Jen 把她的學習單影印了幾份。

run errands

· go to a bank on an errand
去銀行辦事

· send sb on errands
派某人跑腿

· be on an errand
正在跑腿中

跑腿，辦雜事 如果要辦的事不止一件，可以說 run a couple of errands。

● Do you have a busy weekend planned?
● Not really. I need to **run some errands**.

　　●你的週末計畫很忙碌嗎？　●還好，我要辦幾件雜事。

▶ My boss always makes me run errands.
我老闆總是要我跑腿。
I'm going to run some errands in my new car.
我要開我的新車去辦點雜事。

neglect one's work

· lie down on the job
（工作時）摸魚，打混
（如果是在學校的話，可以說 play truant）

· goof off on the job
遊手好閒，逃避工作

疏忽工作 neglect 的意思是「pay little attention」（不太注意）。

● Why were those guys fired?
● They had begun to **neglect their work**.

　　●為什麼那些人被解雇了？　●他們開始疏忽工作。

▶ I can't leave and neglect my work.
我沒辦法離開並忽略我的工作。
This bad grade is because you neglected your work.
你得到這麼差的成績是因為疏於學習。

1 職場・學校

2 電腦・網路

3 社交生活

4 日常生活

5 訊息・理解

6 想法・態度

7 情緒・狀況

8 行為舉止

9 時間地點・副詞片語

be on strike

· nationwide strike
全國性的罷工
· public sector strike
公務員罷工

罷工中 「計畫罷工」的說法是 plan/organize a strike。strike 也可以換成 walkout，意思相同。

● The workers in Paris **were on strike**.
● I heard they closed the subway.

●巴黎的勞工之前在罷工。　●我聽說他們關閉了地鐵。

▶ The whole company will be on strike tomorrow.
全公司明天都會罷工。
The workers on strike marched down the street.
罷工的勞工們沿著街道遊行。

---

 copy 的各種意義

　　隨著電腦的普及，copy 這個已經成為十分常用的單字。但如果把 copy 當成名詞使用呢？這時 copy 代表由原稿複製而成的「副本」，或是書報雜誌等的「一份、一本、一冊」。因此，如果想跟空服員要一份報紙，我們可以說「Can I get a copy of the New York Times?」；如果想要一份今天的會議行程表，則可以說「Can I have a copy of the schedule for today's meeting?」。讓我們再回到 copy 的動詞用法。見到祕書，想要她幫忙影印的時候，我們可以說「I need you to copy these documents.」。如果有某個文件不能影印，否則有觸法之虞時，則可以說「Don't copy that. It's against the law.」。

---

33 會議
have a meeting

1-32.mp3

have a meeting

· have a meeting
scheduled for…
在（時間）有個會議
· There's a meeting
scheduled for…
在（時間）有個會議
· have an important
meeting in…
在（某處）有個重要的會議

開會 have 也可以換成另一個動詞 hold，意思相同。

● Why are you taking me to the board room?
● **There is a meeting** there for all directors.

●你為什麼要帶我到會議室？　●那邊有個主管會議。

▶ I have an important meeting in ten minutes. I've got to run. 我十分鐘後有個重要的會議，我得趕緊過去。
You've got a meeting at three. 你三點有個會議。

schedule a meeting

· schedule a meeting
  with sb
  安排和某人開會的時間
· be set for + 時間
  （會議）定在某個時間

安排會議 後面加上 with sb，可以說明和誰一起開會。

● What time is **the meeting scheduled** for?
● It will be at 5 P.M. this afternoon.
  ●會議安排在幾點進行？　●今天下午五點。

▶ Schedule a meeting with my secretary.
  安排跟我的祕書開會的時間。
  I need to schedule a meeting with you.
  我需要安排跟你開會的時間。

go to a meeting

· attend a meeting
  參加會議
· show up at the
  meeting
  出席會議
· participate in a
  meeting/seminar/
  conference
  參加會議

參加會議 go to 可以換成 attend。meeting 可以換成 seminar，表示參加研討會。

● **Are** you **going to the staff meeting** tonight?
● I might show up at the end of the meeting.
  ●你今晚會參加員工會議嗎？　●會議快結束的時候我可能會到。

▶ Are you going to attend the meeting?
  你會去參加會議嗎？
  I can't believe you never showed up at the meeting.
  我真不敢相信你完全沒有出席會議。

be in a meeting

· be at a seminar
  正在參加研討會
· be busy with meetings
  忙著開會
· be in the middle of a
  meeting
  開會中

開會中 in 可以換成 in the middle of，意思相同。

● Is Louis in the office today?
● He is, but he **is in a meeting** right now.
  ●Louis 今天在辦公室嗎？　●他在，不過他正在開會。

▶ He's in a meeting right now.
  他正在開會。
  I'm in a meeting all morning, but I'm free after two
  o'clock. 我整個早上都在開會，不過我下午兩點之後沒事。

start the meeting

· close/finish a meeting
  結束會議
· call a meeting
  召集會議
· a meeting begins
  會議開始
· begin the meeting
  開始會議

開始會議 也可以說 begin the meeting，意思一樣。

● Do you know what time **the meeting begins**
  tomorrow morning?
● I was told that it would start at ten-thirty.
  ●你知道明天早上會議幾點開始嗎？　●有人跟我說十點半開始。

▶ Let's start the meeting after lunch.
  我們午餐後開始開會吧。
  It's time to get started with the meeting.
  是時候開始會議了。

1 職場・學校
2 電腦・網路
3 社交生活
4 日常生活
5 訊息・理解
6 想法・態度
7 情緒・狀況
8 行為舉止
9 時間地點・副詞片語

cancel a meeting

- · miss a meeting
  錯過會議
- · leave in the middle of the meeting
  在會議途中離開
- · be late to the meeting
  開會遲到

取消會議 也常用被動態 be cancelled，表示被取消。

- ● The manager had to leave suddenly.
- ● That means we must **cancel the meeting**.
  - ● 主管忽然必須離開。　● 那意味著我們一定要取消會議了。

▶ I couldn't believe that Jack left in the middle of the meeting. 我真不敢相信 Jack 在會議途中就離開了。
  I don't want to be late to the meeting again.
  我不想再開會遲到了。

take notes for a meeting

- · keep the minutes
  做紀錄
- · do the minutes for a meeting
  做會議紀錄
- · summarize the meeting
  總結會議

記錄會議內容 summarize a meeting 則表示為會議做總結。

- ● Would you stay and **take notes for the meeting**?
- ● Sure, I've got my notebook computer right here.
  - ● 你可以留下來做會議紀錄嗎？
  - ● 當然可以，我手邊就有筆記型電腦。

▶ Our secretary usually takes notes for our meetings.
  我們的祕書通常會幫我們做會議紀錄。
  Who will take notes for the meeting?
  誰會負責做會議紀錄？

 各式各樣的會議類型

　　說到會議，第一個浮現在腦海裡的應該就是 meeting 這個字吧？不過，依照會議的性質、規模和參加者身分的不同，還有以下各種類型。

　　conference：由政黨或企業等因為利害關係而聚集在一起的人召開，也許需要花上好幾天的大規模正式會議。

　　convention：集會、大會。集合了業界中的專家們所開設的大規模會議。會議頻率通常為一年一次。

　　brainstorming：集體研討會、腦力激盪。也是會議類型的一種，所有與會人依序提出意見，從中選出最好的一個點子之後結案。

　　presentation：發表會、簡報

　　其他還有 staff meeting（員工大會）、shareholders' meeting（股東大會）、sales meeting（銷售會議），budget meeting（預算會議）等等。

34 | 簡報，報告
write a report

1-34.mp3

1 職場・學校

2 電腦・網路

3 社交生活

4 日常生活

5 訊息・理解

6 想法・態度

7 情緒・狀況

8 行為舉止

9 時間地點・副詞片語

write a report

· write this report
  寫這份報告
· receive a monthly report
  收到月報
· finish (up) the report
  完成報告

寫報告 report 可以指在學校寫的報告，也可以指公司的報告書。

● What if we don't **finish the report** before tomorrow morning?
● Then we'll have to face an angry boss.
  ● 如果我們明天早上之前沒把報告完成，會怎麼樣？
  ● 那我們就要面對憤怒的老闆了。

▶ Here is the report that I wrote for you.
  這是我寫給你的報告。
  It'll take you about ten minutes to finish the report you are working on. 你大概還需要十分鐘才能完成你在做的報告。

put together a report

· put one's presentation together
  準備簡報

整理報告 put together 有「組合（零件）」的意思。在此引申為「匯整內容，做成一份報告」。

● What has that team been working on?
● They are trying to **put together a report**.
  ● 那個團隊在忙什麼？ ● 他們正努力整理出一份報告。

▶ We put together a report in five hours.
  我們在五小時之內整理了一份報告。
  I need you and Gene to put together a report.
  我需要你和 Gene 去整理一份報告。

give a speech

· make a speech
  演講
· a speech on/about
  關於…的演講

發表演說 give 也可以換成 make 或 deliver。

● I don't want to **give a speech** in the meeting.
● Why? I think you are an excellent speaker.
  ● 我不想在會議上演講。 ● 為什麼？我覺得你是個很棒的演說家。

▶ I have to make a speech tonight.
  我今晚要發表演說。
  Did he ask you to make a speech at the conference?
  他有要求你在會議上發表演說嗎？

prepare for one's presentation

· have a presentation to give in + 時間
在多少時間之後有一場簡報

· be ready for the presentation
準備好要發表簡報

準備簡報 為了讓簡報順利進行而做事前準備。

● Is everything **ready for the presentation**?
● Let me make sure.
　●簡報都準備妥當了嗎？　●讓我確認一下。

▶ I must prepare for my presentation.
　我必須準備我的簡報。
　Jill spent hours preparing for her presentation.
　Jill 花了好幾個小時準備她的簡報。

work on one's presentation

· practice one's presentation with a laptop
用筆記型電腦練習某人的簡報

· prepare the projector for the presentation
為簡報準備投影機

準備某人的簡報 準備要報告的內容。

● How long will you **work on your presentation** for the boss?
● I'm going to be up all night writing it.
　●你會花多久時間準備對上司的簡報？　●我會熬夜一整晚寫內容。

▶ I worked on my presentation for the meeting.
　我準備了要在會議上發表的簡報。
　Each student worked on his presentation for the class.
　每個學生都準備了自己的課堂報告。

give a presentation on

· complete/finish a presentation
完成簡報

· wind up a briefing successfully
成功地結束簡報

發表關於…的簡報 give 也可以換成 do 或 make，意思相同。

● What is the subject of today's meeting?
● Someone **is giving a presentation on** cooking.
　●今天會議的主題是什麼？　●有人要發表關於烹飪的報告。

▶ Our teacher is giving a presentation on science.
　我們老師正在發表科學報告。
▶ Let's get together after I finish giving the presentation.
　等我報告完，我們聚一下吧。

do a presentation

· do a presentation on/about
進行關於…的簡報

· make the presentation
做簡報

· make a lot of presentations
做很多場簡報

進行簡報 在會議室中，站在人群面前進行簡報。

● I **did a presentation** at the museum.
● What topic did you talk about?
　●我在博物館進行了一場簡報。　●你談的主題是什麼？

▶ Mrs. Cliff did a presentation for the audience.
　Cliff 女士為觀眾們做了一場簡報。
▶ I just don't think I can do this presentation today!
　我覺得我今天沒辦法發表簡報！

cancel the presentation

· complete the presentation
  完成簡報

取消簡報 和取消會議一樣，動詞都是 cancel。

● Many people are absent because of the storm.
● We will need to **cancel the presentation**.

　●很多人因為暴風雪而缺席了。　●我們需要取消簡報。

▶ He cancelled the presentation because he didn't prepare. 他因為沒有準備，所以取消了簡報。
The speaker decided to cancel the presentation.
這位演說者決定取消簡報。

present the report

· present one's idea
  發表某人的意見

發表報告 present 可以理解為「 do the presentation of 」。

● I need to **present a report** in the morning.
● Have you prepared your materials?

　●我今天早上需要發表一份報告。　●你準備好資料了嗎？

▶ Joe presented his ideas to the class.
Joe 向課堂上的同學發表他的意見。
How much time do you need to present the report?
你需要多少時間發表報告？

---

35 交易，簽約，做生意
deal with

1-35.mp3

deal with

· sign a deal with
  和⋯簽約

和⋯做交易 這個片語通常引申為「交易」以外的意思。deal with sb 表示與人相處，而 deal with sth 則是處理、應付事情。

● Did they **sign the deal** yet?
● No, they're still waiting for a house inspection.

　●他們簽約了嗎？　●還沒，他們還在等房屋檢查。

▶ We made a deal with an overseas company.
我們和一間海外公司做了一筆生意。
I'm sure that he'll return our calls and sign a deal with us. 我相信他會回電給我們並且簽約。

1 職場・學校
2 電腦・網路
3 社交生活
4 日常生活
5 訊息・理解
6 想法・態度
7 情緒・狀況
8 行為舉止
9 時間地點・副詞片語

close a deal

- cut/strike/make a deal
  簽署合約
- complete a deal
  完成交易
- blow a deal
  搞砸交易

結案，成交 這裡的 close 指圓滿達成契約協議。

- This is amazing! We may **close the deal** tonight.
- Settle down, we have to think straight.

  ●這太棒了！我們今晚也許能成交。　　●冷靜點，我們必須好好思考。

▶ You told me you were going to Chicago to close a deal.

  你跟我說你要去芝加哥結案。

  I hope that she doesn't blow the deal tomorrow.

  我希望她明天不會把交易給搞砸。

open an account

- land the Holdman account
  獲得 Holdman 這個客戶
- have an account with
  在…有戶頭
- get an account
  得到客戶

開戶，開始交易 這邊的 account 可以指 business account，也就是客戶。

- Tony just has **opened the first account** in China.
- That'll really open up the Chinese market to us.

  ●Tony 剛開始和第一位中國客戶做生意。

  ●那真的會幫我們打開中國市場。

▶ I need to talk to you about the Halverson account.

  我需要跟你談談 Halverson 這個客戶。

  Tom opened an account at the stockbroker's firm.

  Tom 在證券公司開了一個戶頭。

lose an account

- handle one's account
  處理某人的客戶

失去客戶 相對於 get an account 而言，表示失去客戶。

- Why does Sarah look so upset?
- She **lost one of her big accounts**.

  ●Sarah 為什麼看起來那麼苦惱？　　●她失去了一個大客戶。

▶ We're looking for someone to handle our account in India. 我們正在尋找一位可以處理我們印度客戶的人。

  Why do you think we lost the Miller account?

  你為什麼覺得我們失去了 Miller 這個客戶？

sign a contract for

- be under contract
  有合約關係
- make a contract with
  和…簽約
- get/win the contract
  得到合約

簽…的合約 直譯為「在合約上簽名」，因此就是「簽約」的意思。

- I guess he **got the contract**.
- I thought he was in a particularly good mood.

  ●我猜他得到合約了。　　●我覺得他心情特別好。

▶ I'm pleased to announce that we won the contract.

  我很高興宣布我們得到合約了。

  Sally came by and said that she didn't get the contract.

  Sally 順道過來說她沒有得到那個合約。

1 職場・學校

2 電腦・網路

3 社交生活

4 日常生活

5 訊息・理解

6 想法・態度

7 情緒・狀況

8 行為舉止

9 時間地點・副詞片語

lose the contract

失去合約 沒有取得新的合約，或者失去了原有的合約。

- I'm not kidding, we **lost the contract**.
- What are we going to tell the boss?

  ●我不是在開玩笑，我們失去這個合約了。　●我們該怎麼跟老闆說？

▶ The firm lost their contract in Japan.

這間公司失去了他們在日本的合約。

If you fail again, you'll lose the contract.

如果你再失敗，你會失去這個合約。

trade in A with B

· trade in rice with
Thailand
和泰國做白米買賣

和 B 做 A 的生意 get into trade 則表示開始交易。

- What kind of sales do you do?
- I **trade in** clothing **with** the Brazilians.

  ●你做的是什麼樣的業務？　●我和巴西人做服飾買賣。

▶ The companies trade in tea with China.

這些公司和中國做茶葉買賣。

We trade in cars with the Middle East.

我們和中東做汽車貿易。

trade in A for B

· trade in a used car for
a new model
將中古車折價貼現，換一
台新款的

貼補差額後把 A 換成 B trade-in value 是指二手商品的剩餘價值。

- I **traded in** my old phone **for** a new one.
- Wow. That looks really cool!

  ●我把我的舊手機貼了一些錢，換了一台新的。

  ●哇，新手機看起來真酷！

▶ I want to trade in my computer for a smart phone.

我想要把我的電腦貼一些錢，去換一支智慧型手機。

He'll trade in his motorcycle for a car next year.

他明年要把他的摩托車貼一些錢，拿去換汽車。

---

 deal with 的追加說明

　　不止是在商業範圍，deal 這個字也常以各種意義廣泛運用在日常生活中，是個很重要的單字。它雖然常以名詞形態出現，不過動詞片語 deal with 也很常用。deal with 有許多意思，最常見的就是「應付、處理」問題，以及「做生意」（do business with）。cope with（對付、處理）也是類似的用法，同樣代表去處理一件棘手的事或問題，但通常用在成功、有效的狀況下。She's hard to deal with 表示她這個人很難相處、很難對付。I can't deal with the raw stuff 就不能說是生食很難對付了，而是「我沒辦法生吃食物」的意思。I can deal with it 則是表示有能力處理一件事。

36 打折
go on sale

1-36.mp3

have a sale

· have a sale on sth
  舉行某物的打折拍賣

舉行打折拍賣 後面加上 on sth 可以說明打折商品的種類。
- There are a lot of people outside the store.
- The store **is having a big sale** today.
  - 有好多人在這間店外面。　● 這間店今天在舉行大拍賣。

▶ The florist was having a sale on lilacs.
   這間花店的紫丁香有打折。
   I've got to go save 50%. Barney's is having a sale.
   我要去省 50% 的錢。Barney's 正在打折。

be on sale

· be on sale
  販賣中，打折中
· be for sale
  待售（沒有打折的意思）
· be a rip-off
  是假貨

在打折 可以表示商品販賣中，也可以表示正在打折。
- We can't afford a new washing machine.
- They**'re going on sale** next week.
  - 我們買不起新的洗衣機。　● 下禮拜會打折。

▶ The digital TVs are on sale.
   數位電視在打折。
   Many items are on sale before Christmas.
   耶誕節前，很多商品都在打折。

get sth on sale

· get sth at a bargain
  sale
  在特價拍賣時買到某物

以折扣價格買到某物 也就是在打折的時候買下某物。
- Honey, this is for you. I **got it on sale**.
- You're so sweet.
  - 親愛的，這是送你的。我在折扣時買到的。　● 你真貼心。

▶ Kelly got a Rolex watch on sale.
   Kelly 在打折時買到一隻勞力士。
   I got it on sale at a department store.
   我在百貨公司打折時買到的。

give a discount

- give a 10 percent discount
  給予 10% 的折扣

給予折扣 相反的，得到折扣的那方則是 get a discount。

- Can you **give me a discount** for paying cash?
- Let me talk to my boss.

  ●我付現的話，可以打折嗎？　●讓我跟我老闆説一下。

▶ You'll get a discount if you pay in cash.
  如果付現的話，你將獲得折扣。
  I can only give you a discount if you buy more than ten.
  買超過十個我才能給你折扣。

use ten percent off coupon

- 'buy one get one free' sale
  買一送一特賣

使用九折券 說明了折價券的折扣內容。

- We can order the toys online.
- Let's **use a ten percent off coupon**.

  ●我們可以在網路上訂購玩具。　●我們用九折券吧。

▶ The ten percent off coupon is for this site.
  這張九折券是供這個網站使用的。
  We need to find a ten percent off coupon.
  我們需要找到一張九折券。

1 職場・學校
2 電腦・網路
3 社交生活
4 日常生活
5 訊息・理解
6 想法・態度
7 情緒・狀況
8 行為舉止
9 時間地點・副詞片語

37 購買 buy sth for...

1-37.mp3

buy sth for...

- buy sb sth
  買某物給某人
- I'm just browsing.
  我只是看看。
- be a good buy
  （某物）很划算

購買 for 後面接人或活動，表示「為了…購買」；如果接價格，表示以某個價格購買。改成 at 的話，則表示購買的地點。

- I'm in charge of **buying the beer for** the party.
- That sounds like an expensive responsibility!

  ●我負責買派對要用的啤酒。　●聽起來是個很花錢的任務！

▶ I need to buy a gift for my mother.
  我需要買個禮物給媽媽。
  I bought it at the duty-free counter at the airport in Chicago. 我在芝加哥機場的免稅品商店買到這個。

get sth at/from

· pick up sth
買某物

· free of charge
免費

· for nothing (= for free)
免費

在某處買了某物 說明一件商品購買的地點。

● I wanted to **pick up** some of the golf balls you had on sale.

● I'm sorry we're sold out.

●我想要買幾顆你們在打折的高爾夫球。 ●不好意思，我們賣完了。

▶ I got this dress at Macy's.

我在 Macy's 買了這件洋裝。

She got make-up from the Internet.

她在網路上買了化妝品。

purchase a new BMW

· make a purchase
購買

買一台新的 BMW purchase 是比 buy 更正式的說法。

● Did you **purchase** the house you were looking at?

● Yes, we did. It's a done deal.

●你們買了之前在看的房子嗎？ ●嗯，買了，已經成交了。

▶ I'd like to purchase 20 computer software programs.

我想要買 20 套電腦軟體程式。

We'll call you if we decide to purchase life insurance.

如果我們決定要買壽險，我們會打電話給你。

make an online purchase

· purchase sth over the Internet
在網路上購買某物

· buy sth online at…
在（某個網站）購物

線上購物 在網路上購買商品。

● Many people want to **make online purchases**.

● Yeah, I like shopping on the Internet.

●很多人都想在網路上購物。 ●是啊，我喜歡在網路上買東西。

▶ Have you ever purchased anything over the Internet?

你在網路上買過東西嗎？

Why don't you buy her something online at Amazon?

你為什麼不在 Amazon 的網站上買東西給她呢？

send away for

· send for
訂購，派人請…來

· place an order for…
下…的訂單

郵購 原本是郵購的意思，隨著網路的普及，這個慣用語也漸漸用來表示網路購物了。

● I **sent away for** some new glasses.

● Are you sure they will fit you?

●我用郵購訂了幾副新眼鏡。 ●你確定它們適合你嗎？

▶ The students sent away for their books.

學生們用郵購方式買了書。

Did you send away for this picture?

你郵購了這幅畫嗎？

1 職場・學校
2 電腦・網路
3 社交生活
4 日常生活
5 訊息・理解
6 想法・態度
7 情緒・狀況
8 行為舉止
9 時間地點・副詞片語

38 販賣 be sold out

1-38.mp3

sell sth for...

- sell sth for + 價格
  以某個價格賣出某物
- sell sth at the price of...
  以某個價格賣出某物
- sell sb sth
  賣某物給某人（sell sth to sb）

以某個價格賣出某物 for 的後面接賣價。

- Did you compare the prices of the 55 inch LED TVs at the site?
- Yeah, one vendor **sells it at the price of** 3,000 dollars.
  - 你在那個網站上比較過 55 吋液晶電視的價格了嗎？
  - 嗯，有一間店賣三千美元。

▶ He's not going to sell his car for one thousand dollars.
他不會用一千美元賣掉他的車。
He was born to sell things. He could sell an Eskimo ice.
他是天生的銷售員。他連愛斯基摩的冰都賣得出去吧。

be sold out

- be sold at a certain price
  以特定價格出售
- （商品）sell well
  商品賣得很好

賣完，售罄 在這種狀況下，商店的櫥窗上會貼出「SOLD OUT」。

- Can I get one of those necklaces?
- I'm sorry, but they **are all sold out**.
  - 那些項鍊，我可以買一條嗎？ ● 不好意思，但它們已經賣完了。

▶ It's going to sell quickly.
那會賣得很快。
The store sold out of the new computer game.
那間店的新電腦遊戲賣光了。

carry + 商品

- （商店）sell sth
  某商店有賣某物

有售，販賣 carry 的後面接商品名稱，表示店裡有賣某個東西。

- Do you **carry** ink cartridges?
- Yes, are you looking for a particular kind?
  - 你們賣墨水匣嗎？ ● 有，你在找特定的種類嗎？

▶ The grocery store carries our favorite foods.
那間雜貨店有賣我們最喜歡的食物。
I'm sorry, we don't carry that brand.
不好意思，我們沒賣那個牌子。

have sth in stock

· sth be out of stock
  某物沒有庫存

有某物的庫存 有庫存是 in stock，沒有庫存則是 out of stock。
- This is a hot sale item nowadays.
- Do you **have** any more **in stock**?
  - 這東西最近很熱賣。　●你們還有更多庫存嗎？

▶ I'll check to see if we have any in stock.
  我去確認看看我們還有沒有任何庫存。
  Let me see if we have that kind in stock.
  我來看看我們有沒有那種的庫存。

sell sth on the Internet

在網路上販賣某物 在網路上販賣，介系詞可以用 on 或 over。
- How did Don sell his sports car?
- He **sold** the car **on the Internet**.
  - Don 是怎麼賣掉他的跑車的？　●他在網路上賣掉的。

▶ It's a good idea to sell used books over the Internet.
  在網路上賣二手書是個好主意。
  He's trying to sell socks on the Internet.
  他試著在網路上賣襪子。

39 退換貨 exchange A for B

1-39.mp3

send the wrong order

· return the wrong order
  退回送錯的貨品

送錯貨 因為過程中的失誤而錯送了其他顧客訂的東西。
- Has your package come in the mail yet?
- No, the company **sent the wrong order**.
  - 你收到你的包裹了嗎？　●沒有，那間公司送錯了。

▶ It was returned when they sent the wrong order.
  他們送錯貨的時候，貨品就被退回了。
  Be careful not to send the wrong order.
  小心不要送錯商品。

take sth back

· return + 貨品
　退貨

將某物帶回購買處退貨 也可以說 return sth。

- This radio broke after only two days.
- **Take it back** and get a refund.

　●這台收音機才買兩天就壞了。　●把它拿回店裡退錢。

▶ Mom took our present back to the store.
　媽媽把我們的禮物拿回去店裡退貨了。
　Let's take these sneakers back.
　我們把這雙球鞋拿回去退貨吧。

exchange A for B

· make an exchange
　換貨

把 A 換成 B 如果不指明是換成什麼，可以改成 for something else。

- Did you return the present you got?
- Yeah, I **exchanged it for** a new coat.

　●你把收到的禮物拿去退貨了嗎？　●嗯，我換了一件新大衣。

▶ Do you want to return the item or just exchange it?
　你想要退貨還是換貨？
　I'd like to exchange this for something else.
　我想要把這個換成其他東西。

refund for sth

· have/get a refund for sth
　得到某物的退款
· refund sb money
　退給某人錢
· refund in full
　全額退款

某物的退款 退回貨品時拿回來的錢。

- Can I **get a full refund for** this?
- Certainly, if you have your receipt.

　●我可以獲得這個的全額退款嗎？　●當然，只要你有收據就行。

▶ Rico got a refund for the broken stove.
　Rico 得到了他壞掉的爐子的退款。
　Can I have a refund for this shirt?
　我這件襯衫可以退錢嗎？

get one's money back

· would like one's money back
　想要把某人的錢拿回來

把錢拿回來 表示得到店家退款，或者收回借款。

- **I'd like my money back**, please.
- Was there a problem with this item?

　●我想要退款。　●這件商品有什麼問題嗎？

▶ Gina got her money back from her friend.
　Gina 從她朋友那邊拿回了錢。
　They wouldn't give me my money back.
　他們不會把錢還我的。

1 職場・學校
2 電腦・網路
3 社交生活
4 日常生活
5 訊息・理解
6 想法・態度
7 情緒・狀況
8 行為舉止
9 時間地點・副詞片語

40 投資
invest in

invest in

- invest in real estate
  投資不動產
- invest in the stock market
  投資股票市場

投資⋯ 如果用名詞形，則說「make an investment」。

- I'm not sure what to do with my money.
- You should **invest in** our company.
  - 我不知道該怎麼處理我的錢。　●你應該投資我們公司。

▶ Many people don't want to invest in stocks.
很多人不想要投資股票。
I decided to invest in real estate.
我決定投資不動產。

invest one's money in

- invest my savings in this company
  把我的存款投資在這間公司上
- invest his capital in mines
  將他的資產投資在礦業上
- investment bank
  投資銀行

把某人的錢投資於⋯ in 後面可以接公司名稱或投資的地點。

- My father **invested his money in** Samsung.
- Did he make a lot of profit?
  - 我爸爸把錢投資在三星上。　●他有得到很多利潤嗎？

▶ He invested his money in his own business.
他把錢投資在自己的事業上。
You can invest your money in bonds.
你可以把錢投資在債券上。

play the market

- invest in the stock market
  投資股票

在股市進行投機買賣 雖然有點令人意外，但這裡的動詞是用 play。

- You always read about stocks.
- Well, I enjoy **playing the market**.
  - 你總是在讀跟股票有關的東西。　●因為我很喜歡玩股票。

▶ They lost their money playing the market.
他們玩股票賠了錢。
Frieda plays the market with her salary.
Frieda 用她的薪水玩股票。

put money into...

把錢投資在… into 後面接名詞或動詞 -ing 形。

- Should I **put money into** this company?
- Yes, I think it's a safe thing to do.

  ●我該把錢投資在這間公司嗎？　●嗯，我覺得這是個安全的做法。

▶ We plan to put money in investments.

我們計畫把錢拿去投資。

Sam put his money into buying a house.

Sam 把錢用來買房子。

lose one's money

- lose a lot of money in the stock market
  在股票市場賠很多錢
- lose money in mutual funds
  投資共同基金賠錢

輸錢，賠錢　後面可以接動詞 -ing 形，表示因為做了某件事而賠錢。

- William's family **lost all of their money**.
- It is very risky to invest in the stock market.

  ●William 一家人賠掉了所有的錢。　●投資股票是很冒險的。

▶ She lost some of her money on Wall Street.

她在華爾街（指美國股市）賠了一些錢。

We all lost our money investing in mutual funds.

我們都因為投資共同基金賠了錢。

41 節約，省錢
save money

1-40.mp3

save money

- save money for a rainy day
  未雨綢繆
- spare no efforts
  不遺餘力

省錢　save 這個動詞可以表示省錢或者省時（save time）。意義相近的動詞 spare 常接「no ＋名詞」，表示「不吝惜…」。

- Are you traveling to Hawaii?
- No, we're trying to **save money**.

  ●你們會去夏威夷旅行嗎？　●不會，我們在努力省錢。

▶ I stopped smoking to save money!

我為了省錢而戒煙了！

The duty-free shop is a good place to save money.

免稅店是個省錢的好地方。

1 職場・學校
2 電腦・網路
3 社交生活
4 日常生活
5 訊息・理解
6 想法・態度
7 情緒・狀況
8 行為舉止
9 時間地點・副詞片語

cut back on

- cut back on spending
  減少支出
- cut down on cigarette
  減少抽菸

削減…，減少… 減少成本或支出。如果是為了健康而少做某事，則說 cut down on。

- Let's **cut back on** eating out.
- But I really like eating in restaurants.
  - ●我們減少外食的次數吧。　●可是我真的很喜歡在餐廳吃飯。

▶ Maybe next month we can cut back on a few things.
也許下個月我們可以在一些事情上減少支出。
We're going to cut back on shopping too.
我們也要減少購物。

cut off

- cut corners
  （費用等）去除不必要的部分
- » cf. cut it out!
  別鬧了！停止！
  （= knock it out）

切斷，削減 意為 shorten by cutting。cut out 則是 remove by cutting 的意思。

- How did Shelly save money this year?
- She had to **cut off** all of her extra expenses.
  - ●Shelly 今年怎麼省錢的？　●她削減了所有額外開銷。

▶ He is cutting corners to save cash.
他削減經費以節省現金。
Jerry cut off one of his buttons.
Jerry 剪掉了一顆扣子。

waste money

浪費錢 「浪費時間」可以說 waste one's time。

- Many people like to go to nightclubs.
- They **are** just **wasting money**.
  - ●很多人喜歡去夜店。　●他們只是在浪費錢。

▶ Don't waste your money on candy.
別把你的錢浪費在買糖果上面。
They waste money buying comic books.
他們浪費錢買漫畫書。

conserve sth

- conserve goods/
  resources
  節省商品／資源
- energy conservation
  節省能源

節省某物 節省使用物品或資源的意思。

- We don't have much food left.
- We'll have to **conserve** food until tomorrow.
  - ●我們的食物所剩不多了。　●在明天之前，我們必須節省食物。

▶ The family conserved money because of the bad economy. 由於經濟不景氣，這個家庭節約用錢。
Let's conserve our energy until the race.
在比賽之前，讓我們儲備體力吧。

42 賺錢
make money

1-42.mp3

1 職場・學校

2 電腦・網路

3 社交生活

4 日常生活

5 訊息・理解

6 想法・態度

7 情緒・狀況

8 行為舉止

9 時間地點・副詞片語

make money

· make a little money
  賺一點錢
· make more money
  賺更多錢

賺錢 加上 some / a little，表示賺了一點錢。加上 more/extra 的話，就表示賺更多錢。

● I want to **make money** and be comfortable.

● You need to work hard to become rich.

● 我想要賺錢，過舒適的生活。　● 你需要努力工作變有錢。

▶ Some people make money easily.
有些人賺錢很容易。
How can we make some money?
我們該怎麼賺錢？

earn a lot of money

· earn a good salary
  領很好的薪水

賺很多錢 跟 make a fortune 是一樣的意思。

● James **earned a lot of money** as a lawyer.

● We should have gone to law school.

● James 當律師賺了很多錢。　● 我們當初真該念法學院的。

▶ You won't earn a lot of money working here.
你在這邊工作賺不了什麼錢的。
Korea earned a lot of money exporting items.
韓國靠出口商品賺了很多錢。

make a living

· earn a living
  謀生
· do for a living
  為了生活而工作

賺生活費，謀生 動詞 make 也可以換成 earn。

● How will you **make a living**?

● I think I'll become a teacher.

● 你要怎麼謀生？　● 我想我會當老師。

▶ I work my butt off to make a living.
我十分努力工作賺錢謀生。
I have to earn a living and pay the rent.
我必須賺錢謀生並支付房租。

make a fortune

· make a killing
  大賺一筆

賺一大筆錢，變成有錢人 fortune 除了「運氣」以外，也有「財產」的意思。make 也可以換成 have，表示很有錢。

- Bill Gates got rich selling his software programs.
- That's right. He **made a fortune** on them.
  - 比爾蓋茲藉由銷售他的軟體程式，變成了大富翁。
  - 沒錯，他靠軟體賺了很多錢。

▶ You're too lazy to make a fortune.
  你太懶了，賺不了大錢。
  Rob made a fortune while living overseas.
  Rob 住在國外時賺了一大筆錢。

rake in money

迅速或大量地取得錢財 rake 原意為「耙」，因而這個片語表示「像是在耙樹葉一般，把錢通通掃進來」。

- Your business is doing very well.
- That's right. We're **raking in the money**.
  - 你們的事業十分順利。　　● 沒錯，我們很賺錢。

▶ Bob rakes in money with his new job.
  Bob 靠著新工作賺進很多錢。
  A few years ago brokers were raking in money.
  幾年前，股票經紀人賺了很多錢。

cash in on

靠…賺錢 除了「賺錢」的含義以外，這個片語也帶有「利用」的意思。

- Johnny Depp does a lot of advertisements.
- I guess he's **cashing in on** his fame.
  - 強尼戴普拍了很多廣告。　　● 我想他靠他的名氣賺了很多錢吧。

▶ Rindy cashed in on her banking knowledge.
  Rindy 靠著她的銀行知識賺了很多錢。
  I'd like to cash in on the gold coins I have.
  我想用我的金幣來賺點現金。

get rich

· become a millionaire
  成為百萬富翁
· be well-off/well-to-do
  富裕，富有

變有錢 get 的後面接形容詞，表示「變得…」的意思。

- How did Sally **get rich**?
- She owned a real estate company.
  - Sally 怎麼變有錢的？　　● 她擁有一間不動產公司。

▶ Most people dream about getting rich.
  大多數的人都夢想可以變有錢。
  I failed to get rich since I started working in the stock market. 我開始在股票市場工作之後，就沒辦法變有錢了。

have a lot of money

· have enough money to…
有足夠的錢去做…

有很多錢 所有人的夢想和願望。也可以說 have so much money。

● Your uncle always has nice cars.
● That's because he **has a lot of money**.

●你的叔叔總是有很好的車。　●那是因為他有很多錢。

▶ My new boyfriend has a lot money.
我的新男友很有錢。

People in this apartment building have a lot of money.
住在這棟公寓大樓裡的人很有錢。

get the money to buy

得到錢去買… 想要買某樣東西，但錢不夠，另尋財源的狀況。

● I need to **get the money to buy** a car.
● Maybe I can lend you some.

●我需要弄到錢去買車。　●也許我可以借你一點。

▶ Terry got the money to buy a shop.
Terry 得到了買店面的錢。

Kara got the money to buy Christmas presents.
Kara 得到了買耶誕禮物的錢。

43 | 花錢，支付 spend money

1-43.mp3

spend money -ing

· spend one's money -ing
把某人的錢花在…

把錢花在… 這裡的 -ing 是用來說明錢的用途。

● Where did all of your money go?
● We **spent our money** vacationing.

●你們的錢都去哪了？　●我們把錢用來度假。

▶ The church spends money helping others.
這間教會花錢幫助他人。

It's easy to spend more than you have.
人很容易入不敷出。

1 職場·學校
2 電腦·網路
3 社交生活
4 日常生活
5 訊息·理解
6 想法·態度
7 情緒·狀況
8 行為舉止
9 時間地點·副詞片語

spend money on

- spend one's salary
  quickly
  花薪水花得很快

把錢花在… 如果要表示花很多錢，可以說 spend a lot of money on sth。

- Did the police catch you driving fast?
- Yeah, I have to **spend money on** the ticket I got.
  - 警察有抓到你開快車嗎？ ● 有啊，我得花錢付罰單。

▶ The family spent its money on food and rent.
  這個家庭把錢花在食物和租金上。
  I don't like to spend money on jewelry.
  我不喜歡花錢買珠寶。

waste one's money

- waste one's money on
  sth
  浪費某人的錢在某事物上
- waste one's money
  -ing
  浪費某人的錢做某事

浪費某人的錢 後面可以接 on sth 或 -ing 說明錢的去向。

- Many people are buying i-phones.
- Don't **waste your money** on them.
  - 很多人買 i-phone。 ● 別浪費你的錢買那個。

▶ Louis wasted his money gambling. Louis 浪費他的錢賭博。
  They wasted their money on lottery tickets.
  他們浪費錢買樂透。

be broke

- be flat broke
  窮翻了
- be out of money
  沒有錢
- be low on money
  錢很少

破產，很窮 broke 也可以換成 penniless（身無分文）。

- Come on, let's go out tonight.
- I can't go anywhere. I **am broke**.
  - 來嘛，我們今天晚上出去玩吧。 ● 我哪裡都不能去，我窮翻了。

▶ The older couple is always broke. 那對老夫妻總是很窮。
  Helen was broke after she paid the doctor.
  Helen 付完醫藥費後變得很窮。

Cash or charge?

- charge sth on Visa
  用 Visa 信用卡購物
- I'll charge it, please.
  我要用信用卡支付。
- Cash, please.
  我要付現。

現金還是信用卡？ charge 有「請求支付款項」或是「先記帳，日後再請款」的意思。charge 在這裡是指信用卡。

- Will that be **cash or charge**, sir?
- I'm going to pay cash.
  - 先生，請問您要用現金還是信用卡支付？ ● 我要付現。

▶ This is the total you owe. Cash or charge?
  這邊是總金額。您要用現金還是信用卡支付？
  Will you use cash or charge to pay your bill?
  你會用現金還是信用卡付帳單？

pay in cash

· pay by check
以支票支付

· pay in Taiwan dollar
用台幣支付（表示用某種貨幣支付，介系詞用 in）

付現 「用現金」的介系詞是 in。如果是用支票或信用卡，介系詞是 by 或 with。

● Will you **pay** for this **in cash** or **by check**?

● Let me pay for it with my credit card.

　●你要付現還是以支票支付？　●讓我用信用卡支付吧。

▶ I'd like to pay in cash. How much is it?

　我想要付現，這多少錢？

　I'm going to pay for this with a check.

　我要用支票支付。

pay sth on one's credit card

· buy sth on credit
賒帳／用信用卡買某物

· buy sth with one's credit card
用信用卡買某物

用某人的信用卡支付某物 buy sth on credit 表示用信用卡買某個東西。

● I'd like to **buy** this **with my credit card**.

● I'm sorry but we don't accept credit cards.

　●我想要用信用卡買這個。　●不好意思，我們不接受信用卡。

▶ No one buys the newspaper with a credit card.

　沒有人用信用卡買報紙。

　I'd like to buy a car on credit.

　我想要用信用卡買車。

take credit cards

· accept credit cards
接受信用卡

· accept/take checks
接受支票

接受信用卡 用來表示店家是否接受以信用卡付帳。

● This store doesn't **take checks**.

● OK. I have some cash.

　●這間店不接受支票付款。　●OK，我有一些現金。

▶ Do they accept checks?

　他們收支票嗎？

　We take credit card only, no checks.

　我們只收信用卡，不收支票。

pay the bill

· pay the fine
付罰金

· pay one's rent
付某人的租金

· pay one's utility bill
付某人的水電瓦斯費

付帳 至於 pay the price 這個片語，它不是指付具體的價錢，而是「付出代價」。

● How would you like to **pay the bill**?

● I'd like to put it on my credit card.

　●你想要怎麼付帳？　●用信用卡。

▶ I'd like to pay the bill, please.

　我要結帳，謝謝。

　I can't afford to pay my rent this month.

　我這個月付不出房租。

1 職場・學校
2 電腦・網路
3 社交生活
4 日常生活
5 訊息・理解
6 想法・態度
7 情緒・狀況
8 行為舉止
9 時間地點・副詞片語

pay for

· pay tuition
付學費
· pay money for
為了…而付錢
· pay sb money
付錢給某人

支付…的款項 for 後面接要支付的事物。

● We would like to **pay for** your airline ticket.
● That's wonderful. I don't know how to thank you.

●我們會幫你出機票錢。　●太棒了，我不知道該怎麼謝謝你們。

▶ Can you pay for our dinner? 你可以付我們的晚餐錢嗎？
Charlie needs to pay me the money he owes.

Charlie 需要還我他欠我的錢。

make a payment

· make a payment for…
支付…的款項
· make monthly
payments to…
每個月付款給…

支付 payment 是 pay 的名詞形。後面接 for sth 表示付款原因。

● How can you afford your new car?
● I **make a payment** for it every month.

●你怎麼買得起你的新車？　●我每個月都付款。

▶ She made a payment on her credit card. 她用信用卡付款。
I can't afford to make the payments on this. 我付不起這個。

get behind on payments

· get behind with the
payments for one's
car
汽車付款逾期

付款逾期 be in arrears 的意思也一樣，但口語比較少用。

● I **got behind on the payments** to my account.
● You're going to owe even more money.

●我帳戶該支付的款項逾期了。　●你要欠更多錢了。

▶ It's easy to get behind on payments these days.
最近很容易付款逾期。
The Visa can't be used because we got behind on
payments. 因為我們付款逾期，所以這張 Visa 信用卡不能使用。

pay off one's debt

· pay sb back
償還某人
· pay sb back with
interest
連本帶利償還某人

清償債務 與 pay back 的意思相同。

● Students owe a lot of money after graduation.
● They need to **pay off their debt**.

●學生們畢業後欠很多錢。　●他們需要付清貸款。

▶ It will take years to pay off this debt.
這筆債要很多年才付得完。
When can you pay off your debts? 你什麼時候能把債務付清？

be due on

在…到期 due 後面加上時間副詞（片語），表示到期的時間。

● When is this report going to be finished?
● Well, it **is due** next Monday.

●這份報告什麼時候會完成？　●這個嘛，繳交期限是下星期一。

▶ The library books are due on Saturday.
圖書館借來的這些書，星期六到期。
The bills are due on the first day of the month.
這些帳單的繳交期限是月初第一天。

44 借錢，負債
get a loan

1-44.mp3

1 職場‧學校

2 電腦‧網路

3 社交生活

4 日常生活

5 訊息‧理解

6 想法‧態度

7 情緒‧狀況

8 行為舉止

9 時間地點‧副詞片語

owe to sb

- owe A to B
  欠 B（人）A（物）
- I owe you one.
  我欠你一次。

欠某人債 owe A to B 意為向 B 借了 A。A 也可以是欠對方的「人情」。

- I heard you **owe a lot of money to** your father.
- Yes, I had no choice but to borrow it from him.
  ● 我聽說你欠你爸爸一大筆錢。　● 是啊，我沒辦法，只能跟他借。

▶ How much do I owe you for the gas? 我欠你多少瓦斯費？
  Thanks for your help. How much do I owe you?
  謝謝你的幫忙。我欠你多少？

borrow some money from

- borrow sth from
  跟…借某物

向…借錢 borrow 的後面不一定是錢，也可以是別的東西。

- I need to **borrow some money**.
- Oh, sure! How much?
  ● 我需要借點錢。　● 當然可以！要多少？

▶ I allowed him to borrow my car. 我允許他借我的車。
  I'm going to borrow some money from my sister.
  我要跟我姐姐借點錢。

lend sb money

- lend money to sb at
  5% interest
  以 5% 的利息借某人錢
- lend sb sth
  借某人某物

借某人錢 同樣的，lend 的後面也不一定是錢，可以是別的東西。

- Larry is broke this week.
- I can **lend him some money**.
  ● Larry 這星期窮翻了。　● 我可以借他一些錢。

▶ Abby lent her brother money for his bills.
  Abby 借她弟弟錢，讓他付帳單。
  Can you lend me some money until payday?
  在發薪日之前，你可以借我一些錢嗎？

loan sb money

- loan sb sth
  借某人某物

借某人錢 loan 當動詞使用，意思和 lend 相同。

- How did Dick buy this BMW?
- His parents **loaned him money** to get it.
  ● Dick 怎麼買這台 BMW 的？　● 他爸媽借他錢買的。

▶ I ran out of money. Can you lend me some?
  我沒錢了，你可以借我一點嗎？
  Can you lend me $10,000 for a few months?
  你可以借我一萬美金幾個月嗎？

get a loan

- get a loan from a bank
  向銀行貸款
- give A a loan
  貸款給 A
- apply for a loan
  申請貸款
- take out a loan
  貸款

貸款 後面加上 from a bank，表示是向銀行取得的貸款。

- Will you be able to buy that new house?
- Yeah, I'll **get a loan** from a bank.
  - 你能買那間新房子嗎？　●可以，我會跟銀行貸款。

▶ Jay got a loan from his bank to pay for school.
  Jay 跟銀行貸款以支付學費。
  Joan applied for a loan to start a business.
  Joan 為了創業而申請了貸款。

---

45 | 收支平衡 make ends meet

1-45.mp3

make ends meet

使收支平衡，量入為出 使收入和支出打平。表示雖然沒有賺到錢，但也沒有虧錢的安穩狀態。

- Did you sell your gold jewelry?
- Yes, I'm just trying to **make ends meet**.
  - 你賣掉你的金飾了嗎？　●是啊，我努力讓收支平衡。

▶ Tom works three jobs to make ends meet.
  為了使收支平衡，Tom 同時做三份工作。
  We need to save money to make ends meet.
  我們需要省錢，使收支平衡。

make a profit

- make a huge profit
  獲利豐厚
- earn record-breaking profits
  賺進破紀錄的利潤

獲得利潤 也可以說 turn a profit，意思一樣。

- We need to **make a profit** at this shop.
- Let's try and attract more customers.
  - 我們需要讓這間店獲利。　●讓我們試著吸引更多顧客吧。

▶ The company failed for it didn't make a profit.
  因為沒有獲利，所以這間公司倒閉了。
  The stocks for our firm made a profit this year.
  我們公司的股票今年賺了錢。

be in the red

· be in the black
　有盈餘

負債，虧損 源於帳簿上表示虧損的赤字。有盈餘時是黑字，也就是 in the black。

- We're in the red again this month.
- We need to find a way to get out of this slump.

　●我們這個月又虧錢了。　　●我們得找個方法擺脫不景氣。

▶ The business was in the red for the whole year.
　這個企業一整年都在虧損。
　With low sales, the store was in the red.
　由於銷售量低，這間店處於虧損狀態。

be over budget

· be beyond one's
　budget
　超出某人的預算
· be on a tight budget
　預算很緊

超過預算 把 be 換成 go 的話，則是表示超過預算的過程。

- This apartment building looks very expensive.
- They were millions of dollars over budget.

　●這間公寓看起來很貴。　　●它們超過預算好幾百萬。

▶ Hollywood movies are always over budget.
　好萊塢電影總是超出預算。
　We went over budget on our expenses.
　我們在支出上超過了預算。

reduce the cost

· reduce the cost of
　sth/-ing
　降低某事物的費用或成本
· reduce operating
　costs
　降低營運成本

削減成本 後面接 of sth 可以說明減少成本的對象。

- These school books are so expensive.
- I wish we could reduce the cost of buying them.

　●這些課本好貴。　　●我希望我們能少花點錢買這些課本。

▶ The store reduced the cost of the jackets.
　這間商店削減了外套的成本。
　Can you reduce the cost of school?
　你可以降低學費嗎？

start cost-cutting measures

· cost effective
　符合成本效益的
· propose a budget cut
　提議縮減預算

開始成本削減措施 動詞 start 也可以換成 begin。

- Our store is losing a lot of money.
- We need to begin some cost cutting measures.

　●我們的店損失很多錢。　　●我們需要開始採用一些成本削減措施。

▶ They undertook cost cutting measures to save money.
　他們著手進行成本削減措施以節省金錢。
　Many countries are trying to start cost cutting measures.
　很多國家開始試著進行成本削減措施。

1 職場・學校
2 電腦・網路
3 社交生活
4 日常生活
5 訊息・理解
6 想法・態度
7 情緒・狀況
8 行為舉止
9 時間地點・副詞片語

can't afford to

· can't afford+N
買不起某物

無法負擔，付不起 can't afford 後面接名詞或 to do。

- I **can't afford to** buy a new coat.
- I can give you one of my brother's coats.

  - 我買不起新大衣。　- 我可以給你一件我哥哥的大衣。

▶ I can't afford to buy you a house.
  我沒辦法買一間房子給你。
  How much can you afford to spend?
  你付得起多少錢？

get into debt

· be in (deep) debt
負（很多）債

負債 相反的，付清債務則是 get out of debt。

- How did you **get into debt**?
- I had too many credit cards that I used.

  - 你怎麼會負債？　- 我用了太多張信用卡。

▶ Leon got into debt because of school costs.
  Leon 因為學費而負債。
  Some families got into debt by buying expensive homes.
  有些家庭因為購買了昂貴的房子而負債。

 ## make both ends meet

　　每個月都讓如履薄冰般的上班族心頭一驚的一句話，想必是 make ends meet 吧。這個慣用語是說「賺到剛剛好能夠支付所有生活費的錢」（get just enough money for all one's needs），也就是「努力不背負債務」（keep one's head above water）。我們可以想成家計簿或收支表上，最下面（end）總支出和總收入的數字剛好吻合（meet）、打平的狀態。說「I can barely make ends meet.」表示自己勉強維持收支平衡。而最近許多大學畢業後，暫時找不到工作的社會新鮮人們，則可以說「After college, I couldn't find a job and had a hard time making ends meet.」來表示自己的狀況。

46 銀行（開戶，匯兌）
make a deposit

1-46.mp3

open a new account

· open a new bank account
開新的銀行帳戶

開新帳戶 把帳戶關閉則是 close the account。

● I'm going to the bank this morning.
● Are you planning to **open a new account**?
　●我今天早上要去銀行。　●你打算開新戶頭嗎？

▶ We'll give you a bonus if you open a new account.
　如果你開新的帳戶，我們會給你一項優惠。
　Many people opened new accounts at the bank.
　許多人在銀行開了新戶頭。

take money out of one's account

· take money in cash from a bank
從銀行提領現金

從某人的帳戶裡把錢領出來

● I need to **take money out of my account**.
● Let's stop at this bank machine.
　●我需要從我帳戶裡領錢出來。　●那我們在提款機這邊停一下吧。

▶ Paula took money out of her account for the ticket.
　Paula 為了買票，從帳戶裡領了錢。
　He decided not to take money out of his account.
　他決定不要從自己的帳戶裡領錢。

withdraw money from a bank

· overdraw
透支（= have an overdraft）

從銀行提款 動詞 withdraw 也可以換成 draw，意思相同。

● Where is your sister going?
● She wants to **withdraw money from the bank**.
　●你姐姐要去哪？　●她要去銀行領錢。

▶ I had no time to withdraw money from the bank.
　我沒有時間去銀行領錢。
　We withdrew money from the bank to pay for our trip.
　我們從銀行領錢支付我們的旅費。

1 職場・學校
2 電腦・網路
3 社交生活
4 日常生活
5 訊息・理解
6 想法・態度
7 情緒・狀況
8 行為舉止
9 時間地點・副詞片語

99

make a cash deposit

· deposit a check into one's account
把支票存進某人的戶頭

進行現金存款 deposit 意為「存款」，也可以當成及物動詞使用
（ex. deposit money）。

● Hello, how can I help you?
● I'd like to **make a cash deposit**.

   ● 您好，需要什麼幫助嗎？   ● 我想要現金存款。

▶ You can make a cash deposit at the ATM.
   你可以在 ATM 進行現金存款。
   Sam made a cash deposit after selling his car.
   Sam 賣掉他的車之後，把現金存起來了。

transfer money to one's account

把錢轉到某人的帳戶 這是 transfer A to B 的句型。

● How did you sell the computer on the Internet?
● The buyer **transferred money to my account**.

   ● 你怎麼在網路上賣電腦的？   ● 買家把錢轉到我的帳戶。

▶ I transferred money to my son's account.
   我把錢轉到兒子的帳戶。
   You need to transfer money to the company's account.
   你需要把錢轉到公司的帳戶。

cash in traveler's check

· get A cashed
兌現 A

兌現旅行支票 cash in 是兌換成等值現金的意思。

● We'll need more money when we travel.
● Oh, we can **cash in our traveler's checks**.

   ● 我們旅行時會需要更多錢。   ● 噢，那我們可以把旅行支票兌現。

▶ Mike cashed in two traveler's checks in Holland.
   Mike 在荷蘭兌現了兩張旅行支票。
   Let's find a bank to cash in a traveler's check.
   我們找間銀行兌現旅行支票吧。

enter one's account number

· verify an account balance
確認帳戶餘額
· start Internet banking
開始（使用）網路銀行

輸入某人的帳戶號碼 進行 Internet banking（網路銀行業務）會
需要的手續。

● Why isn't this bank's website working?
● I think you need to **enter your account number**.

   ● 這銀行的網站為什麼不動？   ● 我想你需要輸入你的帳戶號碼。

▶ Enter your account number in this space.
   在這個空格輸入你的帳戶號碼。
   Kelly entered her account number on the site.
   Kelly 在網站上輸入了她的帳戶號碼。

1 職場·學校

2 電腦·網路

3 社交生活

4 日常生活

5 訊息·理解

6 想法·態度

7 情緒·狀況

8 行為舉止

9 時間地點·副詞片語

exchange foreign currency

· break a one hundred dollar bill into twenties
把一張百元鈔換成（五張）二十元鈔票

換外幣 這裡的 foreign currency 是指外幣。
- I need to **exchange some foreign currency**.
- I can help you do that.
  - 我需要換些外幣。　● 我可以幫你。
▶ They exchanged foreign currency while in Europe.
他們在歐洲的時候換了外幣。
Every airport has a place to exchange foreign currency.
每個機場都有可以換外幣的地方。

purchase US dollars with Korean won

用韓元買美金 即「支付韓元，換得美金」之意。
- Where can I **purchase US dollars with Korean won**?
- Try the Foreign Exchange Bank over there.
  - 我可以在哪裡用韓元購買美金？　● 試試看那邊的外匯銀行吧。
▶ Tracey purchased British pounds with US dollars at the airport. Tracey 在機場用美金購買了英鎊。
Purchase US dollars with Taiwan dollars before your vacation. 你去度假前，要用台幣購買美金。

47 入學，上學
go to college

1-47.mp3

apply to Harvard

· apply to many colleges
申請許多大學

申請（進入）哈佛大學 apply to 後面接學校或機關，apply for 後面則是接要申請的職位或學位。
- Are you going to **apply to Harvard**?
- No way. I can't afford the tuition.
  - 你會申請哈佛大學嗎？　● 不可能，我付不起學費。
▶ Very few students get in after they apply to Harvard.
申請哈佛大學的學生只有很少數會錄取。
Drake applied to Harvard Medical School.
Drake 申請了哈佛醫學院。

go to college

· go to law school
  念法學院

上大學　跟 go to school 一樣，「上」大學也是用 go 這個動詞。

● What are your plans for the future?
● I'll **go to college** for the next four years.

　●你未來有什麼計畫？　●我接下來四年會去上大學。

▶ I went to college in California.

　我（過去）在加州上大學。

　Where does he plan to go to college?

　他打算去哪裡上大學？

get into Harvard

錄取哈佛大學　get 是個萬能的動詞。這裡加上介系詞 into，變成錄取的意思。

● Why are John's parents so happy?
● They just found out he **got into Harvard**.

　●John 的父母為什麼那麼開心？　●他們剛得知他錄取了哈佛。

▶ You'll never get into Harvard with your grades.

　以你的成績，是永遠進不了哈佛的。

　Less than ten percent of applicants get into Yale.

　只有不到 10% 的申請者能錄取耶魯大學。

enter high school

· enter a good
  university
  進入好大學

進高中　表示開始就讀高中。

● When did you **enter high school**?
● I started high school back in 2003.

　●你哪時候進高中的？　●我 2003 年開始讀高中的。

▶ Vera will enter high school this year.

　Vera 今年會上高中。

　He was fourteen when he entered high school.

　他剛進高中的時候是 14 歲。

be admitted to Yale

· be accepted into
  ＋ 大學名稱
  被某大學錄取

· gain admission to
  ＋ 大學名稱
  錄取某大學

錄取耶魯大學　to 的後面接大學的名稱。

● **Were** you **admitted to Harvard**?
● No, I had to apply to other schools.

　●你有錄取哈佛大學嗎？　●沒有，我必須申請其他學校。

▶ Only one of my classmates was admitted to Princeton.

　我只有一個同學錄取了普林斯頓大學。

　They said I'll never be admitted to Yale.

　他們說我永遠不會被耶魯錄取。

attend a good university

· attend the same high school as sb
和某人念同一間高中

上好大學 attend class 則是「上課」的意思。

- It's important to **attend a good university**.
- I know. It helps people get high-paying jobs.

  ●上好大學很重要。　●我知道，上好大學有助於獲得高薪工作。

▶ My friend Laura attended a good university.
我的朋友 Laura 上了一間好大學。

My kids to attend a good university.

I told my kids to attend a good university.
我告訴我的孩子要上好的大學。

fail the entrance exam

入學考試落榜 fail 可以當及物動詞，後面接考試的名稱。

- John has been up drinking all night.
- Oh, God, he's going to **fail the entrance exam**.

  ●John 喝了一整晚的酒。　●噢，天啊，他入學考試會考砸的。

▶ Ray failed the entrance exam three times before he gave up. 在放棄之前，Ray 在入學考試落榜了三次。

Don't fail the entrance exam for the university.
不要在大學入學考試落榜。

pay one's tuition

付某人的學費 tuition 是指為了接受教育支付的費用。

- The cost of school keeps going up.
- It's so difficult to **pay our tuition**.

  ●學費一直在漲。　●付學費真困難。

▶ You must pay your tuition before attending classes.
你上課前必須付學費。

The students pay their tuition in the main office.
學生們在總辦公室支付學費。

1 職場・學校
2 電腦・網路
3 社交生活
4 日常生活
5 訊息・理解
6 想法・態度
7 情緒・狀況
8 行為舉止
9 時間地點・副詞片語

48 休學，輟學
quit school

1-48.mp3

drop out of school	**輟學** dropout 則是名詞，意為「中輟生」。
	●Bill **dropped out of school** this year.
	●He'll have trouble finding work.
	●Bill 今年輟學了。　●他找工作會很困難。
	▶ Work hard and don't drop out of school.
	努力讀書，不要輟學。
	Jane dropped out of school after failing several exams.
	Jane 在幾科考試被當之後輟學了。
quit (attending) school	**休學** attending 可以省略。因為 quit 接名詞或動名詞當受詞，所以 attend 要加上 -ing。
	●Where is Billy Joe at these days?
	●I don't know. He **quit attending school**.
	●Billy Joe 最近去哪了？　●我不知道，他休學了。
	▶ The lazy students just quit attending school.
	懶惰的學生們休學了。
	He quit school so he could take a job.
	他為了獲得一份工作而休學。
leave school · expel sb from school 　把某人開除學籍	**休學** leave school 雖然有休學的意思，但依照文意，有時也可以視為「畢業」。
	●Wally will **leave school** to start a business.
	●I think that's a bad idea.
	●Wally 將會休學並且創業。　●我覺得那是個壞主意。
	▶ My friend left school when she was 17.
	我朋友在她 17 歲那年休學了。
	You can't leave school until you graduate.
	你在畢業之前都不能休學。

104

be expelled from school

· expel sb from school
  把某人開除學籍

被開除學籍 expel 是「驅逐、趕走」的意思。

● Jeff **was expelled from** school today.
● He always caused a lot of trouble.

  ● Jeff 今天被學校開除學籍了。　● 他總是惹出很多麻煩。

▶ Several students were expelled from school for cheating.
  幾名學生因為作弊而被開除學籍了。
  Sam was expelled from school after the fight.
  Sam 在打架事件發生後被開除學籍了。

---

49 | 畢業
graduate from

1-49.mp3

1 職場・學校

2 電腦・網路

3 社交生活

4 日常生活

5 訊息・理解

6 想法・態度

7 情緒・狀況

8 行為舉止

9 時間地點・副詞片語

---

graduate from

· a graduate
  畢業生

· undergraduate
  大學生

畢業於… 後面加上 with straight A's，表示以全 A 的優秀成績畢業。

● When did you **graduate from** high school?
● I graduated about five years ago.

  ● 你什麼時候從高中畢業的？　● 我大約五年前畢業的。

▶ I think my secretary graduated from your university.
  我想我的祕書是在你的大學畢業的。
  When did you graduate from university?
  你什麼時候從大學畢業的？

---

finish law school

· finish grad school
  完成研究所的學業

· finish medical school
  完成醫學院的學業

完成法學院的學業 finish 的後面接畢業的學院名稱。另外，研究所是 grad(uate) school。

● How long does it take to **finish law school**?
● It takes about three or four years.

  ● 完成法學院的學業要多久時間？　● 大約三到四年。

▶ It may take five years to finish grad school.
  完成研究所的學業，可能會花上五年。
  Aaron finished medical school when he was 30.
  Aaron 在 30 歲的時候完成了醫學院的學業。

go back to school

回學校讀書，復學 go back 可以換成 return。

- I need more education to get a better job.
- You'll have to **go back to school**.
  - ●我需要接受更多教育，以獲得更好的工作。
  - ●那你必須回學校讀書。

▶ Billy went back to school when he was thirty.
Billy 在 30 歲的時候回到學校讀書。
Many older people are going back to school.
很多年長的人回到學校讀書。

have been to university

· only have a high school education
只有高中學歷
· went to law school
上了法學院

上過大學 以完成式表示經驗。

- What kind of education do you have?
- I **went to university** for a few years.
  - ●你接受過怎樣的教育？　●我上大學念了幾年書。

▶ Only a few of the factory workers have been to university. 只有一些工廠工人上過大學。
She had been to university before starting her job.
她開始工作之前上過大學。

---

50 | 讀書，上課
take a course

1-50.mp3

study hard

· study all night
通宵讀書
· do a lot of studying
讀很多書

認真讀書 比較級 study harder 表示更認真讀書。後面可以加上 to do 表示讀書的目的。

- I'm aware of John's poor grades.
- Should we help him to **study harder**?
  - ●我發覺 John 的成績很差。　　●我們應該幫助他更認真讀書嗎？

▶ Everyone studied hard for the final exam.
每個人都為了期末考而認真讀書。
You need to study hard to get good grades.
你需要認真讀書以獲得好成績。

study for the test

· study for the entrance
  exam
  準備入學考試

為了準備考試而讀書 如果是為了入學考試而讀書，可以說 study for the entrance exam。

- Let's **study for the test** together.
- OK, but I want to eat dinner first.

  ●我們一起準備考試吧。　●好啊，但我想先吃晚餐。

▶ Did you study for the test in English class?

  英文課的考試，你準備了嗎？

  Oh no! I forgot to study for the test.

  噢不！我忘了讀書準備考試。

study English

· study math
  學習數學
· improve one's foreign
  language skills
  提升某人的外語能力

學習英文 study 的後面可以接上各式各樣的學科名稱。

- We **study English** three times a week.
- It's pretty difficult, isn't it?

  ●我們一星期學三次英文。　●那很困難，不是嗎？

▶ Many elementary students study English.

  很多小學生學習英文。

  I studied English before going overseas.

  出國之前我學了英文。

take a course

· take a driving lesson
  上駕駛課
· take an intensive
  English course
  上密集的英文課程

修課 要說明是什麼課，可以在 course 前面加上課程的名稱。

- Did you **take a course** at the college?
- Yes, it was a course on artwork.

  ●你在大學修了課嗎？　●是的，那是個跟藝術品有關的課程。

▶ I'll take a course with my favorite professor this year.

  我今年將會修我最喜歡的教授的課。

  When can we take a course together?

  我們什麼時候可以一起上課？

learn sth quickly

· fast learner
  學東西很快的人
· late bloomer
  大器晚成的人

學習某事的速度很快 learn 的後面也可以接 how to do，表示學習做某事的方法。

- How is my son doing in your class?
- He has **learned** the subject **quickly**.

  ●我的兒子在你的課堂上表現如何？　●他學這個科目學得很快。

▶ Juan learned English quickly.

  Juan 學英文學得很快。

  I hope to learn about math quickly.

  我希望能很快學會數學。

1 職場・學校
2 電腦・網路
3 社交生活
4 日常生活
5 訊息・理解
6 想法・態度
7 情緒・狀況
8 行為舉止
9 時間地點・副詞片語

major in

主修⋯ 也可以說 specialize in。in 的後面接主修的學科。
- Many students want to **major in** liberal arts.
- Science and math are more difficult to study.
  - ●很多學生想主修文科。　●科學和數學比較難學。

▶ Ellie majored in communication studies.
  Ellie 主修傳播研究。
  Britt can't decide what to major in.
  Britt 無法決定該主修什麼。

go study in America

· study at a university overseas
  在國外念大學

去美國留學 也就是 go abroad to study in America 的意思。
- Why is Byung Chul learning English?
- He wants to **go study in America**.
  - ●Byung Chul 為什麼在學英文？　●他想要去美國留學。

▶ They both went to study in America last year.
  他們兩個去年都去美國留學。
  Students need a lot of money to go study in America.
  學生需要很多錢才能去美國留學。

hit the books

· I have to hit the books tonight.
  我今晚必須努力 K 書。

讀書 用來強調非常認真讀書，一頭栽進書堆裡的感覺，和我們常說的「K 書」有異曲同工之妙。
- Are you coming out with us?
- No, I need to **hit the books** tonight.
  - ●你要跟我們一起出去嗎？　●不行，我今晚得 K 書。

▶ Cindy hit the books after failing the exam.
  Cindy 考試當掉之後非常認真讀書。
  You need to hit the books more often.
  你需要更常認真讀書。

resume one's studies

· give up one's studies
  放棄學業

重新開始讀書 這邊的 resume 並不是指履歷表，而是「重新開始、繼續」的意思。
- I heard you're getting out of the hospital soon.
- Yes, and I hope to **resume my studies**.
  - ●我聽說你很快就要出院了。　●是啊，我希望繼續我的學業。

▶ They resumed their studies after the summer break.
  放完暑假後，他們回到學校繼續讀書。
  There was no time to resume our studies.
  我們沒有時間再繼續讀書了。

1 職場・學校
2 電腦・網路
3 社交生活
4 日常生活
5 訊息・理解
6 想法・態度
7 情緒・狀況
8 行為舉止
9 時間地點・副詞片語

 I'm a fast learner

　　我們習慣的文法是以動詞為重心，例如說某人對某件事很拿手，會說他「擅長做某事」。但在這個情況下，英文是以名詞為重心，會說他是「擅長做某事的人」。語言不同，思考模式和習慣用法也會有所不同，這就是一個例子。

You cook well => You're a good cook. 你是個擅長烹飪的人。
I can learn fast => I'm a fast learner. 我是個學習速度很快的人。
She kisses well => She's a good kisser. 她是個接吻高手。
Do you drive well => Are you a good driver? 你是擅長開車的人嗎？

51 | 上課時間
sign up for

1-51.mp3

sign up for

・sign up for one's classes
　登記／報名某人的課程
・have math class this morning
　今天早上有數學課
・class scheduled for + 時間
　某時間要上的課

註冊，登記，報名 表示報名某項課程時常用的片語。後面可以接 class, course 或課程的名稱。

● I **signed up for** my classes this morning.
● Which ones will you be taking?
　●我今天早上登記完課程了。　●你會修哪些課？

▶ There's only a week to sign up for our classes.
　我們只有一週的時間選課。
　Is this the office where I can sign up for my classes?
　這是選課登記的辦公室嗎？

skip class

・miss the class
　錯過上課
・pass the class
　修完課程

蹺課 skip school 則是指逃學。

● How did they get in trouble?
● They tried to **skip class** and got caught.
　●他們怎麼惹上麻煩的？　●他們想蹺課結果被抓到。

▶ We skipped class and played computer games.
　我們蹺課去玩電腦遊戲。
　Perry skipped class on the day of the test.
　Perry 在考試當天蹺課。

109

be absent from

· play hooky
  逃學
· play truant from
  逃避（學校等）

缺席… be absent from school 表示曠課，be absent from work 則是曠職。

● **Was** Wendy **absent from** school?
● No, she came to classes today.

  ●Wendy 沒來學校嗎？　●有啊，她今天有來。

▶ Some people were absent from church today.
  有些人今天沒來教會。
  I was absent from class because I was sick.
  我因為生病，所以沒上課。

leave school early

· leave school/work
  early to do
  提早離開學校／公司去做
  某事
· school has been
  canceled
  學校停課了

提早離開學校，早退 在公司則說 leave work early。

● Why did you **leave school early** today?
● I wanted to go and meet my girlfriend.

  ●你今天為什麼提早離開學校？　●我想要去見我女朋友。

▶ The freshman left school early today.
  這位大一學生今天早早就離開了學校。
  I decided not to leave school early.
  我決定不要提早離開學校。

after school

放學後 表示公司下班後則是說 after work。

● When do the sports teams practice?
● They usually get together **after school**.

  ●球隊哪時候練習？　●他們通常下課後集合。

▶ We've still got to study after school.
  我們放學後還是要念書。
  Do you have any plans after school?
  你放學後有什麼計畫嗎？

52 功課，作業
do one's homework

1-52.mp3

do one's homework

· have one's homework done
  做完某人的作業

做某人的作業 homework 也可以換成 assignment，但前者感覺比較口語。

● I **did my homework** on the subway.
● Me too. Now it is all finished.

● 我在地鐵上做了作業。　● 我也是，現在都做完了。

▶ I forgot to do my homework!
我忘記做作業了！
The teacher was happy we did our homework.
老師很高興我們做了作業。

finish one's homework

· complete one's assignment
  完成某人的作業／任務

做完某人的作業 finish 換成 complete 也可以表示完成的意思。

● Where's your daughter right now?
● She is in the kitchen, **finishing her homework**.

● 你女兒現在在哪裡？　● 她在廚房寫作業。

▶ It took an hour to finish my homework.
我花了一小時做完作業。
They will finish their homework later tonight.
他們今晚稍晚會把作業做完。

help sb with one's homework

· get some help with one's homework
  在作業方面得到一些幫助
· finish one's homework
  完成某人的作業

幫某人做作業 這是 help A with B 的句型。

● I don't think Bob is very smart.
● You should **help him with his homework**.

● 我不覺得 Bob 很聰明。　● 你應該幫他做作業。

▶ Mr. Sampson helped me with my homework.
Sampson 先生幫我做作業。
Our best student helps others with their homework.
我們最優秀的學生幫其他人做作業。

1 職場・學校

2 電腦・網路

3 社交生活

4 日常生活

5 訊息・理解

6 想法・態度

7 情緒・狀況

8 行為舉止

9 時間地點・副詞片語

write a paper

· write a report
　寫報告
· write a book report
　寫讀書心得

寫報告 paper 通常是指學期末繳交的報告。如果是畢業論文，則說 thesis 或 dissertion。

● We have to **write a paper** for history class.
● What are you going to do it on?

　●我們必須寫歷史課的報告。　●你的主題是什麼？

▶ I wrote a paper for my science teacher.
　我寫了一份報告給我自然科學課的老師。
　She will write a paper in two days.
　她兩天後會寫報告。

submit the report

交報告 submit 也可以換成 turn in 這個慣用語。

● I can't **submit this report**.
● I know. It's full of mistakes.

　●我不能交出這份報告。　●我知道，這裡面一堆錯誤。

▶ Submit this report in the morning.
　今天早上把這份報告交出來。
　Let's submit this report to our boss.
　我們把這份報告交給老闆吧。

---

53 | 測驗，考試
take the test

1-53.mp3

---

take the test

· get to the exam
　應考

考試 take 的後面可以接 test 或 quiz。

● I want a driver's license.
● You'll need to **take the license test**.

　●我想要駕照。　●你需要去考駕照。

▶ Are you ready to take the test?
　你準備好要考試了嗎？
　What time did Anthony get to the exam?
　Anthony 什麼時候考試的？

cheat on one's exam

- cheat on one's mid-term exam
  在某人的期中考作弊
- skip the final exam
  缺考期末考

考試作弊 cheat on wife 則是指背著妻子和其他人發生關係。

- I heard Kim say you **cheated on your exam**.
- Is that what she said?

  ●我聽 Kim 說你考試作弊。　●她是那樣說的嗎？

▶ He was thrown out of school for cheating on his exam.
他因為考試作弊而被退學了。

Never try to cheat on the entrance exam.
絕對不要嘗試在入學考試作弊。

pass the exam

- pass the bar exam
  通過律師考試

通過考試，考試及格 前面加上 barely，可以表示勉強通過。

- I was up drinking all night.
- You'll never **pass your exam**.

  ●我喝酒喝了一整晚。　●你絕對無法通過考試的。

▶ Do you think she'll pass the exam?
你覺得她會通過考試嗎？

You will pass the exam if you study.
你如果讀書的話，考試就會及格。

fail the exam

- mid-term exam week
  期中考週
- final exam week
  期末考週

考試不及格 fail 的後面接考試的名稱。

- How did you do?
- I think I **failed the exam**.

  ●你考得怎樣？　●我覺得我不及格。

▶ I'm so worried that I might fail the exam.
我很擔心我考試可能會不及格。

It's no wonder she failed the exam.
她考試不及格一點也不意外。

fail the class

- fail math class
  數學被當

某科被當 class 也可以換成 course，意思相同。

- Do you think Frank can pass?
- No, he's certain to **fail the class**.

  ●你覺得 Frank 能過嗎？　●不，他這科一定會被當。

▶ Neil was always absent and he failed the class.
Neil 總是缺席，所以這科被當了。

At least ten percent of students will fail the class.
這科至少有 10% 的學生會被當。

1 職場・學校

2 電腦・網路

3 社交生活

4 日常生活

5 訊息・理解

6 想法・態度

7 情緒・狀況

8 行為舉止

9 時間地點・副詞片語

54 分數，成績
get a good grade

1-54.mp3

get an A in class

· get an F in math
  數學課得到 F 的成績
· get all A's this
  semester
  這學期得到全 A 的成績

在某科得到 A 也可以說 get a good grade 表示得到好成績。

● Your sister is pretty smart.
● She **got an A in science class**.

　●你姐姐非常聰明。　　●她在自然科學課上拿到 A。

▶ Ryan needs to get an A in class. Ryan 需要在課堂上拿到 A。
　I hope you do really well on the exam. 我希望你考得非常好。

get an F on one's report

某人的報告得到 F report 前面可以加上科目名稱，說明是哪一科的報告。

● Why are you so upset?
● I **got an F on my history paper**.

　●你為什麼那麼沮喪？　　●我歷史報告拿了 F。

▶ The teacher said I got an F on his paper.
　老師說我在他課堂上的報告拿了 F。
　You'll get an F on your paper unless you change it.
　你如果不修改報告內容的話，會拿到 F 的。

get a good grade

· have a bad grade
  得到壞成績
· get ... on the exam
  在考試中得到⋯

得到好成績 相反的，得到壞成績就是 get a bad grade。

● You've been studying very hard.
● I need to **get a good grade** on this exam.

　●你這陣子非常努力念書。　　●我需要在這場考試得到好成績。

▶ I got the highest grade on the exam. 我在考試中得到最高分。
　I got 99% on the exam. 我考試得到 99 分。

have one's exam result

· get the result from
  one's exam
  得到某人考試的成績
· show sb one's low
  test score
  給某人看某人的壞成績

有某人的考試成績 動詞也可以換成 see，表示看到成績。

● I **have the class's exam results**.
● Could we see them please?

　●我手邊有班上的考試成績。　　●我們可以看嗎？拜託。

▶ Tomorrow you will have your exam result.
　明天你就會知道你的考試結果。
　They were upset when they had their exam results.
　他們得知考試結果後十分苦惱。

give sb low grades

· give sb the highest grade
給某人最高的評分

給某人低分 grade 是指 A, B, C… 的分級，score 則是指分數。

● Is Johnny getting a scholarship?
● No, the teachers **gave him low grades.**

 ●Johnny 會拿到獎學金嗎？　●不會，老師給了他低分。

▶ Ms. Perry gave me a low grade.

 Perry 老師給了我低分。

 The math teacher gave everyone low grades.

 數學老師給了所有人低分。

 也可以表示「年級」的 **grade**

　　在學校裡，grade 除了表示成績以外，也可以指「年級」。例如一年級就叫 first grade 或 grade one。美國的「年級」是從國小到高中連續計算的，台灣的「國中三年級」相當於美國的「九年級」，英文稱為 ninth grade 或 grade nine。在美國，從國小到國中總共有八個學年，所以 ninth grade 已經是高中一年級了。

　　I will be a 10th grader next month. 我下個月就是十年級生了。

　　I'm studying in grade 4. 我正在唸四年級。

1 職場・學校
2 電腦・網路
3 社交生活
4 日常生活
5 訊息・理解
6 想法・態度
7 情緒・狀況
8 行為舉止
9 時間地點・副詞片語

CHAPTER 2

Computer & Networking

與電腦、網際網路、交通等相關的慣用語

01 電腦
fix the computer

2-01.mp3

---

turn on the computer

· reboot a computer
  重新啟動電腦

開電腦 「打開」電器用品或電燈等的電源時，都說「turn on」。

● I need to use the Internet.
● Let me **turn on the computer**.
　● 我需要用網路。　● 讓我把電腦打開。

▶ Turn on the computer before we start.
　在我們開始之前，先把電腦打開。
　Please go and turn on the computer. 請去把電腦打開。

---

use the computer

· use Windows 8
  使用 Windows 8 系統

用電腦 如果用的是別人的電腦，可以說 use one's computer。

● Is it okay for me to **use your computer** tonight?
● Sure. I don't need it until tomorrow.
　● 今晚我可以用你的電腦嗎？　● 當然可以。我明天才會用到。

▶ Rick needs to use the computer now. Rick 現在需要用電腦。
　Can I use your computer when you're gone?
　你不在的時候，我可以用你的電腦嗎？

---

be done with the computer

· shut off/down the computer
  關電腦

用完電腦 be done with 可以用在許多狀況下，例如事情做完了、和某人分手、該看的東西都看完了、用完某樣東西等等。

● I'll **be done with the computer** in just a minute.
● Take your time. I'm in no rush.
　● 我再一分鐘就會用完電腦。　● 慢慢來，我不急。

▶ Are you done with the computer? 你用完電腦了嗎？
　He shut down his computer and cleared his desk.
　他關了電腦並且清空桌子。

---

upgrade one's computer

· upgrade the video card
  升級顯示卡

升級某人的電腦 藉由升級 CPU、記憶體、顯示卡等等，使電腦效能提高。

● Why are you buying a new notebook?
● I decided to **upgrade my old computer**.
　● 你為什麼要買新的筆電？　● 我決定升級我的舊電腦。

▶ You should upgrade your old computer.
　你應該升級你的舊電腦。
　I had my computer upgraded. 我把我的電腦升級了。

be down

- crash
  電腦（系統）故障／當機
- break down
  （電腦或機械等）故障
- be frozen
  電腦當機

當機，故障 down 原意為「在下面」，但也有「沮喪的」、「老舊的」、「不健康的」等許多比喻性的含意。

- Why can't you find the file?
- I'm sorry, but our system **is down**.
  - 你們為什麼找不到檔案？　●抱歉，我們的系統故障了。

▶ My computer crashed this morning and I lost everything.
我的電腦今天早上當機，結果我所有東西都沒了。
My computer is frozen! 我電腦當機了！

sth be not working

- be not working properly
  沒有正常運作
- do not work
  不能用

故障 如果主詞是電腦，則可解釋為當機。

- Is there a problem with the computer?
- Yeah, the mouse **doesn't work** properly.
  - 這電腦有什麼問題嗎？　●嗯，滑鼠沒辦法正常使用。

▶ The computers aren't working. 這些電腦故障了。
I'm not sure if this computer program will work.
我不確定這電腦程式能不能運作。

(computer) fail

（電腦）故障 fail 本來是「失敗」的意思，在這裡指電腦故障。

- The computer system **failed**.
- Call a technician right now, I'm on my way.
  - 電腦系統故障了。　●馬上打電話給技術人員，我隨後就到。

▶ Why did my computer just fail? 我的電腦為什麼故障了？
The computer failed because of a virus.
這台電腦因為電腦病毒而故障了。

call a computer specialist

- call a computer technician
  找電腦技術人員來

找電腦專家來 call 的後面可以接任何想要請來的專家。

- I can't see what the problem is.
- We will have to **call a specialist**.
  - 我不知道問題在哪裡。　●我們需要找專家來。

▶ Will called a specialist to fix it. Will 找了專家來修它。
I'll call our computer specialist. 我會找我們的電腦維修人員來。

fix the computer

修電腦 除了修東西，也有 fix the problem（解決問題）的說法。

- Is it important to **fix this computer**?
- It can't wait. Fix it as quickly as you can.
  - 修這台電腦很重要嗎？　●不能再等了。用你最快的速度修好它。

▶ I'll help you fix your computer. 我會幫你修電腦。
Do you know anything about fixing computers?
你對修電腦有什麼概念嗎？

1 職場・學校

2 電腦・網路

3 社交生活

4 日常生活

5 訊息・理解

6 想法・態度

7 情緒・狀況

8 行為舉止

9 時間地點・副詞片語

change the printer's ink cartridge

· (printer) be out of ink
  （印表機）沒有墨水了

換印表機墨水匣 cartridge 這個字平常比較少用，但它是印表機常見的耗材。

- There is no writing on this paper.
- It's time to **change the printer's ink cartridge**.
  - ●這張紙上沒印出什麼東西。　●該換印表機的墨水匣了。

▶ Change the printer's ink cartridge before we start.
  在我們開始前，先更換印表機的墨水匣。
  No one changed the printer's ink cartridge.
  沒有人換印表機的墨水匣。

---

02 | 使用電腦 load the file

2-02.mp3

---

set up the computer

設定／安裝電腦 為了開始使用電腦而進行安裝或設定等。

- I need help **setting up the computer**.
- I'll give you a hand after lunch.
  - ●我需要有人幫忙安裝電腦。　●吃完午餐後我會幫你。

▶ Tell your brother to set up the computer.
  叫你哥哥去安裝電腦。
  She set up the computer on her desk.
  她把電腦安裝在她桌上。

install the program

· uninstall the program
  解除安裝程式
· install the software
  again
  再次安裝軟體

安裝程式 安裝程式的時候特別會使用 install 這個動詞。

- What is Bob doing to his computer?
- He's trying to **install the Windows 7 program**.
  - ●Bob 在對他的電腦做什麼？　●他在試著安裝 Windows 7。

▶ They installed all of the software on every computer.
  他們把所有軟體安裝到每一台電腦上。
  Do you know how to install the new version of Windows? 你知道該怎麼安裝新版 Windows 嗎？

load the file

· load software onto one's computer
在某人的電腦上載入軟體

（在電腦上）載入檔案 load 的反義詞是 save。save the file 表示儲存檔案。

● You shouldn't **load that program** on your computer.

● What's wrong with the program?

　●你不該在你的電腦載入那個程式。　●那個程式有什麼問題？

▶ Just load the file and we can start.
　把這個檔案叫出來，我們就可以開始了。
　It will take a minute to load the file.
　載入這個檔案要花一分鐘。

run the program

· update the software
更新軟體

執行程式 run 的原義是讓某物跑動，引申為「使⋯運作」。

● I don't think this computer can **run the program**.

● Yeah, it's a pretty old computer.

　●我覺得這台電腦跑不動這個程式。　●是啊，這台電腦蠻舊了。

▶ I'll teach you how to run the program.
　我會教你怎麼執行這個程式。
　Sally is going to run the program tonight.
　Sally 今晚要跑這個程式。

download the program

· upload the program
上傳程式
· download a file
下載檔案
· download sth on one's smart phone
將某物下載到某人的智慧型手機

下載程式 download 的反義詞是 upload（上傳）。

● Are you coming with us?

● Yes, I just need to **download a file** and I'll be right there.

　●你要跟我們一起來嗎？
　●要，我只需要下載一個檔案，然後我馬上就會過去。

▶ I'm going to download them on my smart phone.
　我要把它們下載到我的智慧型手機裡。
　I went to my favorite sites and downloaded lots of music and games. 我去了我最喜歡的網站，並下載了許多音樂和遊戲。

unzip the file

· zip a file
壓縮檔案
· open the files
打開檔案
· open the junk mail folder
打開垃圾郵件資料夾

解壓縮檔案 壓縮檔通常稱為 zip file，所以在 zip 前面加上表示反義的 un-，就是「解壓縮」的意思。

● Why isn't this file opening?

● You have to **unzip the file** first.

　●這個檔案為什麼打不開？　●你必須先解壓縮檔案。

▶ The instructions say to unzip the file.
　操作指南說要解壓縮檔案。
　Unzip the file you just downloaded.
　解壓縮你剛才下載的檔案。

1 職場・學校
2 電腦・網路
3 社交生活
4 日常生活
5 訊息・理解
6 想法・態度
7 情緒・狀況
8 行為舉止
9 時間地點・副詞片語

delete one's files

- throw away one's files in the garbage
  把某人的檔案丟到資源回收桶

刪除某人的檔案 delete 是電腦操作方面很常用的詞，換成 remove, erase 也是一樣的意思。

- People will be angry if they see our report.
- We need to **delete our files**.
  - 如果別人看到我們的報告，他們會生氣的。
  - 我們需要把檔案刪掉。

▶ Peter accidentally deleted his files.
  Peter 不小心把他的檔案刪掉了。
  He says that someone erased the report from his computer. 他說有人把報告從他的電腦裡刪掉了。

save the file

- save the file as...
  將檔案存為…（某種檔案型態）
- save the file in one's computer
  將檔案存進某人的電腦
- save the file on a USB drive
  將檔案存進 USB 隨身碟

存檔 使用電腦時，要隨時記得存檔，否則突然碰上停電（blackout），或電腦不動（not working）的時候就糟糕囉～

- I think we have finished everything.
- **Save the file** before you shut off the computer.
  - 我想我們完成所有東西了。　● 關電腦之前先存檔吧。

▶ Save the file so we can check it again.
  將檔案存檔，這樣我們之後就可以再確認。
  Let's save the file containing our homework.
  我們把包含我們作業的檔案存檔吧。

recover the data

- recover a deleted/erased file
  救回已刪除的檔案

救回資料 重要檔案遺失（be gone）時必須嘗試的補救辦法。

- My computer broke last night.
- I hope you can **recover the data** on it.
  - 我的電腦昨天壞了。　● 我希望你能救回裡面的資料。

▶ The computer repairman recovered the data.
  電腦維修人員把資料救回來了。
  Can you recover the data on this disk?
  你可以把這台硬碟上的資料救回來嗎？

back up the documents

- back up the documents on a USB drive
  把文件備份到 USB 隨身碟
- copy the file
  複製檔案

備份文件 backup 也可當名詞使用。backup drive（備份用硬碟）也是常見的說法。

- This system is very user-friendly.
- It even reminds you to **back up important documents**.
  - 這個系統非常容易使用。　● 它甚至會提醒你備份重要文件。

▶ I used a USB drive to back up the documents.
  我用 USB 隨身碟來備份文件。
  He forgot to back up the documents yesterday.
  他昨天忘了備份文件。

1 職場・學校

2 電腦・網路

3 社交生活

4 日常生活

5 訊息・理解

6 想法・態度

7 情緒・狀況

8 行為舉止

9 時間地點・副詞片語

03 電腦問題，病毒
have a virus

2-03.mp3

have a virus

中毒 導致電腦變慢、變遲鈍的兇手。

● Why is my computer screen flashing?

● I think your computer **has a virus**.

　●我的電腦螢幕為什麼在閃？　●我想你電腦中毒了。

▶ Randy's computer got a virus from a website.
Randy 的電腦被一個網站感染病毒。
The computer was fixed after it had a virus.
這台電腦中毒之後修好了。

be infected with a virus

被病毒感染 infect 意為「感染」，這裡使用的是被動態。

● What's wrong with your computer?

● It **was infected with a virus**.

　●你的電腦怎麼了？　●它被感染病毒了。

▶ The system failed after it was infected with a computer virus. 這個系統感染到電腦病毒後，就當掉了。
It was repaired after being infected with a virus.
它中毒過後被修好了。

(the file) be gone

· lose everything on the hard drive
失去硬碟上所有檔案

（檔案）不見，消失 做到一半的檔案消失不見，想必是個惡夢。

● Can you save the reports I wrote?

● I'm sorry, but **the files are gone**.

　●你可以把我寫的報告存起來嗎？　●我很抱歉，但檔案不見了。

▶ The files were gone after the virus hit.
中毒之後，檔案不見了。
After the computer crashed, the files were gone.
電腦當機之後，檔案不見了。

123

check for viruses

· check for computer errors
  檢查電腦是否有錯誤

檢查是否有（電腦）病毒 感覺電腦不太正常時會做的事。

● What is this program used for?

● It **checks for viruses** on your hard drive.

　●這軟體是用來做什麼的？　●它會檢查你的硬碟裡有沒有病毒。

▶ I need a software to check for viruses.

　我需要軟體來確認是否有病毒。

　Did you check for viruses after using the Internet?

　你用完網路後有掃毒嗎？

format the disk

· have the computer formatted
  把電腦格式化

格式化硬碟 故障或病毒感染完全沒救時採取的最終手段。

● Can we hurry up a little bit?

● It takes time to **format the disk**.

　●我們可以稍微快一點嗎？　●硬碟格式化是需要時間的。

▶ Carlos said he would format the disk.

　Carlos 說他會把硬碟格式化。

　Let's format the disk before we start.

　在我們開始前，先把硬碟格式化吧。

run an anti-virus program

· buy an anti-virus program
  買防毒程式

執行防毒程式 為了保護電腦不受病毒侵害，必須安裝的軟體。

● What can we do to fix this?

● **Run an anti-virus program** on your computer.

　●我們能怎樣解決這個問題？　●在你電腦上執行防毒程式。

▶ The computer worked better when I ran an anti-virus program. 我執行防毒程式時，電腦運作得比較好。

　I just ran a virus scan on your computer.

　我剛才掃瞄了你電腦的病毒。

clean out the virus

清除病毒 藉由防毒軟體等，將病毒刪除，並且修復中毒檔案。

● Can you make do with my computer?

● Sure, if you **cleaned out that virus**.

　●你可以將就一下用我的電腦嗎？　●當然，只要你清空病毒就行。

▶ I was not able to clean out the virus.

　我無法清除病毒。

　Sheila cleaned out the virus on her laptop.

　Sheila 把她筆記型電腦上的病毒都清光了。

1 職場・學校

2 電腦・網路

3 社交生活

4 日常生活

5 訊息・理解

6 想法・態度

7 情緒・狀況

8 行為舉止

9 時間地點・副詞片語

 奇特的英文發音

　　有些英語母語人士的發音，和我們平常學到的不同。「anti-」便是最具代表性的例子之一，有些母語人士會唸成 [æntaɪ]；同理，semi- 也有人唸成 [sɛmaɪ]。還有 either 前面的「ei」，我們學到的發音是 [i]，但有些母語人士會唸成 [aɪ]，這些人也會把 neither 的「nei」唸成 [naɪ]。也有人受到加拿大式英語的影響，把 often 的「t」唸出來。

04 網路 have access to

2-04.mp3

log in/on to

・log on to Messenger
登入 MSN
・log on to the Internet
登入網路
・log off/out
登出

登入　雖然是英文，但在我們的生活中已經很常用了。log in 和 log on to 是一樣的意思。

● How do I use this e-mail account?

● You have to **log in** right there.

　● 我該怎麼使用這個電子郵件帳號？　● 你必須在那裡登入。

▶ Use the box on the screen to log in. 用螢幕上的框框來登入。
You must log in to use a library computer.
你必須登入才能使用圖書館的電腦。

get connected to

・hook up / connect to
the Internet
連上網路
・get on the Internet
上網
・tap into the Internet
上網

連上（網路）　如果要說連上網路，受詞是 the Internet。

● Why isn't the computer working?

● I tried to **connect to the Internet**, but I did it wrong.

　● 這台電腦為什麼不動？　● 我試著連上網路，但我弄錯了。

▶ We got connected to the Internet at the coffee shop.
我們在咖啡店連上網路。
I will get connected to the Internet soon.
我很快就會連上網路。

search the Internet

- surf the Net
  瀏覽網路
- google sth/sb
  使用 Google 來搜尋某事物／某人

搜尋網路 可以說是現代人的嗜好之一吧？連 google 這個單字都可以當成動詞、表示「搜尋」的意思了。

- How did you find your new car?
- I **searched the Internet** for a good deal.

  ●你怎麼找到你的新車的？　●我搜尋網路找划算的交易。

▶ Don't surf the Internet during business hours.
  上班的時候不要瀏覽網路。

  Younger people are using the Internet to express their opinions. 年輕一輩的人使用網路來表達他們的意見。

have access to

- can't access the site
  無法連上網站
- block access to harmful sites
  封鎖有害網站的存取權限
- find Internet access
  尋找可以上網的地方

有…的使用權限 形容詞 accessible 表示某事物「可以使用」，反義詞 unaccessible 則表示不能使用。

- Many people use computers in the library.
- That's because they **have access to** the Internet there.

  ●很多人在圖書館使用電腦。　●因為他們可以在那裡使用網路。

▶ I must have access to a new computer.
  我必須使用新電腦。

  John had access to his e-mail account.
  John 有權限使用他的電子郵件帳號。

go online

- go online to Yahoo's website
  上 Yahoo 網站
- shop online
  線上購物

上線，上網 後面接上「to...」，可以說明連上什麼網站。

- How often do you **go online**?
- Usually I'm on the Internet a few times a day.

  ●你多久上網一次？　●我通常一天會上幾次網。

▶ Jim went online to research the book.
  Jim 上網研究那本書。

  I go online when I need to email people.
  當我需要寄電子郵件時，我就會上網。

do research on the Internet

- type the keyword in the search bar
  在搜尋欄位打入關鍵字

在網路上進行研究 指的其實就是搜尋資料這件事。

- Why do students go online so much?
- Many of them **do research on the Internet**.

  ●為什麼學生這麼常上網？　●很多人在網路上做研究。

▶ Danny did research on the Internet for class.
  Danny 為了他的課在網路上搜尋資料。

  I did research on the Internet to find the best price.
  我在網路上進行研究，尋找最好的價格。

visit one's blog

· read about sth in one's blog
在某人的部落格讀關於某事物的文章
· write sth on one's blog
在某人的部落格寫些東西
· visit website
拜訪網站

拜訪某人的部落格 看部落格或網站，動詞是 visit。

● I'm going to use the Internet.
● You should **visit my blog**.

　　●我要上網。　　●你該看看我的部落格。

▶ We visited Dave's blog and read his comments.
我們拜訪了 Dave 的部落格，並且閱讀他的評論。
No one visits my blog anymore.
再也沒有人來我的部落格參觀了。

click the right button

· (a message) pop up
（訊息）跳出

點滑鼠右鍵 常用來開啟功能選單的動作。

● **Click the right button** to open the file.
● OK, just give me a minute.

　　●點右鍵打開這個檔案。　　●好，等我一下。

▶ I clicked the right button on the icon.
我在圖示上點了右鍵。
Click the right button when you want to start.
當你想要開始的時候，就點右鍵。

use Internet banking

· pay sth through Internet banking
透過網路銀行來付某事物的款項

使用網路銀行 Internet banking 也可稱為 online banking。

● How do you pay your bills?
● I always **use Internet banking**.

　　●你怎麼付帳單的？　　●我都用網路銀行。

▶ Helen saved her money using Internet banking.
Helen 用網路銀行來省錢。
They used Internet banking to transfer funds.
他們用網路銀行將資金轉帳。

1 職場・學校
2 電腦・網路
3 社交生活
4 日常生活
5 訊息・理解
6 想法・態度
7 情緒・狀況
8 行為舉止
9 時間地點・副詞片語

post sth on the Internet

· write sth on the Internet
在網路上寫些東西

· posting of one's personal views
某人個人觀點的文章

在網路上發表某事物（如文章、圖片）

● I'm going to post a message on the Internet.
● What kind of message is it?

●我要在網路上發一篇訊息。　●怎樣的訊息？

▶ Pam posted her phone number on the Internet.
Pam 把她的電話號碼放上網路。
The company posted an ad for a job on the Internet.
這間公司在網路上刊登了一則徵人廣告。

post one's opinion

· write bad things about…
對於…寫些不好的事

發表某人的意見　後面接 about sth 可以說明是關於什麼的意見。

● What have you been typing?
● I posted my opinion about the government.

●你在打什麼？　●我發表了自己對於政府的意見。

▶ Sam posted his opinion about the election.
Sam 發表了自己對於選舉的意見。
Janie posted her opinion about the article.
Janie 發表了自己對於那篇文章的意見。

post sth in a chat forum

在論壇發表某事物　chat forum 稱為論壇，是讓大家發表並討論意見的地方。

● I just posted my address in a chat room.
● I think you should delete it quickly.

●我剛才在一個聊天室寫了我的地址。　●我想你應該快點刪掉。

▶ Jeff posted his opinion in a chat forum.
Jeff 在一個論壇發表了他的意見。
Never post your phone number in a chat forum.
絕對不要在論壇寫出你的電話號碼。

react to an Internet article

對網路文章做出反應 對一篇文章留言評論之類的行為。

- How did Kevin **react to the Internet article**?
- He didn't like what it said.
  - Kevin 對於那篇網路文章的反應是什麼？
  - 他不喜歡那篇文章的說法。

▶ Many people reacted angrily to the Internet article.
許多人憤怒地回應那篇網路文章。
They didn't react to the Internet article.
他們沒有回應那篇網路文章。

troll on the Internet

· troll
在網路上發表沒有水準的
言論，刻意點燃戰火的人

在網路上發表挑釁的言論 troll 是指在網路上發表無聊言論，
刻意點燃戰火的人，也就是所謂的網路小白。

- This person keeps posting nasty things.
- He's **just trolling on the Internet**.
  - 這個人一直在發表討人厭的文章。　● 他只是在當網路小白。

▶ A troll on the Internet tries to make people angry.
網路小白試圖讓人生氣。
I think trolls on the Internet need to be banned.
我認為需要禁止網路小白發言。

cyber bullying

· cyberbully
網路惡霸

網路霸凌 bully 意為欺負弱者的惡霸，可以當動詞用。前面加上
了「cyber」，指的是在網路上欺負別人。

- Why was your daughter so upset?
- Someone **was cyber bullying** her on the Internet.
  - 你女兒為什麼那麼沮喪？　● 有人在網路上欺負她。

▶ The student's problems came from cyber bullying.
那個學生的問題是網路霸凌造成的。
The cyber bully was not allowed to use the computer.
那個網路惡霸被禁止使用電腦。

use a false name

使用假名 有些人在網路上使用假名是為了做壞事。

- Who started those rumors about you?
- Someone **using a false name** on the Internet.
  - 誰開始散佈你那些謠言的？　● 一個在網路上用假名的人。

▶ He used a false name to post in the chatting forum.
他用假名在網路論壇上發表文章。
Able uses a false name to chat with women.
Able 用假名跟女人聊天。

1 職場·學校
2 電腦·網路
3 社交生活
4 日常生活
5 訊息·理解
6 想法·態度
7 情緒·狀況
8 行為舉止
9 時間地點·副詞片語

use a nickname　使用暱稱　不是指平常稱呼朋友的「綽號」，而是在網路上的 ID。

● Does Dan use his name when he posts?
● Never. He always **uses a different nickname**.
　● Dan 發表文章的時候，是用他的名字嗎？
　● 沒有，他總是用另一個暱稱。

▶ Many people use nicknames in chatrooms.
　許多人在聊天室使用暱稱。
　Harold used a nickname to give his opinion.
　Harold 使用暱稱發表他的意見。

 什麼是 nickname？

　　nickname 一般而言是把較長的本名簡化而成的暱稱。以男性的名字為例，
Richard 會變成 Rick，Robert 變 Bob，Andrew 變 Andy，Nicolas 變 Nick，
Thomas 變 Tom，Joseph 變成 Joe。而女生的話，Samantha 變成 Sam，Cynthia
變成 Cindy，Katherine 變成 Kate，而 Susan 變成 Sue，諸如此類。這種稱呼被
認為可以增加親近感。本篇的 Nickname 則是指在網路上使用的名稱。

06 電腦遊戲 play computer games

 2-06.mp3

play computer games

· play computer games with one's friends
　跟某人的朋友一起玩電腦遊戲
· like computer games
　喜歡電腦遊戲

玩電腦遊戲　如果只玩一款電腦遊戲，可以說 play a computer game，記得要加上冠詞 a。

● What did you do last night?
● I **played computer games** all night.
　● 你昨晚做了什麼？　● 我玩了一整晚的電腦遊戲。

▶ I'm not interested in playing computer games.
　我對於玩電腦遊戲沒有興趣。
　I forgot how much fun it is to play computer games.
　我都忘了玩電腦遊戲有多好玩了。

play some online games

玩線上遊戲　雖然是一個人坐在電腦前，卻能和網路上其他許多玩家一起互動的遊戲。

- Let's **play some online games** together.
- My favorite game is World of Warcraft.

　●我們一起來玩些線上遊戲吧。　●我最喜歡的遊戲是「魔獸世界」。

▶ Tim played some online games for hours.
　Tim 玩線上遊戲玩了好幾個小時。
　Do you like playing online computer games?
　你喜歡玩線上電腦遊戲嗎？

spend too much time playing computer games

· be a much better player of + 遊戲名稱 (than A)
　玩某個遊戲玩得（比 A 還）好

花太多時間玩電腦遊戲

- I am really tired this morning.
- You **spent too much time playing computer games**.

　●我今天早上真的好累。　●你花太多時間玩電腦遊戲了。

▶ My cousin spends too much time playing computer games. 我的堂弟花太多時間玩電腦遊戲。
　Don't spend too much time playing computer games.
　別花太多時間玩電腦遊戲。

be addicted to computer games

· be addicted to the Internet
　沉迷於網路

沉迷於電腦遊戲　對於現實世界的事情一點都不在意，只顧著玩電腦遊戲而廢寢忘食。

- I think I'm **addicted to computer games**.
- You should spend time doing other things.

　●我覺得我很沉迷於電腦遊戲。　●你該花點時間做別的事情。

▶ He's addicted to computer games and plays daily.
　他沉迷於電腦遊戲，每天都玩。
　Helen is still addicted to computer games.
　Helen 仍然沉迷於電腦遊戲。

forbid computer games

· stop playing computer games
　停止玩電腦遊戲

禁止電腦遊戲　如果某人已經進入網路中毒的境界，這是必須採取的措施。

- Can we play computer games now?
- Sorry, but my parents **forbid computer games**.

　●我們現在可以玩電腦遊戲嗎？
　●抱歉，但我的父母禁止玩電腦遊戲。

▶ The library forbids playing computer games.
　那間圖書館禁止玩電腦遊戲。
　Some schools forbid computer games.
　有些學校禁止玩電腦遊戲。

1 職場・學校
2 電腦・網路
3 社交生活
4 日常生活
5 訊息・理解
6 想法・態度
7 情緒・狀況
8 行為舉止
9 時間地點・副詞片語

07 | 網路聊天
meet online

2-08.mp3

meet online

· meet sb on the Internet
在網路上遇見某人

在網路上遇見 透過通訊軟體、聊天室或特定的社群網站遇到聊天對象。

● Gina and her boyfriend **met online**.

● I think he's a really nice guy.

●Gina 和她的男朋友是在網路上認識的。 ●我覺得他是個很好的人。

▶ You can't trust people you meet on the Internet.
你不能相信在網路上認識的人。

I went on a date with the guy I met online.
我和那個在網路上認識的男生出去約會。

meet sb at a chat room

· connect to a chat site
連上聊天網站

· get on a chat site
上聊天網站

在聊天室遇見某人 早期流行的網路交友方法。

● I'm going to **meet my friends in a chat site**.

● Let me see who is online with you.

●我要跟我的朋友在聊天網站見面。 ●讓我看看有誰也在線上。

▶ Aaron met new people in a chat room.
Aaron 在聊天室認識了新朋友。

Nowadays, kids are meeting on the Internet in chat rooms. 現在的孩子們會約在網路聊天室見面。

do a lot of chatting on the Internet

· be addicted to online chatting
沉迷於線上聊天

· be video chatting online
進行線上視訊聊天

常在網路上聊天 如果單純聊天而不進一步發展關係，或許也能避免不少麻煩。

● Do you **do a lot of chatting on the Internet**?

● No, I'm only online a few times a week.

●你常在網路上聊天嗎？ ●沒有，我一週只會上幾次網。

▶ My girlfriend does a lot of chatting on the Internet.
我的女朋友很常在網路上聊天。

Many people do a lot of chatting on the Internet.
許多人常在網路上聊天。

add sb to one's Messenger (list)

把某人加到 MSN 把人加到自己的好友名單。

- Are you going to chat with Abe?
- Sure, I'll **add him to my Messenger list**.

    ●你會和 Abe 聊天嗎？　　●當然，我要把他加到我的 MSN。

▶ Kelly added Bill to her Messenger list.

Kelly 把 Bill 加到了她的 MSN。

Should I add Max to my Messenger list?

我該把 Max 加進我的 MSN 嗎？

use instant messenger for

- instant message (IM)
  即時通訊軟體的訊息
- send an instant message to
  發送即時訊息給…
- via instant message
  透過即時訊息
- » cf. Jim IMed (instant messaged) me about the party

為了…使用即時通訊軟體 IM (instant message) 可以當成動詞。

- I **use instant messenger for** contacting my sister.
- Do you do that every day?

    ●我用即時通訊軟體和我妹妹聯絡。　　●妳每天用嗎？

▶ We send instant message to our overseas friends.

我們發送即時訊息給國外的朋友們。

Sam just got an instant message from his wife.

Sam 剛收到他太太傳來的即時訊息。

---

08 | Twitter，Facebook find sb on Facebook

2-08.mp3

tweet sth

發表推特文章 在 Twitter 上發表短篇訊息。Twitter 是國外非常流行的社交網站，除了可以在個人頁面發表短篇訊息以外，也能追蹤好友並且互傳訊息。在 Twitter 上發表訊息的動作稱為 tweet（推文）。

- Do you ever **tweet** about your day?
- Yes, I let my friends know what I'm doing.

    ●你有在推特上談論過日常生活嗎？。
    ●有，我讓我的朋友們知道我在做什麼。

▶ Some celebrities tweet about their lifestyle.

有些名人在推特上談論他們的生活方式。

He took extra time to tweet the details.

他多花了些時間推文說明細節。

1 職場・學校
2 電腦・網路
3 社交生活
4 日常生活
5 訊息・理解
6 想法・態度
7 情緒・狀況
8 行為舉止
9 時間地點・副詞片語

update one's Facebook profile

· join Facebook
加入臉書
· via Facebook
透過臉書

更新某人的臉書個人檔案

● I never see Lisa these days.

● She is always **updating her Facebook profile**.

　● 我這陣子都沒有看到 Lisa。　● 她一直都有在更新她的臉書頁面。

▶ I joined Facebook last year.
我去年開始使用臉書。
The students got together via Facebook.
學生們透過臉書聚集在一起。

find sb on Facebook

在臉書上找到某人

● An old girlfriend **found me on Facebook**.

● Are you going to meet up with her?

　● 有個前女友在臉書上找到我。　● 你要和她見面嗎？

▶ I found many classmates from high school on Facebook.
我在臉書上找到很多高中同學。
Tommy hopes to find new friends on Facebook.
Tommy 希望在臉書上找到新朋友。

delete one's Facebook account

刪除某人的臉書帳號

● I had to **delete my Facebook account**.

● Were you worried about your private information?

　● 我必須刪掉我的臉書帳號。　● 你擔心你的個人資料問題嗎？

▶ All of my kids deleted their Facebook accounts.
我的孩子們都把他們的臉書帳號刪掉了。
You must delete your Facebook account as soon as possible. 你必須盡快刪除你的臉書帳號。

09 電子郵件帳戶
have an email account

2-09.mp3

set up email accounts

· set up an anonymous email account
建立匿名的電子郵件帳戶
· delete e-mail accounts
刪除電子郵件帳戶

建立電子郵件帳戶 email account 指帳戶，而 email address 是指電子郵件位址。

● Where should I **set up an email account**?
● Many people use Yahoo for email.

　●我該在哪裡建立我的電子郵件帳戶？
　●很多人用 Yahoo 寄電子郵件。

▶ Let's keep in touch. My email address is abc11@aol.com. 我們保持聯絡吧。我的 email 是 abc11@aol.com。
Do you know her email address?
你知道她的 email 嗎？

have an email account

· have a Gmail account
有 Gmail 的帳號
· access one's Yahoo account
使用某人的 Yahoo 帳號

有電子郵件帳戶 申請成功之後，擁有帳戶的狀態。

● Do you **have an email account**?
● Yes, let me give you the address.

　●你有電子郵件帳戶嗎？　　●有，我給你我的 email。

▶ I have had an email account for 10 years.
我有一個用了十年的電子郵件帳戶。
Steve has a secret email account.
Steve 有一個私密的電子郵件帳戶。

change one's email address

· (My email address) has been changed to…
（我的 email）改成了…
· change one's address from A to B
把某人的地址從 A 改成 B

更換某人的電子郵件位址

● I'm going to **change my email address**.
● Tell me your new address so I can send you a mail.

　●我要換個 email。　　●告訴我新的位址，這樣我才能寄信給你。

▶ She changed her e-mail address because of spam.
因為垃圾信的關係，她換了 email。
Dad is going to change his email address.
爸爸要換個 email。

1 職場・學校
2 電腦・網路
3 社交生活
4 日常生活
5 訊息・理解
6 想法・態度
7 情緒・狀況
8 行為舉止
9 時間地點・副詞片語

give sb one's email address

· exchange email addresses
  交換 email
· know one's email address
  知道某人的 email

把電子郵件位址給某人 現代人保持聯絡的方式。

● How can I stay in touch with Rick?
● **Give him your email address**.
    ●我該怎麼跟 Rick 保持聯絡？　●把你的 email 給他。

▶ Darryl gave Sam his email address.
    Darryl 把自己的 email 給 Sam。
    Did you give me your email address?
    你有給我你的 email 嗎？

add sb's address to a mailing list

· delete one's name from one's mailing list
  將某人從某人的寄件清單中刪除

把某人的電子郵件位址加到寄件清單 個人為了寄信給同一群人，會使用 mailing list，電子報和廣告信的發送者也會使用。

● Why do I get so much spam email?
● Someone **added your address to a mailing list**.
    ●為什麼我收到這麼多垃圾信件？
    ●有人把你的 email 加進寄件清單了。

▶ They will add his address to a mailing list.
    他們會把他的 email 加進寄件清單。
    Don't add my address to your mailing list.
    別把我的 email 加進你的寄件清單。

10 收發電子郵件 check one's email

2-10.mp3

check one's email

· check the email
  檢查電子郵件
· access one's email
  存取／看某人的電子郵件

檢查某人的電子郵件 打開信箱檢查是不是有新的信件。

● Hurry up, we're going to be late.
● Let me **check my email** first.
    ●快點，我們要遲到了。　●讓我先檢查我的電子郵件。

▶ I'd like to know how I can access my email.
    我想知道要怎麼看我的電子郵件。
    I check my email about as regularly as I brush my teeth.
    我檢查電子郵件的頻率大概跟刷牙一樣規律。

send sb an email

· send a quick email to let sb know that…
立刻寄封簡單的電子郵件讓某人知道⋯
· send an email to the wrong address
把郵件寄到錯誤的電子郵件位址
· send a message by email
用電子郵件寄信

寄電子郵件給某人 send 的反義詞是 receive（接收）。

● Does Sally know about the meeting?
● Yes, I **sent her an email** yesterday.
　●Sally 知道開會的事嗎？　●知道，我昨天寄了 email 給她。

▶ Send an email right now so that she gets it before noon.
現在馬上寄電子郵件給她，讓她在中午之前收到。
Who did you send that email to?
你把那封電子郵件寄給誰了？

send sth to one's Naver email

寄⋯到某人的 Naver 電子郵件信箱 Naver 可以換成任何電子郵件服務的名稱。

●I **sent an attachment to your Naver email**.
● Really? I didn't receive anything.
　●我寄了一個附加檔案到你的 Naver 信箱。
　●真的嗎？我什麼都沒收到。

▶ Hank sent the file to Bart's Gmail account.
Hank 寄了檔案到 Bart 的 Gmail 帳戶。
Don't send anything to my Yahoo email account.
別寄任何東西到我的 Yahoo 信箱。

drop an email

· drop sb an email to say…
寄電子郵件告訴某人⋯
· contact sb by email
藉由電子郵件聯絡某人

寄電子郵件 跟 drop a line（寄簡短訊息）一樣，寄電子郵件也可以用動詞 drop 來表現。

●Today is Athena's 40th birthday.
●I'll **drop her an email** to say happy birthday.
　●今天是 Athena 的 40 歲生日。　●我會寄電子郵件跟她說生日快樂。

▶ Drop Ned an email about the job.
寄電子郵件給 Ned 說有關工作的事。
Drop me an email to let me know how things are.
寄電子郵件給我，讓我知道事情的狀況。

email sb about

· email at help@mentors.com
寄電子郵件到
help@mentors.com
· block unwanted email
封鎖不想要的郵件
· open unknown emails
打開不知名人士寄的郵件

寄給某人關於⋯的電子郵件 注意這邊的 email 是動詞。

●**Email me to** let me know how you're doing.
●I will. But I don't have your email address.
　●寄電子郵件給我，讓我知道你過得怎樣。
　●我會的。但我沒有你的 email。

▶ We shouldn't open any email from people we don't know. 我們不該打開不認識的人寄的任何電子郵件。
See you later. Don't forget to email me.
晚點見。別忘了寄電子郵件給我。

1 職場・學校
2 電腦・網路
3 社交生活
4 日常生活
5 訊息・理解
6 想法・態度
7 情緒・狀況
8 行為舉止
9 時間地點・副詞片語

forward one's email to

· forward the message to…
  轉寄訊息給…

轉寄某人的電子郵件給… 快速傳遞訊息的簡單方式。

● Al's email said he'll be late to class.
● **Forward his email to** his teacher.

  ●Al 的電子郵件説他上課會遲到。
  ●把他的電子郵件轉寄給他的老師。

▶ Forward the manager's email to everyone.
  把經理的電子郵件轉寄給所有人。
  Forward this email to the police.
  把這封電子郵件轉寄給警察。

get an email from

· get email
  收到電子郵件（*在比較口語的情況下，可以不加冠詞 an）
· get one's email
  收到某人寄的電子郵件

收到…寄來的電子郵件 用 from… 説明寄件者是誰。電子郵件開頭的「From:」也會註明寄件者的 email。

● I **got an email from** Julie today.
● How are her classes at school?

  ●我今天收到一封 Julie 寄的電子郵件。　●她在學校的課上得怎樣？

▶ I got an email from him early this afternoon.
  我今天下午稍早的時候收到他的電子郵件。
  I got an email from a friend in the US.
  我收到美國的朋友寄來的電子郵件。

receive one's email

· receive one's email of June 21
  收到某人 6 月 21 日寄的電子郵件

收到某人的電子郵件 和 get 比起來，receive 這個説法比較適合正式場合。

● Did you get the note I sent?
● Sure, I **received your email**.

  ●你收到我寄的通知了嗎？　●當然，我收到你的電子郵件了。

▶ I didn't receive Tracey's email.
  我沒有收到 Tracey 的電子郵件。
  Did you receive an email from your teacher?
  你有收到老師寄的一封電子郵件嗎？

(an email) got through to sb

· (an email) be sent out to…
  （電子郵件）被寄到…

（電子郵件）寄到了某人那邊 電子郵件是主詞。

● The Internet was down for two hours.
● My email still **got through to** my girlfriend.

  ●網路壞了兩個小時。
  ●我的電子郵件還是有成功寄到我女朋友那邊。

▶ The email got through to everyone on the list.
  這封電子郵件成功寄給了名單上的每個人。
  Each email got through to the addressee.
  每封電子郵件都成功寄到各自的收件人那邊。

read one's email

讀某人的電子郵件 這裡的 one's 是表示收件人。

- Are you finished yet?
- I need time to **read my email**.
  - 你完成了嗎？　●我需要時間讀我的電子郵件。

▶ Michelle read her email at the airport.
  Michelle 在機場看了她的電子郵件。
  I read my email several times a day.
  我一天會看幾次電子郵件。

1 職場・學校

2 電腦・網路

3 社交生活

4 日常生活

5 訊息・理解

6 想法・態度

7 情緒・狀況

8 行為舉止

9 時間地點・副詞片語

---

11 附加檔案，退信
attach the file

2-11.mp3

---

attach the file

- attach a file to the email
  把檔案附加到電子郵件上
- read the attached file
  閱讀附加檔案

附加檔案 附加上去的檔案稱為 attached file 或 attachment。

- How can I get this information to Barry?
- **Attach the file** to an email for him.
  - 我該怎麼把這個訊息給 Barry？
  - 把檔案附加到電子郵件上寄給他。

▶ Attach the file you just finished.
  把你剛完成的檔案附加上去。
  Attach the files so I can look at them.
  把檔案附加上去讓我看。

open the attached file

- download the attached file
  下載附加檔案

打開附加檔案 因為病毒猖獗，所以要特別小心的動作。

- Are you going to email that information?
- Yes, just **open the attached files** I send.
  - 你會用電子郵件寄出那個訊息嗎？
  - 對，只要把我寄的附加檔案打開就好了。

▶ I couldn't open the attached file.
  我打不開附加檔案。
  Open the attached files to see our photos.
  打開附加檔案看我們的照片。

139

get a lot of junk email

收到很多垃圾信件 沒經過自己許可就自己寄來的大量廣告郵件,是現代人的困擾之一。

- I **get a lot of junk email** in my inbox.
- Me too. I really hate that stuff.
  - 我的收件匣收到很多垃圾信件。
  - 我也是。我真的很討厭那堆東西。

▶ Ray got a lot of junk email from overseas.
  Ray 收到很多國外寄來的垃圾信件。
  Do you get a lot of junk email at Hotmail?
  你在 Hotmail 會收到很多垃圾信件嗎?

get returned

- (email) be returned to sb
  (電子郵件)被退回給某人
- return to one's inbox
  回到某人的信箱
- get rejected
  被退回

被退回 由於收件位址打錯或收件人帳號問題,導致信件被退回。

- Have you contacted Mary yet?
- No, my emails to her **get returned**.
  - 你聯絡 Mary 了嗎? ● 沒有,我寄給她的信被退回來了。

▶ All of these emails got returned.
  這些電子郵件都被退回來了。
  This email got returned right away.
  這封電子郵件馬上就被退回來了。

go to one's junk file

- (a junk email) arrived in the inbox
  (垃圾信件)進了收件匣
- put into a junk email folder
  放進垃圾信件匣

被系統丟進垃圾信件匣 junk 本身就是「垃圾」的意思。

- I never got the email Dick sent.
- Maybe it **went to your junk file**.
  - 我總是收不到 Dick 寄的電子郵件。
  - 也許它被歸類為垃圾信件了。

▶ Twenty or thirty emails go to my junk file daily.
  我的垃圾信件匣每天會收到二、三十封郵件。
  The invitation went to Tina's junk file.
  邀請函進了 Tina 的垃圾信件匣。

1 職場・學校

2 電腦・網路

3 社交生活

4 日常生活

5 訊息・理解

6 想法・態度

7 情緒・狀況

8 行為舉止

9 時間地點・副詞片語

12 回覆電子郵件
answer one's email

2-12.mp3

answer one's email

· answer one's email ASAP
盡速回覆某人的電子郵件

回覆某人的電子郵件 這裡的 answer 仍然有回答問題的意思。

● I have to **answer my email**.

● How much time will that take?

　●我必須回覆電子郵件。　●會花多久時間？

▶ She answers her email every morning.
她每天早上回覆電子郵件。
I'm sorry I didn't answer your e-mail.
很抱歉我沒有回覆你的電子郵件。

respond to one's email

· respond earlier
早點回覆

回覆某人的電子郵件 同樣是回覆的意思，但 respond 是不及物動詞，要加上介系詞 to 才能接受詞。

● Did you **respond to Robin's email**?

● No, I haven't had time to do that.

　●你回覆 Robin 的電子郵件了嗎？　●還沒，我還沒有時間回。

▶ Annie responded to my email. Annie 回覆了我的電子郵件。
I can't respond to Fran's email. 我無法回覆 Fran 的電子郵件。

receive a response

· thank you for your quick response
謝謝您的迅速回覆

收到回覆 response 是 respond 的名詞形。

● Has Angie emailed you back yet?

● No, I have not **received a response** from her.

　●Angie 回信給你了嗎？　●沒有。我還沒收到她的回信。

▶ She did not receive a response from her boyfriend.
她沒有收到她男朋友的回覆。
We didn't receive a response from Jim after his computer broke. Jim 電腦壞掉之後，我們就沒有收到他的回覆了。

send a reply to sb

· reply to sb soon
很快回信給某人

· prompt reply to one's email of + 日期
對某人在某天寄的電子郵件的快速回覆

· answer sooner
早點回覆

回信給某人 除了當名詞以外，reply 也可以當成及物動詞來用。

● Did you see the email Shane sent?

● I've already **sent a reply to** him.

　●你看到 Shane 寄來的電子郵件了嗎？　●我已經回信給他了。

▶ The company sent a reply to her. 那間公司回了信給她。
You need to send a reply to your partner.
你需要回信給你的搭檔。

141

write back

- write sb whenever one can
  不論何時，只要方便就寫信給某人
- write with regard to one's email of + 日期
  回覆某人在某天寄的電子郵件（with regard to 是「關於…」的意思）

回信 後面加上 when you can 是請對方有空時回信，是一種婉轉的請求方式。

- I sent an email to my boyfriend in the army.
- Tell him to **write back** when he can.
  - ●我寄了封電子郵件給我在當兵的男朋友。
  - ●叫他方便的時候要回信。

▶ There was no time to write back. 沒有時間回信。
  I wrote back to my grandmother. 我回信給我奶奶。

---

13 信件，備忘錄
drop a line

2-13.mp3

---

write to sb

- write (sb) a letter
  寫信（給某人）
- mail/post a letter to…
  寄信給…
- mail sth (for…)
  寄某樣東西（給…）

寫信給某人 雖然已經很少人手寫信件，但習慣上還是會用 write 這個動詞。

- Did you ever **write to** a movie star?
- I wrote to Tom Cruise but never got an answer.
  - ●你寫信給電影明星過嗎？
  - ●我寫給湯姆克魯斯過，但從來沒有收到回信。

▶ She stayed up for a few hours and wrote a letter to her mother. 她熬夜了幾小時，寫了封信給她母親。
  I was up all night writing this letter to her.
  我熬夜一整晚寫了這封信給她。

---

write an apology letter

- write a long letter to sb
  寫封很長的信給某人
- write home frequently
  常常寫信回家

寫道歉信 apology 和 letter 都是名詞，結合成一個複合名詞。

- I heard you had a fight with Kate.
- I plan to **write an apology letter** to her.
  - ●我聽説你跟 Kate 吵了一架。　●我打算寫封道歉信給她。

▶ Madge wrote an apology letter to Guy.
  Madge 寫了封道歉信給 Guy。
  You need to write an apology letter.
  你需要寫一封道歉信。

drop a line

- drop a line to...
  寫信給…
- drop a line as soon as...
  一…就立刻寫信

寫簡短的信 a line 的本意是「一行文字」。a line 也可以換成 a note。

- Don't forget to **drop me a line**.
- I'll make sure that I keep in touch.

  ●別忘了寫封信給我。　●我一定會保持聯絡。

▶ Drop me a line when you get the chance.

  你方便的時候，寫封信給我。

  Drop me a line to let me know how you're doing.

  寫封信讓我知道你過得怎樣。

answer a letter

- get/receive a letter
  收到信件
- reply a letter
  回信

回信 跟電子郵件一樣，回信可以用 answer 這個動詞。

- Did you write back to Patrick?
- No, I never **answered his letter**.

  ●你回信給 Patrick 了嗎？　●沒有，我從來沒有回他的信。

▶ Mr. Barnes answers every letter that he gets.

  Barnes 先生會回每一封他收到的信。

  She will answer the letter in the morning.

  她將會在早上回信。

send a fax

- send sth to sb by fax
  傳真某物給某人
- get the fax (from)
  （從…）收到傳真

寄傳真 fax 可以當動詞使用，例如「fax sth to sb」、「fax sb sth」或「fax + 地方副詞」等等。

- I can mail the report to you.
- Just **send a fax** of it.

  ●我可以把報告寄給你。　●傳真給我就可以了。

▶ I've been trying to fax to your office all day.

  我一整天都在試著傳真到你的辦公室。

  I will fax them to you tomorrow morning before 12:00.

  我會在明天中午 12 點前傳真給你。

send sb a postcard

- send off a letter
  寄信
- send sb a letter of acceptance
  寄錄取通知給某人
- receive one's letter of acceptance
  收到某人的錄取通知

寄明信片給某人 雖然用明信片傳遞訊息已經有點不合時宜，但還是有很多人喜歡在旅遊時寄紀念明信片。

- My friend **sent me a postcard** from her vacation.
- Is she traveling through Egypt now?

  ●我朋友度假時寄了張明信片給我。　●她現在在埃及旅行嗎？

▶ Tim sent his friends nice postcards.

  Tim 寄了漂亮的明信片給他的朋友們。

  I plan to send off a letter to the newspaper.

  我打算寄信給報社。

1 職場・學校

2 電腦・網路

3 社交生活

4 日常生活

5 訊息・理解

6 想法・態度

7 情緒・狀況

8 行為舉止

9 時間地點・副詞片語

write a note to sb

- write a note and put it on…
  寫張便條並且把它放在…
- take a note
  記筆記
- leave a note
  留個便條

寫便條給某人 sb 可以移到 a note 前面，這時候要去掉介系詞 to，例如 write me a note 或 write one's family a note 等。

- How did Carey quit her job?
- She **wrote a note to** her boss.

  ● Carey 怎麼辭職的？　● 她寫了張便條給她老闆。

▶ I'll write a note to my mom tonight.
  我今晚會寫張便條給我媽。
  I'll send a note around letting everyone know.
  我會寄通知讓大家知道。

 有兩個受詞的動詞

　　有些動詞可以接兩個受詞，write 就是其中之一，例如 write her a letter。這類動詞通常都有「把 A 給 B」的意思，其中的 A 稱為直接受詞，B 稱為間接受詞。在上面的例子裡，a letter 是直接受詞（「寫」的動作直接影響的對象），her 是間接受詞（收到寫出來的東西的人）。兩個受詞的位置也可以對調，但別忘了對調之後要在間接受詞前面加上適當的介系詞，例如 write a letter to her。

---

14 打電話 give a call

2-14.mp3

give sb a call

- give (sb) a ring/buzz
  打電話（給某人）
- call (sb) up
  打電話（給某人）

打電話給某人 除了 call 以外，也可以換成 ring 或 buzz（原意是電話鈴聲）。

- Let's have dinner sometime.
- OK. **Give me a call.**

  ● 我們找個時間一起吃晚餐吧。　● 好，打電話給我。

▶ Feel free to give me a call if you have any questions.
  有問題的話，儘管打電話給我。
  Why didn't you give me a ring yesterday?
  你昨天為什麼沒有打電話給我？

call sb

· call 911
  打 911（美國的報警兼緊急求助電話）
· call security
  打電話給保全

打電話給… call 的後面除了人名以外，還可以接 911、security（保全）、the police、the hotel 等等。

● The bank is being robbed!
● I'll **call 911** and get the police!
  ●銀行被搶了！ ●我打 911 叫警察來！

▶ Call the hotel and book a room.
  打電話到飯店訂房。
  Call the store and see when they open.
  打電話到店裡問他們幾點開門。

call back

· call back later
  稍後回電話
· return one's call
  回某人的電話

回電話 打電話找人而某人不在，對方稍後回電話稱為 call back，自己再打一次電話也是 call back。

● Could you tell her to **call back** after lunch?
● I'll tell her right now.
  ●可以請你轉告她午餐時間後回電嗎？ ●我現在就跟她說。

▶ That's okay. I'll call back later in the afternoon.
  沒關係，我下午晚點會再打電話。
  Hi Jason, it's Nick. I'm returning your call.
  嗨，Jason，我是 Nick。我是要回你的電話。

make a call

· make an international call
  打一通國際電話
· make an important call
  打一通重要的電話
· make a quick call
  打一通簡短的電話

打電話 相反的，接電話則是 take a call。

● I've got to **make a call** right now.
● Here, you can use my cell phone.
  ●我現在必須打個電話。 ●你可以用我的手機。

▶ I have to go make a call, I'll be back.
  我必須打個電話，我稍後回來。
  She took out her phone and made a call.
  她拿出手機打了一通電話。

be calling to ask

· be calling to talk to sb
  打電話和某人說話
· call to tell sb S+V
  打電話告訴某人…
· call to see if S+V
  打電話詢問是否…

為了詢問…而打電話 習慣上會先說 I'm calling to... 表明打電話的動機。

● Chris, I'm **calling to ask** you for a favor.
● I'll do my best, what would you like?
  ●Chris，我打電話是想請你幫忙。 ●我會盡力的。你想要我做什麼？

▶ I'm calling to ask you for a favor.
  我打電話是想請你幫忙。
  I'm just calling to see if you received the payment.
  我打電話是想確認你是否收到款項了。

1 職場・學校
2 電腦・網路
3 社交生活
4 日常生活
5 訊息・理解
6 想法・態度
7 情緒・狀況
8 行為舉止
9 時間地點・副詞片語

15 接電話，掛電話
take the call

2-15.mp3

---

take the call

· take the call in one's office
在某人的辦公室裡接電話
· take this call
接這通電話

接電話 要說「接某人的電話」，則是用 take one's call 來表示。

● Your mom is on the line.
● I can't **take her call** right now.
　●你媽在（電話）線上。　●我現在沒辦法接她的電話。

▶ Would you excuse me for a second while I take this call?
你可以讓我接一下電話嗎？
I will take the call in my office.
我會在我的辦公室裡接這通電話。

---

get the phone

· answer the phone
接電話
· get a call saying that...
接到一通說…的電話

接電話 get off the phone 則是掛電話的意思。

● Hey, someone is calling us.
● I'll **get the phone** and see who it is.
　●嘿，有人打電話給我們。　●我來接看看是誰。

▶ Sally got the phone when it rang. Sally 接了響起的電話。
I'm sorry, but I couldn't get the phone.
我很抱歉，但我無法接這通電話。

---

get through to

· get through to sb on the phone
用電話聯絡上某人
· get through to the warehouse
用電話聯絡上倉庫

打通電話 to 的後面接想打通的對象或地點等等。

● Did you **get through to** your brother?
● No, he never picked up the phone.
　●你聯絡上你哥哥了嗎？　●沒有，他一直不接電話。

▶ It was hard to get through to the office.
那間辦公室的電話很難打通。
I got through to my parent's house. 我打電話到我父母的家。

---

have got another call

· be getting another call
接到另一通電話

有另一通電話 口語中常把表示「擁有」的 have 說成 have got。

● Hold on, I've got another call.
● Don't keep me waiting for you.
　●等等，我有另一通電話。　●別讓我一直等。

▶ I have another call. Can I call you back later?
我有另一通電話，我可以稍後再打給你嗎？
Can you hold on a moment? I have another call.
你可以等一下嗎？我有另一通電話。

get off (the phone)

· hang up
　掛斷（電話）
· hang up on sb
　掛某人電話（通常指不想
　繼續說下去，忽然掛掉電
　話的情形）

掛掉（電話） the phone 後面可以加上 with sb，表示結束和某人的通話。

● Would you please get off the phone?
● Why? I can use it if I want to.
　●可以請你掛電話嗎？　●為什麼？我想用就用。

▶ Please hang up the phone.
　請把電話掛掉。
　Don't hang up. Just listen.
　別掛斷，聽我說。

---

16 能接／不能接電話
be available

2-16.mp3

---

a phone call for

找…的電話 「有某人的電話」則是 There is a phone call for sb。

● There's a phone call for you.
● Thank you. I'll take it in my office.
　●有你的電話。　●謝謝，我在我的辦公室接。

▶ Hey Cindy! Phone call for you!
　嘿，Cindy！妳的電話！
　Excuse me. There's a phone call for you.
　不好意思，有你的電話。

have a phone call

· I have a call for sb
　我有一通找某人的電話
· You have a call from…
　你有通…打來的電話

有電話 後面接 for sb 是指打給某人的電話，接 from sb 則是指某人打來的電話。

● Did you need to see me?
● Yeah, you have a phone call.
　●你要見我嗎？　●對，你有通電話。

▶ I have a call on the other line. I'll have to say good bye.
　我有另一通電話要接，得跟你說再見了。
　You have a call from Mr. Thomas.
　你有通 Thomas 先生打來的電話。

1 職場·學校
2 電腦·網路
3 社交生活
4 日常生活
5 訊息·理解
6 想法·態度
7 情緒·狀況
8 行為舉止
9 時間地點·副詞片語

be available

· be free right now
現在有空

有空的，能接電話的 除了接電話以外，也可以表示在場、能做某事的狀態。

● Is Michael **available**?

● I'm sorry, he's just stepped out.

● Michael 在嗎？　● 抱歉，他剛走出去。

▶ They will be available in an hour.
他們一小時後就會有空。
I'd like to speak with Anthony, if he is available.
如果 Anthony 方便的話，我想跟他講電話。

sb be on line 3

· It's sb on the line
某人在（電話）線上
· pick up on line one
接一線的電話

某人在 3 線上 公司裡通常有很多條電話線路，想請別人接起某線電話時可以這樣說。

● It's your mom on the line.

● Please take a message. I'm busy now.

● 你媽媽在線上。　● 請幫我記下她的留言，我現在很忙。

▶ It's your boyfriend on the line.
你男朋友在線上。
Is Jessica still on the line?
Jessica 還在講電話嗎？

be not in

· step out of the office
走出辦公室

不在 對方要找的人剛好不在位子上，就可以這樣說。

● Hello, could I speak to Jason Lane?

● Sorry, but he's **not in** right now.

● 你好，我可以跟 Jason Lane 講話嗎？　● 不好意思，但他現在不在。

▶ Susan stepped out of the office and can't take your call.
Susan 離開了辦公室，沒辦法接你的電話。
My boss is not in, but maybe I can help you.
我的老闆現在不在，但也許我能幫你的忙。

17 通話中的等待
be on the phone

2-17.mp3

1 職場・學校
2 電腦・網路
3 社交生活
4 日常生活
5 訊息・理解
6 想法・態度
7 情緒・狀況
8 行為舉止
9 時間地點・副詞片語

be on the phone

· The (phone) line is busy
電話忙線中
· be on the other line
正在講另一通電話

通話中 後面可以接 to sb 表示通話對象，接「for + 時間」表示時間長短。加上 still 變成 be still on the phone，強調還在講話中。

● Is Jimmy at home right now?
● Sorry, but he's **on the phone**.
●Jimmy 現在在家嗎？　●抱歉，他正在講電話。

▶ Linda was on the phone for hours.
Linda 講了好幾個小時的電話。
Quiet! I'm on the phone right now.
安靜點！我正在講電話。

hold the line

· hold the line and tell the operator
不掛斷電話，並且告訴總機…
· have been on hold for + 時間
已經在電話上等了…

不掛斷電話 後面可以接上 for a second，請對方「稍等一下」。

● Could you just **hold the line** for a second?
● Sure.
●您可以稍等一下嗎？　●當然。

▶ You'll need to hold the line until I finish.
在我做完之前，不要掛斷電話。
I've been on hold for 10 minutes already.
我已經在電話上等了十分鐘了。

hang on

· hold on
不掛斷電話
· hold on a minute
稍等一下
· hold on a second
稍等一下

不掛斷電話 請別人不要掛斷的時候，也可以說 wait 或 be patient。

● Excuse me, is there someone there who can speak English?
● **Hold on.** I'll get the manager.
●不好意思，您那邊有人會說英文嗎？　●稍等一下，我請經理過來。

▶ Hang on a minute. I'll get him.
稍等一下，我去叫他來。
Can you hang on? I've got another call.
你可以等我一下嗎？我有另一通電話。

give (sb) a message

- leave a (voice) message
  留（語音）留言給某人
- leave a message saying…
  留言說…
- take a message
  幫別人記下留言

留言給某人 沒辦法直接和對方談話，退而求其次留下留言。

- I'm sorry he's out on business.
- Can I **leave a message** for him?
  ● 我很抱歉，他出去辦事了。　● 我可以留言給他嗎？

▶ Could I take a message?
  我可以幫您留言嗎？
  She didn't answer her phone. I left a message.
  她沒有接電話。我留言（在答錄機上）了。

have A call B

- spell one's name
  拼某人的名字

讓 A 打給 B 對方（B）要找的人（A）不在，所以請 A 之後打電話給 B。

- I'll **have her call** you back as soon as she gets in.
- Thank you.
  ● 她一進來我就請她回電給你。　● 謝謝。

▶ Just have him call me, okay?
  叫他打給我，好嗎？
  If she finds it, have her call me immediately.
  如果她找到了，叫她立刻打給我。

---

18 | 轉接電話
put A through to B

2-18.mp3

put A through to B

- put a phone call through to A
  把電話轉接給 A

把 A 打來的電話轉給 B 轉接電話的普遍說法。

- Phone call for you. Are you available?
- Sure, **put it through to** my office.
  ● 你的電話。你有空接嗎？　● 當然。把它轉到我的辦公室吧。

▶ Would you put me through to the manager, please?
  可以請您幫我把電話轉給主管嗎？
  I'll put you through right away.
  我現在立刻幫您轉接。

put sb on the phone

讓某人接電話 把電話轉給某人接。

- I want you to **put mom on the phone**.
- Sorry, but she's busy right now.
  - ●麻煩請媽媽來接電話。 ●抱歉，她現在在忙。

▶ Put your manager on the phone.
  把電話轉給你的主管。
  You should put Lucy on the phone.
  你應該把電話轉給 Lucy 接。

transfer this call to...

- switch the phone to sb
  將電話轉給某人
- switch A over to B
  將 A 電話轉給 B
- direct one's call
  轉接某人的電話

把電話轉接給… transfer 也可以換成 switch 或 direct。

- I'd like to talk to Taylor Walker, please.
- Hold the line please, and I will **transfer** you.
  - ●我想跟 Taylor Walker 說話，謝謝。
  - ●請不要掛斷電話，我幫您轉接。

▶ American Airlines. How can I direct your call?
  這裡是美國航空，請問您想要將電話轉接到哪裡？
  What a noisy line! I'll switch to another.
  電話雜音好吵，我換支電話打。

get A for B

- give me A
  幫我轉接 A

將 B 的電話轉接給 A 口語中常見的用法，通常是很熟的朋友間會使用的表達方式。

- I'd like to speak with Joanna, please.
- I'll **get her for** you.
  - ●我想要跟 Joanna 說話。 ●我幫你把電話轉給她。

▶ Just a moment. Let me get the manager for you.
  稍等一下，我幫你把電話轉給主管。
  Give me Natalie in sales, please.
  請幫我轉接業務部的 Natalie。

reach sb at

- contact sb
  聯絡某人
- would like to contact sb
  想要聯絡某人（和某人通話）
- Where can I reach him?
  我該怎麼聯絡他？

打某支電話聯絡某人 at 的後面接某人的聯絡電話。reach 也可以改成 contact。

- How can I get in touch with you?
- You can **reach me at** 010-3794-5450 any time.
  - ●我該怎麼跟你聯絡？ ●你可以隨時打 010-3794-5450 找我。

▶ How should I contact you to arrange another meeting?
  我該怎麼聯絡你以安排另一場會議？
  My name is Lee, and I would like to contact Sam.
  我是 Lee，我想要跟 Sam 聯絡。

1 職場・學校

2 電腦・網路

3 社交生活

4 日常生活

5 訊息・理解

6 想法・態度

7 情緒・狀況

8 行為舉止

9 時間地點・副詞片語

19 | 收訊不好
be cut off

2-19.mp3

have a bad connection

· (this) must be a bad connection
收訊很差

· (the lines) be crossed
（線路）被干擾

收訊不好，連線有問題 講電話時聽到沙沙聲之類的情況。

● I think we **have a bad connection**.
● Maybe I should call you back.

●我覺得收訊不太好。　●我重新打一次電話給你吧。

▶ There must be a bad connection. 收訊很差。
I'm still here, but we have a really bad connection.
我還在線上，不過收訊實在很差。

get bad reception

· get good reception
收訊狀況良好

收訊不好 reception 可以指電話的收訊，特別是手機的收訊。

● I've been calling your cell.
● Well, we **get bad reception** on the elevator.

●我一直在打你的手機號碼。　●我們在電梯裡，收訊不好。

▶ Jim got bad reception while he was hiking.
Jim 在登山健行的時候收訊不好。
He said his cell phone wasn't getting good reception.
他說他手機的收訊不好。

have trouble hearing sb

· sound far away
（電話中的聲音）聽起來很遙遠

· be noise on one's line
某人的電話有雜音

聽不清楚某人說的話 have trouble doing sth 表示做事有困難。

● You **sound far away**.
● My cell phone's reception isn't good.

●你的聲音聽起來好遙遠。　●我手機的收訊不好。

▶ I'm having trouble hearing you. Can you repeat that?
我聽不太清楚你說什麼，可以再說一次嗎？
There's noise on my line. 我這邊的電話有雜音。

break up

（訊號）中斷 常用進行式，表示訊號快要中斷，也就是「斷斷續續」的意思。

● Your voice isn't very clear.
● I think this line **is breaking up**.

●你的聲音不太清楚。　●收訊斷斷續續的。

▶ The cell phone call began to break up.
手機的收訊開始斷斷續續的。
You're breaking up! 你的聲音聽起來斷斷續續的。

be cut off

· (battery) be dying
  （電池）快沒電了
· (the phone) go dead
  （手機）沒電了
· It eats up batteries.
  這很耗電。

通話被切斷 可以用來表示手機沒電等被迫中斷通話的情況。

● Did you break your cell phone?
● No. My battery **went dead** and it stopped working.

  ●你手機壞掉了嗎？　　●沒有啦，電池沒電，所以手機不能用了。

▶ The phone is dead.
  這手機沒電了。
  Here is the number in case we get cut off, 212-555-1234. 我把電話號碼給你以防斷線，電話是 212-555-1234。

1 職場·學校

2 電腦·網路

3 社交生活

4 日常生活

5 訊息·理解

6 想法·態度

7 情緒·狀況

8 行為舉止

9 時間地點·副詞片語

20 其他電話慣用語
wait for one's call

2-20.mp3

wait for one's call

· expect one's call (from)
  等某人（從…打來）的電話

等某人的電話 wait for（等待）後面接名詞（片語），是很基本的表達方式。

● Mr. Johnson, please. It's Bob from New York.
● He**'s expecting your call**. I'll connect you.

  ●請轉接 Johnson 先生。我是紐約的 Bob。
  ●他在等您的電話。我這就為您轉接。

▶ I spent all night waiting for her call.
  我等她電話等了一整晚。
  She was waiting for your call. Hold on a moment.
  她在等你的電話。請稍候。

use the phone

用電話 常以 May I use the phone? 的形式出現。

● Do you mind if I **use your phone**?
● Sure, go ahead.

  ●你介意我用你的電話嗎？
  ●當然不，請用。（在美國口語中，有許多人會用 Sure 表示對方「可以用電話」，但在正式的情況下應該回答 No，表示「不介意」。）

▶ Excuse me, I have to use the phone.
  不好意思，我需要用電話。
  Why can't you use the phone in here?
  你為什麼不能用這裡的電話？

talk on the phone

· say on the phone
  用電話說

講電話 可以表示講電話或者講手機。

● What did Danny **say on the phone**?
● Something's come up and he can't attend the meeting.

  ● Danny 在電話裡說了什麼？
  ● 發生了一點事情，所以他沒辦法參加會議。

▶ I really hate to talk on the phone.
  我真的很討厭講電話。
  We talked on the phone for a long time.
  我們講電話講了很久。

recognize one's voice

· recognize sb/sth
  認出某人／某物

認出某人的聲音 講電話的時候沒辦法看到對方的面貌，所以用聲音來認人。

● It's me, Tom.
● Sorry, Tom. I didn't **recognize your voice**.

  ● 是我，Tom。 ● 抱歉，Tom，我沒認出你的聲音。

▶ I recognized my mom's voice.
  我認出了我媽媽的聲音。
  Everyone recognized the actor's voice.
  每個人都認出了那位演員的聲音。

have the wrong number

打錯電話 意思是「手邊的電話號碼是錯的」，以致打錯電話。

● May I speak to Jerry, please?
● You must **have the wrong number**.

  ● 我可以跟 Jerry 講話嗎？ ● 你一定是打錯電話了。

▶ I'm afraid you have the wrong number.
  恐怕你打錯電話了。
  I'm sorry, you've got the wrong number.
  很抱歉，你打錯電話了。

dial the wrong number

· dial the wrong number
  (by mistake)
  （不小心）撥錯電話
· call the wrong number
  打錯電話

打錯電話 特別強調打電話的時候撥錯號碼。

● Is this the Lewis Movie Theater?
● No, you **have dialed the wrong number**.

  ● 是 Lewis 電影院嗎？ ● 不是，你撥錯電話了。

▶ I dialed the wrong number after drinking several beers.
  我喝了幾罐啤酒以後，打錯電話了。
  Maybe you dialed the wrong number when you called her. 也許你打給她的時候按錯號碼了。

call sb over

· be on call
待命

打電話叫某人過來 打電話請對方過來，以便當面交代事情或一起做事。

● Do you want to go to a movie?

● I'd like to, but I'm on call today.

　●你想去看電影嗎？　●我很想，但我今天要待命。

▶ Call your friend over here.

　打電話叫你朋友來這裡。

　I'm on call at the hospital all weekend.

　我整個週末都在醫院待命。

21 手機
text sb

2-21.mp3

call sb's cell phone

· call sb on your cell phone
用你的手機打電話給某人

打電話到某人的手機 sb 的部分可以是代名詞、人名或職稱。

● Paula never came to dinner.

● Let's call her cell phone.

　●Paula 一直沒來吃晚餐。　●我們打她的手機吧。

▶ I called my supervisor's cell phone.

　我打了電話到我主管的手機。

　Call me on your cell phone when you are free.

　你有空的時候打手機給我。

reach sb on one's cell phone

· contact sb on one's cell phone
用自己的手機聯絡某人

用自己的手機聯絡某人 one's 和主詞一致，也就是用主詞自己的手機打給某人。

● Have you talked to Andre today?

● No, I couldn't reach him on my cell phone.

　●你今天有跟 Andre 講過話嗎？　●沒有，我打手機找不到他。

▶ Bonnie reached her sister on her cell phone.

　Bonnie 用手機打電話給她姐姐。

　He reached the police on his cell phone.

　他用手機打電話給警察。

1 職場·學校
2 電腦·網路
3 社交生活
4 日常生活
5 訊息·理解
6 想法·態度
7 情緒·狀況
8 行為舉止
9 時間地點·副詞片語

be on a cell phone

· talk on a cell phone
　講手機

在講手機 在用手機講電話的狀態。

- My roommate is driving me crazy.
- Yeah, she talks all night **on her cell phone**.
  - ●我室友快把我搞瘋了。　●是啊，她整晚都在講手機。

▶ Let Gary talk on your cell phone. 讓 Gary 用你的手機講。
　She is on a cell phone, talking to Mom.
　她正在用手機和媽媽講電話。

answer one's cell phone

· (cell phone) be ringing
　（手機）鈴聲在響

接手機 這裡的 one 和接手機的人一致。

- Why didn't you **answer your cell phone**?
- I forgot it at home today.
  - ●你為什麼不接手機？　●我今天把手機忘在家裡了。

▶ He's not answering his cell phone. 他不接手機。
　Your cell phone's ringing. 你的手機在響。

turn off the cell phone

· use one's cell phone
　用某人的手機
· borrow a cell phone
　借手機
· prohibit the use of cell phones
　禁止使用手機

關掉手機 如果手機是因為沒電而自動關機，可以說 The phone switched off.。

- Can you call a taxi for me?
- Sure, I'll **use my cell phone**.
  - ●你可以幫我叫台計程車嗎？　●當然，我用我手機幫你叫車。

▶ I'm sorry to trouble you, but could I borrow a cell phone? 不好意思打擾你，我可以借支手機嗎？
　I turned my cell phone off. 我關了我的手機。

have one's phone on vibrate

· be set to vibrate
　（手機）設在震動模式
· (phone) be on silent mode
　（手機）設在靜音模式

把手機設為震動模式 這是 have + 受詞 + 受詞補語的句型。

- We must be quiet during the movie.
- I **have my cell phone on vibrate**.
  - ●我們看電影的時候必須保持安靜。　●我把我的手機設成震動。

▶ The students had their phones on vibrate.
　學生們把手機設為震動。
　I always have my phone on vibrate. It's more polite.
　我總是把手機設成震動模式，這樣比較有禮貌。

keep one's cell phone charged

· charge the cell phone
　為手機充電

使手機保持充電狀態 charge 是「充電」的意思。

- My phone isn't working again.
- You need to **keep your cell phone charged**.
  - ●我的手機又不動了。　●你要把手機保持在充電狀態。

▶ Keep your cell phone charged. 把你的手機保持在充電狀態。
　I forgot my cell phone charger. 我忘了帶手機充電器了。

miss a call

· get caller-ID
  取得來電者的號碼

沒接到電話 手機或室內電話有未接來電的時候，畫面上顯示的來電號碼稱為 caller ID。

- I **missed a call** when I was in the movie.
- Was it someone whose number you recognize?
  - 我看電影的時候漏接了一通電話。　● 是你認得的號碼嗎？

▶ Did you miss a call just now?
  你剛才是不是漏接了電話？
  Mark missed a call from his girlfriend.
  Mark 漏接了他女朋友打的電話。

send sb a text message

· send sth to sb in a text message
  用簡訊把某資訊傳給某人

· get a text message saying…
  收到一封簡訊說…

傳簡訊給某人 收到簡訊則是 get a text message。

- Are you ready to leave yet?
- Wait, I need to **send Ted a text message**.
  - 你準備好要走了嗎？　● 等等，我需要傳個簡訊給 Ted。

▶ Did you see that I sent you a text message?
  你有看到我傳簡訊給你嗎？
  I can't remember, but I'll send it to you in a text message later. 我記不得了，但我稍後會傳簡訊給你。

text sb

· text message sb
  傳簡訊給某人

傳簡訊給某人 text message 簡稱為 text，因為經常使用而衍生出動詞的用法。

- How often do you **text message** your friends?
- Oh, I do that all day long.
  - 你多常傳簡訊給朋友？　● 噢，我一整天都在傳。

▶ She didn't call or text me all week.
  她一整個禮拜都沒有打電話或傳簡訊給我。
  Most exchanges take place by email or text message.
  大部分的交易透過電子郵件或簡訊進行。

1 職場・學校
2 電腦・網路
3 社交生活
4 日常生活
5 訊息・理解
6 想法・態度
7 情緒・狀況
8 行為舉止
9 時間地點・副詞片語

22 | 智慧型電視／手機，iPad
own a Smart 3D TV

2-22.mp3

---

own a smart 3D TV

· interactive functions built into Smart TV 智慧型電視內建的互動功能

擁有智慧型 3D 電視

● Don't you want to **own a Smart 3D TV**?
● Not yet. I will buy one when we don't have to use 3D goggles.

　● 你不想擁有一台智慧型 3D 電視嗎？
　● 我還不想。等我們不必用 3D 眼鏡的時候，我才會買。

▶ Let's use the webcam through our Smart TV's screen.
我們用智慧型電視的螢幕進行視訊對話吧。
It is interesting to do Internet banking with our Smart TV.
用智慧型電視使用網路銀行很有趣。

---

install applications on a Smartphone

· delete specific applications on a Smartphone 刪除智慧型手機上的特定程式

在智慧型手機上安裝應用程式

● Which **applications** did you **install on your Smartphone**?
● Applications like Smartbanking, twitter, YouTube and so on.

　● 你在智慧型手機裡裝了哪些應用程式？
　● Smartbanking、twitter、YouTube 之類的程式。

▶ I can use my Smartphone as a camcorder or fax machine if I want.
如果我想的話，我能把我的智慧型手機當成攝錄影機或傳真機使用。
I enjoy exploring the various functions of my Smartphone.
我喜歡發掘我智慧型手機裡的多種功能。

---

car linked to a Smartphone

與智慧型手機技術結合的汽車

● Which would you prefer, a hybrid car or a car equipped with a Smartphone?
● I'd prefer a **car linked to a Smartphone** because it could prevent car crashes.

　● 你比較喜歡油電兩用車還是配備智慧型手機的車種？
　● 我喜歡與智慧型手機技術結合的車，因為可以避免車禍。

▶ We can use Smartphone technology to improve auto safety. 我們可以利用智慧型手機的技術來提升汽車安全性。
I love using Smartphone features on the dashboard screen. 我喜歡在儀表板螢幕上使用智慧型手機的功能。

1 職場·學校

2 電腦·網路

3 社交生活

4 日常生活

5 訊息·理解

6 想法·態度

7 情緒·狀況

8 行為舉止

9 時間地點·副詞片語

download e-books from an iBookstore

從 iBookstore 下載電子書
- Why do you want to buy an iPad?
- Mainly because I'll be able to read e-books by **downloading them from an iBookstore**.
  - 你為什麼想買 iPad？
  - 主要是因為這樣我就可以從 iBookstore 下載電子書來閱讀了。

▶ I can print NYT articles from my iPad using AirPrint.
我可以用 AirPrint 把我 iPad 上的紐約時報文章印出來。
We can do more effective multitasking on iPads.
我們可以利用 iPad 進行更有效率的多工處理。

---

23 | 塞車 get held up

2-23.mp3

---

get caught in traffic

· be caught in rush hour traffic
被困在尖峰時間的車潮中
· be caught in a shower
被困在陣雨中

困在車陣中 get/be caught in 是被…困住的意思，後面也可以接陣雨、大雪等惡劣天氣。

- How come you're so late?
- I **got caught in rush hour traffic**.
  - 你怎麼這麼晚到？　●我被困在尖峰時間的車潮中了。

▶ I'm going to be a bit late. I got caught in traffic.
我會稍微晚到。我被困在車陣中了。
Maybe he got caught in traffic because of the bad weather. 也許他是因為天候不佳，所以碰上塞車了。

get held up

· be/get held up behind a traffic accident
被困在車禍回堵的車陣中
· be/get held up by a traffic jam
因為塞車而被耽擱
· get held up at work
被工作耽擱了

被（車潮等）困住 除了表示被塞車耽擱以外，也可以說 traffic is held up 表示交通發生阻塞。

- Why didn't you come to the picnic?
- I'm sorry. We **got held up** in town.
  - 你們為什麼沒有來野餐？　●抱歉，我們在市區塞車了。

▶ They got held up at the airport.
他們被困在機場。
I got held up behind a traffic accident on the highway.
我被困在高速公路車禍回堵的車陣中。

be stuck in traffic

· get stuck in traffic on
the way
在半路上塞車
· (road) be blocked
（道路）被堵住
· (the traffic or cars) be
backed up
（車流或車輛）塞住了

被困在車陣中 be stuck 意為「被困住，動彈不得」。

● The traffic was so bad this morning.
● You can say that again. I **was stuck** for over an
hour!

　　●今天早上的交通很糟。　　●我同意。我塞車塞了超過一小時！

▶ I'm sorry I'm late again. I got stuck in traffic.
　　抱歉我又遲到了，我碰上了塞車。
　　It looks like we're stuck in traffic.
　　看來我們被困在車陣中了。

be a big traffic jam

· be bumper to bumper
塞車（車子一輛接著一
輛，貼得很近的狀態。主
詞是車輛或 traffic。）
· during rush hour
在尖峰時段
· put up with a traffic
jam
忍受塞車

塞車塞得很嚴重 後面接「on + 道路」可以說明哪裡在塞車。

● How come she didn't show up?
● She's probably just late **because of a big traffic
jam.**

　　●她怎麼沒有來？　　●她可能是因為大塞車所以遲到了。

▶ I decided to walk and avoid driving in the rush-hour
traffic. 我決定走路，避開尖峰時段的車潮。
　　There was a big traffic jam on the highway.
　　高速公路塞車塞得很嚴重。

beat the traffic

· beat the rush hour
traffic
避開尖峰時段的車潮
· fight the traffic
對抗塞車

避開塞車 beat 有「搶先」的意思，也就是說趕在塞車之前出發。

● I usually try to get to the office by 6:45 to **beat the
traffic.**
● Then what time do you leave home for work?

　　●我通常在 6:45 之前到辦公室，避開塞車。
　　●那你都幾點出門上班？

▶ I had no idea that traffic was this bad in Paris.
　　我都不知道巴黎的交通這麼糟。
　　It was raining and there was a lot of traffic.
　　剛才下了雨，所以塞車塞得很嚴重。

24 交通事故
have a car accident

2-24.mp3

1 職場・學校

2 電腦・網路

3 社交生活

4 日常生活

5 訊息・理解

6 想法・態度

7 情緒・狀況

8 行為舉止

9 時間地點・副詞片語

have a car accident

· have an accident on the way here
來這裡的路上出了車禍
· have a small accident
出了小車禍
· have a fender-bender
發生了小擦撞

出車禍 也可以簡化為 have an accident。

● I **had a small accident** when I was driving your car, dad.

● I'll never let you drive my car again.

● 爸,我開你的車的時候出了點車禍。

● 我再也不會讓你開我的車了。

▶ Sam, have you ever had a car accident before?
Sam,你曾經發生過車禍嗎?
I had a fender-bender on the way here.
我來這裡的路上發生了小擦撞。

get into a car accident

· be in a car accident
出車禍
· be involved in a car accident
被捲入車禍中

出車禍 get into 表示捲入、陷入某種狀況。

● I **was in a car accident** this morning.

● Oh no! Are you okay?

● 我今天早上出了車禍。   ● 噢不!你沒事吧?

▶ I got into a car accident a few days ago.
我幾天前發生了車禍。
Did you hear she got into a car accident today?
你聽說她今天發生車禍了嗎?

get hit by a car

· be/got run over by a car
被車輾過
· bring about/cause a traffic accident
造成車禍
· avoid accidents
避免車禍

被車撞到 get 可以換成 be,意思相同。

● Watch how fast I can drive.

● You're going to **cause a traffic accident**!

● 你看我能開多快。   ● 你這樣會造成車禍的!

▶ He got hit by a car and tumbles on the asphalt.
他被車撞到,摔到柏油路上。
Alice caused a traffic accident on the bridge.
Alice 在橋上引發了車禍。

wreck a car

- damage someone's car
  弄壞某人的車
- crash a car
  把車撞壞
- fall asleep at the wheel
  開車時睡著

撞壞車子 車子當主詞時，可以說 The car is wrecked in an accident. 。

● Jim **crashed his car** and is in the hospital.
● What a shame!

　● Jim 撞壞了他的車，現在人在醫院。　　● 真不幸！

▶ Don't fall asleep behind the wheel.
　開車時別睡著。
　I think someone damaged your car in the parking lot.
　我想有人在停車場弄壞了你的車。

die in a car accident

- be killed in a traffic accident
  車禍身亡
- lose one's life in a traffic accident
  車禍身亡
- be injured in a traffic accident
  車禍受傷

車禍身亡 fasten the seatbelt（繫安全帶）可以降低車禍死亡率。

● I heard that John **was injured in a car accident**.
● Is he still in the hospital?

　● 我聽說 John 在車禍中受了傷。　　● 他還在醫院嗎？

▶ My good friends died in a car accident.
　我的好友在車禍中過世了。
　Many people die in car accidents.
　許多人因車禍死亡。

---

25 汽車
take a taxi

2-25.mp3

get in

- get out (of)
  下車（普通轎車）
- get off
  下車（公車或火車）
- hop in
  搭乘

上車 一般小客車的上下車是用 get in/out 表示。至於公車、火車等地板比較高，門口可能有階梯的車，則說 get on/off。

● Please let me know where to **get off** to get to Bloomingdale's.
● You can just **get off** at the next stop.

　● 請告訴我去 Bloomingdale's 百貨要在哪裡下車。
　● 你可以在下一站下車。

▶ Is this where we get on the train to New York?
　往紐約的火車是在這邊搭嗎？
　Take the subway for two stops and get off at Paddington Station. 搭地鐵過兩站，在 Paddington 站下車。

take a taxi

· catch a taxi
  攔計程車
· hail a cab
  （揮手）攔計程車
· call a taxi
  （用電話）叫計程車

搭計程車 take 可以換成 get，taxi 可以換成 cab。

● Can you **get me a taxi**, please?
● I'd be glad to.
  ●你可以幫我叫台計程車嗎？　●我很樂意。

▶ We'll grab a taxi to the hotel and get some rest.
  我們要叫台計程車回飯店休息。
  Why don't you take a taxi with me and stay overnight at my place? 你何不跟我一起坐計程車回家，在我家待一晚呢？

pull up

· pull up at the traffic light
  在紅綠燈前停下
· pull up to…
  把車停在…

停車 例如車輛因為遇到紅燈而需要停車的狀況。

● Where should I park my car?
● **Pull up** in front of the apartment building.
  ●我該把車停在哪裡？　●停在那棟公寓大樓前面。

▶ You should pull up a little further.
  你該把車停得再遠一點。
  I pulled up to Mr. Lane's house.
  我把車停在 Lane 先生家。

pull over

· pull over on the shoulder
  把車停在路肩
· pull sb over and give sb a speeding ticket
  叫某人停車，開超速罰單給他

停車 特別指遇到臨檢，或者讓人下車的情況。

● Hey, **pull over**. I want to talk to the girl walking down the road.
● What for? She's too fat and ugly.
  ●嘿，車子停一下，我想跟在那邊走路的女孩子說句話。
  ●為什麼？她太胖了，人又醜。

▶ She saw her husband pull up in front of a hotel.
  她看到她丈夫把車停在飯店前。
  I got pulled over for speeding this morning.
  我今天早上因為超速被警察攔下來取締了。

put on one's brakes

· step on the brakes
  踩剎車
· slam on the brakes
  猛力地踩剎車
· slow down
  放慢速度

踩剎車 原意是使煞車裝置貼上車輪的碟盤，進而減速。

● Why don't you **slow down** a bit?
● I like to drive fast.
  ●你為什麼不開慢一點？　●我喜歡開快車。

▶ I don't know how to put on the brakes.
  我不知道怎麼踩剎車。
  She put on the brakes too quickly.
  她踩剎車踩得太快了。

1 職場・學校
2 電腦・網路
3 社交生活
4 日常生活
5 訊息・理解
6 想法・態度
7 情緒・狀況
8 行為舉止
9 時間地點・副詞片語

26 汽車保養
run out of gas

2-26.mp3

get locked out of the car

· lock the door
  鎖門
· lock myself out
  把我自己鎖在門外

被鎖在車外 如果是被反鎖在房間外面，可以說 get locked out of my room。

● I **got locked out of my car**.
● Did you call the locksmith?

　●我被鎖在車外了。　●你有打電話給鎖匠嗎？

▶ Lisa got locked out of her car downtown.
Lisa 在市中心時，被鎖在車外了。
Did you ever get locked out of your car?
你曾經被鎖在車外嗎？

fasten one's seatbelt

· wear a seatbelt
  繫上安全帶
· unfasten/undo one's seatbelt
  解開安全帶

繫好某人的安全帶 口語中常說 buckle up。

● Please **wear your seatbelt** in my car.
● Is this really necessary?

　●在我的車上請繫好安全帶。　●這真的有必要嗎？

▶ Please fasten your seatbelt, we're going for a ride.
請繫好你的安全帶，我們要去兜風了。
You'd better buckle up in case we get stopped at a police checkpoint.
你最好把安全帶繫好，以免我們在檢查站被警察攔下來。

won't start

· (the brakes) don't work
  （剎車）失靈，沒有用

（車輛等）發不動 例如汽車沒電的時候，就會發生這種情形。

● My car **won't start**. What should I do?
● Why don't you call a repair shop?

　●我的車發不動，我該怎麼辦？　●何不打電話給修車店呢？

▶ Darryl's car won't start, so he must fix it.
Darryl 的車發不動，他必須修好它。
Carol's new car won't start today.
Carol 的新車今天發不動。

have a flat tire

· (tire) blow out
  爆胎
· (tire) be punctured
  輪胎被戳破
· (tire) be low
  輪胎快沒氣了

輪胎沒氣 就是我們常說的「爆胎」。

● Why is the car making that noise?
● I think we **have a flat tire**.
  ●這車子為什麼發出那種聲音？　●我想輪胎漏氣了。

▶ Thomas had a flat tire on the freeway.
  Thomas 在高速公路上爆胎了。
  We had a flat tire while driving to New York.
  我們開車去紐約的途中爆胎了。

have car trouble

· have a big trouble
  with one's car
  某人的車有很大的問題

車子有問題 其他還有像是 have trouble doing... 、have trouble with sth 的用法。

● We **had car trouble** on our trip.
● Were you able to fix it?
  ●在旅行途中，我們的車子出了問題。　●你們有辦法修好嗎？

▶ Renee had car trouble this summer.
  今天夏天 Renee 的車子出了問題。
  He was late because he had car trouble.
  他因為車子有問題而遲到了。

make repairs to + 車輛

· being repaired
  正被修理
· repair the car
  修車
· get one's car repaired
  把某人的車送修

修理… make 也可以換成 carry out 或 do，意思相同。

● I plan to **get my car repaired** next weekend.
● How long will it take to get it fixed?
  ●我打算下週末把我的車子送修。　●修好要花多久時間？

▶ Do you know anything about repairing a car?
  你對修車有什麼概念嗎？
  The repairs on your car are going to be really expensive.
  你這台車修起來會很貴。

wash one's car

· go to an automatic car
  wash
  去自動洗車店
· get one's car washed
  讓某人的車被洗

洗車 如果是讓別人洗，可以說 get one's car washed。

● Cheryl's car looks quite dirty.
● Tell her to **wash her car**.
  ●Cheryl 的車看起來很髒。　●叫她去洗車。

▶ It's time to wash our cars.
  該洗我們的車了。
  I'm planning to wash my car this afternoon.
  我打算今天下午洗我的車。

1 職場・學校
2 電腦・網路
3 社交生活
4 日常生活
5 訊息・理解
6 想法・態度
7 情緒・狀況
8 行為舉止
9 時間地點・副詞片語

put gas in the car

- fill it up with regular unleaded
  加滿一般無鉛汽油
- fill it up with premium
  加滿特級汽油

加油 這裡的 gas 是 gasoline 的口語簡稱，並不是指瓦斯。

● Hello. What would you like?

● Regular unleaded. Please **fill it up.**

　●您好，您要加哪種油？。　　●一般的無鉛汽油，請幫我加滿。

▶ Put gas in the car before it runs out.
　在油用完之前去加油。
　I need to stop to put gas in the car.
　我需要停車加油。

run out of gas

- be out of gas
  油用完了
- be short of gas
  油快用完了
- find a gas station
  找加油站

用完汽油 run out of 表示用完某種平時常用的東西，是很重要的慣用語。

● Did you have a problem while driving yesterday?

● Yeah, I **ran out of gas.**

　●你昨天開車有碰到什麼問題嗎？　　●有啊，我油用完了。

▶ We're about to run out of gas.
　我們快沒油了。
　I ran out of gas. Where can we fill up?
　我沒油了，我們可以去哪裡加油？

tune up

- change the oil
  換油

調整（引擎等） 本來是指幫樂器調音，引申為引擎的調整。

● What would you like done to your car?

● Would you **change the oil,** please?

　●你的車需要什麼服務？　　●可以請你幫我換油嗎？

▶ This car runs poorly and needs a tune up.
　這台車開起來狀況很差，需要調整一下。
　Would you change the oil, please?
　可以請你幫我換油嗎？

1 職場・學校

2 電腦・網路

3 社交生活

4 日常生活

5 訊息・理解

6 想法・態度

7 情緒・狀況

8 行為舉止

9 時間地點・副詞片語

27 開車
give a ride

2-27.mp3

give a ride

- give A a ride (to…)
  載 A（到…）
- give A a ride home
  載 A 回家

載人一程 在英式英語中，則會說 give a lift。

- Are you going downtown right now?
- Yes I am. Get in and I'll **give you a ride**.
  - 你現在要去市中心嗎？　● 是啊，上車吧，我載你一程。

▶ How about I give you a ride home? 要不要我載你回家？
  Do you want me to give you a ride to the airport?
  你要我載你到機場嗎？

get a ride

- get a ride with sb
  搭某人的車
- need a ride
  需要接送
- hitch a ride
  搭便車

讓人接送，搭便車 把 give 改成 get，就變成讓人載的意思。

- I need to **get a ride home**.
- I can call a taxi for you.
  - 我需要有人載我回家。　● 我可以幫你打電話叫計程車。

▶ Can I get a ride with you? I'm going to the station.
  我可以搭你的車嗎？我要去車站。
  It's too dangerous to hitch a ride these days.
  這陣子搭便車太危險了。

ride a bicycle

- ride a bicycle to work
  騎腳踏車上班
- ride the bus to work
  搭公車上班

騎腳踏車 除了騎腳踏車和摩托車以外，ride 也可以指搭乘公車等大眾運輸工具。

- You know how to **ride a bike**, don't you?
- Of course!
  - 你會騎腳踏車，不是嗎？　● 當然會！

▶ Is it hard to learn how to ride a bike? 學騎腳踏車很難嗎？
  I started to ride the bus to work this week.
  我這星期開始搭公車上班。

drive very fast

- drive a little faster
  開得再快一點
- drive a lot/much faster
  開得快很多
- be speeding
  超速行駛

開得很快 比起 drive faster，還是 drive more safely 比較好吧…

- Why are you acting so nervous?
- I think you **drive very fast**.
  - 你為什麼表現得那麼緊張？　● 我覺得你開得很快。

▶ Harold drove very fast to get to his house.
  Harold 開車回家開得很快。
  Most teenagers drive very fast.
  大多數的青少年開車開得很快。

167

have/take a drive

· have a long drive before we get to…
抵達…之前，有很長的路要開
· take a drive in the countryside
在鄉間兜風

兜風 也可以單純表示開車到某個地方。

● We **have a long drive to** Washington.
● Let's get some rest before we leave.
　●我們要開很遠的車到華盛頓。　●我們出發前先休息一下吧。

▶ Leo took a drive to the beach. Leo 開車去海邊。
I took a drive and got some fresh air.
我開車去兜風，呼吸一點新鮮空氣。

go for a drive

· go for a ride
去兜風
· take sb for a drive/ride
帶某人去兜風

兜風 drive 也可以換成 ride，意思相同。

● Why don't we **go for a drive**?
● That's a great idea. I'm a little bored.
　●我們何不去兜個風？　●好主意，我感覺有點無聊。

▶ They went for a drive on Sunday. 他們星期天開車兜了風。
I took him for a ride. 我開車帶他去兜風。

drive one's car home

· drive to work
開車上班
· drive sb home
開車載某人回家

開某人的車回家 drive 後面也可以接人，表示載某人回家。

● I really did drink too much.
● Let me **drive you home**.
　●我真的喝太多了。　●讓我開車載你回家吧。

▶ Mary drove my car home. Mary 開我的車回家。
I drive to work. It takes about 30 minutes to get to the office. 我開車上班，到辦公室大概要花 30 分鐘。

take this exit

· miss the exit
錯過出口
· change lanes
改道（切換車道）
· use the turn signal
打方向燈

走這個出口 從高速公路的出口下交流道。

● Which direction is the airport in?
● You have to **take this exit**.
　●機場在哪個方向？　●你要走這個出口。

▶ Take this exit to go home. 走這個出口回家。
I'm going to take this exit on the highway.
我要從這個出口下高速公路。

be a good driver

· be good at driving
擅長開車

開車技術很好 開車技術很糟的人則是 a bad driver。

● Watch out! You almost hit that car!
● Relax, I'm a good driver.
　●小心點！你差點撞上那台車了！　●放輕鬆，我開車技術很好。

▶ Your sister is a good driver.
你姐姐開車技術很好。
You're such a good driver.
你開車技術真好。

drink and drive

- drunk driver
  酒醉駕車的駕駛人
- drunk driving
  酒醉駕車
- doze off while driving
  開車時打瞌睡
- nod off at the wheel
  開車時打瞌睡

酒後駕車 也就是 driving under the influence，簡稱 DUI。

● Why are the police gathered at the bridge?
● They are trying to catch people who **drink and drive**.

●警察為什麼聚集在橋那邊？　●他們想抓酒後駕車的人。

▶ Does Taiwan have a tough drinking and driving policy?
台灣的酒後駕車政策很嚴格嗎？
Korea introduced a strike-out system for drunk drivers.
韓國採用了酒駕者的「三振制度」（一年酒駕三次就吊銷駕照）。

1 職場・學校

2 電腦・網路

3 社交生活

4 日常生活

5 訊息・理解

6 想法・態度

7 情緒・狀況

8 行為舉止

9 時間地點・副詞片語

28 駕照，違反交通規則
get a ticket

2-28.mp3

get one's driver's license

- pass the driving test
  通過駕駛考試
- renew one's driver's license
  更新某人的駕照

拿到駕照 一般情況下，只說 license 也可以表示駕照。

● Robert can't drive, can he?
● Yes, he just **got his license**.

●Robert 不會開車對嗎？　●他會呀。他剛拿到駕照了。

▶ Is it hard to get your driver's license?
考駕照很難嗎？
I just got my driver's license today!
我今天剛拿到駕照！

get a ticket

- give sb a ticket
  開某人罰單
- get a traffic ticket
  收到交通罰單

被開罰單 雖然也可以表示獲得門票或車票，但也常指被開單。

● **I'm giving you a ticket** for speeding.
● Please give me a break.

●我要開一張超速罰單給你。　●放我一馬吧。

▶ I got a ticket while I was driving here.
我之前在這裡開車時，被開了罰單。
Did you get a ticket?
你有收到罰單嗎？

be fined + 罰金 + for a traffic violation

· be fined + 罰金 + for speeding
  因為超速被罰款…

因為違反交通規則被罰款…

- Why are you so unhappy today?
- I **got fined $200 for** driving too fast.
  - 你今天為什麼這麼不開心？　- 我開車太快被罰了兩百美元。

▶ My dad was fined $100 for a traffic violation during the holiday. 我爸爸在假期時因為違反交通規則，被罰了一百美元。
  The student was fined over $500 for traffic violations.
  這名學生因為違反交通規則，被罰了超過五百美元。

have one's license suspended

· get a license suspension
  被吊扣駕照

駕照被吊扣　have sth p.p. 表示「某物被…」的意思。

- Why isn't Cindy driving her car?
- She **had her license suspended** again.
  - Cindy 為什麼沒有開車？　- 她的駕照又被吊扣了。

▶ Brian's had his license suspended for drinking and driving. Brian 因為酒後駕車而被吊扣駕照。
  Thousands of people get license suspensions every year. 每年都有數千人被吊扣駕照。

have one's license revoked

· be revoked for one year
  被吊銷一年

駕照被吊銷　駕照被吊銷的話，日後就得重考駕照了。

- Does Brett take the bus to work?
- Yeah, he **had his driver's license revoked**.
  - Brett 是搭公車上班嗎？　- 是啊，他的駕照被吊銷了。

▶ Drunks usually have their licenses revoked.
  酒醉駕駛的人通常會被吊銷駕照。
  I'd be in trouble if I had my license revoked.
  如果我的駕照被吊銷，我會有麻煩的。

29 停車
park one's car

1 職場・學校

2 電腦・網路

3 社交生活

4 日常生活

5 訊息・理解

6 想法・態度

7 情緒・狀況

8 行為舉止

9 時間地點・副詞片語

park one's car

· park one's car on the street
把某人的車停在街上
· park one's car here
把某人的車停在這裡
· park somewhere else
在別的地方停車

停某人的車 park 也可以不接受詞，直接表示「停車」的意思。
● How much does it cost to **park here**?
● The parking charge is $4.50 per hour.
　●在這邊停車要多少錢？　●停車費每小時 4.5 美元。

▶ Is it all right to park my car here?
我可以把車停在這裡嗎？
I don't think it's very nice of you to park here.
我覺得你在這裡停車不太好。

pull into a parking lot

· pull out of a parking lot
把車開出停車場
· park in the parking lot
停在停車場

把車停在停車場 pull 後面也可以接車子當受詞。
● Where is the best place to park?
● **Pull into this parking lot**.
　●把車停在哪裡最好？　●停到這個停車場。

▶ I parked in a parking lot so I could call her.
為了打電話給她，我把車停到停車場。
Be careful when you pull out of the parking lot.
開出停車場的時候小心點。

park in one's parking space

· there are no parking spaces…
（某處）沒有停車位

把車停在某人的停車格 要表達「沒有停車位」，可以說 There are no parking spaces. 。
● Someone **parked in my parking space**.
● Let's get them to move their car.
　●有人把車停在我的位子。　●我們去叫他們把車開走。

▶ Someone parked in my parking space.
有人把車停在我的位子。
There are no parking spaces near the school.
學校附近沒有停車位。

171

valet bring up one's car

· hand the valet the ticket
給泊車的人停車券

泊車的人把車開來 「valet」指的是在停車場中代客泊車的人。

● I'm ready to go home now.
● The valet will **bring up your car**.
  ●我準備好要回家了。　●泊車的人會把你的車開過來。

▶ She handed the valet a ticket to get her car.
  她給泊車的人停車券,以便取車。
  A valet brought up our car from the lot.
  泊車的人把我們的車從停車場開來。

tow a car

· tow a car to the garage
把車拖到汽車維修廠
· tow-away zone
拖吊區(禁止停車的區域)
· write sb a parking ticket
開給某人一張違規停車罰單

把車拖走 加上 to the garage 指拖到汽車維修廠(不是指車庫)。

● Can I park here for a while?
● No. Someone will come and **tow your car**.
  ●我可以在這裡停車一下嗎?　●不行,有人會來拖吊你的車。

▶ The man will tow the old car away.
  這位男子會把那台舊車拖走。
  The police will tow a car that is in the wrong place.
  警察會把停錯地方的車子拖走。

---

30 | 公車,火車,地鐵 take a bus

2-30.mp3

catch a train

· catch a bus bound for...
搭乘前往…的公車
· catch a bus to Chicago
搭乘往芝加哥的公車
· catch a bus into town
搭乘往市中心的公車

搭火車 後面可以接「to / bound for / going to + 目的地」。

● Are you leaving so soon?
● Yeah, I've **got a bus to catch**.
  ●你這麼快就要走了嗎?　●嗯,我有公車要搭。

▶ Tara caught a bus going to Toronto.
  Tara 搭了一台往多倫多的公車。
  The cheapest way to travel is to catch a bus.
  旅行最便宜的方式,就是搭公車。

take a bus

- take a bus going to...
  搭乘前往…的公車
- take a bus to one's work
  搭公車去上班
- take bus number 45
  搭 45 號公車

take the train

- take the train for/to...
  搭乘前往…的火車
- take the red line
  搭乘紅線
- take the subway for one stop
  坐地下鐵坐一站
- take the subway to work
  坐地下鐵去上班

go by bus

- go (to A) by train
  搭火車去（A）

get on the bus

- ride the bus
  搭公車
- use a bus/the subway
  使用公車／地下鐵

搭公車 和 catch a train 一樣，可以在後面追加說明目的地。

- It's going to be hard to find a parking spot.
- Let's **take a bus** instead of driving.
  ● 停車位會很難找。　● 我們不要開車，改搭公車吧。

▶ I have to take a bus to the subway.
  我必須搭公車到地鐵站。
  The great thing about taking the bus is I never have to worry about parking!
  搭公車的好處就是我永遠不需要擔心停車的事！

搭火車 train 泛指各種列車，可以指捷運列車，但通常指火車。

- How did you get to Seoul?
- I **took the train** from Busan.
  ● 你怎麼去首爾的？　● 我從釜山搭火車。

▶ Just take the red line and get off at the third stop.
  搭乘紅線，然後在第三站下車。
  Does it bother you to take the train instead of an airplane? 不搭飛機改搭火車，會不會讓你覺得不便？

搭公車去 用「by + 交通工具」說明交通方式的時候不加冠詞。

- Have you got any plans for the break?
- I'm going to my hometown **by bus**.
  ● 你休假有什麼計畫嗎？　● 我要搭巴士回老家。

▶ Can I get there by bus?
  我能搭公車到那裡嗎？
  Why don't you go by train?
  你為什麼不搭火車？

上公車 也可以用 board 這個動詞表示坐上大眾運輸工具。

- Excuse me, is this where we **get on the bus** to Chicago?
- No, you have to go to the next terminal.
  ● 不好意思，去芝加哥的公車是在這邊搭嗎？
  ● 不是，你要去隔壁的總站搭。

▶ She got on the bus near her house.
  她在她家附近上了公車。
  Where did you get on the bus?
  你在哪裡上車的？

1 職場・學校
2 電腦・網路
3 社交生活
4 日常生活
5 訊息・理解
6 想法・態度
7 情緒・狀況
8 行為舉止
9 時間地點・副詞片語

get off at...

· get off at the third stop
在第三站下車

· get off at the next stop
在下一站下車

在…下車 把 get on 的 on 換成 off，就變成相反的意思了。

● What's the fastest way to get to Kwangwhamoon?

● Take the Line Number 3 and **get off at** Gyeongbokgung Station.

●到光化門最快的方法是什麼？　●搭三號線，然後在景福宮站下車。

▶ Take Line Number 2 and get off at Century Park Station.
搭二號線，然後在世紀公園站下車。

Take bus number 9000 and get off at the third stop.
搭 9000 號公車，然後在第三站下車。

transfer trains at...

· change trains for A at B
在 B 轉搭前往 A 的車

· transfer from bus to subway
從公車轉乘地下鐵

在…轉車 transfer 也可以不接受詞，直接表示「轉車」的意思。

● Can I ride this train to London?

● No, you need to **transfer trains at** the next stop.

●我可以搭這班火車去倫敦嗎？　●不行，你要在下一站轉車。

▶ Ellen transferred trains at the depot.
Ellen 在火車站轉乘。

We should transfer trains at the Berlin station.
我們應該在柏林站轉車。

be in the subway

· be a long subway ride to one's house
到某人的家要搭地鐵很久

· while riding the subway
搭乘地下鐵時

· leave sth in the subway
把某物忘在地下鐵

· get a seat in the subway
在地鐵找到座位

在搭地下鐵 美國的地鐵叫 subway，英國則是 underground（口語稱為 tube）。台灣稱為 MRT（mass rapid transit，大眾捷運），近年改用歐洲的說法，稱為 metro。

● Are Karen and John coming to our party?

● Yes, but they **are still in the subway**.

●Karen 和 John 會來參加我們的派對嗎？

●會，不過他們還在搭地下鐵。

▶ The old woman was in the subway station.
那位老太太在地下鐵車站。

Many small restaurants are in the subway tunnel.
在地鐵的地下街有許多小餐廳。

read on the subway

· fall asleep on the subway
在搭地下鐵時睡著

· yield a seat to sb on the subway
在地鐵上讓座給某人

在地鐵上閱讀 搭地鐵或公車的時候，除了發呆以外，也可以讀我們出版社的書啊…

● What do you do on the way to work?

● I **read** novels **on the subway**.

●你上班通勤時會做什麼？　●我在地鐵上讀小説。

▶ Vera fell asleep on the subway and missed her stop.
Vera 搭地下鐵的時候睡著，錯過了她該下車的站。

We yielded a seat to the old woman on the subway.
我們在地鐵上讓座給那位老太太。

1 職場・學校

2 電腦・網路

3 社交生活

4 日常生活

5 訊息・理解

6 想法・態度

7 情緒・狀況

8 行為舉止

9 時間地點・副詞片語

31 | 飛行 miss the flight

2-31.mp3

catch the flight

- catch the flight to New York
  搭乘去紐約的班機
- catch the two-fifteen flight
  搭乘 2 點 15 分的飛機
- catch the connecting flight to…
  趕搭前往…的銜接班機

搭飛機 搭飛機的時候，flight（航班）這個字比 plane 更常用。

- We need to **catch the flight** to Miami.
- OK, let's go buy our tickets.
  ●我們需要搭飛機去邁阿密。　●好，我們去買票吧。

▶ I caught the flight to New York City. 我搭了飛機去紐約。
　We need to make sure we catch the flight.
　我們要確定我們搭得了飛機。

take a flight

- take the early flight
  搭早班飛機
- take a flight to…
  搭飛機去…
- take a long airplane flight
  搭乘長途班機

搭飛機 後面可以接「to + 地點」說明目的地。

- My girlfriend **took a flight** to see her family.
- Where does her family live?
  ●我女朋友搭飛機去見她的家人。　●她家人住在哪裡？

▶ You can't take a flight to Tokyo from here.
　你無法從這裡搭機到東京。
　The tour group took a flight to Paris.
　這個旅行團搭飛機去了巴黎。

board the plane

- be flying to…
  飛往…

登機 board 最早是指上船，但現在可以指搭乘其他大眾運輸工具。

- If you have your boarding pass, you can **board the plane** now.
- Is there a place that I can store my carry-on?
  ●如果您有登機證，您可以現在登機。
  ●有地方可以放我的隨身行李嗎？

▶ You can board the plane now. 您現在可以登機了。
　I'm flying to Boston next Saturday. 我下週六要飛波士頓。

miss the flight

- miss one's plane
  錯過某人的班機

錯過班機 miss 在這裡指「沒有搭上」，也可以接其他大眾運輸工具來用。

- I need to pack my suitcase.
- Hurry! You're going to **miss the flight**.
  ●我需要打包行李。　●快點！你快要錯過班機了。

▶ I missed the flight to Beijing. 我錯過了去北京的班機。
　It costs a lot of money to miss the flight.
　錯過班機會損失很多錢。

check baggage

- check in luggage
  託運行李
- have luggage to
  check in
  有行李要託運
- pick up one's luggage
  領某人的行李
- take one's carry-on
  拿某人的隨身行李

託運行李 check 是 check in 的省略說法。不需託運、隨身攜帶的行李叫 carry-on。

- How many pieces of **luggage are** you **checking in**?
- I would like to **check three pieces**.
  - 你要託運幾件行李？　　● 我要託運三件。

▶ You can check in luggage at this desk.
   你可以在這個櫃台託運行李。
   The group had a lot of luggage to check in.
   這個團體有很多行李要託運。

clear customs

- go through customs
  清關，通關
- the customs officer
  海關人員
- have sth to declare
  有東西要申報

清關，通關 指「海關」的時候，customs 固定用複數形。

- Do you **have anything to declare**?
- No, we only have personal belongings.
  - 你有任何東西要申報？　　● 沒有，我們只有個人隨身物品而已。

▶ As soon as we clear customs, we're going to catch a
   cab. 我們一完成通關，就要去招計程車。
   The customs officer asked me if I had brought any food
   with me. 海關人員問我是否帶了任何食物在身上。

suffer from jet lag

- recover from jet lag
  調好時差

受時差所苦 適應了時差、恢復正常的時候，可以說 recover from jet lag。

- Go easy on them today because they **have jet lag**.
- The first day will be pretty relaxed.
  - 今天對他們寬容點吧，他們有時差。　　● 第一天會很輕鬆的。

▶ I'm still suffering from jet lag.
   我還有時差的問題。
   I'm so sleepy. I'm still recovering from jet lag.
   我好想睡。我還沒從時差中完全恢復。

---

 customs 是指「海關」還是「習慣」？

　　custom 這個字本來是「習慣、風俗」的意思，但在我們的日常生活中，如果是複數的 customs，則是指海關。例如 go to customs 是「去通關」，而 clear customs 則是「完成通關」。如果因為某些問題而把人扣留在海關，則是 keep sb at customs。特別要注意的是，表示海關的 customs 是不加 the 的。

32 迷路，問路
get lost

2-32.mp3

1 職場・學校
2 電腦・網路
3 社交生活
4 日常生活
5 訊息・理解
6 想法・態度
7 情緒・狀況
8 行為舉止
9 時間地點・副詞片語

be lost

· get lost
  迷路（如果是命令句的話，意思是「滾開」）
· get sb lost
  害某人迷路

迷路 主詞是人。動詞可以換成 become，強調變得迷路的過程。
- Excuse me, I think I'm lost. Is this Sunae-dong?
- Yes, it is. Where do you want to go?
  - 不好意思，我好像迷路了。這邊是藪內洞嗎？
  - 是的，你想去哪裡呢？

▶ If you get lost, just give me a call.
  如果你迷路了，打電話給我。
  Can you help me? I'm lost.
  你可以幫我嗎？我迷路了。

draw sb a map

· bring (along) a map
  帶地圖
· find A on the map
  在地圖上找 A
· give sb directions to…
  指引某人到…
· ask for directions
  問路

畫地圖給某人 也可以說 give sb directions（指引），注意這裡的 directions 是複數。
- It's easy to find the National Theater.
- Could you **draw me a map**?
  - 國家劇院很好找。　- 你可以畫張地圖給我嗎？

▶ I don't know, but we can find it on a map.
  我不知道，但我們可以在地圖上找。
  Why don't you stop and ask for directions?
  你何不停下來問路呢？

be located in

· be located nearby
  位於附近
· be in a suburb of
  (Taipei)
  在（台北）的市郊

位於… locate 的意思是「把某設施設置在某地」，被動形就是「某設施位於某地」的意思。
- Where's the tourist information center?
- It's **located in** our lobby.
  - 旅客諮詢中心在哪裡？　- 它位於我們的大廳。

▶ It's located about 10 kilometers from Madrid.
  它位於距離馬德里約十公里遠的地方。
  You are in a suburb of Taipei.
  你在台北的市郊。

be situated in

位於… 意思與 be located 相近。後面可以接 in, near, at 等等。

- Where is the national art museum?
- The museum **is situated in** the center of Barcelona.
  - ●國立美術館在哪裡？　●它座落於巴塞隆納的中心。

▶ The Italian restaurant is situated in my neighborhood.
這間義大利餐廳在我家附近。
The police station is situated at the end of the street.
警察局位於這條街的盡頭。

take 20 minutes by car

- A be 10 km west of B
  A 位在 B 西方 10 公里處
- be a 10 minute walk (from here)
  （從這裡）要走十分鐘
- be about 10 minutes' ride from...
  距離…大約十分鐘的車程

開車要花 **20 分鐘** 說明到目的地要花的時間。

- Where is the historical museum?
- It's about **20 minutes' ride from** here.
  - ●歷史博物館在哪裡？　●在距離這邊開車約 20 分鐘的地方。

▶ It should take 50 minutes by car.
開車應該要花 50 分鐘。
The bank is a ten minute walk from the bus stop.
從公車站走到銀行要十分鐘。

---

33 詳細說明方向 go this way

2-33.mp3

go this way

- go that way
  走那條路
- go one's way
  （事件、形勢等）對某人有利
- » cf. go one's own way
  照自己的意思做，一意孤行

走這條路 要對方往某個方向走。也常省略成 This way.。

- Which path would you like to take?
- I think we should **go this way**.
  - ●你要走哪條路？　●我想我們該走這邊。

▶ You can go this way to reach the store.
你可以走這條路到那間店。
We went this way on our first date.
我們第一次約會時走了這條路。

go straight

· go straight through…
直走穿過…

· go straight up to…
直走到…

· go straight until S+V
直走到…為止

· keep going straight until you reach…
在抵達…之前一直直走

take this road for + 時間

· take this road for about five minutes
走這條路走大約五分鐘

· get across the street
穿越馬路

go south 2 blocks

· go south to…
往南走到…

· go west until sb gets to…
往西走直到某人抵達…

· follow those signs
跟著那些標誌

turn to the left

· turn (to the) left at the corner
在那個街角左轉

· turn to the left when you come to…
當你抵達…之後左轉

· turn right at the first traffic light
在第一個紅綠燈右轉

直走 如果要說「走到底」的話，可以加上 down，例如 Go straight down this street.。

● Could you tell me how I get to the subway?

● **Go straight** ahead until you see the sign.

●請問我該怎麼去地鐵站？　●直走到看見標誌為止。

▶ Let me repeat that, first go straight then take a left at the light. 讓我再重複一遍，先直走，然後在紅綠燈左轉。
Go straight for five blocks. You can't miss it.
直直走過五個街區，不會太難找的。

走這條路走… 用時間來表示距離的方式。

● Excuse me, where is the Hilton Hotel?

● **Take this road for** about ten minutes and it's on your right.

●不好意思，希爾頓飯店在哪裡？
●走這條路大約十分鐘，在右手邊。

▶ Take this road until it ends and then turn right.
走這條路走到底，然後右轉。
Take this road until you reach the traffic lights.
走這條路到看到紅綠燈為止。

往南走兩個街區 棋盤格道路劃分的建築物區塊稱為 block。

● How do I get to Kyobo Bookstore?

● **Go west three blocks** and it's on the left.

●我該怎麼去教保書店？　●往西走三個街區，在左手邊。

▶ Go west for three blocks and turn left.
往西走三個街區，接著左轉。
I think if you follow those signs, you'll get there.
如果你跟那些標誌走，我想就會到了。

左轉 也可以直接說 turn left。

● Is the computer shop around here?

● Sure, just **turn left** when you reach the corner.

●電腦店在這附近嗎？　●對，你走到那個街角左轉就是了。

▶ Just go straight and turn left.
直走然後左轉。
Turn left at the intersection. You'll see it.
在那個路口左轉，你就會看到了。

1 職場・學校
2 電腦・網路
3 社交生活
4 日常生活
5 訊息・理解
6 想法・態度
7 情緒・狀況
8 行為舉止
9 時間地點・副詞片語

34 說明位置與其他
be next to

2-34.mp3

be on one's left

· be on one's right
  在某人的右邊
· be on the right side of
  在…的右邊

在某人的左邊 告訴對方到了附近以後，目的地在哪一邊。

● Which way is the stock exchange?
● It's two miles ahead, **on your left hand side**.
   ●股票交易所在哪邊？　●前面兩英里左右，在你的左手邊。

▶ The waiting room is around the corner on your left.
   等候室在你左手邊附近。
   The headquarters is on the right side of this map.
   總部位於這張地圖的右邊。

be next to

· be close to…
  接近…
· be right there
  就在那邊
· be in the other
  direction
  在另一個方向

在旁邊 表示目的地在哪個顯眼的地標旁邊。

● My car **is next to** the post office.
● Let's walk there and go for a drive.
   ●我的車在郵局旁邊。　●我們走過去，然後開車兜風吧。

▶ The store is just next to your building.
   那間店就在你那棟大樓旁邊。
   The store is across the street, next to the station.
   那間店在對街的車站旁邊。

go the right way

· Coming through!
  請讓開！
· Clear the way!
  請讓路！
· move out of one's
  way
  讓路給某人

走對路 也可以用來比喻「做正確的行為」。

● Turn right at the next traffic light.
● Are you sure we**'re going the right way**?
   ●在下一個紅綠燈右轉。　●你確定我們走的路是對的嗎？

▶ I have hot coffee. Please move out of my way.
   我手上有熱咖啡，請不要擋到我的路。
   We moved out of her way because she was running.
   因為她在跑步，所以我們讓開了。

180

get into an elevator

- ride the elevator to the 2nd floor
  搭電梯到二樓
- be going down
  （電梯）往下

搭電梯 電梯服務人員會說 Going up/down. 表示電梯往上／往下。

- I want to go to the top of the Empire State Building.
- Let's **get into an elevator** and go up.
  - 我想去帝國大廈的頂樓。　　● 我們搭電梯上去吧。

▶ Kevin has to get into an elevator to go to his apartment.
  Kevin 要搭電梯才能到他的公寓。

  I got into an elevator to reach Steve's office.
  我搭電梯去 Steve 的辦公室。

get on the escalator

- take the escalator down to…
  搭手扶梯下去…
- ride the escalator up toward…
  搭手扶梯上去…

搭手扶梯 也可以說 take/ride the escalator。

- Let's **get on the escalator** and go upstairs.
- Sure, I want to see the shops up there.
  - 我們搭手扶梯上樓吧。　　● 好啊，我想看看上面的店。

▶ You should take the escalator down to get to the sports section. 你要搭手扶梯下去，才能到運動服飾區。

  Go down the escalator and you're there.
  搭手扶梯下去，你就到了。

 考驗介系詞能力的「地標指示法」

　　很多書都會教讀者遇到老外問路要怎麼指示方向，什麼左轉、右轉、turn left、turn right 的，還要想想應該走過幾個街區。這種說明「怎麼走」的方法，雖然能直接表達通往某個地方的流程，但如果要去的地方很遠、路線很複雜的時候，就連母語人士都會覺得這種表達方式很麻煩，聽的人也不見得能完全了解。要是對方想去的地方附近有明顯的地標，就可以直接說明那個地方和地標之間的相對位置關係。想要熟練這種表達位置的方式，最重要的就是熟悉各種介系詞的意義。

in front of A	在 A 的前面
behind A	在 A 的後面
across from A	在 A 對面
between A and B	在 A 與 B 之間

　　當然，也可以比較籠統地說 be close to A（接近 A），但比較適合用在真的很接近、絕對不會找不到的情況下。

1 職場・學校

2 電腦・網路

3 社交生活

4 日常生活

5 訊息・理解

6 想法・態度

7 情緒・狀況

8 行為舉止

9 時間地點・副詞片語

Social life with others

和人見面、道別等社交生活中的慣用語

get a minute

· get/have a second
　有一點時間
· wait a second
　等一下
· Hold on a minute/
　second!
　等一下！

有一點時間 也可以說 have a minute。minute 是指很短的時間。

● Do you **have a minute**?
● Well yeah, sure, what's up?
　●你有一點時間嗎？　●有啊，怎麼了嗎？

▶ I need to talk to you, if you have a minute.
　如果你有點時間的話，我要跟你談一下。
　Hold on a second. I have a question for you.
　等一下，我有問題要問你。

have the time to

· have time for+N
　有時間做（某事）

有時間做… 但要注意 Do you have the time? 是問對方知不知道現在的時間。

● The plane is not due to arrive for another hour.
● Then we **have time for** another drink.
　●飛機還要一小時才會抵達。　●那我們有時間再喝點東西。

▶ Do you have time to talk about the meeting tomorrow?
　你有時間討論明天的會議嗎？
　Do you have time to talk for a bit?
　你有時間說個話嗎？

have no time to

· not have much time
　沒有很多時間
· not have much free
　time to do
　沒有很多空閒時間可以
　做…
· have no time available
　沒有時間

沒時間做… to 接動詞原形。改成 for 的話，後面要接名詞。

● You should come out with us.
● I **have no time to** hang out these days.
　●你應該和我們一起出去。　●我最近沒時間閒晃。

▶ I have no time to waste. Please give me a break.
　我沒時間可以浪費，你饒了我吧。
　I have no time to go there.
　我沒時間去那邊。

be available to

- Are you available?
  你有空嗎／你單身嗎？
- be available on
  在…可取得
- (be) available for+N/to
  do
  （人）有空做…

**have time to
do before...**

- have a couple of
  hours before S+V
  在…之前有幾個小時
- have a few hours
  before
  在…之前有幾個小時
- have an hour free
  有一小時的空閒時間

有空閒做… available 用在人身上的時候，表示有空閒的時間。
Are you available to...? 可以用來問有沒有空見面、講電話、幫忙…
等等。

- Do you need to visit a dentist?
- Yeah. Who **is available** now?
  - 你需要看牙醫嗎？ - 是啊，現在哪位醫生有空？
- ▶ I'm not sure if I am available on Friday.
  我不確定我星期五有沒有空。
  I'd like to speak with Mark, if he is available.
  如果 Mark 有空的話，我想跟他說話。

在…之前有時間去做 預定行程開始之前有空的狀況。

- The movie starts at eight.
- We **have time to** eat **before** it begins.
  - 電影八點開始。 - 在開場前我們有時間去吃個東西。
- ▶ We have a couple of hours before school ends.
  距離放學還有好幾個小時。
  I have a few hours before I need to go home.
  在我得回家之前，我還有幾小時。

---

02 騰出時間
make time

3-02.mp3

make time to

- make some time to do
  /for sth
  騰出一些時間做…

騰出時間做… to do 也可以換成「for + 名詞」。

- I'm going to see my grandmother this weekend.
- It's good you **make time to** visit her.
  - 我這個週末要去看我的外婆。 - 你能抽出時間去看她真是太好了。

- ▶ Make time to pack up your suitcase.
  騰出時間打包你的行李。
  I'll make time to come down and see you.
  我會抽空下去看你。

1 職場・學校
2 電腦・網路
3 社交生活
4 日常生活
5 訊息・理解
6 想法・態度
7 情緒・狀況
8 行為舉止
9 時間地點・副詞片語

take time out to | 騰出時間做… 可以直接照字面的意思想成「拿出時間」做事。

- I'm going to **take time out to** do some shopping.
- Oh good, let's go shopping together.
  - 我要抽出時間逛一下街。 ● 太好了，我們一起去逛街吧。
- ▶ She took time out to plant a flower garden.
  她抽出時間去種植花園。
  We'll take time out to visit some old friends.
  我們會抽出時間拜訪一些老朋友。

put in + 時間名詞 | 投入（多少時間） 也有 put in energy（投入精力）的說法。

- How long have you been working here?
- We **put in** seven hours so far.
  - 你們在這裡弄了多久了？ ● 到目前已經花了七小時。
- ▶ Workers must put in thirty years before retiring.
  勞工在退休前要工作三十年。
  The baseball players put a lot of energy into playing.
  這些棒球選手投入了很多精力在比賽上。

spare time for | 為了…騰出時間 也可以說 make time for。for 接名詞或動名詞。

· spare some time for -ing
  騰出時間做某事

- I can **spare some time for** hiking.
- Well, let's go to the mountains this weekend.
  - 我可以騰出一些時間健行。 ● 那麼，我們這週末去山上吧。
- ▶ He spared some time for helping the old woman.
  他騰出一些時間幫助那位老太太。
  You should spare some time for relaxing.
  你應該騰出一些時間放鬆。

arrange time for | 安排…的時間 set the time 則是指調整手錶、時鐘的時間。

· arrange time for -ing
  安排…的時間
· arrange time for sb to do
  為某人安排時間做某事

- I would like to interview that musician.
- We can **arrange a time for** you to meet him.
  - 我想要訪問那位音樂家。 ● 我們可以幫你安排時間跟他見面。
- ▶ The farmers arranged time for harvesting red peppers.
  農夫們安排時間採收辣椒。
  I need to arrange time for our Christmas party.
  我需要安排耶誕派對的時間。

03 花時間，浪費時間，省時間 spend time

3-03.mp3

1 職場・學校

2 電腦・網路

3 社交生活

4 日常生活

5 訊息・理解

6 想法・態度

7 情緒・狀況

8 行為舉止

9 時間地點・副詞片語

spend time (on) -ing

- spend a lot of time (on) -ing
  花很多時間做某事
- spend (more) time with
  與…共度（更多）時間
- spend a spare time
  度過閒暇時間

花時間做… 在口語中，通常會省略 on。

- What did you do with your friends?
- We **spent time** talking and drinking coffee.
  - 你和朋友們做了什麼？　● 我們花時間聊天、喝咖啡。

▶ I'm planning to spend a lot of time on the beach.
我打算花很多時間待在海邊。
We spend too much time commuting back and forth to work. 我們花太多時間通勤上下班。

spend + 時間名詞 -ing

- spend + 時間名詞 + -ing (with sb)
  花多少時間（和某人一起）做某事
- spend + 時間名詞 + at
  花多少時間在…上
- spend the day in bed
  一整天都待在床上

花多少時間做某事 也可以接金錢，表示做某事的代價。

- This report looks pretty good.
- I **spent hours** writing it.
  - 這報告看起來很不錯。　● 我花了好幾個小時寫。

▶ I think we will spend a few days in that area.
我想我們會在那個區域待上幾天。
Don't you spend Christmas with your family?
你耶誕節不跟家人度過嗎？

use one's time effectively

- make good use of one's time
  好好利用時間

有效率地運用某人的時間 make effective use of sth 意為「有效率地運用某物」。

- You spend hours playing computer games.
- Yeah, I need to **use my time more effectively**.
  - 你花好幾小時玩電腦遊戲。
  - 是啊，我需要更有效率地運用我的時間。

▶ Peter uses his time very effectively.
Peter 非常有效率地運用他的時間。
All students must use their time effectively.
所有學生都必須有效率地運用時間。

187

be up + 時間副詞片語 + -ing

- be up all night playing computer games
  熬夜一整晚玩電腦遊戲
- be in + 地點 + for + 時間 + doing research
  在某地花多少時間做調查

熬夜多久做某事 另外，up and doing sth 是努力做某事的意思。
- Susan **was up for** an hour exercising.
- She's always in good physical condition.
  - Susan 熬夜一小時運動。　　●她的身體狀況一直很好。

▶ Jim was up all night playing computer games.
Jim 熬夜一整晚玩電腦遊戲。
The campers were up for hours singing songs.
這些露營的人熬夜唱了好幾小時的歌。

be worth one's time

值得某人花時間 後面可以接 to do 表示花時間做什麼。
- Should we go watch the parade today?
- No, it's **not worth our time** to do that.
  - 我們今天應該去看遊行嗎？　　●不，那不值得我們花時間去看。

▶ The seminar was really worth my time.
我花時間去那場研討會真的很值得。
Irma's party was worth our time.
Irma 的派對令我們不虛此行。

waste one's time

- waste one's time -ing
  浪費某人的時間做某事
- waste time on sth
  浪費時間做某事
- waste of time
  時間的浪費

浪費某人的時間 後面可以接 on sth 或 doing sth 表示做什麼。
- I have something you really should buy.
- I don't want it. Don't **waste my time**.
  - 我有個你真的應該買的東西。　　●我不想要，別浪費我的時間。

▶ The traffic jams waste everyone's time.
塞車浪費所有人的時間。
Using the Internet all day long wastes your time.
上網一整天會浪費你的時間。

save time

- time saving
  省時的

省時間 另外，save the day 是轉危為安、挽救局面的意思。
- Is this the best way to drive to work?
- No, I'll show you a way to **save time**.
  - 這是開車上班的最佳路線嗎？
  - 不是，我來告訴你一條省時的路線。

▶ I tried to save time so I could finish faster.
我試圖節省時間，好能更快完成。
The computer program will save time for you.
那個電腦程式可以幫你省時。

1 職場・學校

2 電腦・網路

3 社交生活

4 日常生活

5 訊息・理解

6 想法・態度

7 情緒・狀況

8 行為舉止

9 時間地點・副詞片語

 -ing 的用法

　　-ing 除了用在現在進行式以外，還有很多種用法。其中一種是當作現在分詞，把兩個句子簡化為一句。例如 There is a cold (which is) going around the office.（感冒在辦公室裡流傳），其中的現在分詞片語 going... 是修飾 a cold，使用這種句型就不用同時說 There is a cold. 和 The cold is going around the office 了。再舉一個例子，I saw John. 和 John walked in the rain. 也可以合併為 I saw John walking in the rain.（我看見 John 走在雨中）。諸如此類的用法可以讓英文的表達顯得更成熟，請大家嘗試使用看看。

04 耗費時間 take time

3-04.mp3

take time -ing

· take time to do
做…花時間
· take time for sb to do
某人做…會花時間

做…花時間 主詞要用虛主詞 it。注意動詞不能用 cost。

● It's easy to fall down on the snow and ice.
● It will **take time** getting to the subway station.
　●在冰雪上很容易跌倒。　　●走到地鐵站要花些時間了。

▶ It'll take time to repair that computer.
　修電腦會花點時間。
　It will take time for him to drive here.
　他開車到這裡來會花點時間。

take + 時間 + to

· take + 時間 + (for A) + to do
做…花（A）多少時間
· take (A) a long time to do
做…花（A）很長的時間

做…花多少時間 要表示花某人時間，可以說 take sb... 或在 to 前面加上 for sb。

● I thought you were going to leave.
● It **took me a while to** find my keys.
　●我以為你要離開了。　　●找鑰匙花了我一點時間。

▶ It takes time to cook a big meal.
　煮頓大餐很花時間。
　It took an hour to walk home.
　走路回家花了一小時。

take long to

· take a long time
  to do...
  做…花很多時間
· take way too much
  time to...
  做…花太多時間
· It won't take long
  to do...
  做…不會花太多時間

做…花很長的時間 take a while 則是「花一點時間」。

● How long will it take to have the interview?
● It won't **take long** at all.
  ●舉行面試會花多久時間？　●不會太久。

▶ It'll take a long time to paint the house.
  漆房子會花很多時間。
  It won't take long to set up the new computer.
  安裝新電腦不會花很多時間。

it didn't take
long before

· take a great deal of
  time
  花許多時間

沒多久就… before 的後面接完整的子句（S+V）。

● Did Heather and Ralph break up?
● Yes, but **it didn't take long before** they were back
  together.
  ●Heather 和 Ralph 分手了嗎？　●對，不過他們沒多久就復合了。

▶ It didn't take long before the thunderstorm began.
  沒多久就開始下起大雷雨。
  It didn't take long before he finished his ice cream.
  他沒多久就把冰淇淋吃完了。

last for + 時間

· last + 時間
  持續多少時間
· last four weeks
  持續四個星期

持續多少時間 也可以不加 for，把 last 當成及物動詞來用。

● Is this a good cell phone to buy?
● It will probably **last for** a few years.
  ●這支手機值得買嗎？　●這可能可以用個幾年。

▶ The movie will last for two hours.
  電影會演兩小時。
  I bet you he won't last a month in prison.
  我跟你打賭他不會在監獄裡待上一個月。

1 職場・學校

2 電腦・網路

3 社交生活

4 日常生活

5 訊息・理解

6 想法・態度

7 情緒・狀況

8 行為舉止

9 時間地點・副詞片語

05 關於時間的慣用語 It has been…

3-05.mp3

It has been + 時間 + since

· have been a long time since S+V
自從…已經很久了

自從…已經多少時間了 後面接過去式或現在完成式子句。

● Have you seen Gina lately?
● **It has been** a few years **since** I've seen her.

●你最近有看到 Gina 嗎？　●我好幾年沒看到她了。

▶ It has been a week since our last rainstorm.
距離上次的暴風雨已經過了一星期。
It has been six months since he joined the army.
他加入軍隊已經六個月了。

It's about time S+V

· It's high time S+V
現在是…的最佳時機

差不多該… 雖然沒有確切的計畫，但現在是個好時機。

● **It's about time** we got a raise.
● You're telling me.

●我們差不多該獲得加薪了。　●你說的沒錯。

▶ It's time for you to get married.
該是你結婚的時候了。
It's high time he finds a good job.
現在是他找到好工作的最佳時機。

not A until B

· It was not until…that S+V
直到…才…

在 B 之前不做 A until 的後面接完整的子句。

● I'm getting really hungry now.
● We can't eat **until** Katie arrives.

●我真的越來越餓了。　●Katie 來之前我們都不能吃。

▶ You can not go out until you finish working.
在完成工作之前你都不能出去。
He did not smile until he saw Bonnie.
直到看到 Bonnie，他才終於笑了。

by the time S+V

· every time S+V
　每次…
· Whenever S+V
　不論何時…
· each time S+V
　每次…

到…的時候 by the time 可以視為連接詞，意義接近 when。

● Is it possible for me to become rich **by the time** I'm thirty?
● It would be difficult, but you can never tell.

　●我三十歲的時候有可能變有錢嗎？　●很難吧，但也很難説。

▶ By the time Karen arrives, we will be ready.
　Karen 到的時候，我們就會準備好了。
　Every time I turn around, Hal is looking at me.
　每次我轉身，Hal 都在看著我。

when I was young

· when you were young
　在你小時候
· at one's time of life
　在某人那樣的年齡
· at one's age
　在某人的年齡（at the age of...）

我小的時候 也可以說 as a child。

● Do you know anything about playing the violin?
● I studied the violin for a few years **when I was young**.

　●你懂得拉小提琴嗎？　●我小時候學小提琴學了幾年。

▶ I lived in the country when I was young.
　我小時候住在鄉下。
　I would play the violin when I was young.
　我小時候會拉小提琴。

06 計畫
have a plan

3-06.mp3

have a plan

· have other plans
　有別的計畫
· have got plans for that evening
　那個傍晚已經有別的計畫

有計畫 後面可以接 for sth 或 to do sth，表示計畫的內容。

● You should go out with us on Friday night.
● I'd like to, but I **have other plans**.

　●你星期五晚上該和我們一起出去。　●我很想，但我有別的安排。

▶ We have a plan to retire early.
　我們計畫早點退休。
　I've got other plans for this evening.
　我今天傍晚已經有別的計畫了。

have no plans to

· not have any special plan
沒有任何特別的計畫
· have sth planned
計畫好某事

沒有…的打算 也可以說 have no plans for sth。

● Are you going home for the holiday?
● No, I **have no plans to** travel home.
　●你放假會回家嗎？　●不會，我沒有這個打算。

▶ They have no plans to go out tonight.
　他們今天晚上沒打算出門。
　We have no plans to visit Joe and Elaine.
　我們沒有要去拜訪 Joe 跟 Elaine 的打算。

make a plan

· make a plan for+N/to do
為了…做計畫
· work out a plan
制定計畫
· draw up a plan
制定計畫

做計畫 也可以用複數，改成 make plans。

● I don't know what I want to study.
● You should **make a plan** for your future.
　●我不知道我想學什麼。　●你應該為自己的未來做計畫。

▶ They made a plan to meet in a week.
　他們計畫一週後見面。
　Alan made a plan to complete the report.
　Alan 定了完成報告的計畫。

plan to

· plan on -ing
計畫做…
· plan anything for…
為…做好一切打算

打算… 也常常以進行式 be planning to 的形式出現。

● I heard that you **plan to** quit your job.
● All I need is a better job.
　●我聽說你打算辭職。　●我只是需要更好的工作。

▶ What do you plan to do this weekend?
　你這週末打算做什麼？
　She's planning on getting married this year.
　她計畫今年結婚。

go as planned

· go according to plan
依照計畫進行

依照計畫進行 go as scheduled 則是指按照計畫時程進行。

● Did you have a good time on your date?
● No, it really didn't **go as planned**.
　●約會開心嗎？　●不，完全沒照計畫進行。

▶ The English class didn't go as planned.
　英文課沒照計畫進行。
　If everything goes as planned, we're going to making a killing. 如果一切都照計畫進行，我們會大賺一筆。

1 職場·學校
2 電腦·網路
3 社交生活
4 日常生活
5 訊息·理解
6 想法·態度
7 情緒·狀況
8 行為舉止
9 時間地點·副詞片語

be up to sth

打算做某事 這個片語常常用來表示某人有邪惡的念頭。

- You look like you're up to something.
- I feel like selling my stocks.
    - 你看起來好像有什麼打算。　　●我想賣掉我的股票。

▶ I think those teenagers are up to something.
我覺得那些年輕人好像有什麼陰謀。
Angelina is always up to something.
Angelina 總是心懷不軌。

keep to a plan

- fulfill a plan
  履行計畫
- change of plan
  計畫的改變

按照計畫 也可以說 stick to a plan，更強調對計畫的堅持。

- Maybe we shouldn't go on a vacation.
- Let's keep to our plan and just go.
    - 也許我們不該去度假。　　●我們還是照原定計畫去吧。

▶ Bart can never keep to a plan.
Bart 總是不照計畫做事。
It was hard, but I kept to my plans.
那很不容易，但我還是依照原定計畫做了。

be under consideration

考慮中 介系詞 under 也出現在 under construction（施工中）這個慣用語裡。

- Will your father allow you to go on the trip?
- He said that it is under consideration.
    - 你父親會允許你去旅行嗎？　　●他說他在考慮中。

▶ The plans for the new building are under consideration.
那棟新大樓的計畫還在考慮中。
A new menu for the cafe is under consideration.
那間咖啡店考慮要推出新菜單。

07 預定，打算
be going to

3-07.mp3

be going to

· be about to do
即將做某事

將要… 相對於 will，be going to 常有「很快會做」的感覺。
- Aren't you afraid he's **going to** be angry?
- Who cares what he thinks?

  ●你不怕他會生氣嗎？　●誰管他怎麼想？

▶ I wonder how it's going to turn out.
我想知道這件事會發展成怎樣。
I'm going to work on this stuff at home tonight.
我今天晚上要在家處理這件事。

be supposed to

應該… 也可以表示「有義務這麼做」的意思。
- You're **supposed to** pick up Sarah.
- Well, I'd better leave now.

  ●你該去接 Sarah 了。　●嗯，我最好現在離開。

▶ Do you know what time we're supposed to leave?
你知道我們什麼時候該離開嗎？
We're supposed to visit my parents tonight.
我們今晚應該拜訪我的父母。

be scheduled to

· be planned to do
被計畫做…

預定… 和 be planned to 意思相近。
- When **is** your flight **scheduled for**?
- At 6 a.m. I've got to wake up early.

  ●你的班機是幾點？　●早上六點。我得早起了。

▶ The bus is not scheduled to leave for another 45 minutes. 這班公車要 45 分鐘後才會開車。
When is he scheduled to arrive at the airport?
他預定什麼時候到機場？

1 職場・學校
2 電腦・網路
3 社交生活
4 日常生活
5 訊息・理解
6 想法・態度
7 情緒・狀況
8 行為舉止
9 時間地點・副詞片語

be due to

預定… due to sth 則是「因為某事」的意思。

- The plane **is** not **due to** arrive for another hour.
- Then we have time for another drink.

●那班飛機預定一小時後才會抵達。　●那我們有時間再喝點東西了。

▶ Kerry can't be here due to getting sick.

Kerry 因為生病所以不能來。

The bus was late due to breaking down.

那班公車因為故障而誤點了。

be bound to

一定會… 和 be very likely to、be obliged to 意思相近。

- Dan is a very slow runner.
- I think he **is bound to** lose the race.

●Dan 跑得很慢。　●我想他一定會輸掉這場賽跑。

▶ You're bound to get fat from eating so much.

你吃這麼多，一定會變胖。

This new car is bound to become popular.

這款新車一定會受歡迎。

be expected to

· Are you expecting?
你懷孕了嗎？

被預期… 當預期心態很強烈時，也會有 should 或 must 的意思。

- How much was your new dress?
- It was three times what I had **expected to** pay.

●你的新洋裝多少錢？　●是我預期的三倍。

▶ Everyone is expected to bring a present.

每個人都需要帶一份禮物。

Brian is expected to enter Harvard University.

預料 Brian 會進哈佛大學。

earlier than (sb) expected

· earlier than usual
比平常更早

比（某人）預期的還早 expected 也可以換成 planned/ scheduled。

- Did you get the package I sent you?
- Yes, it came **earlier than I expected**.

●你收到我寄給你的包裹了嗎？　●有，比我預期的還早到。

▶ Sally graduated from high school earlier than expected.

Sally 比預期的更早從高中畢業了。

She went to the office a little earlier than usual.

她比平常早一點到了辦公室。

196

ahead of schedule

· be + 時間 + ahead of
  schedule
  比預定的早了多少時間

超前計畫 也可以說 ahead of time，意思相同。

- Where did my school bus go?
- It left the stop **ahead of schedule**.
  - 我的校車去哪了？　●它比預定時間還早離站。

▶ The building was finished ahead of schedule.
  這棟建築比計畫的還早完工。
  Our train arrived ahead of schedule.
  我們的火車比預定時刻提早抵達了。

behind schedule

· be + 時間 + behind
  schedule
  比預定的晚了多少時間
· behind time
  （火車等）誤點

進度落後 前面的動詞可以是 be 或 fall。

- Why do I have to stay late tonight?
- Everyone has to stay late tonight because we're
  behind schedule.
  - 為什麼我今天晚上得待到那麼晚？
  - 因為我們進度落後，所以每個人都得待到那麼晚。

▶ We are behind schedule on this work.
  我們這件工作的進度落後了。
  The project was stopped for being behind schedule.
  這個計畫因為進度落後，所以被中止了。

on schedule

· be right on schedule
  完全如期進行
· arrive on schedule
  按預定時間抵達

如期，準時 according to schedule 是指「根據／按照計畫」。

- Is Flight 187 arriving at six o'clock?
- Yes, that flight is **on schedule**.
  - 187 號班機會在六點抵達嗎？　●是的，它會準時抵達。

▶ It's difficult to keep the work on schedule.
  這份工作很難如期執行。
  My father arrived at my house on schedule.
  我父親按預定時間到了我家。

1 職場・學校
2 電腦・網路
3 社交生活
4 日常生活
5 訊息・理解
6 想法・態度
7 情緒・狀況
8 行為舉止
9 時間地點・副詞片語

08 行程
have a schedule

3-08.mp3

set up a schedule

· set up
建立，決定（計畫等）

制定計畫表 後面接 for/of... 可以說明是什麼的計畫。
- I'm visiting ten countries in Europe.
- You should **set up a schedule** of things to see.
  ●我要拜訪十個歐洲國家。 ●你該做個觀光計畫。

▶ I set up a schedule for this weekend.
我為這個週末定了個計畫表。
Did Jeff set up a schedule for his schoolwork?
Jeff 替他自己的作業排好計畫了嗎？

set a date

· set a date to do/
for sth
決定日期去做…

決定日期 動詞 set 也可以改成 fix，意思相同。
- I've got to schedule an appointment with the surgeon.
- Well, make sure you let me know when you **set a date**.
  ●我該跟外科醫生約時間看診。 ●你確定日期後記得告訴我。

▶ Harry and Melinda set a date to get married.
Harry 跟 Melinda 定了婚期。
We've set a date for the festival.
我們決定了慶祝活動的日期。

check one's schedule

· check the schedule
確認行程

確認某人的行程 沒確認自己的行程就約時間，如果造成撞期就糗大囉。
- When are you free to talk with me?
- Mmm, let me **check my schedule**.
  ●你什麼時候有空跟我聊聊？ ●嗯，讓我確認一下我的行程。

▶ I went there to check the schedule.
我去那裡確認行程。
Just let me check the schedule and I'll get back to you.
讓我確認一下行程，我會再打電話給你。

have a schedule

- have a tight schedule
  行程很緊湊
- have a set schedule
  有定好的行程
- know sb's schedule
  知道某人的行程

有（事先的）計畫 I have nothing on my schedule. 是沒有計畫，也就是有空的意思。

- ● Let's just go shopping this afternoon.
- ● I can't. I **have a schedule** to keep.
  ●我們今天下午去逛街吧。　●我不行，我有計畫了。

▶ Greg has a schedule of his classes.
Greg 有他的課表。

The soldiers have a schedule of their training.
軍人們有訓練計畫表。

schedule the meeting

- schedule an appointment
  安排一場會面

排定會議 schedule 作為動詞使用，可以接「會議」、「約會」等受詞。

- ● Can you introduce me to your boss?
- ● Leave it to me. I'll **schedule an appointment**.
  ●你可以向我介紹你的老闆嗎？　●交給我吧，我來排個時間見面。

▶ Please schedule a meeting for Monday morning.
請在星期一早上安排一場會議。

I'm calling to find out if the meeting has been rescheduled. 我打電話是要詢問會議有沒有改時間。

change one's schedule

- changes in the schedule
  行程的變更
- move up the meeting schedule
  將會議提前

更改某人的行程 要說更改某件事的時間，可以很簡單地說 reschedule sth。

- ● Are you going to join us for dinner?
- ● No, I can't **change my schedule**.
  ●你會和我們一起吃晚餐嗎？　●不，我沒辦法更改行程。

▶ Abe will change his schedule to meet his friend.
Abe 會更改行程，去見朋友。

They changed their schedule during the summer.
他們更改了這個夏天的行程。

rearrange one's schedule

- fit sth into one's schedule
  讓某事配合某人的行程

重新安排某人的行程 也可以說 modify one's schedule。

- ● Traffic in Seoul can be a real killer.
- ● I guess I'd better call and **reschedule**.
  ●首爾的交通真的是有夠糟的。　●我猜我最好打個電話重新約時間。

▶ My boss rearranged his schedule on Thursday.
我的老闆重新安排了他星期四的行程。

The tour company rearranged its schedule.
旅行社重新安排了行程。

1 職場・學校
2 電腦・網路
3 社交生活
4 日常生活
5 訊息・理解
6 想法・態度
7 情緒・狀況
8 行為舉止
9 時間地點・副詞片語

There's a... scheduled for...

· There isn't time on one's schedule to do
某人的行程已經滿了，沒有空做某事

有…安排在… 具體說明哪時候有什麼安排的表達方式。

● **There is** a meeting **scheduled for** tomorrow afternoon.
● Our boss wants everyone to attend it.

　●有個會議安排在明天下午。　●我們老闆希望每個人都能參加。

▶ There is a play scheduled for this evening.
有一場戲排在今天傍晚上演。

There is a festival scheduled for Saturday.
有個慶祝活動安排在星期六。

be due (tomorrow)

· be due in January
一月到期
· be due on May 5
五月五號到期
· A is overdue (by+期間)
A 已經過期（多久了）
· meet the due date
趕上到期日

（明天）到期 due 後面接時間副詞片語，表示某件事的截止期限，或是車船預定到達的時間。

● Why are the students working so hard?
● Their project **is due tomorrow**.

　●這些學生為什麼這麼努力？　●他們明天要完成研究計畫。

▶ Our electric bill is due tomorrow.
我們的電費帳單明天到期。

The team's report is due on January 4.
這個團隊一月四號要交出報告。

discuss today's schedule

· develop the new schedule
制定新的行程表
· announce the schedule to…
向…宣布行程

討論今天的行程 adjust the schedule 則是「調整行程」。

● Why were you in a meeting this morning?
● We needed to **discuss today's schedule**.

　●你們今天早上為什麼在開會？　●我們需要討論今天的行程。

▶ The guide discussed today's schedule with the tourists.
導遊和旅客們討論今天的行程。

No one discussed today's schedule with us.
沒有人跟我們討論今天的行程。

1 職場・學校

2 電腦・網路

3 社交生活

4 日常生活

5 訊息・理解

6 想法・態度

7 情緒・狀況

8 行為舉止

9 時間地點・副詞片語

09 遲到，延誤
be late for

3-09.mp3

be late for

- be late to do
  做…遲了
- be late because of the traffic jam
  因為塞車而遲到

…遲到 for 的後面接名詞。如果要接動詞，則說 be late to do…。

- We will **be late for** my doctor's appointment.
- Don't worry, we'll get there on time.
  - ●我們看病會遲到。　●別擔心，我們會準時到那裡的。

▶ I'm worried it's too late for us to get there on time.
我擔心現在已經太晚，我們無法準時到那裡。
I don't want to be late to the meeting again.
我不想再開會遲到。

turn up late for work

- be late for work
  上班遲到

上班遲到 上學遲到則是 late for school。

- Lonnie **turned up late for work** again.
- I'll bet her boss is very angry.
  - ●Lonnie 上班又遲到了。　●我猜她老闆很生氣。

▶ I was late for work on the first day. 我第一天上班就遲到。
You can't be late for work every day. 你不能天天上班遲到。

be + 時間 + late for

- be 2 hours late for
  …遲到兩小時

遲到了多久 如果是早到的話，則說「be + 時間 + early」。

- Do you care if we're late?
- I don't care if we **are a little late for** the party.
  - ●你擔不擔心我們會遲到？
  - ●派對遲到一下下的話，我覺得沒什麼好擔心的。

▶ He was 15 minutes late for class. 他上課遲到了 15 分鐘。
We were an hour late for the movie.
我們看電影遲到了一個小時。

be getting late

- be running late (for)
  （對某事而言）時間晚了
- be running (a bit) late
  時間（有點）晚了

時間晚了 getting 也可以換成 running，意思相同。

- It has been dark for a few hours.
- I guess it **is getting late**.
  - ●天色暗了幾小時了。　●我想時間晚了吧。

▶ It is getting late in the day. 很晚了。
I'd love to, but it's really getting late.
我很想，但時間真的晚了。

be delayed for + 時間

· put off
  推遲（某事）
· keep sb
  耽擱到某人

被延遲／耽擱了多久時間　delayed 也可以換成 postponed 或 put off。

● It's snowing pretty hard tonight.
● Yeah. Will the flight **be delayed**?

　●今晚雪下得蠻大的。　●是啊，班機會誤點嗎？

▶ The flight to Miami is delayed for one hour.
　飛往邁阿密的班機誤點了一小時。
　I don't know what's keeping him.
　我不知道是什麼耽擱到他了。

---

10 | 意圖
mean to

3-10.mp3

be intended to

· intend to do
  想要／打算做…
· go as I intended
  （事情）照我的打算發展

某物的目的是…　接動詞原形。接名詞時說 intended for。

● Why did they build that large hotel?
● It **was intended to** attract wealthy people.

　●他們為什麼蓋了那棟大飯店？　●因為想要吸引有錢人。

▶ The garden was intended to grow flowers.
　這座花園是用來種花的。
　Does your wife intend to work here during your stay?
　在你停留的期間，你太太打算在這裡工作嗎？

mean to

· mean to tell
  打算告訴…
· be meant to do
  （照道理）應該…

有意…　接動詞原形。通常用否定形，表示自己犯錯是不小心的。

● Hey, you just stepped on my toe.
● Sorry, I didn't **mean to** hurt you.

　●喂，你踩到我腳趾頭了。　●抱歉，我不是有意弄傷你的。

▶ They didn't mean to come late.
　他們不是有意遲到的。
　Henry didn't mean to break your watch.
　Henry 不是故意弄壞你的手錶的。

have no intention to

- have no intention of -ing
  沒有做…的打算
- with the intention of -ing
  有著做…的意圖

沒有打算做… to do 也可以換成 of doing。

- Casey invited you to her party.
- I **have no intention of** going there.
  ●Casey 邀請你去她的派對。　●我不打算去那裡。

▶ He has no intention of leaving his house.
  他沒打算出門。
  Seamus has no intention of talking to her.
  Seamus 沒打算跟她說話。

be designed to

被設計來做… 表示某物是為了某個目的而製造的。

- Is this computer program useful?
- It **was designed to** make work easier.
  ●這個電腦軟體有用嗎？　●它是為了使工作更容易而被設計出來的。

▶ This sports car was designed to go fast.
  這台跑車是為了高速行駛而設計的。
  This building was designed to be comfortable.
  這棟大樓是以舒適為目的而建造的。

on purpose

故意 通常表示故意做壞事。用一個字表示的話就是 deliberately。

- Kelly got into a fight last night.
- He did it **on purpose**. He was in a bad mood.
  ●Kelly 昨晚捲入一場打鬥。　●他是故意的。他昨天心情很差。

▶ Bill was late for class on purpose.
  Bill 故意上課遲到。
  I didn't hand in my homework on purpose.
  我故意沒交作業。

1 職場・學校
2 電腦・網路
3 社交生活
4 日常生活
5 訊息・理解
6 想法・態度
7 情緒・狀況
8 行為舉止
9 時間地點・副詞片語

11 見面
get together

get together (with sb)

· get back together
重修舊好
· have a get-together
辦一場聚會

和…見面 接 for sth 可以表示見面的目的，接 and do... 表示見面後要做的事。

● Why don't we **get together** on Saturday?
● Sure. Call me in the morning.
　●我們何不在星期六見個面呢？　●好啊，早上打電話給我吧。

▶ I wonder if we could get together on the 15th.
　我想知道我們能不能在 15 號見面。
　Why don't we get together on Saturday?
　我們何不在星期六見個面呢？

meet sb in person

· meet with
和…見面
· meet a client
和客戶見面

當面見某人 in person 是「親自，直接」的意思。

● Do you like our new President?
● Sure. I've **met him in person**.
　●你喜歡我們的新總統嗎？　●當然，我當面見過他。

▶ Danielle met Brad Pitt in person.
　Danielle 當面見到了布萊德彼特。
　Have we met somewhere before?
　我們之前在哪裡見過面嗎？

run into

· run/come across
巧遇，偶然遇到
· bump into
偶然遇到

巧遇… 後面接人，意思是 meet sb unexpectedly。

● I **ran into** Chris this morning.
● How's he doing?
　●我今天早上巧遇了 Chris。　●他過得怎樣？

▶ He ran into his ex-girlfriend at the market.
　他在市場巧遇了他的前女友。
　We ran into our former math teacher.
　我們偶然遇到我們之前的數學老師。

show up

· turn up
  出現

現身，抵達 表示抵達聚會或約好的地方，與 turn up 意義相同。

- What made you think that I wasn't going to **show up**?
- I just thought you had other more important plans.
  - 你為什麼覺得我不會出席？　●我只是以為你有其他更重要的安排。

▶ How come he didn't show up at the seminar this morning? 他為什麼沒有出席今天早上的研討會？
  I might show up at the end of the meeting.
  我可能會在會議快結束的時候露面。

keep sb company

陪伴某人 意思是 stay with sb who doesn't want to be alone。company 是「陪伴」或「客人」的意思。

- Helen has been in the hospital since yesterday.
- I should go there and **keep her company**.
  - Helen 從昨天住院到現在。　●我應該去陪陪她。

▶ He came by to keep me company.
  他來陪我。
  My mom's dog always keeps her company.
  我媽媽養的狗常常陪在她身邊。

have company

· have company at the moment
  現在有客人
· enjoy one's company
  喜歡和某人作伴

有人陪伴，有客人 company 的前面不能加上冠詞 a 或 the。

- Is it OK if I come over now?
- I'm sorry, but we **have company**.
  - 我現在過去方便嗎？　●不好意思，我們有客人。

▶ We're going to have company this weekend.
  我們這週末有客人。
  They had company when they went out to eat.
  有人陪他們一起出去吃飯。

see each other

· be alone with
  和…單獨在一起

見面 也有「交往」的意思。

- I heard Brett and Wendy **are seeing each other**.
- It's true. They make such a cute couple.
  - 我聽說 Brett 和 Wendy 正在交往。
  - 是真的。他們是對很可愛的情侶。

▶ Bob and his girlfriend decided not to see each other.
  Bob 和他女朋友決定分手。
  They began to see each other during high school.
  他們從高中時期開始交往。

1 職場・學校

2 電腦・網路

3 社交生活

4 日常生活

5 訊息・理解

6 想法・態度

7 情緒・狀況

8 行為舉止

9 時間地點・副詞片語

company 只有「公司」的意思嗎？

　　說到「company」這個單字，大家應該會先想到「公司」吧。更認真學習英文的話，就會知道其實 company 也有「同事」、「朋友」、「同伴」、「客人」等各種涵義。但是，即使已經學過了，在字典上也確實畫了線背下來了，也不一定能夠活用。舉例來說，當我們去旅行時，請外國友人帶我們到處晃了一整天，我們就可以說「I was grateful for Mr. Smith's company on the long journey up to Edinburgh.」。或是公司派我們去陪客戶觀光，帶著他遊覽市區，結束時客戶可能就會說「I enjoyed your company.」來表達對我們的感謝之意。如果把這個 company 誤以為是「公司」，還回答「Thank you very much. The company I work with is very good.」，那可不只是丟了自己的臉，也會讓公司蒙羞的。

　　Company 除了「和某人在一起」（the presence of another person）這種比較抽象的意思之外，也可以表示「陪在身邊、一起度過時間的人」（the people with whom a person spends time）。再舉個例子吧。在一個派對上，看來百般無聊，站在牆邊一動也不動的兩人，他們可能會說：「The people at this party are really boring—present company excepted, of course!」（這個派對的人真無聊——當然，除了我身邊的你以外！）。

12 | 邀請
invite sb to

3-12.mp3

**invite sb to
+ 場所（派對）**

・invite sb for+N
　邀請某人去…
・invite sb to/for dinner
　邀請某人吃晚餐
・be invited to + 場所
　被邀請去某個地方

邀請某人去… to 後面可以接地點或慶祝的場合。

● I **invited** Jerry **to** our wedding.
● That's great! I hope he will come.
　●我邀請 Jerry 來參加我們的婚禮。　●太好了！我希望他會來。

▶ No wonder she didn't invite you to her birthday party.
　難怪她沒有邀請你去參加她的生日派對。
　I am thrilled to be invited to the party.
　我很興奮能受邀參加派對。

invite sb to

· invite sb over
  邀請某人到家裡
· be invited to do
  受邀做…

邀請某人做… 在 invite sb 後面加上 to 和動詞原形說明目的。

● **Were** you **invited to** join the science club?
● Sure. I'm aware of where they will meet.

●你有被邀請加入科學社團嗎？　●當然。我知道他們會在哪裡聚會。

▶ I'll invite you over and explain it to you in English.
　我會邀請你過來，用英文解釋給你聽。
　Paul invited her to have dinner on Christmas Eve at his place. Paul 邀請她在耶誕夜到家裡吃晚餐。

turn down one's invitation

· reply to an invitation
  回覆邀約

拒絕某人的邀約 後面接 politely 表示禮貌地拒絕。

● Are you coming to her New Year's party?
● No, I had to **turn down her invitation**.

●你會去她的新年派對嗎？　●不會，我得拒絕她的邀約。

▶ We turned down David's invitation.
　我們拒絕了 David 的邀約。
　Dick turned down Harriet's invitation.
　Dick 拒絕了 Harriet 的邀約。

make oneself at home

· make oneself comfortable
  輕鬆自在

當成在自己家裡一樣輕鬆 at home 也可以換成 comfortable。

● Wow! This is a great place.
● Thank you. Just **make yourself comfortable**.

●哇！你住的地方好棒。　●謝謝，請隨意。

▶ Make yourself at home while you wait.
　等待的時候請隨意，不用拘束。
　Come in and make yourself at home.
　進來吧，當自己家。

wear out one's welcome

待得太久而不再受到歡迎 wear out 是「磨損，耗盡」的意思。

● I asked my friend to leave my house.
● I guess he **wore out his welcome**.

●我請我朋友離開我家。　●我猜他是待得太久才不受歡迎。

▶ Don't stay too long and wear out your welcome.
　別待太久，以免不受歡迎。
　He wore out his welcome with his bad manners.
　他因為不禮貌而變得不受歡迎。

1 職場‧學校
2 電腦‧網路
3 社交生活
4 日常生活
5 訊息‧理解
6 想法‧態度
7 情緒‧狀況
8 行為舉止
9 時間地點‧副詞片語

13 介紹
would like sb to meet

3-13.mp3

would like A to meet B

- want A to meet B
  希望 A 能見 B
- I've heard so much about you.
  久仰大名。
- I've been dying to meet you.
  我一直很想見你。

想把 B 介紹給 A 是比 introduce 更正式的說法。

- Hello, Sarah. I **want you to meet** my friend, John.
- It's a pleasure. I've heard so much about you.
  - 嗨，Sarah，來見見我的朋友 John。
  - 這是我的榮幸，我久仰大名了。

▶ Mom, I would like you to meet my boyfriend.
  媽，這是我男朋友。
  I'd like you to meet my roommate.
  我想向你介紹我的室友。

This is + (關係) + 人名

- This is + (人名) + speaking
  （在電話中表示身分）
  我是…

這是… 跟我們口語中說的「這位是…」意思一樣。

- **This is** my lovely wife, Susie.
- Nice to meet you.
  - 這是我可愛的妻子，Susie。 ● 很高興見到你。

▶ Danny, this is Jim Tomson. He's a colleague.
  Danny，這是 Jim Tomson。他是我的同事。
  This is my friend, Jennifer.
  這是我朋友 Jennifer。

introduce A to B

- It gives me great pleasure to introduce A
  我很榮幸介紹 A
  （使用於正式場合）

把 A 介紹給 B introduce oneself to... 則是指「把自己介紹給某人」。

- There are cute girls at the bar.
- Let's go over and **introduce ourselves**.
  - 酒吧裡有很多可愛的女孩子。 ● 我們過去介紹一下自己吧。

▶ I'd like to introduce you to Mr. Kim, our president.
  我想把你介紹給我們的總裁 Kim 先生。
  It gives me great pleasure to introduce Mr. Carter.
  我很榮幸介紹 Carter 先生。

(It's) nice to meet you

· It's nice to meet you, too.
我也很高興認識你。

· I'm glad/thrilled to meet you.
很高興認識你。

很高興認識你 在初次見面時表示喜悅之情的典型說法。

● Julie, I want you to meet my friend. This is Allan.

● Hi! **Nice to meet you**.

●Julie，來見見我的朋友。這是 Allan。　●嗨！很高興認識你。

▶ Nice to meet everyone. It's great to be here.
很高興認識大家，能來這裡真是太好了。

It's nice to meet you, too. I've heard a lot about you from my wife. 我也很高興認識你。我從我太太那裡聽過很多你的事情。

know each other

彼此認識 後面接 by one's voice 則是指彼此通過電話。

● Have you ever met Brian?

● Oh yes, we **know each other** well.

●你見過 Brian 嗎？　●喔，有啊，我們很熟。

▶ Sam and Dave know each other from high school.
Sam 和 Dave 從高中時就認識了。

Do you know each other from work?
你們是在工作場合上認識對方的嗎？

---

1 職場·學校
2 電腦·網路
3 社交生活
4 日常生活
5 訊息·理解
6 想法·態度
7 情緒·狀況
8 行為舉止
9 時間地點·副詞片語

14 拜訪
come over

3-14.mp3

come over

· come over to one's place
拜訪某人的家

· come over to do
來做…

· come over here
來這裡

來訪，拜訪 很常用的慣用語。接 to N 可以表示場所，接 to do 表示目的，也可以接 here 等場所副詞。

● When can I **come over to** see you?

● Whenever you like. Just don't forget to bring some food.

●我什麼時候可以去拜訪你？

●什麼時候都可以，只要別忘了帶點食物來。

▶ Feel free to come over to my place.
儘管隨時來我家。

Why don't you come over here and talk to me for a second? 你何不過來和我講幾句話呢？

stop by

- stop off
  逗留，路過拜訪
- stop by any time after...
  在…之後的任何時候拜訪
- stop by one's apartment
  順道去某人的公寓

路過拜訪 特別指在去某處的途中剛好經過，短暫地拜訪一下。

- I'm going to **stop by** the store on the way to work.
- Can you pick me up some snacks?

  ●我上班途中要順道去那間店。 ●你可以幫我買些點心嗎？

▶ We're going to stop by a nightclub.
  我們要順道去夜店。

  I'll stop by your house on my way home.
  我在回家路上會順便去你家。

drop by

- drop by for...
  為了…順便拜訪
- drop in
  順便拜訪
- drop in at + 場所 (on + 人)
  順道拜訪某處（的某人）

（突然地）順便拜訪 常指沒有事先約好，突然拜訪的狀況。

- What brings you here?
- I was in the neighborhood and I thought I'd **drop by**.

  ●你怎麼來了？ ●我剛才在這附近，所以就想拜訪一下。

▶ Let's drop by Tara's apartment.
  我們順道去 Tara 家拜訪吧。

  Feel free to drop by anytime.
  請儘管隨時來訪。

stop over

中途停留 名詞形是 stopover，特別指飛行旅途的中途停留，與 layover 同義。

- Do you have a direct flight to LA?
- No, I have a **stopover** in New York.

  ●你直飛洛杉磯嗎？ ●不是，我會在紐約中途停留。

▶ Our stopover will last 2 hours.
  我們會中途停留兩小時。

  My flight has a stopover in Iceland.
  我的班機會在冰島中途停留。

visit someplace

- visit sb in the hospital
  探某人的病
- be worth visiting
  值得拜訪

拜訪某處 visit 可以接人或地點當受詞。

- We are thinking of coming to **visit** you this summer.
- Fancy that! I'll have to get my guest room all ready!

  ●我們打算今年夏天去拜訪你。 ●太棒了！我得趕緊整理我的客房。

▶ I've been looking forward to visiting the factory.
  我很期待參觀工廠。

  I'm going to visit Tom in the hospital at lunch.
  我午餐時間要去醫院看 Tom。

come to visit

- come and visit (sb for dinner)
  來拜訪（某人並共享晚餐）
- be on a visit to (China)
  正在參訪（中國）
- pay a visit to
  拜訪…

來拜訪 on a visit 意為「拜訪中」、「停留中」。

- You should **come to visit** us in Miami.
- Sure, I can do that in December.
  - 你該來邁阿密拜訪我們。　●好啊，我十二月可以。

▶ When is Grandma going to come to visit?
  奶奶什麼時候要來拜訪？
  Come to visit my hometown in Canada.
  來我加拿大的老家拜訪。

call on

拜訪 call on 也有「請求某人」的意思。

- Did you see your friend from church?
- Yeah, I **called on** her at her house.
  - 你見了你教會的朋友嗎？　●嗯，我去她家拜訪她。

▶ When is a good time to call on you?
  什麼時候拜訪你比較好？
  Let's call on our new neighbor.
  我們去拜訪我們的新鄰居吧。

buzz sb in

- knock on the door
  敲門
- come up to one's apartment
  來某人的公寓

按對講機幫某人開門 按按鈕的時候會發出聲響，所以說 buzz。

- Jerry is standing outside the door.
- You better **buzz him in**.
  - Jerry 站在門外。　●你最好幫他開門。

▶ Sharon didn't buzz the stranger in.
  Sharon 沒有讓那個陌生人進來。
  The doorman buzzed me in.
  那個看門的人讓我進來。

stay for

- stay for a little while longer
  再多待一會兒
- stay for + 期間
  停留（多久）
- stay for + 餐點
  留下來用餐

逗留 for 後面可以接名詞，表示理由或期間。

- It's late and I should go home.
- Please **stay for** a while longer.
  - 很晚了，我該回家了。　●請多待一會兒。

▶ I'm planning to stay for three weeks.
  我預計停留三個星期。
  That's too bad. I was hoping you'd stay for dinner.
  真可惜，我原本還希望你能留下來一起吃晚餐。

1 職場・學校
2 電腦・網路
3 社交生活
4 日常生活
5 訊息・理解
6 想法・態度
7 情緒・狀況
8 行為舉止
9 時間地點・副詞片語

15 等待 wait for

3-15.mp3

wait for

· wait for sb to do
等待某人做⋯
· wait a while
等一下

等待 「for sb」是等人,「for＋時間名詞」則表示等待的期間。

● I need to do my hair before we go.
● I'll **be waiting for** you in the living room.
　●我們離開前,我要整理一下頭髮。　●我會在客廳等你。

▶ Can you wait for me in my room? 你可以在我房間裡等我嗎?
　We have to wait for the bride and groom to cut the cake.
　我們要等新娘和新郎切蛋糕。

wait until

· wait until later
等以後
· wait until S+V
等到⋯
· wait until late at night
without going to bed
等到很晚都沒睡

等到⋯ 想要給人驚喜,或是想要吊人胃口時,可以這麼說。

● Can I open my birthday presents?
● **Wait until** we bring out the cake.
　●我可以打開我的生日禮物嗎?　●等我們把蛋糕拿來再開。

▶ You'll have to wait until I finish my breakfast.
　你得等我吃完早餐。
　I don't think I want to wait until Monday! 我不想等到星期一!

keep sb waiting

一直讓某人等 沒按時做某事,害人浪費時間等待。

● I have been here for twenty minutes.
● I'm sorry. I **kept you waiting** so long.
　●我到這裡已經 20 分鐘了。　●對不起,我讓你等了那麼久。

▶ She kept me waiting for an hour. 她讓我等了一小時。
　Sorry to keep you waiting, I had a call on the other line.
　抱歉讓你久等了,我剛才在講另一通電話。

wait one's turn

· It's my turn to do
輪到我做⋯了

等輪到自己 turn 在這裡表示「次序」、「順序」的意思。

● I have to buy this dress right now.
● Come on lady, **wait your turn**.
　●我現在就要買這件洋裝。　●小姐,幫幫忙,排隊等一下。

▶ The man didn't wait his turn to get on the bus.
　那個男人插隊上了公車。
　I can wait my turn to turn in my exam.
　我可以等到該我交考卷的時候。

take turns

· take turn -ing
  輪流做…
· in turn
  依次

輪流 後面可以直接接 V-ing 表示輪流做什麼。
- The children are very polite.
- They **take turns** playing with toys.
  - 這些孩子很有禮貌。　　● 他們輪流玩玩具.

▶ We took turns using the computer.
  我們輪流用了電腦。
  You'll have to take turns driving.
  你們得輪流開車。

get in line

· wait in line
  排隊等待
· stand in line
  站成一排
· be next in line
  在下個順位

排隊 只想到自己，覺得只有自己急而插隊，稱為 cut in line。
- I can't stand **waiting in lines** like this.
- Me, neither, do you want to leave?
  - 我受不了像這樣排隊等。　　● 我也是。你想離開了嗎？

▶ They got in line at five this morning.
  他們今天早上五點開始排隊。
  You must get in line to buy your food.
  你要買食物就得排隊。

put sb on a waiting list

把某人記在候補名單上 put sb on the wanted list 是「通緝某人」的意思。
- They **put us on a waiting list** for the flight.
- Hopefully you'll get it.
  - 他們把我們加進那班飛機的候補名單。　　● 希望你們排得上候補。

▶ They put us on a waiting list for the flight.
  他們把我們加進那班飛機的候補名單。
  Put me on a waiting list for the tickets.
  請把我加進購票的候補名單裡。

while we wait

當我們等待的時候 while 在這裡接 S+V，但也常接 -ing。
- Gosh, it is so boring sitting here.
- Let's play a game **while we wait**.
  - 天啊，坐在這裡好無聊。　　● 等待的時候，我們來玩個遊戲吧。

▶ We can't smoke while we wait.
  我們等待的時候不能抽菸。
  I'll read you a story while we wait.
  我們等待的時候，我來念個故事給你聽。

1 職場・學校
2 電腦・網路
3 社交生活
4 日常生活
5 訊息・理解
6 想法・態度
7 情緒・狀況
8 行為舉止
9 時間地點・副詞片語

hold on

- Hold it! = Wait! Stop!
  等等！
- hold it a second
  等一下
- hold on a moment
  等一下

等一下 除了在電話裡請對方稍等之外，日常生活裡也很常用。

- The key's stuck in the lock.
- I can fix it. **Hold on**.

  ●鑰匙卡在鎖裡了。　●我可以修好它，等一下。

▶ Hold on, there's a stain on your shirt.

  等等，你襯衫上有塊髒汙。

  Just hold on for a second and I'll find it.

  等一下就好，我會找到它的。

one after another

一個接一個 「隨機地」則是 at random。

- Did everyone go home already?
- Yes, they left **one after another**.

  ●所有人都回家了嗎？　●是的，他們一個接一個離開了。

▶ The teams were defeated, one after another.

  那些隊伍接連被打敗了。

  I met with the students, one after another.

  我一個接一個地跟學生見面。

---

16 打招呼與道別
say hi to

3-16.mp3

say goodbye to

跟…說再見 「good bye」可以連起來寫，也可以在中間空一格，或是在中間加上「-」。

- Are you ready to leave yet?
- I am. **Say goodbye to** your friends.

  ●你準備好要走了嗎？　●嗯。跟你的朋友說再見。

▶ It's time to say good-bye.

  該說再見了。

  I have a call on the other line. I'll have to say good bye.

  我有另一通電話要接，我得掛電話了。

say hi to

- say hi to A for me
  幫我跟 A 問好
- say hello to (A for B)
  （幫 B 跟 A）問好

向某人打招呼／問好 to 後面接問候的對象。

- By the way, Jim said to **say hello to** you.
- Where did you see him?

  ●對了，Jim 要我跟你問好。　●你在哪裡見到他的？

▶ Say hi to your mom and dad.
  跟你父母問好。
  Say hello to your parents for me.
  幫我跟你父母問好。

give one's best to

- remember me to A
  代我向 A 問好

向某人問好 best 可以改成 best regards。

- **Give my best to** everyone at the school.
- I'll tell them you said hello.

  ●幫我跟學校的大家問好。　●我會替你向他們問好的。

▶ Give my best to Uncle John.
  幫我向 John 叔叔問好。
  Give my best regards to him for me when you see him.
  你見到他的時候，幫我跟他問好。

see sb off

- see sb out
  送某人出門

為某人送行 see off 是送行，send-off party 是歡送會。

- I went to the station to **see Patty off**.
- Is she moving to another city?

  ●我去車站為 Patty 送行.　●她要搬到別的城市嗎？

▶ Dad said he would see Anna off.
  爸爸說他會幫 Anna 送行。
  We saw Charlie off when he joined the military.
  Charlie 入伍的時候，我們為他送行。

walk sb to

- walk sb out
  陪某人走到外面

陪某人走到… 這裡的 walk sb 是陪某人一起走的意思。

- It's time for me to drive home.
- I'll **walk you to** your car.

  ●我該開車回家了。　●我陪你走到車那邊吧。

▶ Jason walked Cindy to her home.
  Jason 陪 Cindy 走回家。
  You don't have to walk me home.
  你不必陪我走回家。

1 職場・學校
2 電腦・網路
3 社交生活
4 日常生活
5 訊息・理解
6 想法・態度
7 情緒・狀況
8 行為舉止
9 時間地點・副詞片語

17 約定會面
have an appointment

3-17.mp3

have an appointment

· have a doctor's appointment
跟醫生約了要看診
· have another appointment
有別的約
· have an appointment to do
有個要做…的約

有約 appointment 是指和醫生約診、或者跟髮廊約了做頭髮等情況。情侶約會則是 have a date。

● So what did you do today?
● Oh, I **had an appointment** to get my hair cut.
　● 你今天做了什麼？　● 喔，我今天約了剪頭髮。

▶ I can't. I have an appointment.
　我不行，我有約了。
　You have a dental appointment today.
　你今天跟牙醫有約。

make an appointment

· make an appointment with sb
和某人約見面
· make a dentist appointment
和牙醫約診

約見面 可以接介系詞片語，說明「何時、和誰、為了什麼目的」見面。

● I think that we should make an offer on the property.
● I'll **make an appointment** with the agent for later today.
　● 我想我們該對那棟房子出價。　● 我會跟仲介約今天稍晚見面。

▶ I'm calling to make an appointment with Dr. Laura.
　我打來約 Laura 醫生的診。
　I can't make my 3:30 appointment this afternoon.
　我沒辦法赴我今天下午 3:30 的約。

set up an appointment

· set up an appointment for next week
約個下星期的時間

約見面 後面可以接 with sb 表示對象、接 for... 表示目的或時間。

● Are you going to get checked by a doctor?
● I **set up an appointment** for Monday.
　● 你會接受醫師檢查嗎？　● 我約了星期一。

▶ Let's set up an appointment for an interview.
　我們約個時間面試吧。
　I'd like to set up an appointment for next week.
　我想約個下星期的時間。

keep an appointment

· cancel tomorrow's appointment
  取消明天的約

· miss an appointment
  沒守約

守約 表示按照約定的時間見面。

● You are very late today.

● I had to **keep an appointment** this morning.
  ●你今天好晚。　●我今天早上得赴一個約。

▶ I couldn't keep an appointment with her.
  我沒辦法依約和她見面。
  You need to keep an appointment for next week.
  你要守下星期的那個約。

take a rain check

· give a rain check
  提出延期

· rain check
  球賽因故取消時發放的免費門票

改約其他時間 rain check 原本指的是球賽因大雨被迫取消時發送、讓觀眾可以免費看其他比賽的門票。

● Come on upstairs for some coffee.

● I can't, but I'll **take a rain check**.
  ●上樓喝杯咖啡吧。　●我不行，改天吧。

▶ Sarah took a rain check on the invitation.
  Sarah 將邀請改了期。
  I'm very busy, so I'll take a rain check.
  我很忙，所以改天吧。

1 職場・學校
2 電腦・網路
3 社交生活
4 日常生活
5 訊息・理解
6 想法・態度
7 情緒・狀況
8 行為舉止
9 時間地點・副詞片語

18 聯絡
get in touch

3-18.mp3

get in touch with

· get back in touch (with)
  重新（和某人）取得聯繫

和…取得聯繫 with 後面接取得聯繫的對象。

● I heard that John is coming to town this weekend.

● Did you **get in touch with** him?
  ●我聽說 John 這週末會進城。　●你聯絡上他了嗎？

▶ Where can I get in touch with her?
  我該怎麼聯絡上她？
  I got back in touch with old friends through a web site.
  我透過一個網站重新聯絡上老朋友。

keep in touch with

· stay/be in touch with
  和…保持聯絡

和…保持聯絡 有定期聯絡的狀態。keep 也可以換成 stay。

● What happened to your friend Tim?

● I **keep in touch with** him through e-mail.

　● 你朋友 Tim 怎麼了？　● 我和他用電子郵件保持聯絡。

▶ Would you keep in touch with me?

　你會跟我保持聯絡嗎？

　Let's keep in touch!

　我們保持聯絡吧！

lose touch with

· be out of touch
  with sb
  和某人失去聯絡

和…失去聯絡 lose 是及物動詞，touch 是它的受詞。

● What are all your cousins doing these days?

● I don't know. I **lost touch with** them over the years.

　● 你的堂弟妹們最近過得怎樣？

　● 我不知道。我跟他們好幾年沒聯絡了。

▶ She lost touch with her college classmates.

　她和大學的同學們失去了聯絡。

　I hope we don't lose touch with him.

　我希望我們不會和他失去聯絡。

make contact with

· contact sb
  聯絡某人
· keep in contact with
  和…保持聯絡
· get back in contact
  with
  和…重新取得聯繫

聯絡… 和 touch 一樣，contact 也有聯絡的意思。

● I haven't heard from Joan in a month.

● Let's try to **make contact with** her soon.

　● 我一個月沒跟 Joan 聯絡了。　● 我們快試著跟她聯絡吧。

▶ We made contact with our manager.

　我們聯絡了我們的經理。

　Did you make contact with Tim this weekend?

　你這週末有聯絡 Tim 嗎？

get a hold of

· get through to…
  聯絡上…
· get called in
  被呼叫

聯絡上某人 原始的意思是「得到」，和 obtain 相近。

● Mike never answers his e-mail.

● It's difficult to **get a hold of** him.

　● Mike 從來不回電子郵件。　● 要聯絡上他很難。

▶ She needs to get a hold of a lawyer.

　她需要聯絡上律師。

　I've been trying to get a hold of you all morning!

　我一整個早上都在試著聯絡上你！

19 預約
make a reservation

3-19.mp3

1 職場‧學校
2 電腦‧網路
3 社交生活
4 日常生活
5 訊息‧理解
6 想法‧態度
7 情緒‧狀況
8 行為舉止
9 時間地點‧副詞片語

book a flight

‧ book a flight to + 都市
訂前往某都市的機票
‧ book a flight from A to B
訂從 A 飛往 B 的機票
‧ be booked on flight…
訂了…班機的機票

訂機票 book 當動詞，後面可以接 a seat, a room, a ticket 等受詞。
● American Airlines. How may I direct your call?
● I'd like to **book a ticket** from Chicago to New York.
　● 這裡是美國航空，請問您想將電話轉接到哪裡？
　● 我想要訂一張芝加哥到紐約的機票。

▶ The tickets are going fast so we'd better book some seats right away. 票賣得很快，所以我們最好馬上訂位。
I'm booked on American Airlines flight number 567 to New York. 我訂了美國航空飛往紐約的 567 號班機。

be booked up

‧ sth be booked (up)
某物預訂一空了
‧ sb be booked (up)
某人有很多事要做

訂滿了 飯店、餐廳或機位被預訂一空，沒有任何空位的狀況。
● Why don't you make a reservation on Northwest Airlines?
● I tried, but the flights **are all booked**.
　● 你為什麼不訂西北航空？　● 我試過了，可是班機都被訂滿了。

▶ Every bus to Kaohsiung was all booked up.
往高雄的客運車票都訂滿了。
I tried to leave but the train was booked up.
我試著要離開，但火車票都被預訂一空了。

reserve a room at

‧ reserve a table for + 人數
預訂幾人的桌子
‧ reserve a seat/ticket
訂位／訂票
‧ be reserved
被預訂了

在…訂了一間房間 在餐廳等地看到「reserved」，就表示已訂位。
● Did you plan your vacation yet?
● Yes, we **reserved a room** at Hilton Hotel.
　● 你們為假期做計畫了嗎？　● 嗯，我們在希爾頓飯店訂了房間。

▶ The newlyweds reserved a room at a Hawaiian hotel.
這對新婚夫妻在一間夏威夷的飯店訂了一間房。
Let's reserve a room at one of the cheaper hotels.
我們從比較便宜的飯店裡選一間來訂房吧。

make a reservation

- make a reservation for
  預訂…
- confirm a reservation
  確認預訂
- reconfirm my
  reservation
  再次確認我的預訂

預訂 make a reservation 可以簡化為動詞「reserve」。

- Can I **make reservations**?
- No, it's on a first come, first serve basis.
  - 我可以預訂嗎？　●不行，這裡採先到先服務制。

▶ I want to reconfirm my reservation.
我想要再確認我的預約。
I didn't have time to make a hotel reservation before leaving. 我在離開之前沒有時間訂房。

cancel one's reservations

- change my return date
  更改我的回程日期

取消某人的預訂 可以接 for sth 或 to do… 表示預訂的內容。

- What did you do when the storm came?
- I **canceled my reservations** for the trip.
  - 風暴來襲的時候你做了什麼？　●我取消了旅行的預約。

▶ Cancel my reservations at the hotel.
請取消我的飯店訂房。
I must cancel my reservations to go out to eat.
我得取消我的餐廳預訂。

---

20 交情好壞
make friends with

3-20.mp3

make friends with

- be friends with
  和…是朋友
- Let's just be friends.
  我們當朋友就好。

和…做朋友 因為交朋友是互相的，所以用複數形。

- Did you enjoy your visit to Europe?
- Yes, I **made friends with** some people there.
  - 你的歐洲行玩得開心嗎？　●嗯，我在那裡交了些朋友。

▶ She made friends with everyone in class.
她和班上每個人都是朋友。
I don't want to make friends with anyone here.
我不想和這邊的任何人做朋友。

shake hands (with)

（和⋯）握手　握手是兩個人做的動作，所以 hands 是複數。

- The President visited our school.
- Did he **shake hands with** the students?

　●總統拜訪了我們學校。　●他有和學生們握手嗎？

▶ Dan shook hands with his boss. Dan 和他老闆握了手。
　We shook hands to complete the deal 我們握手完成交易。

get on well

相處得很好　要表示相處的對象，可以接 with sb。

- Does Dave **get on well** with his wife?
- No, they are always arguing.

　●Dave 和他太太處得好嗎？　●不好，他們總是在吵架。

▶ He got on well with his boss. 他和他的老闆處得很好。
　Try to get on well with everyone. 試著和每個人好好相處。

get along

和睦相處　同樣可以接 with sb 表示相處的對象。

- I don't **get along** with my roommate.
- Maybe you should move elsewhere.

　●我和我的室友處得不好。　●也許你該搬去別的地方。

▶ The children got along with each other.
　這兩個孩子彼此處得很好。
　It's easy to get along with your friends. 你朋友很好相處。

get acquainted (with)

（和⋯）認識　acquaintance 表示「認識的人」、「熟人」。

- Why are we having a meeting?
- It's to **get acquainted with** the new workers.

　●我們為什麼要開會？　●為了和新員工們認識。

▶ I got acquainted with her during the bus ride.
　我和她是在坐公車時認識的。
　Let's get acquainted with our new neighbors.
　我們去認識新鄰居吧。

have a good relationship

- have a good/bad relationship with
  和⋯的關係好／不好
- develop relations
  發展關係
- miss the relationship with
  懷念與⋯的關係

關係好　相反的，要表示關係不好，把 good 改成 bad 即可。

- Can we use the classroom after school?
- Sure. I **have a good relationship** with my teacher.

　●我們放學之後可以用這間教室嗎？　●當然，我跟老師關係很好。

▶ She had a good relationship with her parents.
　她和她父母的關係很好。
　I have a good relationship with my principal.
　我和校長的關係很好。

1 職場・學校
2 電腦・網路
3 社交生活
4 日常生活
5 訊息・理解
6 想法・態度
7 情緒・狀況
8 行為舉止
9 時間地點・副詞片語

be on good terms with

· be on bad/poor terms with
　和…的關係不好

和某人的關係／交情好 term 在這裡表示「關係」。

● I heard you visit this restaurant often.
● I **am on good terms with** the staff here.
　●我聽說你常來這間餐廳。　●我和這邊的工作人員關係很好。

▶ Hank is on good terms with his doctor.
　Hank 和他的醫生關係很好。
　I am on good terms with the new supervisor.
　我和新主管的關係很好。

be bonded together

· bond with
　和…團結在一起
· be bonding (with)
　（和…）關係很好
· be social with
　和…相處得很好

很親密 be united/joined together 也是一樣的意思。

● Mary and Jane seem very close.
● They **are bonded together** like sisters.
　●Mary 跟 Jane 看起來很親近。　●她們就像姊妹一樣親密。

▶ My best friend and I are bonded together.
　我最好的朋友和我很親密。
　We are social with the other employees.
　我們和其他員工的關係很好。

go way back

認識很久了 表示是很久以前就認識的老朋友。

● Have you ever met my friend Logan?
● Yes. Logan and I **go way back**.
　●你見過我的朋友 Logan 嗎？　●見過，我跟他是老朋友了。

▶ Their close relationship goes way back.
　他們親近的關係可以追溯到很久以前。
　Janice and Ian's friendship goes way back.
　Janice 和 Ian 的友誼可以追溯到很久以前。

be at odds with

· be out with
　和…的關係不好

和…不一致／意見不合 with 後面可接「人或事物」來說明。

● Why did the company fire Alex?
● His behavior **was at odds with** his job.
　●公司為什麼把 Alex 開除了？　●他的行為牴觸到工作。

▶ Teenagers are often at odds with their parents.
　青少年們通常和父母意見不合。
　Her lies were at odds with the truth.
　她所說的謊和事實大相逕庭。

21 | 對話
talk to

3-21.mp3

1 職場・學校

2 電腦・網路

3 社交生活

4 日常生活

5 訊息・理解

6 想法・態度

7 情緒・狀況

8 行為舉止

9 時間地點・副詞片語

talk to

· talk to sb privately
  和某人私下談話
· talk with
  和…談話
· talk later
  晚點聊

對…說話 to sb 是單向的「對…說」，with sb 則是強調彼此交談的「和…談話」，但實際上的對話常是單向、雙向混合的，所以這兩種說法經常混用。

● Is it okay if I phone after lunch?

● No problem. I'll **talk to** you then.

　　●我午餐後打電話給你可以嗎？　　●沒問題，我到時候再跟你談。

▶ Sorry, I got a date. Talk to you later.

　　抱歉，我有約會。晚點再聊。

　　I need to talk with you. Can you please come out?

　　我得跟你談談，可以請你出來嗎？

talk about

· talk more about
  談更多關於…的事
· I'm talking about…
  我在說關於…的事
· talk about A over dinner
  在晚餐的時候談 A 的事

談和…有關的事 about 可以接人事物等各種話題。

● What do you think about my proposal?

● We need to **talk about** that.

　　●你覺得我的提案怎麼樣？　　●我們得談一下那件事。

▶ Are you ready to talk about it?

　　你準備好要談這件事了嗎？

　　I don't know what you're talking about.

　　我不知道你在說什麼。

have a word with

· have words with
  和…爭吵
· have a quick word with
  和…很快地談一下
· have a talk
  談話

和…談一下 have words with 是「和…爭吵」的意思，千萬別搞混了。

● Umm, Jimmy. May I **have a word with** you?

● Yeah, of course.

　　●嗯，Jimmy，我可以跟你談一下嗎？　　●好，當然可以。

▶ You should have a word with Melanie.

　　你應該和 Melanie 談一下。

　　May I have a word with you?

　　我可以跟你談一下嗎？

223

chat about

· chat with
　和…聊天
· have a chat with
　和…聊天
· have a little chat with
　和…短暫地聊一下

聊關於…的事 chat 是指輕鬆、休閒、非正式的談話。

- Did you meet your friends from grade school?
- Yes, we **chatted about** our lives and families.
  - 你跟你小學同學們見面了嗎？
  - 是啊，我們閒聊了關於生活和家庭的事。

▶ Let's chat about next month's schedule.
　我們來聊聊下個月的行程吧。
　Some people enjoy chatting about the weather.
　有些人喜歡聊天氣。

let me say

· let me see
　讓我看看，讓我想想

（有感而發地）讓我說／我說啊… 用來表達自己想法的發語詞。

- Are you happy about Aurora's performance?
- **Let me say** that it was very disappointing.
  - 你對 Aurora 的表現滿意嗎？　● 我得說非常令人失望。

▶ Let me say that this can be repaired.
　我說啊，這是可以修好的。
　Let me say that you look very nice tonight.
　我說啊，你今晚看起來很棒。

get back to

· get back to sb (on)
　回覆某人（關於…）
· get back to sth
　回到…

稍後再聯絡… 正在忙的時候有人打電話來，或是還沒辦法給對方答案，想跟對方說「我晚點再打給你」、「我晚點再回覆你」時，便可使用這個表現方式。

- I need a decision from you. **Get back to** me.
- I'll call you tomorrow morning.
  - 我需要你的決定，回電話給我。　● 我明天早上會打給你。

▶ I'm sorry I didn't get back to you sooner.
　我很抱歉沒有早點回你電話。
　I'll get back to you on that. I might have other plans.
　我晚點會再回覆你。我可能有別的計畫。

speak to sb about

· speak up
　大聲說
· speak English
　說英文

跟某人談有關…的事 to 後面接人，about 接談論的內容。

- Eddie is making everyone in his class upset.
- I'll **speak to him about** his behavior.
  - Eddie 讓他班上的每個人都很不開心。　● 我會跟他談談他的行為。

▶ Speak to Nicky about being on time.
　跟 Nicky 說要準時。
　I would like to speak to the head of your department.
　我想跟你的部門主管說話。

say something to

· say something about
  說些和…有關的事
· say much about
  說很多關於…的事
· say that S+V
  說…

對…說些事 具體切入談話重點之前也可以使用的發語詞。

● Have you asked about the price of this vase?
● No, I'll **say something to** the clerk before we go.

　●你問了這個花瓶的價錢了嗎？
　●沒有，我會在我們離開前跟店員談談。

▶ I have to say something to all of you.
　我有點事要跟你們所有人說。
　He doesn't say much about it.
　關於這件事他說得不多。

tell sb about

· tell sb some details
  about
  跟某人說關於…的一些細節
· tell sb sth
  跟某人說某事

跟某人說關於…的事 也可以改成第四類句型 tell A B「把 B 這件事告訴 A」。

● Can you **tell me about** the pyramids in Egypt?
● Sure. I visited them a few years ago.

　●你可以跟我說關於埃及金字塔的事嗎？
　●當然可以。我幾年前拜訪過。

▶ Can you tell me about it over the phone?
　你可以用電話跟我說那件事嗎？
　Can you tell me your address?
　你可以告訴我你的地址嗎？

tell sb S+V

· Don't tell me S+V
  別跟我說…
· tell sb how/what/
  why...
  跟某人說…

跟某人說… tell sb 後面除了名詞之外，也可以接子句。

● Can you **tell me** where the toilet is?
● Wait a minute, let me ask someone for you.

　●你能告訴我廁所在哪裡嗎？　●等一下，讓我幫你問人。

▶ I told you! Don't tell me you don't remember!
　我跟你說過了！別跟我說你不記得！
　You didn't tell me your boyfriend smoked.
　你沒跟我說你男朋友抽了菸。

1 職場・學校
2 電腦・網路
3 社交生活
4 日常生活
5 訊息・理解
6 想法・態度
7 情緒・狀況
8 行為舉止
9 時間地點・副詞片語

consult with sb

- consult a lawyer
  諮詢律師
- consult sb about…
  和某人商量…的事

和某人商量 特別常用在「接受某人建議」的情況下。

- Timothy is getting a divorce from his wife.
- He needs to **consult with** his lawyer about it.
  - Timothy 要和他太太離婚。　●他需要和他的律師討論這件事。

▶ I consulted with my parents about my school.
　我和父母商量有關學校的事情。
　She consulted her boyfriend about the party.
　她和她男朋友商量了派對的事。

get counseling

- be in marriage
  counseling
  接受婚姻諮商
- seek counseling
  尋求諮商
- counsel sb to do
  建議某人做…

接受諮商 後面可以加 from，後接機構或提供諮商者。

- Max gets mad very easily.
- He should try to **get counseling**.
  - Max 很容易暴怒。　●他應該試著接受諮商。

▶ She got counseling for her mental problems.
　她因為精神問題接受了諮商。
　Why don't you go and get counseling? I think it would
　really help. 你為什麼不去接受諮商呢？我想會很有幫助的。

discuss A with B

- discuss the problem
  討論這個問題

和 B 討論 A discuss 後面不接任何介系詞，直接接要討論的事。

- The board of directors are going to meet next week.
- What are they going to **discuss**?
  - 下週要召開董事會。　●他們要討論什麼事？

▶ Let's discuss the trip with your mom.
　我們跟你媽媽討論旅行的事吧。
　We need to get together to discuss the proposal.
　我們需要聚一下，討論這個提案。

talk over

商討，討論… over 是「關於…」的意思，後面接要討論的事。

- The club will meet at seven tonight.
- We have to **talk over** our new projects.
  - 社團今晚七點要聚會。　●我們得討論我們的新計畫。

▶ Did you talk over the problems you had?
　你討論了你的問題嗎？
　She talked over her future plans. 她談了她未來的計畫。

take sth up with

· take up sth with sb
  和某人討論某事

和⋯討論（重要的問題） sth 是要討論的問題。

- The toilets smell very bad today.
- You must **take it up with** the cleaning staff.
  - 廁所今天聞起來好臭。　● 你得跟清潔人員談一下。

▶ I took my low salary up with my boss.
  我跟老闆談到我的低薪。
  She took the bad food up with her waitress.
  她對女服務生說食物不好吃。

speaking of

· speaking of which
  說到這個⋯

說到⋯ of 後面接要談論的主題關鍵詞。

- I just joined a health club.
- **Speaking of** health, let's go jogging.
  - 我剛加入了健康俱樂部。　● 說到健康，我們去慢跑吧。

▶ Speaking of your sister, how has she been?
  說到你姊姊，她過得怎樣？
  Speaking of lunch, let's get something to eat.
  說到午餐，我們去買點東西吃吧。

put one's heads together

· be on the table
  公開的，在檯面上

集思廣益 許多人的頭聚集在一起，討論解決方法的樣子。

- It's too difficult to solve this problem.
- Let's **put our heads together** and figure it out.
  - 這個問題太難解決了。　● 讓我們集思廣益，找出解決方法吧。

▶ We put our heads together and created a program.
  我們集思廣益，寫了一個程式。
  We can put our heads together and fix this.
  我們可以集思廣益來解決這個問題。

run it/that by

和⋯說明⋯，和⋯討論⋯ by 後面接說明的對象。

- Do you like my new ideas?
- I need to **run them by** my boss.
  - 你喜歡我的新點子嗎？　● 我需要跟我的老闆說明。

▶ Run it by me one more time.
  再跟我說明一次。
  I'll run it by my wife tonight.
  我今晚會向我太太徵詢意見。

1 職場・學校
2 電腦・網路
3 社交生活
4 日常生活
5 訊息・理解
6 想法・態度
7 情緒・狀況
8 行為舉止
9 時間地點・副詞片語

run sth by sb

　　run sth by sb 意為「向某人諮詢意見」。也就是由於要向 sb 對於 sth 尋求「意見」（opinion），或是徵求「許可」（permission），所以要「針對某件事做解釋或說明」。舉例來說，run that contract by a lawyer 就表示「和律師討論那份合約」。如果說明過後，對方還是不了解，他就會說 run that by me again，表示「再向我解釋一次」。

23 | 離開
leave for

3-23.mp3

go to someplace

- go to the gym
  去健身房
- go to sb's house
  去某人的家
- go to the grocery store
  去雜貨店

去某處 to 的後面接場所或地名。

- ●What did you do last Friday evening?
- ●I **went to** the theater with my boyfriend.
  - ●你上週五晚上做了什麼？　●我跟我男朋友去看電影。
- ▶ Let's go to this Internet cafe to surf the Web.
  我們去這間網咖上網吧。
  I've decided to go to New York without you.
  我決定不用你陪，自己去紐約。

go abroad

- go overseas
  出國
- travel abroad
  出國旅行

出國 study abroad 意為「出國留學」，go abroad on a scholarship 則是「拿獎學金出國」。

- ●I heard a lot of students **are going abroad** these days.
- ●True. It's because we aren't satisfied with our education.
  - ●我聽說最近有很多學生出國留學。
  - ●沒錯，這是因為我們對國內的教育不滿意。
- ▶ I'd like to go abroad for a few years. 我想要出國幾年。
  Have you traveled overseas? 你出國旅行過嗎？

leave for + 地點

· leave + 地點
  離開…
· leave + 地點 + for
  離開…去…
· leave so soon
  很快離開

動身前往… leave 後面可接出發地點，for 後面接目的地。

● Why are you packing your clothes?
● I **leave for** Mexico in the morning.

●你為什麼在打包衣服？　●我早上要出發去墨西哥。

▶ Brad and Andrea leave for their vacation tonight.
  Brad 和 Andrea 今晚會出發去度假。
  I'm going to leave for Canada. 我要出發前往加拿大。

be headed for

· be headed over to
  前往…
· head for
  前往…
· head off to
  前往…
· head out (to…)
  （往…）出發

前往… head 當動詞時，與 go towards 同義。

● By the way, what are you doing tonight?
● I'm **headed to** the library.

●對了，你今晚要做什麼？　●我要去圖書館。

▶ Bette is headed for New York City. Bette 要去紐約。
  We're headed for a large campground.
  我們要去一個很大的營地。

get out of (here)

· Get out of here!
  滾出去！／你少騙人了！
» cf. get off work
  收工下班

離開 對於對方所說的話感到不可置信時，也可以說這句話。

● I thought I told you to **get out of here**.
● You did, but I don't want to.

●我以為我叫你走了。　●你是說了，但我不想走。

▶ Would you like me to get out of here? 你想要我離開這裡嗎？
  I can't wait to get out of here. 我等不及要離開這裡了。

be off to

· take off
  離開，（飛機）起飛
· be leaving
  要離開了
· be gone
  走了，不見了

（急忙地）離開，出發 off 是分離、出發的意思，to 後面接目的地。

● I saw your kids leave in a taxi.
● Yes, they **are off to** their grandmother's house.

●我看見你的孩子們坐上計程車離開。　●是啊，他們要去奶奶家。

▶ Well, I'm off to China in the morning.
  嗯，我早上要去中國。
  I am leaving with my best friend.
  我要和我最好的朋友一起離開。

have been to + 地點

· Where have you been?
  你（之前）去哪了？

去過某處 have gone to 則是指去了以後沒有回來的情況。

● Have you traveled much internationally?
● Yes, I **have been to** 36 different countries.

●你常出國旅行嗎？　●嗯，我去過 36 個不同的國家。

▶ She had been to the Louvre Museum. 她去過羅浮宮。
  Tad has been to the best restaurant in Jakarta.
  Tad 去過雅加達最棒的餐廳。

1 職場・學校

2 電腦・網路

3 社交生活

4 日常生活

5 訊息・理解

6 想法・態度

7 情緒・狀況

8 行為舉止

9 時間地點・副詞片語

while I'm away

・while I'm out
　當我出去的時候
・while I'm gone
　當我離開的時候

當我不在的期間 因為外出或出差而暫時不在的情況。

- Can you water my plants **while I'm away**?
- You need to give me the key to your apartment.
  - ●當我不在的時候，你可以給我的植物澆水嗎？
  - ●你得把你公寓的鑰匙給我。

▶ Don't behave badly while I'm away.
　我不在的時候，不要不守規矩。
　You might have problems while I'm away.
　我不在的時候，你可能會有些問題。

need to be at + 地點

需要到達… 用 need 表現出一種非去不可的感覺。

- I **need to be at** my house in 20 minutes.
- I'll try to drive a little faster.
  - ●我需要在 20 分鐘後趕到家。 ●我會努力開快點。

▶ Fiona needs to be at school today.
　Fiona 今天得去學校。
　You need to be at the bus station soon.
　你得趕緊到公車站。

go up to

・come up to
　來到…
・walk up to
　走向…
・drive up to
　開往…

走上前去… up to 是「到…」的意思，後面接人、事或物。

- I think we have gotten lost.
- Let's **go up to** someone and ask for help.
  - ●我想我們迷路了。 ●我們去找個人尋求協助吧。

▶ Simon went up to her and asked her out.
　Simon 走向她，並且約她出去。
　We're going to go up to Zane's house.
　我們要去 Zane 的房子。

1 職場・學校

2 電腦・網路

3 社交生活

4 日常生活

5 訊息・理解

6 想法・態度

7 情緒・狀況

8 行為舉止

9 時間地點・副詞片語

24 為了做某事而來／去…
come here to

3-24.mp3

---

go + 動詞

· go (out) and + 動詞
　（出）去做…
· go to + 動詞
　去做…

去做… 表示「go and + 動詞」的口語說法。

● **Go do** some work on your school project.
● I will. It's almost finished now.
　●去做點你學校報告的作業。　●我會的，差不多要做完了。

▶ Do you want to go get something to eat?
　你想去買點東西吃嗎？
　Where can I go to check my e-mail?
　我該去哪裡查看我的電子郵件？

---

go -ing

· go shopping
　去逛街
· go camping
　去露營

去做… go 後面接動詞 -ing 形就可以表示要去做什麼。

● What are your plans for this weekend?
● I'm **going hiking** on Sunday.
　●你這個週末有什麼計畫？　●我星期天要去健行。

▶ I'm going jogging tomorrow morning.
　我明天早上要去慢跑。
　Are you ready to go shopping?
　你準備好要去逛街了嗎？

---

go for + N

· go for a walk
　去散步
· go for a swim
　去游泳

去做… go 後面也可以接 for 和名詞表示要做的事。

● Did you have any plans on Sunday?
● I'd like to **go for** a hike in the country.
　●你星期天有什麼計畫嗎？　●我想去鄉間健行。

▶ Would you like to go for a drive?
　你想去兜個風嗎？
　Let's do that now and then go for a coffee.
　我們現在就做那件事，然後去喝杯咖啡。

---

come to

· come and + 動詞
　來做某事
· come for + N
　為了…而來
· come to + 場所
　來（某地）

來做… to 後面接名詞時表示目的地，接動詞原形則表示目的。

● This was the first time I visited a beach.
● Really? I just love **coming to** see the ocean.
　●這是我第一次來海邊玩。　●真的嗎？我真的很喜歡來看海。

▶ Would you like to come for dinner? 你想來吃晚餐嗎？
　I came for the meeting at ten. 我為了十點的會議而來。

231

come here to

· I'm here to do…
　我來這裡做…

來這裡做… 表示為了什麼理由來這裡。

● When did your dad **come to** the States?
● When he was in his thirties.

　●你爸爸什麼時候來美國的？　●在他三十幾歲的時候。

▶ Do you need me to come to your house?
　你需要我去你家嗎？
　I came here to see if I could get a job.
　我來這裡看看是否能得到一份工作。

25 | 去市區
go downtown

3-25.mp3

go downtown

· go downtown to do
　去市區做…
· go into town
　進市區
· get to downtown
　抵達市區

去市區 the downtown area 和 the city center 都是表示市中心。

● How would you like to go to a movie?
● Let's not **go downtown** tonight.

　●你想不想去看電影？　●我們今晚不要去市區吧。

▶ I went downtown to buy groceries.
　我去市區買了雜貨。
　Just go downtown and it's right across from City Hall.
　你到了市區之後，它就在市政府對面。

come downtown

· come downtown to do
　來市區做…
· come to town for
　為了…來市區

來市區 後面可以接 to do 或 for + N 說明目的。

● I heard that John is **coming to town** this weekend.
● Did you get in touch with him?

　●我聽說 John 這個週末會來市區。　●你有和他聯絡嗎？

▶ Let me know when you come downtown.
　你來市區的時候跟我說一聲。
　We came downtown to see a movie.
　我們來市區看電影。

walk downtown

- take sb all over the city
  帶某人繞市區一圈

在市區行走 前面兩個 downtown 都是表示「往市區」，這裡的 downtown 則是表示「在市區」。

- Can I give you a ride somewhere?
- No thanks. I'm going to **walk downtown**.
  - 你要我載你去哪裡嗎？ ● 不用，謝謝。我會在市區裡用走的。

▶ I don't want to walk downtown.
我不想在市區行走。
Jane walks downtown twice a week.
Jane 一週會在市區步行兩次。

be in town

- be in town to do
  在市區做⋯
- stay in town
  待在市區

在市區 in the city 也可以表示「在市區裡」，和 downtown 同義。

- Why are you buying so much food?
- My parents **are in town** this week.
  - 你為什麼要買那麼多食物？ ● 我父母這禮拜會來市區。

▶ I heard the sheriff was in town looking for you this morning. 我聽說今天早上警長來市區找你。
Don't hesitate to give me a ring when you're in town next time. 下次你來市區的時候，請儘管打電話給我。

be out in the suburbs

在郊區 suburb 是「郊區」的意思。

- Where did Kevin and Anna buy a house?
- Their house **is out in the suburbs**.
  - Kevin 和 Anna 在哪裡買了房子？ ● 他們的房子在郊區。

▶ Gordon lived out in the suburbs after moving.
Gordon 搬家後住在郊區。
Our family's house was out in the suburbs.
我們家之前在郊區。

1 職場・學校
2 電腦・網路
3 社交生活
4 日常生活
5 訊息・理解
6 想法・態度
7 情緒・狀況
8 行為舉止
9 時間地點・副詞片語

26 抵達（對方所在之處）
get to

get to + 地點

到達某處 與 get to do（開始做）不同，接名詞表示目的地。

- Could you tell me how I **get to** the subway?
- Go straight ahead until you see the sign.
    - 你可以告訴我該怎麼去地鐵站嗎？
    - 一直直走，直到看到標誌為止。

▶ How will you get to the airport? 你要怎麼去機場？。
　 I cannot wait to get to New York. 我等不及要去紐約了。

get there

· How do I get there?
  我該怎麼去那裡？
· get here
  到這裡

到那裡 「get to + 地點」裡的「to + 地點」替換為地方副詞 there 的說法。

- Isn't there a short cut to get home?
- No, there's only one way to **get there**.
    - 沒有捷徑可以回家嗎？　●沒有，只有一條路可以回去。

▶ I can't get there by one o'clock.
　 我無法在一點的時候到那邊。
　 It takes an hour to get there from here.
　 從這裡到那裡要花一小時。

be there

· be almost there
  就快到那裡了
· be right here
  = be coming
  馬上就過來

到那裡 be just in time for 意為「及時趕上…」。

- Make sure that you arrive on time tomorrow.
- Don't worry. I'll **be there** early.
    - 你明天一定要準時抵達。　●別擔心，我會提早到那裡。

▶ We'll be there in a few minutes. 我們幾分鐘後就會到那裡了。
　 I'll be there as soon as I can. 我會盡快到那裡。

arrive on time

· arrive at the airport
  (early)
  （提早）抵達機場
· arrive at + 時間
  在…抵達

準時抵達 arrive 是表示「抵達」的代表性單字，常以 arrive in/at 的形態出現。

- When is he scheduled to **arrive at** the airport?
- He's supposed to arrive tomorrow after lunch.
    - 他預計什麼時候抵達機場？　●他應該會在明天午餐過後抵達。

▶ I hope the bus will arrive on time. 我希望公車會準時抵達。
　 Make sure that you arrive on time tomorrow.
　 你明天一定要準時抵達。

reach + 地點

抵達某處 reach 相當於 arrive at，後面直接接受詞。

- How long will it take for us to **reach** the Inn?
- It should only take about 20 minutes.
  - ●我們到旅館要花多久時間？　●應該只要 20 分鐘左右。

▶ It takes about 15 minutes for him to reach the office.
他大概要花 15 分鐘才會抵達辦公室。
Keep going straight until you reach the church.
一直直走，到抵達教堂為止。

be on the way

· be on the way to
  在往…的途中
· be on one's way (to)
  在某人（往…）的途中

在半路上 也可以說 on one's way 強調是在某人的路程上。

- When are you leaving?
- I'm **on my way** now.
  - ●你什麼時候要離開？　●我現在要走了。

▶ I was on my way home from work.
我那時候在下班回家的途中。
I left my passport in the taxi on the way to the hotel.
我搭計程車去旅館的時候，把護照忘在車上了。

be on the way back

· be on the way back to
  在回到…的路上
· be on one's way
  back (to)
  在某人回來（到…）的
  路上

在回來的路上 後面加「to + 地點」可以說明是回到哪裡。

- Thanks, I will return soon.
- Bring me a coffee **on your way back**.
  - ●謝謝，我很快會回來。　●回來的路上帶杯咖啡給我。

▶ Larry is gone, but he is on the way back.
Larry 離開了，但他正在回來的路上。
I was just on my way back from Brian's house.
我剛才在從 Brian 家回來的路上。

make it to + 地點

· make it to the
  wedding
  準時參加婚禮
· can('t) make it
  辦得到（辦不到）

準時抵達某處 make it 除了「辦到」以外，也有「抵達」、「來」的意思。

- I won't be able to **make it to** the presentation.
- That's okay. I'll take notes for you.
  - ●我沒辦法參加發表會了。　●沒關係，我會幫你記筆記。

▶ Helen can't make it to Washington DC.
Helen 無法去華盛頓。
We're having a party for Tom. Hope you can make it.
我們要幫 Tom 辦個派對，希望你能來。

1 職場・學校
2 電腦・網路
3 社交生活
4 日常生活
5 訊息・理解
6 想法・態度
7 情緒・狀況
8 行為舉止
9 時間地點・副詞片語

I'm coming

· I'm going
  我會去
· I'm not going
  我不會去

我快到了 接對方所在的地方時，come 有「去」的意思。

● Come on, or we're going to be late.

● **I'm coming** as quickly as I can.

 ● 快點，不然我們會遲到。　● 我正盡速趕去。

▶ I'm coming to your birthday party. 我會去你的生日派對。

 I'm coming to class in ten minutes. 我十分鐘後會去上課。

 ## I'm coming vs. I'm going

　　I'm going 是在有聚會等場合時，表達「我會參加」的說法。而 I'm coming 並不是表示「我會來」，而是「我會去」。對於只知道 go 代表「去」，come 代表「來」的人而言，想必一定非常困惑吧？在英文裡，come 和 go 代表的移動方向是以「說話者」（speaker）和「聽者」（hearer）為基準。舉例來說，如果是移動到說話者或聽者所在的位置（moving to the place where the speaker or hearer is），這種情況下要說 come。若是移動到其他的地點，則會說 go（moving from where one is to another place）。因此，當有人叫你過去時，你會說 I'm coming，而不是 I'm going。請記住，I'm going 前往的地方既不是自己所在的地點，也不是聽者所在的地點，而是在兩者之外的另一個地方。至於 I'm coming 則是表示前往對方所在的位置（where the other person is）。

---

27 | 一起去 go together

3-27.mp3

go together (with)

和…一起去 go together 後面接 with sb 表示一起去的人。

● Would you like to get a drink?

● Sure, let's **go together with** our friends.

 ● 你想去喝一杯嗎？　● 當然好，我們和朋友們一起去吧。

▶ I can't go together with everyone here.
 我沒辦法和這裡的每個人一起去。

 Let's go together and grab dinner.
 我們一起去吃個晚餐吧。

go with

· a condo goes with the job in Manhattan
在曼哈頓的工作有提供公寓（供住宿）

和…一起去 go with 也可以比喻性地表示「選擇某個方案」或「跟某人交往」。

● I'm going to visit Beijing this summer.
● I wish I could **go with** you.

●我今年夏天要去北京。　●真希望我可以跟你一起去。

▶ Do you need me to go with you?
你要我跟你一起去嗎？
I decided I'm going to go with her.
我決定和她交往。

come along with

· be accompanied by/ with
由…陪同

和…一起去 用一個字表示就是 accompany 的意思。come 也可以換成 go。

● I would like to go out for lunch on Friday.
● Sounds good to me. I'll ask Greg to **come along**.

●我星期五想出去吃午餐。　●聽起來不錯，我會找 Greg 一起。

▶ Celia decided to come along with us.
Celia 決定和我們一起去。
Do you want to come along?
你想要一起去嗎？

come outside

· come/go inside
進來／去裡面

· come/go downstairs
來／去樓下

到外面來 go outside 則是「去外面」。

● Martha, I need to take a break from this discussion.
● Sure. Why don't you **go outside** for a while?

●Martha，我想要休息一下再繼續討論。
●好啊，你何不去外面一下呢？

▶ You'd better not go outside. It's too cold.
你最好別去外面，太冷了。
We should go outside and get something to eat.
我們得出去找點東西吃。

go over there

· go there alone
獨自去那邊

· come over here
來這邊

去那邊 表示從現在所在的地方，前往另一個地方。反過來則是 come over here。

● I need you to **come over here** at 5 p.m. tomorrow.
● I'm sorry, I can't. I have another appointment.

●我需要你明天下午五點來這邊。
●很抱歉，我不行，我有另一個約了。

▶ Go over there and buy me some coffee.
去那邊幫我買杯咖啡。
Would you come over here please?
可以請你過來一下嗎？

1 職場・學校

2 電腦・網路

3 社交生活

4 日常生活

5 訊息・理解

6 想法・態度

7 情緒・狀況

8 行為舉止

9 時間地點・副詞片語

28 回來，回去
go back to

3-28.mp3

go back (to)

- go back to do
  回去做…
- come back (to)
  回來（做…）

回去（某處） 除了表示回到某個地方以外，也可以表示繼續之前在做的事或談論的話題。

- What are your plans for next year?
- I'm going to **go back to** live in LA.
  ●你明年的計畫是什麼？　●我要搬回洛杉磯住。

▶ Do you have to go back to work?
你得回去工作嗎？
I'd rather die than go back.
我寧可死掉也不要回去。

get back to

回去… to 後面如果接事物，則是在抽象概念的層面上表示「回到那件事」，和表示「晚點再回覆你」的 get back to sb 不同，請仔細分辨。

- What are we learning how to cook today?
- Today we are going to **get back to** basics.
  ●我們今天要學哪種料理？　●今天我們要回到基礎的部分。

▶ Try to get back to your hometown.
試著回去你的家鄉。
I will get back to the painting eventually.
我最後會回去作畫。

be back + 時間

- be back one hour later
  一小時候回來
- be back any minute
  隨時都會回來
- be right back
  馬上回來
- be back from
  從…回來

多久後會回來 後面可以接 one hour later, in ten minutes 等時間副詞片語。

- Are you going to be long?
- No, I'll **be back** in ten minutes.
  ●你會離開很久嗎？　●不會，我十分鐘後就會回來。

▶ I have a feeling that we will be back here soon.
我覺得我們很快就會回到這裡。
What time do you think she will be back?
你覺得她幾點會回來？

find one's way back

- find one's way back into
回到／回歸…

找到路回來 直譯便是「找到回來的路」。
- We got lost while walking in the forest.
- How did you **find your way back**?
  - 我們在森林裡走路的時候迷路了。　● 你們怎麼找到路回來的？

▶ I hope she'll find her way back to me.
　我希望她會回到我身邊。
　It was difficult to find our way back home.
　很難找到我們回家的路。

return to + 地點

回到某處 在表示「回去」的 return 後面加上 to 接地點，表示回去哪裡。
- The student government meeting is over.
- We have to **return to** our classrooms.
  - 學生會的會議結束了。　● 我們得回教室了。

▶ Why did you decide to quit your job and return to England? 你為什麼決定辭職回到英國？
　How soon will you return to the US?
　你多快會回美國？

---

29 | 回家
go home

3-29.mp3

go home

回去家裡 除了回家（房子）以外，也可以表示回家鄉、回國。
- Just say when and we can go home.
- I'll let you know when I want to go.
  - 你只要說個時間，我們就回家。　● 我想回去的時候會跟你說的。

▶ I'd love to, but I have to go home early tonight.
　我很想，但我今晚得早點回家。
　I wanted to let you know that Sam went home.
　我想跟你說 Sam 回家了。

1 職場・學校
2 電腦・網路
3 社交生活
4 日常生活
5 訊息・理解
6 想法・態度
7 情緒・狀況
8 行為舉止
9 時間地點・副詞片語

get home

· arrive at home
  到家
· I'm home.
  我在家。

到家 把「get to + 地點」裡的「to + 地點」改為副詞 home 的說法。

● John is leaving work right now.
● When will he **get home**?

  ●John 現在要下班了。　●他什麼時候會到家？

▶ It takes around 1 hour for me to get home. I should get going. 我回家要花大約一小時。我得走了。
  When's she getting home?
  她什麼時候會到家？

come home

· come home late
  很晚回家

回來家裡 想強調「回來」的話，可以說 come back home。

● When will Sharon be here?
● She'll **come home** when the movie finishes.

  ●Sharon 什麼時候會到這裡？　●電影結束後她就會回家。

▶ Barry didn't come home until late.
  Barry 很晚才回家。
  Why did you come home so late last night?
  你昨晚為什麼那麼晚回家？

stay (at) home

· stay home all day
  整天都待在家
· stay in
  窩在家裡
· keep at home
  留在家裡
· be home
  在家

待在家 home 的前面有 at 時是名詞，不加介系詞時是副詞。

● My son had to **stay home** from school today.
● Why? Is he sick?

  ●我兒子今天得待在家，不能去上學。　●為什麼？他生病了嗎？

▶ You should stay at home for a few days.
  你應該在家待幾天。
  Do you mind if I stay home tonight and play with the kids? 你介意我今晚待在家陪孩子們玩嗎？

drive home

· take the taxi home
  搭計程車回家
· walk home
  走路回家

開車回家 載別人回家的時候，則說 drive sb home。

● Thanks for your time.
● It was nothing. Have a safe **drive home**.

  ●謝謝你撥出時間。　●沒什麼，開車回家注意安全。

▶ Bart didn't drive home when it was snowing.
  下雪的時候，Bart 沒有開車回家。
  Rachel plans to drive home tomorrow morning.
  Rachel 打算明天早上開車回家。

30

帶某人去⋯，使⋯移動
take…to

3-30.mp3

1 職場・學校
2 電腦・網路
3 社交生活
4 日常生活
5 訊息・理解
6 想法・態度
7 情緒・狀況
8 行為舉止
9 時間地點・副詞片語

take A to + 地點

- take A to B
  帶 A 到 B
- take the suitcase to the car
  把行李箱拿到車上

帶 A 到某處 take sb by car 則表示開車帶某人去某處。

- Wow, it's really late right now.
- Shall I **take you to** your place?

  ●哇，現在好晚了。　●你要我送你回家嗎？

▶ You told me you were going to take me to lunch.
  你說你會帶我去吃午餐的。
  I wanted to take you to one of my favorite restaurants.
  我原本想帶你去我最喜歡的一間餐廳。

pick up

開車接某人 pick up A 或 pick A up 都是正確的，但 A 是代名詞時只能說 pick A up。

- We are on our way to the airport to **pick up** the boss.
- Did you check to see if his flight is arriving on time?

  ●我們正前往機場去接老闆。　●你們有確認他的班機會準時抵達嗎？

▶ I'll pick you up tomorrow at 9 a.m.
  我明天早上九點會去接你。
  Do you need me to pick you up from the airport?
  你需要我去機場接你嗎？

ride with sb to

和某人一起坐車去⋯ with 後面接人，to 後面接目的地。

- Has Pam called a taxi yet?
- No, she'll **ride with Lisa to** the airport.

  ●Pam 叫計程車了嗎？　●沒有，她會坐 Lisa 的車去機場。

▶ Sandra rode with me to the museum.
  Sandra 和我一起搭車去博物館。
  Inga rode with her friends to the festival.
  Inga 和她的朋友們一起搭車去參加慶祝活動。

move over

· move A over to + 地點
　把 A 移到⋯

挪出位子　shift from A to B 意為「從 A 移動到 B」。

● Can you **move over** and give me some space?
● Sure, I'd be glad to give you more room.
　●你可以挪一下，分點空間給我嗎？　●當然，我來挪點空間給你。

▶ No one on the subway would move over.
　地下鐵裡沒有人會挪出座位。
　I asked each person to move over.
　我請每個人都挪過去一點。

move sth outside

· move A into B
　把 A 搬進 B
· move back/forward
　往後／前移動

將某物搬到外面　move A 的後面可以接副詞或介系詞，表示把 A 移動到什麼地方。

● Have you filled this garbage bag?
● Yeah, we can **move it outside**.
　●你把這個垃圾袋裝滿了嗎？　●嗯，我們可以把它移到外面去。

▶ Let's move these chairs outside.
　我們把這些椅子搬到外面去吧。
　You should move the bicycle outside.
　你應該把這台腳踏車搬到外面去。

31 搬家 move to

3-31.mp3

move to

· move to another
　apartment
　搬到另一間公寓
· move to this town
　搬來這個城市
· move out
　搬出去

搬到⋯　to 後面接搬家的目的地。

● I've decided to **move to** Japan this year.
● Really? Are you sure about that?
　●我決定今年要搬到日本。　●真的嗎？你確定了嗎？

▶ Sal wants to move to Brooklyn.
　Sal 想要搬到布魯克林區。
　I may have to move to New York for my job.
　我可能會因為工作得搬到紐約。

move from

- move away
  搬走
- move away from
  從…搬走

從…搬出來 說明搬離的地點。

- The rent is too high at my apartment.
- You should **move from** that place.

  ●我公寓的租金太貴了。　●你應該搬離那邊。

▶ Pam decided to move from her parent's house.
Pam 決定從她父母家中搬出來。

I don't want to move from my hometown.
我不想搬離我的家鄉。

move in

- move in with sb
  和某人一起搬進來／同居
- move abroad
  搬到國外

搬入，同居 move in with sb 是「同居」的意思。

- Marie and Andy will **move in** after they get married.
- Have they planned their wedding yet?

  ●Marie 和 Andy 結婚後會搬進來。　●他們計畫好婚禮了嗎？

▶ You can move in after you pay the rent.
你交房租後就可以搬進來。

We moved in after I got a new job.
我得到新工作後，我們就搬進來了。

move here

- move there
  搬到那裡
- move somewhere else
  搬到別的地方

搬來這裡 move around 則是表示「到處搬來搬去」。

- This city has many international residents.
- People **move here** from all around the world.

  ●這個城市有很多外國居民。　●人們從世界各地搬來這裡。

▶ Cindy decided not to move here.
Cindy 決定不要搬來這裡。

You can move here with your parents.
你可以和你的父母一起搬來這裡。

help sb move to

幫某人搬到… 因為搬家不太可能一個人完成，所以這是很常用的說法。

- Are you going somewhere this morning?
- I must **help Tony move to** a new apartment.

  ●你今天早上要去哪裡嗎？　●我得幫 Tony 搬到新公寓。

▶ We helped the professor move to a new office.
我們幫教授搬到新的辦公室。

Help me move to a better place.
幫我搬到一個更好的地方。

1 職場・學校
2 電腦・網路
3 社交生活
4 日常生活
5 訊息・理解
6 想法・態度
7 情緒・狀況
8 行為舉止
9 時間地點・副詞片語

32 | 停留 stay for

3-32.mp3

stay for + 期間

· stay longer (with)
（和…）待得更久一點

停留多久的時間 口語中，stay 比 remain 更常用來表示停留。

● I'd like to talk more with you.
● You should **stay for** a few more minutes.

　●我想跟你聊更多。　●你該再多留幾分鐘。

▶ I've decided to stay longer. 我決定要待久一點。
Do you need me to stay longer? 你需要我待久一點嗎？

stay another day

· stay overnight
過夜
· stay the night
過夜

再多留一天 stay 後面可以不接介系詞，直接接上時間名詞，表示「暫時留下來」。

● Are you going home tomorrow?
● No, we'll **stay for another day**.

　●你們明天要回家嗎？　●沒有，我們會多留一天。

▶ Are you sure it's okay if we stay another day?
你確定我們可以再多留一天嗎？
It's Mr. Lee in room 607, I need to stay another day.
我是 607 號房的李先生，我要再多住一天。

stay at

· stay at a friend's
home
留宿朋友家
· stay over
留宿，在…過夜

待在…，停留在… at 後面接上地方名詞，表示要停留的地方。

● Where did Tim stay in Chicago?
● He **stayed at** an expensive hotel.

　●Tim 在芝加哥時住在哪裡？　●他住在一間很貴的飯店。

▶ We'll stay at my uncle's house. 我們會留宿在我叔叔的房子。
They didn't stay at the university. 他們沒有留在大學。

stay here

· stay there
待在那裡
· stay inside
待在裡面
· stay outside
待在外面

待在這裡 stay 後面可以加上 here, there 等各種副詞，表示要停留的地方。

● We really like your new house.
● You can **stay here** when you visit me.

　●我們真的很喜歡你的新家。　●你們來找我時，可以住在這裡。

▶ Feel free to stay here as long as you like.
你想在這裡住多久都沒關係。
They will allow us to stay here. 他們會讓我們待在這裡。

stick around

- stick with
  留在…身邊（stay close to）

再多留一會兒 表示比預計的時間再留久一點。
- Are you in a hurry to leave?
- No, I can **stick around** for a while.
  - ●你急著要走嗎？　●沒有，我可以再多留一會兒。

▶ She'll stick around until eleven tonight.
　她今晚會再多待一會兒，到 11 點為止。
　Greg stuck around the nightclub.
　Greg 流連在夜店。

---

33 | 稱呼，名稱
call A B

3-33.mp3

---

call by one's first name

- be on a first name basis
  很親近（可以用名字稱呼彼此）
- be on first-name terms with sb
  和某人很親近
- call sb names
  辱罵某人

叫某人的名字 不是稱呼「Mr. + 姓」，而是親密地直接叫名字。
- Do you know the manager well?
- Yes I do. We **are on a first name basis**.
  - ●你跟主管很熟嗎？
  - ●是啊，我們很熟（熟到可以直接叫名字）。

▶ Don't call our boss by his first name.
　別直接叫我們老闆的名字。
　She called her mom by her first name.
　她直接用名字來稱呼她的母親。

call A B

- call sb a liar
  說某人是個騙子
- call sb a chicken
  說某人是膽小鬼

稱呼 A 為 B B 是人名或其他稱號。
- What is the name of your boss?
- Everyone **calls him Mr. Gibbs**.
  - ●你老闆的名字是什麼？　●大家都叫他 Gibbs 先生。

▶ Sue called Brandon a liar.
　Sue 說 Brandon 是個騙子。
　We call Beth Dr. McKinney.
　我們稱呼 Beth 為 McKinney 博士。

1 職場・學校
2 電腦・網路
3 社交生活
4 日常生活
5 訊息・理解
6 想法・態度
7 情緒・狀況
8 行為舉止
9 時間地點・副詞片語

call sth in English | **用英文稱呼某物** 如果想問某個東西用英文怎麼說，可以問 What's this called in English?。

● What is the word for this thing?

● We **call it an umbrella in English**.

　　●稱呼這個東西的單字是什麼？　　●在英文裡，我們稱它為 umbrella。

▶ What do you call that in English?

　　那個用英文要怎麼說？

　　I don't know how to say it in English.

　　我不知道這個用英文要怎麼說。

be called | **被稱為⋯** 後面接本名、暱稱或其他稱號。

● Does Michael have a nickname?

● He **is called** Micky by his friends.

　　●Michael 有暱稱嗎？　　●他的朋友都叫他 Micky。

▶ This snack is called a Twinkie.

　　這個零食叫「Twinkie」。

　　This kind of pomelo is called "wendan."

　　這種柚子稱為「文旦」。

name sb + 名稱 | **將某人命名為⋯** 這裡的 name 是動詞，句型是 name A B。

· name A after B
　用 B 的名字來為 A 命名
· be named for
　被取名為⋯
· sb named sth
　某人為某物命名

● Leo and Madge have a new child.

● I heard they **named him** Phil.

　　●Leo 和 Madge 剛生了小孩。　　●我聽說他們把他命名為 Phil。

▶ We named our dog Henry.

　　我們把我們的狗命名為 Henry。

　　We'll name the baby Fred.

　　我們把嬰兒命名為 Fred。

34 禮儀
behave oneself

3-34.mp3

1 職場‧學校

2 電腦‧網路

3 社交生活

4 日常生活

5 訊息‧理解

6 想法‧態度

7 情緒‧狀況

8 行為舉止

9 時間地點‧副詞片語

be polite to

· A be polite to B
  A 對 B 有禮貌

· It's polite/impolite to do
  做⋯是有禮貌／無禮的

對⋯有禮貌 主詞和 to 後面接的都是人。

● That man is very powerful.

● We should all **be polite to** him.

  ● 那個男人很有權力。　● 我們都該對他有禮貌。

▶ I am always polite to my grandparents.

  我一向對我的祖父母有禮貌。

  Donald was not polite to his teacher.

  Donald 對他的老師不禮貌。

have good manners

· be well-mannered
  彬彬有禮

· remember one's manners
  注意某人自己的行為舉止

有禮貌 manner 的複數形表示「禮節，禮貌」。

● Everyone loves Danielle's children.

● They **have good manners**.

  ● 大家都很喜愛 Danielle 的孩子們。　● 他們很有禮貌。

▶ All of my classmates have good manners.

  我的同學們都很有禮貌。

  Do your students have good manners?

  你的學生們很有禮貌嗎？

behave oneself

· be on one's best behavior
  行為舉止非常有規矩

· one's behavior is out of place
  某人的行為舉止完全沒規矩

守規矩 behave nicely 則表示「舉止得體」。

● Why is Bart sitting over in the corner?

● He didn't **behave himself** in class.

  ● Bart 為什麼坐在角落？　● 他在課堂上很沒規矩。

▶ I always behave myself when I drink.

  我喝酒的時候一向很注意自己的行為。

  Did Fara behave herself at the party?

  Fara 在派對上行為檢點嗎？

talk back to

· be rude to do...
  ⋯是很粗魯無禮的

頂嘴 talk back to sb all the time 則是表示「總是在頂嘴」。

● It is very rude to **talk back to** teachers.

● Parents must teach children good manners.

  ● 跟老師頂嘴很沒禮貌。　● 父母必須教孩子良好的禮儀。

▶ Brett was punished when he talked back.

  Brett 頂嘴之後被懲罰了。

  Don't talk back to our boss. 別跟老闆頂嘴。

35 | 約會
have a date

3-35.mp3

fix A up with B

・set A up with B
　介紹 B 給 A

介紹 B 給 A 用在介紹異性朋友的狀況。fix 可以改成 set。

● I'm going to **fix you up with** a date.
● I'd rather go to the party all by myself.

　●我要幫你介紹個約會對象。　●我寧可自己一個人去參加派對。

▶ Lisa set Rebecca up with her friend.
　Lisa 介紹她的朋友給 Rebecca。
　Let's set my sister up with a nice guy.
　我們介紹個好男人給我姐姐吧。

have a date

・get a date with sb
　約某人約會
・want a date
　想要有個約會對象
・have a hot date
　有個火熱的約會

有約會 後面接 with sb 可說明約會的對象。

● What are your plans for tonight?
● I **have a date**. We're going out for dinner.

　●你今晚有什麼計畫？　●我有個約會，我們要出去吃晚餐。

▶ I've got a date with Lily this evening.
　我今晚跟 Lily 有個約會。
　Can you believe she had a date with the teacher?
　你能相信她跟那個老師約會過嗎？

date sb

・How was your date?
　你的約會怎樣？
・How did your date go?
　你的約會怎樣？

和某人約會 date 當名詞時代表約會（對象），當動詞時表示約會的行為。

● Did you ever **date** Melissa?
● No, but I was interested in her.

　●你跟 Melissa 約會過嗎？　●沒有，不過我之前對她有興趣。

▶ How can you date that younger guy?
　妳怎麼可以跟那個比你年輕的小夥子約會？
　This is why she doesn't date short guys.
　這就是她不跟矮個子約會的原因。

go out with

- go out with
  和…約會，和…出去
- go out
  約會，出去
- go with
  和…一起去，和…戀愛，
  選擇…

和…約會 隨情況不同，go out with 也可以單純表示和某人出去。

- Will you **go out with** me tonight?
- I'd rather stay home and watch TV.
  - ●你今晚要跟我出去約會嗎？ ●我寧可待在家看電視。

▶ She doesn't want to go out with you.
  她不想和你出去約會。
  It's hard to get women to go out with me.
  很難找到願意跟我出去約會的女人。

go on a date

- go (out) on a date with
  sb last night
  昨晚和某人去約會
- be out on a date
  正在約會

去約會 go 的後面可以加上 out，a date 後面可以加上 with sb 說明對象。

- Wow, you look really nice tonight.
- I'm **going on a date with** a doctor.
  - ●哇，你今晚看起來容光煥發。 ●我要和一個醫生去約會。

▶ He'll go on a date with Melinda.
  他要跟 Melinda 約會。
  How would you like to go out on a date with me?
  要不要和我約會看看？

go out on a blind date

- set sb up on a blind
  date
  安排某人跟他不認識的人
  約會

跟不認識的人約會 blind date 是指由別人安排、雙方互不認識的約會，也可以指「聯誼」。

- I'm **going out on a blind date**.
- Really? Who introduced you to her?
  - ●我要跟不認識的人約會。 ●真的嗎？誰把你介紹給她的？

▶ I'm afraid to go out on blind dates.
  我很怕跟不認識的人約會。
  They met when they went out on a blind date.
  他們是在聯誼的時候認識的。

be seeing sb

和某人在交往 see 的進行式經常表示「交往」的意思。

- Bonnie and Mark seem very close.
- They **have been seeing** each other for a year.
  - ●Bonnie 和 Mark 看起來很親密。 ●他們倆交往一年了。

▶ So you mean now you're not seeing anyone?
  所以你是說你現在沒有跟任何人在交往囉？
  What makes you think he's seeing someone?
  你為什麼覺得他正在和某人交往？

1 職場・學校

2 電腦・網路

3 社交生活

4 日常生活

5 訊息・理解

6 想法・態度

7 情緒・狀況

8 行為舉止

9 時間地點・副詞片語

ask sb out

- ask sb out on a date
  約某人出去約會
- ask sb on a date
  約某人去約會
- get asked out on a
  date by…
  被某人約出去約會

約某人出去 後面可以接 on a date 清楚表示是去約會。

- I think that boy is very cute.
- You should **ask him out**. He'll probably say yes.
  - 我覺得那個男生非常可愛。　● 你該約他出去，他可能會答應。

▶ Wasn't that the same guy who asked you out last week?
  那不就是上星期約你出去的那個男人嗎？

  I just got asked out on a date by my next door neighbor.
  我剛被隔壁鄰居問要不要去約會。

have been on a few dates

- haven't been on a
  date in + 時間
  有多久沒約過會了

約了幾次會 用現在完成式表示到目前為止的約會經驗。

- Are George and Mindy engaged to get married?
- No, but they **have been on a few dates** together.
  - Geroge 和 Mindy 訂婚了嗎？　● 還沒，不過他們約過幾次會。

▶ Sarah has been out on a few dates this month.
  Sarah 這個月出去約了幾次會。

  I have been on a few dates with Lily.
  我跟 Lily 約了幾次會。

go steady with

- meet the girl of one's
  dreams
  遇見夢中情人

和…穩定交往 和某個異性長時間持續交往的狀態。

- Have you asked Andrea out yet?
- No, but I hope to **go steady with** her someday.
  - 你約 Andrea 出去約會了嗎？
  - 沒有，但我希望有天能跟她穩定交往。

▶ I haven't gone steady with anyone.
  我從來沒有跟任何人穩定交往過。

  Patty is going steady with a businessman.
  Patty 目前和一個商人穩定交往。

1 職場·學校
2 電腦·網路
3 社交生活
4 日常生活
5 訊息·理解
6 想法·態度
7 情緒·狀況
8 行為舉止
9 時間地點·副詞片語

36 喜歡，愛
have feelings for

3-36.mp3

like sb better than

喜歡某人勝過… 用比較句型表示喜歡的程度。

● How is your new math teacher?

● I **like her better than** my history teacher.

　● 你的新數學老師怎麼樣？　● 我喜歡她勝過我的歷史老師。

▶ I like her better than any other girl.
　比起任何其他女孩，我更喜歡她。
　He likes Matt better than his other friends.
　比起其他朋友，他更喜歡 Matt。

fall in love with

· fall in love quickly
　很快墜入愛河

和…墜入愛河 表示「戀愛了」最典型的慣用語。

● Brian **fell in love with** a girl from Brazil.

● Where did they meet for the first time?

　● Brian 和一個從巴西來的女孩墜入愛河。
　● 他們初次見面是在哪裡？

▶ My brother falls in love with many girls.
　我哥哥和許多女孩戀愛。
　She fell in love with the tall young man.
　她和那個高個子的年輕男人墜入愛河。

love at first sight

一見鍾情 第一次看到對方就愛上他的狀況。

● Were Tina and Arnold friends before they dated?

● No. It was **love at first sight** for both of them.

　● Tina 和 Arnold 交往之前是朋友嗎？　● 不是，他們倆是一見鍾情。

▶ It was love at first sight when I met my wife.
　我對我太太是一見鍾情。
　It was love at first sight when she saw me.
　她對我是一見鍾情。

have feelings for

- not have any feelings for
  對…沒有任何感覺
- have a strong feeling that S+V
  強烈地感覺…
- take a shine to sb
  愛上某人

對某人有好感 中文也會用「有感覺」表示喜歡某人。

- Are you in love with my sister?
- Yes, I **have feelings for** her.
  - 你愛上我姐姐了嗎？　●嗯，我對她有好感。

▶ He had feelings for his co-worker. 他喜歡上他的同事。
Sandy had feelings for my boyfriend.
Sandy 曾經喜歡上我的男朋友。

have a crush on

- have got a major crush on sb
  瘋狂迷戀某人
- have a huge crush on sb
  瘋狂迷戀某人

迷戀某人 crush 是指瞬間迷戀上某人的狀態。

- You keep looking at Doris tonight.
- I think I **have a crush on** her.
  - 你今晚一直盯著 Doris 看。　●我想我愛上她了。

▶ It's common to have a crush on someone in school.
迷戀上學校裡的某個人是很平常的事。
She had a crush on a boy in her apartment building.
她愛上了一個和她住同一棟公寓的男生。

be crazy about

- be crazy about sth
  對某事瘋狂著迷
- be nuts/mad about
  瘋狂愛上…
- be stuck on
  迷戀…

為某人瘋狂 可以表示深深愛上某個人。

- Angie and Brad spend all of their time together.
- That's because they **are crazy about** each other.
  - Angie 和 Brad 總是形影不離。　●那是因為他們都深愛對方。

▶ I'm crazy about my new girlfriend. 我深愛我的新女友。
Kathy is crazy about her husband. Kathy 深愛她的丈夫。

be drawn to sb

- be attracted to
  被…吸引
- be into sb
  對某人有興趣／著迷

被某人吸引 draw 本來是「拉，拖」的意思，引申為「吸引」。

- The professor is very smart.
- I'm **drawn to** him because of his intelligence.
  - 這位教授很聰明。　●我被他的才智給吸引住了。

▶ Neil was drawn to Stacy's happy personality.
Neil 被 Stacy 開朗的人格吸引住了。
She was drawn to the talented singer.
她被那個很有天分的歌手吸引住了。

fall for sb

愛上某人 for 後面如果接 sth，則表示「被…騙，上…的當」。

- I have heard Barb is in love.
- She **fell for** a man who is much older than her.
  - 我聽説 Barb 戀愛了。　●她愛上了一個年紀比她大很多的男人。

▶ I fell for her while we were dancing.
我們跳舞的時候，我愛上了她。
Tara fell for a boy in her class. Tara 愛上了她班上的一個男孩。

miss sb

想念某人 深愛的人不在身邊時感受到的心情。

- Well, I guess this is goodbye.
- I'm going to **miss** you so much.
  - 嗯，我想是該說再見了。　● 我會很想你的。

▶ I miss Allie more every day.
我每天都更加思念 Allie。
Lisa misses her grandmother.
Lisa 很想念她的奶奶。

be one's type

- show affection toward
  對…展現出好感
- be the love of one's life
  是某人一生的摯愛
- be perfect for each other
  彼此是完美的伴侶
- be meant to be each
  other
  命中註定要在一起

是某人喜歡的類型 type 也可以換成 style。

- Elsie is tall and has dark hair.
- That's great! She **is my type**.
  - Elsie 很高，有烏黑的秀髮。　● 太棒了！她是我的菜。

▶ The handsome actor is my type.
那位英俊的演員是我喜歡的類型。
All of those girls are my type.
那些女孩全都是我喜歡的類型。

---

37 擁抱
give a hug

3-37.mp3

give sb a hug

- run to hug sb
  飛奔去擁抱某人
- hold sb in one's arms
  把某人抱在懷中
- hold sb tight
  緊緊擁抱某人

給某人一個擁抱 free hugs campaign 是主動上街擁抱陌生人的活動。hug 也可以當動詞。

- Go **give** your brother **a hug**.
- I have to wait until he gets off the plane.
  - 去給你哥哥一個擁抱。　● 我得等到他下飛機。

▶ My girlfriend gave me a big hug.
我女朋友給了我一個大大的擁抱。
She gave him a hug before she left.
她離開前，給了他一個擁抱。

1 職場・學校
2 電腦・網路
3 社交生活
4 日常生活
5 訊息・理解
6 想法・態度
7 情緒・狀況
8 行為舉止
9 時間地點・副詞片語

be turned on

- turn sb on
  讓某人感到興奮
- turn sb off
  讓某人倒盡胃口

興奮 意為「開關被打開了」。經常指「sexual switch」被打開，可不能隨便對別人的男女朋友這樣說哦⋯

- Did you like the dress Helen wore?
- Yes, I **was turned on** by it.

  ●你喜歡 Helen 穿的那件洋裝嗎？ ●喜歡，那讓我變得很興奮。

▶ She was turned on by his personality.

  她被他的個性吸引，對他產生了興趣。

  Men are turned on by a woman's face.

  男人會因為女人的容貌而興奮起來。

make love

- make out with
  和⋯親熱
- get it on (with sb)
  （和某人）上床
- get lucky (with sb)
  （和某人）上床
- have intercourse with
  和⋯性交

做愛 這是 have sex 美化過的說法。雖然也可以更明白地說 have intercourse（性交），但除了警方或醫界以外，在日常生活中很少人會說昨天和另一半 have intercourse 吧⋯

- What is your biggest wish?
- I want to **make love to** Ryan on a beach in Acapulco!

  ●你最大的願望是什麼？ ●我想跟 Ryan 在阿卡波可的海灘上做愛！

▶ I want to make love to my girlfriend.

  我想和我的女朋友做愛。

  Did you get lucky with Cynthia last night?

  你昨天和 Cynthia 有上床嗎？

come on to

- make a move on sb
  對某人展開行動
- make a pass at sb
  挑逗／勾引某人
- hit on sb
  搭訕某人
- talk dirty to sb
  對某人開黃腔

挑逗⋯，勾引⋯ 用話語等方式挑逗別人，to 後面接 sb。

- You seem very angry with Rick.
- Yeah. He **came on to** me last night.

  ●你看起來很生 Rick 的氣。 ●是啊，他昨晚想挑逗我。

▶ Don't come on to every girl you know.

  別挑逗每個你認識的女孩。

  He came on to Steph while they worked together.

  昨晚他跟 Steph 一起工作時，挑逗了她。

sleep with

和⋯上床 與其說是睡覺，不如說是做男女之間的運動？

- I hope you didn't **sleep with** Brandon.
- No, I really don't trust him.

  ●我希望你沒有跟 Brandon 上床。 ●我沒有。我實在不相信他。

▶ Be careful about who you sleep with.

  好好選擇你的枕邊人。

  I didn't sleep with your girlfriend.

  我沒有跟你的女朋友上床。

38 分手
break up with

3-38.mp3

1 職場・學校

2 電腦・網路

3 社交生活

4 日常生活

5 訊息・理解

6 想法・態度

7 情緒・狀況

8 行為舉止

9 時間地點・副詞片語

break up with

· break (off) with sb
  和某人分手
· break it off with sb
  和某人分手
· break off one's
  relationship
  結束某人的關係

和…分手 with 後面接分手的對象。

● I heard you had some trouble with your girlfriend.
● I had to **break up with** her. We were fighting a lot.

● 我聽說你跟你女朋友有點問題。
● 我不得不和她分手。我們經常吵架。

▶ It seems like it's time to break up with her.
看來是跟她分手的時候了。
I'm sorry but I have to break up with you.
我很抱歉,但我得跟你分手。

dump sb

· get dumped by
  被…甩掉

甩掉某人 比 break up with sb 更口語化的說法。

● What did Carole do when her boyfriend cheated?
● She **dumped** him and found someone else.

● Carole 的男朋友劈腿時,她怎麼做?
● 她把他甩掉,找了新的對象。

▶ I'd dump my girlfriend for a date with you.
為了和妳約會,我可以跟我女朋友分手。
You should dump her and get someone else.
你該跟她分手,找其他對象。

split up (with)

· be separated from sb
  和某人分開
· sb be over (sb)
  (和某人)結束(It's
  over with sb)
· be through (with sb)
  (和某人)結束

(和…)分手 和中文的「決裂」一樣,本來是「分裂」的意思。

● Fran and Barb are always fighting.
● I'm thinking that they should **split up**.

● Fran 和 Barb 總是在吵架。 ● 我覺得他們應該分手。

▶ It's over between Jen and Terry.
Jen 跟 Terry 之間玩完了。
My girlfriend told me it's over with us.
我的女朋友跟我說我們結束了。

cheat on sb

· cheat on A with B
  背叛 A，和 B 發生關係

背叛某人，劈腿 主詞是劈腿的人，on 後面接被劈腿的人。

● What caused the big fight between them?
● Bill **cheated on** his girlfriend.

　●他們倆為了什麼大吵一架？　●Bill 背叛了他女朋友。

▶ Greg was caught when he cheated on his wife.
　Greg 劈腿的時候被他太太抓包了。
　She cheated on her boyfriend twice.
　她背著她男朋友偷吃了兩次。

break one's heart

· heartbreaker
  令人傷心的人／事物
· broken heart
  （失戀）破碎的心
· get over one's broken
  heart
  從失戀中恢復

傷某人的心 和人分手等情況下感受到的錐心之痛。

● Why are you so sad about your girlfriend?
● She said goodbye and **broke my heart**.

　●你為什麼因為你女朋友那麼傷心？　●她跟我提分手，傷了我的心。

▶ That girl will break his heart.
　那個女孩會傷透他的心。
　Bud breaks many girls' hearts.
　Bud 讓許多女孩心碎。

---

39 | 結婚，離婚 get married to

3-39.mp3

get married to

· be married to
  和…結婚了

和…結婚 雖然和 marry sb 的意思相同，但 get married to 更常用。

● Is that woman your girlfriend?
● No, I'm **married to** her.

　●那位女士是你的女朋友嗎？　●不是，我和她結婚了。

▶ The point is that you're married to Jane.
　重點是，你和 Jane 結婚了。
　Why did you choose to get married to your wife?
　你為什麼選擇和你太太結婚呢？

marry sb

- get hitched (with)
  （和…）結婚
- marry young
  很年輕就結婚

和…結婚　marry 是及物動詞，相當於中文的「嫁給…」或「娶…」。

- Tomorrow I'm going to ask Amanda to **marry** me.
- I'll keep my fingers crossed for you.

　●我明天要跟 Amanda 求婚。　　●我會為你祈禱的。

▶ Kate, will you marry me?

　Kate，你願意嫁給我嗎？

　I can't believe you're going to ask her to marry you!

　我真不敢相信你要跟她求婚！

propose to sb

- accept the proposal
  接受求婚
- plan out wedding for May
  準備五月的婚禮

向某人求婚　求婚的名詞形是 proposal，而 proposition 是指提案或建議。proposition 當動詞時表示「求歡」，要小心使用。

- She said you actually **proposed to** her.
- Well I didn't! I didn't **propose**!

　●她說你真的有跟她求婚。　　●我沒有！我沒有求婚！

▶ What makes you think he's going to propose?

　妳為什麼覺得他會求婚？

　I got a marriage proposal last night.

　我昨晚被求婚了。

be engaged to

- get engaged to sb
  和某人訂婚
- break off an engagement
  取消訂婚

和…訂婚了　訂婚的名詞形是 engagement。

- Are June and Rob still dating?
- Yes, June **is engaged to** Rob.

　●June 和 Rob 還有在約會嗎？　　●是啊，June 和 Rob 訂婚了。

▶ My best friend got engaged to the biggest loser.

　我最好的朋友和那個人生大輸家訂了婚。

　I've never been engaged in my life.

　我這輩子還沒訂過婚。

get pregnant

- get sb pregnant
  讓某人懷孕
- be pregnant with one's second child
  懷了第二胎

懷孕　「不小心懷孕」可以說 get pregnant by mistake。

- What should I do? I **got her pregnant**.
- I knew it. I told you to use a condom.

　●我該怎麼辦？我讓她懷孕了。

　●我就知道，我跟你說過要用保險套了。

▶ Diane got pregnant six months ago.

　Diane 六個月前懷孕了。

　You told me Jessica was pregnant.

　你跟我說 Jessica 懷孕了。

1 職場・學校
2 電腦・網路
3 社交生活
4 日常生活
5 訊息・理解
6 想法・態度
7 情緒・狀況
8 行為舉止
9 時間地點・副詞片語

start a family

組成家庭 表示結了婚、生了小孩的狀態。

- Why did you decide to get married?
- I am ready to **start a family**.
  - ●你為什麼決定結婚？　●我準備好要組成一個家庭了。

▶ People are more focused on their careers than on starting a family. 比起組成家庭，人們更專注在自己的職業上。
  Maybe now is not the right time to be starting a family.
  也許現在不是組成家庭的好時機。

have a baby

- have a baby boy
  有個小男孩
- have a baby girl
  有個小女孩

有了孩子 如果用未來式（will, be going to）或者現在進行式表示未來，則是指「懷孕」。

- Yeah. I mean, we **are having a baby** together.
- Hold on! You got her pregnant?
  - ●是啊，我是說，我們要有自己的孩子了。　●等等！你讓她懷孕了？

▶ We decided to have a baby.
  我們決定要生個小孩。
  Congratulations on having a baby!
  恭喜你們有小寶寶了！

give birth to

- give birth to a baby boy
  生下一個小男孩
- Caesarean section
  剖腹生產
- natural childbirth
  自然分娩

生下…　「生下雙胞胎」則是 give birth to twins。

- Alicia **gave birth to** twins.
- Let's go visit her in the hospital.
  - ●Alicia 生了雙胞胎。　●我們去醫院探望她吧。

▶ Do you remember when I was giving birth to the twins?
  你還記得我生雙胞胎的時候嗎？
  My wife recently gave birth to a beautiful baby daughter.
  我的妻子最近生了個漂亮的女嬰。

expect a baby

- be in labor
  在分娩前陣痛
- labor pains
  產前陣痛
- deliver
  生（孩子）

懷孕，懷胎　和 pregnant 同義，但改用動詞 expect 來表達。

- Heather looks like she is pregnant.
- She **is expecting a baby** in a few months.
  - ●Heather 看起來像是懷孕了。　●她再過幾個月就要生了。

▶ The married couple is expecting a baby soon.
  這對已婚夫婦的小孩快出生了。
  She doesn't have a stomach ache, she's in labor.
  她不是胃痛，是分娩的陣痛。

get a divorce

- be divorced from sb
  和某人離婚
- file for divorce
  訴請離婚
- sign the divorce
  papers
  簽署離婚文件

離婚 divorce 也可以當動詞用。

- I'm worried about Dick. He doesn't look good these days.
- I heard his wife is asking him to **divorce**.
  - 我很擔心 Dick，他最近看起來不太好。
  - 我聽說他太太跟他提出離婚。

▶ It took two months to get a divorce.
  離婚花了兩個月。
  I have no other choice but to file for divorce!
  除了訴請離婚以外，我沒有別的選擇！

---

1 職場・學校
2 電腦・網路
3 社交生活
4 日常生活
5 訊息・理解
6 想法・態度
7 情緒・狀況
8 行為舉止
9 時間地點・副詞片語

40 關聯，連累
get involved in

3-40.mp3

---

get involved in

- be involved with sb
  和某人交往（be in a romantic relationship）

牽涉… 隨著上下文不同，會有不同的意思，最基本的意思是「牽涉…」。

- Why was Nate sent to jail?
- He **got involved in** illegal activities.
  - Nate 為什麼入獄了？   ● 他牽涉一些非法活動。

▶ She's getting more involved in school activities now.
  她現在越來越投入學校的活動了。
  Are you married or involved with anyone?
  你有和任何人結婚或交往嗎？

be related to

- be closely related to
  和…有密切關聯
- A-related+N
  和 A 有關聯的…

和…有親戚關係 也可以說 be relevant to。

- You're **not related to** Kirk Smith, are you?
- Actually, he's my father.
  - 你跟 Kirk Smith 沒有親戚關係吧，有嗎？   ● 事實上，他是我父親。

▶ Are you related to Emily Thompson?
  你和 Emily Thompson 有親戚關係嗎？
  Yes, she is my mother.
  有，她是我母親。

be a party to

和…有關聯，參與… 表示和某個行動或決定有關。

- Jacob **was a party to** cheating.
- Well, we will have to punish him.

  ●Jacob 有參與作弊。　●嗯，我們得懲罰他。

▶ Debbie was a party to the theft.

  Debbie 有參與偷竊。

  I'm not going to be a party to your lie.

  我不會和你的謊言有任何牽連。

step in

· step into
  開始（某事）；介入（某個狀況）

介入…，插手干預… 為了解決某個問題，或是預防問題發生而做出的行動。

- I think Mr. Wilson is retiring soon.
- Who will **step in** to replace him?

  ●我想 Wilson 先生很快就要退休了。　●誰會來接替他的位子？

▶ I will step in and help her.

  我會介入並幫助她。

  You can step in and fix it.

  你可以介入並解決問題。

be engaged in

· be occupied with
  忙於…

從事…，參加… 也可以說 engage oneself in。in 如果改成 to 的話，是「和某人訂婚」的意思。

- Ivan **was engaged in** criminal activity.
- Did the police catch him?

  ●Ivan 參與了犯罪活動。　●警察有抓到他嗎？

▶ I'm engaged in writing a novel.

  我致力於寫小說。

  They were engaged in finishing their homework.

  他們忙著完成他們的作業。

be connected with

· be connected in some way
  以某種形式相關

和…有關 名詞形 connection 是「關聯」的意思。

- Many houses have been broken into.
- I think it's **all connected with** one gang.

  ●很多房子都遭了小偷。　●我想這應該全都和一個幫派有關。

▶ These problems are connected with the economy.

  這些問題和經濟有關。

  My bills are connected with an accident I had.

  這些帳單和我所遭受的一個事故有關。

have to do with

· have got to do with
  和…有關

和…有關　with 後面可以接人或事物。

● What do you want to talk about?
● It **has to do with** our class schedule.

　●你想談什麼？　　●和我們的課表有關係。

▶ What does stress have to do with my sickness?
　壓力和我的病有什麼關係？
　What does that have to do with you?
　那件事和你有什麼關係？

have something to do with

· have got something to do with
  和…有關
· have a lot to do with
  和…有很大的關聯

和…有關　something 換成 a lot 就表示「大有關聯」。

● The new manager is not very good.
● Many problems **have something to do with** him.

　●新的經理不太好。　　●很多問題都跟他有關。

▶ This festival has something to do with the school.
　這個慶祝活動和學校有關。
　Our accident had something to do with the weather.
　我們碰上的意外和天氣有關。

have nothing to do with

· be unconnected with
  和…無關

和…無關　with 後面可以接人、事物或 -ing 等等。

● You made me hurt my leg.
● I **had nothing to do with** hurting you.

　●你害我的腿受傷。　　●我跟你受傷沒有關係。

▶ It's got nothing to do with age.
　這和年齡無關。
　This has nothing to do with me and my family.
　這和我跟我的家人無關。

get mixed up

· get mixed up in sth
  被某事連累（多半指不法
  的事件）

被連累／牽扯　特別常用在被牽連進不法或不正當行為的情況。

● Why was Paul expelled from school?
● He **got mixed up** in drug dealing.

　●Paul 為什麼被退學了？　　●他被牽扯進毒品交易。

▶ The exam papers got mixed up on the desk.
　考卷被亂放在桌上。
　I got mixed up in some really bad stuff.
　我被牽扯進某件很糟的事情裡。

1 職場・學校
2 電腦・網路
3 社交生活
4 日常生活
5 訊息・理解
6 想法・態度
7 情緒・狀況
8 行為舉止
9 時間地點・副詞片語

41 在意，介入
stay out of

3-41.mp3

mind -ing

· mind if S+V
  介意是否…
· Would/Do you mind
  -ing/if S+V?
  你介意…嗎？
· not mind -ing
  不介意…

介意…，反對… 請記住這裡的 mind 有否定的意思。

● **Would you mind if** I take a look around here?
● Not at all, be my guest.
  ●你介意我在這邊到處看看嗎？　●一點也不介意，請便。

▶ Do you mind picking me up tomorrow?
  你介意明天來接我嗎？
  Do you mind if I sit here for a sec? 你介意我在這裡坐一下嗎？

not care if S+V

不在意是否… not care the less 的字面意義是「不會更不在意」，也就是「一點也不在意」的意思。

● What do you think about the situation?
● **I don't care if** we go on strike or not.
  ●你覺得這情勢怎樣？　●我不在意我們要不要罷工。

▶ I don't care if she's fat or thin. 我不在意她胖還是瘦。
  I don't care who he sleeps with. 我不在意他跟誰睡過。

not matter to sb

· It doesn't matter if
  S+V
  是否…無所謂

對某人而言無所謂 matter 是「有關係，要緊」的意思。

● When do you want to get together to talk about it?
● It **doesn't matter to** me.
  ●你什麼時候想聚一下，討論這件事？　●我無所謂。

▶ It doesn't matter what other people think.
  別人怎麼想不重要。
  Don't tell me it doesn't matter. 別跟我說這無所謂。

be none of
one's business

· mind your own
  business
  管好你自己的事
· keep A's nose out of
  B's business
  A 不管 B 的閒事

不關某人的事 對於搞不清楚事情狀況，什麼都要插一腳管事的人，可以這麼說。

● David was curious about how much money you make.
● That **is none of his business**.
  ●David 很好奇你賺多少錢。　●那不關他的事。

▶ Their relationship is none of your business.
  他們的關係不關你的事。
  Our conversation is none of their business.
  我們的對話不關他們的事。

stay out of

· stay out of one's way
  不干涉某人

不管某事 通常用在命令句，要別人少管閒事。

- I think Tom is smarter than his wife.
- Let's just **stay out of** their business.
  - ●我想 Tom 比他太太聰明。　●我們別管他們的事吧。

▶ Stay out of her way when she is upset.
  當她苦惱時，少去煩她。
  I asked you to stay out of this.
  我叫你別管這件事了。

poke one's nose in

· poke/stick one nose into...
  干涉…

干涉，過問（與自己無關的事） 伸著鼻子東聞一下、西聞一下的樣子，引申為干涉的意思。in 可以換成 into。

- Thelma is always talking about other people.
- She **pokes her nose into** other people's lives.
  - ●Thelma 總是在說別人的事。　●她很愛過問別人的生活。

▶ Don't poke your nose in and bother her.
  你別管閒事，不要去煩她。
  I was fine until you poked your nose in.
  一直到你來干涉之前，我都很好。

get one's hands off of

· get one's hands off me
  別碰我
· get one's hands on
  向…伸手，把…弄到手

不碰… 就是字面上的意思：「把手從某事物移開」。of 可以省略。

- **Get your hands off of** my money!
- I was just counting it for you.
  - ●別碰我的錢！　●我只是在幫你數錢。

▶ Get your hands off of that candy!
  別碰那些糖果！
  Get your hands off of my new car!
  別碰我的新車！

regardless of

不管… of 後面可以接名詞、-ing 或是名詞子句。

- Do you like red or white wine with fish?
- I prefer white to red **regardless of** what I'm eating.
  - ●你想用紅酒還是白酒來搭配魚？
  - ●不管是吃什麼，我都偏好白酒勝過紅酒。

▶ He likes to be outdoors, regardless of the weather.
  不論天氣如何，他都喜歡在戶外。
  I feel happy, regardless of having no money.
  儘管沒錢，我還是很開心。

1 職場・學校
2 電腦・網路
3 社交生活
4 日常生活
5 訊息・理解
6 想法・態度
7 情緒・狀況
8 行為舉止
9 時間地點・副詞片語

回答 **Do you mind?** 的方法

　　當我們和 native speaker 用英文對話時，有時候會用「Yes, 不是這樣的」或「No, 是這樣的」的句子來回答否定疑問句，這樣會讓對方感到很困惑。中文和英文的思考模式不同，對於「你還沒吃飯嗎？」這種否定疑問句，中文會先回答對方的猜測是否正確，例如「對，還沒吃」或「不，吃過了」。但在英文裡，回答 Yes 或 No 取決於後面是肯定句或否定句，和問句是肯定還是否定無關，所以 Didn't you have lunch? 的回答會是 No, I didn't 或 Yes, I did，不會出現中文裡肯定和否定混雜的情形。

　　這一節提到的 do you mind if，看起來似乎違反上面的規則：

A: Do you mind if I sit here? 你介意我坐在這裡嗎？
B: No, go right ahead. 不，請坐吧。

　　但 B 的回答其實省略了 I don't mind（我不介意）。如果對於 Do you mind...? 該回答 Yes 還是 No 感到很困惑的話，不妨想想自己是介意（Yes）還是不介意（No）。

42 | 參加，一起做 take part in

3-42.mp3

take part in

· participate in
　參加…

參加… 因為興趣而參加活動或比賽等等。

● You have been running a lot lately.
● I want to **take part in** a marathon.

　●你最近跑得很勤。　●我想參加一場馬拉松。

▶ Did you take part in the game show?
　你有參加那場遊戲展嗎？
　Come and take part in our celebration.
　來參加我們的慶祝活動。

want in

- want out
  想退出（某事）
- be in/out
  參與／退出（某事）

想參與（某事） 相反的，want out 是想退出的意思。

- We're setting up a game of cards.
- Great. I **want in** when you start.
  - 我們正在準備一場撲克牌比賽。
  - 好棒！你們開始的時候，我也要參加。

▶ Things have changed since then. I want in.
情勢從那時候開始就變了。算我一份。
I know what's going on, and I want in.
我知道發生了什麼事，我想要加入。

count sb in

- count sb out
  沒算某人一份，把某人排除在外

算某人一份 count sb out 則是把某人排除在外。

- Would you like to drink some beer?
- Oh yeah. **Count me in**.
  - 你想喝點啤酒嗎？　● 噢，好啊，算我一份。

▶ Count me in to play computer games.
要玩電腦遊戲的話，算我一份。
Why did you count me out?
你為什麼沒算我一份？

join sb for

- join sb for/in…
  和某人一起做…
- join sth
  加入某事
- Welcome aboard.
  歡迎登機／歡迎加入。

和某人一起做… for 後面接要做的事。for 也可以換成 in。

- I'm busy, but **join me for** drinks later.
- What time should I come by?
  - 我很忙，但等等跟我一起去喝杯酒吧。　● 我該幾點過來？

▶ Would you like to join me for a cup of coffee?
你想跟我一起喝杯咖啡嗎？
I want to get into better shape so I joined a gym.
我想要更健康，所以加入了健身房。

be excused from

免於…，不必參加… 這是比較正式的說法。

- Brenda has been very sick.
- She **was excused from** all of her classes.
  - Brenda 病得很嚴重。　● 她獲准不必上任何一堂課。

▶ They are excused from exercising.
他們獲准不參加訓練。
David was excused from the exam.
David 獲准不必考試。

1 職場・學校
2 電腦・網路
3 社交生活
4 日常生活
5 訊息・理解
6 想法・態度
7 情緒・狀況
8 行為舉止
9 時間地點・副詞片語

Everyday Life Activities

一天從起床到就寢，日常生活行為的慣用語

CHAPTER 4

01 睡覺
get to bed

4-01.mp3

go to bed

- go/get to sleep
  去睡覺
- go back to sleep
  去睡回籠覺

上床睡覺 在口語裡常說 hit the sack。

- I just called to talk to you.
- It's 2:00 in the morning. **Go to sleep.**
  - 我打電話只是想跟你說話。　● 現在是凌晨兩點。去睡覺。

▶ I got to bed really late last night. 我昨晚很晚才睡。
  I'm getting ready to go to sleep. 我準備好要睡了。

sleep tight

- sleep well
  睡得很好
- sleep on one's side
  側睡
- sleep like a log/dog
  睡得很沉，睡得很死

睡得很好 常用於祈使句，前面可以加上 Good night 等等。

- You look very tired. Didn't you **sleep well** last night?
- It was so cold that I couldn't sleep.
  - 你看起來很累，昨晚沒睡好嗎？　● 昨晚冷到我睡不著。

▶ I didn't sleep well last night. 我昨晚沒睡好。
  Sleep tight. Have a good rest. 好好睡，好好休息。

fall asleep

- begin to fall asleep
  開始睡著
- fall asleep at the wheel
  開車時睡著

睡著 也可以說 fall into a sleep。

- Don't **fall asleep.** It's only 9:30.
- I'm tired. I worked hard all day.
  - 別睡著，現在才九點半。　● 我好累，我辛苦工作了一整天。

▶ Jason fell asleep while riding the bus.
  Jason 在搭公車的時候睡著了。
  My cousin fell asleep while watching TV.
  我的堂弟在看電視的時候睡著了。

get sleepy

- look sleepy
  看起來很睏
- feel a little sleepy
  覺得有點睏
- yawn
  打哈欠

睏了 同義詞 drowsy 帶有「睏得難以思考」的感覺。

- Oh God, I'm **so sleepy** today.
- You look exhausted. Go and get some rest.
  - 天啊，我今天好睏。　● 你看起來精疲力盡。去休息一下吧。

▶ Everyone got sleepy in the hot classroom.
  在悶熱的教室裡，每個人都變得很睏。
  My father gets sleepy early in the evening.
  我父親晚上很早就想睡了。

take a nap

· take naps
  小睡片刻
· doze off
  （不小心睡著）打瞌睡
  （nod off）

小睡片刻 take 也可以換成 have。nap 也可以當動詞。

● What a day! I'm really tired.
● Do you want to **take a nap** before dinner?

　●好忙的一天！我真的好累。　　●你想在吃晚餐前小睡一下嗎？

▶ I like to take a nap in the afternoon.
　我喜歡在下午睡午覺。
　I think I'm going to take a nap. 我想我要去小睡片刻。

talk in one's sleep

· sleep in one's clothes
  還穿著（外出時穿的）衣
  服就睡著了

說夢話 名詞形是 sleeptalking。sleepwalking 是「夢遊」。

● What's the matter? Why did you wake me up?
● You **were talking in your sleep**.

　●怎麼了？你為什麼把我叫醒？　　●你剛才在說夢話。

▶ John's brother talks in his sleep about school.
　John 的弟弟在睡覺時會說跟學校有關的夢話。
　I talk in my sleep whenever I am tired.
　當我很累的時候，我就會說夢話。

turn in

睡覺 因為平常學到的意思都是「提交…」，或許會覺得很意外，
但這是很道地的說法。

● We have to leave at 4 AM tomorrow.
● I think we'd better **turn in** early tonight.

　●我們明天得在早上四點動身。　　●我想我們今晚最好早點睡。

▶ I'm ready to turn in for the night. 我準備好要睡覺了。
　When is everyone going to turn in? 大家準備什麼時候睡覺？

keep late hours

· keep early hours
  早睡早起
· sleep late
  睡到很晚

晚睡晚起 late 換成 early 當然就是「早睡早起」了。

● The light in Mike's window is always on.
● That's because he **keeps late hours**.

　●Mike 房間的燈總是亮著。　　●那是因為他晚睡晚起。

▶ I'm tired because I've been keeping late hours.
　我因為晚睡晚起了一陣子，變得很累。
　She prefers to keep late hours. 她喜歡晚睡晚起。

---

 sleep with

　　sleep 最基本的意思是為了儲備隔天的體力而去休息、睡覺。但它還有另
一個暗示性的用法，和「性」有關，相當於 have sex。我們平常也會說「和某
人睡過」吧？英文也一樣，是用 sleep with sb 來表達。這個慣用語可以委婉地
表示「沒有結婚，但發生了性關係」的情況。

1 職場・學校
2 電腦・網路
3 社交生活
4 日常生活
5 訊息・理解
6 想法・態度
7 情緒・狀況
8 行為舉止
9 時間地點・副詞片語

get out of bed

· get out of bed on the wrong side
  有起床氣

· get out of the wrong side of the bed
  有起床氣

起床 起床後整理床舖的動作則是 make the bed。

● Arthur is going to be late for work.
● Tell him to **get out of bed** right now.

　●Arthur 上班要遲到了。　●去叫他現在就起床。

▶ I didn't want to get out of bed this morning.
　我今天早上不想起床。
　Get out of bed and get ready for school!
　快點起床，準備去上課！

get up

起床，站起來 get up early 就是「早起」的意思。

● Do you need to **get up** early tomorrow morning?
● Yeah. Please set the alarm for 5 a.m.

　●你明天早上要早起嗎？　●是啊，請把鬧鐘設定在早上五點。

▶ Do you need to get up early tomorrow morning?
　你明天早上要早起嗎？
　Why do you get up so early these days?
　你最近為什麼都那麼早起？

wake up

· wake sb up
  叫某人起床

· wake-up call
  電話叫醒服務（也就是我們常說的 morning call，但英文是不說 morning call 的）

起床，醒來 wake up to sth 則是「意識到／認識到某事」。

● I **wake up** at 5 every morning.
● I don't get up as early as you do.

　●我每天早上都五點起床。　●我不像你那麼早起。

▶ I hope I didn't wake you up this morning.
　希望我今天早上沒有把你吵醒。
　I'd like to request a wake-up call.
　我想要電話叫醒服務。

stay up

· stay up all night
  熬夜一整晚

· be up all night
  一整晚都沒睡

· remain awake (at night)
  一整晚都醒著

熬夜 後面可以接 through the night，表示「徹夜」。

● Did she **stay up** late last night?
● No, she went to bed early.

　●她昨晚熬夜到很晚嗎？　●沒有，她昨天很早就睡了。

▶ Are you going to stay up and watch the sunrise?
　你要熬夜看日出嗎？
　It's not good for you to stay up too late.
　熬夜到太晚對你不好。

1 職場・學校

2 電腦・網路

3 社交生活

4 日常生活

5 訊息・理解

6 想法・態度

7 情緒・狀況

8 行為舉止

9 時間地點・副詞片語

wait up for

熬夜等待… sit up for 和 stay up for 也是一樣的意思。

- Paul won't be back until midnight.
- Let's **wait up for** him to get here.

  ●Paul 要到半夜才會回來。　●我們熬夜等他來吧。

▶ I'll be late so don't wait up for me.

我會晚回來，所以別熬夜等我了。

Wait up for the members of the tour group.

請熬夜等待旅行團的團員。

---

03 | 盥洗
wash up

4-03.mp3

wash up

洗（手） 不接受詞，在美國表示洗手或臉，在英國表示洗碗盤。

- Work was very difficult today.
- Go ahead and **wash up** and get ready for dinner.

  ●今天工作上碰到很多難事。　●去洗個手，準備吃晚餐吧。

▶ John went to the bathroom to wash up.

John 去浴室洗了手。

I'm going to wash up before I join you.

跟你一起走之前，我要先去洗個手。

wash one's face

· wash one's hands
  洗手
· wash one's face
  洗臉
· wash/shampoo one's hair
  洗頭髮

洗臉 wash 當然也可以接受詞，直接表示清洗的部位。

- Dinner is ready to eat now.
- Let's go **wash our hands**.

  ●可以吃晚飯了。　●我們去洗手吧。

▶ Tara washes her face every morning.

Tara 每天早上都會洗臉。

Wash your hands so you don't get sick.

請洗手以免生病。

brush one's teeth

· (dental) floss
  牙線
· gargle
  漱口

刷牙 刷完牙後，再用牙線（floss）做 flossing（用牙線潔牙），效果會更好喔。

● You have such healthy teeth.
● Well, I **brush my teeth** three times a day.

  ●你的牙齒好健康。　●嗯，我一天刷三次牙。

▶ Lisa is brushing her teeth in the bathroom.

  Lisa 正在浴室裡刷牙。

  You should brush your teeth more often.

  你應該更勤加刷牙。

shave one's head

· have one's head
  shaved
  讓人剃頭
· cut oneself shaving
  刮鬍子的時候割到自己
· use the electric shaver
  使用電動刮鬍刀

剃頭 shave 是動詞，表示「剃…」。go unshaven 則是「不刮鬍子」。

● What happened when you joined the military?
● On the first day they **shaved my head**.

  ●你入伍的時候發生了什麼事？

  ●我入伍的第一天，他們就剃了我的頭。

▶ I'm going to shave my head this summer.

  我這個夏天要剃光頭。

  He shaved his head because he was going bald.

  他把頭髮剃光，因為他快要禿頭了。

splash on aftershave

· put on some
  aftershave lotion
  塗抹一點鬍後乳液
· wear lotion on one's
  face
  在臉上擦乳液

噴灑鬍後水 如果是擦保養品，動詞可以用 apply。

● So, you've got a date with Angela tonight.
● Yeah. I'm going to **splash on some aftershave**.

  ●所以，你今晚要跟 Angela 約會。　●是啊，我要噴些鬍後水。

▶ Rick splashed on aftershave this morning.

  Rick 今天早上用了鬍後水。

  My skin felt cooler after I splashed on some aftershave.

  我用了些鬍後水後，皮膚感覺涼爽了點。

trim one's nails

· paint one's nails
  彩繪指甲
· bite one's nails
  咬指甲

修剪指甲 trim 也可以用來表示修剪頭髮、草皮、樹木等行為。

● You should **trim your nails** soon.
● I know. They are getting long.

  ●你差不多該剪指甲了。　●我知道，它們越來越長了。

▶ I took a shower and trimmed my nails.

  我淋了浴，並且剪了我的指甲。

  Tim took a long time to trim his nails.

  Tim 花了很多時間剪指甲。

take a shower

· be in the shower
  淋浴中
· take a bath
  沐浴

淋浴，沖澡 take 可以換成 have。shower 換成 bath 則是指沐浴。

● What happened?
● Nothing. I'm going to **take a shower**.
  ●怎麼了？　●沒事，我要去沖個澡。

▶ I feel like taking a shower.
  我想要沖個澡。
  It's been eight days since I took a shower.
  從我上次沖澡到現在，已經過了八天了。

dry one's hands

· dry one's hair with the towel
  用毛巾把頭髮擦乾
· dry oneself with the towel
  用毛巾擦乾自己

把手弄乾 表示洗手後擦手，或者用 hand dryer（烘手機）烘乾。

● Do you have something I could **dry my hands** with?
● Sure. You can use one of my towels.
  ●你有什麼東西可以讓我把手擦乾嗎？
  ●當然有，你可以用我的毛巾。

▶ He dried his hands after washing them.
  他洗完手之後把手擦乾。
  Jason had to dry his hands on his T-shirt.
  Jason 得用他的 T 恤把手擦乾。

freshen oneself up

· freshen up
  盥洗，使煥然一新

洗臉或手 freshen up 的原意是把某個東西變得更乾淨、更清爽。

● I need to **freshen myself up**.
● There is a bathroom over there.
  ●我需要盥洗一下。　●那邊有間浴室。

▶ You can freshen yourself up at my house.
  你可以在我家盥洗一下。
  Patty freshened herself up before going out.
  Patty 出門前盥洗了一下。

wear one's glasses

· clean one's glasses
  清潔某人的眼鏡

戴眼鏡 wear 改成 put on 的話，則是專指「戴起眼鏡」的動作。

● Jim looks very different today.
● That's because he's **wearing his glasses**.
  ●Jim 今天看起來很不一樣。　●那是因為他戴著眼鏡。

▶ I need to wear my glasses to read books.
  我讀書的時候需要戴眼鏡。
  She wears her glasses during the class.
  她上課的時候會戴眼鏡。

1 職場・學校
2 電腦・網路
3 社交生活
4 日常生活
5 訊息・理解
6 想法・態度
7 情緒・狀況
8 行為舉止
9 時間地點・副詞片語

04 美髮
get one's hair cut

4-04.mp3

---

get one's hair cut

· get/have a haircut
  去剪頭髮

去剪頭髮 表示去理髮廳等場所讓人剪頭髮。這裡的 cut 是過去分詞，表示被動。get 也可以換成 have。

● You look different today.
● I **got my hair cut**. Does it look good?
  ●你今天看來很不同。　●我剪了頭髮。好看嗎？

▶ I'll get my hair cut on Wednesday afternoon.
  我星期三下午要去剪頭髮。
  Did you just get your hair cut?
  你剛剪了頭髮嗎？

---

brush one's hair

· scratch one's head
  搔抓頭髮

梳頭髮 也可以說 comb one's hair。

● Let's go eat some lunch.
● I need to **brush my hair** first.
  ●我們去吃點午餐吧。　●我需要先梳頭髮。

▶ Sarah forgot to brush her hair this morning.
  Sarah 今天早上忘記梳頭髮。
  I brushed my hair before going to work.
  我去上班之前梳了頭髮。

---

get one's hair done

· fix one's hair
  修整頭髮
· change one's hairstyle
  改變某人的髮型
· hate one's hairdo
  不喜歡某人的髮型

去做頭髮 包括剪、燙、造型等美髮服務。

● Where is your mom at today?
● She went to the salon to **get her hair done**.
  ●你媽媽今天去了哪裡？　●她去沙龍做頭髮。

▶ Melissa got her hair done before her wedding.
  Melissa 在她的婚禮前做了頭髮。
  It's getting expensive to get my hair done.
  我去做頭髮越來越貴了。

dye one's hair black

· dye one's hair blond
  把某人的頭髮染成金色

把頭髮染黑　dye 也可以換成當動詞用的 color。

● Barry has quite a bit of gray hair.

● He's planning to **dye his hair black**.

　●Barry 有很多白頭髮。　●他打算把頭髮染黑。

▶ She dyed her hair black after her haircut.
　她剪完頭髮後，把頭髮染黑了。
　I need to dye my hair black to look younger.
　為了看起來更年輕，我需要把頭髮染黑。

go bald

· come off / fall out
  （頭髮）掉落

· lose one's hair
  掉頭髮

· hair loss
  掉髮

· stop the hair from
  falling out
  停止掉髮

變禿頭　動詞 go 也可以換成 become。

● Peter **went bald** when he was 25 years old.

● That's too bad. He looks less attractive now.

　●Peter 25 歲的時候禿頭了。

　●真糟糕，他現在看起來沒那麼吸引人了。

▶ I hope I don't go bald when I'm older.
　我希望我老了之後不會變禿頭。
　My dad went bald when he was in his fifties.
　我爸爸五十幾歲的時候禿了頭。

05 化妝
wear one's makeup

4-05.mp3

wear one's makeup

· wash one's
  makeup off
  卸妝

· wear a new perfume
  噴新的香水

化妝　wear 不止能表示穿衣服，也可以表示塗抹化妝品。

● Why does Dana look so nice?

● She **wore her makeup** to the dance.

　●Dana 為什麼看起來這麼美？　●她化了妝去參加舞會。

▶ Carly wore her makeup when she went shopping.
　Carly 去逛街的時候化了妝。
　She didn't wear her makeup during the meeting.
　她開會的時候沒有化妝。

1 職場・學校
2 電腦・網路
3 社交生活
4 日常生活
5 訊息・理解
6 想法・態度
7 情緒・狀況
8 行為舉止
9 時間地點・副詞片語

put one's makeup on

- put on heavy/light makeup
  化濃／淡妝

化妝 把 wear 換成 put on 的說法，也可以說 put on one's makeup。

- I **put on too much makeup**. I look like a clown.
- No, you don't. But I would remove that eyeliner.
  - ●我妝化太濃了，看起來像個小丑。 ●不會啊，但我會把眼線去掉。

▶ Betty decided not to put her makeup on.
  Betty 決定不要化妝。
  The women put their makeup on in the bathroom.
  那些女士們在浴室裡化了妝。

have makeup on

- have no make-up on
  沒有化妝
- put/wear makeup
  化妝

有化妝 makeup 是 make up 的名詞形，也可以寫成 make-up。

- Most of the girls **have makeup on**.
- They want to look good for the boys.
  - ●那些女孩大部分都有化妝。
  - ●她們想在男孩們面前表現出漂亮的樣子。

▶ She is too young to have makeup on.
  她還太年輕，不該化妝。
  I have makeup on because I'm meeting Larry.
  因為要跟 Larry 見面，所以我化了妝。

do one's makeup

- do one's makeup in the mirror
  在鏡子前面化妝

化妝 動詞 do 可以換成表示「塗抹」的 apply。

- Why has Katie been in the bathroom so long?
- I think she's **been doing her makeup**.
  - ●Katie 為什麼在浴室裡那麼久？ ●我想她是在化妝。

▶ Every morning I do my makeup. 我每天早上都會化妝。
  She'll do her makeup before her date. 她去約會之前會化妝。

fix one's makeup

- check one's makeup
  檢查妝容

補妝 從這幾個例子可以看出來，化妝這件事通常都是以名詞 makeup 表示，要表示動作時在前面加上動詞。

- I need to **fix my makeup** now.
- I'll have a drink while you do that.
  - ●我現在需要補妝。 ●你補妝的時候，我去喝點東西。

▶ She fixed her makeup after getting wet.
  淋濕之後，她補了妝。
  They fixed their makeup before going downtown.
  她們去市區之前補了妝。

06 上廁所
use the bathroom

4-06.mp3

1 職場・學校

2 電腦・網路

3 社交生活

4 日常生活

5 訊息・理解

6 想法・態度

7 情緒・狀況

8 行為舉止

9 時間地點・副詞片語

use the bathroom

· use the public toilet
使用公共廁所
· use the rest room
使用洗手間

使用浴室（廁所） bathroom 除了表示浴室，也可以表示廁所。公共廁所是 public toilet。

● Do you mind if I **use your bathroom**?

● No, go ahead.

● 你介意我用你的廁所嗎？　●不會，去吧。

▶ Let me know if you need to use the bathroom.
你如果需要使用廁所的話，跟我説。
I'll use the bathroom before we leave.
我們離開之前，我要去上廁所。

go to the rest room

· go to the bathroom/
powder room
去廁所
· be in the rest room
在洗手間裡

去洗手間 rest room 多半指餐廳或電影院的洗手間，而 powder room 則是住家裡只有洗手台和馬桶、給客人用的小廁所。

● Hello Peter. Where have you been?

● Hi. I **have been in the bathroom**.

● 嗨，Peter，你去哪了？　●嗨，我剛才在廁所。

▶ I'm going to the bathroom now.
我現在要去廁所。
She arrived earlier and has gone to the powder room.
她早到了，而且去了洗手間。

take a piss

· go for/have a piss/pee
去小便
· hold one's urine
憋尿
· feel nature's call
「感受到自然的呼喚」→
想上廁所
· call of nature
尿意，便意

小便 pee 是小孩子的說法，take a piss 是大人的說法。但就跟中文一樣，還是說「上廁所」（go to the bathroom）比較文雅一點。

● You drank a lot of beer tonight.

● Yeah, and now I need to **take a piss**.

● 你今天晚上喝了好多啤酒。　●是啊，所以我現在要去小便了。

▶ Fred is outside taking a piss.
Fred 在外面小便。
I couldn't find a place to take a piss.
我找不到一個可以小便的地方。

do one's business

- ease oneself
  大便
- relieve oneself/one's bowels
  大便
- have a bowel movement
  大便
- be taken short
  突然有便意

上廁所 排泄也是很重要的工作（？），因此 on business 也有「在上廁所」的意思。

- I'm going in the toilet to **do my business**.
- I'll give you some privacy.
  ●我要去廁所辦點事了。　●我就不打擾你了。

▶ She took a long time to do her business.
她蹲廁所蹲了很久。
I'm going to do my business in the bushes over here.
我要去那邊的灌木叢解決一下。

do number one

- fart in front of...
  在…前面放屁
- break the wind
  放屁
- hold one's gas in
  忍住不放屁
- smell the fart
  聞到屁味

小便 孩子們的口語用法，number two 則是「大便」。

- What's up, Tom?
- I have to **go number two**, mom.
  ●Tom，怎麼啦？　●媽媽，我要去大便。

▶ You don't have to hold in your fart.
你不需要憋著屁。
I want to do number one.
我想去小便。

---

07 穿衣服 get dressed

4-07.mp3

get dressed

- get undressed
  脫衣服
- get sb dressed
  幫某人穿衣打扮

穿好衣服 在口語裡，這個說法比 dress oneself 常用。

- **Get dressed** for the party.
- What time are we going there?
  ●為了派對穿戴打扮一下吧。　●我們幾點要過去？

▶ Now get dressed, we're going to the gym.
把衣服穿好，我們要去健身房。
How long does it take to get dressed?
穿好衣服要多久？

wear a suit

- wear a winter coat
  穿冬天的大衣
- wear size 34
  穿 34 號（尺寸）
- wear one's shoes
  穿鞋子

穿西裝　wear a suit and tie 則表示「穿西裝打領帶」。

- So, where are we going to eat tonight?
- It's a nice restaurant. **Wear a suit**.

  ●所以，我們今晚要去哪裡吃飯？　●是間很棒的餐廳，你要穿西裝。

▶ All workers will wear a suit in the office.
  所有的員工在辦公室裡都穿西裝。
  I plan to wear a suit to the wedding.
  我打算穿西裝去參加婚禮。

put on

- have something on
  穿著…（狀態）

穿上…　wear 是穿著的狀態，put on 則是穿上的動作。

- Should I wear my red dress?
- No, you should **put on** your black skirt.

  ●我該穿我的紅色洋裝嗎？　●不，你該穿上你的黑色裙子。

▶ I'll put on some shorts to exercise.
  我會穿短褲去運動。
  Go ahead and put on something comfortable.
  去穿上舒適的衣服。

take off

脫掉…　undress 是「脫衣服」，不接受詞。naked 則是指「裸體的」。

- It seems to me that the room became hot.
- I know. I have to **take off** my jacket.

  ●我覺得房間變得好熱。　●我知道，我得把外套給脫了。

▶ Take off your coat and sit down.
  把你的大衣脫掉，然後坐下。
  Well, take off your shirt and lie down.
  把你的襯衫脫掉，然後躺下。

try on

試穿…　買衣服之前，為了確定是否真的適合、喜不喜歡而試穿。

- Do you think this coat will fit me?
- Why don't you **try it on**?

  ●你覺得這件大衣會適合我嗎？　●你何不試穿呢？

▶ Can I try on one of these suits?
  我可以試穿這其中的一套西裝嗎？
  Why don't you try it on?
  你何不試穿呢？

1 職場・學校
2 電腦・網路
3 社交生活
4 日常生活
5 訊息・理解
6 想法・態度
7 情緒・狀況
8 行為舉止
9 時間地點・副詞片語

dress up

- get/be all dressed up
  盛裝打扮，穿得很漂亮
- get/be too dressed up
  穿得太正式或太華麗
- be well dressed
  穿著得體

盛裝打扮 為了相親或面試等場合穿得特別隆重的情況。

- Why **are** you **dressed up** tonight?
- I've got a date that I want to impress.
  - ●你今晚為什麼盛裝打扮？　●我有個約會，想讓對方印象深刻。

▶ Why are you all dressed up?
  你們為什麼都盛裝打扮？
  I plan to dress up for the talent show.
  我打算為了才藝表演盛裝打扮。

change one's clothes

- get changed
  換衣服

換衣服 試衣間則稱為 fitting room。

- Can you help me move this furniture?
- Sure, but I need to **change my clothes** first.
  - ●你可以幫我搬這件家具嗎？　●當然，但我得先換衣服。

▶ Bob will change his clothes before leaving.
  離開之前，Bob 會換衣服。
  I'll change my clothes after showering.
  淋浴之後，我會換衣服。

look good on

- A look good/nice in
  that dress
  A 穿那件洋裝很好看

看起來很適合⋯ 主詞不是人，是衣服、眼鏡等被穿戴的物品。

- That shirt **looks good on** you.
- Thank you. I just bought it.
  - ●那件襯衫很適合你。　●謝謝，我剛買的。

▶ Do these glasses look good on me?
  這副眼鏡適合我嗎？
  All clothes look good on her.
  所有的衣服都很適合她。

go well with

與⋯相配 也可以用及物動詞 suit 或 match 表示相配、適合。

- I'm going to wear my black shirt.
- That shirt **goes well with** blue jeans.
  - ●我要穿我的黑襯衫。　●那件襯衫和藍色牛仔褲很搭。

▶ Your hat and gloves go well with your coat.
  你的帽子和手套跟你的大衣很搭。
  Does this scarf go well with my outfit?
  這條圍巾跟我穿的衣服搭嗎？

1 職場・學校

2 電腦・網路

3 社交生活

4 日常生活

5 訊息・理解

6 想法・態度

7 情緒・狀況

8 行為舉止

9 時間地點・副詞片語

 try on vs. try sth

　　try 後面通常接名詞或「to + 動詞」，表示「嘗試不曾做過的事」、「試圖做某事」。如果接的名詞是食物，則表示「吃吃看」，例如 try stinky tofu（吃吃看臭豆腐）。I'll try my best 則是「我會盡我所能」的意思。不過，如果 try 後面接衣物或首飾等要穿戴的東西，就要加上介系詞 on，表示「試穿」，例如 try on this shirt。

08 | 坐 take a seat

4-08.mp3

take a seat

· (Is this seat) Taken?
　（這個位子）有人坐嗎？
· have a seat in the chair
　坐在椅子上

坐下 動詞 take 可以換成 have。
● Can I sit at this table with you?
● Of course you can. **Have a seat.**
　●我可以跟你一起坐在這張桌子嗎？　●當然可以，請坐。

▶ Take a seat and tell me about your day.
　坐下來跟我聊聊你今天過得怎樣吧。
　Please have a seat in the reception area.
　請坐在接待區。

sit by

· sit with one's legs crossed
　翹二郎腿坐著
· sit face to face with…
　和…面對面坐著
· sit side by side with…
　和…肩並肩坐著

坐在…旁邊 by 也可以換成 beside（不是 besides）或 next to 表示「在…旁邊」。
● Is Greg still in the building?
● Yes, but he went to **sit by** his friends.
　●Greg 還在大樓裡嗎？　●對，不過他去和他朋友們坐在一起了。

▶ I can't sit by you right now.
　我現在不能坐在你旁邊。
　Angie decided to sit by Brad in the library.
　Angie 在圖書館裡決定坐在 Brad 旁邊。

sit down

· sit down on the sofa
  坐在沙發上

坐下 比較有禮貌的說法是 please be seated。

● I'm ready to eat some food.
● Sit down and I'll bring it to you.

  ●我準備要吃點東西了。　●坐下吧，我會拿來給你。

▶ Sit down until we are ready to start.
  直到我們準備好開始為止都坐著。
  Is it okay for me to sit down here?
  我可以坐在這裡嗎？

stand up

· stand on one's toes
  踮著腳站著
· stand in a line
  排隊（站成一列）

站起來 如果要清楚表示「離開座位站起來」，可以說 rise from one's seat。

● Stand up and help me move this chair.
● I think you can move it by yourself.

  ●站起來幫我搬這張椅子。　●我想你可以自己搬。

▶ Stand up and let me sit down there.
  站起來，讓我坐那裡。
  Stand up and let me take a look. Lift up your shirt.
  站起來讓我看一下。把你的襯衫拉高。

lie down

· lie down on the bed
  躺在床上
· lie on one's back
  仰躺
· lie on one's face
  臉朝下趴著
· lie back
  往後躺

躺下 lie 後面也可以接地方副詞或介系詞片語，表示躺的地方或者方式。

● Vera has a bad stomach ache today.
● Tell her to lie down for a while.

  ●Vera 今天胃痛很嚴重。　●叫她去躺一下。

▶ I will lie down after I finish working.
  我工作完成之後會躺下。
  Did Jeff lie down and rest tonight?
  Jeff 今晚有躺著休息嗎？

09 | 擤鼻涕
blow one's nose

4-09.mp3

blow one's nose

· have a runny nose
  流鼻涕
· nose bleed
  流鼻血（名詞）
· have a bloody nose
  在流鼻血

擤鼻涕 pick one's nose 則是大家一定會偷偷做的「挖鼻孔」。

● Excuse me, I have to **blow my nose**.
● Oh, did you catch a cold?

   ● 不好意思，我要擤鼻涕。　● 噢，你感冒了嗎？

▶ Kevin blew his nose at the table.
   Kevin 在桌前擤鼻涕。
   Cindy went to the bathroom to blow her nose.
   Cindy 去浴室擤鼻涕。

sweat a lot

· wipe the sweat off/
  from
  擦掉…上的汗
· get sweaty
  變得滿身是汗
· drop sweat
  滴汗

流很多汗 sweat 也可以用來比喻「很努力做某事」。

● I like doing different types of exercise.
● Me too, but I really **sweat a lot**.

   ● 我喜歡做各種運動。　● 我也是，可是我都會流很多汗。

▶ She sweats a lot when the weather gets hot.
   天氣變熱的時候，她會流很多汗。
   I'll try not to sweat a lot when I'm on my date.
   我約會的時候會努力不要流太多汗。

hold a sneeze

· give a sneeze
  打噴嚏
· sneeze a lot
  打很多噴嚏
· make A sneeze
  …害 A 打噴嚏

忍住不打噴嚏 別人打噴嚏的時候，可以說 (God) Bless you! 請他保重。

● I think it's rude to sneeze loudly.
● Is it better to **hold a sneeze** then?

   ● 我覺得大聲打噴嚏很失禮。　● 那憋著不打噴嚏比較好嗎？

▶ It's probably unhealthy to hold a sneeze.
   忍住不打噴涕可能不太健康。
   My sister tries to hold her sneezes.
   我姐姐努力忍住不打噴嚏。

1 職場・學校
2 電腦・網路
3 社交生活
4 日常生活
5 訊息・理解
6 想法・態度
7 情緒・狀況
8 行為舉止
9 時間地點・副詞片語

have a bad breath

· have a body odor
  有體臭

有口臭　口臭可以用 mouthwash（漱口水）或 breath freshener（口腔清新噴霧）去除。

● Why don't you want to date Herb again?

● He **has bad breath**. Can't you smell it?

　● 你為什麼不想再跟 Herb 約會？　　● 他有口臭。你聞不到嗎？

▶ Use some mouthwash because you have bad breath.
　你口臭很嚴重，去用點漱口水吧。
　They had bad breath after eating the garlic.
　他們吃完大蒜之後有口臭。

spit on sb

» cf. Spit it out!
　儘管說吧！

對某人吐口水　spit 的時態變化是 spit-spit-spit，全都一樣。

● So you went to the protest march?

● Yes, but someone **spit on** me.

　● 所以你參加了抗議遊行？　　● 是啊，不過有人對我吐口水。

▶ He spit on me and we got in a fight.
　他對我吐口水，所以我們打了起來。
　The students spit on the unpopular child.
　學生們對著那個不受歡迎的孩子吐口水。

---

10 哭 burst into tears

4-10.mp3

burst into tears

· break into tears
  嚎啕大哭

· with tears in one's
  eyes
  眼淚在眼眶裡打轉

突然哭起來　例如聽到不好的消息，太過震驚而開始大哭。

● What did June do when you broke up with her?

● She **burst into tears**. She was very upset.

　● 你跟 June 分手時，她怎麼了？　　● 她嚎啕大哭，非常難過。

▶ Beth burst into tears when she got a failing grade.
　Beth 拿到不及格的成績時，她嚎啕大哭。
　Nancy was so tired and unhappy that she burst into
　tears. Nancy 太累、太不開心了，所以她突然哭了起來。

be in tears

· shed tears
　流淚
· end in tears
　以流淚收場

在流眼淚，在哭 drop tear 則是「掉眼淚」的意思。

● Was Paul still in his house?
● Yes, but he **was in tears** when I got there.

　●Paul 還在他家嗎？　●嗯，不過我到那裡的時候，他正在哭。

▶ The crowd was in tears after the President spoke.
　總統演講完之後，群眾都流淚了。
　She was in tears when she left her family.
　她流著淚離開家人。

cry a lot

· cry bitter tears
　痛哭
· cry oneself to sleep
　哭著入睡
· make A cry
　讓 A 哭
· cry for joy
　喜極而泣

很常哭 cry one's eyes out 意為「差點把眼珠都哭出來般，哭得很厲害」的樣子。

● Your boyfriend joined the army?
● Yeah, I **cried a lot** after he was gone.

　●你男朋友去當兵了？　●是啊，他走了之後我經常在哭。

▶ You'll cry a lot when you see that movie.
　你看那部電影的時候會一直哭。
　Suzie cried a lot after her mom died.
　Suzie 的母親過世後，她常常在哭。

sob

· weep
　（文學體）靜靜地哭

啜泣 sob out 則是「啜泣／嗚咽地說著…」。

● I can hear Betsy **sob** in her room.
● Go see if you can make her feel better.

　●我可以聽到 Betsy 在她房裡啜泣。　●去看看你能不能安慰她。

▶ Everyone sobbed during the funeral.
　所有人在喪禮上都啜泣著。
　You shouldn't sob when you hurt yourself.
　當你傷到自己時，你不該啜泣。

dry one's tears

· wipe a tear from one's eye
　拭去眼中的淚水

擦乾眼淚「擦乾」汗或眼淚時，動詞可以用 wipe 或 dry。

● It seems like everything is so terrible.
● **Dry your tears.** It will be fine.

　●似乎一切都很糟。　●把眼淚擦乾，會變好的。

▶ Daria dried her tears after crying all night.
　Daria 哭了一整晚之後，把眼淚擦乾了。
　Dry your tears and go take a shower.
　擦乾你的眼淚，去沖個澡。

1 職場・學校

2 電腦・網路

3 社交生活

4 日常生活

5 訊息・理解

6 想法・態度

7 情緒・狀況

8 行為舉止

9 時間地點・副詞片語

11 笑 smile at

smile at

· smile back
（在對方微笑後）回以微
笑
· smile with relief
如釋重負地微笑
· have a big smile
臉上掛著大大的微笑

對…微笑 和 laugh 不同，smile 是帶著笑容但沒出聲的樣子。

● I think the waitress is kind of cute.
● She **smiled at** you. I think she likes you.
　●我覺得那個女服務生蠻可愛的。　●她對你微笑，我想她喜歡你。

▶ Try to smile at the students in class.
　試著對著課堂上的學生們微笑。
　Did you smile at your new teacher?
　你有對你的新老師微笑嗎？

laugh at

· laugh out loud
笑得很大聲
· have a laugh
笑
· have a good laugh
笑開懷

笑…，嘲笑… laugh 除了指「笑出聲」，也可以表示「嘲笑」的
意思。

● What happened when Ron fell down?
● Everyone **laughed at** him.
　●Ron 跌倒的時候，發生了什麼事？　●每個人都嘲笑他。

▶ I laugh at Jim Carrey movies.
　Jim Carrey 的電影讓我大笑。
　We laughed at her arrogant behavior.
　我們嘲笑她自大的行為。

make sb laugh

· can't help laughing
忍不住一直笑
· burst into laughter
突然大笑，爆笑
· burst out laughing
突然大笑，爆笑

讓某人笑 keep sb in stiches 則是「讓某人大笑」。in stiches 本來
是指「像被針刺一樣痛」，後來引申為「笑得很厲害」的意思。

● How can I impress a girl I want to date?
● You can impress a girl if you **make her laugh**.
　●我該怎麼讓我想約會的女孩印象深刻？
　●你如果能讓女孩子笑，你就能讓她印象深刻。

▶ Some jokes will make me laugh.
　有些笑話會讓我笑出來。
　The comic made almost everyone laugh.
　這個漫畫幾乎讓所有人都笑了。

1 職場・學校

2 電腦・網路

3 社交生活

4 日常生活

5 訊息・理解

6 想法・態度

7 情緒・狀況

8 行為舉止

9 時間地點・副詞片語

keep a straight face

- keep one's face straight
（忍住笑）裝出很嚴肅的表情

忍住不笑 hold back one's laughter 也是一樣的意思。

- I can't believe our teacher made that mistake.
- I know. It was hard to **keep a straight face**.
  - ●我真不敢相信我們老師犯了那個失誤。
  - ●我知道，要忍住不笑真難。

▶ Can you keep a straight face when Sam tells jokes?
Sam 說笑話的時候，你能忍住不笑出來嗎？
I can never keep a straight face when I lie.
我說謊的時候總是沒辦法不笑場。

 除了 smile 和 laugh 以外，各種「笑」的表達方式

　　跟中文一樣，英文也有很多表示各種不同笑法的詞彙。例如 chuckle，是因為想到什麼有趣的事情，一個人暗自輕聲竊笑的樣子。而 giggle 則是因為某件可笑或令人驚訝的事，而咯咯笑或傻笑的狀態。至於 grin 則是不發出聲音，露齒而笑的模樣。

---

12 | 大叫 shout to

4-12.mp3

shout to/at

- shout so loud
叫得很大聲
- shout for help
呼喊求助

對…大叫 shout sth out 則是指把某些話大聲喊出來。

- The other hikers are far ahead of us.
- **Shout to** them and tell them to slow down.
  - ●其他健行的人遠遠超前我們。　●對他們喊一下，叫他們放慢速度。

▶ Did you shout to the people in the next building?
你有對隔壁大樓的人大喊嗎？
Shout to our friends over there.
對著我們在另一頭的朋友們大叫。

yell at

· yell out
  大聲叫出…

對⋯吼叫 yell 可以指害怕、生氣或興奮時大叫的樣子。

- Billy was behaving so badly today.
- That's why the teacher **yelled at** him.
  - Billy 今天的行為舉止表現得很不好。　● 所以老師才對他吼了。

▶ We yelled at our unkind classmates.
  我們對著不友善的同學們大吼。
  Don't yell at me for being wrong.
  別因為我做錯事就對著我大吼。

scream

· cry out
  大哭，大叫

尖叫，放聲大哭 scream in anger 表示因為生氣而尖叫。

- Did you hear someone **scream**?
- Yes, I think somebody may be in trouble.
  - 你有聽到誰在尖叫嗎？　● 有，我想可能有人碰上麻煩了。

▶ Annie screamed when she saw the spider.
  Annie 看到蜘蛛時尖叫。
  I'm going to scream if you bother me again.
  如果你再來煩我，我會大叫的。

keep one's voice down

· raise one's voice
  大聲說話，提高音調
· talk in a low/loud
  voice
  小聲／大聲說話
· lower one's voice
  壓低聲音

壓低聲音 lose one's voice 則是「發不出聲音」。

- Hey, what are you doing here?
- **Keep your voice down**. We're in a library.
  - 嘿，你在這邊幹嘛？　● 小聲一點，我們在圖書館裡。

▶ Gene kept his voice down when he talked.
  Gene 壓低聲音說話。
  Keep your voices down during the movie.
  看電影的時候要輕聲細語。

groan with pain

· moan with pain
  痛苦地呻吟

痛苦地呻吟 相反的，groan with pleasure 是因為愉悅發出感嘆的聲音，例如吃到美味的食物等。

- I saw Mark get hurt playing football.
- He **groaned with pain** after being injured.
  - 我看到 Mark 踢足球時受傷了。　● 他受傷之後，很痛苦地呻吟。

▶ The old man groaned with pain as he sat down.
  那位老先生坐下時發出痛苦的呻吟。
  Wendy groaned with pain when she fell.
  Wendy 跌倒時，發出痛苦的呻吟。

13 呼吸 take a breath

4-13.mp3

1 職場・學校
2 電腦・網路
3 社交生活
4 日常生活
5 訊息・理解
6 想法・態度
7 情緒・狀況
8 行為舉止
9 時間地點・副詞片語

take a breath

· take a deep breath
  深深吸一口氣
· take one's breath away
  （因為震撼而）令某人摒息

吸一口氣 catch one's breath 則是「調整／恢復呼吸」。

- I can't continue working here.
- **Take a breath**, you'll be alright.
  - 我沒辦法繼續在這裡工作了。　　● 喘口氣，你會沒事的。

▶ Take a breath before you dive into the pool.
  在你跳進游泳池前，先吸一口氣。
  He took a breath and then began to run.
  他吸了一口氣，然後開始奔跑。

breathe in

· breathe in
  吸氣
· breathe out
  吐氣

吸氣 相反的，breathe out 就是「吐氣」。

- I am so stressed out right now.
- **Breathe in** slowly and relax.
  - 我現在整個人壓力好大。　　● 慢慢吸氣，然後放輕鬆。

▶ Breathe in and out during the exercise.
  運動的時候，要（配合呼吸）吸氣然後吐氣。
  Breathe in while the doctor checks your heart.
  當醫生檢查你的心臟時要吸氣。

hold one's breath

摒住呼吸 可能是為了照 X 光，或是不讓別人發現而摒住呼吸。

- How long can you **hold your breath**?
- I think I can hold it about two minutes.
  - 你可以憋氣多久？　　● 我想我大概可以憋個兩分鐘。

▶ You learn to hold your breath while swimming.
  你游泳的時候，會學會憋氣。
  Okay, this is going to be tough. Hold your breath.
  好，接下來會有點難。摒住你的呼吸。

289

be out of breath

- gasp
  喘氣
- pant
  喘氣

上氣不接下氣 = be breathless = be short of breath = breathe hard = be panting，全都是一樣的意思。

- ● I **am out of breath** from walking home.
- ● That's because you're getting fat.
  - ●我走路回家走得上氣不接下氣。　●那是因為你越來越胖。

▶ Adam was out of breath after the marathon.
跑完馬拉松之後，Adam 上氣不接下氣。

Jim exercises often and is never out of breath.
Jim 很常運動，所以從來不會上氣不接下氣。

sigh with relief

- give a sigh of relief
  如釋重負地呼一口氣

如釋重負地呼一口氣 動詞 sigh 是「嘆氣」的意思。

- ● What happened when the exam finished?
- ● All of the students **sighed with relief**.
  - ●考試完之後怎麼了？　●所有學生都鬆了一口氣。

▶ I'm going to sigh with relief when this report is done.
這份報告完成之後，我會如釋重負地呼一口氣。

Pam sighed with relief when school was canceled.
學校臨時停課時，Pam 如釋重負地呼了一口氣。

---

14 | 居住 live in

4-14.mp3

---

live in

- live in a luxury apartment
  住在一間豪華的公寓
- live in California
  住在加州
- live in that area
  住在那個區域

住在… in 後面接表示地點的名詞。

- ● My family is going to move overseas.
- ● It's hard to believe that you're going to **live in** another country.
  - ●我家要搬到國外去。　●很難相信你們要住在另一個國家。

▶ I live in a small one-bedroom studio.
我住在有一間臥房的小工作室裡。

Can you afford to live in that apartment?
你住得起那間公寓嗎？

live in the neighborhood

- be in the neighborhood
  在近鄰
- live close by
  住得很近
- live in a suburb
  住在郊區

住在近鄰 neighbor 是鄰居，neighborhood 則是指鄰近的區域。

- Is Joseph driving by?
- Yes, he **lives in the neighborhood**.
  - Joseph 會順道開車過來嗎？　●會，他住這附近。

▶ A famous actress lives in the neighborhood.
　有位知名的女演員住在這附近。
　My Uncle Tom lives in the neighborhood.
　我的叔叔 Tom 住這附近。

live all alone

- live together
  住在一起
- live longer
  住得久一點，活得久一點
- live an interesting life
  過著有趣的生活

一個人住 = live by oneself = live on one's own，都是一樣的意思。

- Does your grandmother live with you?
- No, she chose to **live all alone**.
  - 你的外婆跟你一起住嗎？　●沒有，她選擇一個人住。

▶ Lots of college couples live together before marriage.
　很多大學情侶在結婚前同居。
　It's not like we agreed to live together forever.
　這並不是說我們同意要永遠住在一起。

live away from

- live away from home
  不住在家裡
- live away from one's family
  沒有和家人住在一起

離開…居住 live far apart 意為「分開很遠居住」。

- What is the hardest part of going to a university?
- All of the students **live away from** their families.
  - 上大學最困難的地方是什麼？　●所有的學生都離開家人居住。

▶ He lives away from his wife most of the week.
　一整個禮拜他幾乎都沒有跟太太住在一起。
　She lived away from Taiwan for a few years.
　她有好幾年都沒住在台灣。

settle down

- live overseas/abroad
  住在國外
- settle down to reading
  定下心來讀書
- settle down to work
  定下心來做工作

定居，安頓下來 settle down to sth 則是「定下心來做某事」。

- I'm happy that I'm finished with military service.
- Are you going to **settle down** now?
  - 我很開心我服完兵役了。　●你現在準備要安頓下來了嗎？

▶ I'd like to settle down somewhere in the country.
　我想要定居在這個國家的某處。
　Jane and Dick settled down and had some kids.
　Jane 和 Dick 安頓了下來，有了幾個孩子。

1 職場・學校
2 電腦・網路
3 社交生活
4 日常生活
5 訊息・理解
6 想法・態度
7 情緒・狀況
8 行為舉止
9 時間地點・副詞片語

15 租屋
rent a house

rent a house

- rent a larger room
  租比較大的房間
- rent an apartment
  租公寓
- monthly rent
  月租

租屋 rent 意為「付錢租用」，例如租房子、租車、租機器等。

● Why don't you get your own place?

● It's too expensive to **rent a house**.

　●你為什麼不去弄間自己的房子？　●租房子太貴了。

▶ They are going to rent a house in Hawaii.
　他們要在夏威夷租房子。
　Try to rent a house before you buy one.
　在你買房子之前，先試著用租的。

find a house to rent

- a house to rent
  供租用的房子

找房子租 動詞 find 也可以換成 look for。

● Orlando and his wife are divorcing.

● He should **find a house to rent**.

　●Orlando 和他的太太要離婚了。　●他該找間房子租了。

▶ Did she find a house to rent near her job?
　她有在公司附近找到房子租嗎？
　I found a house to rent on your street.
　我在你住的那條街上找到一間房子租。

live in a rental

- live in a monthly
  rented housing
  住在需繳月租的房子

住在租的房子裡 rental fee 是「租金」，monthly rent 則是「月租」。

● How is Helen doing these days?

● She's **living in a cheap rental** unit.

　●Helen 最近過得怎樣？　●她住在一間租金很便宜的房子。

▶ They lived in a rental until they bought a house.
　直到他們買了房子之前，他們都住在租來的房子裡。
　She lives in a rental near a shopping center.
　她住在一間購物中心附近的出租屋。

sign a lease

- the lease expires/runs
  out
  租約到期
- the lease runs/takes
  effect
  租約生效

簽租約 主要是指企業用的建築物、車輛等等的租約。

● How long is your lease for?

● I **signed a lease** for one year.

　●你的租約多久？　●我簽了一年的約。

▶ My lease says I can't have pets. 我的租約上說我不能養寵物。
　The lease expires in six months. 這份租約六個月後到期。

292

be leased in one's name

· lease out
出租…

· lease sth from sb
向某人租用某物

· buy a house
買房子

以某人的名義簽租約 簽約人和使用人不必然是同一個人。

- How can you afford this place?
- It **was leased in my father's name**.

   ●你怎麼租得起這個地方？　●這是用我父親的名義簽約租下的。

▶ She leased the apartment in her boyfriend's name.
   她用她男朋友的名義租了公寓。
   It was all leased in Terry's name. 這都是用 Terry 的名義租的。

---

1 職場・學校

2 電腦・網路

3 社交生活

4 日常生活

5 訊息・理解

6 想法・態度

7 情緒・狀況

8 行為舉止

9 時間地點・副詞片語

16 清洗，打掃
do the dishes

4-16.mp3

---

do the dishes

· wash the dishes
洗碗盤

洗碗盤 dishes 泛指所有需要清洗的碗盤、杯子等等。

- Your kitchen is pretty dirty.
- I know. I don't like **doing the dishes**.

   ●你的廚房好髒。　●我知道，我不喜歡洗碗盤。

▶ I don't like to do the dishes. 我不喜歡洗碗盤。
   Let me help you finish washing the dishes.
   讓我幫你把碗盤洗完吧。

do the laundry

· run the washer
使用洗衣機

· get the laundry
washed
把衣服洗好

洗衣服 就是 wash the clothes 的意思。

- Will you help me load up the truck?
- Not until I **get the laundry washed**.

   ●你可以幫我把東西裝上卡車嗎？　●要等到我把衣服洗好。

▶ I'm going to go do the laundry. 我要去洗衣服。
   You need to do the laundry tomorrow. 你明天得洗衣服。

clean one's room

· clean the apartment
清掃公寓

· need to be cleaned
需要被清掃

· keep it clean
保持乾淨

清掃某人的房間 clean 除了當形容詞以外，也能當動詞。

- I want to go play with my friends.
- Not until you **clean your bedroom**.

   ●我想去跟朋友們玩。　●等到你把你房間打掃乾淨才行。

▶ I cleaned my room before you came.
   在你來之前，我打掃了房間。
   Don't forget to clean your room. 別忘了把你房間打掃乾淨。

293

clean up

· clean this place up
把這邊打掃乾淨

收拾，清掃 表示「打掃／收拾得乾乾淨淨」。

● I can't **clean up** this place alone.
● That's why we're here. We'll help you.
　　● 我沒辦法一個人打掃這邊。
　　● 所以我們才在這裡啊，我們會幫你的。

▶ Didn't you clean up the kitchen?
　　你沒有清理廚房嗎？
　　We need to clean up the room as quickly as possible.
　　我們得盡快把房間打掃乾淨。

wash off

· wash sth off
洗掉某物
· sth wash off
某物會被洗掉

洗乾淨，洗掉 可以接受詞，也可以不接受詞。

● I have been working outside for hours.
● You should **wash off** in the bathroom.
　　● 我在外面工作了好幾小時。　　● 你該去浴室把身體洗乾淨。

▶ That dirt will wash off in the shower.
　　那塊髒污會在淋浴時被洗掉。
　　There was no time to wash off when I finished.
　　當我完成的時候，我沒有時間把自己洗乾淨。

wipe up

· wipe the floor
擦地板

擦掉（灰塵等） wipe 是用抹布把灰塵或水氣抹掉之類的動作。

● Gee, the eggs I was cooking spilled.
● **Wipe up** the mess you made here.
　　● 天啊，我在煮的蛋灑出來了。　　● 把你搞的這一團亂擦乾淨。

▶ You can wipe up the water with a towel.
　　你可以用毛巾把水擦掉。
　　Did he wipe up the soda on the floor?
　　他把地板上的汽水擦掉了嗎？

sweep the floor

掃地 sweep 表示用掃把等工具掃除乾淨。

● The party will be starting in an hour.
● We should **sweep the floor** before people arrive.
　　● 派對一小時後開始。　　● 在人們抵達前，我們應該掃地。

▶ It only takes ten minutes to sweep the floor.
　　掃地只需要花十分鐘。
　　Did you sweep the floor of your bedroom?
　　你掃了你臥室的地板了嗎？

mop up

· mop the floor
  拖地板

（用拖把）拖乾淨… mop 表示「用拖把拖…」。

● The students left a mess in the classroom.
● Well, go mop up whatever they spilled.

　● 那些學生把教室搞得一團糟。
　● 嗯，把他們打翻的東西都拖乾淨。

▶ I didn't mop up the gymnasium.
　我沒有拖體育館的地板。
　Mom mops up the kitchen every morning.
　媽媽每天早上都會拖廚房的地板。

vacuum the mat

用吸塵器吸墊子 vacuum 也可以縮寫成 vac。

● You need to **vacuum the mats** in your car.
● I need to clean everything in my car.

　● 你該把汽車裡的墊子吸一下。　● 我得清理車裡所有的東西。

▶ Vacuum the mat in front of the door.
　去把門前的墊子吸一吸。
　Ask him to vacuum the mat in his bedroom.
　叫他用吸塵器吸他房間裡的墊子。

mow the lawn

割草皮 由此衍生出 lawn mower（割草機）這個名詞。

● You really should go out and **mow the lawn**.
● Yeah, I guess the grass is getting pretty high.

　● 你真的該出去割草皮。　● 是啊，我想草應該長得很高了吧。

▶ Don mowed the lawn every week this summer.
　Don 這個夏天每個禮拜都割草。
　I paid Steve $25 to mow the lawn.
　我付 Steve 25 美元，請他幫我割草。

1 職場・學校
2 電腦・網路
3 社交生活
4 日常生活
5 訊息・理解
6 想法・態度
7 情緒・狀況
8 行為舉止
9 時間地點・副詞片語

故障
break down

4-17.mp3

break down

· break sth down
  砸碎／弄壞某物
· breakdown
  故障（名詞）

故障 表示電腦故障或車子拋錨等無法正常運作的狀態。

● You are late for class.
● It's not my fault I'm late. The bus **broke down**.

　●你上課遲到了。　●會遲到不是我的錯，是公車拋錨了。

▶ Did your car break down again? 你的車又拋錨了嗎？
　I can't believe the bus broke down. 我不敢相信公車拋錨了。

not work well

· work properly
  運作正常
· stop working
  停止運作，故障

運作得不好 運作得很好、很正常則是說 work well/properly。

● Why did you return your new TV?
● It did **not work well** when I used it.

　●你為什麼把新電視退回去了？　●我用的時候，它運作不太正常。

▶ The old car didn't work well.
　這台老爺車開起來不太順。
　Does the machine work well?
　這台機器運作正常嗎？

be out of order

· be out of service
  （機器等）暫停服務
· shut off the electricity
  關掉電源

故障 表示「機器故障」最典型的說法。

● Can you make 20 copies of this paper?
● Sorry, the copier **is out of order**.

　●你可以把這份報告影印 20 份嗎？　●抱歉，影印機故障了。

▶ The juice machines are all out of order.
　這些果汁機都故障了。
　The pay phone was out of order. 這台公共電話故障了。

failure in...

· engine failure
  引擎故障

…的故障 表示整體中某個部分的故障。

● The rocket didn't work properly.
● Yes, there was a **failure in** its engine.

　●火箭沒有正常運作。　●嗯，它的引擎有點故障。

▶ There was a failure in our house's heating system.
　我們房子的暖氣系統有點故障。
　Was there a failure in your plans?
　你的計畫有什麼地方出問題嗎？

call a mechanic

· call a plumber
打電話叫水管工人
· call a serviceman
打電話叫維修人員

打電話叫技師 維修人員可以直接稱為 repairman。

● This car is always breaking down.
● **Call a mechanic** and get it fixed.
　●這台車總是發生拋錨。　●打電話叫技師修好它。

▶ Call a mechanic to help you out.
　打電話請技師幫你。
　Call a mechanic when it gives you problems.
　出現問題時,請打電話找技師。

---

1 職場・學校

2 電腦・網路

3 社交生活

4 日常生活

5 訊息・理解

6 想法・態度

7 情緒・狀況

8 行為舉止

9 時間地點・副詞片語

18 修繕,修理
fix the car

4-18.mp3

---

fix the car

· fix the/one's house
修(某人的)房子
· fix the leak in the sink
修理水槽的漏水

修車 發生故障或無法運作時,「修理」的動作稱為 fix。

● You never **fixed the broken window** in your car.
● That's because I don't have enough money.
　●你都不修你車上破掉的窗戶。　●因為我錢不夠。

▶ What will it cost to fix the car?
　修這台車要花多少錢?
　Can you come into the living room and help me fix the TV? 你可以來客廳幫我修電視嗎?

fix the problem

· fix things
修理東西,解決事情
· fix the problem with one's car
解決某人車子的問題

解決問題 除了 fix,動詞也可以換成 resolve。

● Do you think that she will be able to fix the problem?
● If she can't do it, nobody can.
　●你覺得她能解決這個問題嗎?
　●如果她也解決不了,那就沒人能辦到了。

▶ Did you help Jan fix the problem?
　你有幫 Jan 解決問題嗎?
　No. I have no idea how to help her.
　沒有,我完全不知道該怎麼幫她。

get sth fixed

· get fixed
  被修好
· fix up
  修理…，定下（日期）

請人修理好某物 得到別人的幫助，使某物被修好的意思。

● I **had my car fixed**.

● How much did it cost?

  ●我請人把車子修好了。　●花了多少錢？

▶ The restaurant got the stove fixed.

  餐廳請人把爐子修好了。

  We got the broken window fixed.

  我們請人把壞掉的窗子修好了。

repair the house

· make/do repairs
  修理
· do repairs on the
  house
  修繕房屋
· get A repaired
  請人把 A 修好
· repair the damages
  修復損傷

維修房子 repair 當名詞時用複數，例如 do/make repairs。

● Your roof is leaking water.

● I know. We have to **repair this house**.

  ●你的屋頂在漏水。　●我知道，我們得維修房子了。

▶ Will you repair the house or sell it?

  你會修理房屋，還是會賣掉？

  I need to repair the house before our vacation.

  在我們度假之前，我得把房子修好。

remodel the house

· renovate the house
  裝修房屋

改建房屋 remodel A into B 表示「把 A 改造成 B」。

● Vera bought a 20 year old house.

● She'll have to **remodel her house** soon.

  ●Vera 買了一間 20 年的老房子。　●她很快就得改建房屋了。

▶ It cost a lot of money to remodel the house.

  改建那棟房屋花了很多錢。

  We remodeled the house so it was comfortable.

  我們改建了房子，所以住起來很舒適。

1 職場・學校
2 電腦・網路
3 社交生活
4 日常生活
5 訊息・理解
6 想法・態度
7 情緒・狀況
8 行為舉止
9 時間地點・副詞片語

19 天氣
be sunny

4-19.mp3

be sunny

- be windy
  颳風,多風
- be cloudy
  多雲,陰天
- be fine
  (天氣)好

晴朗 look on the sunny side of things 則是比喻樂觀地看待事物。

- It's going to **be sunny** most of the week.
- Let's plan some outdoor activities.
  - 這整週大部分時間會出太陽。 ● 我們來計畫一些戶外活動吧。

▶ It was sunny yesterday afternoon. 昨天下午很晴朗。
  You told me it was sunny outside. 你說外面有出太陽的。

have beautiful weather

- have bad weather
  天氣不好
- when the weather changes
  當天氣改變時

天氣很好 除此之外,clear, fine, bright, sunny, fair 等形容詞也可以表示天氣好。

- Today is so sunny and warm.
- We **have beautiful weather** often here.
  - 今天很晴朗又溫暖。 ● 我們這邊天氣常常都很好。

▶ They had beautiful weather during their trip.
  他們去旅行的時候天氣很好。
  I hope we have beautiful weather for our picnic.
  我希望我們野餐時天氣會很好。

have unpredictable weather

- be so irregular/erratic
  (天氣)很不規律
- The weather forecast said S+V
  天氣預報說…

天氣難以預測 天氣預報稱為 weather forecast 或 weather report。

- The river flooded in our city.
- I guess you've **had very unpredictable weather**.
  - 河水淹進我們的城市了。 ● 我想你們那邊的天氣真的很難預測。

▶ Georgia has very unpredictable weather in the spring.
  喬治亞州春天的天氣非常難預測。
  Some of the islands had very unpredictable weather.
  有些島嶼的天氣很難預測。

turn cold

- turn hot
  (天氣)變熱
- get cold
  (天氣)變冷
- be freezing to death
  冷到快死掉

變冷 要強調真的非常冷,可以說 freezing cold 或 stone cold。

- Do you know what the weather will be like?
- I've heard it will **turn cold** tomorrow.
  - 你知道接下來的天氣會怎樣嗎? ● 我聽說明天會變冷。

▶ It usually turns cold in October. 十月通常會轉冷。
  Will it turn cold when it gets dark?
  當天色變暗時,天氣會變冷嗎?

have been cold for...

天氣冷了（一段時間） 用現在完成式表示前一陣子的天氣。

- It **has been cold** this week.
- Let's hope it will warm up soon.

  ●這星期都很冷。　●讓我們期待天氣很快會變暖吧。

▶ New York has been cold for a while.

　紐約已經冷了好一陣子。

　We have been cold for the entire time.

　這陣子我們這邊一直很冷。

go up to...degrees

· be...degrees in here
　這邊是⋯度
· be...degrees outside
　外面是⋯度

上升到⋯度 在美國通常是指 ...degrees Fahrenheit（華氏⋯度）。以下的例子都是華氏溫度。

- Did you turn on the heater?
- Sure, it's **gone up to 70 degrees**.

  ●你把電暖器打開了嗎？　●當然，現在上升到 70 度了。

▶ The temperature will go up to 90 degrees today.

　今天氣溫會上升到 90 度。

　The temperatures on the beach went up to 87 degrees.

　海灘上的氣溫上升到 87 度。

miss the sunny weather

· hate cloudy days
　討厭陰天
· if the weather holds
　如果這種天氣持續下去
· weather permitting
　如果天氣許可

想念晴朗的天氣 weather 指某個地區、某個時間點的天氣狀況，而 climate 則是概括表示某區域的長期天氣特徵。

- Do you enjoy being in London?
- No, I **miss the sunny weather** of my home.

  ●你在倫敦開心嗎？　●不，我很想念我家鄉晴朗的天氣。

▶ Joan misses the sunny weather of summer.

　Joan 想念夏天晴朗的天氣。

　We miss the sunny weather we had last week.

　我們想念上週晴朗的天氣。

feel chilly

· get chilly
　變冷
· feel sticky
　（因為天氣濕熱）覺得濕
　濕黏黏的

感覺冷 chilly 是比 cool 冷，又沒有 cold 那麼冷的狀態。

- Could you turn up the thermostat?
- Of course. **Are you feeling chilly**?

  ●你可以把自動調溫器打開嗎？　●當然可以，你覺得冷嗎？

▶ I felt chilly in the bus station.

　我在客運車站覺得很冷。

　We feel chilly when the weather starts to change.

　當天氣開始變化，我們覺得很冷。

have yellow dust storm

· issue a yellow-dust warning
發布沙塵暴警訊

有沙塵暴　「沙塵」也可以說 sandy dust。

● What was the weather like in Seoul?

● We **had a yellow dust storm** that covered everything.

　●首爾的天氣怎樣？　●當時有沙塵暴，籠罩了所有東西。

▶ I hope we won't have a yellow dust storm.
希望我們不會有沙塵暴。
The event will be canceled if we have a yellow dust storm. 如果遇到沙塵暴，那個活動會被取消。

---

20 下雪，下雨 fall heavily

4-20.mp3

(snow) fall heavily

· heavy rain/snow
暴雨／大雪
· (the snow) started to fall
開始下（雪）

（雪）下得很大　雨或雪下得很大是用 heavy 來形容。

● Why did they cancel classes today?

● The snow **fell heavily** on the roads this morning.

　●今天為什麼停課了？　●今天早上下了大雪，路面都是雪。

▶ Snow falls heavily on the higher mountains.
高山上在下大雪。
Snow fell heavily over most of the state.
整個州幾乎都在下大雪。

it starts to rain

· It started snowing
開始下雪

開始下雨　也可以說 it starts raining。

● **It started to rain** late last night.

● The weather was still gloomy this morning.

　●昨天深夜開始下雨。　●今天早上天氣還是陰陰的。

▶ It starts to rain whenever I go outside.
我只要一出門，就開始下雨。
It started to rain as the airplane took off.
飛機起飛的時候開始下雨了。

1 職場・學校
2 電腦・網路
3 社交生活
4 日常生活
5 訊息・理解
6 想法・態度
7 情緒・狀況
8 行為舉止
9 時間地點・副詞片語

be pouring rain

· in the pouring rain
  在大雨中
· It rains all day long.
  整天都在下雨。
· rain cats and dogs
  雨下得很大
· rain hard
  雨下得很大

傾盆大雨 字面上的意思就是「雨像是用倒的一樣」，表示暴雨持續傾瀉而下，所以常用進行式。

● Should we plan the picnic for tomorrow?
● No, it's going to **rain hard** all day.
  ●我們該為明天的野餐作計畫嗎？　●不，明天整天都會下大雨。

▶ It rained hard for the entire week.
  整個禮拜都在下大雨。
  It was pouring rain when I left the bus.
  我下公車時，雨下得非常大。

walk in the rain

· go out in the rain
  在雨天外出
· get caught in the rain
  被雨淋

在雨中散步 在雪中當然就是 in the snow。

● I think I'll go for a **walk in the rain**.
● Make sure you take your umbrella.
  ●我想要在雨中散步。　●記得帶把傘。

▶ Debbie and Jim took a walk in the rain.
  Debbie 和 Jim 在雨中散步。
  It's foolish to go out and walk in the rain.
  下雨天還出門走路很傻。

get wet

· get soaking wet
  全身濕透

淋濕 如果是淋到全身濕透了，可以說 get soaking wet。

● The children **got wet** while walking home.
● Tell them to put on dry clothes.
  ●孩子們在走回家的路上淋濕了。　●叫他們穿上乾的衣服。

▶ You'll get wet if you go outside.
  如果出去的話，你會淋濕的。
  I got wet because of the rainstorm.
  我因為暴雨而被淋濕了。

21 | 用餐
have dinner

4-21.mp3

go out to eat

- eat out
  去外面吃飯

出去吃飯 eat 後面可以直接接出去吃的東西。

- Are you meeting Paul tonight?
- Yeah, we plan to **go out to eat**.

  ●你今晚要跟 Paul 見面嗎？ ●嗯，我們打算出去吃飯。

▶ I love to go out to eat at restaurants.
  我喜歡出去外面餐廳吃飯。
  Let's go out to eat some spaghetti.
  我們出去吃點義大利麵吧。

go to lunch

- go out to lunch
  出去吃午餐
- go (out) for lunch
  （出）去吃午餐
- step out for lunch
  出去吃午餐

去吃午餐 後面可以加上 with sb 表示一起吃飯的對象。

- May I speak to Bill, please?
- He just **stepped out for lunch**.

  ●我可以跟 Bill 說個話嗎？ ●他剛才出去吃午餐了。

▶ Where do you want to go for lunch? 你想去哪裡吃午餐？
  How about going out for lunch? 出去吃午餐如何？

have dinner (with)

- get dinner
  買晚餐
- dinner with…
  和…一起吃晚餐
- eat (some) dinner
  吃（一點）晚餐

（和…）一起吃晚餐 「What's for dinner?」則是詢問「晚餐要吃什麼？」。

- Do you have time to **have dinner**?
- Not really. I think I must be going now.

  ●你有時間吃晚餐嗎？ ●應該沒有，我想我現在得走了。

▶ Do you have time to have dinner? 你有時間吃晚餐嗎？
  Where are you going to eat dinner? 你要去哪裡吃晚餐？

be at lunch

- before/after dinner
  晚餐前／後
- during one's lunch
  hour
  在某人的午餐時間
- on one's lunch hour
  在某人的午餐時間

在吃午餐 at lunch 指「吃午餐時」，詞性是副詞。

- Are you going to visit Danny in the hospital?
- Yes, I am going **at lunch**.

  ●你會去醫院探望 Danny 嗎？ ●會，我會在午餐時去。

▶ Our boss plans to be at lunch with us.
  我們老闆打算和我們一起吃午餐。
  Tammy is at lunch for another hour.
  Tammy 又多吃一小時的午餐。

1 職場・學校

2 電腦・網路

3 社交生活

4 日常生活

5 訊息・理解

6 想法・態度

7 情緒・狀況

8 行為舉止

9 時間地點・副詞片語

303

take sb for dinner

- take A to lunch
  帶 A 去吃午餐
- come over for dinner
  來吃晚餐
- join A for dinner
  跟 A 一起吃晚餐
- ask sb for dinner
  邀某人吃晚餐

帶某人去吃晚餐 因為是「去外面」，所以也可以說 take sb out for dinner。

- What do you want to **have for lunch**?
- How about getting a hot dog?
  ●你午餐想吃什麼？　●買熱狗怎麼樣？

▶ Where are you taking me for lunch?
  你要帶我去哪裡吃午餐？
  It's possible to go outside for lunch.
  可以去外面吃午餐。

---

22 | 吃 grab a bite

4-22.mp3

---

have + 食物 + for dinner

- What's on the menu?
  菜單上有什麼？（有什麼菜可以點？）
- have pizza for lunch
  吃披薩當午餐

吃⋯當晚餐 dinner 也可以換成 lunch 等等。

- What will mom make for us tonight?
- I think we are **having meatloaf for dinner**.
  ●媽媽今天晚上要煮什麼？　●我想我們的晚餐是美式肉餅吧。

▶ I had a big steak for dinner.
  我吃了塊大牛排當晚餐。
  She wants to have vegetables for dinner.
  她想吃蔬菜當晚餐。

have a light meal

- have a big meal
  吃大餐
- eat so much food
  吃很多食物
- have a light lunch
  吃少量的午餐

吃輕食 meal 也可以換成 dinner 或 lunch 等等。

- Can I get you a plate of food?
- Sure, I'd like to **have a light meal**.
  ●要我幫你拿盤食物嗎？　●好啊，我想吃點輕食。

▶ Curtis had a big meal at the airport.
  Curtis 在機場吃了份大餐。
  She had a light meal because she's on a diet.
  她吃了輕食，因為她正在減肥。

grab a bite

- grab some dinner
  隨便吃點晚餐
- grab sb + 食物
  幫某人買東西吃
- want a bite of A
  想吃一口 A
- get a bite to eat
  隨便找個東西吃

隨便吃點東西，充飢 匆匆忙忙、簡單吃點東西的樣子。至於 grab a (cup of) coffee 當然就是喝咖啡了。

- I feel hungry. Let's eat.
- Do you want to **grab some snacks**?
  - 我餓了，我們去吃東西吧。　●你想要隨便吃點零食嗎？

▶ Let's grab a bite to eat.
  我們隨便找點東西吃吧。
  Could you grab me a coffee when you go to the coffee shop? 你去咖啡店的時候，可以幫我帶杯咖啡嗎？

help oneself to + 食物

- want some (more)
  想要（更多）一點…
- treat oneself to
  捨得享受…（食物或衣服等）

自行隨意取用食物 招待別人吃東西時通常會說的話。

- Angela, please **help yourself to** the cake.
- I will. It looks quite delicious.
  - Angela，請自己隨意拿蛋糕吃。　●我會的，它看起來很好吃。

▶ Help yourself to the cake.
  請自行取用蛋糕。
  He helped himself to a bottle of beer.
  他自己拿了罐啤酒喝。

come and get it

- Dinner is served.
  晚餐準備好了。（管家的說法）

來吃（東西） 準備好食物要人來吃的時候會說的話。

- Everything is ready. **Come and get it.**
- This food looks like it will be good to eat.
  - 食物都準備好了。快來吃吧。　●這食物看起來很好吃。

▶ Dinner is served. Come and get it.
  晚餐準備好了，來吃吧。
  Take anything you want. Come and get it.
  你想拿什麼就拿什麼，來吃吧。

1 職場・學校
2 電腦・網路
3 社交生活
4 日常生活
5 訊息・理解
6 想法・態度
7 情緒・狀況
8 行為舉止
9 時間地點・副詞片語

23 喝
take a drink

have a drink

· get/take a drink
  喝杯酒
· have (a few) drinks
  with
  和…喝幾杯
· have a drink together
  一起喝杯酒

喝一杯 a drink 雖然也可以指水或果汁，但一般而言通常是說酒。

● I've really got to go home now.
● **Have a drink** with me before you leave.
  ●我現在真的得回家了。　●離開前陪我喝一杯。

▶ Have a drink with us after work. 下班後跟我們喝一杯。
  You're not allowed to have drinks out here.
  你不能在外面這裡喝東西。

go for a drink

· meet/come by for a
  drink
  見面／順道過來喝杯酒
· go out drinking
  出去喝酒
· buy A a drink
  請 A 喝一杯酒

去喝杯酒 booze 是酒的口語說法，喝酒則是「hit the booze」。

● How about **going out for a drink** tonight?
● Yes, let's do that.
  ●今晚要不要出去喝杯酒？　●好啊，就這麼辦。

▶ How about going out for a drink tonight?
  今晚要不要出去喝杯酒？
  What do you say to getting together for a drink?
  要不要一起去喝杯酒？

drink a lot of alcohol

· drink coffee
  喝咖啡
· drink a few beers
  喝幾杯啤酒
· don't drink
  別喝酒

喝很多酒 a lot of 換成 too much 就是「喝太多酒」。

● My uncle **drinks a lot of alcohol**.
● That sounds very unhealthy.
  ●我舅舅喝很多酒。　●聽起來非常不健康。

▶ I drank a lot of alcohol with my friends.
  我和我朋友們喝了很多酒。
  Don't let me drink too much beer. 別讓我喝太多啤酒。

get a beer

· have a few beers
  during our lunch break
  午休的時候喝幾杯啤酒
· have a nice cold beer
  喝一杯很棒的冰啤酒
· go drink some beer
  去喝些啤酒

喝啤酒 flat beer 則是放得太久而沒氣的啤酒。

● Where are you going tonight?
● I'm going to **have a beer** with Brad.
  ●你今晚要去哪？　●我要跟 Brad 喝啤酒。

▶ Did you have a beer with those guys?
  你有和那些人喝啤酒嗎？
  I feel like going for a beer. 我想去喝杯啤酒。

pour + 酒 + into one's glass

· pour sb some wine
  倒點酒給某人
· spill one's coffee (on)
  把某人的咖啡灑出來（濺在…）
· spill wine all over one's dress
  把酒灑在某人整身洋裝上

把酒倒進某人的杯子 酒可以換成其他飲料，容器也可以替換。
- Can I have some of that wine?
- Sure, **pour some into your glass**.
  ●我可以喝那瓶酒嗎？　●當然，倒一些到你的杯子吧。

▶ He poured juice into the glass.
  他把果汁倒進杯子裡。
  Please pour it into my glass.
  請把它倒進我的杯子。

have some more soda

多喝點汽水 soda 泛指汽水、可樂等碳酸飲料。
- You must be thirsty. **Have some more soda**.
- Thank you. I need to drink a lot.
  ●你一定渴了，多喝點汽水吧。　●謝謝，我需要喝很多。

▶ Have some more soda with your burger.
  多喝點汽水配你的漢堡吧。
  Have some more soda with me.
  跟我一起多喝點汽水吧。

make a toast

· Bottoms up!
  乾杯！
· Here's to…!
  為…乾杯！

敬酒 動詞 make 也可以換成 propose。後面可以加上 to sth/sb 表示敬酒的原因或對象。
- Let's **make a toast** to everyone here.
- Cheers everybody! Drink up!
  ●我們向這邊所有人敬酒吧。　●大家乾杯！一飲而盡！

▶ Everyone made a toast to the married couple.
  每個人都向那對結婚的夫妻敬酒。
  Did you make a toast to your boss?
  你有向你老闆敬酒嗎？

freshen up

· Say when
  （添酒時）夠了的話請說一聲

添酒 原意是「使…變得煥然一新」，除了指「盥洗」以外，也可以指「重新把酒添滿」。
- Can I **freshen up** your drink?
- Sure. I'm drinking cocktails tonight.
  ●要我再為您添些酒嗎？　●好，我今晚喝的是雞尾酒。

▶ The waiter will freshen up our drinks.
  服務生會把我們的酒添滿。
  Could you freshen up my tonic water?
  可以請你把我的通寧水添滿嗎？

1 職場・學校
2 電腦・網路
3 社交生活
4 日常生活
5 訊息・理解
6 想法・態度
7 情緒・狀況
8 行為舉止
9 時間地點・副詞片語

make a toast to vs. Here's to...

　　有些人會因為開心（happiness）或成功（success）等理由而提議要舉杯敬酒。這時便可使用 make a toast 這個慣用語來表達，我們也可將其中的動詞 make 替換為 propose 使用。最常見的慣用說法是「I'd like to make a toast（我想要敬酒）」，後面接 to sb (for...) 可以說明要祝賀的對象和理由。舉例來說，如果要敬林先生酒的話，可以說 I'd like to make a toast to Mr. Lin；如果要感謝 Bill 所做的一切努力，則可以說 I'd like to propose to Bill for all the hard work he's done。我們最常在美國電影或影集中聽見這句話的時候，應該是在婚禮的場景吧？例如向新婚夫妻敬酒說的「I'd like to propose to the newly married couple」，或是說「Let's have a toast to the wonderful bride」來向美麗的新娘子敬酒等。但這個表現方式通常是用在婚禮或是宴會等，比較 formal 而且有許多人聚集的場合上。若是屬於輕鬆而且小規模的聚會，一般則是使用 Cheers, Bottom up 或者 Here's to your health 的句型，說著 Here's to...（為了…）或 Let's drink to... 並乾杯。

24 | 喝醉 get drunk

4-24.mp3

drink too much

· be a heavy drinker
　是個酗酒的人
· be on the booze
　暴飲
· be off the booze
　戒酒

喝太多 drink like a fish 表示大喝特喝，喝了很多酒的樣子。

● Why does my head hurt so much today?
● You **drank too much** beer last night.

　●為什麼我今天頭那麼痛？　●你昨晚喝太多啤酒了。

▶ It's really unhealthy to drink too much.
　喝太多酒很不健康。
　He really did drink too much.
　他真的喝太多了。

get tipsy

微醺 tipsy 意為有點醉的微醺狀態。get 也可以換成 feel。

- That was the best party we ever had.
- Yeah, most of the guests **got tipsy**.
    - 那是我們舉辦過最棒的派對。　　●是啊，大部分的賓客都有點醉了。

▶ I need to go home. I feel tipsy.
   我得回家了，我覺得有點醉。
   She got tipsy after a few shots of whisky.
   喝了幾杯威士忌後，她有點醉了。

get a hangover

- relieve hangovers
  消除宿醉
- have an awful hangover
  宿醉很嚴重
- wake up with a terrible hangover
  在嚴重宿醉中起床

宿醉 「宿醉很嚴重」時，可以說「have a huge hangover」。

- I have never seen Peter drink that much.
- I bet he **has a huge hangover** today.
    - 我從來沒看 Peter 喝那麼多過。　　●我猜他今天一定宿醉得很嚴重。

▶ John got a hangover after drinking vodka.
   John 喝了伏特加後宿醉了。
   You'll get a hangover if you drink too much.
   你喝太多酒的話，會宿醉的。

get drunk

- get/feel tipsy
  微醺

喝醉 口語中常用表示「裝載」的單字 load，說「be loaded」表示「喝醉了」。

- You **seem a little drunk** tonight.
- It has been a while since I had beer.
    - 你今晚看來有點喝醉了。　　●我離上次喝啤酒已經有一陣子了。

▶ I heard you were drunk and broke a window yesterday.
   我聽說你昨天喝醉，還把一片窗戶打破了。
   How did Ted get so drunk on Friday night?
   Ted 星期五晚上怎麼會喝得那麼醉？

drink and drive

- drive drunk
  酒後駕車
- a drunk driver
  酒後駕車的人
- DUI (Driving Under the Influence)
  酒後駕車
- while under the influence
  在酒醉的狀況下

酒後駕車 名詞形是「drunk driving」。

- Why are the police stopping cars?
- They want to catch people who **drink and drive**.
    - 警察為什麼在把車子攔下來？　　●他們想要抓酒後駕車的人。

▶ The accident happened when he was drinking and driving. 事故發生在他酒後駕車的時候。
   It is illegal to drink and drive in this country.
   在這個國家，酒後駕車是違法的。

1 職場・學校
2 電腦・網路
3 社交生活
4 日常生活
5 訊息・理解
6 想法・態度
7 情緒・狀況
8 行為舉止
9 時間地點・副詞片語

25 餐廳，點餐
have the same

4-25.mp3

eat at

· eat at home
  在家吃飯

· go out to a Mexican
  restaurant
  去一間墨西哥餐廳

在…吃飯 eat in 是 eat out 的反義詞，表示「在家吃飯」。

● Would you like to go out to lunch with me?

● Sure. Do you like to **eat at** Vietnam restaurant?

　　●你想跟我一起出去吃午餐？　　●好啊，你想去越南餐廳吃飯嗎？

▶ Would you like to eat at McDonald's? 你想去吃麥當勞嗎？
  Do you like to eat at Happy Noodles?
  你喜歡去 Happy Noodles 吃飯嗎？

I'll have + 食物

我要吃… ，請給我… 在餐廳點餐時的說法，意思就是「I'd like to order…」。

● Can I get you some food to eat?

● **I'll have** a sandwich and some milk.

　　●我可以為您上些什麼菜呢？　　●我想要一份三明治和一點牛奶。

▶ I'll have a salad and a burger. 我要一份沙拉和一個漢堡。
  I'll have a steak and some potatoes.
  我要一份牛排和一些馬鈴薯。

have the special

點特餐 相對於特餐，一般的餐點稱為 regular menu。

● Do you want to **have the special**?

● No, I'm going to order something different.

　　●你想要點特餐嗎？　　●不，我要點些別的。

▶ I'll have the special with some French fries.
  我要點特餐，還有一些薯條。
  Let's have the special for lunch. 我們點特餐當午餐吧。

order the steak

· order one's food
  點某人的食物

· order a pizza
  點披薩

· take/get an order
  接受點餐

點牛排 服務員接受點餐則稱為「take/get an order」。

● **I ordered the steak** with peas.

● That sounds delicious. I want the same thing.

　　●我點了還有豌豆的牛排。　　●聽起來很好吃，我要一樣的。

▶ Order the steak. You'll love it. 點牛排，你會喜歡的。
  I didn't order the steak for breakfast.
  我沒有點牛排當早餐。

have the same

・Make it two!
　來兩份（一樣的）吧！

點一樣的　same 跟 future、Internet 一樣，前面要加冠詞 the。

● Give me some bacon and eggs.
● I'll **have the same** as you.

　●給我一些培根和蛋。　●我要和你一樣的。

▶ Do you want to have the same thing?
　你想要一樣的嗎？
　I'll have the same as she's having.
　我要和她正在吃的那個一樣的餐點。

come with

・What comes with...?
　…附有什麼？

附有⋯　come 前面的主詞是「主要的商品」。

● All of our specials **come with** a salad and dessert.
● Okay, I think I'll have special number 2, please.

　●我們所有特餐都有附一份沙拉和甜點。
　●好的，那我要點二號特餐。

▶ Does this vacation come with a free car rental?
　這個假期旅遊包套附有免費租車嗎？
　The pie comes with a scoop of ice cream.
　這個派附有一球冰淇淋。

would like steak rare

・would like steak medium
　想要牛排半熟
・How would you like + 食物？
　你想要你的⋯怎麼煮？

想要牛排三分熟　牛排有 rare, medium（半熟）, well done（全熟）等熟度，可依個人喜好來點餐。另外，形容牛排嫩可以說 tender，牛排老了則是 tough。

● How do you want your steak?
● I **would like my steak cooked medium**.

　●你的牛排要幾分熟？　●我想要半熟。

▶ Dad would like his steak rare.
　爸爸的牛排要三分熟。
　She would like her steak medium.
　她的牛排要半熟。

would you care for...?

・What would you like to order/eat?
　您想要點什麼？
・I will have the usual.
　我要點跟平常一樣的。
　（照舊）

您想要⋯嗎？　care for 在否定／疑問句中表示「喜歡」的意思。

● I would like to have a hot dog.
● **Would you care for** some mustard on it?

　●我想要一份熱狗。　●您想要在上面加些芥末嗎？

▶ Would you care for some salad dressing?
　您想要一些沙拉醬嗎？
　Would you care for some chocolate ice cream?
　您想要一些巧克力冰淇淋嗎？

1 職場・學校
2 電腦・網路
3 社交生活
4 日常生活
5 訊息・理解
6 想法・態度
7 情緒・狀況
8 行為舉止
9 時間地點・副詞片語

find a store that sells

· a place that serves...
有賣…的地方

找一間有賣…的店 在找某個特定產品時的說法。

● I need to **find a store that** sells smoked salmon.
● Try that big gourmet deli.
  ●我需要找間有賣煙燻鮭魚的店。　●去那間很大的熟食店看看。

▶ Where can I find a store that sells t-shirts?
  哪裡能找到賣 T 恤的店？
  Frank found a store that sells peanut butter.
  Frank 找到一間有賣花生醬的店。

wait on

· wait on sb
服務某人
· get waited on
得到服務
· wait on sth
等待某事

（餐廳／商店）服務… Are you waited on? 意為「有人在服務您了嗎？」

● Go **wait on** those customers.
● They aren't ready to order yet.
  ●去服務那些顧客。　●他們還沒準備好要點餐。

▶ The waitress will wait on you soon.
  女服務生很快就會服務您。
  No one came to wait on us.
  沒有人來服務我們。

26 在餐廳結帳 pay for dinner

4-26.mp3

pay for dinner

· pay the cost or bill
支付費用或帳單
· buy lunch
買午餐

付晚餐錢 支付任何東西都可以說「pay for sth」。

● Did Harry make you **pay for dinner**?
● He tried to get me to pay for it, but I refused.
  ●Harry 讓你付了晚餐錢嗎？　●他試圖讓我付，但我拒絕了。

▶ Who's going to pay for dinner?
  誰要付晚餐錢？
  Can you pay for dinner? I can't afford it.
  你可以付晚餐錢嗎？我付不起。

pick up the tab

· foot the bill
  付帳
· tip…
  給…小費
· leave a tip for
  給…小費

付帳 這邊的 tab 是指餐廳的帳單。

● Michael said that he'd **pick up the tab**.
● In that case I'll have another drink.
  ●Michael 説他會付帳。　●這樣的話，我還要再點一杯飲料。

▶ I don't have enough money to pick up the tab.
  我的錢不夠付帳。
  She picked up the tab for everyone.
  她幫所有人付了帳。

split the bill

· go Dutch
  各付各的
· go fifty-fifty with
  和…各付一半

分開結帳 當然也可以說 go Dutch。

● Let's **split the bill**.
● That sounds like a good idea.
  ●我們分開結帳吧。　●聽起來是個好主意。

▶ We split the bill among five people.
  我們五個人分開結帳。
  They split the bill for their dinner.
  他們分開付了晚餐錢。

be on sb

· It's on me.
  我請客。
· be on the house
  店老闆請客

由某人買單 主詞可以是 it 或 this one 等要買單的東西。

● This one **is on** me.
● Thanks a lot! I'll pay for lunch tomorrow.
  ●這個我來付吧。　●謝謝！明天的午餐就由我來買單。

▶ Order anything you want because it's on me.
  隨意點吧，我會買單。
  Let's go out for dinner and drinks on me.
  我們出去吃晚餐吧，我請你飲料。

be one's treat

· It's my treat.
  我請客。
· That will be my treat.
  這次由我請客。

由某人請客 treat 也可以當動詞，句型是 treat sb to sth。

● How much do we owe for the meal?
● Forget it, it's **my treat** tonight.
  ●這一餐我們要付多少？　●別在意，今晚我請客。

▶ My father says it's his treat.
  我爸爸説他請客。
  Let's go to a fancy restaurant. It's my treat.
  我們去間很棒的餐廳吧，我請客。

1 職場・學校
2 電腦・網路
3 社交生活
4 日常生活
5 訊息・理解
6 想法・態度
7 情緒・狀況
8 行為舉止
9 時間地點・副詞片語

27 外帶
For here or to go?

4-27.mp3

For here or to go?

· Is that for here or to go?
你的餐點要在這邊吃，還是要帶走？

要在這邊吃，還是帶走？ 也可以省略 For，直接說「Here or to go?」。

● Is that **for here or to go**?
● To go, please.

　●你的餐點要在這邊吃，還是要帶走？　　●我要帶走。

▶ Is your food for here or to go?
　你的餐點要在這邊吃，還是要帶走？
　I'll take it home with me. 我要帶回家。

Is this to go?

· get some food to go
買一些食物外帶
· Can I get it to go?
我可以外帶這個嗎？
· I'd like + 食物 + to go
我想要外帶…

這要外帶嗎？ 也可以說「Do you want it to go?」。

● I have your order. **Is this to go**?
● No, I'm going to sit down and eat.

　●您的點餐已完成，您是要外帶嗎？　　●不，我要坐在這裡吃。

▶ Is this to go home with you? 您的餐點要外帶回家嗎？
　Your food is ready. Is this to go?
　您的餐點已經好了，要外帶嗎？

have + 食物 + delivered

· take-out food
外帶的食物

讓食物被外送 後面接 to... 可以表示外送的地點或對象。

● What food are you having at the party?
● We're **having pizza delivered** to my house.

　●你們在派對上要吃什麼？　　●我們會叫披薩外送到我家。

▶ Let's have some Chinese food delivered.
　我們叫一些中式料理的外送吧。
　Ben had his groceries delivered.
　Ben 叫人把他買的食品雜貨送到家。

pick up

· pick up some food for dinner
買點食物當晚餐吃
· bring some food home
帶點食物回家

買（食物） 去超市買生活用品、食物稱為「grocery shopping」。

● Can you **pick up** dinner on the way home?
● I'm sorry, I don't have time to get it.

　●你回家的路上可以買晚餐嗎？　　●抱歉，我沒有時間去買。

▶ Pick up some snacks for us to eat. 去買點零食來給我們吃。
　I'm going to pick up a coffee, do you want one?
　我要去買杯咖啡，你要嗎？

get doggie bag

- ask for a doggie bag
  要求打包
- leftover
  剩下的食物

打包剩下的食物 brown bag 則是指帶出門吃的午餐，因為歐美人士通常會裝在棕色的紙袋裡。

- Could we **have a doggie bag**?
- Sure. Do you want all of it put in the doggie bag?

  ●我們可以打包嗎？　●當然可以，你們想要全部都打包嗎？

▶ I got a doggie bag for the leftover food.
  我把剩下的食物打包。
  Get a doggie bag from our waitress.
  從我們的女服務生那邊拿打包的食物。

---

28 食慾
be full

4-28.mp3

---

feel hungry

- be starving
  餓扁了

覺得餓 I could eat a horse 是表示「非常餓」的口語說法。

- I'm so hungry I could eat a horse.
- Let me buy you dinner. You've been working so hard these days.

  ●我餓到可以吃掉一頭牛。
  ●我請你吃晚餐吧，你最近工作很辛苦。

▶ It's just that I'm not hungry right now.
  只是我現在真的不餓。
  You must have been hungry.
  你一定餓了。

be full

- be stuffed
  很撐
- have enough
  吃得夠多了

飽了 吃了太多，再也吃不下的意思。

- How about something for dessert?
- I am too full to eat anything else.

  ●要不要吃點什麼當甜點？　●我太飽了，沒辦法再吃任何東西。

▶ John was full after eating at the buffet.
  John 吃完自助餐以後很飽。
  Gerry is full and wants to lie down.
  Gerry 很飽，想要躺下。

1 職場・學校
2 電腦・網路
3 社交生活
4 日常生活
5 訊息・理解
6 想法・態度
7 情緒・狀況
8 行為舉止
9 時間地點・副詞片語

have good appetite

- not have much of an appetite
  沒什麼食慾
- not have any appetite
  沒有任何食慾
- lose one's appetite
  失去食慾

胃口好 表示自己在流口水，可以說「My mouth waters / is watering」。

- My son is always eating something.
- Yes, he **has a very good appetite**.
  - ●我兒子總是在吃東西。　●是啊，他的胃口非常好。

▶ I have a good appetite and want to eat.
我胃口很好，想要吃東西。
Gina never has a good appetite.
Gina 的胃口總是不好。

look delicious

看起來很美味 tasty 和 yummy 也都是表達「美味」的詞彙。

- The wedding cake **looks absolutely delicious**!
- I am dying for a piece.
  - ●這個結婚蛋糕看起來絕對很好吃！　●我超想吃一塊。

▶ These cookies look delicious.
這些餅乾看起來很好吃。
Everything in the bakery looks delicious.
這間麵包店的所有東西看起來都很好吃。

taste good

- taste bitter
  嚐起來苦苦的
- taste the same
  嚐起來一樣
- taste like
  嚐起來像…

好吃 東西十分好吃，彷彿在口中融化開來的樣子，可以用「melt in one's mouth」來表達。

- Does seaweed **taste good**?
- Some people like its flavor.
  - ●紫菜好吃嗎？　●有些人喜歡它的味道。

▶ The chocolate ice cream tastes good.
巧克力冰淇淋很好吃。
This old rice does not taste good.
這些放太久的米不好吃。

29 | 烹飪 cook dinner

4-29.mp3

1 職場・學校
2 電腦・網路
3 社交生活
4 日常生活
5 訊息・理解
6 想法・態度
7 情緒・狀況
8 行為舉止
9 時間地點・副詞片語

cook dinner

- cook a meal
  煮飯
- cook breakfast
  做早餐
- cook Korean food
  做韓國料理

做晚餐 cook 後面可以接三餐、餐點、食材當受詞。
- How will we get something to eat?
- Mom is going to **cook dinner** for everyone.
  - 我們該怎麼解決晚餐？ ● 媽媽會煮晚餐給大家吃。
- ▶ I need to cook dinner before it gets late.
  我得趁天色變暗前煮晚餐。
  Jane loves to cook Italian food. Jane 喜歡做義式料理。

cook something for dinner

- cook rice for dinner
  為了晚餐而煮飯

煮點東西當晚餐吃 也可以換成其他名詞，指明煮的東西。
- What are you doing in the kitchen?
- I'm going to **cook something for dinner**.
  - 你在廚房裡做什麼？ ● 我要煮點東西當晚餐吃。
- ▶ Please cook something for my dinner.
  請煮點東西給我當晚餐。
  She'll cook something for lunch soon.
  她很快就會去煮點東西當午餐。

cook sth for

- cook sb sth
  煮某種東西給某人吃
- cook sb lunch
  做午餐給某人吃

為了…煮某樣東西 cook 是指「用火烹調料理」，所以受詞不能是沒有加熱的食物。例如做壽司是 make the sushi。
- My father-in-law is coming over today.
- You should **cook dinner** for him.
  - 我的岳父今天會過來。 ● 你應該煮晚餐給他吃。
- ▶ I cooked spaghetti for Sunny. 我煮了義大利麵給 Sunny 吃。
  She cooked treats for all of her friends.
  她煮菜款待她所有的朋友們。

make dinner for...

- make some food
  煮些食物
- make (A) some breakfast
  做些早餐（給 A 吃）
- make some coffee for...
  煮點咖啡給…喝

做晚餐給…吃 make 這個動詞可以表示製作、準備食物或飲料。
- Well, I must be off. Got to **make dinner for** the kids.
- What are you making tonight?
  - 嗯，我得走了，要去做晚餐給孩子們吃。 ● 你今晚要煮什麼？
- ▶ It's time to make dinner for the guests.
  該是做晚餐給客人們吃的時候了。
  We can make dinner for Jason. 我們可以做晚餐給 Jason 吃。

317

fix sb sth

· fix dinner
  準備晚餐
· fix oneself + 食物
  做…來吃

幫某人準備某樣東西 fix 有多種涵義，在口語裡也有「準備餐點或飲料」的意思。

● Kevin is waiting in the living room.
● **Fix** him some coffee while he waits.
  ●Kevin 在客廳裡等著。　●在他等待的時候，幫他準備點咖啡。

▶ I'm going to fix myself a drink.
  我要幫自己弄杯飲料來喝。
  You should fix them some coffee.
  你該幫他們準備點咖啡。

---

30 各種烹飪法
boil the stew

4-30.mp3

---

roast

· roast the chicken
  烤雞
· bake a cake
  烤蛋糕（bake 是指用烤箱烤糕點）
· bake better cookies
  烤出更好的餅乾

烤…，炙… 用火或烤爐來烤肉類或蔬菜的方法。

● Why is everyone so busy in the kitchen?
● We're going to **roast** a turkey today.
  ●為什麼每個人都在廚房那麼忙？　●我們今天要烤一隻火雞。

▶ I love to roast nice pieces of meat.
  我喜歡烤上等的肉片。
  Have some of my fresh baked cookies.
  吃點我剛烤好的餅乾吧。

boil the stew

· boil water
  將水煮沸
· steam the vegetables
  蒸蔬菜

燉煮食物 boil 是用沸水去煮，steam 則是用熱蒸氣去蒸。

● We had to **boil the stew** all night.
● I'll bet it will taste great.
  ●我們得燉一整晚。　●我想那一定會很好吃。

▶ Boil the stew so it's ready to eat.
  把菜燉一燉，準備開動了。
  She boiled the stew for several hours.
  她把菜燉煮了幾個小時。

knead the dough

· knead the dough
　揉麵團
· mix the batter
　攪勻麵糊

揉麵團 注意 knead 的「k」不發音，而 dough 的發音是 [do]。

● You have big muscles in your arms.
● That's because I **knead dough** all day long.
　● 你的手臂肌肉很大。　● 那是因為我整天都在揉麵團。

▶ Knead the dough before baking the bread.
　在烤麵包前，先揉麵團。
　You must knead the dough for ten minutes.
　你必須揉麵團揉十分鐘。

grill meat

· grill the bacon
　烤培根
· grill chicken
　烤雞

烤肉 grill 是把魚或肉放在鐵網上，用火直接烤的烹調方式。

● Let's **grill hamburgers** for dinner tonight.
● That sounds like a great idea.
　● 我們今晚烤漢堡當晚餐吃吧。　● 聽起來是個好主意。

▶ Our neighbors grill steaks every weekend.
　我們的鄰居每個週末都會烤牛排。
　Let's grill some salmon to eat.
　我們烤點鮭魚吃吧。

slice the meat

· stir
　攪拌
· chopping board
　砧板

將肉切片 slice 是切成薄片，chop 則是切碎。

● Can I help you make dinner?
● Sure. **Slice the meat** on the counter.
　● 我可以幫你做晚餐嗎？　● 當然可以，把長桌子上的肉切片吧。

▶ Slice the ham for our sandwiches.
　把火腿切片，做我們的三明治。
　You have to slice the meat for us.
　你得幫我們把肉切片。

1 職場・學校
2 電腦・網路
3 社交生活
4 日常生活
5 訊息・理解
6 想法・態度
7 情緒・狀況
8 行為舉止
9 時間地點・副詞片語

31 抽菸 give up smoking

4-31.mp3

smoke a cigarette

· have a smoke
  抽菸
· second-hand smoking
  二手菸

抽菸 chain smoking 是「抽個不停」，heavy smoking 則是「抽很多菸」。

● I forgot that he **smokes cigarettes**.
● I'll ask him to smoke outside.
  ●我忘了他抽菸。　●我會叫他去外面抽。

▶ I'm going outside to smoke a cigarette. 我要去外面抽根菸。
  You're not allowed to smoke in restaurants.
  你不可以在餐廳裡吸菸。

light a cigarette

· borrow one's lighter
  借某人的打火機

點燃香菸 把菸熄掉是 put out，把菸蒂揉成一團熄滅是 stub out。

● Can you **light a cigarette** for me?
● I'm sorry, but I have no lighter.
  ●你可以幫我點菸嗎？　●抱歉，但我沒有打火機。

▶ Let me light a cigarette first. 讓我先點根菸。
  She lit a cigarette in the bathroom. 她在廁所點了根菸。

smoke heavily

· be addicted to
  smoking
  對抽菸上癮
· chain smoker
  抽菸抽個不停的人

抽很多菸 a light smoker 是指菸抽得不多的人。

● Why does this office smell so bad?
● One of my co-workers **smokes heavily**.
  ●為什麼這辦公室的空氣這麼糟？　●我有一位同事抽很多菸。

▶ Dave got cancer because he smoked heavily.
  Dave 因為抽很多菸，得了癌症。

▶ If you smoke heavily, you'll be unhealthy.
  如果你抽很多菸，你會變得不健康。

cut down on smoking

· reduce smoking
  減少抽菸

減少抽菸的量或次數 cut down 後面可以接想要降低或減少的東西，例如 drinking, expenses, fat 等等。

● I can't run as fast as I used to.
● Try to **cut down on** your smoking.
  ●我沒辦法跑得像以前一樣快了。　●試著少抽點菸。

▶ Phil cut down on smoking because of the cost.
  Phil 因為想省錢，所以減少了抽菸的量。
  The doctor said to cut down on smoking.
  醫生說要少抽點菸。

give up smoking

- stop/quit smoking
戒煙

戒菸　stop smoking 也是「戒菸」，stop to smoke 則是「為了抽菸而停止（走路或手邊的事等）」。

- Wow, Tom, you look really good.
- I **gave up smoking** about a year ago.
  - ●哇，Tom，你看起來氣色很好。　　●我大約一年前戒了菸。

▶ You have to stop smoking. It is going to kill you some day. 你得戒菸，它總有一天會要了你的命。
She helped many people quit smoking.
她幫助很多人戒了菸。

---

32 度假
go on a vacation

4-32.mp3

---

take a vacation

- get a vacation
取得假期
- look forward to a vacation
期待假期
- take a holiday and go to…
取得休假去…

度假　take a leave of absence 則是「請假」的意思。

- I'm **looking forward to** our **vacation**.
- We should have a great time.
  - ●我很期待我們的假期。　　●我們會玩得很開心的。

▶ Why don't you go to Thailand for your vacation?
你為什麼不去泰國度假呢？
I can't wait for my vacation to begin.
我等不及假期開始了。

go on a vacation

- go on a vacation with…
和…一起度假
- go on a holiday
去度假
- be here on a vacation
在這裡度假

度假　vacation 也可以換成 holiday，表示比較短的假日。

- Shall we **go on a vacation** together?
- I'm not sure. Let's talk about it.
  - ●我們該一起去度假嗎？　　●我不確定，來討論一下吧。

▶ You'll be sorry if you don't come on a vacation with me.
你如果不跟我一起去度假，你會後悔的。
I'm thinking of going on a vacation.
我正在考慮要去度假。

1 職場・學校
2 電腦・網路
3 社交生活
4 日常生活
5 訊息・理解
6 想法・態度
7 情緒・狀況
8 行為舉止
9 時間地點・副詞片語

go away (for + 時間)

· be away on (a)
  vacation/leave
  在休假

不在（一段時間） go away 可以表示離開到外地超過一天。

● Hello, is Mr. Jones in the office?

● No, he's **away on a vacation**.

    ●嗨，Jones 先生在辦公室嗎？   ●不，他去度假了。

▶ Let's go away for a few days.

    我們離開幾天吧。

    We went away during the winter break.

    我們在寒假時，離開了一陣子。

join sb on vacation

· meet sb while I was
  vacationing in + 地點
  當我在…度假時，我遇見
  某人

和某人一起度假 另外，口語中的 tag along 則是指雖然沒被邀請，還是跟著參加的行為。

● When will you see Tim and Trish?

● We'll **join them on their vacation**.

    ●你們什麼時候會見到 Tim 和 Trish？   ●我們會跟他們一起去度假。

▶ The students joined the teacher on a vacation.

    學生們和老師一起去度假。

    We'll join another family on a vacation.

    我們會跟另一個家庭一起去度假。

be on leave

· be on vacation/holiday
  休假中

· during one's vacation
  在某人休假期間

休假中 產假稱為 maternity leave 或 maternal leave。

● I saw Jim working in the office today.

● That's weird. He is supposed to **be on a vacation**.

    ●我今天看到 Jim 在辦公室工作。   ●真奇怪，他應該在休假的。

▶ I'll take care of your dog when you're on vacation.

    你去度假的時候，我會照顧你的狗。

    I met Herman when he was on leave.

    我在 Herman 休假的時候見到他了。

33 休息
take a break

4-33.mp3

take a break

- take a ten-minute break
  休息十分鐘
- take a coffee break
  喝個咖啡休息一下
- need a break
  需要休息一下

after a break

- after a short break
  短暫休息一下之後
- during the school break
  在學校放假期間

have/take...off

- take/get time off
  休息
- take the rest of the day off
  一天中剩下的工作時間都請假
- on one's days off
  在某人的休假日

be off

休息一下 由於一般通常會休息個五分鐘，所以 take five 同樣也有「休息一下」的意思。

- Shall we **take a break** now?
- No, let's keep going.
  - 我們現在要不要休息一下？　●不行，我們繼續走吧。

▶ Why don't you take a break? 你為什麼不休息一下？
Take a break from your work. 從工作中休息一下。

休息一下之後 短暫休息的時間稱為 break time。

- The concert will continue **after a break**.
- Let's stand up for a few minutes.
  - 演唱會會在休息一下之後繼續。　●我們站個幾分鐘吧。

▶ We'll return to classes after a break.
我們休息一下再回來上課。
The TV show will be on after a break.
電視節目會在廣告休息時間後開始。

休假 表示「休息一段時間」的意思。

- Why don't you **take** the rest of the day **off** and go home?
- God bless you!
  - 你為什麼不現在直接請假回家呢？　●保重！

▶ Will he have the Christmas holiday off?
他耶誕節會放假嗎？
I have the whole week off. 我整個星期都休假。

休假，不上班 be on duty 則是在執勤、在上班的意思。

- I see your brother is around these days.
- He **is off** from school until January.
  - 我最近常看到你哥哥。　●他一直到一月都不用去學校。

▶ They are off from work today. 他們今天不上班。
I am off until later this afternoon. 我到今天下午前都在休假。

323

get some rest

· take a rest
  休息一下
· take time to relax
  花時間放鬆
· kill time
  殺時間

休息一下 如果看到很累的人，就可以這樣對他們說。

- It's getting to be pretty late.
- I'm going upstairs to **get some rest**.
  - ●時間很晚了。　●我要上樓休息一下。

▶ Go home and get some rest. 回家休息一下。
  I'll take a nap and get some rest.
  我要睡個午覺，休息一下。

---

34 | 去旅行 take a trip

4-34.mp3

---

go travel

去旅行 「go and V」省略 and 的說法，意思和 go traveling 一樣。

- I'm itching to **go travelling** again.
- When was the last time you went travelling?
  - ●我又心癢癢想去旅行了。　●你上次去旅行是什麼時候？

▶ She'll go travel after she graduates. 她畢業之後會去旅行。
  I want to go travel around Europe. 我想要環遊歐洲。

travel to...

· travel with a tour
  group
  跟旅行團一起旅行
· travel here from China
  從中國來這裡旅行
· travel overseas on
  vacation
  休假時去海外旅行

去…旅行 to 後面接目的地，也可以加 with 接一起旅行的人。

- How was your summer vacation?
- Great! We **traveled to** five countries in Europe.
  - ●你的暑假過得怎樣？　●很棒！我們去歐洲五個國家旅行。

▶ I love to travel to other countries on my vacations.
  我喜歡在休假時去別的國家旅行。
  He is excited to travel overseas.
  他很興奮要去海外旅行。

travel around

· travel around the
  world
  環遊世界
· travel all over the
  world
  環遊世界

環遊…，遊遍… 環遊全世界就是 around the world。

- Have you **traveled around** the US?
- No, I spent most of my time in New York.
  - ●你有遊遍美國嗎？　●沒有，我大部分的時間都待在紐約。

▶ You should travel around the country. 你應該環遊國內一周。
  Sam promised to travel around Asia. Sam 答應了要環遊亞洲。

go on a trip to

· go on a journey
  去旅行
· take off on a trip
  去旅行

去…旅行　go on a business trip 是「出差」，go on a honeymoon 則是「去度蜜月」。

● Where do you want to visit most?
● I want to **go on a trip to** Australia.
  ●你最想去什麼地方？　●我想去澳洲旅行。

▶ The class went on a trip to the zoo.
  這個班級去動物園旅遊。
  Our family went on a trip to Sweden.
  我們家去瑞典旅遊。

take a trip to/around

· take a one-day trip
  去一日遊
· take a trip around the
  world
  環遊世界
· be on a group tour
  跟團旅遊

去…旅行　後面接旅行的目的地。

● Let's **take a trip around** Italy.
● Won't that be really expensive?
  ●我們去義大利玩一趟吧。　●不會很貴嗎？

▶ I took a trip around Greece last year.
  我去年環遊了希臘。
  The girls took a trip to the beach.
  女孩們去海邊旅遊。

start the trip

· plan the trip
  計畫旅行

開始旅行　在口語中，hit the road 也可以表示開始旅行。

● Have you planned your vacation yet?
● Yeah, we'll **start the trip** in London.
  ●你們計畫好你們的假期了嗎？　●嗯，我們會從倫敦開始旅行。

▶ Wendy started the trip early in the morning.
  Wendy 今天早上很早的時候啟程了。
  You can't start the trip without money.
  你沒有錢就不能去旅行。

set off for

出發去…　表示「出發」的說法還有 begin a journey 和 start off。

● Are you all ready to begin your vacation?
● Sure. I'll **set off for** Hawaii soon.
  ●你們都準備好要開始放假了嗎？
  ●當然，我馬上要動身去夏威夷了。

▶ Her mom set off for the high school.
  她媽媽出發前往那所高中。
  Each person set off for a different place.
  每個人都各自動身前往不同的地方。

1 職場・學校
2 電腦・網路
3 社交生活
4 日常生活
5 訊息・理解
6 想法・態度
7 情緒・狀況
8 行為舉止
9 時間地點・副詞片語

leave on a long trip

- come along on the trip
  去旅行
- leave on a trip
  overseas
  動身去海外旅行

去旅行很長一段時間 road trip 也是長期旅行，但特別用在坐車旅行的情況。

- Bill has got five suitcases with him.
- He's going to **leave on a long trip** tomorrow.

  ●Bill 帶了五個行李箱。　●他明天要開始一趟長期旅行。

▶ Clancey left on a long trip last month.

  Clancey 上個月開始了一趟長期旅行。

  We'll leave on a long trip as soon as possible.

  我們會盡快開始一趟長期旅行。

show sb around

- guide sb around…
  帶某人參觀…的周遭

帶某人到處逛逛 around 後面可以接要逛的地方。

- I grew up in Los Angeles.
- Could you **show me around** the city?

  ●我是在洛杉磯長大的。　●你可以帶我逛逛這個城市嗎？

▶ The kind man showed me around.

  那個親切的男人帶我到處逛。

  I can show you around this place.

  我可以帶你逛這個地方。

do some camping

- camp in the woods
  在樹林中露營
- be on a camping trip
  去露營旅行
- go backpacking
  帶背包旅行

去露個營 「露營」一般的說法是 go camping。

- Where are you off to this weekend?
- We're going to **do some camping** in the
  mountains.

  ●你們這週末要去哪裡？　●我們要去山上露個營。

▶ You can do some camping this spring.

  你可以在今年春天去露個營。

  Norman did some camping with his friends.

  Norman 和他的朋友們去露了營。

35 玩樂
hang out

4-35.mp3

1 職場・學校

2 電腦・網路

3 社交生活

4 日常生活

5 訊息・理解

6 想法・態度

7 情緒・狀況

8 行為舉止

9 時間地點・副詞片語

hang out (with)

· hang around with
和…一起消磨時間

（和…）度過／消磨時間　表示不特別去做什麼事情，一起打發時間。

● What did you do Saturday night?

● I **hung out with** an old friend of mine.

　● 你星期六晚上做了什麼？　● 我和一位老朋友打發時間。

▶ Stay a little longer and hang out with me.
再待久一點，和我一起玩。

Do you know of any cool places to hang out?
你知道什麼不錯的地方可以打發時間的嗎？

enjoy -ing/N

很享受…，…很開心　enjoy 後面接動詞 ing 形或名詞。

● Did you **enjoy walking** around today?

● Yes, but I'd like a guide tomorrow.

　● 你今天四處漫步還開心嗎？　● 嗯，但我明天想要有個導遊。

▶ I enjoyed talking with you. 和你談話我很開心。

Enjoy your stay in Chicago. 在芝加哥玩得開心點。

enjoy oneself very much

· enjoy oneself at the concert
很享受演唱會，看得很開心

過得很開心　表示因為餐點、電影或假期而過得很開心。

● How did you like the new restaurant?

● We **enjoyed ourselves very much** there.

　● 你覺得那間新餐廳怎麼樣？　● 我們很喜歡那邊。

▶ It's high time we took a vacation and enjoyed ourselves.
我們抓緊時機請了假，並且玩得十分開心。

I hope you enjoy yourself today. 我希望你今天玩得開心。

have fun

· have a little bit of fun
過得有點開心

· sound like a lot of fun to
去做…聽起來非常有趣

玩得開心　也可以加上 a lot of 或 much 強調「玩得很開心」。

● Oh boy, we're going to **have fun** tonight!

● What are you guys doing?

　● 噢，我們今晚將會玩得非常開心！　● 你們要做什麼？

▶ I want you to feel free to have fun while you're on vacation. 我希望你在假期中盡量玩得開心。

I'd rather have fun than save money.
比起省錢，我寧可過得開心。

be fun -ing

- be fun to do
  做某事很有趣
- be (just) for fun
  （只是）為了好玩
- be a fun time (for)
  （對某人而言）很有趣

做某事很有趣 fun 後面可以接 to do 或 -ing。

- It **was really fun** attending the school reunion.
- Now I wish I had gone with you.
  - 參加同學會真是太有趣了。　● 現在我真希望我有跟你一起去。

▶ It was fun playing basketball today. 今天打籃球很開心。
  It is fun riding bikes to school. 騎腳踏車上學很有趣。

have a good time (at)

- have a nice day
  擁有愉快的一天
- have a great time
  with...
  和…一起度過很開心的時光
- have a good time at
  the musical
  看音樂劇度過開心的時光

（在…）過得很開心 「Have a good time!」是「玩得愉快！」的意思，也可以說「Have a good one!」或「Have a nice day!」。

- Sandy is back from her date.
- I wonder if she **had a good time**.
  - Sandy 約會回來了。　● 我想知道她是否玩得開心。

▶ I wonder if she had a good time. 我想知道她是否玩得開心。
  You'll have a good time at the nightclub.
  你在夜店會玩得很開心的。

fool around (with...)

- goof around
  消磨時間
- » cf. goof off
  沒有事情做，遊手好閒的人；摸魚打混的人

遊手好閒，亂搞 mess with 也是一樣的意思。

- Who was making all of that noise?
- Some kids **were fooling around** with each other.
  - 誰在製造那些噪音？　● 有些孩子在互鬧對方。

▶ Don't fool around with my car. 別亂玩我的車。
  I'm going to fool around with this computer.
  我要來玩這台電腦。

waste time

- screw around
  遊手好閒

浪費時間 後面可以接動名詞表示浪費時間做什麼事。

- Shall we drive up to Seoul?
- Let's fly. I don't want to **waste time**.
  - 我們應該開車上首爾嗎？　● 我們坐飛機吧。我不想浪費時間。

▶ You shouldn't waste time watching TV.
  你不該浪費時間看電視。
  Kara always wastes time in the morning.
  Kara 早上總是浪費時間。

take sb on a picnic

- go on/for a picnic
  去野餐
- have a picnic + 地方副詞片語
  在…野餐

帶某人去野餐 「去野餐」可以說「go on a picnic」。

- Have you planned any activities for your mom?
- I think I'll **take her on a picnic**.
  - 你有幫你媽媽計畫什麼活動嗎？　● 我想我會帶她去野餐。

▶ Let's take everyone on a picnic! 我們帶所有人去野餐吧！
  Mr. Park took us on a picnic. Park 先生帶我們去野餐。

live it up

- have a blast with
  和…玩得十分開心

花錢盡情享受生活 可以單獨使用，或加上 at 或 in 接場合。

- Should I go on a date with Pierre?
- **Live it up.** Go have fun with him.
  - ●我該跟 Pierre 去約會嗎？　●要享受人生呀！跟他去玩個開心吧。

▶ We decided to live it up at the casino.
  我們決定在賭場盡情享樂。
  Did you live it up at your birthday party?
  你在自己的生日派對上玩得痛快嗎？

1 職場・學校
2 電腦・網路
3 社交生活
4 日常生活
5 訊息・理解
6 想法・態度
7 情緒・狀況
8 行為舉止
9 時間地點・副詞片語

36 看電視或電影
watch a movie

4-36.mp3

watch a movie

- watch action movies
  看動作片
- watch the sports
  channel on TV
  看電視上的體育頻道
- watch baseball games
  看棒球比賽

看電影 在口語中，watch 也可以換成 catch 來說，意思一樣。

- I can't **watch a movie** without popcorn.
- Don't be so picky.
  - ●我看電影不能沒有爆米花。　●別挑剔了。

▶ We went to watch a movie at the shopping mall.
  我們去購物中心看電影。
  Would you like to go watch a movie?
  你想去看個電影嗎？

see a new movie

- see a movie tonight
  今晚看部電影

看一部新電影 watch 是集中注意力去觀看，see 則是指「看到」。所以 see a movie 通常單純指「看電影這件事」或「看電影的經驗」。

- Shall we watch something on TV?
- No, I want to **see a new movie.**
  - ●我們要不要看點電視？　●不要，我想看一部新電影。

▶ They went out to see a new movie.
  他們出去看一部新電影。
  Did you ever see the movie "The Fan?"
  你有看過《The Fan》這部電影嗎？

329

go to a movie

- go to a cinema
  去電影院（看電影）
- get to the movie theater
  去電影院

去看電影 用單數形，但冠詞如果改成 the，就要用複數形 the movies。

- Why don't we **go to the movies** tonight?
- Why don't you get lost?
  ●我們今晚何不去看電影呢？　●你怎麼不滾開？

▶ How about we go to a movie tonight?
  我們今晚去看個電影怎樣？
  How often do you go to the movies?
  你多久去看一次電影？

listen to music

- listen to music on a cell phone
  用手機聽音樂
- listen to music with headphones
  用耳機聽音樂
- listen to classical music
  聽古典樂

聽音樂 hear 是「聽到」，listen to 才能表示集中注意力去聽。

- Did you come here to dance?
- No, I just came to **listen to music**.
  ●你來這邊跳舞的嗎？　●不，我只是來聽音樂的。

▶ The audience sat down to listen to music.
  觀眾們坐下來聽音樂。
  I would listen to music when I rode the subway.
  我搭地鐵時會聽音樂。

turn A off

- turn off the light
  關燈
- turn the TV off
  關電視
- turn A on
  打開 A

把 A 關掉 表示關掉電視、電器或瓦斯。「打開」則是 turn on。

- I'm going to bed in a while.
- **Turn the lights off** when you do.
  ●我等等要去睡了。　●你去睡的時候把燈關掉。

▶ It's okay to turn off the radio.
  關掉廣播沒關係。
  I'm not sure how to turn on this phone.
  我不太確定該怎麼把這電話打開。

turn A up

- turn A down
  把 A 的音量調小

把 A 的音量調大 把音量調小則是說 turn down。

- I can't hear the television.
- **Turn the volume up** a little.
  ●我聽不到電視的聲音。　●把音量調大一點。

▶ Turn the heat up before it gets cold.
  在變冷之前，把暖氣溫度調高吧。
  Turn the radio up so we can dance.
  把廣播的聲音調大，我們才能跳舞。

tune in

- stay in tune
  鎖定頻道不轉台
- put on some dance music
  播放一些舞曲

將廣播或電視轉到某個頻道 後面可以加上 to 接頻道或節目。

- What are your plans this evening?
- I'm going to **tune in** to my favorite show.
  - 你今晚的計畫是什麼？　● 我要看我最愛的電視節目。

▶ Are you going to tune in to the program?
  你要轉到那個節目去嗎？
  You should tune in and watch it.
  你應該轉到那個頻道並且觀看它。

hit play

- hit pause
  按暫停鍵
- push the power button on the remote control
  按遙控器上的電源鍵
- surf the channel
  一直轉台

按播放鍵 因為按遙控器的時候燈號會閃爍，所以遙控器（remote control）又稱為 flicker。

- How can I start the DVD player?
- **Hit play** on the front panel.
  - 我該怎麼啟動 DVD 播放器？　● 按一下前面面板的播放鍵。

▶ It didn't start because you didn't hit play.
  因為你沒有按播放鍵，所以它沒有開始。
  Hit play on the CD player and the music will come on.
  按下 CD 播放器上的播放鍵，音樂就會開始播放了。

get a ticket

- get a ticket for the concert
  買演唱會的票
- get tickets
  買票
- get good seat
  買到好位子（的票）

買票 後面接 for 和表演或比賽的名稱，可以說明是哪種票。

- I **got a ticket** for the Lakers game.
- Let's go to the game together.
  - 我買了張湖人隊球賽的票。　● 我們一起去看比賽吧。

▶ Did you get a ticket for the flight?
  你買了機票嗎？
  Laura got a ticket for the concert.
  Laura 買了演唱會的票。

have an exhibit

- exhibit pictures
  展覽圖畫
- exhibit works of art
  展覽藝術品

有展覽 exhibit 也很常當動詞用，意為「展示」。

- Why are you going to the museum?
- It **has an exhibit** with items from the Titanic.
  - 你為什麼要去博物館？　● 那邊有鐵達尼號的物品展覽。

▶ The school had an exhibit with student art.
  學校辦了學生的藝術作品展覽。
  Our gallery has an exhibit with famous photos.
  我們的畫廊有一場展出知名照片的展覽。

1 職場・學校
2 電腦・網路
3 社交生活
4 日常生活
5 訊息・理解
6 想法・態度
7 情緒・狀況
8 行為舉止
9 時間地點・副詞片語

37 | 開派對 have a party

have a party

· have a farewell/going-away party
開歡送派對
· have a party at one's house
在某人家裡開派對
· have a barbecue party
開烤肉派對

開派對 後面可以接 with sb 說明一起開派對的人，接 for sb 則表示是為誰開的。

● **I'm having a party** tonight. Can you come?
● I'm sorry, I can't. I have to study for my exams.
　●我今晚要開派對，你能來嗎？　●抱歉不行，我得讀書準備考試。

▶ We're having a party for Tom. Hope you can make it.
　我們要幫 Tom 開個派對，希望你能來。
　He might have a party at home.
　他可能會在家開派對。

hold a party

· host a housewarming party
主辦喬遷宴
· host the party
主辦派對

舉辦派對 potluck 則是指每個人分享一道菜的派對。

● We'll **hold a party** for everyone on Friday.
● Can I bring my boyfriend to it?
　●我們星期五會為所有人舉辦一場派對。　●我可以帶我男朋友去嗎？

▶ When will you hold a party for your mom?
　你什麼時候會為你媽媽舉辦派對？
　It takes a large place to hold a party.
　舉辦派對要有很大的場地。

throw a party

舉辦派對 give a party 也是一樣的意思。

● I'm going to **throw a party** this Friday.
● We have a test on Monday. I wonder how many people will come.
　●我這禮拜五要辦一場派對。
　●我們星期一有個考試，我不知道有多少人會來。

▶ Shouldn't we give a party for him?
　我們不該幫他辦個派對嗎？
　Helen threw a party in her new apartment.
　Helen 在她的新公寓辦了派對。

organize a party

· organize the staff
  party
  準備員工派對
· plan a surprise party
  計畫一場驚喜派對

準備派對 動詞 organize 也可以換成 arrange。

● Can you help **organize a surprise party** for Helen?
● Sure. When do you want to have it?
  ●你可以幫忙準備為 Helen 辦的驚喜派對嗎？
  ●當然，你打算哪時候辦？

▶ The class is organizing a surprise party for Mr.
  Thompson. 這個班級正在為 Thompson 老師準備驚喜派對。
  Jack organized a surprise party for his best friend.
  Jack 為了他最好的朋友準備了一場驚喜派對。

go to the party

· go to the festival
  去參加慶祝活動
· leave the party
  離開派對

去參加派對 明明沒被邀請，卻闖進去當不速之客，則稱為 crash
a party。

● **Are** you **going to the party** tomorrow night?
● If Scott goes, I'll go too.
  ●你會去明天晚上的派對嗎？　●如果 Scott 去的話，我也會去。

▶ Hey Bob, do you feel like going to a party?
  嘿，Bob，你想去個派對嗎？
  I went to a party last night.
  我參加了一場派對。

come to the party

· come with A to the
  party
  跟 A 一起來參加派對

來參加派對 在派對上一定會有些掃興的人，這種人稱為
partypooper。

● I need to know whether you're **coming to the
  party**.
● I'm still not sure.
  ●我得知道你會不會來參加派對。　●我還是不確定。

▶ How many people came to the party?
  有多少人來參加派對？
  Are you coming to the party tonight?
  你今晚會來參加派對嗎？

attend one's party

· attend one's wedding
  參加某人的婚禮
· meet at a party
  在派對上見面或認識

參加某人的派對 attend 除了表示參加會議，也可以表示參加派
對，語感比較正式。

● How did you two get together?
● We **met at a party** in California.
  ●你們倆怎麼在一起的？　●我們是在加州的一場派對碰面的。

▶ Didn't we meet at a party a few years ago?
  我們幾年前是不是在一場派對見過面？
  I can't attend your party on Wednesday night.
  我無法參加你星期三晚上的派對。

1 職場·學校
2 電腦·網路
3 社交生活
4 日常生活
5 訊息·理解
6 想法·態度
7 情緒·狀況
8 行為舉止
9 時間地點·副詞片語

celebrate one's birthday

· celebrate one's (first) anniversary
  慶祝某人的（一週年）紀念日

· celebrate the holiday
  慶祝節日

慶祝某人的生日　celebrate 可以接生日、紀念日或耶誕節等節日當受詞。

● What is the special event tomorrow?
● We're going to **celebrate Daniel's birthday**.

　●明天的特別活動是什麼？　●我們要慶祝 Daniel 的生日。

▶ We went to a bar to celebrate her birthday.
　我們去一個酒吧慶祝她的生日。
　I forgot to celebrate my brother's birthday.
　我忘了慶祝我哥哥的生日。

start one's birthday celebration

· come to the celebration
  來參加慶祝活動

開始某人的生日派對　celebration 是名詞，指慶祝活動或慶典。

● Did you sing 'Happy Birthday' to Hank?
● Not yet. Let's **start his birthday celebration**.

　●你有對 Hank 唱生日快樂歌嗎？
　●還沒，我們開始進行他的生日派對吧。

▶ We started her birthday celebration early.
　我們提早開始了她的生日派對。
　Terry started his birthday celebration after work.
　Terry 下班後開始了他的生日派對。

fall on

落在（某一天）　主詞是紀念日、生日或節日，on 的後面接「星期幾」或日期。

● What day is Christmas Eve this year?
● I think it will **fall on** a Saturday.

　●今年的耶誕夜是星期幾？　●我想應該是星期六。

▶ Joe's birthday fell on a Wednesday.
　Joe 的生日在星期三。
　The lunar new year's day falls on a different day each year. 每年的農曆新年都落在不同的日子。

38 健康
keep in shape

4-38.mp3

1 職場・學校

2 電腦・網路

3 社交生活

4 日常生活

5 訊息・理解

6 想法・態度

7 情緒・狀況

8 行為舉止

9 時間地點・副詞片語

keep in shape

· be in good[bad] shape
〔不〕健康，身材很好
· be in good condition
很健康
· shape up
表現變好，身體變健康

維持健康 keep one's health 也是「維持健康」的意思。

● How are you able to **keep in shape**?

● I go jogging almost every day.
　●你為什麼能維持健康？　●我幾乎每天慢跑。

▶ It is difficult to keep in shape. 維持健康很困難。
　Those women do aerobics to keep in shape.
　那些女士作有氧運動維持健康。

feel a lot healthier

· look unhealthy
看起來不健康
· get healthy
變健康
· be in good health
很健康
· be out of health
不健康

覺得健康多了 要表示「健康」，除了 be healthy，也可以說 be in health。

● How is your new diet going?

● It has made me **feel a lot healthier**.
　●你的新減肥計畫進行得怎樣？　●它讓我感覺健康多了。

▶ Heather felt a lot healthier after exercising.
　運動過後，Heather 覺得健康多了。
　Some of the workers are not in good health.
　有些員工的健康狀況不佳。

ruin one's health

· keep one's health
維持健康

損害健康 be bad/good for one's health 表示「有害／有益健康」。

● Mike has been drinking too much alcohol.

● I think he's going to **ruin his health**.
　●Mike 一直以來喝太多酒了。　●我想他會傷害自己的健康。

▶ The disease ruined Maria's health. 疾病損害了 Maria 的健康。
　Cigarette smoking ruins people's health.
　抽煙會損害人們的健康。

get well

· be in failing health
變得健康狀況不佳
· one's health fails
某人的健康狀況變得不佳
· get severe
變嚴重

從疾病中復原 這裡的 well 是形容詞，表示「健康的」。變得更好則可以說 get better。

● Simon has been in the hospital for a week.

● I think he will **get well** soon.
　●Simon 在醫院待了一個星期。　●我想他很快會復原。

▶ How long did it take you to get well?
　你花了多久的時間復原？
　I hope you get well soon. 我希望你能盡快復原。

keep fit

- keep oneself fit
  保持體態
- keep fit by exercising
  藉由運動保持體態

保持體態 fit 除了「適合」的意思以外，也引申為「健康」的意思，現在常常指「身材好」。

- This video will help you **keep fit**.
- Does it have different exercises?

  ●這個影片能幫助你保持體態。　●那裡面有不同的運動方法嗎？

▶ Eat a healthy diet and keep fit.
吃健康的飲食來保持體態。
Linda kept fit for her boyfriend.
Linda 為了她的男朋友而保持體態。

---

39 | 病痛
get hurt

4-39.mp3

---

get hurt

- 身體部位 + hurts
  …痛
- hurt oneself
  傷到自己→受傷
- get ill/sick
  生病

受傷 hurt 的動詞三態變化是 hurt-hurt-hurt，這裡的 hurt 是過去分詞，用了 get + pp 的句型。

- It looked like you injured your leg.
- I'm pretty sure I did. **It hurts!**

  ●你看起來傷到腿了。　●我很確定是受傷了。很痛！

▶ My ear really hurts.
我的耳朵真的很痛。
I've got a terrible headache today and my back hurts.
我今天頭痛得厲害，背也很痛。

be allergic to

- feel lousy
  覺得身體不舒服

對…過敏 to 後面接造成過敏的東西。

- Come here and try some of this.
- I can't. I'm **allergic to** peaches.

  ●過來吃看看這個。　●不行，我對桃子過敏。

▶ Maybe you're allergic to something in the room.
也許你對這房間裡的某個東西過敏。
I'm allergic to peanuts.
我對花生過敏。

contract the disease

· contract a virus
　感染病毒
· have trouble with…
　…方面有問題
· prevent a disease
　預防疾病

感染疾病 contract 除了簽約以外，也有感染病毒或疾病的意思。

● How was your overseas church trip?
● One of our members **contracted a disease**.
　●你的教會海外之旅如何？　●我們其中一位成員染上了疾病。

▶ I don't know when I contracted this disease.
　我不知道我什麼時候感染這個病的。
　Do you think he contracted the disease while in Africa?
　你覺得他是在非洲的時候染上疾病的嗎？

have pain (in)

· feel pain in
　覺得…痛
· have got a pain in my
　side
　我身體的側邊在痛
· have a sore throat
　喉嚨痛

…痛 可以加 in 接身體感到疼痛的部位。have 也可以換成 feel。

● Why are you walking so slowly?
● I **have a pain in** my foot today.
　●你為什麼走得那麼慢？　●我今天腳痛。

▶ Mom has pain in her hand.
　媽媽的手在痛。
　Older people have pain in their joints.
　老年人的關節會痛。

develop into

· develop + 病名
　患病
· 病名 + develop
　疾病逐漸形成

演變為某種疾病 develop 的原意是「發展」，主詞是病痛的時候就是「逐漸形成」或「變嚴重」的意思。

● Why is Andy in the hospital?
● His cold **developed into** pneumonia.
　●Andy 為什麼在醫院？　●他的感冒演變成肺炎。

▶ The doctor thinks it will develop into a serious illness.
　醫生認為這會演變成很嚴重的疾病。
　The scratch developed into a painful problem.
　這個抓傷演變成疼痛問題。

1 職場・學校
2 電腦・網路
3 社交生活
4 日常生活
5 訊息・理解
6 想法・態度
7 情緒・狀況
8 行為舉止
9 時間地點・副詞片語

40 | 受傷
break one's leg

get injured

· get hit by a car
  被車撞
· be seriously wounded
  （因為刀槍等）受重傷

受傷 injure 通常指因為意外或自然災害受傷，wound 是刀槍傷。

● I used to play football for my university.
● It's so easy to **get injured** doing that.
    ● 我以前代表大學踢足球。　● 踢足球很容易受傷。

▶ Annie got injured in the car wreck. Annie 在車禍中受傷了。
  I heard that John was injured in a car accident.
  我聽說 John 在車禍中受傷了。

break one's leg

· trip over/down
  絆倒

摔斷腿 break 表示「造成骨折」。leg 可以換成其他身體部位。

● How did you **break your leg**?
● It happened when I was skiing.
    ● 你怎麼摔斷腿的？　● 是我滑雪的時候發生的。

▶ Joan broke her leg last summer. Joan 去年夏天摔斷了她的腿。
  That's when I broke my leg. 那就是我摔斷腿的時候。

hurt one's ankle

· hurt one's knee -ing
  在…的時候傷到膝蓋

傷到腳踝 hurt 與 injure 類似，表示因為意外造成傷害。

● I **hurt my ankle** while I was running.
● How long will it take to heal?
    ● 我跑步的時候傷到了腳踝。　● 要多久才會痊癒？

▶ Henry jumped and hurt his ankle.
  Henry 跳了下去，傷到他的腳踝。
  This is how she hurt her leg. 她就是這樣傷到腿的。

sprain one's neck

· foot is cramping
  腳正在抽筋
· become paralyzed
  變得麻痺
· fracture a rib
  折斷肋骨
· have got a really stiff
  neck
  脖子非常僵硬

脖子扭到 也可以說 have a stiff neck，就是脖子僵硬、很難轉動的樣子。

● My legs **have been cramping up**.
● Since when?
    ● 我的腿一直在抽筋。　● 從什麼時候開始的？

▶ I got a cramp in my thigh. 我的大腿抽筋了。
  Sarah sprained her neck when she fell.
  Sarah 跌倒的時候扭到脖子。

scrape up one's knees

- get a scrape on…
  擦傷…
- get a mild scratch
  得到輕微的擦傷
- get this scratch
  得到這個擦傷
- feel so itchy
  覺得很癢

擦傷膝蓋 運動選手穿的有厚墊的護膝，稱為 knee pads。

- My son **scraped up his knees**.
- Was he playing in the park?

  ●我兒子擦傷了膝蓋。　●他在公園玩嗎？

▶ Hal scraped up his knees when he fell down.
  Hal 跌倒的時候，擦傷了膝蓋。
  Rollerskaters frequently scrape up their knees.
  穿輪鞋溜冰的人常常會擦傷膝蓋。

41 | 感冒
catch a cold

4-41.mp3

catch a cold

- catch a cold from…
  被…傳染感冒
- There's a cold going around
  感冒正在流行

得到感冒 也可以說 get a cold。

- What's wrong with you?
- I **caught a cold** yesterday.

  ●你怎麼了？　●我昨天感冒了。

▶ Many children caught colds at school.
  很多孩子在學校得到感冒。
  Stay inside or you'll catch a cold.
  待在室內，不然你會感冒。

have a bad cold

- have a slight cold
  得了小感冒
- have a head cold
  得了鼻炎

患了重感冒 get over one's cold 意為「從感冒中痊癒」。

- Can you help me? I **have a cold**.
- Sure. I've got some medicine.

  ●你可以幫我嗎？我感冒了。　●當然，我有一些藥。

▶ She is at home because she has a bad cold.
  她患了重感冒，所以待在家裡。
  Take some vitamin C if you have a bad cold.
  如果你患了重感冒，吃點維他命 C 吧。

1 職場・學校

2 電腦・網路

3 社交生活

4 日常生活

5 訊息・理解

6 想法・態度

7 情緒・狀況

8 行為舉止

9 時間地點・副詞片語

have a fever

· run a fever
  發燒

· have a runny nose
  流鼻水

發燒 發燒很嚴重用 high 表示體溫高，「have a high fever」就表示發高燒。

● The kid has a runny nose and is coughing a lot.
● Does he **have a fever**?

  ●孩子流鼻水又一直咳嗽。　　●他有發燒嗎？

▶ You feel hot. I think you have a fever.
  你摸起來熱熱的，我想你發燒了。
  Pam took aspirin because she has a fever.
  Pam 發燒了，所以她吃了阿斯匹靈。

have got the flu

· be sick with the flu
  患了流行性感冒

得了流行性感冒 flu 是 influenza 的縮寫，和一般的感冒不同，症狀嚴重得多，中文稱為「流行性感冒」。如果只是普通感冒，卻說 I got the flu，大家會被嚇得落荒而逃的。

● Kerry **has got the flu**.
● She needs to get some rest.

  ●Kerry 得了流行性感冒。　　●她需要休息一下。

▶ Many people have got the flu this winter.
  今年冬天很多人得了流行性感冒。
  These hospital patients have got the flu.
  這些醫院的患者們得了流行性感冒。

come down with

得了… with 後面接病名。

● Where's Bill today?
● He **came down with** a cold and called in sick.

  ●Bill 今天去哪了？　　●他得了感冒，所以打電話請了病假。

▶ I must be coming down with a cold.
  我一定得了感冒了。
  Lisa came down with malaria in Indonesia.
  Lisa 在印尼得了瘧疾。

42 頭痛
have a headache

4-42.mp3

1 職場・學校

2 電腦・網路

3 社交生活

4 日常生活

5 訊息・理解

6 想法・態度

7 情緒・狀況

8 行為舉止

9 時間地點・副詞片語

have a headache

・give A a headache
讓 A 頭痛

頭痛 have 也可以換成萬用動詞 get。

● I **have a severe headache** and I need some medicine.
● Do you want Tylenol or aspirin?
　●我的頭痛得很厲害，我需要一點藥。　●你想要泰諾還是阿斯匹靈？

▶ I've got a splitting headache. 我頭痛欲裂。
　I can't work because I have a headache.
　我因為頭痛無法工作。

suffer from headaches

受頭痛之苦 splitting headache 的意思是頭痛到像要裂開一樣。

● I've **suffered from headaches** since I was young.
● Is there any treatment you use?
　●我從年輕的時候就一直犯頭痛。　●你有接受任何治療嗎？

▶ We suffered from headaches because of the noise.
　我們因為噪音而飽受頭痛之苦。
　They suffered from headaches after drinking too much.
　他們喝太多酒之後，飽受頭痛之苦。

feel heavy

・heavy-headed
頭重重的

覺得重重的 形容因故導致身體狀況不佳時，哪裡覺得重重的狀態。主詞是覺得沉重的部位。

● You know, my arms **feel heavy**.
● I think you need to get some sleep.
　●我的手臂覺得好重。　●我想你該去睡點覺。

▶ His heart felt heavy when he left his girlfriend.
　他離開女朋友的時候，覺得心很沉重。
　The runner's feet felt heavy during the race.
　那位跑者在比賽中覺得腳很沉重。

have a migraine

· come down with a
  migraine
  得了偏頭痛

有偏頭痛　have 也可以換成 get。migraine 是很常用的字。
- Why are you holding your head?
- I **have a migraine** and my head hurts.
  ●你為什麼抱著頭？　●我有偏頭痛，我的頭好痛。

▶ Tess has a migraine and needs some medicine.
  Tess 有偏頭痛，需要一點藥。
  I have a migraine every few months.
  我每隔幾個月就會來一次偏頭痛。

**complain of
a headache**

抱怨頭痛　「慢性頭痛」則是 chronic headache。
- What happened to your daughter?
- She **has been complaining of a headache**.
  ●你女兒怎麼了？　●她一直在抱怨頭痛。

▶ Tom complained of a headache before class.
  Tom 在上課前說他頭痛。
  Has anyone here complained of a headache?
  這裡有人說自己頭痛嗎？

---

43 身心崩潰
have a breakdown

4-43.mp3

have a breakdown

· suffer from insomnia
  受失眠之苦

· nervous prostration
  精神疲憊

精神崩潰　have a nervous breakdown 的簡略說法。因為以前的人認為精神狀態和神經有關，所以加上了形容詞 nervous（神經的）。
- Why did Karen stop working here?
- I heard she **had a nervous breakdown**.
  ●Karen 為什麼不在這裡工作了？　●我聽說她精神崩潰了。

▶ Zelda had a nervous breakdown and was hospitalized.
  Zelda 因為精神崩潰住了院。
  Relax or you'll have a nervous breakdown.
  放輕鬆，不然你會精神崩潰。

have high blood pressure

· check one's blood pressure
  量血壓

有高血壓 用一個字表示高血壓，就是 hypertension。

● I always **have high blood pressure**.
● You need to have a healthier life.

　　●我總是有高血壓。　　●你需要過更健康的生活。

▶ He has high blood pressure and can't eat salt.

　　他有高血壓，不能吃鹽。

　　Let me check your blood pressure.

　　讓我量一下你的血壓。

have heart failure

· have a heart attack
  心肌梗塞發作
· be at risk of cardiac arrest
  有心跳停止的危險

患有心臟衰竭 heart attack 是心肌梗塞，cardiac arrest 是心跳停止，兩者都可以用在 have... 的句型。

● What caused Leo to die?
● He **had heart failure**.

　　●是什麼原因造成 Leo 死亡？　　●他患有心臟衰竭。

▶ Tim had heart failure while at work.

　　Tim 在工作的時候心臟衰竭。

　　She had heart failure and passed away.

　　她患有心臟衰竭，因此過世了。

have a stroke

患有中風 動詞 have 也可以換成 suffer。

● What causes people to **have a stroke**?
● It can be caused by smoking cigarettes.

　　●什麼原因會導致人們中風？　　●抽菸會導致中風。

▶ Ray couldn't talk after he had a stroke.

　　Ray 中風之後就不能說話了。

　　Many older people have a stroke.

　　許多老年人都患有中風。

pass out

· black out
  （眼前一黑）昏倒
· faint
  昏倒

昏倒 用一個字來說就是 faint。另外，pass away 意為「去世」，pass up 則是「放棄（機會）」。

● It was so hot outside today.
● I know. The heat made me **pass out**.

　　●今天外面好熱。　　●我知道，那熱度害我昏倒了。

▶ Cheryl passed out when she heard the news.

　　聽到那個消息時，Cheryl 昏倒了。

　　I'll pass out if I see someone bleeding.

　　如果我看到有人在流血，我會昏倒。

1 職場・學校
2 電腦・網路
3 社交生活
4 日常生活
5 訊息・理解
6 想法・態度
7 情緒・狀況
8 行為舉止
9 時間地點・副詞片語

44 頭部器官的問題
have a sore throat

have bad/poor eyes

· be a little nearsighted
  有點近視
· be farsighted
  遠視
· go blind
  失明

視力不好 「視力好」則是 have good eyesight。

● Can you see the deer in the distance?
● No, I can't. I **have bad eyesight.**
  ●你可以看到遠處那隻鹿嗎？　●不行，我視力很差。

▶ The accident was caused by poor eyesight.
  事故是因為視力不佳造成的。
  He had bad eyesight and couldn't enter the military.
  他因為視力不佳，無法加入軍隊。

have eye trouble

· have red eyes
  眼睛充血發紅
· have an eye infection
  有眼部感染

有眼睛方面的問題 have sore eyes 則是「眼睛疼痛」。

● I used to **have eye trouble** as a kid.
● Is that why you wear glasses?
  ●我小時候有眼睛方面的問題。　●那就是你戴眼鏡的原因嗎？

▶ Danni is seeing the doctor because she has eye trouble.
  Danni 因為有眼睛方面的問題，所以要去看醫生。
  Alan has eye trouble and needs an operation.
  Alan 有眼睛方面的問題，需要動手術。

have toothaches

· pull the tooth
  拔牙
· have a cavity
  有蛀牙
· get the braces
  去做牙套

牙齒痛 可以在 toothaches 前面加上 bad, terrible, appalling 等形容詞表示痛得很厲害。

● Would you like some tea or coffee?
● No, I **get toothaches** when I drink hot things.
  ●你想要一點茶或咖啡嗎？　●不要，我喝熱的會牙痛。

▶ Rick gets toothaches after eating candy.
  Rick 吃了糖果之後，就會牙痛。
  His teeth are bad and he has toothaches.
  他的牙齒很差，也有牙痛。

have an ear infection

- have en ear trouble
  有耳朵方面的問題
- one's ears are burning
  某人的耳朵灼痛
- one's ears are ringing
  某人的耳朵耳鳴

感染耳疾 因為感染造成的發炎也可以用 infection 來表達。

- Oh, my ear hurts so much!
- I think you **have an ear infection**.
  ●噢！我的耳朵好痛！ ●我想你的耳朵感染細菌了。

▶ Nick got an ear infection after he went swimming.
  Nick 去游泳之後感染了耳疾。
  The doctor said Mark has an ear infection.
  醫生說 Mark 感染了耳疾。

have a sore throat

- be stuffed up
  （鼻子）塞住

喉嚨痛 have a hoarse throat 則是指「喉嚨嘶啞」。

- I caught a cold this week.
- I'll bet you **have a sore throat**.
  ●我這禮拜得了感冒。 ●你一定有喉嚨痛吧。

▶ He had a sore throat due to smoking.
  他因為抽菸，所以喉嚨痛。
  I have had a sore throat for three days.
  我喉嚨痛了三天。

---

45 胃不舒服
have an upset stomach

4-45.mp3

have an upset stomach

- suffer from indigestion
  受消化不良之苦
- one's stomach is upset
  某人胃不舒服
- feel bloated
  覺得肚子脹氣

胃不舒服 如果只是有點消化不良，可以說 have indigestion。

- Both of my kids **have an upset stomach**.
- That's because they ate too much junk food.
  ●我兩個孩子的胃都不舒服。 ●那是因為他們吃太多垃圾食物了。

▶ He had an upset stomach after breakfast.
  他吃完早餐後胃就不舒服。
  Eating new foods can give you an upset stomach.
  再吃新的食物會讓你的胃不舒服。

1 職場 · 學校
2 電腦 · 網路
3 社交生活
4 日常生活
5 訊息 · 理解
6 想法 · 態度
7 情緒 · 狀況
8 行為舉止
9 時間地點 · 副詞片語

get food poisoning

· be poisoned by food
  得到食物中毒

得到食物中毒 get 也可以換成 suffer from。

● **Have** you ever **gotten food poisoning**?
● Yes, I had it once when I was overseas.
  ●你曾經食物中毒過嗎？　●有，我在國外時有過一次。

▶ Owen got food poisoning and threw up.
  Owen 食物中毒，而且吐了。
  The group got food poisoning at the restaurant.
  這個團體在餐廳食物中毒。

have stomach cramps

· have a cramp in one's
  stomach
  胃抽筋／絞痛
· muscle cramps
  肌肉痙攣
· have/get a cramp
  抽筋

胃抽筋／絞痛 cramp 是「抽筋」，也就是肌肉痙攣。

● I have to stop running right now.
● Do you **have a cramp** in your stomach?
  ●我得立刻停止跑步。　●你的胃抽筋了嗎？

▶ He had stomach cramps after eating.
  吃東西之後，他的胃就絞痛。
  I have a cramp in my stomach that hurts.
  我胃抽筋了，很痛。

have diarrhea

· have the runs
  拉肚子
· be constipated
  有便秘

拉肚子 「便秘」是 constipation，所以「處在便秘的狀態」是 be constipated。

● **Are** you **suffering from diarrhea**?
● No, but I have a stomachache.
  ●你有在拉肚子嗎？　●沒有，但我胃痛。

▶ Kate had diarrhea after eating spicy food.
  Kate 吃完辣的東西之後，就拉肚子了。
  Some international travelers have diarrhea.
  有些國際觀光客會拉肚子。

throw up

· vomit
  吐
· feel sick to one's
  stomach
  想吐
· feel nauseated
  覺得噁心想吐

吐 比起 vomit，口語比較常說 throw up。

● My stomach is very upset right now.
● Let me know if you have to **throw up**.
  ●我的胃現在非常不舒服。　●如果你想吐的話跟我說。

▶ She was sick but she didn't throw up.
  她生病了，但她沒有吐。
  I threw up many times because I had the flu.
  我因為流行性感冒吐了很多次。

46 其他疾病
get diabetes

4-46.mp3

have/get diabetes

· die from diabetes
因為糖尿病去世

有糖尿病 「家族有糖尿病史」的說法是 one's family has a history of diabetes。

● Why do you always carry food with you?

● I **have diabetes**, so I need to eat a lot.

● 你為什麼總是帶著食物？　● 我有糖尿病，所以我需要吃很多。

▶ Some famous people have diabetes.
有些知名人士患有糖尿病。
Her diet changed because she has diabetes.
她因為患有糖尿病而改變了飲食。

have side effects

· develop complications
產生併發症

有副作用 後面可以加上 from，接產生副作用的原因。

● I'm **having side effects** from my surgery.

● Is it causing you a lot of pain?

● 我的手術有副作用。　● 手術讓你很痛嗎？

▶ Pam had side effects from her medication.
Pam 因為她的藥物而得到副作用。
Do people have side effects from drinking?
人們會因為喝酒得到副作用嗎？

be swollen

· get swollen
變腫

· reduce the swelling
消腫

腫大 動詞 swell 的過去分詞。「消腫」可以說 reduce the swelling, let the swelling go down 或 make the swelling go down。

● We've been walking along for hours.

● I know. My feet **are very swollen**.

● 我們已經走好幾個小時了。　● 我知道，我的腳很腫。

▶ Christian's eye was swollen after the fight.
打架過後，Christian 的眼睛腫起來了。
If your legs are swollen, lie down for a while.
如果你的腿腫了，就躺一下吧。

1 職場・學校

2 電腦・網路

3 社交生活

4 日常生活

5 訊息・理解

6 想法・態度

7 情緒・狀況

8 行為舉止

9 時間地點・副詞片語

347

have a rash

· 身體部位 + break out in a rash
　…起疹子
· have a heat rash on
　…起熱疹
· get hives
　得蕁麻疹

起疹子 break out in a rash 也是一樣的意思。

● What are the signs of poison ivy?
● **A rash and itching.** Do you think you have it?
　●常春藤中毒的徵狀是什麼？　●起疹子和發癢。你覺得你有嗎？

▶ I have a rash on the palm of my hand.
　我的手掌起了疹子。
　Most babies have a rash on their fannies.
　大部分嬰兒的屁股都會起疹子。

pop some pimples

擠青春痘 pop 是弄破的意思。pop 也可以換成表示「擠壓」的 squeeze。

● Teenagers often **pop their pimples.**
● I think that might leave a scar.
　●青少年常常擠青春痘。　●我想那會留疤的。

▶ He popped some pimples while looking in the mirror.
　他看著鏡子，擠了幾顆青春痘。
　The doctor said not to pop your pimples.
　醫生叫你不要擠青春痘。

---

47 服藥 take one's medicine

4-47.mp3

pick up one's prescription

· prescribe some medicine
　（在處方上）開一些藥

領處方箋 prescribe 是「開處方」，prescription 則是「處方箋」。

● I'm here to **pick up my prescription.**
● Here it is.
　●我來這邊拿我的處方箋。　●給你。

▶ You can pick up your prescription at the pharmacy.
　你可以在藥局領你的處方箋。
　Where can I pick up my prescription?
　我可以在哪裡領我的處方箋？

take one's medicine

· take a dose of…
  服用一劑…
· take a pill
  吃一顆藥

吃藥　藥草製成的藥劑稱為 herbal medicine。
- ●Here, **take this medicine**.
- ●Will it help me get rid of my cold?
  - ●來，吃這個藥。　●這會幫我治好感冒嗎？

▶ Don't forget to take your medicine.
  別忘了吃你的藥。
  I took my medicine three times a day.
  我一天吃了三次藥。

take vitamins

· take some medicine
  for indigestion
  吃一點消化不良的藥
· take some cold
  medicine
  吃一點感冒藥
· take a painkiller
  吃止痛藥

吃維他命　take 後面可以接各種口服藥物，請善加活用。
- ●Is your stomach feeling better now?
- ●Yes. I **took some medicine for indigestion**.
  - ●你現在覺得胃好點了嗎？　●嗯，我吃了一點消化不良的藥。

▶ He took some cold medicine after the meal.
  他用餐後吃了一點感冒藥。
  Let's take some vitamins for our health.
  我們吃點維他命增進健康吧。

take medication

· put sb on medication
  對某人施行藥物治療
· be on medication
  for…
  接受（某種疾病）的藥物
  治療

接受藥物治療　medicine 指的是藥物，medication 則是「用藥物進行治療的行為」。
- ●I've been feeling very sick lately.
- ●**Are** you **taking any medication**?
  - ●我最近覺得很不舒服。　●你有接受任何藥物治療嗎？

▶ You should take medication for your headache.
  你應該接受藥物治療你的頭痛。
  Henry took medication in the hospital.
  Henry 在醫院接受了藥物治療。

swallow a pill

吞藥片　藥水是 liquid medicine，藥粉則是 powdered medicine。
- ●Here, you have to **swallow these pills**.
- ●Are they going to make me feel better?
  - ●來，你得把這些藥吞下去。　●這些藥會讓我舒服一點嗎？

▶ I can't swallow pills easily.
  我不太會吞藥片。
  Swallow this pill for your allergies.
  為了治療你的過敏，把這個藥吞下去。

1 職場・學校
2 電腦・網路
3 社交生活
4 日常生活
5 訊息・理解
6 想法・態度
7 情緒・狀況
8 行為舉止
9 時間地點・副詞片語

48 治療疾病
cure a disease

4-48.mp3

cure a disease

- cure sb (of + 病名)
  治療某人（的某種病）
- cure for + 病名
  …的治療法

治療疾病 受詞可以是病患或疾病。

- Has Danny been in the hospital yet?
- Yeah, they **cured his cancer**.
  - Danny 住院了嗎？　●嗯，他們治療了他的癌症。

▶ The doctors have drugs to cure malaria.
  醫生有藥可以治療瘧疾。
  We don't know how to cure stomach cancer.
  我們不知道該怎麼治療胃癌。

treat the headache

- treat a patient
  治療病患
- treat sb with + 藥物
  用…治療某人
- treatment
  治療（法）

治療頭痛 動詞除了 treat，也可以用 cure 或 remedy。

- What is the best way to **treat a headache**?
- Most people just take two aspirin.
  - 治療頭痛最好的方法是什麼？　●大多數的人就是吃兩片阿斯匹靈。

▶ My grandma has a special way to treat a headache.
  我的奶奶有特別的方法可以治療頭痛。
  You can treat a headache by putting ice on it.
  你可以把冰塊放在頭上來治療頭痛。

get over

- get over a cold
  從感冒中復原

（從疾病中）復原 受傷的「復原」則是說 heal (up)。

- I hope you **get over** your illness soon.
- Me too. I really hate being sick.
  - 希望你能很快從疾病中復原。
  - 我也這麼希望，我真的很討厭生病。

▶ Did Inez get over her cold?
  Inez 的感冒好了嗎？
  It takes a long time to get over the flu.
  流行性感冒要很久才能復原。

wear a cast

- wear a bandage
  纏著繃帶
- walk on crutches
  用拐杖走路

打了石膏 後面可以接「around + 身體部位」表示石膏打在哪邊。

- Why **are** you **wearing a cast** around your foot?
- I hurt my leg when I fell off my bike.
  - 你的腳為什麼打了石膏？　　●我從腳踏車跌下來的時候傷到了腳。

▶ Kevin had to wear a cast around his arm.
  Kevin 的手臂必須打石膏。
  She wore a cast around her broken bones.
  她摔斷的骨頭那邊打了石膏。

go away

（病痛等）消失 用「走開」比喻疾病消失。

- Many students start to cough in the winter.
- It will **go away** when nicer weather comes.
  - 很多學生到了冬天就開始咳嗽。
  - 天氣變好的時候，症狀就會消失了。

▶ A cold will go away in about a week.
  感冒大約會在一週後復原。
  My sore throat went away after a while.
  過了一陣子之後，我喉嚨的疼痛就消失了。

apply some ointment to

- apply a heating pad to
  在…放上暖墊

在…塗上藥膏 除了指塗抹化妝品，apply 也可以指塗抹藥膏。

- My husband's knee has been hurting.
- Why don't you **apply some ointment to** it?
  - 我先生的膝蓋一直很痛。　　●你們何不塗點藥膏呢？

▶ I'll apply some ointment to this rash.
  我會在發疹的地方塗點藥膏。
  The doctor said to apply some ointment to your skin.
  醫生說要塗點藥膏在你的皮膚上。

get acupuncture

- get acupuncture on one's neck
  讓人針灸脖子
- apply acupuncture on…
  在（身體部位）針灸

接受針灸 可能是個有點困難的單字，但跌打損傷師父所使用的「針灸」便是「acupuncture」。

- I heard you are using oriental medicine.
- Yes. It's very effective to **get acupuncture**.
  - 我聽說你在使用東方療法。　　●是啊，針灸非常有效。

▶ Melvin got acupuncture for his stomach problems.
  Melvin 為了治療他的胃部毛病而接受針灸。
  You should get acupuncture for your headaches.
  你應該接受針灸治療你的頭痛。

1 職場・學校
2 電腦・網路
3 社交生活
4 日常生活
5 訊息・理解
6 想法・態度
7 情緒・狀況
8 行為舉止
9 時間地點・副詞片語

leave one's stomach empty

· drink sth on an empty stomach
在空腹的狀態下喝某物

保持空腹 這是 leave sth adj 的句型。「在空腹的狀態下」則是 on an empty stomach。

● Was that your stomach making noise?

● Yeah, I **left my stomach empty** this morning.

●那是你的胃發出的聲音嗎？　●是啊，我今天早上是空腹的狀態。

▶ It's not healthy to leave your stomach empty.
讓你的胃空腹不是件健康的事情。

There was no time to eat so I left my stomach empty.
因為沒時間吃東西，所以我就空腹了。

stop the bleeding

· I've got a bleeder.
我這邊有個出血的患者。

止血 bleeder 指「在流血的人」，因此也可以說 stop the bleeder（幫流血的人止血）。

● That is a huge cut on your hand.

● I need your help to **stop the bleeding**.

●你手上有個很大的割傷。　●我需要你幫忙止血。

▶ It took ten minutes to stop the bleeding.
止血花了十分鐘。

That bandage will stop the bleeding.
那個繃帶可以止血。

 出人意料的 cast 和 apply

　　這兩個單字都是我們很熟悉的基本單字。我們都知道 cast 是「投、擲」，apply 是「申請」，但在這一節學到的意思卻是「石膏」和「塗抹」。類似的單字還有 contract（感染…）、ground（禁止…外出）、delivery（生產）、literature（廣告文案）和 book（預約…）等等。

49 接受診斷
have a checkup

1 職場・學校

2 電腦・網路

3 社交生活

4 日常生活

5 訊息・理解

6 想法・態度

7 情緒・狀況

8 行為舉止

9 時間地點・副詞片語

have a checkup

- get a check-up
接受檢查（定期檢查則是 regular check-up）

接受檢查 做身體檢查的意思。也可以說 have a medical check up / examination。

● What brings you to the doctor's office today?

● I need to **have my yearly checkup**.

● 你今天怎麼來診所了？　● 我需要做年度檢查。

▶ You must have a checkup before playing sports.
你做運動前，一定要先接受檢查。

My grandparents have a checkup every year.
我的祖父母每年都會接受檢查。

examine a patient

- have + 身體部位 + examined
讓…被檢查

檢查病患 see a patient 也是「看診，檢查」的意思。

● What is taking the doctor so long?

● He needs time to **examine a patient**.

● 這醫生為什麼花這麼多時間？　● 他需要時間檢查病患。

▶ The nurse couldn't examine a patient.
這位護士無法檢查病患。

Let me examine a patient before we start.
在我們開始前，讓我先檢查一位病患。

see a doctor

- consult a doctor
看醫生

看醫生 也可以說 consult a doctor，但 see a doctor 還是比較常用。

● The rash on my skin keeps getting worse.

● Hurry and go to **see a doctor**.

● 我皮膚上的疹子越來越嚴重了。　● 趕快去看醫生。

▶ I need to go to see a doctor. 我需要去看醫生。
Shelly saw a doctor about her cough.
Shelly 因為咳嗽問題而去看醫生。

go to a doctor

- go to a doctor for a check up
去找醫生做檢查
- go to a doctor for an overhaul
去找醫生做精密檢查
- go to the dentist
去看牙醫

去看醫生 去找醫生當然就是去看病的意思。

● I have been feeling tired all the time.

● You need to **go to a doctor** about that.

● 我一直都覺得很累。　● 你需要看醫生解決這個問題。

▶ Have you gone to a doctor recently? 你最近有去看醫生嗎？
He only goes to a doctor when he's very ill.
他只有在病得非常嚴重的時候才會去看醫生。

take sb to the doctor

- be rushed to the emergency room
  被緊急送往急診室
- take someone's temperature
  量某人的體溫

帶某人去看醫生 也可以用 take A to the hospital 來表達。

- Can you **take Monica to the doctor's office**?
- Sure, when does she want to go?
  - 你可以帶 Monica 去診所嗎？ ● 當然，她想什麼時候去？

▶ He took his wife to the doctor.
他帶他太太去看醫生。
I'll take my father to the doctor today.
我今天會帶我爸爸去看醫生。

be in the hospital

- be in the hospital giving birth
  在醫院生產

住院 也可以用動詞 hospitalize（使住院接受治療），說法是 be hospitalized。

- What made Charlie so sick?
- He's **been in the hospital** with cancer.
  - Charlie 為什麼病得那麼重？ ● 他因為癌症住院。

▶ Larry is in the hospital with a stomach bug.
Larry 因為肚子痛而住院。
How long will you be in the hospital for?
你會住院多久？

get surgery

- perform an operation
  施行手術
- undergo surgery
  接受手術

接受手術 後面可以加 on 接要動手術的部位。

- Freddy **got surgery** on his heart this year.
- I heard that is a dangerous operation.
  - Freddy 今年接受了心臟手術。 ● 我聽說那是個危險的手術。

▶ Did she get laser surgery on her eyes?
她接受了眼睛雷射手術嗎？
You need to get surgery before it's too late.
你需要接受手術，以免太遲。

get A x-rayed

- take an x-ray
  照 X 光

讓 A 照 X 光 用的是「get + A + pp」的句型，而且把 x-ray 當成動詞使用。

- Arnold hurt his leg playing soccer.
- Go **get his leg x-rayed** quickly.
  - Arnold 踢足球時傷到了他的腿。 ● 趕快讓他的腿照 X 光。

▶ Get your head x-rayed when you have a chance.
你有機會的話，去照頭部 X 光。
Did you get Brandon's foot x-rayed?
你照了 Brandon 腳的 X 光了嗎？

1 職場・學校

2 電腦・網路

3 社交生活

4 日常生活

5 訊息・理解

6 想法・態度

7 情緒・狀況

8 行為舉止

9 時間地點・副詞片語

go through physical therapy

接受物理治療 「物理復健治療」則是 physical rehab treatment。

● My mom had to **go through physical therapy**.

● Has it helped her to feel better?

　●我媽媽必須接受物理治療。　●治療有讓她覺得比較好嗎？

▶ She needs to go through physical therapy for her hand.
她的手需要接受物理治療。

　Many injured people go through physical therapy.
許多受傷的人都接受物理治療。

have plastic surgery

· get a nose job
　接受隆鼻手術
· get a boob job
　接受隆胸手術

接受整形手術 cosmetic surgery 也是「整形手術」的意思。

● Is it a good idea to **have plastic surgery**?

● Only after someone is forty years old.

　●接受整形手術是個好主意嗎？　●對四十歲以後的人才值得吧。

▶ Sue had plastic surgery on her nose.
Sue 的鼻子做了整形手術。

　He had plastic surgery to become more handsome.
他為了變得更帥，去做了整形手術。

50 | 運動 work out

4-50.mp3

go for a walk

· take a walk
　散步
· take a long walk
　走很遠的路

去散步 walk 也可以當及物動詞，walk sb 指「陪某人一起走」。

● Where are you going?

● I want to **take a walk** around the park.

　●你要去哪裡？　●我想在公園裡四處走走。

▶ How about we take a walk tonight?
我們今晚散個步怎麼樣？

　I don't want to go for a walk in the rain.
我不想在雨中散步。

355

go on a hike

· go hiking
  去健行
· take a long hike
  長途健行

去健行 健行步道則是 a hiking trail。

● What is the chess club doing tomorrow?
● We **are all going on a hike**.
  ●西洋棋社團明天要做什麼？ ●我們都要去健行。

▶ Fall is the best time to go on a hike.
  秋天是最棒的健行季節。
  Would you like to go on a hike with me?
  你想跟我一起去健行嗎？

go to a gym

· go to a gym to work
  out
  去健身房做運動
· go to a gym 4 days a
  week
  每週有四天去健身房

去健身房 get the gym 則是「接受健身課程」。

● Care to have a few drinks with me?
● I'm sorry, but I have to **go to the gym** now.
  ●想跟我去喝幾杯嗎？ ●抱歉，但我現在要去健身房了。

▶ I try to go to the gym three times a week.
  我試著一星期去三次健身房。
  He went to a gym located in his neighborhood.
  他去一間在他家附近的健身房。

work out

· work out all night
  做整晚的運動

運動 work out regularly 是「定期運動」。workout 也可以當名詞。

● Why are you sweating so much?
● I just finished **working out**.
  ●你為什麼流那麼多汗？ ●我剛做完運動。

▶ Morning is her favorite time to work out.
  早上是她最喜歡做運動的時間。
  If you work out, you will become stronger.
  如果你做運動，你會變得更強壯。

exercise every day

· exercise regularly
  定期運動

每天運動 take exercise 也是做運動的意思，這裡的 exercise 是名詞。

● I have no energy and feel sick.
● This is why you need to **exercise**.
  ●我沒有力氣，覺得不舒服。 ●所以你需要運動。

▶ I exercise before going to work.
  去上班之前，我會做運動。
  The only way to lose weight is to exercise and eat right.
  減肥唯一的方法是運動並且吃正確的食物。

run two miles

· run for five miles
  跑五英里
· be a fast runner
  是個很快的跑者
  →跑得很快

跑兩英里 跑步的距離可以直接當受詞。也可以說「run for + 距離」。

● Lisa looks like she's in good condition.
● She **runs at least two miles** every day.
  ●Lisa 看起來狀況很好。　●她每天都跑至少兩英里。

▶ They plan to run two miles before they come home.
  他們打算在回家前跑兩英里。
  I don't think I could run ten miles these days.
  我不覺得我最近能跑十英里。

run in the marathon

· run in one's first
  marathon
  第一次跑馬拉松
· run the entire 42 km
  跑完全程 42 公里
· finish the marathon
  跑完馬拉松

跑馬拉松 表示「在馬拉松比賽裡跑步」。

● Why did Randolph come to New York City?
● He's here to **run in the marathon**.
  ●Randolph 為什麼來紐約市？　●他來這裡跑馬拉松。

▶ Jen has trained hard to run in the marathon.
  Jen 為了跑馬拉松而努力訓練。
  Most people aren't strong enough to run in a marathon.
  大多數的人都沒有強壯到能跑馬拉松。

play golf

· practice one's golf
  swing
  練習揮桿
· play tennis
  打網球

打高爾夫球 a golf club 是高爾夫球桿，a golf course 則是高爾夫球場。

● Does your father enjoy being retired?
● Yeah, he **plays golf** almost every day.
  ●你爸爸很享受退休嗎？　●是啊，他幾乎每天都打高爾夫球。

▶ We're going to watch some pros play golf.
  我們要去看一些專業選手打高爾夫球。
  Did you play golf on your vacation?
  你度假的時候有打高爾夫球嗎？

1 職場・學校
2 電腦・網路
3 社交生活
4 日常生活
5 訊息・理解
6 想法・態度
7 情緒・狀況
8 行為舉止
9 時間地點・副詞片語

work out 是在外面工作的意思嗎？

　　已經學過的簡單單字，我們常常會認為它們就只有一種意思，因為大多數的人都懶得查字典，要不然就是一板一眼地死背單字，而失去了聯想力。字典不只能用來查沒看過的單字，還能讓我們發現常用單字的其他意思。

　　沒有人不知道 work 這個單字。但除了「工作」以外，很多人不知道它還有「運動」的用法。要是提到「運動」，大概就只會想到 exercise 這個字吧。聽到有人容光煥發地說他每天「work out」，或許還會以為他是每天在戶外工作才這麼健康呢！雖然大家都說笨蛋沒藥醫，但只要我們保持求知慾，並且深入學習英文單字的多重涵義，至少不會因為無知而鬧笑話。

　　為了身體健康（physical fitness），最近有許多上班族開始上健身房。除此之外，在網球場打網球，還有家庭主婦為了消除贅肉而做的瘦身操，這些都可以稱為「work out」，也就是「為了健康、維持體態或鍛鍊體力而做的運動」。想要達到效果，當然得定期（regularly）去做才行。至於像 gym、fitness clubs（健身俱樂部）這種 work out 的地方，我們稱為 workout spot。work 和 out 連起來，就是表示「運動」的名詞。

---

51 | 減肥
go on a diet

4-51.mp3

go on a diet

· be on a diet
　在減肥
· start a new diet
　重新減肥

節食減肥　diet 可以表示一般的日常飲食，也可以表示減肥時的特殊飲食。

● My mom has gotten kind of heavy.
● She needs to **go on a diet** for a while.
　●我媽媽變得有點胖。　　●她需要減肥一陣子。

▶ Many people go on a diet after the holidays.
　許多人在假期過後減肥。
　I went on a diet before my wedding.
　我在婚禮前開始減肥。

get fat

· get a little fat
  變得有點胖

變胖 fat 是個很直接的字，負面意義很明顯，所以用在別人身上的時候要小心。

● Stella **got fat** after eating a lot of ice cream.
● She has to eat fruits and vegetables instead.
  ● Stella 因為吃了很多冰淇淋，所以變胖了。
  ● 她得改吃水果和蔬菜。

▶ I would be unhappy if I got fat.
  如果我變胖了，我會很不開心。
  No wonder they're getting so fat.
  難怪他們變那麼胖。

put on some weight

· gain weight
  變重
· watch one's weight
  注意某人的體重

變重了些 如果是因為放假時大吃大喝變胖，就可以說 put on holiday weight。

● It's difficult to lose weight over the age of 40.
● Most middle aged people **put on some weight**.
  ● 四十歲以後很難減肥。　● 大多數的中年人都會變重一點。

▶ Randy put on some weight while he was a student.
  Randy 當學生的時候胖了一些。
  My girlfriend thinks she has put on some weight.
  我的女朋友覺得她變重了些。

lose weight

· lose some weight
  輕了一點

減重 「變瘦」則是 become thin/slim。

● I wish I could **lose some weight**.
● It's what's inside that counts.
  ● 我希望我能輕一點。　● 內在美才重要。

▶ It's so hard to lose weight.
  減肥真的好難。
  It looks like you've lost weight lately.
  你最近看起來變輕了。

join a health club

· lift the weight
  舉重
· do/practice yoga
  做／練習瑜珈
· do stretching
  做伸展運動

加入健康俱樂部 health club 也可以稱為 fitness club。

● How can I get into better shape?
● Why don't you **join a health club**?
  ● 我該怎麼讓體態更好看？　● 你何不加入健康俱樂部呢？

▶ Harry joined a health club in January.
  Harry 一月加入了健康俱樂部。
  I lost some weight because I've joined a gym to work out. 我加入了健身房去做運動，所以瘦了一點。

1 職場・學校
2 電腦・網路
3 社交生活
4 日常生活
5 訊息・理解
6 想法・態度
7 情緒・狀況
8 行為舉止
9 時間地點・副詞片語

Information & Understanding
Understanding

聆聽、觀看、理解等與訊息相關的各種慣用語

CHAPTER 5

01 | 聽
hear sb -ing

5-01.mp3

hear from

- hear from sb recently
  最近接到某人的消息
- hear from the bank
  接到銀行的聯絡

接到…的消息 就是「receive news or information from」的意思，表示接到某個人或團體的信或電話。

● I'll give you a call when things cool down.

● I look forward to **hearing from** you.

  ●事情冷靜下來的時候，我會打電話給你。　●期待聽到你的消息。

▶ How have you been? I haven't heard from you in a while.

  你過得怎樣？我有一陣子沒聽到你的消息了。

  I'm looking forward to hearing from you soon.

  我期待很快就能收到你的回音。

hear of

- hear much of...
  聽到很多關於…的消息

聽說（某個人事物） 表示知道關於某個事物的事情，可以說 know about sth。have not heard of sth 則表示「沒聽說過某事」。

● Have you seen the new war movie?

● No, I've **never heard of** it.

  ●你看過那部新的戰爭片嗎？　●沒有，我從來沒聽說過。

▶ Lynn heard of a popular beauty shop.

  Lynn 聽說有一間很受歡迎的美容沙龍。

  I can't believe it. I never heard of such a thing.

  我真不敢相信，我從來沒聽過這樣的事。

hear about

- hear more about sth/
  what S+V
  聽到更多關於某事的事
- hear about sth second
  hand
  間接聽到關於某事的事

聽到關於…（的詳細資訊） 至於 hear of 就只是表示聽說過而已。

● Nice to meet you, Sam.

● I've **heard so much about** you.

  ●Sam，很高興認識你。　●我聽過很多關於你的事。

▶ I heard about your daughter.

  我聽到有關你女兒的事。

  I heard about your wedding the other night.

  我之前某個晚上聽到關於你婚禮的事。

  Did you hear about the man who died yesterday?

  你有聽過昨天去世的那位男子的事情嗎？

not hear anything about

- not hear of any of...
  沒聽說任何的…
- not hear anything of...
  沒聽說任何的…

沒有聽到任何關於…的消息 用 not...any... 的句型表示強烈的否定。

- I **haven't heard anything about** the money.
- Yeah, I hope they give it to us soon.
  - 我沒有聽到關於那筆錢的任何消息。
  - 是啊，希望他們能快點把錢給我們。

▶ Are you sure? I haven't heard anything about that.
  你確定嗎？我沒聽過關於那件事的任何消息。
  Have you heard any of the current popular music?
  你聽過任何一首現在的流行音樂嗎？
  I've never heard of anyone dying from lack of sex.
  我從來沒聽說過有人因為性行為不足死掉。

hear that S+V

- I heard (that)
  我聽說…

聽到… hear 後面接子句當受詞時，可以接 if SV, that SV 或 what, who, how 等複合關係代名詞起始的子句。

- Did you **hear if** Mark got the job?
- Judging by the look on his face, I'd say yes.
  - 你有聽說 Mark 是否找到工作了嗎？
  - 從他臉上的表情看來，我想是的。

▶ I heard that the weather there is very nice.
  我聽說那裡的天氣很好。
  I heard that he moved to Philadelphia. 我聽說他搬到費城了。

hear the news

- hear sth on the radio
  在廣播上聽到某事
- hear sb loud and clear
  大聲且清楚地聽到某人的話

聽到新聞／消息 要表示是在電視上看到的，可以在後面加上 on TV；如果是從某人那裡聽說的，可以加上 from sb。

- **Have** you **heard the news** about Greg?
- No, did something happen to him?
  - 你聽說關於 Greg 的消息了嗎？ ● 沒有，他怎麼了嗎？

▶ We all heard the news about the earthquake.
  我們都聽說了關於地震的消息。
  The television is where many people hear the news.
  電視是許多人得知新聞的來源。

hear sb -ing

- hear sb do
  聽到某人做…
- hear sb say
  聽到某人說…

聽到某人在… -ing 也可以換成動詞原形。

- I **heard** you and Justin **talking**.
- Talking about what?
  - 我聽到你和 Justin 在說話。 ● 說什麼？

▶ Have you ever heard him talk about his father?
  你有聽他談過他父親嗎？
  I didn't hear you come in. 我沒聽到你進來了。

1 職場・學校
2 電腦・網路
3 社交生活
4 日常生活
5 訊息・理解
6 想法・態度
7 情緒・狀況
8 行為舉止
9 時間地點・副詞片語

hear sb out

· Hear me out!
  聽我把話說完！

聽某人把話說完 不打斷某人的話，好好聽他說完的意思。

● Stop lying to me. I'm not stupid.
● Please **hear me out**. I can explain this.

　●別再騙我了。我不是傻子。　　●請聽我把話說完，我可以解釋的。

▶ Hear us out and then we can talk.
　聽我們把話說完，然後我們可以談談。
　I didn't even hear her out.
　我甚至沒把她的話聽完。

be + 形容詞 + to hear that...

· be sorry to hear that
  聽到那件事覺得很遺憾
· be pleased to hear that...
  聽到…覺得很開心

聽到…覺得很… 可以用來表示聽到某個消息覺得很遺憾或驚訝等等。

● Andy's ex-girlfriend just got married.
● He **was sorry to hear that** she didn't love him.

　●Andy 的前女友剛結了婚。　　●他聽說她不再愛他，覺得很難過。

▶ I'm glad to hear you're all right.
　聽到你一切都好，我很開心。
　I'm sorry to hear that he was injured.
　聽到他受傷我很遺憾。

listen to

· listen to music
  聽音樂
· listen to what I say
  聽我說
· I'm listening.
  我在聽。

（專注地）聽… hear 比較像是「聲音不經意傳到耳朵裡」，而 listen 則是「專注地聽」，to 後面可以接人或事物。

● I'm sorry, but let me explain why I did it.
● I really don't have time to **listen to** you now.

　●我很抱歉，但讓我解釋我那麼做的理由。
　●我現在真的沒有時間聽你說話。

▶ I like listening to new age music.
　我喜歡聽新世紀音樂。
　I'm listening to the MP3 files from a Mentors' book.
　我正在聽一本 Mentors 出版社的書附的 MP3 檔案。

from what I hear

· Not that I have heard
  我聽說的不是那樣

就我所聽到的 表示「根據我所聽到的訊息，情況是…」。

● Is Mrs. Carlson going to continue working?
● **From what I hear**, she plans to retire.

　●Carlson 太太會繼續工作嗎？　　●就我所知，她打算要退休。

▶ From what I hear, that's going to take a while.
　我所聽到的消息是，那會花上一點時間。
　From what I hear, it's supposed to rain tomorrow.
　就我所聽到的，明天應該會下雨。

1 職場・學校

2 電腦・網路

3 社交生活

4 日常生活

5 訊息・理解

6 想法・態度

7 情緒・狀況

8 行為舉止

9 時間地點・副詞片語

be all ears

· be all thumbs
  手拙

全神貫注地聽，傾聽 就是表示用全部的聽力仔細聽。

● Do you know Jerry and Tina are going to get a divorce?

● Oh my God, is that true? Why? I'm all ears.

  ●你知道 Jerry 和 Tina 要離婚了嗎？

  ●天啊，那是真的嗎？為什麼？我洗耳恭聽。

▶ That's unbelievable. Tell me what you know. I am all ears. 那真讓人難以置信。跟我說你知道什麼，我洗耳恭聽。

When she has a problem, everyone's all ears.

當她有困難的時候，每個人都傾聽她的需要。

---

 hear vs. listen

　　雖然 hear 跟 listen 都是「聽」，但 hear 的聽是不經意地聽到，也就是聲音自然傳入耳朵的狀態。相反的，listen 則是集中精神（pay attention）去聽。還要注意 listen 是不及物動詞，後面要加上介系詞 to 才能接受詞。

---

02 | 看，觀察 look at

5-02.mp3

see sb -ing

· see sb do
  看到某人做…

· not see sb in years
  很多年沒看到某人

看到某人做… -ing 也可以改成動詞原形，但 -ing 形比較有「目擊正在…的一刻」的動態感。

● Are you still dieting? I **saw you eating** some cake.

● I gave up. I couldn't turn away delicious food.

  ●你還在減肥嗎？我看到你吃了一些蛋糕。

  ●我放棄了，我無法抗拒美味的食物。

I saw him working in the office today.

我今天看到他在辦公室工作。

You saw her dancing in the street?

你看到她在街上跳舞？

watch sb -ing

- watch sb do
  看某人做…
- watch TV
  看電視

觀看某人做… see 比較偏向「偶然看到」，watch 則是有意識地觀看動作的進行。

- Why did you come here today?
- I want to **watch Heather act** in the play.
  - 你今天為什麼來這裡？　● 我想看 Heather 在這場戲劇中演出。

▶ I like to watch baseball games.
  我喜歡看棒球比賽。
  I'm not tired yet. I think I will watch TV.
  我還不累，我想我會看電視。

look at

- take a look (at)
  看一看
- take a look around
  在附近看看

注視… 表示有意識地朝著某個人事物的方向看。

- **Look at** this. It's a picture of my boyfriend.
- Wow, he looks like a movie star.
  - 看看這個，這是我男朋友的照片。　● 哇，他看起來好像電影明星。

▶ She is afraid to look at snakes.
  她很怕盯著蛇看。
  Do you mind if I take a look around here?
  你介意我在這附近看看嗎？

wait and see

- wait and see what happens
  等著看會發生什麼事
- wait and see how S+V
  等著看會怎麼…

靜觀事物的發展 因為無法確定接下來的進展，所以決定靜候、觀望。

- When will the festival begin?
- We need to **wait and see.**
  - 慶祝活動什麼時候會開始？　● 我們得等等看。

▶ Let's wait and see how things go.
  我們靜觀其變，看事情會怎麼發展吧。
  Just wait and see what she has to say.
  等著看她要說什麼吧。

lose sight of

沒再看見…，錯失… 表示「從視線中消失」，也就是失去了某個人事物的蹤影。

- Where did Miranda go?
- I don't know. I **lost sight of** her.
  - Miranda 去哪裡了？　● 我不知道，我沒看到她了。

▶ Don't lose sight of the goals you have in life.
  別錯失你人生中的目標。
  He lost sight of his girlfriend at the mall.
  他在購物中心跟女友走丟了。

03 知道 get to know

5-03.mp3

know sth

- know (all) about
  知道關於…（所有）的事
- know of
  聽說過關於…的事
- know sb by sight
  = recognize
  認得某人（的外貌）

（直接）得知…，知道… 如果是 know sb，就是中文說的「認識某人」。

- I'd like to buy some antiques.
- I **know** a lovely antique shop in New York.
  - 我想買些古董。　●我知道紐約有間很可愛的古董店。

▶ I know his phone number and e-mail address.
  我知道他的電話號碼和電子郵件位址。
  Who is she? What do we know about her?
  她是誰？我們知道關於她的什麼？

get to know

- need to know
  需要知道
- happen to know
  剛好知道

得以認識… 表示因緣際會認識某個本來不認識的人，或者因為體驗了某事物而開始了解它。

- Can you recommend a good therapist to me?
- Yes, I **happen to know** a very good psychiatrist.
  - 你可以推薦我好的治療師嗎？
  - 好啊，我剛好知道一個很棒的心理醫生。

▶ You can take this opportunity to get to know her well.
  你可以藉這個機會深入認識她。
  Do you happen to know if there is a good restaurant around here? 你知道這附近有沒有好餐廳嗎？

know the answer

- know the answer to
  that question
  知道那個問題的答案
- know the whole story
  知道所有來龍去脈
- know the truth
  知道真相

知道答案 answer 後面可以加上 to sth，說明是某事的答案。

- The teacher might not **know the answer**.
- It doesn't hurt to ask.
  - 老師可能不知道答案。　●問問看也不會怎樣。

▶ Please just level with me. I want to know the truth.
  請對我坦白，我想知道真相。
  I think I know the answer to this question.
  我想我知道這個問題的答案。

1 職場・學校

2 電腦・網路

3 社交生活

4 日常生活

5 訊息・理解

6 想法・態度

7 情緒・狀況

8 行為舉止

9 時間地點・副詞片語

367

know that S+V

· know what to do
  知道要做什麼
  →知道怎麼做

· want to know what
  S+V
  想知道…什麼

· want sb to know
  that...
  想要某人知道…

知道… that 也可以換成 what, which, how, why 等等。

● We're playing cards. Want to join us?

● Sure. I **know how to** play this game.

  ●我們在玩撲克牌。想加入我們嗎？　●當然好。我知道怎麼玩。

▶ You know how to ride a snowboard, don't you?

  你會玩滑雪板，不是嗎？

  I want to know what the boss said.

  我想知道老闆說了什麼。

have some knowledge of

· have good
  knowledge of
  對…有豐富的知識

· be knowledgeable
  about
  對…有豐富的知識

懂一點… 請記住 knowledge 是 know 的名詞形。形容詞 knowledgeable 的意思是「博學的，有知識的」。

● How can I repair my car?

● Nick **has some knowledge of** car repair.

  ●我該怎麼修我的車子？　●Nick 懂一點修車。

▶ I have some knowledge of foreign cultures.

  我知道一些外國文化。

  I have some knowledge of computers. I can write programs. 我懂一點電腦。我會寫程式。

be aware of

· be aware that S+V
  知道…

· be aware of what...
  知道…

察覺…，知道… aware 前面可以加上 well, fully 等副詞，表示程度。

● **Are** you **aware of** what she said about you?

● No. Did she say something bad?

  ●你知道她說了你什麼嗎？　●不知道。她說了什麼壞話嗎？

▶ You were both aware of the situation.

  你們倆都知道狀況怎樣。

  Are you aware of what's going on with Jim?

  你知道 Jim 過得怎樣嗎？

be familiar with

· be familiar to sb
  被某人認得

熟悉… 可以接人或事物當受詞。A be familiar to B 則表示 B 認得 A，但 A 不認識 B。

● Have you met Bonnie's family?

● No, I'm **not familiar with** them.

  ●你見過 Bonnie 的家人嗎？　●沒有，我跟他們不熟。

▶ I'm familiar with this area.

  我對這區域很熟。

  She's familiar with all phases of this business.

  她通曉這項產業的所有層面。

as far as I know

· as you know
  如你所知
· as you see
  如你所見
· as you can see
  由此可見

就我所知 在說一件自己也不是很了解的事情時，會先說這句話。

● As far as I know, they sent it yesterday.
● Then it should arrive later today.

　●就我所知，他們是昨天寄的。　●那應該今天晚一點會到。

▶ As far as I know, he didn't show up at the party.
　就我所知，他沒有在派對上露面。
　As you know, a lot of people are not familiar with Indian food. 如你所知，很多人不熟悉印度料理。

realized that

· take a/the hint
  領會、看出暗示
· give a hint
  給暗示

了解… 表示了解、領悟到以前不知道的事情。

● Why did you decide to go back home early?
● I realized that I was much happier here with my family.

　●你為什麼決定早點回家？
　●我了解到我還是在這裡陪家人快樂得多。

▶ She came to realize that she was stupid.
　她開始了解自己的愚蠢。
　I realize now that it was a mistake.
　我現在了解那是個錯誤。

notice sth/sb

· notice S+V
  注意到…
· notice A -ing
  注意到 A 做…
· start to notice that
  S+V
  開始注意到…

注意到… 可以表示因為看到或聽到而發現的意思。

● She has an eye for expensive antiques.
● I noticed that.

　●她對昂貴的古董很有眼光。　●我注意到了。

▶ I started to notice that I was making an improvement.
　我開始注意到我正在改善中。
　You'll notice that things are done differently here.
　你會注意到事情在這裡的做法不一樣。

1 職場・學校

2 電腦・網路

3 社交生活

4 日常生活

5 訊息・理解

6 想法・態度

7 情緒・狀況

8 行為舉止

9 時間地點・副詞片語

04 不知道
have no idea

5-04.mp3

not know sth

· not know about
　不知道關於⋯的事

不知道⋯ know 是單純表示「知道」，know about 則是「知道關於⋯的事」。

● My uncle died suddenly last week.
● I **didn't know that.** I'm so sorry for your loss.
　● 我叔叔上週突然死了。
　● 我不知道這件事。我很遺憾你失去了親人。

▶ I have an idea, but I don't know the exact figure.
　我有個想法，但還不知道具體的模樣。
　I mean it. I didn't know about that.
　我說真的，我不熟悉那件事。

not know how to

不知道該怎麼⋯ 使用的是「疑問詞 + to do」當名詞的句型。

● Jerry was happy to see you tonight.
● I know, but I **didn't know what to** say to him.
　● Jerry 今晚很高興能看到你。
　● 我知道，但我不知道該跟他說什麼。

▶ I don't know how to thank you.
　我不知道該怎麼謝你。
　I don't know what to do.
　我不知道該做什麼。

not know that S+V

不知道⋯ 不知道的事情是一個句子時，可以在 know 後面接 that 子句、what 子句或 if 子句。

● I **don't know if** my homework is correct.
● Why don't I check it for you?
　● 我不知道我的作業寫得對不對。　● 要不要我幫你檢查？

▶ I don't know what I'm going to do.
　我不知道我該做什麼。
　I don't know if it's such a good idea.
　我不知道這個主意有沒有那麼好。

370

have no idea

- have no idea how to do...
  不知道該怎麼做…
- have no idea how S+V...
  不知道是怎麼…的
- not have the slightest idea
  壓根沒有主意

不知道 這裡的 idea 不是「想法」的意思，而是 knowledge 的意思。I got an idea 或 come up with an idea 裡的 idea 才是「點子，提案」的意思。

- How was your trip to Toronto?
- You **have no idea how** exciting it was.
  ●你的多倫多之旅如何？ ●你不知道那有多刺激。

▶ I had no idea you were from New York.
  我不知道你是從紐約來的。
  I have no idea what you're talking about.
  我不知道你在說什麼。

not have a clue

- not have a clue what/where/why/how...
  完全不知道…
- not see any reason why S+V
  不了解為什麼…

完全不知道 clue 意為「線索」。「沒有一點線索」就是完全不知道、一點也不知道的意思。

- Has Peter ever been to Boston?
- I **don't have a clue**.
  ●Peter 有去過波士頓嗎？ ●我完全不知道。

▶ I don't have a clue where we are.
  我完全不知道我們在哪裡。
  He doesn't see any reason why you were so upset.
  他完全不了解你為什麼那麼生氣。

know nothing about

- not know anything about
  對於…完全不知道
- not know the first thing about...
  對於…一無所知
- not know the half of...
  對於…不太清楚

對於…什麼都不知道 不用 not，而是用有否定意義的 nothing 來表示「什麼都不知道」。

- Did those kids break the window?
- No, they **know nothing about** it.
  ●那些孩子把窗戶打破了嗎？ ●沒有，他們什麼都不知道。

▶ You don't know anything about her, do you?
  關於她，你什麼都不知道，對嗎？
  I don't know the first thing about the stock market.
  我對股票市場一無所知。

not know for sure

不太確定 sure 也可以換成 certain，意思一樣。

- How long is the storm going to last?
- Maybe an hour. I **don't know for sure**.
  ●這場暴風雪會持續多久？ ●也許一小時吧，我也不清楚。

▶ I think she might be a little late but I don't know for sure.
  我想她會遲到一下，但我也不是很確定。
  I really don't know for sure, but I'm willing to give it a try.
  我真的不太確定，但我願意試試看。

1 職場・學校
2 電腦・網路
3 社交生活
4 日常生活
5 訊息・理解
6 想法・態度
7 情緒・狀況
8 行為舉止
9 時間地點・副詞片語

without one's knowing

- without knowing what to do
  不知道該怎麼做
- without knowing A
  不知道 A

沒讓某人發覺 在某人不知道的情況下做了某些事。

- Did the teacher catch you skipping class?
- No, I skipped class **without her knowing**.

   ●老師有抓到你蹺課嗎？   ●沒有，我沒讓她發現我蹺課。

▶ Linda left the party without my knowing.

   Linda 離開了派對，沒讓我發覺。

   The thief stole the money without anyone knowing.

   小偷神不知鬼不覺地偷走了錢。

You got me

- Search me.
  我不知道。
- Beat me.
  我不知道。

你問倒我了 除了「你抓到我了」以外，也用來表示被對方的問題問倒了。

- Is George coming over today?
- **You got me**. I haven't heard anything.

   ●George 今天會過來嗎？   ●你問倒我了，我什麼也沒聽說。

▶ I don't know. You got me.

   我不知道，你考倒我了。

   What will happen? You got me.

   會發生什麼事？你考倒我了。

not that I know of

- Not that I remember
  就我所記得的並非如此

據我所知並非如此 know of 也可以換成 remember, recall 等動詞來使用。

- Are you allergic to any kinds of medication?
- **Not that I know of.**

   ●你對任何藥物過敏嗎？   ●據我所知沒有。

▶ Not that I know of, but I'll go and check.

   據我所知並非如此，但我會去檢查看看。

   Not that I know of. Why?

   據我所知不是這樣。你為什麼這麼問？

1 職場・學校

2 電腦・網路

3 社交生活

4 日常生活

5 訊息・理解

6 想法・態度

7 情緒・狀況

8 行為舉止

9 時間地點・副詞片語

05 問問題，詢問 ask about

5-05.mp3

ask (sb) about

· ask about sth/sb/-ing
問關於…的事
· ask sb about sth/sb/
-ing
問某人關於…的事

（跟某人）問關於…的事 about 後面接名詞或動詞 -ing 形。

● Who should I **ask about** extending my vacation?
● Me, I'm the one in charge.

　●我該跟誰詢問延長休假的事情？　●我，我是負責的人。

▶ Why did you ask me about my marriage?
你為什麼問起我的婚姻？
I'm told they asked about us.
我被告知他們問起了我們的事。

ask (sb) a question

· ask some questions
about
問一些關於…的問題

問（某人）問題 a question（一個問題）也可以換成 a few questions 或 some questions 表示「幾個問題」。

● Can I **ask you a few questions**?
● You can ask me anything you want to.

　●我可以問你幾個問題嗎？　●你想問什麼都可以。

▶ Can I ask you a question? It's urgent.
我可以問你一個問題嗎？這很急。
Feel free to ask me any questions you might have.
如果你有任何問題，儘管問。

ask sb why/what...

· ask sb if S+V
問某人是否…

問某人… 要問的問題可以用「疑問詞 S+V」的形態來表達。

● My boss **asked me if** I planned to change jobs.
● So, what did you say to him?

　●我的老闆問我是不是打算換工作。　●那你跟他說了什麼？

▶ The bank teller asked me if I wanted to open an account. 銀行行員問我是否想開戶。
She asked me what I did for a living.
她問我的職業是什麼。

have a question

· have a question for sb
  有問題要問某人
· have a question
  about sth
  有關於某事的問題
· call into question...
  質疑…

有問題（要問） 後面可以加上 about sth 表示是什麼問題。

● You got a sec? I **have a question** for you.
● Sorry, how about later? I have an appointment.
  ●你有時間嗎？我有個問題想問你。
  ●抱歉，等一下可以嗎？我有一個約。

▶ Excuse me, I have a question for you.
  不好意思，我有個問題要問你。
  Do you have some questions to ask me?
  你有些問題要問我嗎？

answer one's question

· answer sb
  回答某人
· answer me this
  回答我這個（問題）

回答某人的問題 answer sb 其實也是一樣的意思。

● Why didn't you **answer my question**?
● Okay, I will give you an answer soon.
  ●你為什麼不回答我的問題？　●好吧，我會很快給你答案。

▶ You didn't answer my question.
  你沒回答我的問題。
  Just answer me this: Why did we break up?
  你只要回答我這個問題：我們為什麼分手？

give sb an answer

· give (sb) a firm answer
  給（某人）確切的答案
· get an answer
  得到答案

給某人答案 answer 當名詞的時候，可以和 give, get 等動詞連用。

● Could you **give me an answer** by tomorrow?
● Sure, I'll let you know by then.
  ●你明天前可以給我一個答案嗎？　●當然，我到時候會告訴你。

▶ I'd like to give you an answer after work.
  我想下班後再給你答案。
  You don't have to give me an answer right now.
  你不需要現在就回答我。

wonder if S+V

想知道是否… wonder 這個字有感覺不確定，所以「納悶、想知道」的意思。

● I **wonder if** Tammy is still angry that she was fired.
● Well, that was five years ago.
  ●不知道 Tammy 是不是還因為被炒魷魚而生氣。
  ●嗯，那是五年前的事了。

▶ I wonder if he will finish the report on time.
  我懷疑他會不會準時完成報告。
  I am curious whether I will get a raise next year.
  我很好奇我明年會不會加薪。

1 職場・學校

2 電腦・網路

3 社交生活

4 日常生活

5 訊息・理解

6 想法・態度

7 情緒・狀況

8 行為舉止

9 時間地點・副詞片語

be curious about

· be curious about
  how...
  好奇如何…

· be curious to know...
  好奇想知道…

· be curious whether
  S+V
  好奇是否…

對…好奇 也可以用 curious 加上 to know / to see / to hear 等與獲得訊息有關的動詞。

● What I'm **curious about** is whose USB it was.

● It was my USB.

　●我好奇的是，這是誰的 USB？　●那是我的 USB。

▶ You're not curious what he wrote about you?

　你不好奇他寫了你什麼嗎？

　I'm just curious about how she talked you into doing
　that. 我只是好奇她是怎麼説服你做那件事的。

---

06 確認，檢查
check out

5-06.mp3

check out

· Check it out!
  來看看吧！

· checkout
  結帳處

檢查，結帳離開，將書借出 想一探究竟而去確認的行為。除此之外，也有很多約定俗成的意思。

● I'd like to **check out** now.

● Could you tell me your room number please?

　●我想要退房。　●可以請您告訴我您的房號嗎？

▶ Check out all the houses decorated with lights for
　Christmas. 看看那些為了耶誕節而裝上燈飾的房子。
　We need to check out your office. 我們需要檢查你的辦公室。

check in

· check in one's
  baggage
  （在機場）託運行李

登記入住，辦理登機手續 表示「登記進入」的意思，是旅館和機場的慣用語。

● We have to **check in** our bags at least half an hour
　before our flight.

● Let's do that now and then go for a coffee.

　●我們最晚要在飛機起飛前半小時辦理登機手續。

　●我們現在就去吧，然後去喝杯咖啡。

▶ Is it too early to check in? 現在登記入住會太早嗎？
　She checked in yesterday and paid with a credit card.
　她昨天登記入住，並且用信用卡付款

go over

- go over sth
  檢視某物
- » cf. go over to a place
  去某個地方
- check over
  檢視…

審查…，檢視… go over to 則是「去（某處）」的意思。

- Why did Jeremy call the meeting?
- He wants to **go over** our future plans.

  ●Jeremy 為什麼召開這場會議？　●他想審查我們未來的計畫。

▶ They didn't go over the schedule.

他們沒有檢視時間表。

Let's sit down and go over the budget.

我們坐下來審查預算吧。

check on

- check up on
  確認…（的狀態）

確認… 確認是否有異常、是否正常運作、是否安全、是不是事實等等。受詞可以是人或事物。check up on 也是一樣的意思。

- The chair I ordered has not yet arrived.
- I can **check on** your order for you.

  ●我訂的椅子還沒來。　●我可以幫你確認你的訂單狀態。

▶ Sam ran forward to check on what was going on.

Sam 跑去前面確認發生什麼事。

I checked on him but he's a little busy today.

我去看了他，但他今天有點忙。

run a check

- run a check on sth/sb
  檢查，測試…

做檢查，做測試 run 也可以換成 carry out, make 或 do 等動詞。

- Is all of this information correct?
- We should **run a check** to make sure.

  ●這些資訊都是正確的嗎？　●我們應該做檢查來確認。

▶ I can run a check on the new employees.

我可以測試新進員工。

They ran a check on each person.

他們測試了每個人。

let me check

- Let me check sth
  讓我確認看看某事
- Let me check if S+V
  讓我確認是否…

讓我確認看看 自發性地要去確認某件事時，可以這麼說。check 後面可以接名詞或 if S+V 表示要確認的事物。

- Do you know when the next train leaves?
- Just a moment. **Let me check**.

  ●你知道下班車什麼時候出發嗎？　●等等，讓我確認一下。

▶ Let me check your temperature.

讓我量一下你的體溫。

Let me see if I can reschedule the appointment.

讓我看看我是否能重新安排這個約會。

check to see if S+V

· check and see (if)
　確認看看（是否…）
· check if S+V
　確認看看是否…
· see if
　看看是否…

確認看看是否… 把 check if 和 see if 結合成 check to see if 的表達方式。

● Is your boss in the office?
● I'll **check to see if** he came in.
　●你的老闆在辦公室裡嗎？　●我去確認看看他進來了沒有。

▶ I'm just checking to see if she's okay.
　我只是想看看她好不好。
　I'll see if she wants to come back.
　我去看看她想不想回來。

look over

檢查…，瀏覽… 帶有「很快速地檢查過一遍」的意思。

● James gave me the report this morning.
● Let's **look over** what it says.
　●James 今天早上給了我這份報告。　●我們看一看它寫了什麼吧。

▶ Karen looked over the new rules.
　Karen 看了一遍新的規定。
　You need to look over this e-mail.
　你該看看這封電子郵件。

look into

深入檢查…，調查… examine carefully 的意思。可以接名詞或動詞 -ing 形當受詞。

● Did you ever **look into** that stock I told you about?
● I did and I bought some of it.
　●你有去研究我之前跟你說過的那支股票嗎？
　●有，而且我買了一些。

▶ Let's look into getting a dog.
　我們研究看看要怎麼領養一隻狗吧。
　We have to look into the matter right now.
　我們必須立刻調查這件事。

look up

· look (sth) up in the
　dictionary
　查字典（找某個字）

查找… 表示在書、字典或電腦上查詢想要的資訊。

● I don't know what this word means.
● Let's **look it up** in the dictionary.
　●我不知道這個字是什麼意思。　●我們查查字典吧。

▶ We can look up his name in the phone book.
　我們可以在電話簿裡找他的名字。
　I want to look up a friend who lives in Berlin.
　我想找一位住在柏林的朋友。

1 職場・學校
2 電腦・網路
3 社交生活
4 日常生活
5 訊息・理解
6 想法・態度
7 情緒・狀況
8 行為舉止
9 時間地點・副詞片語

make sure

- make sure of
  確認⋯
- make sure that S+V
  確認⋯

確認 常用來提醒別人要記得確認某事。

- ●**Make sure** that you log off when you're through.
- ●Don't worry, I will.
  - ●用完之後，要記得登出。　●別擔心，我會的。

▶ We need to make sure that the CEO is able to attend.
   我們需要確認那位 CEO 可以出席。
   I'll make sure that I'll keep in touch.
   我會記得保持聯絡。

get sth straight

- get things straight
  把事情弄清楚
- straighten out
  澄清⋯，清理⋯
- Let me get this
  straight.
  讓我弄清楚這件事。

把某事弄清楚 常常以「Let me get it straight」的句型來表達。

- ●Let me **get this straight**, you don't love me?
- ●That's right!
  - ●讓我把事情搞清楚。你不愛我嗎？　●沒錯！

▶ Let me get this straight. He tried to hit you?
   讓我把事情搞清楚。他試圖打你嗎？
   Let's just get one thing straight. I don't want to date you.
   我就直說了，我不想跟你約會。

let me repeat that

讓我再說一遍 想再把某件事強調一次時可以用的說法。

- ●So can I buy a new sports car?
- ●No! **Let me repeat that**. No!
  - ●所以我可以買新的跑車嗎？　●不行！我再說一次，不行！

▶ I'm leaving. Let me repeat that. I'm gone.
   我要走了。讓我再說一次，我走了。
   Let me repeat that, first insert your card then turn the
   key. 讓我再說一次，先把你的卡插進去，然後轉動鑰匙。

you said S+V

- You told me (that) ...
  你跟我說過⋯
- I thought you said
  S+V
  我以為你說過⋯
- I guess you're talking
  about...
  我猜你在說的是⋯

你說過⋯ 通常會拉高音調，強調對方說過某件事，用意是要搞清楚事實究竟是怎樣。

- ●**You said** I'm such a loser?
- ●I'm so sorry, but everyone knows that.
  - ●你說我真的很失敗？　●我很抱歉，但大家都知道啊。

▶ You said that you liked me! How could you do this to
   me? 你說過你喜歡我的！你怎麼可以這樣對我？
   You told me that you didn't like the secretary.
   你說你不喜歡那個祕書的。

see to it that...

- see (to it) that S+V
  記得要…
- see to it
  記得一定要做到

記得要… 和 make sure 的意思類似，通常是有事拜託別人，請對方一定要做到。

- I can give you the money tomorrow.
- **See to it that** you do.

  ●我明天可以給你錢。　●你一定要記得給我。

▶ See to it Candy gets this package.

　一定要讓 Candy 拿到這個包裹。

　See to it the computer gets turned off.

　一定要記得確認電腦有關機。

---

07 傳聞
hear a rumor

5-07.mp3

rumor has it that

- There is a rumor that S+V
  有傳聞說…
- There is a rumor going around the office/campus that S+V
  辦公室／校園裡有傳聞說…
- It is wildly rumored that S+V
  …的傳聞甚囂塵上

有傳聞說… 表示自己聽到了什麼傳聞。

- **Rumor has it that** you'll be promoted next month.
- Right. I'll become a vice president.

  ●有傳言說你下個月會升職。　●對，我會當上副總裁。

▶ Rumor has it that we are going to get a 20% cut.

　有傳聞說我們會被減薪 20%。

　There is a rumor that Christine is pregnant.

　有八卦說 Christine 懷孕了。

hear a rumor

- hear a rumor that S+V
  聽到傳聞說…
- hear some negative rumors about
  聽到一些關於…的負面謠言

聽到傳聞 可以在後面加上 about N 或 that S+V，說明 rumor 的內容。

- Annie, I **heard a rumor** that you got married.
- That's not true. I'm so embarrassed.

  ●Annie，我聽到傳聞說妳結婚了。　●那不是真的，我覺得好尷尬。

▶ I heard a rumor that the store's going to shut down.

　我聽到傳聞說這間店要關了。

　I heard some negative rumors about the election.

　我聽到一些關於選舉的負面謠言。

1 職場・學校

2 電腦・網路

3 社交生活

4 日常生活

5 訊息・理解

6 想法・態度

7 情緒・狀況

8 行為舉止

9 時間地點・副詞片語

start rumors

- spread rumors
  散播謠言
- spread gossip about
  散播關於…的八卦
- hear an interesting
  piece of gossip about
  聽到一個關於…的有趣八
  卦

散播謠言 也可以用單數形 start a rumor。

- They've been spreading rumors about us.
- We've got to get even.
  - 他們散播跟我們有關的謠言。　●我們得報仇。

▶ I heard you were spreading gossip about my divorce.
  我聽說你在散佈我離婚的謠言。
  Do you want me tell you the rumor people spread?
  你要我告訴你大家都在傳什麼八卦嗎？

get wind of

- get wind of the
  possibility (that) S+V
  聽到風聲說可能會…
- hear sth through the
  grapevine
  從小道消息聽說某事
- A little bird told me
  (that S+V)
  我聽小道消息說…

聽到…的風聲 跟中文一樣，用「風」比喻來路不明的傳言。

- Is it true that Richard is going to quit?
- I think so. I just **got wind of** it.
  - Richard 是真的要辭職嗎？　●我想是真的，我剛聽到風聲。

▶ I got wind of the possibility that the store would be sold.
  我聽到風聲說這間店可能會被賣掉。
  I heard through the grapevine that you're going to move.
  我聽到小道消息說你要搬家。

travel fast

- (Rumors) get around
  fast
  （謠言）散播得很快

（謠言等）散播得很快 主詞可以是 word, good news, bad news 等等。

- Did you hear Rex got engaged?
- Yes I did. Good news **travels fast**.
  - 你聽說 Rex 訂婚了嗎？　●有，真是好事傳千里啊。

▶ Word of her accident traveled fast.
  她出意外的消息傳得很快。
  News of the baby's birth traveled fast.
  小寶寶出生的消息傳得很快。

1 職場・學校

2 電腦・網路

3 社交生活

4 日常生活

5 訊息・理解

6 想法・態度

7 情緒・狀況

8 行為舉止

9 時間地點・副詞片語

08 消息，情報 find out

5-08.mp3

inform sb of sth

- inform sb (that) S+V
  通知某人…
- be informed of
  被通知／告知…

通知某人某事 of 也可以換成 about。

- I'm here to tell you that we're cutting 100 jobs.
- Why didn't you **inform** us earlier?
  - 我是來跟你們說，我們要砍掉一百個職位。
  - 你為什麼不早點通知我們？

▶ Sandy informed us she was quitting school.
Sandy 通知我們說她要休學。
She came by to inform us of her resignation.
她順道來通知我們她辭職了。

get information on

- give sb the information
  給某人資訊
- find the information for sb
  幫某人找資訊
- hide the information from sb
  對某人隱藏資訊

獲得關於…的資訊 on 也可以換成 about。

- Please **get me some information on** the company.
- What kind of information do you need?
  - 請給我一些關於那間公司的資訊。 ● 你需要哪種資訊？

▶ When we get any new information, I'll let you know.
如果我們得到任何新消息，我會告訴你。
I'm just trying to find some information on the city.
我只是試著找一些關於那個城市的資訊。

find out

- find out about sth/sb
  查明…
- find out what S+V
  查明…什麼

發現…，查明… 也就是「取得關於…的資訊」（get information about...）。

- How did you **find out** about this concert?
- There was a newspaper ad describing it.
  - 你怎麼發現這個音樂會的？ ● 報紙上有音樂會的廣告。

▶ When you find out the results, please give me a call.
當你查出結果，請打個電話給我。
I'm calling to find out if the meeting has been postponed. 我打電話來確認這個會議是否被延期了。

keep sb posted

· keep sb posted on
  how S+V
  隨時告訴某人…得如何

隨時告訴某人消息 post 原本是「張貼訊息」的意思。「一直 post 某人」就是持續告訴某人消息。

● Paula was taken to the hospital today.
● **Keep us posted on** what happens to her.

　●Paula 今天被送去醫院了。　●請隨時告訴我們她的狀況。

▶ Keep me posted on how she's doing.
　隨時告訴我她過得怎樣。
　I've got to go. I'll keep you posted, okay?
　我得走了，我會隨時通知你，好嗎？

fill sb in on

· fill in the blank
  填空格
· fill in the form
  填寫表格

告訴某人關於…的詳情 特別常用在對方沒參與某件事，或者不知道整體的情形，所以要為對方補充資訊的情況。fill in 最常用的意思是「填寫（資料）」。

● I have a lot to tell you about the meeting.
● You'll have to **fill me in** later because I'm busy now.

　●關於那場會議，我有很多要跟你說。
　●你等一下再告訴我，因為我現在很忙。

▶ Well, I'll be happy to fill in the blanks.
　嗯，我很樂意填寫這些空格。
　Please fill in all the information on the form.
　請將所有資料填在表格上。

give (sb) a message

· get the message
  收到訊息
· have a message
  有訊息

傳達訊息（給某人） 可以表示把字條送到某人手上、告訴某人電話留言的內容等等。

● My phone may **have a message** from them.
● Hurry and tell me what it says.

　●我手機上可能有他們傳來的訊息。　●趕快告訴我上面說什麼。

▶ I'll give her the message as soon as she gets in.
　她一進來，我就會把訊息傳達給她。
　Would you please give him a message for me?
　你可以幫我傳個話給他嗎？

have news for

· have good news for...
  有好消息要跟…說
· have some bad news
  有些壞消息
· hear the bad news
  聽到壞消息

有消息要跟…說 for 後面接人，表示「給某人的消息」。此外，news 的前面常常會加上 good 或 bad 表示是好消息或壞消息。

● I **have some bad news for** you.
● Oh? Give it to me straight.

　●我有些壞消息要跟你說。　●哦？就直說吧。

▶ Here's good news for you. 有好消息要跟你說。
　I've got news for you. You're going to be promoted!
　我有消息要跟你說。你要升職了！

read sth in the newspaper

· read/see in the (news) paper that S+V
在報紙上讀到／看到…（的消息）

· read a newspaper article which said that...
讀到一篇說…的報紙報導

· read about A in the newspaper
在報紙上讀到與 A 有關的新聞

在報紙上讀到某事 注意介系詞是 in，「（某些內容）在書上」也是說 in a book。

● I **read in the newspaper** that the economy is bad.

● That's right. Business is bad for everyone.

　　●我在報紙上讀到經濟狀況很差的消息。

　　●是啊，對每個人來說景氣都很差。

▶ I just read it this morning in the newspaper.
我今天早上才在報紙上看到這件事。

I read in the newspaper that Brad Pitt got married.
我在報紙上看到布萊德彼特結婚了。

see on the news that

在電視新聞上看到… 和 on TV 一樣，介系詞是 on。

● Why are you joining a gym?

● I **saw on the news that** exercise builds muscles.

　　●你為什麼要加入健身房？　　●我看到新聞說運動可以增加肌肉。

▶ I saw on the news that hiking is becoming popular.
我看到新聞說最近開始流行登山健行。

I saw on the news that arctic ice is melting.
我看到新聞說北極的冰在融化。

find A on the Internet

在網路上找到 A 要表示搜尋的過程，則可以說 search for A。

● I **found something on the Internet** for our report.

● What information did you get?

　　●我在網路上找到一些我們報告可以用的東西。

　　●你找到了什麼資訊？

▶ I found a cheap price on the Internet.
我在網路上找到了便宜的價格。

I found his website on the Internet.
我在網路上找到了他的網站。

1 職場・學校

2 電腦・網路

3 社交生活

4 日常生活

5 訊息・理解

6 想法・態度

7 情緒・狀況

8 行為舉止

9 時間地點・副詞片語

09 誤會
get sb wrong

5-09.mp3

get sb wrong

· Don't get me wrong
別誤會我

誤會某人 動詞 get 也可以換成 take。

● Do you really hate my shoes?
● Don't **get me wrong**. I think they are OK.

　●你真的討厭我的鞋嗎？　●別誤會我，我覺得還 OK。

▶ Don't get me wrong, I'd love to work with you.
　別誤會我，我很想跟你一起共事。
　Don't get me wrong. I'm trying to help you.
　別誤會我，我在努力幫你。

take sth the wrong way

· Don't take this the wrong way (, but...)
別誤會（，但…）

誤解某事物 the wrong way 可以表示「錯誤的路」或者「錯誤的方法」。

● Why is Tanya so angry at you?
● She **took** something I said **the wrong way**.

　●Tanya 為什麼對你那麼生氣？　●她誤解了我說的話。

▶ Don't take what I say the wrong way.
　別誤解我說的話。
　Don't take this the wrong way, but how old are you?
　我沒有別的意思，但請問你幾歲？

take it personally

· Don't take it personally.
不要當作是針對你；我不是針對你。

當作是針對自己 通常以 Don't take it personally 的形式出現，表示接下來要說的話可能會讓對方不太高興，希望對方不要當成人身攻擊。

● What did she say about me?
● Don't **take it personally**, but she said you were a jerk.

　●她怎麼說我的？　●別太放心上，她說你是個混帳。

▶ Don't take it personally, but I really don't like your new haircut. 我不是針對你，但我真的不喜歡你的新髮型。
　I can't help but take it personally.
　我就是忍不住對號入座。

mean no offense

- I really didn't mean any offense
  我真的無意冒犯
- I didn't mean any harm
  我無意冒犯
- No offense
  無意冒犯
- None taken
  我不介意（表示自己沒有因為聽到什麼話而不開心）

無意冒犯 也可以把 offense 換成 harm 使用。

- I don't want to be your friend. **No offense.**
- Gee, that's too bad.
  ●我無意冒犯，但我不想當你的朋友。　　●噢，真是太糟了。

▶ No offense, but I've got to go back home.
  我沒有惡意，但我得回家了。
  I think that coat isn't a good match for you. No offense.
  我無意冒犯，但我覺得那件大衣跟你不太搭。

have no hard feelings

- No hard feelings on my part
  我沒有生氣
- There were no hard feelings
  （某人）沒有生氣

不覺得生氣 常常用來表示「我沒有生氣」，希望對方不要誤會自己。

- I'm sorry that we argued.
- **There are no hard feelings on my part.**
  ●很抱歉我們吵架了。　　●我沒有生氣。

▶ It was a mistake, and he has no hard feelings.
  那是個誤會，而且他也不覺得生氣。
  No hard feelings about you leaving me behind.
  我沒有因為你丟下我而生氣。

didn't mean to

- I didn't mean to offend you
  我不是有意冒犯你的
- I didn't mean to insult you
  我不是有意侮辱你的
- I didn't mean it
  我不是有意的

無意做… 表示不是有意做某件事，希望對方不要誤會。也可以直接說 didn't mean it，用 it 代替不定詞來表示某個行為。

- How could you do this to me?
- I really **didn't mean to** make you miserable.
  ●你怎麼可以這樣對我？　　●我真的無意讓你那麼悲慘。

▶ I'm sorry! I didn't mean to do that!
  我很抱歉！我不是有意那麼做的。
  I didn't mean to hurt you.
  我無意傷害你。

mistake A for B

將 A 誤認為 B 不論是錯認了人或事物，都適用這個片語。

- Why are you eating the tomato sauce?
- Oh my, I **mistook** the tomato sauce **for** soup.
  ●你為什麼在吃番茄醬？　　●我的天啊，我把番茄醬當成湯了。

▶ Jerry mistook a stranger for one of his friends.
  Jerry 把一位陌生人誤認為他的朋友。
  He was so drunk that he mistook the student for his wife. 他喝得太醉，把那位學生誤認為他太太。

1 職場・學校
2 電腦・網路
3 社交生活
4 日常生活
5 訊息・理解
6 想法・態度
7 情緒・狀況
8 行為舉止
9 時間地點・副詞片語

be a misunderstanding

· There's a little misunderstanding
有一點誤會

是個誤會 常常用在 there is... 的句型裡表示「有誤會」，這時候可以把 be 改成 seem to be 或 must have been 表示推測。

● What do you think about Pam?
● I think she's completely innocent and it's **all a big misunderstanding**.
　● 你覺得 Pam 怎麼樣？
　● 我覺得她是清白的，這整件事是個很大的誤會。

▶ There seems to be some kind of misunderstanding.
看來有些什麼誤會。
This can't be happening. This is a misunderstanding.
這不可能發生的。這是個誤會。

cause a misunderstanding

· avoid any possible misunderstanding
避免任何可能的誤會
· produce a misunderstanding
產生誤會

造成誤會 cause 的受詞經常是不好的結果。

● Can I drink some beer in the park?
● No, it might **cause a misunderstanding**.
　● 我可以在公園喝點啤酒嗎？　● 不行，那樣可能會造成誤會。

▶ Jason's rude manners caused a misunderstanding.
Jason 粗魯的行為造成了誤會。
Different customs can cause misunderstandings.
不同的習俗會造成誤會。

be a little mix-up

· be confused
困惑的

有點混亂 用在 There is... 的句型，mix-up 可以換成 confusion。

● This isn't the food I ordered.
● I'm sorry sir. There **was a little mix-up**.
　● 這不是我點的食物。　● 先生不好意思，我們搞混了。

▶ There was a little mix-up during the concert.
音樂會進行途中有點混亂。
There was a little mix-up when I traveled overseas.
我在國外旅行的時候發生了一點混亂。

1 職場・學校

2 電腦・網路

3 社交生活

4 日常生活

5 訊息・理解

6 想法・態度

7 情緒・狀況

8 行為舉止

9 時間地點・副詞片語

10 起疑心
have doubts about

5-10.mp3

doubt sth

· not doubt that S+V
  不懷疑…
· doubt if S+V
  懷疑是否…
  →覺得…不太可能

對某事起疑 doubt 如果接子句，可以翻譯成「覺得…不太可能」。

● **I doubt** you will be able to get baseball tickets.

● Well, I'm going to try anyway. It won't hurt.

  ●我懷疑你是否能弄到棒球賽門票。

  ●嗯，總之我就試試看，試試看也不會怎樣。

▶ I doubt that it's possible.

  我覺得那不太可能。

  I doubt if you noticed, but I was late again today.

  我覺得你可能沒注意到，但我今天又遲到了。

have doubts about

· have doubts that S+V
  對…有懷疑
· be doubtful
  懷疑

對…有懷疑 doubt 當名詞用，後面接 about sth 或 that S+V 說明懷疑的事。

● Are Aarron and Emily going to get married?

● I think they **have doubts about** their relationship.

  ●Aarron 和 Emily 會結婚？ ●我覺得他們對這段關係有些質疑。

▶ I have doubts about my new boss.

  我不是很信任我的新老闆。

  He has doubts about Claire's cooking skills.

  他對 Claire 的廚藝有疑問。

have no doubt about

· have no doubt (that)
  S+V
  確信…

對…深信不疑 「沒有 doubt」就是「很確定」的意思。

● Are you sure our basketball team will win?

● I **have no doubt about** the outcome.

  ●你確定我們的籃球隊會贏嗎？ ●我對這個結果深信不疑。

▶ Tim had no doubt about his future plans.

  Tim 對於他未來的計畫非常確定。

  I have no doubt you'll get better.

  我很確定你的狀況會變好。

there is no doubt of

· There's no doubt of/about
　…是無庸置疑的
· without a doubt
　無庸置疑
· No doubt.
　當然。

…是無庸置疑的 of 可以換成 about，或者直接在 no doubt 後面接子句。

● She's an excellent musician.

● **No doubt.** She's talented and she practices a lot.

　●她是一位傑出的音樂家。　●當然。她既有天分又經常練習。

▶ There is no doubt we'll get there on time.

　我們一定會準時抵達那裡。

　There is no doubt about it, he's going to file for bankruptcy. 無庸置疑地，他會提出破產申請。

suspect that...

· suspect sth
　懷疑某事

懷疑…，猜想… 感覺可能有什麼不好的事，或者心中對於事實真相有些猜測時會用的說法。

● Did the police catch the bank robber?

● No. I **suspect that** he'll rob another bank.

　●警察抓到銀行搶匪了嗎？　●沒有，我猜他還會再搶另一間銀行。

▶ Jane suspects that Tommy likes her.

　Jane 懷疑 Tommy 喜歡她。

　I suspect that my daughter has been drinking.

　我懷疑我女兒有在喝酒。

---

11 | 說實話 tell the truth

5-11.mp3

tell (sb) the truth

· to tell you the truth
　說真的…
· frankly speaking
　老實說…
· to be frank with you
　老實跟你說…

（對某人）說實話 正所謂「真相只有一個」，truth 通常只會以 the truth 的形態出現。

● Should I **tell him the truth**?

● Just do the right thing.

　●我該跟他說實話嗎？　●做正確的事（說實話）就對了。

▶ You better tell him the truth.

　你最好跟他說實話。

　Why didn't you just tell her the truth?

　你為什麼不直接跟她說實話呢？

be honest with

- be honest about sth
  對某事坦白
- to be honest (with you)
  坦白說…
- be honest with sb and say that...
  坦白地對某人說…

對⋯誠實 對人誠實可以說 with sb，對某事坦白則是 about sth。

- How can I say I don't love Jane?
- Just **be honest with** her.
  - ●我怎麼能對 Jane 說我不愛她？　●就坦白跟她說吧。

▶ Stop saying that. You have to be honest with me.
  別再那樣說了。你得對我誠實。
  I'm going to be honest with you.
  我要跟你坦白。

give it to sb straight

- tell it like it is
  實話實說
- Give it to me straight.
  有話直說。

對某人直說 特別常用在祈使句 Give it to me straight. 裡。

- How will you tell Jim that his mom died?
- I'll have to **give it to him straight**.
  - ●你要怎麼跟 Jim 說他媽媽去世了？　●我得跟他直說。

▶ Give it to me straight. I can't wait to hear about that.
  有話直說。我等不及要聽了。
  How about you give it to me straight?
  你何不跟我直說呢？

level with sb (on sth)

- get something off one's chest
  將某事一吐為快

向某人坦白（某事） 通常表示說出某個不好的消息，或不願意透露的事實。

- Please just **level with me**. I want to know the truth.
- I'd like to, but I can't. This is a secret.
  - ●請跟我坦白，我想知道真相。
  - ●我很想，但我不能這麼做。這是個祕密。

▶ I think it's time to level with you.
  我想是時候跟你坦白了。
  I really need to level with you. I am very unhappy.
  我真的得跟你老實說，我非常不開心。

come clean with sb

- spit it out
  把話坦白說出來

對某人坦白承認 帶有「把祕密都說出來」的意思，通常表示曾經隱瞞自己犯下的錯誤。

- You have to **come clean with** Judith.
- I just can't tell her how I feel.
  - ●你必須對 Judith 坦白。　●我就是沒辦法告訴她我的感受。

▶ You've got to come clean with me.
  你得對我坦白承認。
  You have got to come clean with her! This is not right!
  你得對她坦白承認！這樣不對！

1 職場・學校
2 電腦・網路
3 社交生活
4 日常生活
5 訊息・理解
6 想法・態度
7 情緒・狀況
8 行為舉止
9 時間地點・副詞片語

12 祕密
keep a secret

5-12.mp3

keep a secret

- keep sth a secret
  將某事保密
- keep a secret from
  對…保密（不讓…知道）
- keep a secret about
  保守一個關於…的祕密

保守祕密 也可以說 keep sth a secret，就是讓某事保持在祕密的狀態。

- Can I trust you to **keep a secret**?
- Sure, you can count on me.
  - 我可以相信你會保密嗎？　●當然，你可以相信我。

▶ Could you keep a secret?
  你可以保密嗎？
  Don't worry. I can keep a secret.
  別擔心，我會保密的。

keep quiet

- keep quiet about
  保守關於…的祕密
- keep sth quiet
  將某事保密

緘口不語，保密 後面也可以加上 about 接保密的事情。

- Tell me what Joseph did last night.
- OK, but you need to **keep quiet** about it.
  - 告訴我 Joseph 昨晚做了什麼。　●好，但你得保密。

▶ Keep quiet about the money I gave you.
  別對任何人提起我給你的錢。
  Why do you keep quiet about it?
  你為什麼對那件事什麼也不說？

keep one's mouth shut

- Keep this to yourself.
  不要把這件事告訴別人。

保守祕密 直譯就是「閉著嘴」的意思。後面也可以加上 about 接保密的事情。

- Is this a secret?
- Yes it is. **Keep your mouth shut.**
  - 這是祕密嗎？　●對，所以閉緊你的嘴巴。

▶ Paul should really keep his mouth shut.
  Paul 真的應該閉上他的嘴。
  You keep your mouth shut about the document.
  關於這份文件的內容，你對誰都不能說。

won't say a word

- won't say a word about/to
关於／對…一個字都不會說
- won't breathe a word
一個字都不會說
- won't tell anyone at all
不會告訴任何人
- can't tell anyone about
不能告訴任何人關於…

（關於某件事）一個字都不會說 後面可以接「to＋人」表示不會對某人說。

- Don't ruin the surprise party.
- I **won't say a word**.

  ●別把驚喜派對搞砸了。　●我一個字都不會說的。

▶ I promise I won't say a word.

  我保證我一個字都不會說。

  You can trust me. I won't say a word.

  你可以相信我。我一個字都不會說的。

watch one's tongue

- hold one's tongue
說話小心點

小心說話 表示對方的言辭不太恰當，或者提醒對方不要洩密。

- I think my teacher is kind of nasty.
- **Watch your tongue**. You're going to be punished.

  ●我覺得我的老師有點下流。　●說話小心點，你會被處罰的。

▶ Watch your tongue, or I'll beat you up.

  說話小心點，否則我會揍扁你。

  Hold your tongue! The walls have ears!

  說話小心點！隔牆有耳！

between you and me

- This is just between you and me.
這是你我之間的祕密。

是你我之間的祕密 也可以說 between ourselves，表示世界上只有彼此知道這件事。

- Honey, this is just **between you and me**.
- Sure, I won't say a word.

  ●親愛的，這是我們倆的祕密。　●當然，我一個字都不會說的。

▶ This secret meeting is between you and me.

  這場祕密會議只有你我知道。

  Let's keep this between you and me and Jason.

  這是你、我和 Jason 間的祕密。

cover up

- cover up for
為了保護…而掩蓋事實
- My lip's are sealed.
我會保密。
- Your secret is safe with me.
我會保密。
- take it to one's grave
到死都保密

掩蓋…，掩飾… 將某事隱藏起來不讓人發現，相當於 conceal 或 hide。經常用在為了保護某人而壓下某事的情況。

- Did your boss get punished for his mistake?
- No, he **covered up** everything that happened.

  ●你老闆有因為他的失誤而被懲罰嗎？

  ●沒有，他掩蓋了所有發生過的事情。

▶ Don't worry. Your secret's safe with me.

  別擔心，我會幫你保密的。

  You're making up new lies to cover up the old ones.

  你現在是為了圓過去的謊扯新的謊。

1 職場・學校
2 電腦・網路
3 社交生活
4 日常生活
5 訊息・理解
6 想法・態度
7 情緒・狀況
8 行為舉止
9 時間地點・副詞片語

have a big mouth

大嘴巴 表示守不住心裡的祕密，很容易隨便跟別人說。英文的說法不是 be a big mouth，而是 have a big mouth（有一張大嘴巴）。

- I want to tell you some gossip.
- You've got a big mouth.
  - ●我想跟你說一些八卦。　　●你真是大嘴巴。

▶ You have a really big mouth. I told you not to say anything! 你真的是個大嘴巴。我叫你什麼都不要說的！
Pat has a big mouth. Be careful of what you're saying.
Pat 是個大嘴巴。（跟他）說話要小心。

let on

- let on to sb
  向某人洩密
- let on that S+V
  洩密說…
- let the secret slip
  把祕密說溜嘴
- let the cat out of the bag
  洩露祕密

洩密　「向別人洩漏祕密」還有 reveal sth、tell what sb know 或 hint sth 等說法。

- Marsha has been pregnant for three months.
- She never **let on** to me about that.
  - ●Marsha 已經懷孕三個月了。　　●她從來沒跟我說過這件事。

▶ Don't let on that you know her age.
別洩漏你知道她年齡的祕密。
He didn't let on that he was a gangster.
他沒有洩漏自己是個流氓的祕密。

hide the truth

- have nothing to hide
  沒有需要隱藏的事
  →光明磊落

隱藏真相　除了隱藏某些發生過的事情以外，也可以表示隱藏自己內心的情感。

- Herman has been to jail in the past.
- Really? He **hid the truth** from all of us.
  - ●Herman 過去坐過牢。　　●真的嗎？他對我們所有人隱瞞了這件事。

▶ You need to hide the truth from your family.
你需要對你的家人隱藏真相。
Mike hid the truth about his divorce.
Mike 隱藏了自己離婚的事實。

13 說謊
tell a lie

5-13.mp3

tell a lie

- tell a lie to do
  為了做…而說謊
- tell a white lie
  說善意的謊言

說謊 這裡的 lie 是名詞。lie 當動詞時有「躺臥」和「說謊」的意思。「說謊」的時態變化是 lie-lied-lied-lying,「躺臥」的時態變化則是 lie-lay-lain-lying,請區分清楚。

- Is Melissa really from a rich family?
- No she isn't. She **told a lie** to us.
  ●Melissa 真的是出生在有錢人家嗎? ●不是,她對我們說了謊。

▶ If you tell a lie to your dad, he'll get angry.
  你如果對你爸爸說謊,他會生氣。
  You shouldn't tell a lie to a client.
  你不該對客戶說謊。

lie to sb

- lie about
  對於…說了謊

對某人說謊 lie 當動詞時,後面可以加 to 接被騙的人。發現自己被騙,可以說「You lied to me!」。

- Don't **lie to** me. I'm not that stupid.
- I'm not kidding. I'm dead serious.
  ●別騙我。我沒那麼笨。 ●我不是在開玩笑。我很認真的。

▶ If you lie to me, I will lie to you.
  如果你騙我,我也會騙你。
  Don't lie to me. I've seen you kissing him.
  別騙我,我看到你親他了。
  I'm sorry that I lied to you before.
  我很抱歉先前騙了你。

be a liar

- call sb a liar
  說某人是個騙子

是個騙子 美國社會把說謊這件事看得很嚴重,所以不能亂用 liar 這個字。

- He promised to make me rich.
- He's **a liar**. Don't fall for it.
  ●他答應會讓我變有錢的。 ●他是個騙子,別上當了。

▶ We should watch out for Jack. He's a liar.
  我們應該小心 Jack。他是個騙子。
  Peter has been saying that you're a liar.
  Peter 一直說你是個騙子。

1 職場・學校
2 電腦・網路
3 社交生活
4 日常生活
5 訊息・理解
6 想法・態度
7 情緒・狀況
8 行為舉止
9 時間地點・副詞片語

pretend to do

- pretend not to do
  假裝不做…
- pretend that S+V
  假裝…

假裝做… 表示為了騙人或捉弄人而裝成某種樣子。

- How can we get a day off?
- Here's my plan. We'll **pretend** we're sick.
  - ●我們怎樣才能得到一天休假？　●這是我的計畫：我們要裝病。

▶ Don't try to pretend you're best friends with the boss.
別裝作你們是老闆最好的朋友。
We'll just pretend like it never happened.
我們會裝作這件事從來沒發生過。

---

14 辯解
give an excuse

5-14.mp3

---

give an excuse

- give sb an excuse for...
  給某人一個…的理由
- give sb lousy excuses
  給某人很爛的藉口
- give sb the same old excuses
  給某人老掉牙的藉口
- give one excuse after another
  說一個又一個的藉口

給理由／藉口 可以說 give sb an excuse for... ，表示對象以及要辯解的事情。

- What do you think of John's **excuse**?
- To be frank, I don't buy it at all.
  - ●你覺得 John 的理由怎樣？　●老實說，我一點也不信。

▶ She gave another excuse for not paying me.
她又給了另一個不付我錢的藉口。
The student gave her teacher an excuse for being late.
那位學生對她的老師說了遲到的理由。

have no excuse

- There's no excuse for
  …沒有什麼藉口好說
- have good excuses
  有好理由

沒有藉口 後面可以接 for sth 說明做錯的事。

- Why did you fail your exam?
- I should have studied harder. I **have no excuses**.
  - ●你為什麼考試不及格？　●我應該更用功讀書。我沒有藉口。

▶ I had an excuse for being late.
我有遲到的理由。
There's no excuse for it.
那沒有什麼藉口好說的。

make an excuse

· No more excuses.
  不要再找藉口了。
· find an excuse for
  對於…找個理由

找理由／藉口 和 give an excuse 的意思很接近，但 make an excuse 是指想辦法找理由的過程。

● Did Larry get drunk and get into a fight?
● Yes, but he'll **make an excuse for** his behavior.

●Larry 喝醉然後捲入一場打架中嗎？
●是啊，但他會為自己的行為找個藉口的。

▶ He always finds an excuse for anything that he does.
  對於他做的任何事情，他總是可以找到理由。
  Jamie made an excuse for being late.
  Jamie 找了個遲到的藉口。

don't give me that

少來這套，別狡辯了 聽到對方很爛的理由或藉口時，就可以這麼說，表示「我一點也不信」。

● I can't work with that guy.
● **Don't give me that.**

●我沒辦法跟那個人一起工作。　●少來這套。

▶ Don't give me that. I know all the details.
  少來這套，我知道所有細節。
  Don't give me that. I'm mad at you.
  別狡辯了，我對你很火大。

explain oneself

為自己的行為辯解 除了為做錯的事辯解，也可以表示「明確表達自己的立場」。

● I don't want to talk to you at all.
● Come on, let me **explain myself**.

●我一點也不想跟你說話。　●拜託，讓我解釋。

▶ She took an hour to explain herself.
  她花了一小時為自己辯解。
  He couldn't explain himself to his parents.
  他無法向父母親為自己辯解。

1 職場・學校

2 電腦・網路

3 社交生活

4 日常生活

5 訊息・理解

6 想法・態度

7 情緒・狀況

8 行為舉止

9 時間地點・副詞片語

15 理由 have a reason

5-15.mp3

have a reason for

· have no reason to
沒有做…的理由
· have (got) reasons for/
to...
對於…有理由

對於…有理由 for 後面接名詞。如果要接動詞的話，可以說 have a reason to do。

● Do you **have a reason for** acting so badly?
● I'm sorry, but I am in an angry mood.
  ● 你有理由解釋行為那麼糟糕的原因嗎？
  ● 我很抱歉，但我現在情緒很憤怒。

▶ Andy didn't have a reason for breaking the mirror.
   Andy 沒有打破鏡子的理由。
   She has no reason to hurt me.
   她沒有理由傷害我。

have a good reason for

· have every reason to
有充分理由做…

對於…有好理由 have 也可以換成口語的 have got。

● Please excuse me for being late.
● You'd better **have a good reason for** this.
  ● 請原諒我遲到。　● 你最好有個好理由。

▶ Tom had a good reason for leaving the party.
   Tom 有離開派對的好理由。
   They have a good reason for entering university.
   他們有進大學的好理由。

give a reason for

· give sb a reason
給某人一個理由
· give sb a good reason
why S+V
給某人一個為何…的好理
由

給一個…的理由 要接動詞的話，可以說 give a reason to do。

● You must **give a reason for** your dirty clothes.
● I was out wrestling with my friends.
  ● 對於你的髒衣服，你一定要給我個理由。
  ● 我在外面跟朋友玩摔角。

▶ He gave a reason for sending the flowers.
   他給了個送花的理由。
   Did you give a reason for insulting the manager?
   你有說明侮辱主管的理由嗎？

what's the reason for

· What's the reason
  (that) S+V?
  …的理由是什麼？
· What's the reason
  (why) S+V?
  …的理由是什麼？

…的理由是什麼？ 也可以說 what's the reason that S+V。

- ●**What's the reason for** the big mess?
- ●The children have been playing in the kitchen.

  ●為什麼這邊搞得一團亂？　●孩子們在廚房裡面玩。

▶ What's the reason for the cold weather this week?
  這個星期天氣這麼冷的理由是什麼？
  What's the reason why she quit suddenly?
  她突然辭職的理由是什麼？

there are reasons for

· There are some
  reasons why S+V
  …是有些理由的
· There are a lot of
  reasons for...
  …有很多理由

…是有理由的 reasons 的前面可以加上 several, many 等數量形容詞修飾。

- ●Why did you change your major at university?
- ●**There are many reasons for** that.

  ●你為什麼換了大學的主修？　●有很多理由。

▶ There are a lot of reasons for that.
  那有很多理由。
  Is there any reason that Koreans eat this soup?
  韓國人喝這種湯有什麼理由嗎？

there's no reason for

· There's no reason
  to do
  沒有理由去做…
· There's no reason
  why/that S+V
  …沒有理由

…沒有理由 reason 後面可以接 to do, for sth, that S+V 等等。

- ●Is there any reason why we shouldn't hire him?
- ●**There's no reason** that I know of.

  ●有任何我們不該雇用他的理由嗎？　●我找不出理由。

▶ There's no reason that anyone should work during the
  holiday. 任何人都沒有理由要在假日工作。
  There's no reason to complain.
  沒有理由好抱怨。

one of the reasons for

· for some reason
  不知道為什麼
· for some reason or
  other
  不知道為什麼
· for personal reasons
  基於個人原因
· for no reason
  沒有理由地

…的理由之一 如果要說是「…的理由的一部分」，則可以說
part of the reason。

- ●We have to pay a lot more rent money.
- ●**Part of the reason for** the increase is that utility
  fees are rising.

  ●我們得付高出許多的租金。
  ●租金增加的理由，一部分在於水電費漲價。

▶ For some reason I feel very sleepy today.
  不知道為什麼，我今天非常睏。
  Part of the reason for this is that we spent too much
  money. 之所以會這樣，一部分的原因是我們花太多錢了。

1 職場‧學校

2 電腦‧網路

3 社交生活

4 日常生活

5 訊息‧理解

6 想法‧態度

7 情緒‧狀況

8 行為舉止

9 時間地點‧副詞片語

how come S+V

· How come?
  為什麼？

怎麼…？　意思和 Why 相似，不同的地方在於，how come 直接接
S+V 就能形成問句，不需要將 be 動詞或助動詞提前。

● **How come** he didn't show up last night?

● I'm not sure. Maybe he was ill.

　●他昨晚怎麼沒有出現？　　●我不確定，也許他病了吧。

▶ How come you don't live with your mom?
　你怎麼不跟你媽媽一起住？

　How come you never said anything to me?
　你怎麼什麼話都沒跟我說過？

that's because...

· That's because he
  drove drunk.
  那是因為他酒醉駕駛。

· It's because S+V
  那是因為…

那是因為…　用來帶出之前提到的某件事的原因。例如有人問到
某人被吊銷駕照的原因，就可以說 That's because he drove drunk.
（那是因為他酒後駕駛。）

● Why is the refrigerator not working?

● **That's because** my sister pulled out the plug.

　●冰箱為什麼不動了？　　●那是因為我姊姊把插頭拔掉了。

▶ That's because I didn't want you to get upset about it.
　那是因為，我不希望你因為那件事覺得不開心。

　That's because you don't understand that.
　那是因為你不懂那件事。

that's why...

· That's why he lost his
  driver's license.
  那就是他失去駕照的原
  因。

那就是…的原因　跟 that's because 相反，用來帶出之前提到的某
件事的原因。延續酒後駕駛的例子，如果說到某人酒後駕駛，就可
以說 That's why he lost his driver's license.（那就是他失去駕照的原
因。）

● That business is really cut-throat.

● **That's why** I decided to quit.

　●那個產業真是太殘酷了。　　●所以我才決定辭職。

▶ I hate you and that's why I'm leaving.
　我討厭你，所以我才要離開。

　That's why I wanted to talk to you.
　那就是我想和你談談的理由。

(it's) not that S+V, but that S+V

不是…而是… 想澄清真正的理由時可以使用的表達方式。

- ●Andrea is the most unhappy person I know.
- ●**It's not that** she's angry, **but that** she has a lot of stress.

  ●Andrea 是我認識過最不開心的人。　●她不是生氣，而是壓力很大。

▶ It's not that I like work, but that I need money.
  我不是喜歡工作，而是需要錢。
  It's not that he fell down, but that he slipped on the ice.
  他不是跌倒，而是在冰上滑了一跤。

because S+V

· only because S+V
  只因為…
· because of
  因為…

因為… 表示原因的典型句型。如果原因是名詞的話，則說 because of sth。

- ●Look, don't get so upset at me.
- ●I'm angry **because** you're just not listening.

  ●嘿，別那麼生我的氣。　●我生氣是因為你根本沒在聽。

▶ I brought my friend because I didn't want to come alone.
  我帶了朋友，是因為我不想一個人來。
  I'm happy because tomorrow is a holiday.
  我很開心，因為明天是假日。

since S+V

因為… as 也可以接 S+V 表示原因，但不如 since 常用。

- ●We must buy some food **since** we ate everything.
- ●Alright, let's head to the grocery store.

  ●我們一定要買點食物，因為我們把東西都吃光了。
  ●好吧，我們去雜貨店吧。

▶ We'll be late since you got us lost.
  因為你害我們迷路了，所以我們會遲到。
  I'm so tired since we stayed awake all night.
  我好累，因為我們一整晚沒睡。

due to

· owing to
  因為…
· thanks to
  託…的福，多虧…（後面
  接感謝的對象或事物）
· on account of
  因為…，由於…

因為… 和口語中最常用的 because of 句型不同，due to 和 owing to 這兩個介系詞片語都是用在比較 formal（正式）的場合，例如公告等。

- ●Why did the health club close?
- ●It closed **due to** having very few members.

  ●那間健康俱樂部為什麼關門了？
  ●因為會員人數很少，所以才關門的。

▶ We're going inside due to the rainy weather.
  因為下雨，所以我們要去室內。
  Thanks to you I'm not single anymore.
  多虧有你，我再也不是孤單一人了。

1 職場・學校
2 電腦・網路
3 社交生活
4 日常生活
5 訊息・理解
6 想法・態度
7 情緒・狀況
8 行為舉止
9 時間地點・副詞片語

16 説明
make clear

5-16.mp3

explain sth to sb

· explain that S+V
  解釋…
· explain sth (more in detail)
  （更詳細地）解釋某事
· explain oneself to sb
  向某人解釋自己的意思或行為

向某人解釋某事 除了 explain oneself 以外，explain 後面絕對不能直接接人當受詞。

● I've got to tell you something.
● No, no. You don't have to **explain yourself** to me.
    ● 我一定要告訴你一件事。
    ● 不，不用，你不必跟我解釋自己的行為。

▶ Would you mind explaining it to me?
  你可以跟我解釋一下嗎？
  Let me explain why I did it.
  讓我解釋我為什麼那麼做。

give an explanation of

· owe sb an explanation
  欠某人一個解釋

提出一個…的解釋 give 後面可以加上「人」，也就是要解釋的對象。

● Steve told me he wants to break up.
● I hope he'll **give you an explanation of** that.
    ● Steve 跟我說他想分手。　● 我希望他會給你一個解釋。

▶ He's going to give an explanation of the problem.
  他會對這個問題提出一個解釋。
  I am confused by the teacher's explanation.
  我被老師的解釋搞得很困惑。

go into details

· tell details about/on
  詳細說明…
· give specifics
  詳細說明
· give the details of...
  詳細說明…
· give sb all the details
  對某人詳細說明

詳細說明 後面可以加上 about 或 on，接要解釋的事情。

● I have some real estate you should look at.
● Can you **tell me some details about** it?
    ● 我手上有個你應該看看的房產。
    ● 你可以告訴我房子的一些細節嗎？

▶ Jerry gave specifics about his plans.
  Jerry 詳細說明了他的計畫。
  Tell us the details of your wedding.
  跟我們說你婚禮的詳細內容。

1 職場・學校

2 電腦・網路

3 社交生活

4 日常生活

5 訊息・理解

6 想法・態度

7 情緒・狀況

8 行為舉止

9 時間地點・副詞片語

make clear

· make it clear that S+V
把…解釋清楚
· Do I make myself
clear?
我說得夠清楚了嗎？

把⋯解釋清楚 與 clarify 同義。make oneself clear 則表示把自己的想法解釋清楚。

● My parents want to know which university I'll attend.

● You should **make clear** the one you prefer.

● 我父母想知道我會去哪間大學。

● 你應該跟他們說清楚，你比較喜歡哪間。

▶ He tried to make his opinion clear.
他試圖將他的意見表達清楚。
Let me make myself clear. This is a mistake.
讓我解釋清楚。這是個誤會。

account for

· account for one's actions
說明某人自身的行動
· give a brief/full account
簡短地／完整地說明

說明⋯，對⋯負責任 如果 account for 後面接數字，表示「佔…的數量」。

● You need to **account for** the money you spent.

● I can show you every bill I paid.

● 你需要說明你所花掉的錢。　● 我可以讓你看我付過的每張帳單。

▶ Pat couldn't account for his late arrival.
Pat 無法說明他遲到的原因。
I'll give a brief account for the meeting.
我將對這場會議做個簡短的說明。

---

17 理解 get it

5-17.mp3

understand sth/sb

· understand why S+V
了解為什麼…
· now I understand why
+ 結果
現在我了解為什麼…了

了解⋯ understand that S+V 的句型也很常用。

● Do you know what I'm saying?

● Sorry, I don't **understand**.

● 你知道我在說什麼嗎？　● 抱歉，我不懂。

▶ I don't understand what you mean.
我不了解你的意思。
I'm sorry, I can't understand what you said.
我很抱歉，我不了解你所說的。

make oneself understood

讓人了解自己的意思　常以 make oneself understood in English 的形式出現，意思是「用英文表達自己的想法」。

- Can you **make yourself understood** in Japanese?
- No, not yet.

  ●你可以用日文表達自己的意思嗎？　●不，還不行。

▶ Sarah made herself understood when I met her.

我遇見 Sarah 的時候，她讓我了解她的想法。

Can you make yourself understood?

你可以讓我了解你的想法嗎？

get it

- Did you get it?
  你懂了嗎？
- I made nothing of it.
  我無法理解。

理解　這是很常見的口語用法。聽了別人說的話，想表達「我明白了」，可以說 (I) Get it. 或 (I) Got it.，兩者的意思沒什麼不同。

- What's wrong with you today?
- I don't **get it**. This stuff is too hard.

  ●你今天是怎麼了？　●我不知道，這東西太難了。

▶ I don't understand why they don't get it.

我不懂他們為什麼不懂。

All right. I get it. I see what's going on here.

好吧，我懂了，我知道這邊的狀況了。

get across (to sb)

- get across one's points
  解釋清楚自己的意見
- see sth through
  負責某事到最後，看透某事物

使自己被理解　come across 也是一樣的意思。get sth across / get across sth 則是把某事解釋清楚。

- Did you explain everything to Lucy?
- Yeah, I think I **got it across to** her.

  ●你跟 Lucy 解釋一切了嗎？　●嗯，我想我讓她理解了。

▶ I'm just trying to get across my points.

我只是試圖解釋清楚我的意見。

He saw the project through until it was finished.

他負責這個計畫到完成為止。

follow sb

- impossible to follow you
  無法理解你的意思
- I don't follow you.
  我不懂你在說什麼。

理解某人的意思　經常以否定形出現，表示無法理解對方的話。

- I didn't understand what Henry was saying.
- It was difficult to **follow** him.

  ●我不懂 Henry 在說什麼。　●他的話很難理解。

▶ I didn't follow the teacher's lesson.

我沒有跟上老師講的課。

I can't follow you. Please speak more slowly.

我不懂你在說什麼。請說慢一點。

18 意義
stand for

5-18.mp3

it means that S+V

· be meant to do...
  有義務做…，是用來做…
· be meant for sth
  適合某事物

意思是… 被動態 be meant to do sth 是「有義務做某事」、「是用來做某事」的意思，be meant for sth 則是「適合某事物」的意思。

● Jane cleaned out her desk today.
● **It means that** she's not coming back.
  ●Jane 今天清空了她的桌子。　●意思是她不會回來了。

▶ This machine was meant to do copying.
  這台機器是用來影印的。
  That means that I can start drinking right now.
  那就是説我現在可以開始喝酒了。

what do you mean by...?

· What do you mean by that?
  你那是什麼意思？
· What do you mean S+V?
  你說…是什麼意思？

你…是什麼意思？ by 後面接 that 或動詞 -ing 形。

● You gained some weight.
● **What do you mean by** that? Am I fat?
  ●你胖了一點。　●你那是什麼意思？我胖嗎？

▶ What do you mean you have no more money?
  你説你已經沒有錢了是什麼意思？
  What do you mean you're going to London?
  你説你要去倫敦是什麼意思？

you mean...?

· Are you telling me/
  saying that S+V
  你是在跟我說…嗎？
· You mean the day
  after tomorrow?
  你的意思是後天嗎？

你的意思是…嗎？ I mean... 則是重新解釋之前說過的話時會用的句型。

● I think you won first prize.
● **You mean** that I beat everyone else?
  ●我想你得了第一名。　●你是説我打敗了其他所有人嗎？

▶ You mean you don't want to work for me anymore?
  你是説，你不想繼續在我手下工作了嗎？
  Are you saying you want to stay together?
  你們是説，你們想要在一起嗎？

1 職場・學校
2 電腦・網路
3 社交生活
4 日常生活
5 訊息・理解
6 想法・態度
7 情緒・狀況
8 行為舉止
9 時間地點・副詞片語

stand for sth

- be symbolic of
  象徵…（symbolize）
- imply sth/that...
  暗示…，暗指…

代表某事物　常常用來說明某個縮寫或符號代表什麼意思。

● Tell me what this means.
● It is a symbol that **stands for** quiet.
　●跟我說這是什麼意思。　●這是代表安靜的符號。

▶ This is symbolic of impressionist art. 這象徵著印象派藝術。
　He implied that we were lazy. 他暗指我們很懶。

put it

- put it simply
  簡單地說

表達　是 express it 的口語說法。

● How would you **put it**?
● Just tell them you need a bigger salary.
　●如果是你，會怎麼表達？　●就跟他們說你需要更多薪水。

▶ To put it simply, I'm moving away. 簡單來說，我要搬走了。
　I decided to put it very honestly. 我決定非常誠實地說。

19　重要
put A before B

5-19.mp3

be important

- It's important that.../to
  do...
  …很重要
- be essential to do
  有必要做…

重要　常用的句型是 It's important that... / to do...。

● Jamie, how come you never told me that?
● I thought that it **wasn't important to** you.
　●Jamie，你怎麼從來沒告訴我那件事？　●我以為那對你不重要。

▶ It's important to live together as a family.
　像家人一樣住在一起很重要。
　Why is it so important to you? 為什麼那對你那麼重要？

make much of

- make much of the fact
  that...
  很重視…的事實

重視…　make little of 則是「輕視，等閒視之」的意思。

● Larry looks so handsome today.
● People **are making much of** his new haircut.
　●Larry 今天看起來真帥。　●人們都很重視他的新髮型。

▶ My boss made much of the fact that I left early.
　我老闆把我早下班的事看得很重。
　The teacher made much of the fact that he cheated.
　老師對於他的作弊行為非常重視。

come first

- Work comes first.
  工作至上。
- My children always come first
  我的孩子總是最重要的
- first-come-first-serve basis
  不接受預訂，先到者先得的制度

⋯是最重要的 come 的主詞可以是人或事物等。

- When you work at this company, punctuality **comes first**.
- That's pretty much the same for all companies.
  - 當你在這間公司工作時，嚴守時間是最重要的。
  - 所有公司差不多都是這樣。

▶ Work comes first for the older generation.
  對老一輩的人來說，工作是最重要的。
  I stayed home because my children always come first.
  我待在家裡是因為孩子是我的第一優先。

put A before B

把 A 看得比 B 更重／更優先 也就是「比起 B，A 的 priority 更高」的意思。

- What is the philosophy of your company?
- I always tell my employees to **put** honesty **before** benefit.
  - 貴公司的哲學是什麼？
  - 我總是告訴員工們要把誠信看得比利益更重。

▶ Lisa puts others before herself most of the time.
  Lisa 通常都把其他人看得比自己更重要。
  I had to put studying before relaxing.
  我得把讀書看得比放鬆更重要。

give sth top priority

把⋯列為第一優先 字面上的意思就是選出一樣最重要的事，放在第一順位。

- We have to get this homework done.
- You're right. We should **give it top priority**.
  - 我們得把這份作業完成。
  - 你說得對，我們應該把它列為第一優先。

▶ I'd like you to give this top priority. 我希望你優先處理這件事。
  I'd like to make it my top priority.
  我想把這件事當成我的第一優先。

sth matters

- it doesn't matter (to me)
  （對我而言）沒關係，不重要

某事很重要 後面可以接 to sb 表示「某事對某人很重要」。

- Your kitchen is very clean.
- Keeping the area where you eat clean **matters**.
  - 你的廚房很乾淨。 ● 保持自己用餐環境的清潔很重要。

▶ It matters to me. We should try to conserve things.
  這對我而言很重要。我們應該努力節省物品。
  How can you say that it doesn't matter to me?
  你怎麼可以說那對我而言不重要？

1 職場・學校
2 電腦・網路
3 社交生活
4 日常生活
5 訊息・理解
6 想法・態度
7 情緒・狀況
8 行為舉止
9 時間地點・副詞片語

make a difference

- make a difference to
  對…有影響力
- make a huge
  difference to the game
  對比賽有很大的影響

有影響力，造成改變 反義的說法就是 make no difference。

● You are always kind to poor people.
● I want to **make a difference** in their lives.
  ●你總是對窮人很親切。　●我希望能為他們的生活創造一點改變。

▶ You can make a big difference.
  你可以創造很大的改變。
  She tried to make a difference by doing something for you. 她想要為你做點什麼，試圖創造一點改變。

first of all

- first thing's first
  要事第一

首先 類似的慣用語還有 above all。後面除了接「要優先做的事」以外，也可以接「最重要的事」。

● I wonder if we could get together on the 5th.
● **First of all**, let me check my schedule.
  ●不知道我們 5 號能不能見面。　●先讓我確認我的行程。

▶ First of all, we haven't been introduced. I'm Jim Morris.
  首先，我們還沒彼此介紹過。我叫 Jim Morris。
  First of all, Tony and I are not back together.
  首先，我跟 Tony 沒有復合。

last but not least

最後但也同樣重要的一點 在演說或文章的最後，想要再次喚起人們注意力的說法。

● **Last but not least**, let's discuss our vacation.
● I was thinking I'd like to go to Miami.
  ●最後但也同樣重要的是，讓我們討論我們的假期吧。
  ●我在想著要去邁阿密。

▶ Last but not least, we need to talk about the rent.
  最後但也同樣重要的一點，我們需要談一下租金。
  Last but not least, my family is coming to visit us.
  最後但也同樣重要的是，我的家人要來拜訪我們。

20 弄丟，掉東西
leave sth in...

5-20.mp3

leave sth in/at/on...

· leave one's passport in the taxi
把某人的護照留在計程車上

把某物留在… in, at, on 後面接名詞。

● I **left** my cell phone **in** the car.
● We'd better go back to the parking lot.
　●我把手機留在車上了。　●我們最好回去停車場。

▶ Herman left his passport in the taxi.
　Herman 把他的護照留在計程車上了。
　Dad left his glasses at the restaurant.
　爸爸把他的眼鏡留在餐廳了。

leave sb -ing

任由某人… 表示丟下某人，讓他一直做某件事，或者保持某個狀態。

● Willis **left** his girlfriend **crying** at home.
● What a terrible way to break up.
　●Willis 把他的女朋友丟在家裡，任她哭泣。
　●真是糟糕的分手方式。

▶ Linda left the children playing in the room.
　Linda 讓孩子們在房間玩耍。
　I left them studying at the library.
　我把他們丟在圖書館念書。

lose sth

· lose weight
減重→變瘦
· lose one's wallet
弄丟某人的錢包
· lost and found
失物招領處

弄丟某物 被動態是 sth is lost（某物不見了）。

● What are you looking for?
● I **lost** some money around here.
　●你在找什麼？　●我在這附近掉了錢。

▶ Michelle lost weight this summer.
　Michelle 這個夏天瘦了。
　Did you lose your wallet at the beach?
　你把錢包掉在海邊了嗎？

1 職場・學校
2 電腦・網路
3 社交生活
4 日常生活
5 訊息・理解
6 想法・態度
7 情緒・狀況
8 行為舉止
9 時間地點・副詞片語

miss sth

· be going to miss you
  會想念你

想念某事 miss -ing 則是「想念做某事」。

● I **miss** living in New York.
● Yes, it's quite an exciting place.
  ● 我懷念住在紐約的時候。　● 是啊，那是個挺刺激的地方。

▶ Sharon misses seeing her best friend.
  Sharon 想見到她的摯友。
  They miss going camping every year.
  他們每年都想要去露營。

put sth in

· put sth over there
  把某物放到那裡

把某物放進… in... 也可以換成其他介系詞片語或地方副詞。

● Is this your pencil?
● Yeah, just **put** it **in** my bag.
  ● 這是你的鉛筆嗎？　● 嗯，就把它放進我的包包吧。

▶ Put the books over there.
  把書放到那裡。
  Put the candy in a bowl.
  把糖果放在碗裡。

21 | 主張 insist on

5-21.mp3

insist on sth

· insist on one's own
  way
  堅持自己的方式
· if you insist (on it)
  如果你堅持

堅決主張某事 insist 有堅持的意思，insist one's way 則是「堅持自己的方式→堅持己見」。

● I thought Dave was off work today.
● He is, but he **insists on** going in to his office.
  ● 我以為 Dave 今天休假。　● 他是啊，但他堅持要進辦公室。

▶ Harry insisted on a big dinner tonight.
  Harry 堅持今晚要吃大餐。
  Olivia insists on paying for the tickets.
  Olivia 堅持要付票錢。

argue that S+V

- argue with sb
  和某人爭執
- argue about sth
  對於某事起爭執
- argue against
  據理反對…

主張… argue against 則是「據理反對…」的意思。

- I'm sorry that we **argued**.
- There are no hard feelings on my part.
  - ●很抱歉我們吵架了。　●我沒有生氣。

▶ Let's not argue about it.
  我們別吵這個了。
  You should have argued with them about it.
  你當時該跟他們爭論這件事的。

claim that S+V

- claim sth/to do...
  聲稱…
- lay/make claim to...
  要求…
- claim all the credit for
  success
  把成功的功勞都攬在身上

聲稱…，主張… claim 後面除了接子句以外，也可以接名詞或 to do 當受詞。

- Melissa **claims that** Brian started a fight.
- That's not true. Brian is a nice guy.
  - ●Melissa 聲稱 Brian 挑起了一場爭執。
  - ●那不是真的。Brian 是個好人。

▶ Jack claimed that she started the fight.
  Jack 聲稱她挑起了紛爭。
  Ray claimed he acted in a Hollywood movie.
  Ray 聲稱他演過好萊塢電影。

make one's point

- make one's point that
  S+V
  闡明…的主張
- make one's case
  (that...)
  陳述自己的主張
- You made your point!
  你說得夠清楚了！

闡明主張，證明自己的論點正確 也可以說 make one's point that S+V。

- Do you need me to explain more?
- No, I think you **made your point**.
  - ●你需要我多做解釋嗎？　●不用，我想你已經說得夠清楚了。

▶ It took a long time for Tina to make her point.
  Tina 花了很多時間闡明自己的論點。
  Nick made the case that he should skip school.
  Nick 說明自己需要蹺課的原因。

urge that

- urge sb to do
  催促某人去做…

催促…，力勸… urge sb to do 意為「催促某人去做…」。

- The snow is falling very quickly.
- The people on the news **are urging that** people don't drive.
  - ●雪下得很急。　●新聞力勸人們不要開車。

▶ I urged her to break up with her boyfriend.
  我力勸她跟她的男朋友分手。
  I urge that you go get some rest.
  我要求你去休息一下。

1 職場・學校
2 電腦・網路
3 社交生活
4 日常生活
5 訊息・理解
6 想法・態度
7 情緒・狀況
8 行為舉止
9 時間地點・副詞片語

22 提議
Why don't you...

suggest -ing

- suggest sb to do
  建議某人去做…
- suggest sth to sb
  向某人建議某事
- suggest that S+V
  建議…

提議做… suggest 後面可以接名詞、-ing 或 that S+V。

- What will you do on your blind date?
- I'll **suggest** going to an Italian restaurant.
  - 你聯誼那天要做什麼？　● 我會提議去一間義大利餐廳。

▶ Can you suggest a good restaurant in the area?
  你可以推薦那個區域的好餐廳嗎？
  She suggested that we rent a car for the weekend.
  她建議我們週末租一台車。

make a suggestion

- have a better
  suggestion
  有更好的提議
- put a suggestion in
  the box
  把建議投入意見箱
- listen to a suggestion
  聽取建議

給建議 後面可以接 to sb 表示對象，或者接 about sth 表示建議的內容。

- I want to **make a suggestion** about your clothes.
- Do you think I should change them?
  - 我想對你的衣服給點建議。　● 你覺得我該換掉它們嗎？

▶ Why don't you make a suggestion to your boss?
  你為什麼不對你老闆提個建議？
  No one takes my brilliant suggestions seriously.
  沒有人認真看待我優秀的建議。

propose that S+V

- propose a toast
  敬酒
- propose marriage
  求婚
- make proposal of/for
  提出…的提案

提議… 跟 suggest 比起來，propose 是更積極的提案。

- I **propose** we combine these two projects into one.
- What do you mean, exactly?
  - 我提議把這兩個計畫合併成一個。　● 你的意思究竟是什麼？

▶ I'd like to propose a toast to your new job.
  我想為你的新工作敬酒。
  What do you think about my proposal?
  你覺得我的提案怎麼樣？

offer A B

· make (sb) an offer
  （對某人）提議／出價
· have an offer from
  從…得到工作機會

對 A 提供 B offer to do 意為「提議做…」。

● Why did you choose to take the job?
● They **offered** a high salary **to** me.

　　●你為什麼選擇接受這份工作？　　●他們開了很高的薪水給我。

▶ Are you going to offer me a chance to work here?
　你會給我個機會，讓我能在這裡工作嗎？
　I think we need to make an offer on the house.
　我想我們需要對房子出價。

put forward sth

· proposals put forward
  by sb
  由某人提出的提案

提出某事物 sth 可以是 idea 或 proposal 等等。

● Renee **put forward** her ideas.
● Did you think they were worthwhile?

　　●Renee 提出了她的想法。　　●你覺得她的想法有價值嗎？

▶ The proposals were put forward by our staff.
　這些提案是由我們的員工提出的。
　He put forward a plan for the future.
　他提出了未來的計畫。

go ahead and

去…吧 用祈使句鼓勵對方做某事。

● Can I try to fix this computer?
● **Go ahead and** see if you can make it work.

　　●我可以試著修這台電腦嗎？　　●試試看你能不能修好它吧。

▶ Go ahead and turn up the TV.
　去把電視音量調大。
　Why don't you go ahead and start the meeting?
　你何不開始這場會議呢？

feel free to

· feel free to contact me
  不用客氣儘管聯絡我
· don't hesitate to do
  不要猶豫去做…
  →儘管做…

儘管去… 相當於 don't hesitate to do，請對方照自己的意思隨意去
做某事。

● Thank you for your help with this report.
● If there's anything else you need, **feel free to** ask.

　　●謝謝你幫忙做這份報告。
　　●如果你還有任何需要，儘管要求沒關係。

▶ Feel free to stay here as long as you like.
　你想在這裡待多久都可以。
　Feel free to pick out whatever you need.
　儘管拿任何你需要的東西。

1 職場・學校
2 電腦・網路
3 社交生活
4 日常生活
5 訊息・理解
6 想法・態度
7 情緒・狀況
8 行為舉止
9 時間地點・副詞片語

how about + N/-ing?

· How about S+V?
　…怎麼樣？
· How about you?
　那你呢？
· What about N/-ing?
　…怎麼樣？

…怎麼樣？　除了名詞以外，how about 後面還可以接 S+V。

● **How about** three o'clock?
● Perfect. I'll meet you there.

　●三點怎麼樣？　●太好了，我們那邊見。

▶ How about coming over to my place tonight?
　今晚來我家怎麼樣？
　How about we talk about this over dinner?
　我們吃晚餐時討論這件事怎麼樣？

why don't you...?

· Why don't we do...?
　我們何不…？
· Why don't I do...?
　我來做…吧。（Let me do...）

你何不…？　雖然是疑問句型，但事實上是在向對方提出建議。

● **Why don't we** buy a new big screen TV?
● Will you stop? We can't afford that!

　●我們何不買個新的大螢幕電視呢？
　●你別再説了好嗎？我們買不起！

▶ Why don't you go find your mother and talk to her?
　你何不去找你母親，跟她談談？
　Why don't you let me walk with you?
　你何不讓我陪你走呢？

Why not?

　　Why not? 有兩種意思，一種就跟字面上一樣，單純詢問對方「為什麼不行、為什麼辦不到？」等等的理由（please, explain your negative answer）。另一種則是對於別人的提議，表達「有何不可？」（I can't think of any reason not to do），也就是強烈地表達 yes 的意思。

　　A: Do you want to come with us for drinks? 你想跟我們一起去喝酒嗎？
　　B: Why not? 有何不可呢？
　　A: I'll come by your office when I'm through. 那我事情處理完後，會順道來
　　　　　　　　　　　　　　　　　　　　　　你辦公室。

23 記得
remind A of B

5-23.mp3

1 職場・學校

2 電腦・網路

3 社交生活

4 日常生活

5 訊息・理解

6 想法・態度

7 情緒・狀況

8 行為舉止

9 時間地點・副詞片語

remember sb -ing

· remember to do
  記得去做…
· remember -ing
  記得做了…
· as long as I remember
  只要我記得

記得某人做過… 用來表示「記得過去所做的事」。

● Jack can't find his keys.
● I **remember** him setting them down.
  ● Jack 找不到他的鑰匙。　● 我記得他有把鑰匙放下。

▶ Remember to shut off the light when you leave.
  當你離開時，記得把燈關掉。
  How can you not remember us kissing in the street?
  你怎麼能不記得我們在街上接吻過？

remember that

· remember when S+V
  記得當…的時候

記得… remember 後面可以接 that S+V 表達比較長的內容。

● Bill always seems to be sleepy.
● **Remember that** he works all night long.
  ● Bill 總是看起來很想睡。　● 別忘了他得工作一整晚。

▶ Remember when we visited Hollywood?
  你記得我們去好萊塢的時候嗎？
  I remember how nervous I was for my first interview!
  我還記得我第一次面試時有多緊張！

keep sth in mind

· keep/bear sth in mind
  把某事牢記在心
· keep in mind that S+V
  把…牢記在心
· keep your family in
  mind
  把你的家人放在心上

牢記在心 keep 也可以換成 bear。也可以接子句，句型是 keep in mind that S+V。

● Let's buy a lot of Christmas presents.
● **Keep it in mind that** we have to save money.
  ● 我們買很多耶誕節禮物吧。　● 別忘了我們得省錢。

▶ Keep in mind that Mindy is always late.
  別忘了 Mindy 總是會遲到。
  Please keep in mind that this is your last chance.
  請牢記這是你最後的機會。

413

look back on sth

· look back on the past
  回首過往

回顧某事 也就是 think about 過去發生的事情。

● I like to **look back on** my school days.
● Yeah, we had a lot of good friends then.
  ●我喜歡回顧我的校園時光。　●是啊，我們那時候有很多好朋友。

▶ Vera looked back on her childhood with happiness.
  Vera 開心地回顧她的童年。
  Try not to look back on the past.
  試著不要回首過往。

remind A of B

· that reminds me of...
  那使我想起…
· recall sth (to one's mind)
  想起某事

使 A 想起 B A 一定是人或團體，B 則是想起的事物。

● The building looks very strange.
● Yes, its shape **reminds** everyone **of** a cell phone.
  ●這棟大樓看起來很怪。
  ●是啊，看到它的形狀，每個人都會想到手機。

▶ You remind me of my daughter.
  你讓我想起我的女兒。
  You remind me of myself when I was an intern.
  你讓我想起之前還在實習的我。

refresh one's memory

· refresh one's
  memory of
  喚醒某人…的記憶
· search one's memory
  搜尋某人的記憶

喚醒某人的記憶 refresh 是「更新」的意思，引申為使記憶變得清晰的意思。

● I can't remember our trip to Canada.
● Really, you'd better **refresh your memory**.
  ●我記不得我們的加拿大之旅。　●你真的該喚醒你的記憶了。

▶ You need to refresh your memory of happier times.
  你需要喚回快樂時光的記憶。
  Why don't you refresh your memory of your early
  childhood? 你何不喚醒你幼年時光的記憶呢？

ring a bell

· Ring a bell?
  記得嗎？

喚起記憶 口語的說法，表示某個名稱讓人有印象，就像鈴聲忽然響起一樣。

● Does that name **ring a bell**?
● I'm sure I went to school with her brother years
  ago.
  ●你對那個名字有印象嗎？　●我確定我幾年前跟她哥哥一起上學。

▶ Jeffery Tabor's name rings a bell.
  Jeffery Tabor 的名字我有印象。
  I grew up in Friendsville. Does that place ring a bell?
  我在 Friendsville 長大的。這個地名你有印象嗎？

have a good memory

· have a bad memory
  記憶力不好
· know/learn...by heart
  背下…

記憶力好　後面可以接 of sth 表示記憶的內容。

● How did you remember that?
● Oh, I **have a very good memory**.

　●你怎麼記得那件事？　●噢，我的記憶力很好。

▶ My grandfather has a bad memory now that he's old.
　我爺爺年事已高，記憶力變得不好。
　He knows all of the poems by heart.
　他背下了所有的詩。

if my memory serves

如果我沒記錯　這是一個正式的說法。當不確定某件事的正確性，想要小心地表達時，就可以使用。

● Where do you keep the bottle opener?
● **If my memory serves**, it's in that drawer.

　●你把開瓶器放在哪裡？　●如果我沒記錯，應該在那個抽屜裡。

▶ If my memory serves, we've met before.
　如果我沒記錯的話，我們之前見過面。
　If my memory serves, it's almost your birthday.
　如果我沒記錯的話，你的生日快到了。

---

24 | 忘記 forget to

5-24.mp3

forget about

· Forget about it.
  算了吧。
· be forgetful
  健忘

忘掉…　忘掉過去的事情。about 後面接名詞。

● Will we be getting some ice cream?
● **Forget about** it. We're going straight home.

　●我們要不要去吃點冰淇淋？　●算了吧，我們要直接回家。

▶ I forgot about our date. I'm so sorry.
　我忘記我們有約，很抱歉。
　Don't let me forget her birthday.
　別讓我忘記她的生日。

1 職場・學校
2 電腦・網路
3 社交生活
4 日常生活
5 訊息・理解
6 想法・態度
7 情緒・狀況
8 行為舉止
9 時間地點・副詞片語

forget to

· forget to mention that
S+V
忘了提到…

· don't forget to do
別忘記去做…

忘記去做… 表示忘記去做本來打算要做的事。

● Don't **forget to** fill out those forms today.
● I'll leave them on your desk before I go.
　● 今天別忘了要把那些表格填好。
　● 我離開前會把它們放在你的桌子上。

▶ Please don't forget to make a backup of those files.
　請別忘了備份那些檔案。
　I forgot to tell you that the boss called.
　我忘了跟你說，老闆打了電話來。

forget that S+V

· forget the time when
S+V
忘記當…的時候

忘記… forget 可以接名詞或 that 子句當受詞。

● Brenda and Fred are getting married.
● I **forgot that** they were dating.
　● Brenda 和 Fred 要結婚了。　● 我忘了他們有在約會。

▶ Did you forget that you had that suitcase?
　你忘了你有那個行李箱嗎？
　How come you forgot that I told you this?
　你怎麼忘了我告訴你這件事？

almost forget

· almost forget to do
差點忘記要做…

· almost forget that...
差點忘記…

· totally forget
完全忘記

差點忘記 差一點就忘記，但最後還是想起來了。

● Christmas day will be here soon.
● I **almost forgot** to buy Christmas presents.
　● 耶誕節快到了。　● 我差點忘了要買耶誕禮物。

▶ Helen almost forgot to come.
　Helen 差點忘了要來。
　Kevin totally forgot about the meeting.
　Kevin 完全忘了開會的事。

before I forget

趁我忘記之前 用在怕自己會忘掉，所以趕緊先說的狀況。

● You still owe me twenty dollars.
● Let me give it to you now, **before I forget**.
　● 你還欠我二十塊。　● 我現在給你吧，趁我忘記之前。

▶ Before I forget, Angie wants to see you.
　趁我忘記之前先說，Angie 想要見你。
　Before I forget, we need to order some supplies.
　趁我忘記之前先說，我們需要訂一些用品。

slip one's mind

- sth completely slipped one's mind
  某事完全被某人忘記了
- slip one's memory
  被某人忘記

被某人忘記 mind 也可以換成 memory。主詞是被忘記的事。

- ● Did you clean up the break room?
- ● Oh my gosh, that **slipped my mind**.
  ● 你把休息室打掃乾淨了嗎？　　● 噢，我的天啊，我忘記那件事了。

- ▶ Her birthday party completely slipped my mind.
  我完全把她的生日派對給忘了。
  The dentist appointment slipped Joan's memory.
  Joan 把跟牙醫的約診給忘了。

put sth behind sb

- manage to put sth behind sb
  試圖把某事拋在某人腦後
- put today behind you
  把今天的事拋在你腦後

把某事拋在某人腦後 表示暫時忘掉某件麻煩、討厭的事。

- ● You had some money problems, right?
- ● I did, but I **put them behind me**.
  ● 你有些金錢上的問題對嗎？　　● 是沒錯，但我把它們拋在腦後了。

- ▶ We managed to put that trouble behind us.
  我們試圖把那個問題拋在腦後。
  Let's just put today behind us. 我們把今天的事拋在腦後吧。

be on the tip of my tongue

一時想不起來 話已經到嘴邊了，卻一時想不起來，說不出口。

- ● What word do you use for this?
- ● I'm sorry, but the words **are on the tip of my tongue**.
  ● 你會用什麼字來形容這個？　　● 抱歉，但我一時想不起來。

- ▶ The old phrase was on the tip of my tongue.
  我一時想不起那個老諺語。
  Rob tried to remember, but it was on the tip of his tongue. Rob 努力回想，但他一時想不起來。

let it go

忘掉它 字面上的意思是「讓它走」，引申為「忘掉」的意思。

- ● Nicole had a terrible divorce last year.
- ● Well, I hope she's been able to **let it go**.
  ● Nicole 去年離婚的過程很不愉快。　　● 嗯，我希望她能忘掉這件事。

- ▶ Let it go. It's all in the past. 忘了吧。都過去了。
  At some point, you just got to let it go, right?
  有一天你總該放手，對吧？

---

 forget to do vs. forget doing

　　forget sth 和 forget that/how S+V 是「忘記某件事」，而 forget to do sth 則是「忘記要做某事」。如果要說「忘記做過某件事」，則說 forget doing sth。和 forget 意思相反的 remember，用法也是一樣，後面接不定詞 to do 表示要做的事，接動名詞 doing 則表示以前做過的事。

1 職場・學校
2 電腦・網路
3 社交生活
4 日常生活
5 訊息・理解
6 想法・態度
7 情緒・狀況
8 行為舉止
9 時間地點・副詞片語

Thoughts & Attitude

能夠傳達自己想法和態度的各種慣用語

CHAPTER 6

01 思考，意見
think of

6-01.mp3

think of

· think of sb/sth
　想到／考慮…
· think about sb/sth
　思考…

想到…，考慮… 問句 What do you think of...? 則是「你對…有什麼想法？」的意思。

● What do you **think of** cloning humans?
● It is totally crazy. It seems immoral to me.
　●你對於複製人有什麼想法？　●這太瘋狂了。我覺得不道德。

▶ What do you think of the new guy?
　新來的那個男生，你覺得怎樣？
　Give me a few days to think about it.
　給我幾天考慮一下。

think of -ing

考慮要去做… 常用進行式，表示之後打算要做的事。

● What are you doing tonight?
● I **was thinking of** going to the new jazz bar near my house.
　●你今晚要做什麼？　●我考慮要去我家附近新開的爵士酒吧。

▶ Are you thinking of applying for a loan?
　你在考慮要申請貸款嗎？
　I am thinking about becoming an airline pilot.
　我在思考以後成為一位飛機駕駛員。

think S+V

· think so
　這麼覺得
· think positively about
　積極地思考…

認為… think 可以接 that 子句，但 that 常常省略。

● I don't **think that** I have the time to finish it.
● Come on, you have the time. Go for it!
　●我覺得我沒有時間完成它。　●拜託，你有時間的。放手一搏吧！

▶ Do you think that she will be able to fix the problem?
　你覺得她能解決問題嗎？
　I think that Angie is the most generous person.
　我覺得 Angie 是最慷慨的人。

give sth some thought

- give no thought (to...)
  沒有考慮過…，沒花心思在…上

考慮看看某事 常以 give it some thought 的型態出現。

- I don't know if I can do that.
- Well, just **give it some thought**.
  ●我不知道我是否做得到。　●嗯，就考慮看看吧。

▶ He gave no thought to the topic of his report.
  他對於自己報告的主題完全沒用心。
  You should give it some thought. 你應該考慮看看。

find sth + 形容詞

- find sb/sth interesting
  覺得…很有趣
- find sth difficult
  覺得…很難
- find it hard/easy to do
  覺得…做起來很難／簡單

認為／覺得某事… sth 後面可接形容詞或動詞 -ing 形。

- What's taking so long?
- I'm **finding** our homework **difficult**.
  ●什麼事花了那麼多時間？　●我覺得我們的功課很難。

▶ Jenna found James very interesting. Jenna 覺得 James 很有趣。
  Jim found hiking up the mountain difficult.
  Jim 覺得登山健行很難。

have sth in mind

- have sth serious in mind
  在想某件嚴肅的事情
- » cf. have sth on one's mind
  擔心，考慮太多

心裡有…的想法 表示已經決定了某件事或者有了某個意見。

- Where will the wedding take place?
- I **have** a nice restaurant **in mind**.
  ●婚禮會在哪裡舉行？　●我在考慮一間不錯的餐廳。

▶ Sit down, I have something serious in mind to discuss.
  坐下，我有些嚴肅的事想要討論。
  Fiona had the trip in mind. Fiona 想去旅行。

at the thought of

- tremble at the thought of
  一想到…就發抖
- be in one's thought
  在某人的心中

一想到… of 後面接名詞或動名詞。

- That food was absolutely terrible.
- Yeah, I feel sick **at the thought of** it.
  ●那食物糟透了。　●是啊，我一想到就想吐。

▶ Dorothy trembled at the thought of the argument.
  Dorothy 一想到那場爭執就發抖。
  Your mother is in all of our thoughts. 你母親在我們大家心中。

be a good idea to

- It's a good idea to...
  做…是個好主意
- My idea is to...
  我的想法是去做…

做…是個好主意 to 後面接動詞原形。

- It would **be a good idea to** leave now.
- Let's get out of here together.
  ●現在離開是個好主意。　●我們一起走吧。

▶ I really don't think that's a good idea.
  我真的不覺得那是個好主意。
  Don't you think it is a good idea to monitor your employees? 你不覺得監控你的職員們是個好主意嗎？

1 職場・學校
2 電腦・網路
3 社交生活
4 日常生活
5 訊息・理解
6 想法・態度
7 情緒・狀況
8 行為舉止
9 時間地點・副詞片語

have a different opinion

· have a good
  opinion of
  對於…有好見解
· have no opinion of
  對於…沒有意見

有不同的意見　表示對於某事的看法不同。

- ●Did you tell Stan about your idea?
- ●Yes, but he **had a different opinion** of things.
  - ●你跟 Stan 說了你的想法了嗎？　　●有，但他對事情有不同的意見。

▶ Everybody had a different opinion.
　每個人都有不同的意見。
　I have no opinion on civil rights.
　我對於民權沒有意見。

give one's opinion on

· in one's opinion
  就某人的意見

針對…給意見　對某件事表達個人意見。

- ●What do you think of going to church?
- ●I don't want to **give my opinion on** that.
  - ●你對於上教會有什麼想法？　　●我不想對這件事發表意見。

▶ In my opinion, we need a better boss.
　就我個人的意見，我們需要一個更好的老闆。
　Jesse gave her opinion on the new coat.
　Jesse 對於那件新大衣給了她的意見。

if you ask me

如果你問我的意見　謹慎地表達個人意見的說法。

- ●Brett says he can't work any more.
- ●**If you ask me**, he's just being lazy.
  - ●Brett 說他沒辦法再工作下去了。　　●要我說的話，他只是懶惰。

▶ If you ask me, I'd move in with him.
　要我說的話，我想搬去跟他住。
　If you ask me, she is dying to get people's attention.
　如果你問我，我會說她死命想要得到他人的注意。

the way I see it

· the way I look at
  this is
  我對這件事的看法是…
· from what I've seen
  依我所見

依我看來　用來說明自己對於情況的看法。

- ●George just got a visa for England.
- ●**The way I see it**, he plans to move there.
  - ●George 剛拿到英國簽證。　　●依我看來，他打算搬到那裡。

▶ From what I've seen, there are many problems.
　依我所見，那有很多問題。
　The way I see it, you've got no choice on that.
　就我看來，對於那件事，你沒有選擇的餘地。

1 職場‧學校

2 電腦‧網路

3 社交生活

4 日常生活

5 訊息‧理解

6 想法‧態度

7 情緒‧狀況

8 行為舉止

9 時間地點‧副詞片語

feel that way

· feel that way about...
  對於…覺得那樣
· look at...differently
  對於…有不同的看法

那樣覺得，那樣想 way 是「方式」的意思。

● I think you're the most beautiful woman in the world.
● Really? I'm surprised you **feel that way**.

●我覺得你是世界上最美的女人。　●真的嗎？我很驚訝你那樣想。

▶ I'm not at all surprised they feel that way.
我一點也不驚訝他們會那樣想。
Not all married women feel that way.
不是所有已婚女性都會那樣想。

what's sb like?

· What does sb look like?
  A 的外型／長相怎樣？

某人怎麼樣？ 用來詢問某人的個性或特質。

● **What's** your new professor **like**?
● He's smart and he makes us work hard.

●你的新教授怎麼樣？　●他很聰明，而且讓我們努力用功。

▶ What does your brother look like?
你哥哥長得怎樣？
What does Frank look like? Is he cute?
Frank 長得怎樣？他可愛嗎？

What is...like? vs. What does...look like?

「What is + 名詞 + like?」和「How is + 名詞？」同義，是用來問某個事物怎麼樣。和「What does + 名詞 + look like?」比較後會更清楚。「What is + 名詞 + like?」可以用來問各方面的性質，但「What does + 名詞 + look like?」則是單純詢問外觀怎麼樣。舉例來說，What does your new house look like? 是在詢問房子的外觀，而 What is your new house like? 則可以回答房子住起來如何等等。

02 | 考慮
consider -ing

6-02.mp3

---

consider

- consider -ing
  考慮…
- all things considered
  考慮到一切→整體而言

考慮 意思是 think carefully。consider 可以接名詞或動詞 -ing 形當受詞。

- What should I do with these extra clothes?
- **Consider** giving them away.
  - 我該怎麼處理這些多的衣服？　●考慮看看把它們送出去吧。

▶ All things considered, you had fun tonight.
　整體而言，你今晚玩得很開心。
　I'm considering leaving your father.
　我在考慮離開你父親。

take sth into consideration

- give sth a lot of consideration
  對於某事考慮很多

考慮某事 把某事列入 consideration（考慮的事）的意思。

- You should try to become a lawyer.
- I'll **take** your advice **into consideration**.
  - 你應該努力成為一位律師。　●我會考慮你的建議。

▶ She gave the job offer a lot of consideration.
　她對於那份工作機會做了很多考慮。
　I'll take your arguments into consideration.
　我會考慮你的論點。

take sth into account

- take account of sth
  考慮某事

考慮某事 在判斷或決定某事時，考量某些要素的意思。

- Did Bill follow your suggestions?
- No, but he **took** them **into account**.
  - Bill 有遵從你的建議嗎？　●沒有，但他有考慮過。

▶ Olga should take the future into account.
　Olga 應該考慮到未來。
　That's the first thing you have to take into account.
　那是你必須考量的第一件事。

424

1 職場・學校

2 電腦・網路

3 社交生活

4 日常生活

5 訊息・理解

6 想法・態度

7 情緒・狀況

8 行為舉止

9 時間地點・副詞片語

after careful consideration

深思熟慮後 在做出某個決定前，考慮了很多的樣子。

● What did you decide to do?

● **After careful consideration**, we decided to buy it.

●你們決定怎麼做？　●經過深思熟慮後，我們決定買它。

▶ After careful consideration, here's what I've decided.
深思熟慮後，這是我的決定。

After careful consideration, I've decided that I'm getting married. 深思熟慮後，我決定要結婚。

be under consideration

・in consideration of
考慮到…

考慮中，檢討中 be under 表示「在某種情況下」。還在考慮的情況下，就是還不能決定的意思。

● Have they accepted my new idea?

● No, it's **under consideration** right now.

●他們接受了我的新點子嗎？　●還沒，現在還在考慮中。

▶ We can't help you, in consideration of everything.
考慮到各種因素，我們無法幫你。

A new highway is now under consideration.
一條新高速公路的建案正在檢討中。

---

03 慎重思考，再考慮
think over

6-03.mp3

think over

・think over sth
慎重思考某事

・think it over
慎重思考

・think twice
再次思考

慎重思考 做出決定前慎重考慮的意思。也可以用 think twice 來表達。

● I need to **think over** my choices.

● You'll have to decide soon.

●我需要仔細考慮我的選擇。　●你得快點決定。

▶ You think it over. Call me back.
你好好思考一下吧。再回電給我。

You need to think carefully before starting your own business. 在開創自己的事業之前，你需要慎重思考。

have second thoughts

· have second thoughts about+N/-ing
對…改變主意
· Don't give it a second thought.
別多心了。

改變主意，有疑慮 對於一件事有其他的想法，表示開始產生疑慮，或者想要改變之前的決定。

● Don't **give it a second thought**. I'm always glad to help.
● Thanks so much.

● 別多心了，不論何時我都樂意幫忙。　● 真的非常感謝。

▶ We had second thoughts about renting the apartment.
我們對於租那間公寓有疑慮。
Jim is having second thoughts about going to China.
Jim 正在重新考慮去中國的事。

on second thought

重新考慮之後 改變心意時會說的話。

● Let's go out to eat at a restaurant tonight.
● **On second thought**, we should stay home and save money.

● 我們今晚去餐廳吃飯吧。　● 重新考慮的話，我們該待在家裡省錢。

▶ On second thought, she decided to move.
重新考慮之後，她決定搬家。
On second thought, we should call Brad.
重新考慮的話，我們應該打電話給 Brad。

reconsider

· reconsider one's decision
重新考慮某人的決定
· reconsider one's plans
重新考慮某人的計畫

重新考慮 重新考慮已經決定的事。通常接 plan, decision 當受詞。

● The accident made me **reconsider** my plans.
● Did you decide to do something else?

● 這場事故讓我重新考慮了我的計畫。　● 你決定要去做別的事嗎？

▶ Take some time to reconsider your decision.
花點時間重新考慮你的決定。
I'll need to reconsider the offer you made.
我需要重新考慮你的提議。

sleep on it

· let me sleep on it
讓我對此深思熟慮一下
· need more time to think
需要更多時間思考

深思熟慮 睡在 it 上面，就是把問題放在心中，思考一晚再說。

● So, did you decide to rent the apartment?
● I need to **sleep on it** before making a decision.

● 所以，你決定租那間公寓了嗎？
● 做出決定前，我需要深思熟慮一番。

▶ Let me sleep on it and give you an answer tomorrow.
讓我考慮一晚，明天給你答案。
Jill needs more time to think your proposal.
Jill 需要更多時間來思考你的提案。

1 職場・學校
2 電腦・網路
3 社交生活
4 日常生活
5 訊息・理解
6 想法・態度
7 情緒・狀況
8 行為舉止
9 時間地點・副詞片語

04 | 視為 take A for B

6-04.mp3

consider A (as) B

· consider yourself lucky
覺得你自己運氣好
· consider oneself (to be) N
認為自己是⋯
· consider oneself lucky/fortunate
覺得自己運氣好

把 A **視為** B consider A as B 的 as 可以省略。

● Have you known Tim a long time?
● I **consider** him my best friend.
　●你認識 Tim 很久了嗎？　●我把他當成我最好的朋友。

▶ Consider yourself lucky for avoiding the work.
　能夠避掉那份工作，你該覺得自己幸運。
　She considers chocolate the best flavor.
　她認為巧克力是最棒的口味。

regard A as B

· regard sb/sth as N
認為⋯是⋯
· be widely regarded as
被廣泛地認為是⋯
· be (highly) regarded
（非常）受重視

認為 A 是 B A 可以是人或事物。

● I **regard** Alfred **as** a genius.
● Yes, he's the smartest guy in class.
　●我認為 Alfred 是個天才。　●是啊，他是班上最聰明的人。

▶ Most people regard artwork as worthwhile.
　大多數的人認為藝術品是有價值的。
　He regarded the meeting as a waste of time.
　他認為這場會議浪費時間。

think of A as B

· think of oneself as N
覺得自己是⋯
· think sb (to be) N/adj
覺得某人是⋯
· look upon A as B
把 A 視為 B

覺得 A 是 B A 可以是人或事物。

● It sure feels cold outside today.
● I **think of** winter **as** unpleasant.
　●今天外面真的感覺很冷。　●我覺得冬天很討厭。

▶ They looked upon homework as boring.
　他們覺得作業很無聊。
　We think of ghosts as scary. 我們覺得鬼很嚇人。

take A for B

· take him for a fool
誤以為他是個傻子
· What do you take me for?
你把我當成怎樣的人了？

把 A **錯認為** B 誤以為 A 是 B 的表達方式。

● Mr. Johnson has a lot of money.
● Really? We **took** him **for** a poor person.
　●Johnson 先生有很多錢。　●真的嗎？我們以為他是窮人。

▶ They took Cami for a fool. 他們誤以為 Cami 是個傻子。
　I took his story for a lie. 我誤以為他的故事是謊話。

come across as

- come across as
  + 形容詞
  看起來像…

- deem sb as
  認為某人是…

看起來像… come across 雖然有「偶然遇見」的意思，但後面如果加上「as＋形容詞」，則解釋為「有…的印象」。

- Why did you get angry at Rachel?
- She **came across as** very unkind.
  - 你為什麼生 Rachel 的氣？　● 她非常不客氣。

▶ Taylor came across as being very self-confident.
Taylor 給人自信滿滿的印象。

Aaron was deemed as being the best student.
Aaron 被視為最棒的學生。

---

05 | 突然想到
hit on

6-05.mp3

---

occur to sb that

- It occurred to me that
  我想起…

- It never occurred to
  me that
  我從來沒想過…

某人想起… 常用的句型是 it occurred to me that...。

- **It occurred to me that** Bill doesn't have his cell phone.
- You're right, hopefully we don't have to get in touch with him.
  - 我想起 Bill 沒帶手機。　● 你說的對。希望我們不會需要和他聯絡。

▶ It occurred to me I've made sacrifices over the past six years. 我想起過去六年來我做了一些犧牲。

It suddenly occurred to me Tom was using me all that time. 我突然想到 Tom 總是在利用我。

dawn on sb that

- it dawned on me that
  S+V
  我忽然明白…

- it dawned on her that
  S+V
  她忽然明白…

某人忽然明白… 同樣的，常以 it dawned on me that... 的形式出現。

- Why did Karen quit her job?
- **It dawned on her that** she was wasting her time.
  - Karen 為什麼辭職了？　● 她忽然了解她是在浪費時間。

▶ It dawned on me that I forgot my wallet.
我忽然發覺我忘了我的皮夾。

It dawned on her that she missed her appointment.
她忽然想起她錯過了約會。

hit on

· hit on a new idea
  想出一個新點子

發現…，想出… 主詞是人，有「突然想到」的意思。

● How did you figure out the math problem?

● We **hit on** the answer after a few hours.

  ● 你們怎麼解出那個數學題的？　● 我們在幾小時之後想出了答案。

▶ He hit on a new idea at the meeting.
  他在會議上想出了新的點子。
  I hit on the plan of creating a website.
  我想出了做網站的計畫。

come to mind

· come to think of
  這樣一想，現在想想看
· bring/call...to mind
  使…浮現在腦中

浮現在腦中 某件事沒來由地忽然進入思考中的意思。

● That law firm is full of nothing but ambulance chasers.

● **Come to think of it**, they do have a bad reputation.

  ● 這間律師事務所，都是些勸事故受害者打官司賺訴訟費的律師。
  ● 這樣一想，他們的名聲的確不好。

▶ You can say the first thing that comes to mind.
  你可以把第一個浮現在腦中的想法說出來。
  Come to think of it, you should take a day off.
  這樣想想，你該休一天假。

make sb think of

· It got me thinking of/
  that...
  這讓我想到／覺得…

使某人想到／覺得… 並非突然想起，而是因為某個人事物才想起來的。

● It is so beautiful outside today.

● It **makes me think of** last summer.

  ● 今天外面天氣真好。　● 讓我想到去年夏天。

▶ It got me thinking that he could become a doctor.
  這讓我覺得，他可以成為一名醫生。
  You made me think that you still loved me.
  你讓我覺得你還愛我。

1 職場・學校
2 電腦・網路
3 社交生活
4 日常生活
5 訊息・理解
6 想法・態度
7 情緒・狀況
8 行為舉止
9 時間地點・副詞片語

06 推測
take a guess

6-06.mp3

guess that S+V

- guess right/wrong about
  猜對／錯…
- guessing game
  猜謎遊戲

猜測… 表示有點不確定的說法，意思和 I think... 相近。

- What's gotten into you?
- **I guess** I'm just tired of this dumb job.
  ●你怎麼了？　●我想我只是厭倦這份愚蠢的工作。

▶ She guessed right about my age. 她猜對了我的年齡。
I guess you're a little stressed out right now.
我猜你現在有點壓力過大。

take a guess

- take a guess at...
  猜猜看…
- take a guess that S+V
  猜測…
- Take a guess!
  猜猜看！

猜猜看 guess 當名詞時，會搭配動詞 take 使用。

- What year of school are you in?
- **Take a guess.** Let's see if you know.
  ●你是哪個年級的？　●猜猜看，看你知不知道。

▶ She took a guess about the store's closing time.
她猜了這間店的關門時間。
You can take a guess how old I am. 你可以猜猜看我多大。

suppose that S+V

- Let's suppose that
  讓我們假設…
- I suppose
  我想想…
- Suppose/Supposing that S+V
  假設…

猜想…，假設…，讓… 除了「猜想」、「假設」以外，也可以表示含蓄的邀約，意思與 let 相近。

- **Suppose that** we go out together.
- Oh, I don't think that's a good idea.
  ●我們一起出去吧。　●噢，我不覺得這是個好主意。

▶ Let's suppose that he is coming tonight.
讓我們假設他今晚會來。
Do you suppose that's real? 你覺得那是真的嗎？

must have + pp

- must be
  一定是…

一定…了 must 除了表示義務，也可以表示十分確定的推測。

- I'm about to buy a brand new house.
- Really? You **must be very excited**.
  ●我準備要買一間全新的房子。　●真的嗎？你一定很興奮。

▶ You must have been busy preparing all of this food.
準備這所有的食物，你一定很忙。
He must have lost his keys sometime this afternoon.
他一定是今天下午的某個時候把鑰匙弄丟了。

should be/do

應該是… 同樣表示推測，但心裡的把握比 must 略低。

- I can't wait to see the results of the test.
- They **should be** here by Monday.
  - 我等不及想看測驗的結果。　　●星期一應該就會寄來了。

▶ We should be in the city by nine.
我們應該會在九點抵達市區。
The waiter should be bringing us our meal soon.
服務生應該很快就會把我們的餐點送來。

---

07 | 預期
...than I thought

6-07.mp3

1 職場・學校
2 電腦・網路
3 社交生活
4 日常生活
5 訊息・理解
6 想法・態度
7 情緒・狀況
8 行為舉止
9 時間地點・副詞片語

be expected to

- expect that S+V
  預期…
- expect (A) to do
  期待做…／預期 A 會做…

被預期… 省略 by sb 的被動句型，to 後面接動詞原形。

- It's **expected to** be sunny today.
- Great. Let's do something outside.
  - 今天預測會是個晴天。　　●很好，我們來做點戶外活動吧。

▶ The nurses say you're expected to make a full recovery.
護士們說你應該可以完全康復。
Don't expect that to happen anytime soon!
不要期望那會很快發生！
I expect Pam to arrive any moment in his new BMW.
我猜 Pam 隨時都可能開著他的新 BMW 抵達。

come to expect

- exceed one's
  expectations
  超過某人的預期
- beyond one's
  expectations
  超乎某人的預期
- meet the expectations
  滿足期待

逐漸習慣… 「逐漸會去期望某件事」，表示習慣某件事發生。

- Kelly is never on time for appointments.
- We've **come to expect** that she'll be late.
  - Kelly 從來不會準時赴約。　　●我們已經習慣她遲到了。

▶ It's exceeded all my expectations.
這超過了我所有的預期。
Women have expectations. And you didn't meet them.
女人都有期待，而你沒有達到這些期待。

431

have expectations

- have the expectation of N/that S+V
  有…的期待
- be filled with expectations
  充滿期待

有期待 使用 expect 的名詞形 expectation，後面可以直接接 S+V 表示期待的內容。

- Your son seems to be really smart.
- We **have expectations** he'll become a scientist.
  ●你兒子看起來真的很聰明。　●我們期待他成為一位科學家。

▶ Sam has expectations she'll become rich.
  Sam 期待她變有錢。

I happen to know that Will has really high expectations for this birthday. 我偶然得知 Will 對這次生日有很高的期待。

...than I thought

- harder than I thought
  比我所想的還難
- better than I thought
  比我所想的還好

比我所想的還… 前面用形容詞或副詞的比較級。thought 也可以換成 imagined（想像）等動詞過去式。

- Your apartment is bigger **than I thought**.
- Yeah, there's a lot of room in here.
  ●你的公寓比我想的還大。　●是啊，這邊有很多空間。

▶ You're not stupid. You're meaner than I thought.
  你不笨，你比我想的還卑鄙。

My teacher is a lot smarter than I imagined.
  我的老師比我想像的還要聰明得多。

...than I expected

- ...as you expected
  如你所預期的…

比我預期的還… expected 也可以換成 had expected，強調是以前有過的想法。

- How was your date last night?
- She was more cute **than I expected**.
  ●你昨晚的約會如何？　●她比我預期的還可愛。

▶ That's actually less than I expected it would be.
  那事實上比我預期的還少。

Isn't it as good as you expected?
  這不是跟你預期的一樣好嗎？

...than sb bargained for

比某人預料中還… bargained for 是「預料到」的意思。

- Did you buy a new notebook computer?
- Yes, it was more expensive **than I bargained for**.
  ●你買了新的筆記型電腦嗎？　●是啊，比我預料中貴。

▶ The trip was longer than we bargained for.
  這趟旅行比我們預期的還長。

The movie was funnier than she bargained for.
  這部電影比她預料的還有趣。

1
職場・學校

2
電腦・網路

3
社交生活

4
日常生活

5
訊息・理解

6
想法・態度

7
情緒・狀況

8
行為舉止

9
時間地點・副詞片語

not hold one's breath

不抱太大期望 「不摒息以待」，也就是別抱什麼期望的意思。

- I'm going to be very rich someday.
- Yeah, **don't hold your breath** for that to happen.
  - ●我有一天會變得非常有錢。 ●是喔，別太期待那會發生吧。

▶ Don't hold your breath for the economy to improve.
別對經濟改善抱太大的期望。
If you are waiting for him to apologize, don't hold your breath. 如果你在等他道歉，別太期待了。

---

 expect 是「懷孕」？

expect 的基本意義是「期待」，常見的句型有 expect sb to do，或者被動句型 be expected to do「被期望去做…」。但 expect 還有一個會讓我們大吃一驚的字義，就是「懷孕」。She's expecting a baby. 意為「懷了一個小孩（期待嬰兒出生）」，「孕婦」則稱為 expectant mother。

---

08 | 相信，依靠 believe in

6-08.mp3

believe that S+V

- believe it or not
  信不信由你
- It's believed that.../to be...
  人們相信…

相信… 這是 believe 最常見的用法。被動態 be believed to... 則是「（被）人們相信…」的意思。

- Do you know where mom is?
- I **believe that** she is cooking something.
  - ●你知道媽媽在哪裡嗎？ ●我相信她正在煮東西。

▶ He believed that the car would be fast.
他相信這台車會跑得很快。
I believe that we should all support our boss.
我相信我們都應該支持我們的老闆。

believe in

- believe in God
  相信神

相信⋯ 和 have faith in 同義，表示信任某個人事物。

- I don't **believe in** our boss.
- I know. I don't trust him either.
  - ●我不相信我們的老闆。　●我知道，我也不信任他。

▶ Do you believe in ghosts?
你相信有鬼嗎？
Is it still possible to believe in love at first sight?
現在還能相信一見鍾情嗎？

trust sb

- trust sb to do
  信賴某人會做⋯
- trust sb at sb's word
  相信某人的話
- trust that S+V
  相信⋯

信賴某人　trust sb to do 則是相信某人會做某事。

- Is Will taking care of that work?
- Yeah, I **trust** him to do a good job.
  - ●Will 負責那份工作嗎？　●是啊，我相信他會做得很好。

▶ I'm sorry, but I don't trust you guys.
抱歉，但我不相信你們。
I'm going to trust you to break up with Jessica.
我相信你會和 Jessica 分手。

depend on

- depending on
  取決於⋯
- It depends.
  視情況而定。

依靠⋯，取決於⋯ on 後面可以接人或事物。

- Could you tell me where the closest subway station is?
- **It depends.** Where do you want to go?
  - ●你可以告訴我最近的地鐵站在哪裡嗎？
  - ●要看情況。你想去哪裡？

▶ I have a responsibility to those who depend on us.
我對那些依賴我們的人有責任。
I usually read a book each month, depending on how busy I am. 我通常每個月讀一本書，取決於我有多忙。

count on

- count on (A) -ing
  預期⋯／期待 A 做⋯
- count on A to do
  期待 A 去做⋯
- rely on
  依賴⋯

依靠⋯，相信⋯ on 後面可以接人或事物。

- Please get it done right away.
- Don't worry, you can **count on** me.
  - ●請馬上把它完成。　●別擔心，你可以相信我。

▶ You can count on me for a good recommendation.
相信我吧，我會幫你寫一封很好的推薦信。
I feel like I can count on him.
我覺得我可以依靠他。

fall back on

依靠… 表示碰到困難時能夠依靠的人或事物。

- How is your family doing?
- It's lucky we have extra money to **fall back on**.

  ●你的家人過得怎樣？　●我們很幸運有多的錢可以支持生活。

▶ You have good friends to fall back on.
  你有好朋友們可以依靠。
  She fell back on her good reputation.
  她仰賴於她的好名聲。

have faith in

· have no faith in
  不相信…
· put a lot of faith in
  非常信任…

相信… faith 表示強烈的信任感。

- Is Erin a good carpenter?
- I **have faith in** her ability to build things.

  ●Erin 是個好木匠嗎？　●我對於她建造東西的能力深信不疑。

▶ I know you put a lot of faith in me, Jim.
  Jim，我知道你非常信任我。
  My father doesn't have any faith in me.
  我父親對我一點信心也沒有。

lose faith in

不再相信… 因為某些原因，從本來 have faith 的狀況變得不再信任，就是失去了（lose）faith。

- Are you still friends with Aurora?
- No, I **lost faith in** her when she lied to me.

  ●你跟 Aurora 還是朋友嗎？
  ●不，她騙了我的時候，我就不信任她了。

▶ Don't lose faith in your parents.
  別對你的父母失去信心。
  Jenny lost faith in the church she attended.
  Jenny 對自己上的教會失去了信任。

buy

· I don't buy it.
  我不信。

相信（某人說的話） 常用的說法是 can hardly buy your story（很難相信你說的話）。

- Like I said, the train was delayed.
- Well, I don't **buy it**.

  ●就像我說的，火車誤點了。　●嗯，我不相信。

▶ I don't buy her story about being kidnapped.
  我不相信她說自己被綁架。
  When he says he's a genius, I don't buy it.
  當他說他是個天才，我並不相信。

1 職場・學校
2 電腦・網路
3 社交生活
4 日常生活
5 訊息・理解
6 想法・態度
7 情緒・狀況
8 行為舉止
9 時間地點・副詞片語

09 希望
hope to

hope S+V

· hope for
希望…（接名詞）

· hope so/not
希望如此／希望不是

希望… hope 單純表示希望某件事發生，wish 則常常用來表示祝福，或搭配與現實相反的假設語氣，表示雖然希望如何，但事與願違，或可能性很低。

● Thank you for the gift you sent on my birthday.

● Oh, it was my pleasure. **I hope** you like it.

　● 謝謝你送我的生日禮物。　● 噢，那是我的榮幸。希望你喜歡。

▶ We hope they will attend our party.

　我們希望他們會參加我們的派對。

　The win-win situation is what we all hope for.

　雙贏的局面是我們大家都希望的。

have hope for

· have high hopes for
對…有很大的期望

· have any hope of -ing
對於…有任何期望

對…抱有希望 hope 前面可以加上形容詞 high 或 big，表示期望很高。

● You lost a lot of money this year.

● I **have hope for** a better time next year.

　● 你今年損失了很多錢。　● 我希望明年狀況會變好。

▶ I have big hopes for her. She's going to be a doctor.

　我對她抱有很大的希望。她會成為一位醫生。

　I had high hopes for a relationship with you.

　我很希望能和你交往。

　Mom has no hope of starting a relationship with him.

　媽媽完全不期望和他發展關係。

there is hope of

· there is hope of -ing
有…的希望

· there is no hope of -ing
沒有…的希望

有…的希望 of 後面接名詞或動詞 -ing 形。

● An airplane crashed near the mountain.

● **There is hope of** rescuing some people.

　● 一架飛機在山附近墜毀了。　● 有希望能夠救出一些人。

▶ There is no hope of getting an A in the class.

　在這個班上，不用抱希望能拿到 A。

　There is hope of finding the wallet you lost.

　有希望能夠找到你掉的皮夾。

in hopes of

- in hopes that S+V
  抱著…的希望
- hopefully, A will
  但願 A 會…

抱著…的希望 後面接名詞。也可以說 in hopes that S+V。

- Stanley and Jennifer are dating now.
- She is dating him **in hopes of** getting married.

  ●Stanley 和 Jennifer 現在在約會。　●她是希望結婚而跟他約會的。

▶ We came in the hopes that we'd meet your parents.

我們來是希望能見到你的父母。

Hopefully, Lindy will be home soon.

但願 Lindy 會很快回家。

wish to

- wish sb sth
  祝某人…
- I wish you the best
  我祝你順利
- make a wish (for)
  （為…）許願

希望… 祝福別人的時候可以用 wish sb sth 的句型，例如 wish you a merry Christmas（祝你耶誕快樂）或 wish him a happy birthday（祝他生日快樂）。

- I'll be starting my new job next week.
- **I wish** you all the best at your new job.

  ●我下星期要開始新工作了。　●希望你新工作順利。

▶ We wish to apologize for the late arrival of this train.

我們想對這班火車誤點致歉。

I wish you good luck.

祝你幸運。

look forward to

- look forward to meeting with you
  期待與你見面

期待… 「翹首盼望」的意思。to 後面接名詞或動詞 -ing 形。

- I'll give you a call when things cool down.
- I **look forward to** hearing from you.

  ●等事情冷靜下來後，我會打電話給你。　●我期待你的來電。

▶ I look forward to talking with you this afternoon.

我期待今天下午與你談話。

I'm looking forward to English class.

我期待英文課。

dream of

夢想… 表示像夢一樣，可能性不高，卻又希望美夢成真。

- I **dream of** working in the movie business.
- You should take film classes at university.

  ●我夢想能在電影業界工作。　●你應該在大學修電影課。

▶ Sal dreams of owning his own shop.

Sal 夢想能擁有一間自己的店。

In fact, little girls dream of big, white weddings.

事實上，小女孩們夢想著盛大的白色婚禮。

1 職場・學校
2 電腦・網路
3 社交生活
4 日常生活
5 訊息・理解
6 想法・態度
7 情緒・狀況
8 行為舉止
9 時間地點・副詞片語

該用 hope 還是 wish 呢？

雖然 hope 和 wish 在中文裡都翻譯成「希望」，但只有 wish 能使用 wish sb sth 的句型來表示祝福，例如 I wish you a merry Christmas。

另外，I wish (that)... 和 I hope (that)... 的使用情況也不同。I wish (that)... 常常用在與事實相反的情況，表示事與願違，這時候要使用與事實相反的假設語氣。例如「我真希望我知道他的電話號碼（但我不知道）」，就會說 I wish + I knew his number（與現在事實相反的假設語氣，動詞用過去式）。相反的，I hope (that)... 則用在事情有可能發生的情況下，以「我希望知道他的電話號碼」這個例子而言，說法就是 I hope + I know his number（單純陳述可能發生的事，用現在式）。

10 | 負責任 take charge of

6-10.mp3

be responsible for

· be responsible to sb
　對某人負責
· hold/find sb
　responsible for sth
　認為某人要對某事負責

對⋯有責任 for 後面接事情。如果是對人負責，則是 be responsible to sb。

● My mother-in-law **was responsible for** breaking up our marriage.
● How did she do that?

　●我岳母要對破壞我們的婚姻負責。　●她是怎麼做的？

▶ I don't hold her responsible for the accident.
　我不認為她要對事故負責。
　We all should be responsible for our own children.
　我們都該對我們自己的孩子負責。

take responsibility for

· share the responsibility of -ing
分擔做…的責任
· accept responsibility for...
承擔…的責任

負起…的責任 responsibility 前面加 full 或 complete 修飾，則表示「負全責」。

● You need to **take responsibility for** your mistakes.
● But I didn't do anything wrong.

●你需要對你的錯誤負責。　●但我沒有做錯任何事。

▶ You have to take full responsibility for your behavior.
你必須對你的行為負起全責。
We take some responsibility for whatever our child does.
我們對於我們小孩做的任何事都有一些責任。

take charge of

· take control of
掌管…

負責…，掌管… charge 也可以換成 control，意思一樣。

● Our boss is out sick this morning.
● OK, I'll **take charge of** the office.

●我們老闆今天早上請病假。　●好，我會負責辦公室。

▶ I took control of the business when my father died.
我父親去世後，我掌管了事業。
Sally will take charge of planning the party.
Sally 會負責計畫派對。

be in charge of

· be in full charge of
對…負全責

主管…，負責… 負責掌管公司的某個部門，或是正在進行中的案子等。

● Who's **in charge of** buying the supplies?
● The secretary is getting all of that stuff.

●誰負責買備品？　●祕書會把東西都買好。

▶ Who is in charge of customer service?
誰負責顧客服務？
I'd like to talk to the person in charge of parking permits.
我想跟負責停車證的人說話。

take on

承擔（事情、責任等） 受詞通常是 work 或 responsibility。

● Can you help me with decorating?
● Sorry, I can't **take on** any extra work.

●你可以幫我裝飾嗎？　●抱歉，我不能再接更多工作了。

▶ We took on a few new students in class.
我們班上接納了幾位新學生。
She's all set to take on more responsibility in the office.
她準備好要承擔辦公室裡更多的責任了。

1 職場・學校
2 電腦・網路
3 社交生活
4 日常生活
5 訊息・理解
6 想法・態度
7 情緒・狀況
8 行為舉止
9 時間地點・副詞片語

take over

· take over sth
  接任／接管某事
· take sth over
  接任／接管某事

接任…，接管… 「負擔某個職責」的意思，與 take control of 同義。

● I'm going to **take over** as class president.
● Did you win a student election?

  ● 我會接任班長的職務。　● 你贏了學生選舉嗎？

▶ Who is going to take over the company? 誰會接管公司？
  You can take over the meeting. 你可以接手會議。

take the blame

· take the blame for sth
  承擔某事的責任

負責任 用在對批評或指責負起責任的情況。

● Who caused the car wreck?
● Brody **took the blame for** the accident.

  ● 誰造成了車禍事故？　● Brody 承擔了事故的責任。

▶ You should take the blame for that problem.
  你應該承擔那個問題的責任。

  I took the blame when I spilled the wine.
  當我把酒灑出去時，我道了歉。

 ## 讓人頭大的 **charge**，一次學會各種不同的用法！

　　字彙是英文讓人覺得困難的理由之一。特別是那些我們不熟悉，不知道居然還擁有這樣或那樣字義的字彙們，更是頭號兇手。雖然應該深入學習，但因為我們把英文當成外語來學，所以常常知其一不知其二，對於沒看過的用法困惑不已。

　　charge 就是令人困惑的單字之一。當動詞的時候，除了「索取費用」（ask in payment）以外，還有「起訴，指責」（accuse）、「攻擊」（attack）、「命令，委以責任」（give as a duty or responsibility）或「充電」（take in and store electricity）等各種意義。

　　這一章中「in charge of」的 charge 就是從「委以責任」的字義衍生出來的名詞用法，有「care, control, responsibility」等意義，所以 in charge of 就是「負責…」（have the responsibility for）的意思。

　　當 sales department（業務部）的經理出差，自己代為管理部門的時候，就可以說「The sales department is in/under my charge while the manager is away.」，或者以人為主詞，用「I am in charge of the sales department while...」來表達。當董事長路過，看到負責人的位子空空如也，就可能會不悅地問「這裡是誰負責的？」（Who is in charge of this office?）

　　再補充一些說法。「I'd like to speak to the person in charge」意為「我想跟負責人說話」。「take charge of」則是「負責」。對於丈夫去世後，一肩挑起家業的女主人，可以這麼說：「She took charge of the family business after her husband died.」。

11 有義務
have a duty to

6-11.mp3

have duty to

· have a duty to sb
  對某人有義務
· have a duty to do
  有義務做…
· fulfill one's duty to
  履行做…的義務

有義務做… duty 是指法律上或道德上應該做的事。

● A guy in my office is stealing supplies.
● You **have a duty to** tell someone about it.

　●我辦公室有一個人會偷辦公用品。　●你有義務告訴某個人這件事。

▶ Policemen have to fulfill their duty to protect people.
　警察必須履行他們保護人民的義務。
　She has a duty to protect her children.
　她有義務保護她的孩子們。

be obliged to

· under the obligation to
  有做…的義務

不得不…，被迫… 是 formal 的說法。be 可以換成 feel，表示感覺上非做不可。

● You met up with Ann last night?
● Yeah, I **was obliged to** buy her dinner.

　●你昨晚和 Ann 見面了？　●嗯，我不得不買晚餐給她。

▶ I think we're obliged to have a drink.
　我想我們只好喝一杯了。
　She was obliged to attend her firm's annual softball
　game. 她不得不參加她公司的年度壘球比賽。

be liable for

· be liable for taxes
  有繳稅的義務

有…的義務 主要用在稅金、費用等金錢的義務上。

● I'd like to rent this apartment.
● You'll **be liable for** any damage you cause.

　●我想租這間公寓。　●那你要對你造成的房屋損傷負責。

▶ Every adult is liable for paying taxes.
　每個成年人都有義務繳稅。
　You are liable for repaying the loan.
　你有義務償還貸款。

1 職場・學校
2 電腦・網路
3 社交生活
4 日常生活
5 訊息・理解
6 想法・態度
7 情緒・狀況
8 行為舉止
9 時間地點・副詞片語

441

owe it to oneself to

· owe it to sb to take care of sb
應該幫某人照顧某人

應該（為自己）做⋯ owe 是「欠」的意思，表示有義務做。

● I've been in love with Howard for years.
● You **owe it to yourself to** do something about it.
　● 我和 Howard 交往了很多年。　● 你應該對這段關係做些努力。

▶ Beth owes it to her sisters to take care of their mom.
　Beth 應該幫她的姊妹照顧媽媽。
　I owe it to myself to do some work on my house.
　我的房子該做些整修。

play one's part

盡本分 play a part/role in... 則是「在⋯中扮演角色／對⋯有影響」的意思。

● We all have to **play our part in** the wedding.
● Are you going to help the bride?
　● 我們都必須在婚禮中各司其職。　● 你要幫忙新娘嗎？

▶ You need to play your part on the ball team.
　你需要在球隊中盡職。
　He played his part in the band.
　他在樂團中盡自己的本分。

---

12 | 有必要，沒必要 be in need of

6-12.mp3

---

need to

· need sth
需要某事物
· need healthy habits
需要健康的習慣
· need sb to do
需要某人做⋯

需要做⋯ 另一個句型是 need sb to do sth「需要某人去做某事」。

● I **need you to** copy the minutes and distribute them.
● To everybody or just the board members?
　● 我需要你影印會議記錄並且分發。
　● 發給每個人還是只給董事會成員？

▶ I think you need to talk with the boss about it.
　我想你需要跟老闆討論這件事。
　I need you to sign the document.
　我需要你簽署文件。

don't need to

- don't have to do
  不必做…
- there's no need to
  不需要做…

不需要做… need 也可以換成 have to，但意思會變成「不必做…」。

- Have you asked to borrow her phone?
- I **don't need to** borrow a phone now.
  - ●你跟她借手機了嗎？　●我現在不需要借手機。

▶ I don't need to pay for it.
  我不需要付那個的錢。
  You're right, I don't have to apologize.
  你是對的，我不必道歉。

be in need of

- be in need of help
  需要幫助
- be needed
  被需要→是需要的

需要… 如果只說 sb is in need，那就是某人有困難或很窮困的意思。

- Can I get something for you?
- I **am in need of** something to eat.
  - ●我可以幫你買點什麼嗎？　●我需要一點東西吃。

▶ They are in need of help studying.
  他們學習上需要幫助。
  I have patients in need of medical attention right now.
  我有病患需要立刻接受治療。

be necessary for

- it is necessary for sb to do
  某人必須做…
- it is necessary that S+V
  必須…
- that won't be necessary
  那沒有必要

必須… 另一種句型是 It is necessary to do…。

- There is a fire in the building.
- It **is necessary for** everyone to leave.
  - ●那棟大樓裡失火了。　●每個人都必須離開。

▶ Was it necessary to show up at my office?
  我必須到辦公室嗎？
  It is necessary for this contract to be valid.
  必須讓這個合約生效。

all I need/want is

- All I need is love.
  我只需要愛情。
- could use+N
  需要／想要…

我需要的只是… 「某物是我需要的一切」，也就是說只要這個就夠了。

- Your room has a desk and a small bed.
- Great. **That's all I need** to study.
  - ●你的房間有張桌子和小小的床。　●很好。我讀書時只需要這些。

▶ Now all you need is your speech.
  現在你該做的事就是演講。
  All you need is a woman who likes men.
  你只需要一個喜歡男人的女人就好了。

1 職場・學校
2 電腦・網路
3 社交生活
4 日常生活
5 訊息・理解
6 想法・態度
7 情緒・狀況
8 行為舉止
9 時間地點・副詞片語

13 確信，自信
be sure of

6-13.mp3

be sure of

· be sure of the answers
  對答案很確定
· feel quite sure that S+V
  對於…相當確定

確定… 後面接名詞。of 可以換成 about，be 可以換成 feel。

- I'm sure he wants to live with you.
- You're sure? You're absolutely sure?
  - ●我確定他想跟你一起住。　●你確定？你百分之百確定？
- ► You seem sure about the decision.
  你看起來對這個決定很有把握。
  I'm sure she's going to be all right. 我確定她會沒事的。

be sure to

一定要做… 常用在祈使句，提醒對方一定要做某事。

- **Be sure to** call me right after you get there.
- Don't worry. I will.
  - ●你到那裡以後一定要打電話給我。　●別擔心，我會的。
- ► Be sure to finish this work before the weekend.
  一定要在週末前完成這件工作。
  I'll be sure to tell him what we need.
  我一定會跟他說我們需要什麼。

be certain that S+V

· be certain of...
  確信…
· feel certain about sth
  對某事感到確定

確信… 也可以說 be certain of sth。

- I'm going to Susan's party tonight.
- **Be certain that** you bring some wine.
  - ●我今晚要去 Susan 的派對。　●記得帶點酒去。
- ► I'm certain that he didn't break the window.
  我確信他沒有打破窗戶。
  I feel certain this has been a very difficult period for you.
  我相信現在對你而言是個很困難的時期。

be bound to

· be bound to do
  一定會做…
· bound for + 地名
  （大眾交通工具）開往…

一定會做… be bound 本來是「被綁住」的意思，引申為「一定」。

- It's **bound to** be hot tomorrow.
- Let's wear shorts and T-shirts.
  - ●明天一定會很熱。　●我們穿短褲和 T 恤吧。
- ► Joey is bound to be here soon. Joey 一定會很快到這裡。
  This bus is bound for Chicago. 這班公車開往芝加哥。

be confident that

- be confident about
  對⋯有信心
- be/feel convinced of
  確信⋯

對⋯有信心 也可以把 confident 改成名詞，說「have confidence in sth」。

- I **am confident that** I'll get into Princeton.
- How can you be sure about that?

●我有信心會上普林斯頓大學。　●你怎麼能確定？

▶ I feel totally confident that you're going to pass the exam. 我完全相信你會通過考試。

We are confident we'll be able to handle this.
我們有信心能處理這件事。

assure sb that S+V

- assure A of B
  向 A 保證 B，
  使 A 相信 B
- be assured of/that...
  對於⋯放心

向某人保證⋯ Be assured that... 則是「請放心⋯」的意思。

- Tammy wants us to visit her.
- **Assure her that** we will come by.

●Tammy 希望我們去拜訪她。　●向她保證我們會順道過去。

▶ Be assured that the restaurant is good.
請放心，那間餐廳很好。

He tried to assure me of his honesty.
他試圖讓我相信他是誠實的。

guarantee that S+V

- guarantee sb sth
  向某人保證某事
- guarantee to do
  保證去做⋯

保證⋯ 跟 assure 比起來，guarantee 的語感更強烈、更正式一點。

- Have you finished the work yet?
- No, but I **guarantee that** it will be finished tonight.

●你完成那個工作了嗎？　●還沒，但我保證今晚會完成。

▶ Stan guaranteed that he would win the race.
Stan 保證他會贏得那場比賽。

We guarantee that you will like the result.
我們保證你會喜歡這個結果。

be destined to

- be destined for
  （大眾交通工具）開往⋯

註定會⋯，註定要⋯ destiny 是「命運」的意思，destine 則是「註定」。這個慣用語的意思是「像命運一樣無法避免」。

- William seems to be very smart.
- He **is destined to** do something important.

●William 看起來非常聰明。　●他註定要做些重要的事。

▶ They are destined to get married.
他們註定要結婚。

I was destined to spend my life here.
我註定要在這裡生活。

1 職場・學校

2 電腦・網路

3 社交生活

4 日常生活

5 訊息・理解

6 想法・態度

7 情緒・狀況

8 行為舉止

9 時間地點・副詞片語

bet S+V

- bet sb + 錢 (that) S+V
  跟某人賭多少錢，一定
  會…
- bet on the result of
  the match
  賭這場比賽的結果

打賭（一定會）… 跟中文一樣，表示有自信到可以賭一把的程度。主詞通常是 I。

- **I'll bet you** $100 you won't get an A.
- You're on. I studied hard for this test.
    - 我跟你賭一百塊，你一定不會拿到 A。
    - 好啊，我很努力讀書準備考試。

▶ I'll bet it will be expensive to fix. 我打賭這修起來一定很貴。

  I bet he has a huge hangover today. 他今天一定宿醉很嚴重。

---

14 有勇氣，失去勇氣
have the courage

6-14.mp3

have the courage to

- work up the courage
  to do
  提起勇氣去做…
- lose the courage to do
  失去做…的勇氣
- have enough courage
  to do
  有足夠的勇氣做…

有勇氣做… 和中文的說法幾乎一樣。courage 的形容詞形是 courageous（有勇氣的）。

- Who will lead our group?
- Cathy **has the courage to** lead us.
    - 誰會領導我們的團隊？ ● Cathy 有勇氣領導我們。

▶ It took a lot of courage to fight him. 和他爭吵需要很多勇氣。

  I need to work up the courage to ask her for a date.
  我需要提起勇氣，約她去約會。

take a lot of courage

- It takes (sb) a lot of
  courage to do
  做…需要（某人）很大的
  勇氣

需要很大的勇氣 主詞通常是虛主詞 it，後面接用不定詞（to do）表示的行為。要表示行為的主詞，可以說 take sb a lot of courage to do... 或 take a lot of courage for sb to do...。

- My cousin works with lions and tigers.
- It **takes a lot of courage to** do that job.
    - 我堂弟的工作是照顧獅子和老虎。
    - 要有很大的勇氣才能做那份工作。

▶ It will take a lot of courage to do that.
  做那件事需要很大的勇氣。

  It took a lot of courage for her to try again.
  她花費許多勇氣再試一次。

get up the nerve (to...)

· have the nerve to do
有勇氣做…

提起勇氣（做…）　nerve 在這裡是「膽子」的意思。

● Why haven't they gotten married yet?

● They **haven't gotten up the nerve to** talk to their parents.

　　●他們為什麼還沒結婚？　●他們還沒有勇氣跟他們的父母談。

▶ Tim had the nerve to talk back to his teacher.
Tim 大膽跟老師頂嘴。

You need to get up the nerve to quit your job.
你需要提起勇氣辭掉工作。

takes balls to do

· takes balls to quit a job
辭掉工作需要勇氣
· takes guts (to do)
做…需要勇氣

做…需要勇氣　balls 是指男性的生殖器官，引申為勇氣，是口語中常見的說法。如果感覺有點不雅，也可以改成 It takes guts。guts 本來是腸子的意思，因為古人把它當成勇氣的來源，所以也指勇氣。

● He caught the thief as he was running away.

● It **takes balls to** run after a thief.

　　●他抓到逃跑中的小偷。　●去追小偷這件事需要勇氣。

▶ It takes balls to quit a good job.
辭掉一份好工作是需要勇氣的。

It takes guts to work in a prison.
在監獄工作是需要勇氣的。

get cold feet

· cold feet before interview
面試前的退縮

退縮　表示 lose courage，沒辦法繼續做下去的意思。

● So they didn't get married?

● No, the bride **got cold feet**.

　　●所以他們沒結婚？　●沒有，新娘退縮了。

▶ Donna got cold feet before her job interview.
Donna 在接受工作面試前退縮了。

Many people get cold feet before a big decision.
許多人面臨重大決定時會退縮。

1 職場・學校

2 電腦・網路

3 社交生活

4 日常生活

5 訊息・理解

6 想法・態度

7 情緒・狀況

8 行為舉止

9 時間地點・副詞片語

15 有名
be famous for

6-15.mp3

be famous for

· be famous for+N/-ing
　因…而有名
· be famous as a
　teacher
　以身為教師而有名
· be notorious for
　因…惡名昭彰

因…而有名 意思相反的慣用語是 be notorious for 「因…惡名昭彰」。

● Who is that tall man?
● He **is famous for** being a basketball player.
　　●那個高個子的男人是誰？　　●他是知名的籃球選手。

▶ The criminal is notorious for killing people.
　這名罪犯因殺人而惡名昭彰。
　You know what the British people are famous for?
　你知道英國人以什麼聞名嗎？

be known for

· be known to do
　因為做…而知名
· be known for its
　excellent cuisine
　因極佳的料理而知名

因…而知名 known 前面可以加 well 修飾，表示「很知名」。

● He's **known for** his smooth talk.
● I'll keep that in mind when I run into him.
　　●他因為很會花言巧語而出名。
　　●下次我碰到他時，我會記住你說的話。

▶ This restaurant is known for its spaghetti.
　這間餐廳的義大利麵很有名。
　The electoral system is known for being corrupt.
　這個選舉制度因腐敗而為人所知。

be a well-known...

· be a well-known
　entertainer
　是知名的藝人
· be a well-known liar
　是眾所周知的騙子

是眾所周知的… famous 專指因為好事而有名，well-known 則可以表示好或不好的名聲。

● John is **a well-known** gambler.
● Does he win a lot of money?
　　●John 是個眾所周知的賭鬼。　　●他贏很多錢嗎？

▶ Britney Spears is a well-known entertainer.
　布蘭妮是知名的藝人。
　You're a well-known liar. I don't trust you anymore.
　你是個眾所周知的騙子。我不再相信你了。

be renowned for

· be renowned for wines
因酒而聞名
· win renown as a fair judge
因為是個公正的法官而有名望

因…有名 因為特別的專長或實績而有聲譽。

● Have you been to this restaurant before?
● Yes, it's **renowned for** the food it serves.

●你以前來過這間餐廳嗎？　●有，這間餐廳的餐點很有名。

▶ California is renowned for producing white wines.
加州以生產白酒而著名。
Nick won renown as a fair judge in court.
Nick 因為是個公正的法官而有名望。

have a reputation for

· have a good reputation for...
擁有…的好名聲
· establish one's reputation
建立聲望

有…的名聲 reputation 前面可以加上 good 或 bad 表示名聲好壞。

● Why did you buy a Hyundai car?
● They **have a good reputation for** running well.

●你為什麼買現代的車子？　●他們車子的性能是出名的好。

▶ Tom established a reputation as an honest man.
Tom 建立了誠實的名望。
I have a good reputation for finishing on time.
我因為準時完成而有名。

---

16 受歡迎，流行
be popular with

6-16.mp3

be popular with

· be popular with tourists
受遊客的歡迎→是遊客喜歡去的地方
· be the most popular
是最受歡迎的
· become popular
變得受歡迎→開始流行

受…歡迎 become popular 則是「變得受歡迎」，也就是開始流行的意思。

● Rolex makes very nice watches.
● They **are popular with** people who are rich.

●勞力士製作非常棒的手錶。　●它們很受有錢人喜愛。

▶ The Eiffel Tower is popular with tourists.
遊客很喜歡去艾菲爾鐵塔。
Jan is the most popular girl in our school.
Jan 是我們學校最受歡迎的女生。

1 職場・學校
2 電腦・網路
3 社交生活
4 日常生活
5 訊息・理解
6 想法・態度
7 情緒・狀況
8 行為舉止
9 時間地點・副詞片語

be in

- be out
  不流行
- be in fashion
  流行
- be out of fashion
  不流行
- come back into the
  fashion
  重新開始流行

流行　這裡的 in 是 in fashion 的意思。不流行當然就是 out (of fashion) 了。

- Louis Vuitton bags **are in** this year.
- I hope my boyfriend buys me one.
  ●LV 的包包今年很流行。　　●我希望我男朋友會買一個給我。

▶ Long skirts are out this spring.
  長裙今年春天不流行了。
  Blue jeans are always in.
  藍色牛仔褲總是很流行。

up to date

- out of date
  過時的（= not modern, not current, not timely）

最新的，入時的　意思和 current, timely, modern 相近。

- Sally wants to find a new boyfriend.
- It's time for her to buy some **up to date** clothes.
  ●Sally 想找個新男友。　　●她該買些時下流行的衣服了。

▶ The milk in the fridge is out of date.
  冰箱裡的牛奶過期了。
  This is the most up to date computer software.
  這是最新的電腦軟體。

catch on

流行　catch on to sth 則是「了解某事」的意思。

- I see many people wearing NBA hats.
- That style **has really caught on**.
  ●我看到很多人戴 NBA 的帽子。　　●那造型真的很流行。

▶ New fashions catch on every year.
  每年都會有新的流行。
  Short hairstyles for women are catching on.
  女性正在流行短髮。

set trend

- trend setter
  領導潮流的人

領導潮流　形容詞是 trendsetting「領導潮流的」。

- Many people like that pop singer.
- She **sets fashion trends for** young women.
  ●很多人喜歡那位流行歌手。　　●她領導了年輕女性的潮流。

▶ I think this jewelry will set a new trend.
  我覺得這個珠寶會引領新的流行。
  Madonna has been a trend setter for many years.
  瑪丹娜是多年來的流行先驅。

17 聰明
use one's head

6-17.mp3

1 職場・學校
2 電腦・網路
3 社交生活
4 日常生活
5 訊息・理解
6 想法・態度
7 情緒・狀況
8 行為舉止
9 時間地點・副詞片語

have got brains

· have got no brains
不聰明

· brain power
腦力

聰明 這裡的 brains（頭腦）是 intelligence（智力）的意思。

● Harvey spends all day studying.
● He's **got brains** and wants good grades.
　　● Harvey 一整天都在讀書。　　● 他很聰明，而且他想得到好成績。

▶ John has got no brains and will never succeed.
　　John 不聰明，永遠不會成功。
　　Brain power has made it a wealthy country.
　　腦力使它變成一個富國。

use one's head

用腦 head 也可以換成 brain。常常用在祈使句裡。

● I forgot to take a coat with me.
● **Use your head!** It's winter outside!
　　● 我忘了帶外套。　　● 用點腦好嗎！現在外面是冬天！

▶ Carrie knows what she's doing.
　　Carrie 知道她在做什麼。
　　Two heads are better than one.
　　三個臭皮匠勝過一個諸葛亮。

look smart

· look smart for one's age
以某人的年紀而言看起來很聰明

· intelligent-looking
看起來聰明的

看起來聰明 smart 的同義字有 intelligent, sensible, clever 等等。

● The student in the first seat **looks smart**.
● Oh yes, she's a very intelligent girl.
　　● 坐在第一個位子的那個學生看起來很聰明。
　　● 噢，沒錯，她是個非常聰明的女孩。

▶ The president is very intelligent-looking.
　　總裁看來非常聰明。
　　I couldn't find anyone who looks smart.
　　我找不到任何看起來聰明的人。

know better than to

· should know better than to try to fool me
應該知道不能愚弄我

知道不該… 知道有比做某事更好的行為,也就是不應該做某事的意思。

● I was asked to leave my apartment.
● You **know better than to** pay your rent late.

●我被要求搬離我的公寓。　●你知道不能遲交房租吧。

▶ The businessman should know better than to try to fool me. 那位商人應該知道不能愚弄我。

The girls should know better than to walk alone late at night. 女孩們應該知道晚上不要獨自行走。

too clever to do sth

· too clever to do such a thing
太聰明而不會做這種事

太聰明而不會做某事 too...to...「太…而不會…」是很常用的句型。

● Did Sal lose money on the stock market?
● No, he's **too clever to** lose money.

●Sal 在股票市場賠了錢嗎?　●沒有,他太聰明了,不會賠錢。

▶ The children were too clever to do such a thing.
孩子們太聰明了,不會做這種事。

Joan was too clever to get caught skipping school.
Joan 太聰明了,不會被抓到蹺課。

---

18 發牢騷,表達不滿
complain about

6-18.mp3

complain about

· complain to sb about
向某人抱怨…
· complain that S+V
抱怨…
· have nothing to complain about
沒什麼好抱怨的

抱怨… 也可以說 complain of。complain to sb 則是表示「向某人抱怨」。

● My neighbor's TV is too loud.
● **Have** you **complained about** the noise?

●我鄰居的電視太吵了。　●你跟他們抱怨過噪音嗎?

▶ She complained to me about her parents.
她跟我抱怨她的父母親。

My wife complains all the time.
我的妻子總是在抱怨。

make a complaint about

- without complaint
  沒有怨言

抱怨…，投訴… 經常用在因為產品或服務不佳而提出投訴的狀況。

- I heard you had a problem at your hotel.
- Yes, we **made a complaint about** the service.
  - 我聽説你們在飯店出了點問題。
  - 是啊，我們對他們的服務提出了客訴。

▶ My grandmother does all the cooking without complaint.
  我的祖母毫無怨言地煮了所有的菜。
  I want to make a complaint about this product.
  我想投訴這個產品。

be dissatisfied with

- be dissatisfied with one's service
  對某人的服務不滿意
- dissatisfied look
  不滿的臉色

對…不滿意 unsatisfied 看起來和 dissatisfied 很像，但它是表示需求沒有完全滿足、還需要更多的意思。

- Why did Carol get a new phone?
- She **was dissatisfied with** the one she had.
  - Carol 為什麼買了新的手機？　● 她對之前那支不滿意。

▶ I'm dissatisfied with the service in this restaurant.
  我對這間餐廳的服務不滿意。
  My husband gave me a dissatisfied look.
  我先生給了我一個不滿的臉色。

express one's discontent

- growing discontent
  漸增的不滿
- speak out against
  公開指責…

表達不滿 後面可以接 with/at/over sth 表示對什麼不滿。

- This food is really terrible.
- I'm going to **express my discontent** to the waiter.
  - 這食物真的很糟。　● 我要跟服務生表達我的不滿。

▶ There's growing discontent with the government.
  對政府的不滿逐漸高漲。
  Kyle spoke out against the fight.
  Kyle 公開指責這場爭吵。

grumble about sth

- grumble about school food
  對學校的食物發牢騷
- grumble at employees
  對著員工發牢騷

對於某事發牢騷 grumble 的本義是自己一個人碎碎唸。

- Jack **is always grumbling about** something.
- He's a very unhappy man.
  - Jack 總是在對什麼事情發牢騷。　● 他是個很不開心的人。

▶ We grumbled about the taste of the school food.
  我們對於學校食物的口味發了牢騷。
  Our boss grumbled at the employees in the meeting.
  我們老闆在會議上對員工發了牢騷。

1 職場・學校
2 電腦・網路
3 社交生活
4 日常生活
5 訊息・理解
6 想法・態度
7 情緒・狀況
8 行為舉止
9 時間地點・副詞片語

19 無視，輕視
think less of

6-19.mp3

neglect sb/sth

· neglect to do
忘記做…
· neglect one's baby
疏於照顧／沒有好好照顧
某人的嬰兒
· neglect one's duty
怠忽職守

忽視… 和中文的「忽視」一樣，neglect 本來是「沒看到」的意思，因而產生出「沒注意到」的意思。

● The owner **has neglected** the house for years.
● He will have to repair it soon.
● 屋主好幾年沒管這間房子了。　● 他必須盡快修理房子。

▶ We neglected to turn off the lights when we left.
我們離開時忘了關燈。
Tina had problems when she neglected her baby.
當 Tina 疏於照顧自己的嬰兒時，出了問題。

think less of

· think nothing of
覺得…沒什麼，不把…放
在心上
· Think nothing of it.
別放在心上。

瞧不起… think nothing of 則是「覺得…沒什麼」、「不把…放在心上」或「一點也看不起…」的意思。

● I **think less of** Tim since he got his third divorce.
● Yeah, I wonder why his marriages failed.
● 我瞧不起 Tim，因為他離了第三次婚。
● 是啊，我想知道為什麼他的婚姻都失敗了。

▶ Antonio thinks nothing of lending his friends money.
Antonio 覺得借錢給朋友沒什麼。
I'm glad to do it. Think nothing of it.
我很樂意做。別放在心上。

look down on sb

· look down on people
看輕人們
· feel superior to
感覺比…優越

鄙視／瞧不起某人 相反的，「尊敬」是 look up to。

● One of our classmates isn't responsible.
● People **look down on** her because of that.
● 我們有位同學很不負責任。　● 大家就是因為那樣才看不起她。

▶ Those who are wealthy sometimes look down on people. 有錢的人有時候會瞧不起別人。
I looked down on Ray for stealing things.
我因為 Ray 偷東西而鄙視他。

make light of sth

· make light of one's problem
輕鬆看待某人的問題

· make little of...
輕視／瞧不起…

對某事不以為意 彷彿某件事很輕微、很輕鬆的意思。

● Greg has been sick for a month.

● I know, but he **makes light of** his illness.

●Greg 病了一個月。　　●我知道，但他不把自己的病放在心上。

▶ It's important to make light of your problems.
輕鬆看待你的問題是很重要的。

I made little of the information I was given.
我輕視了別人給我的資訊。

leave sb out in the cold

· be left out in the cold
被排除在外

· give sb the cold shoulder
冷淡對待某人

把某人排除在外；不告訴某人情況 就像字面上的意思一樣，彷彿把某人關在門外吹冷風的感覺。

● Has anyone from NY called you yet?

● No, they **have left me out in the cold**.

●有任何人從紐約打電話給你嗎？　　●沒有，他們不讓我知道消息。

▶ He was left out in the cold when the plan changed.
當計畫變更時，他被蒙在鼓裡。

They decided to leave Cathy out in the cold.
他們決定把 Cathy 排除在外。

---

20 卑鄙，可恥
play dirty

6-20.mp3

be mean to sb

· mean trick
卑劣的惡作劇

· gross
（口語）噁心的

對某人刻薄 mean 的動詞用法很常見，但在這裡是形容詞，而且意思不同。

● The kids **were mean to** Teddy.

● Yeah, but I don't feel sorry for him.

●那些孩子對 Teddy 很刻薄。　　●是啊，但我不覺得他可憐。

▶ It was a mean trick to steal her money.
偷她的錢真的是個很卑劣的惡作劇。

The smell near the toilet was gross.
廁所附近的味道很噁心。

1 職場・學校
2 電腦・網路
3 社交生活
4 日常生活
5 訊息・理解
6 想法・態度
7 情緒・狀況
8 行為舉止
9 時間地點・副詞片語

be nasty

- nasty fellow
  卑鄙的人
- be nasty to sb
  對某人行為卑劣

卑鄙，下流，噁心，脾氣不好 主詞是場所時，表示髒亂。
nasty 的本義是「骯髒，齷齪」。

- Allie's room **is really nasty**.
- Tell her she must clean it up.
  ● Allie 的房間真的很髒。　● 叫她一定要打掃乾淨。

▶ Ralph is a nasty fellow when he drinks too much.
Ralph 喝太多酒的時候，脾氣會變得很不好。
The old shower in the house is nasty.
這間房子的舊淋浴間很髒。

be so cheap

很小氣 表示不肯多花錢。另外，cheap 形容東西的時候，除了表示「便宜」，還常常有「廉價、粗劣」的意思。

- Are you going to pay for my dinner?
- Don't **be so cheap**. Pay for yourself.
  ● 你要幫我付晚餐錢嗎？　● 別那麼摳門，自己付自己的。

▶ Carl is so cheap that he doesn't buy presents.
Carl 很小氣，他不買禮物的。
My uncle was so cheap that he never went on vacation.
我叔叔很寒酸，他從來不去度假。

play dirty

- treat sb poorly
  對某人很差
- behave shamelessly
  行為無恥

耍骯髒的招數 特別常用來表示在比賽中搞小動作的情況。

- No one likes the members of that team.
- I've heard they **play dirty**.
  ● 沒有人喜歡那個隊伍的隊員。　● 我聽說他們會耍賤招。

▶ Sharon was treated poorly at her new school.
Sharon 在新學校受到很差的對待。
Don't play dirty when you're on the soccer field.
在足球場上不要耍骯髒的招數。

what a shame to

做…真是太可惜／可恥 除了表示可恥，還常常引申為做某事很不應該、很可惜的意思。

- Our refrigerator stopped working yesterday.
- **What a shame to** ruin all of that food!
  ● 我們的冰箱昨天壞了。　● 浪費了那些食物真是太可惜了！

▶ What a shame to sit and do nothing all day!
一整天只是坐著什麼事都不做，真是太可惜了！
What a shame to deceive a girl!
欺騙女孩子真是太可恥了！

1 職場・學校
2 電腦・網路
3 社交生活
4 日常生活
5 訊息・理解
6 想法・態度
7 情緒・狀況
8 行為舉止
9 時間地點・副詞片語

21 做傻事
do a stupid thing

6-21.mp3

do a stupid thing

· do something foolish
做些傻事
· it is stupid of sb to do
某人做⋯很笨

做傻事 stupid 跟中文裡的「笨」一樣，會讓人有被侮辱的感覺，不能隨便說。

● I **did a stupid thing**. I lost my wallet.
● Really? How much money was in it?
　●我做了件蠢事。我把皮夾弄丟了。　●真的嗎？裡面有多少錢？

▶ Don't drink too much and do something foolish.
別喝太多酒，然後做出些傻事。
She did a stupid thing when everyone was watching.
她在眾目睽睽之下做了件傻事。

make a fool of oneself

· make a fool of sb
愚弄／欺騙某人

出醜 因為做了蠢事「讓自己像個傻瓜」的意思。

● Did you enjoy going to the party with Brad?
● No, he **made a fool of** himself there.
　●你和 Brad 去派對玩得開心嗎？　●不，他在那裡出了醜。

▶ I made a fool of myself when I forgot what to say.
我忘記該說什麼的時候真的很糗。
Danny made a fool of himself last night.
Danny 昨晚出了醜。

play dumb

· play dead
裝死

裝傻 play 後面接形容詞的時候，是「裝作」的意思，相當於 pretend to be。

● I don't know how the vase was broken.
● Don't **play dumb** with me. You know!
　●我不知道這花瓶怎麼破的。　●別跟我裝傻，你知道的！

▶ We played dumb when the teacher asked us questions.
老師問我們問題時，我們裝作不知道。
Many criminals play dumb with the police.
許多罪犯對警察裝傻。

be ridiculous

· Don't be ridiculous!
別胡說八道了！
· be silly
愚蠢

荒謬，可笑 並不是很幽默的意思，而是因為莫名其妙、很蠢而引人嘲笑。

● Do you like the decorations in my house?
● No, I think they **are ridiculous**.
●你喜歡我家裡的裝飾嗎？　●不喜歡，我覺得它們很可笑。

▶ The tie David wore was ridiculous.
David 戴的領帶很可笑。
The band's new song is silly.
這個樂團的新歌很蠢。

talk nonsense

胡言亂語 就是說些沒有 sense（意義）的話。

● Maybe I should quit going to university.
● Don't **talk nonsense**. You have to continue.
●也許我應該從大學退學。　●別胡言亂語了。你必須念下去。

▶ Cecil talks nonsense when he drinks too much.
Cecil 喝太多時會胡言亂語。
Will you please stop talking nonsense to everyone?
可以拜託你不要再跟大家胡言亂語了嗎？

22 忍耐，無法忍受 put up with

6-22.mp3

lose patience

· lose control of one's temper
控制不住脾氣
· have no patience
沒耐性

失去耐性 lose one's temper 則是「發脾氣」。

● Why did you get so angry with Aurora?
● I **lost patience** in dealing with her.
●你為什麼那麼生 Aurora 的氣？　●我沒有耐性再應付她了。

▶ Adam seems to lose patience very easily.
Adam 看起來很容易失去耐性。
The teacher lost patience when the students kept talking. 學生一直說話，讓老師失去了耐性。

be impatient with

· be impatient with her
  對她沒耐心
· run out of patience
  用光耐心

對…沒耐心 be impatient to do 則是「迫不及待做…」。

- He is often impatient with his little sister.
- He **is impatient with** his friends too.
  - 他常常對自己的妹妹沒耐心。 ● 他對自己的朋友也很沒耐心。

▶ Calm down and don't be impatient with her.
  冷靜下來，別對她沒耐心。
  I've run out of patience with you!
  我對你的耐心已經用光了！

not stand sb/sth

· not stand -ing
  無法忍受做…
· not stand sb -ing
  無法忍受某人做…
· I can't stand any
  more.
  我忍不下去了。

無法忍受… 這裡的 stand 是 tolerate 的意思，也可以接動詞 -ing 形當受詞。

- I **cannot stand** the smell of garlic.
- Really? I love the way it smells.
  - 我無法忍受大蒜的氣味。 ● 真的嗎？我喜歡它的氣味。

▶ Sheila can't stand dating short guys.
  Sheila 無法忍受和矮個子的男人約會。
  I can't stand his singing.
  我無法忍受他的歌聲。

not take it anymore

無法再忍受 就是「have had enough」（受夠了）的意思。

- So you decided to stop going to church?
- Right. I could **not take it anymore**.
  - 所以你決定不再去教會了？ ● 對，我無法再忍受了。

▶ Stop talking. I cannot take it anymore.
  別再說了。我無法再忍受了。
  He quit because he could not take it anymore.
  他因為再也忍受不了，所以辭職了。

put up with

· can no longer put up
  with...
  無法再忍受…
· can't tolerate sth
  無法忍受某事

忍受… 相當於 tolerate，後面可以接人或事物當受詞。

- Is your shower still broken?
- Yes, we can't **put up with** it anymore.
  - 你的淋浴間還是壞的嗎？ ● 是啊，我們無法再忍受了。

▶ They can no longer put up with the cold temperatures.
  他們無法再忍受寒冷的氣溫了。
  Tom can't tolerate the slow Internet service.
  Tom 無法忍受慢吞吞的網路。

1 職場・學校
2 電腦・網路
3 社交生活
4 日常生活
5 訊息・理解
6 想法・態度
7 情緒・狀況
8 行為舉止
9 時間地點・副詞片語

take sth lying down | **默默容忍** 彷彿躺下來一樣，對於不合理的對待完全不反抗。通常以否定形式出現。

- Was Eric fired from his job?
- Yes, but he won't **take the firing lying down.**
  - Eric 被炒魷魚了嗎？　●嗯，但他不會甘願吞下這口氣的。

▶ I don't plan to take the insult lying down.
  我不打算默默忍受這個侮辱。
  Ginger can't take the bad news lying down.
  Ginger 無法忍受這個壞消息。

control oneself | **自制** 克制憤怒、悲傷等情緒，不把情緒顯露出來。

· hang in there
　堅持下去

- I'm really feeling very angry today.
- **Control yourself.** Don't get too upset.
  - 我今天真的覺得非常生氣。　●克制一下，別太生氣。

▶ Hang in there. It will be better tomorrow.
  撐住吧，明天會變好的。
  He controlled himself during the argument.
  在爭吵中，他克制著自己。

---

 hang in there

　　用來激勵面臨困難或困境的人們。hang 的意思是「掛」，in there 則是「在那邊」，引申為「堅持下去」的意思。例如某人又被老闆罵了，想鼓勵他撐下去，就可以說「Hang in there!」。同樣的句子也適用於為災民打氣等類似的情況。「Stick with it!」的意思也是一樣。

A: I don't think I can run around the track another time.
　我覺得我沒辦法再跑一圈。
B: Hang in there! Just one more lap.
　撐住啊！只要再跑一圈就好了。
A: Okay, but then I'm taking a nice long break.
　好吧，但跑完以後我要好好休息一陣子。

23 反對，拒絕
go against

6-23.mp3

go/be against

- be/go against sb/sth
  反對…
- be against the law
  違法
- be contrary to
  和…相反

反對…，違反… 和 be contrary to 的意思相近。

- Everyone in class wants to take the exam today.
- You can't **go against** your classmates.
  - 班上每個人都想今天考試。　●你無法違抗你的同學們。

▶ Stealing things is against the law.
偷東西是違法的。
I am against the new proposal.
我反對新的提案。

oppose sb/sth

- be opposed to
  反對…

反對… 被動態的 be opposed to 比較常用，一樣表示「反對」的意思。

- I'm going to **oppose** George in the election.
- Well, I hope you are able to win.
  - 這次選舉，我要投反對票給 George。　●嗯，希望你能獲勝。

▶ We are opposed to cloning humans.
我們反對複製人。
The driver was opposed to the special traffic law.
這位駕駛人反對特別交通法。

object to sb/sth

- object that S+V
  反對…
- make/find/raise an objection to/against
  反對…
- have an objection to
  反對…

反對… object 當名詞是「物體」的意思，在這裡則是動詞「反對」的意思。

- I **object to** the way you've treated students.
- Do you think I treated them badly?
  - 我反對你對待學生們的方式。　●你覺得我待他們很差嗎？

▶ He raised an objection to the new taxes.
他對於新的稅金提出反對。
The judge had an objection to the lawyer's speech.
法官對律師的辯護提出異議。

461

disagree with

- disagree with sb/sth
  反對…的意見
- disagree with sb on sth
  和某人對某事意見不一
- agree to disagree
  同意各方可持有不同的意見

與…意見不一致 也可以用 disagree 的名詞形，說 have a disagreement with。

- We **disagreed with** Brooke about the report.
- Yes, I think Brooke was mistaken too.
  - 對於這份報告，我們和 Brooke 意見相左。
  - 嗯，我也覺得 Brooke 弄錯了。

▶ Let's just agree to disagree about this.
  對於這一點，我們就同意大家保留不同意見吧。
  I disagree with the schedule you gave me.
  我不同意你給我的行程表。

say no to

- say no
  說不
- say no to drugs
  對毒品說不

對…說不，拒絕… 常用在反對 drug（毒品）或 racism（種族主義）的標語上。

- I don't want to help my friend skip class.
- You can **say no to** her if she asks you to help her.
  - 我不想幫我的朋友蹺課。　● 如果她要你幫忙的話，你可以拒絕她。

▶ She said no when I asked her to marry me.
  我要她嫁給我的時候，她拒絕了。
  Say no to drugs or you will ruin your life.
  對毒品説不，否則你會毀掉你的人生。

the other way around

- on the contrary
  相反的，另一方面

相反 經常用來表示實際情況和先前所說的相反。

- I heard that you lied to Peter.
- It's **the other way around**. Peter lied to me.
  - 我聽説你騙了 Peter。　● 正好相反，是 Peter 騙了我。

▶ On the contrary, you are wrong.
  相反的，你是錯的。
  I didn't fail. It's the other way around.
  我沒有失敗，事實正好相反。

refuse to do

拒絕做… 拒絕他人的邀約、請求或提案等等。

- Are you still angry at Mark?
- Yeah, I **refuse to** answer his calls.
  - 你還在生 Mark 的氣嗎？　● 嗯，我拒接他的電話。

▶ She refused to go swimming with me.
  她拒絕跟我去游泳。
  I refused to complete the assignment.
  我拒絕完成這項任務。

1 職場・學校

2 電腦・網路

3 社交生活

4 日常生活

5 訊息・理解

6 想法・態度

7 情緒・狀況

8 行為舉止

9 時間地點・副詞片語

there's no way to

· There's no way that
  S+V
  沒有方法能…
· There is no telling S+V
  很難猜測…，無法預料…

沒有方法能做…，做…不可能 字面的意思是「沒有方法」，
也就是不可能辦到。

● **There's no way to** get home tonight.
● Let's try to find a hotel.
　　●今晚沒辦法到家了。　　●我們試著找間旅館吧。

▶ There's no way to find it.
　　不可能找到它的。
　　There's no telling what their date will be like.
　　很難預測他們的約會會怎麼樣。

draw the line at

在…劃定界限 表示能接受到什麼程度為止。

● Can I call you at any time tonight?
● I **draw the line** at calls after 9 pm.
　　●我今晚什麼時候打電話給你都可以嗎？　　●我最晚只接電話到九點。

▶ It's true that she dated him, but they broke up.
　　她確實有和他約會，但他們分手了。
　　I draw the line at working without a salary.
　　我拒絕做不支薪的工作。

---

24 贊成，同意
agree with

6-24.mp3

agree with

· make an agreement
  with
  和…達成協議
· be in agreement with
  和…意見一致
· couldn't agree with sb
  more
  不能同意某人更多→完全
  同意某人

同意… 如果同意的是「事物」而不是人，就要說 agree to。

● We should try to improve our school.
● I **agree with** you. What should we do first?
　　●我們應該努力改善我們的學校。　　●我同意。我們應該先做什麼？

▶ The company made an agreement with another firm.
　　這間公司和另一間公司達成了協議。
　　What I'd like to say is we agreed on a plan.
　　我想說的是，我們對一項計畫取得了共識。

be for sb/sth

· be in favor of -ing
支持／同意做…
· be of the same opinion
意見相同

贊成… 「反對」則是 be against。

● Do you favor the new law about pollution?

● Yes, I'm **all for** that law.

　●你贊成那項關於污染的新法規嗎？　●嗯，我完全贊成那條法規。

▶ I'm in favor of walking to the park.

　我贊成走路去公園。

　We're of the same opinion on the movie we'll watch.

　我們對於要看的電影意見相同。

be with

· be with sb on
對於…同意某人的看法
· Are you with me?
你懂我的意思嗎？

同意…，站在…那一邊 在慣用語 Are you with me? 裡，則表示「了解」的意思。

● Do you think Karen and Anna will help us?

● Yes, they **are both with** us.

　●你覺得 Karen 和 Anna 會幫我們嗎？

　●我覺得會，他們都站在我們這邊。

▶ We're with Tom on his project.

　對於 Tom 的案子，我們和他的想法相同。

　I'll go talk to the teacher. Are you with me?

　我要去跟老師談談。你懂我的意思嗎？

approve of

· approve of my choice
贊同我的選擇
· be approved for use in sth
經核准用於某事
· get approval from
得到…的認可

贊成… approve of sb doing sth 意為「贊成某人做某事」。

● Did you introduce your boyfriend to your parents?

● Yes. They told me that they **approve of** him.

　●你向你父母介紹男朋友了嗎？　●有，他們跟我說，他們認可他了。

▶ Everyone approves of my choice of a sports car.

　大家都贊同我對跑車的選擇。

　This heater is approved for use in bedrooms.

　這台電暖器經核准能在臥室使用。

take one's side

· be on one's side
站在某人那邊
· Time is on no one's side.
時間對每個人都是公平的。

同意／支持某人 take sides with sb 則是「偏袒某人」的意思。

● Do you agree with what Helen said?

● Yes, I'll **take her side** in the argument.

　●你同意 Helen 說的嗎？　●是啊，在爭論中，我是站她那邊的。

▶ My husband told me he is on my side.

　我丈夫跟我說，他是站在我這邊的。

　We all get old. Time is on no one's side.

　我們都會變老。時間對每個人都是公平的。

go along with

· go along with one's views
  同意某人的看法

同意… 字面上的意思是「和…一起走」，引申為看法相同。

● Terry wants us to go out tonight.
● That's great. I'll **go along with** her on that.
  ●Terry 希望我們今晚能出去。　●很棒，我贊成她的意見。

▶ It's difficult to go along with the president's ideas.
  很難同意總裁的想法。
  He didn't go along with me on this.
  對於這件事，他的意見和我不同。

have a point

· You've got a point (here).
  你說的有道理。

有道理 也就是說對方的話是個 good idea 或 good suggestion。

● My father told me to quit smoking.
● He **has a point**. You'll be healthier.
  ●我父親要我戒菸。　●他說的有道理。你會變得更健康。

▶ That's right. You've got a point.
  沒錯。你說的有道理。
  I have a point to make about our workplace.
  對於我們的工作場所，我有一點意見。

meet (sb) halfway

· compromise with sb
  和某人妥協

和某人妥協 「在半路見面」，比喻各讓一步、互相妥協。

● Jim and Harry could not agree.
● I hope Jim **met Harry halfway**.
  ●Jim 和 Harry 無法同意對方。　●我希望 Jim 和 Harry 妥協。

▶ I decided to meet her half way.
  我決定和她妥協。
  She compromised with her husband on the decision.
  對於這個決定，她和她丈夫妥協了。

talk the same language

· You can say that again.
  你說的沒錯。（表示非常同意）

意見相同，意氣相投 表示意見相同，或者想法和嗜好很接近的意思。

● Let's go grab a few beers.
● Yeah, now we**'re talking the same language**.
  ●我們去喝幾杯啤酒吧。　●很好，我們現在志同道合了。

▶ You can say that again. I totally agree.
  你說的沒錯。我完全同意。
  Steve and I don't even talk the same language.
  Steve 和我的意見一點也不相同。

1 職場・學校
2 電腦・網路
3 社交生活
4 日常生活
5 訊息・理解
6 想法・態度
7 情緒・狀況
8 行為舉止
9 時間地點・副詞片語

see eye to eye

· see eye to eye with sb on sth
  對於某事和某人意見一致
· say yes to
  同意…
· Same here.
  我也是。
· I'll drink to that.
  我同意。（強烈同意）

看法一致 彼此的眼睛互相對看，比喻看法相同。

● You really seem to like your boss.
● It's true. We usually **see eye to eye** on things.
  ●你看起來真的很喜歡你的老闆。
  ●是真的，我們對事物的看法經常相同。

▶ I'd say yes to a raise in my salary.
  我同意調漲我的薪水。
  Let's have a good new year. I'll drink to that.
  我們過個很棒的新年吧。我同意。

---

25 小心
be careful of

6-25.mp3

---

be careful of

· be careful to do
  小心地做…
· be careful about -ing
  小心地做…
· Be careful.
  小心。

小心… be careful to do 意為「小心地做…」。

● **Be careful of** people selling things on the subway.
● I know. Some of the items are really junk.
  ●小心在地鐵賣東西的人。　●我知道。那些東西有的根本是垃圾。

▶ Be careful about driving too fast.
  小心開車不要太快。
  Be careful when you are out after dark.
  天黑後，出門要小心。

with care

· handle with care
  小心搬運，小心拿

小心地，謹慎地 這裡的 care 是名詞，前面可以加形容詞 great 強調「很小心地」。

● That package has a glass vase in it.
● I'll handle it **with care**.
  ●那個包裹裡有個玻璃花瓶。　●我會小心搬運它的。

▶ Mom makes each meal with care.
  媽媽精心料理每一餐。
  We drove with care during the storm.
  我們在暴風雪中謹慎地駕駛。

pay attention to

- not to pay attention to rumors
  不去管謠言

注意… 也可以說 give attention to。

- **Pay attention to** this part of the textbook.
- Are we going to be tested on it?
  - ●注意課本上的這部分。　●這裡考試會考嗎？

▶ I told you not to pay attention to rumors.
我跟你說過不要去管謠言。
Pay attention to the things I tell you.
注意那些我告訴你的事情。

keep one's eye on

- keep your eye on your surroundings
  留意你的周遭

小心留意… 不移開目光，一直留意、照顧的意思。與 keep watching 同義。

- How can I become a better baseball player?
- **Keep your eye on** where the ball goes.
  - ●我該怎樣才能成為更好的棒球選手？　●注意球的去向。

▶ Keep your eye on your surroundings in the forest.
在森林中，留意你的周遭。
I'll keep my eye on the younger students.
我會留意比較年輕的學生。

look out

- Look out!
  小心！
- look out for cars
  小心車子
- look out for
  小心…，留意找…

小心…，注意… 和 watch out 意思相同。

- I'm going to visit several different countries.
- **Look out for** thieves near your hotel.
  - ●我要拜訪幾個不同的國家。　●留意旅館附近的小偷。

▶ Look out for cars when you cross the street.
當你過馬路時，小心車子。
Look out for the construction site.
小心建築工地。

watch out

- watch (out) for sth
  （為了避免不好的事）
  小心某事物

小心，警戒 給對方忠告，要對方注意周遭時可使用。

- We're going out to a nightclub tonight.
- **Watch out** if Dave starts drinking whiskey.
  - ●我們今晚要去夜店。　●當 Dave 開始喝威士忌時，要小心。

▶ Watch for the water that spilled on the floor.
小心灑在地上的水。
Watch out when you cross the bridge.
過橋時小心點。

1 職場・學校

2 電腦・網路

3 社交生活

4 日常生活

5 訊息・理解

6 想法・態度

7 情緒・狀況

8 行為舉止

9 時間地點・副詞片語

be cautious about

· be cautious about
  sth/-ing
  對…小心／謹慎

對…小心／謹慎 為了避開一些可預測的危險、危機而保持警戒。

● I'm planning to invest my money in stocks.
● **Be cautious about** where you put the money.

  ● 我打算把錢投資在股票上。　● 對於投資的地方謹慎點。

▶ Be cautious about riding a motorcycle.
  騎摩托車時謹慎點。

  Be cautious about meeting people on-line.
  見網友時小心點。

---

 keep one's eye on

　　keep one's eye on... 和 have one's eye on... 的意思有點不同。keep one's eye on... 是「因為無法相信，或是因為擔心而特別關注」的意思。而 have one's eye on sth 則是因為喜歡而「盯著某個東西看」。至於 have an eye for sth 則是用來形容對於貴重物品或好東西有「能分辨、鑑賞的眼力」。最後，I only have eyes for you. 則是戀人間所說的話，代表「我只看著你」（I'm loyal to you only），用來表達自己對對方的一片真心。至於為什麼用複數的 eyes，可能是為了表達不會東張西望吧…。

　ex. Your secretary seems like a spy. Keep your eye on her.
　　　你的祕書看起來像是間諜。要留意她。
　　　My wife has an eye for the paintings. 我妻子很會看畫。

26 可能性，傾向
be likely to

1 職場・學校

2 電腦・網路

3 社交生活

4 日常生活

5 訊息・理解

6 想法・態度

7 情緒・狀況

8 行為舉止

9 時間地點・副詞片語

---

be likely to

· be more likely to do
比較有可能做…

很有可能… likely 前面可以加上 more 或 less 表達可能性高低。

● Jonas has a very good singing voice.

● He **is likely to** become a successful singer.

　● Jonas 的歌喉很棒。　● 他很有可能成為一位成功的歌手。

▶ They are likely to attend the meeting together.
他們很有可能一起出席會議。
I am likely to travel to Washington D.C. next month.
我下個月很有可能會去華盛頓特區旅行。

---

be unlikely to

· be less likely to do
比較不可能做…

不太可能… 表示可能性低，但也不是完全不可能。

● I studied for hours to take this test.

● You **are unlikely to** do poorly on it.

　● 我為了這場考試唸了很多個小時的書。　● 你不太可能考壞的。

▶ My uncle is unlikely to visit our house.
我叔叔不太可能拜訪我們家。
They are unlikely to play computer games.
他們不太可能去玩電腦遊戲。

---

tend to

· have a tendency to do
有做…的傾向

傾向於做…，常常會做… 沒有做某事的傾向是 tend not to。

● I don't trust anything that Rachel says.

● She also **tends to** lie to me.

　● 我不相信 Rachel 說的任何事。　● 她也常會騙我。

▶ That dog tends to bark all night long.
那隻狗常常會吠一整個晚上。
Dave tends to drive fast in his car. Dave 傾向於開快車。

---

be apt to

傾向於做…，容易做… 用法和意義幾乎和 tend to 一樣。

● Simon has been very nice to me.

● I think he**'s apt to** ask you out on a date.

　● Simon 一直對我很好。　● 我想他有可能會約妳去約會。

▶ It's apt to start snowing this afternoon.
今天下午有可能會開始下雪。
She's apt to go home and take a nap. 她有可能會回家午睡。

be subject to

- be subject to sth
  容易遭受某事
- be disposed to+N
  有…的傾向（常用於正式場合）

容易遭受… 主要用於受到負面影響的狀況下。to 後面接名詞。

- I think there are too many cars parked on this street.
- They **are subject to** tickets if the police see them.
  - 我覺得街上停了太多車。　● 如果警察看到的話，它們都要吃罰單。

▶ You are subject to the rules of your parents.
  你要遵守你父母的規矩。

  Everything at the meeting was subject to discussion.
  會議中所有事項都是討論對象。

---

27 有價值，沒價值 be worth -ing

6-27.mp3

be worth + N/-ing

- be not worth the trouble
  不值得花工夫
- be worth a try
  值得一試
- It's not worth it.
  這不值得。

有…的價值 be worth little 意為「價值很低」。

- Is this old coin valuable?
- No, it **is worth** very little.
  - 這個舊硬幣有價值嗎？　● 沒有，它價值很低。

▶ It may be worth a try.
  那可能值得一試。

  It's not worth the trouble to complete the report.
  不值得花工夫來完成這份報告。

be worth + 金額

- 金額 + worth of sth
  價值多少錢的某物（用金額計算數量）

值多少錢 worth 後面接具體的金額表示價值的說法。

- I heard Sam's father gave him some gold coins.
- Yes, they **are** probably **worth** thousands of dollars.
  - 我聽說 Sam 的爸爸給了他一些金幣。
  - 是啊，那些可能值好幾千美元。

▶ That car will be worth at least $11,000.
  那台車至少值 11,000 美元。

  Can you give me $10 worth of gas?
  可以幫我加 10 美元的油嗎？

470

be worthy of + N

· be worthy of praise
  值得稱讚
· be worthy of
  confidence
  值得信任

值得⋯的 be worthy to be pp 意為「值得受到⋯」。

- Is this medicine useful for an upset stomach?
- Sure, it's **worthy of** use.
  - ●這藥對腸胃不適有用嗎？ ●當然，這值得一試。

▶ His good deeds are very worthy of praise.
  他的善行非常值得稱讚。
  Her boss decided Jenna was worthy of confidence.
  她老闆判斷 Jenna 是值得信任的。

be of no use

沒有用 of use 就是 useful 的意思。加上 no 變成 of no use，相當於 useless。

- Would you like to borrow my dictionary?
- No, it **is of no use** to me.
  - ●你想借我的字典嗎？ ●不想，它對我沒有用。

▶ The small shoes were of no use to the giant.
  這雙小鞋子對那位巨人沒有用。
  The DVD was of no use to anyone.
  這片 DVD 對任何人都沒有用。

good for nothing

· good-for-nothing
  husband
  一無是處的丈夫

完全沒用的；沒用的人 totally useless 的意思，當名詞或形容詞用。

- Ben is really a **good for nothing**.
- He makes me pay for his meals.
  - ●Ben 真的很沒用。 ●他要我幫他付飯錢。

▶ Mary is still yelling at her good-for-nothing husband.
  Mary 還在對她一無是處的丈夫大吼。
  That good for nothing is always late.
  那個沒用的人總是遲到。

1 職場・學校

2 電腦・網路

3 社交生活

4 日常生活

5 訊息・理解

6 想法・態度

7 情緒・狀況

8 行為舉止

9 時間地點・副詞片語

28 有興趣
get interested in

6-28.mp3

be interested in

· get interested in
  對⋯產生興趣

對⋯有興趣 如果要表示沒興趣，可以說 be indifferent to。

● I'm **interested in** the new golf class.
● Me too! Why don't we join together this Saturday?

  ●我對新的高爾夫球課有興趣。
  ●我也是！我們何不這週六一起加入呢？

▶ Are you interested in working some overtime?
  你想加一點班嗎？
  She's not interested in working for us.
  她沒興趣在我們公司上班。

have an interest in

· lose interest in
  對⋯失去興趣
· have no interest in
  對⋯沒興趣

對⋯有興趣 這裡的 interest 是名詞，「興趣」的意思。

● Would you like to go to an art gallery?
● No, I don't **have an interest in** art.

  ●你想去藝廊嗎？　●不想，我對藝術沒興趣。

▶ Bill has an interest in taking photos. Bill 對拍照有興趣。
  I have an interest in the stock market. 我對股票市場有興趣。

take an interest in

· take such an
  interest in
  對⋯非常有興趣
· show an interest in
  對⋯展現興趣
· express an interest in
  對⋯表示興趣

對⋯產生興趣，關心⋯ 常常說 take such an～來加強語氣。

● Albert is a very smart man.
● He **took an interest in** books at an early age.

  ●Albert 是個非常聰明的男人。　●他從很小就對書有興趣。

▶ You must take an interest in your children.
  你必須關心你的孩子。
  I took an interest in the football game. 我對足球比賽有興趣。

share the same interests

· draw/attract interest
  引起興趣

有共同的興趣 mutual interest 則是「彼此共通的興趣」。

● Judy and Harry seem very happy together.
● They **share many of the same interests**.

  ●Judy 和 Harry 在一起看起來非常開心。　●他們有許多共同的興趣。

▶ My best friend and I share the same interests.
  我最好的朋友和我有共同的興趣。
  The classmates share the same interests.
  同學們有共同的興趣。

be into

· be into sth/-ing
  對某事有興趣
· I'm so into you.
  我很喜歡你。

對…有興趣，熱中於… 彷彿陷在裡面一樣，很入迷的樣子。
be not into 就是沒興趣。

● Do you want to go to that hip new bar after work?
● I'm into it.

　● 下班後你想不想去那間時髦的新酒吧？　● 我有興趣。

▶ Frank is into collecting postcards.
　Frank 熱中於收集明信片。
　I am into riding motorcycles.
　我很喜歡騎摩托車。

go in for

對…有興趣，參加… 「喜歡某個活動」的意思。也有「參加考試或比賽」的意思。

● Would you like to come to the club?
● No, I don't **go in for** drinking alcohol.

　● 你想來夜店嗎？　● 不想，我不喜歡喝酒。

▶ My girlfriend goes in for shopping.
　我女朋友很喜歡購物。
　Carl goes in for watching sports on TV.
　Carl 很喜歡在電視上觀看運動比賽。

be intrigued by

對…好奇，對…著迷 intrigue 是及物動詞，「激起好奇心」的意思。被動態的 be intrigued by 表示「被…激起好奇心」。

● Why do you read mystery novels?
● I **am intrigued by** their stories.

　● 你為什麼讀推理小說？　● 我對推理小說的故事很著迷。

▶ I was intrigued by the girl's beauty.
　我被那女孩的美貌迷住了。
　Tammy was intrigued by the sports car.
　Tammy 對那台跑車著迷。

have a lot in common with

· have something in
  common
  有某個共同點
· have a little in
  common
  有少許共同點
· have nothing in
  common
  沒有共同點

和…有很多共同點 a lot 也可以換成其他數量名詞，表示相同的程度。

● Are Canada and the US similar countries?
● They **have a lot in common with** each other.

　● 加拿大和美國是相似的國家嗎？　● 它們之間有許多共同點。

▶ Samantha has a lot in common with her friends.
　Samantha 和她朋友們有許多共同點。
　I don't think we have anything in common.
　我不覺得我們有任何共同點。

1 職場・學校
2 電腦・網路
3 社交生活
4 日常生活
5 訊息・理解
6 想法・態度
7 情緒・狀況
8 行為舉止
9 時間地點・副詞片語

be into

　　be into 是把進入的概念引申為「很有興趣」、「很熱中」、「很著迷」。介系詞除了表示空間概念以外，還有許多引申的抽象意義，即使出現沒看過的使用方式，有時候還是可以用基本的意義猜到意思。如果覺得很麻煩的話，就把不一樣的用法背起來吧！當你得知平常看起來很純潔的女朋友，居然愛看 A 片，就可以說「I can't believe you are so into porn movies.」。be into 也可以表示對人的愛意，例如對心愛的另一半說「I'm so into you.」。

29 想做某事
would like to

6-29.mp3

would like to

想要做… would like 是 want 的意思，語氣比 want 更客氣。would like sth 就等於 want sth，would like sb to do... 則是「希望某人做某事」。

- I've heard about the Great Wall of China.
- **Would you like to** go and visit it?
  - ●我聽說過中國的萬里長城。　●你想去參觀嗎？

▶ I'd like you to think about that.
　我希望你能考慮那件事。
　I'd like a nice notebook computer.
　我想要一台好的筆記型電腦。

want to

· want+N
　想要…
· want sb to do
　想要某人做…

想要做… 比 would like to 輕鬆、隨意的說法。日常生活中對親朋好友只要說 want 就好了，用 would like 反而太過禮貌，像是刻意保持距離一樣。

- Everyone **wants you to** sing a song.
- I'm not going to sing tonight.
  - ●每個人都希望你唱首歌。　●我今晚不會唱歌。

▶ What do you want to have for lunch? 你中午想吃什麼？
　You want me to lie to my boss? 你想要我對我老闆説謊？

feel like -ing

· I don't feel like -ing
  我不想做…
· I don't feel like that.
  我不想做那件事。

想要做… 也有 feel like + N 的說法。feel like + N 除了表示「有做…的心情」以外,也有「感覺像…」的意思。

● Do you **feel like** shopping with me?
● Sure! I need to buy some new clothes.

　●你想跟我去逛街嗎?　●當然!我需要買些新衣服。

▶ I feel like having a nice cold beer right now.
　我現在想喝杯好喝的冰啤酒。
　So what do you feel like having for lunch?
　所以你中午想吃什麼?

be willing to

願意做… 名詞 willingness 則是「意願」的意思。

● Now let's talk turkey.
● We**'re willing to** pay you half the asking price.

　●現在讓我們認真地討論吧。　●我們願意支付要價的一半。

▶ I'm willing to do anything to help her career.
　我願意做任何事來幫助她的事業。
　I'm willing to work on Saturdays until my vacation.
　直到我去度假前,我星期六都願意工作。

can't wait to

· can't wait until...
  等不及(某個時間點)

等不及做… 非常想做某事,迫不及待的意思。

● I'll bring my girlfriend to dinner tonight.
● We **can't wait to** meet her.

　●我今晚會帶我女朋友來吃晚餐。　●我們等不及想見她。

▶ I can't wait for vacation.
　我等不及想放假。
　I can't wait for the new computer game.
　我等不及想要那個新的電腦遊戲。

be anxious to

· be anxious about/for
  擔心…

渴望做… anxious about sth 則是「擔心某事」的意思。

● Have the exam results been announced?
● No, I'm **anxious to** see my score.

　●考試結果公布了嗎?　●還沒,我很想看到我的分數。

▶ Mom is anxious to finish paying the taxes.
　媽媽很想趕快繳完稅。
　I'm so anxious to hear your decision.
　我非常想聽到你的決定。

1 職場・學校
2 電腦・網路
3 社交生活
4 日常生活
5 訊息・理解
6 想法・態度
7 情緒・狀況
8 行為舉止
9 時間地點・副詞片語

would rather do

- would rather not do
  寧可不要做…
- would rather S+V
  寧願…
- would rather V1 than V2
  比起 V2 寧可 V1

寧可做… 沒有意願做另一件事，相較之下不如做這件事。通常用來委婉地拒絕對方的邀請。

- Let's go to a movie tonight.
- I **would rather** stay home and watch TV.
  ●我們今晚去看電影吧。 ●我寧可待在家裡看電視。

▶ I'd rather not meet you for dinner. 我寧可不跟你一起吃晚餐。
  I'd rather take the subway. 我寧可搭地鐵。

be in the mood to

- have a good mind to do
  很想做…

有做…的心情，想做… 也可以說 be in the mood for + N。

- Why do you want to go to a club?
- I **am in the mood to** dance tonight.
  ●你為什麼想去夜店？ ●我今晚想跳舞。

▶ We are in the mood for some good Korean food.
  我們想吃點好吃的韓國料理。
  I have a good mind to quit working here.
  我想要辭掉這邊的工作。

 ## would like to 和 like to

　　I'd like 就是 I would like 的縮寫。I like 是說明自己的興趣或傾向，I'd like 則是目前想要／想做某事的意願。另外，I like 後面可以接名詞、to do 或 -ing，但 I'd like 沒有後面接 -ing 的說法。I'd like sth 則常常用在餐廳點菜的狀況，表示「我想要（某道菜）」。

1 職場・學校

2 電腦・網路

3 社交生活

4 日常生活

5 訊息・理解

6 想法・態度

7 情緒・狀況

8 行為舉止

9 時間地點・副詞片語

30 愛好 be one's favorite

6-30.mp3

be one's favorite

· do one's own thing
做最喜歡的事，做最拿手的事

是某人的最愛 注意 favorite 可以當名詞或形容詞。

● I really love the Argentina soccer team.
● That's great! Who **is your favorite** player?

　●我真的很喜歡阿根廷足球隊。　●太棒了！誰是你最喜歡的球員？

▶ LA Dodgers is my favorite team.
洛杉磯道奇隊是我最喜歡的球隊。
Documentaries are also one of my favorite things to watch. 紀錄片也是我最喜歡觀看的類型之一。

have similar taste in

· have different tastes in
對於…的嗜好不同

對於…有相似的嗜好 taste 也可以換成 preference（偏好）。

● Are your son and daughter alike?
● They **have similar tastes in** the food they like.

　●你的兒子和女兒相像嗎？　●他們喜歡的食物很類似。

▶ We have similar tastes in our hobbies.
我們在興趣上有相似的嗜好。
They have similar tastes in clothing styles.
他們對於衣服款式的嗜好相似。

be one's style

· That's not my style.
那不是我的風格。

是某人的風格 中文也借用了這個說法：「…是我的 style」。

● Cheryl always wears black clothes.
● She told me that**'s her style.**

　●Cheryl 總是穿黑衣服。　●她跟我說那是她的風格。

▶ It's my style to come late to parties.
晚到派對會場是我的風格。
This shirt is your style. 這件襯衫很合你的風格。

be one's thing

是某人的愛好 喜歡到像是擁有某個東西的感覺。

● Why do you wear so much jewelry?
● That**'s my thing.** I think it looks good.

　●你為什麼戴那麼多珠寶？　●我喜歡這樣。我覺得很好看。

▶ Meeting new people is Linda's thing. Linda 喜歡認識新朋友。
Playing basketball is Steven's thing. Steven 喜歡打籃球。

be not one's cup of tea

不合某人的口味 用茶比喻喜歡的事物。常以否定形出現，表示不合口味。香港人也會說某個東西不是「我杯茶」。

● Did you enjoy salsa dancing?

● I hated it. It's **not my cup of tea**.

　　● 你喜歡 salsa 舞嗎？　● 我討厭。那不合我胃口。

▶ Blind dates are not my cup of tea.
　我不喜歡聯誼。
　This Russian food is not my cup of tea.
　這道俄國菜不合我的口味。

31 習慣 have a habit of

6-31.mp3

have a habit of

· have a habit of -ing
  有…的習慣
· make a habit of sth/
  -ing
  養成…的習慣

有…的習慣 後面接 -ing，表示習慣做某事。

● What kind of habit do you have?

● I **have a habit of** staying up late.

　　● 你有什麼習慣？　● 我有熬夜的習慣。

▶ You have a bad sleeping habit.
　你睡覺的習慣很差。
　You should not make a habit of it.
　你不該養成那種習慣。

get into the habit of

· turn into a habitual
  activity
  變成習慣

養成…的習慣，產生…的習慣 fall into the habit of 也是一樣的意思。

● I am afraid that I am too tired these days.

● **Get into the habit of** working out on regular basis.

　　● 我最近恐怕太累了。　● 養成定期做運動的習慣吧。

▶ I fell into the habit of having a nap after lunch.
　我養成了午餐後睡午覺的習慣。
　Don't fall into the habit of drinking too much.
　別養成喝太多酒的習慣。

in one's spare time

· as a hobby
　作為興趣

在空閒時間 spare time 可以換成 leisure time（閒暇時間）。

- These paintings are beautiful.
- I did them **in my spare time**.
  - ●這些畫很美。　●我在空閒時間畫的。
- ▶ She'll visit her mom in her spare time.
  她有空的時候會去看她媽媽。
  Marco collects toys as a hobby.
  Marco 收集玩具當作興趣。

be not one's habit to

· be not in the habit of
　-ing
　沒有做…的習慣
· be a good habit to do
　做…是個好習慣

做…不是某人的習慣 也可以解釋成「某人不是會做…的人」。

- Can you give some money to this charity?
- It's **not my habit to** donate money.
  - ●你可以捐點錢給這個慈善機構？　●我沒有捐錢的習慣。
- ▶ Saving money is a good habit to practice.
  省錢是個值得實踐的好習慣。
  Studying is a good habit to develop.
  學習是個值得培養的好習慣。

kick the habit

· kick the habit of -ing
　戒掉做…的習慣

戒掉習慣 主要用在壞習慣上。kick 換成 break 也是一樣的意思。

- Smoking makes me cough a lot.
- You should **kick the habit**.
  - ●抽菸讓我常常咳嗽。　●你應該戒掉這個習慣。
- ▶ It took months for Dad to kick the habit.
  爸爸花了幾個月戒掉那個習慣。
  I was able to kick the habit of getting up late.
  我能夠戒掉晚起床的習慣。

1 職場・學校

2 電腦・網路

3 社交生活

4 日常生活

5 訊息・理解

6 想法・態度

7 情緒・狀況

8 行為舉止

9 時間地點・副詞片語

32 似乎
seem to

6-32.mp3

seem to

· seem that S+V
  似乎…

似乎… seem 後面也可以直接接形容詞，表示看起來如何。

● What is Brian's favorite food?
● He **seems to** like ice cream the best.
   ● Brian 最喜歡的食物是什麼？　　● 他似乎最喜歡冰淇淋。

▶ It seems that George doesn't want to study.
   George 似乎不想唸書。
   She seems to be ready to start. 她看來準備好要開始了。

seem like

· seem like+N
  看起來像…
· seem like S+V
  看來…

看來… 後面接 S+V。seem like sth 則是指「看起來像某物」的意思。

● Are you ready to start our trip?
● Yes, it **seems like** we can leave.
   ● 你準備好要開始我們的旅行了嗎？　　● 是的，看來我們可以出發了。

▶ It seems like his mood is good. 看來他的心情很好。
   She seems like she will quit school. 她看起來會休學。

look like S+V

· look like+N
  看起來像…
· look like S+V
  看起來像…

看起來像… look 除了表示「看」以外，也有「看起來」的意思。

● It **looks like** Marshall ate too much.
● He always does that.
   ● Marshall 看來像是吃太多了。　　● 他總是這樣。

▶ You look like you are hungry. 你看起來很餓。
   It looks like snow will fall tonight. 今晚看起來會下雪。

be like

好像… 用在 It's like S+V 的句型。

● Have you eaten at the new restaurant?
● Sure. **It's like** my mom's cooking there.
   ● 你去那間新餐廳吃過飯了嗎？
   ● 當然，那裡的菜就像我媽媽煮的一樣。

▶ It's like prices go higher every year. 價格好像每年都會上漲。
   It's like work is becoming more difficult.
   工作好像越來越困難了。

feel like S+V

· feel like S+V
感覺好像…

· feel like+N
感覺像是…

· feel like -ing/N
想做…

感覺好像… 比 seem like 和 look like 更偏重個人感受的說法。

- I **feel like** such a loser. I have no friends.
- That's not true. I'm your friend.
  - 我覺得自己像個輸家。我沒有朋友。
  - 那不是真的。我是你的朋友呀。

▶ I feel like he doesn't like me.
我感覺他不喜歡我。
I feel like fast food is making me fat.
我覺得速食讓我變胖。

sound like S+V

· (It/That) Sounds like
N/S+V
聽起來像…

· Sounds like a plan.
（某個提議）聽起來不
錯。

· sound + 形容詞
聽起來…

聽起來好像… sound 後面可以接形容詞，表示「聽起來…」。

- It **sounds like** a storm is coming.
- I hear thunder in the distance too.
  - 聽起來好像暴風雨快來了。　● 我也有聽到遠方的雷聲。

▶ You sound angry with your boyfriend.
妳聽起來對你男朋友很生氣。
You sound sick today. Are you OK?
你今天聲音聽起來生病了，你還好嗎？

have the feeling that

· have a hunch that
S+V
有…的預感

有…的感覺，覺得… have 也可以換成 get 來用。

- Barney came over to talk to me.
- I **have the feeling** he'll ask you out on a date.
  - Barney 過來跟我說了話。　● 我感覺他會約你去約會。

▶ Jimmy had a hunch that we were here.
Jimmy 有預感我們在這邊。
We had a feeling that the movie was exciting.
我們覺得這部電影很刺激。

give sb the impression that

· give sb a bad
impression
給某人壞印象

· get the impression
that...
感到…的印象

給某人…的印象 「有…的印象」則是 have the impression that...。

- You shouldn't be so quick to judge!
- I know, but she **gave me a bad impression**.
  - 你不應該這麼快下判斷！　● 我知道，但她給我很不好的印象。

▶ Our teacher gave the impression he was bored.
我們老師給人無聊的印象。
Did you get the impression that he was lying?
你覺得他在騙人嗎？

1 職場・學校
2 電腦・網路
3 社交生活
4 日常生活
5 訊息・理解
6 想法・態度
7 情緒・狀況
8 行為舉止
9 時間地點・副詞片語

it figures that S+V

· It figures that he is German
他應該是德國人

· That figures.
有道理。不出所料。

…合理，…不意外　that 後面接對於情況的預測或判斷。

● Julia stole all of the money we had.
● **It figures that** she took everything.

● Julia 偷了我們所有的錢。　●她拿了所有東西也不意外。

▶ It figures that Karl is German.

Karl 應該是德國人。

He never called you? That figures.

他從來沒打電話給你？不出所料。

---

33 | 我説…
The point is that...

6-33.mp3

---

the point is that S+V

· That is my point.
那是我要講的重點。

重點是…　形容詞 pointless 則是「沒有意義」的意思。

● **The point is that** we need to fix this garage.
● I know, but we don't have enough money.

● 重點是我們需要修這個車庫。　● 我知道，但我們的錢不夠。

▶ The point is I don't need this right now.

重點是，我現在不需要這個。

The point is Andy wants to be with her.

重點是，Andy 想跟她在一起。

what I'm trying to say is that...

· What I'm saying is that S+V
我想說的是…

我想說的是…　也可以說 what I want to say 或 what I would like to say。

● You think you are going to move to England?
● **What I'm trying to say is that** I can get a job there.

● 你想要搬到英國？　● 我想説的是，我可以在那裡找到工作。

▶ What I'm trying to say is that he's rich.

我想説的是，他很有錢。

That is what I'm trying to say.

那就是我想説的。

what I'd like to say is that...

我想說的是⋯ 和 what I'm trying to say is... 一樣，用來強調自己主要想表達的事情。

- **What I'd like to say is** he hurt me.
- Tell us why he did that to you.

　●我想說的是，他傷害了我。　　●告訴我們他為什麼那樣對你。

▶ What I'd like to say is the job finished today.

　我想說的是，這份工作今天完成了。

　What I'd like to say is that you're a really great guy.

　我想說的是，你真的是個很好的人。

I mean that S+V

· See what I mean?
　明白我的意思嗎？

我的意思是⋯，我是說⋯ 用在話講到一半，想重新把自己的意思解釋清楚，或者想強調重點的情況。

- Don't try to take care of me. **I mean**, I'm okay.
- Are you sure you're okay?

　●別費心照顧我。我是說，我沒事的。　　●你確定你沒問題嗎？

▶ I mean she's a workaholic.

　我的意思是，她是個工作狂。

　I mean which country you come from.

　我是問你從哪個國家來的。

you know,

· you know what
　你知道嗎？／我跟你說⋯

呃⋯ 跟 you see 一樣，沒什麼特別的意思，是在想接下來要說什麼的時候，用來避免沉默的發語詞。

- I'd like to go out tonight.
- **You know**, we could go to a nightclub.

　●我今晚想出去。　　●呃，我們可以去夜店。

▶ You know what? The store is probably closed.

　我說啊，那間店八成關了。

　You know, we might as well go home.

　那個，我們也該回家了。

1 職場·學校

2 電腦·網路

3 社交生活

4 日常生活

5 訊息·理解

6 想法·態度

7 情緒·狀況

8 行為舉止

9 時間地點·副詞片語

34 想出
come up with

6-34.mp3

come up with

· cf. come down with
　染上（疾病）

想出… 表示想出某個特別的點子或提議。

● Let me see what you**'ve come up with.**

● It's not much, but it's a start.

　●讓我看看你想出了些什麼。　●不是很多，但至少是個開始。

▶ You'd better come up with something better than that.
　你最好想出比那還好的東西。
　We'd better come up with a good plan soon!
　我們最好快點想出個好計畫！

make up

· make up a story
　編造故事

編造（故事等） make up 也有「化妝」的意思，是不是表示化妝也有創造假象的成分呢…

● I think Kelly has been lying to us.

● But why would she **make up** a story?

　●我覺得 Kelly 在騙我們。　●但她為什麼要捏造故事呢？

▶ I need to make up an excuse for dad.
　我需要編個理由給爸爸。
　Don't make up a lie. Tell me the truth.
　不要說謊。告訴我事實。

cook up

· cook up some story
　杜撰故事

編造（故事等） 像煮菜一樣，把事情變成完全不同的樣子。

● What have Kyle and Stan been doing?

● They **are cooking up** plans for this week.

　●Kyle 和 Stan 在幹嘛？　●他們在編造這週的計畫。

▶ We need to cook up something to increase business.
　我們需要編造些什麼來增加業績。
　I don't know, but I can cook up something.
　我不知道，但我可以編出些什麼。

1 職場・學校

2 電腦・網路

3 社交生活

4 日常生活

5 訊息・理解

6 想法・態度

7 情緒・狀況

8 行為舉止

9 時間地點・副詞片語

think up

想出… 想出某個想法、點子或辯解的理由等等。

- The story you wrote is very interesting.
- It took a long time to **think it up**.

　●你寫的那個故事非常有趣。　　●把故事想出來花了很長的時間。

▶ Let's try to think up something new.

　我們努力想出點新東西吧。

　Tina couldn't think up an idea for the class project.

　對於課堂上的研究計畫，Tina 想不出點子。

invent an excuse

編造出理由 invent 是「發明」的意思，引申為「無中生有」。

- I don't have a good reason for being late.
- You will just have to **invent an excuse**.

　●我沒有好理由可以解釋遲到。　　●你就是得編個理由。

▶ She always invents excuses for not paying me.

　她總是在編造不付我錢的理由。

　Be honest and don't invent some excuse.

　誠實點，不要找理由。

---

35 | 肯定與否定
no longer

6-35.mp3

sure thing

當然 相當於 of course 或 certainly。

- Yeah, we have to make an effort to stay in touch.
- **Sure thing.** Bye!

　●是啊，我們得努力保持聯繫。　　●當然。再見！

▶ Sure thing, she is coming over now.

　當然（她會來），她現在正在過來。

　Can you give me a hand moving it? Sure thing.

　你可以幫我搬這個嗎？當然。

of course

當然 否定形是 of course not「當然不」。

● Please excuse us for a moment.

● **Of course.** You can call me when you're ready.

　　● 請等我們一下。　　● 當然好，你們可以等好了之後叫我一聲。

▶ Of course. Make yourself at home.

　　當然，當自己家吧。

　　Of course. I won't tell anybody.

　　當然，我不會跟任何人說。

definitely

肯定地，當然 和 certainly 或 absolutely 同義。

● Have you ever been in big trouble?

● **Definitely.** Many times.

　　● 你碰過大麻煩嗎？　　● 當然，很多次了。

▶ Am I pessimistic? Absolutely not.

　　我悲觀嗎？當然不。

　　Certainly. I'll give him the message when he gets in.

　　當然好，他進來的時候我會把訊息告訴他。

not...at all

一點也不… 表示「連一點點的程度也沒有」，是強烈的否定句型。

● It looks like you **don't** like your meal **at all**.

● No, it's just that I'm not hungry right now.

　　● 你看來一點也不喜歡你的餐點。　　● 不是，只是我現在不餓。

▶ A designated driver is someone who doesn't drink at all.

　　指定駕駛是完全不喝酒的人。

　　（註：指定駕駛是指在派對上不喝酒，負責載別人回家的人。）

　　It's not at all what I expected.

　　這完全不是我預期的。

no longer

不再… 意思相當於 not...any more。

● As of today, we **no longer** have a travel allowance.

● Who told you that?

　　● 從今天開始，我們再也沒有出差費了。　　● 誰跟你說的？

▶ Ralph is not here any more.

　　Ralph 再也不在這裡了。

　　She's no longer working on the project.

　　她不再參與這個計畫了。

1 職場・學校

2 電腦・網路

3 社交生活

4 日常生活

5 訊息・理解

6 想法・態度

7 情緒・狀況

8 行為舉止

9 時間地點・副詞片語

not necessarily

・not entirely
並非完全如此

不必然⋯ 雖然可能性很高，卻不是 100% 會發生，表示輕微的否定。

● You're **not necessarily** going to pass this class.

● Well, I still don't feel like studying.

　● 你這一門課不見得會及格。　● 嗯，我還是不想讀書。

▶ This is not necessarily the best hotel room.
　這不見得是最好的飯店客房。

　Karl is not necessarily going to show up tonight.
　Karl 今晚不一定會現身。

out of the question

不可能，不可以 不用問就知道不可能的意思。

● Come on, you can lend me some money.

● No way. It is **out of the question**.

　● 拜託啦，你可以借我一點錢。　● 不行，不可以。

▶ Traveling to North Korea is out of the question.
　去北韓旅行是不可能的。

　Taking a holiday then is out of the question.
　那時候要休假是不可能的。

徹底解析 sure !

　　到現在還只知道 sure 是「確定」的意思可不行哦。sure 除了當形容詞，並且衍生出 be sure to, make sure 等慣用語以外，在口語裡還可以當副詞。口語中的 sure 常常用來代替 yes，是一種輕鬆的肯定說法；別人跟自己道謝的時候，也可以說 sure 表示「不用謝」、「沒什麼」。別總是像機器人般只會說 yes，也試著輕鬆簡單地用用看「sure」吧。

　　當副詞用的 sure 甚至可以取代 surely，例如「It sure is hot out there」就是「外面真的很熱」的意思，「Man, I sure miss Julie」則是說「啊，我真的好想 Julie」。不過，這完全是口語的說法，在寫文章的時候還是得乖乖用 surely 才恰當。

Emotions & Situations

開心、生氣、各種狀況的慣用語

CHAPTER 7

01 開心，心情好
be happy with

be happy with

· be happy to do
  樂意做…
· be happy for sb
  為某人感到開心
· make sb happy
  讓某人開心

對…滿意 be happy 後面可以接 with/about/for sth 或 to 不定詞。

● I wanted to let you know I'm getting divorced.
● But why? You **seemed so happy with** your husband.

　●我想告訴你，我要離婚了。
　●但為什麼呢？你看起來對你先生很滿意啊。

▶ Are you happy with that?
　你對那個滿意嗎？
　You sound happy about your meeting.
　你聽起來對會議感到很滿意。

be glad to

· be glad that S+V
  因為…而高興
· be pleased to do/
  with+N
  因為…而高興

因為…而高興 be pleased 是比 be glad 更莊重的說法。

● She told me that she feels much better.
● I'm **glad to** hear that.
　●她跟我說她感覺好多了。　●我很高興聽到她這麼說。

▶ I'd be glad to do your homework.
　我很樂意做你的作業。
　I'm glad you like it.
　我很高興你喜歡它。

be pleased to

· be pleased with+N
  對…感到高興
· be pleased that S+V
  對…感到高興
· be satisfied with
  滿足於…

因為…而高興 常使用在英文書信或演講中，屬於比較 formal 的說法。

● Are you sure I can stay in your house?
● We'd **be pleased to** have you stay with us.
　●你確定我可以住在你家嗎？　●我們很樂意讓你跟我們一起住。

▶ They were pleased to be invited to the wedding.
　他們很開心受邀參加婚禮。
　He was pleased to take Betty to the dance.
　他很高興帶 Betty 去參加舞會。

be nice to

· be good/great
  -ing/to do
  做…很好／很棒
» cf. be good/nice
  talking to you
  （談話結束後）很高興能
  跟你說上話

做…很好，做…很高興 be nice to... 通常指未來或當下的行為，be nice -ing 則通常指已經完成的行為。

● Mary, it's **so nice to** see you again.
● What are you doing here?
　●Mary，真高興再次見到你。　●你在這裡做什麼？
▶ It would be nice to do something this afternoon.
　今天下午如果能做點什麼的話就太好了。
　Good night, it was very nice to meet you.
　晚安，真的很高興見到你。

be excited about

· be/get excited to do
  對於要做…很興奮
· be/get thrilled to do
  對於要做…很興奮

對…很興奮 excited 的前面可以加上 very, really, so, a little 來表示興奮的程度。

● They **are excited about** going overseas.
● I think it will be a fun trip.
　●他們對於出國很興奮。　●我想那會是趟有趣的旅行。
▶ Are you excited about celebrating Christmas?
　你對於慶祝耶誕節感到興奮嗎？
　I'm so excited to see you again.
　我很興奮要再次和你見面。

feel good about

· feel good about
  oneself
  心情好

因為…心情很好 about 後面接名詞或 -ing，說明心情好的原因。

● Why did you give the homeless man money?
● I **feel good about** helping poor people.
　●你為什麼給那個流浪漢錢？　●幫助窮困的人讓我覺得心情很好。
▶ Kendra felt good about completing the marathon.
　Kendra 跑完了全程的馬拉松，心情很好。
　Did Sam feel good about finishing his work?
　Sam 對於完成了工作感覺開心嗎？

feel much better

· feel better about (A
  -ing)
  對於（A 做了…）感覺好
  了點
· feel much better now
  現在覺得好多了
· make A feel better
  about...
  讓 A 對於…覺得好多了

覺得好多了 表示從壞心情中恢復，或者身體從病痛中恢復健康。

● I certainly hope you **are feeling better**.
● I am. Thank you so much.
　●我真的希望你現在開心點了。　●我有，非常謝謝你。
▶ She was just trying to make you feel better.
　她只是在試著讓你開心一點。
　I'll feel much better in the morning.
　等到早上我就會覺得好多了。

feel comfortable with

· feel comfortable with
  sb -ing
  對於某人做⋯感到自在
· feel/be uncomfortable
  with
  對於⋯覺得不自在

對⋯感到自在 comfortable 除了表示身體感覺舒服，也可以指心情自在。

● I'd like you to sing a song for us.
● I **feel uncomfortable with** so many people here.
　●我希望你為我們唱首歌。　●這邊人太多了，我覺得不自在。

▶ Do you feel uncomfortable with those shoes?
　你覺得那雙鞋不舒服嗎？
　He feels comfortable with his kind boss.
　親切的上司讓他覺得很自在。

be in a good mood

· be in a bad mood
  心情不好
· be in a mood to do...
  有想做⋯的心情

心情好 mood 是指一時的情緒。moody person 則是情緒起伏很大的人。

● I wonder if the boss is still angry with me.
● He seems to **be in a good mood** today.
　●不知道老闆是不是還在生我的氣。　●他今天看起來心情很好。

▶ Gina was in a good mood after eating lunch.
　吃完午餐後，Gina 的心情很好。
　They are in a good mood because they are together.
　他們因為在一起，所以心情很好。

have a good feeling

· have a bad feeling
  about
  對於⋯感覺不好

感覺好 have a good feeling about/toward sb 則是「對某人有好感」。

● Do you like the girl who joined our class?
● Yes. I **have a good feeling** about her character.
　●你喜歡轉來我們班上的那個女生嗎？　●嗯，我很喜歡她的個性。

▶ I have a good feeling about the exam I took.
　對於那場考試，我感覺還不錯。
　He had a good feeling about his blind date.
　他對於他的聯誼覺得很開心。

1 職場・學校
2 電腦・網路
3 社交生活
4 日常生活
5 訊息・理解
6 想法・態度
7 情緒・狀況
8 行為舉止
9 時間地點・副詞片語

02 傷心，憂鬱，心情不好
feel sad about

7-02.mp3

feel/be sad about

· feel so bad about
對於…感到非常傷心
· feel blue
感覺憂鬱
· It's sad that...
…很令人難過

對於…感到傷心 也可以說 It's sad that S+V。

● I **feel sad about** my uncle dying.
● Yes, he was a good man and we'll miss him.
　● 我對於叔叔過世感到很傷心。
　● 嗯，他是個好人，我們會想念他的。

▶ Jane felt sad about the movie's ending.
Jane 對於電影的結局感到很傷心。
I feel sad when the Christmas holiday ends.
耶誕假日結束讓我很難過。

feel terrible about

· be terrible at...
很不擅長…

對於…感覺很糟 feel terrible 後面也可以接 that S+V 句型。

● You look kind of sick today.
● I **feel terrible**. I have a sore throat.
　● 你今天看起來有點不舒服。　● 我感覺很糟。我喉嚨痛。

▶ She felt terrible about lying to Steve.
她對於欺騙 Steve 感覺很不好。
I feel terrible about embarrassing the teacher.
讓老師難堪，我感覺很糟。

be unhappy with

· be unhappy with
one's boss
對老闆不滿
· be unhappy working
here
在這裡工作不開心

對…不開心／不滿意 with 可以換成 about 或 at。或者也可以直接在 unhappy 後面接 -ing。

● Why do you want to break up with me?
● I'm **feeling unhappy with** you.
　● 你為什麼想跟我分手？　● 我跟你在一起不開心。

▶ I'm unhappy with James and my marriage.
我對於 James 和我的婚姻不滿意。
I'm not happy with my job.
我不喜歡我的工作。

feel/get depressed

· look so depressed
  看起來好沮喪

感覺沮喪／消沉 depressed 前面可以加上 so 或 a bit 修飾，後面可以接 about sth 說明原因。

● What is wrong with you these days? Are you ill?
● No, I'm just a bit **depressed about** my life.
  ● 你最近怎麼回事？你生病了嗎？
  ● 沒有，我只是對自己的人生有點沮喪。

▶ Do you feel depressed about working here?
  在這裡工作讓你很沮喪嗎？
  He feels depressed about being dumped by Sheila.
  被 Sheila 甩了，他覺得很沮喪。

get frustrated with

· look frustrated
  看起來很挫折
· feel frustrated
  覺得很挫折

對…感到挫折 對於無法如己意而感到十分挫折或焦躁。

● Why did you leave the meeting so suddenly?
● I **was frustrated with** you! You talk too much!
  ● 你為什麼那麼突然離開會議？ ● 你讓我覺得好煩！你說太多話了！

▶ I'm frustrated with my lack of options.
  因為沒有什麼選擇，讓我覺得很挫折。
  She's frustrated with her computer's problems.
  她對於自己電腦的問題感覺很挫折。

feel bad about

· feel bad about -ing
  對於做…覺得難過
· make A feel bad
  讓 A 覺得難過
· not feel well/good
  覺得不開心或不舒服

對於…覺得難過 feel bad 也可以指身體「覺得不舒服」。

● Does she still **feel bad**?
● Well, apparently she does.
  ● 她心情還是不好嗎？ ● 嗯，很明顯是的。

▶ Don't feel bad about that. You earned that.
  別對那件事不開心了。你是自作自受。
  It looks like she doesn't feel well.
  她看起來心情不好。

be/feel left out of

· feel rejected/
  excluded/isolated
  感覺被排斥
· be/feel miserable
  覺得不幸或悲哀
· be pathetic
  可憐，可悲

被排除在…之外 彷彿被當成局外人一樣的感覺。

● Karen's brother seems upset about something.
● He **was left out of** Karen's wedding.
  ● Karen 的哥哥好像在生什麼氣。 ● 他感覺像是 Karen 婚禮的局外人。

▶ I was left out of the card game.
  我沒能加入牌局。
  Nobody calls me these days. I feel so left out.
  最近沒有人打電話給我。我感覺好像被排除在外。

hurt sb's feelings

傷某人的心 字面上的意思就是「傷害某人的感情」。

- Is Harry sad because I broke up with him?
- I'm sure that you **hurt his feelings**.
  - Harry 是因為我跟他分手所以難過的嗎？
  - 我很確定你傷了他的心。

▶ It hurt my feelings that I wasn't invited.
沒有被邀請讓我很傷心。
It hurt Mom's feelings that we forgot her birthday.
我們忘了媽媽的生日，讓她很難過。

under the weather

· be/feel under the
  weather
  感覺不舒服

不舒服 身體有點不舒服、有點生病的感覺。

- Why is our boss so late today?
- He's at home because he's **under the weather**.
  - 我們老闆今天為什麼這麼晚？　●他因為不太舒服，所以待在家。

▶ I couldn't go to Penghu because I was under the
weather. 我身體不太舒服，所以不能去澎湖。
Terry is under the weather and is lying in bed.
Terry 不太舒服，正躺在床上。

miss sb/-ing

· miss sb -ing
  想念某人做…（的時候）

想念某人／懷念做某事 因為見不到面或再也無法做某事而感到想念。

- Well, I guess this is goodbye.
- I'm going to **miss** you so much.
  - 嗯，我想是該說再見了。　●我會很想你的。

▶ I will miss you coming to visit me.
我會想念你來看我的時光。
You have no idea how much I miss her.
你不知道我有多想她。

1 職場・學校
2 電腦・網路
3 社交生活
4 日常生活
5 訊息・理解
6 想法・態度
7 情緒・狀況
8 行為舉止
9 時間地點・副詞片語

03 | 生氣
get upset

get upset about

- I'm so upset that S+V
  …讓我很煩
- upset sb
  讓某人很煩

因為…覺得煩 因為煩惱而有點抓狂，但也不到 angry 的程度。
如果比 angry 還要生氣，就會說 furious。

- **Are** you **upset about** something?
- I feel awful. I got fired today.
  - ●你在煩什麼嗎？　●我感覺很糟。我今天被炒魷魚了。

▶ I'm really upset that he did that.
  他那麼做真的讓我很煩。
  I'm so upset that you forgot our anniversary.
  我真的很討厭你忘掉我們的紀念日。

get/be angry with

- be angry at/with sb
  生某人的氣
- be angry about sth
  生某事的氣
- be angry about sb
  -ing
  因為某人做了…而生氣
- be angry because/that
  S+V
  因為…而生氣

對…生氣 說明生氣的理由用 at, over, about，對某人生氣則用 at
或 with。

- Why **are** you so **angry with** me?
- Because you always take his side.
  - ●你為什麼這麼生我的氣？　●因為你總是站在他那邊。

▶ I don't have any reason to be angry at you.
  我沒有任何生你氣的理由。
  The problem is that the boss is still angry with you.
  問題是老闆還在生你的氣。

get/be mad at

- get/be mad at sb
  生某人的氣
- get/be mad about
  sth/-ing
  生某事的氣
- get/be mad about sb
  為某人瘋狂

對…生氣 be mad about sb 反而是「為某人瘋狂」，很喜歡某人的
意思。

- I'm mad at my boss.
- Oh? Why is that?
  - ●我很氣我老闆。　●哦？為什麼呢？

▶ I got mad at him because he took my money.
  因為他拿走了我的錢，所以我很生他的氣。
  Don't worry, I'm not going to get mad.
  別擔心，我不會生氣的。

make sb angry

· make A feel bad
  讓 A 心情不好

讓某人生氣 雖然也可以用及物動詞 infuriate 或 enrage 表達「激怒…」的意思,但都是文章用語,口語裡不常說。

● How was your trip to Ottawa last December?
● Terrible. Some unkind people **made me angry**.
  ● 你去年 12 月的渥太華之旅如何?
  ● 糟透了。有些不友善的人讓我很生氣。

▶ This messy room will make your father angry.
  這亂七八糟的房間會讓你父親生氣的。
  The careless driver made everyone angry.
  那位漫不經心的司機讓每個人都很生氣。

be pissed off

· be/get pissed off with/
  at
  對於…非常生氣

氣炸了 不適合用在正式場合,感覺有點粗野的說法,但也因為這樣,所以很能傳達「氣得要命」的感覺。

● I heard that Bob was fired today.
● It's true. He **is really pissed off**.
  ● 我聽説 Bob 今天被炒魷魚了。　● 是真的。他氣炸了。

▶ I heard that Sam is really pissed off at you.
  我聽説 Sam 真的很你的氣。
  I just got fired today and I'm really pissed off.
  我今天被炒了魷魚,快氣死了。

lose one's temper

· lose one's temper
  with...
  對於…發脾氣
· lose one's cool
  (with...)
  發脾氣(←→keep one's
  cool)

發脾氣 temper 在這裡是「冷靜,沉著」的意思,「失去 temper」感覺有點像是中文裡的「失控」。

● The boss is going to **lose his temper** when he sees this report.
● I know. It has too many mistakes in it.
  ● 老闆看到這份報告會發脾氣的。　● 我知道,裡面有太多錯誤了。

▶ She lost her temper when her boyfriend lied.
  當她男朋友説謊時,她發了脾氣。
  I lost my temper because she was so late.
  因為她很晚到,所以我發了火。

1 職場・學校
2 電腦・網路
3 社交生活
4 日常生活
5 訊息・理解
6 想法・態度
7 情緒・狀況
8 行為舉止
9 時間地點・副詞片語

drive sb crazy

· drive somebody up the wall
  讓某人大發脾氣
· go crazy
  瘋了→很生氣

把某人搞瘋 drive 是「驅使」的意思。這裡的 crazy 就是 angry 的意思，也可以換成 mad, insane, nuts 等等。

● Can you shut off that radio? It's **driving me crazy**.

● Why are you so sensitive to noise?

  ●你可以把廣播關掉嗎？那快把我逼瘋了。

  ●你怎麼對雜音那麼敏感？

▶ The traffic jam was driving everyone crazy.

  塞車把每個人都搞瘋了。

  The media really went crazy covering that case.

  媒體非常瘋狂地報導那個事件。

get on one's nerves

惹惱某人 被煩到發怒的意思。

● What is the most difficult thing about being married?

● Husbands and wives can **get on each other's nerves**.

  ●結婚最困難的事是什麼？ ●夫妻可能會惹惱彼此。

▶ The slow Internet connection got on my nerves.

  慢吞吞的網路連線讓我很不耐煩。

  Does Sharon ever get on your nerves?

  Sharon 惹毛過你嗎？

get worked up

· get/be worked up about/over
  為⋯生氣或激動
· burn somebody up
  使某人發火（= make sb hit the ceiling / hit the roof）

激動，生氣 這是被動態，可以改成主動態 ...work sb up（⋯讓某人激動）。

● My son went to a pop music concert last night.

● Many kids **were worked up** about the singers.

  ●我兒子昨晚去了一場流行樂的演唱會。

  ●很多孩子為那些歌手瘋狂。

▶ Don't get worked up over your argument with him.

  別為了和他的爭執生氣。

  My parents got worked up over my poor grades.

  我父母因為我糟糕的成績而大為光火。

04 擔心 worry about

7-04.mp3

1 職場・學校

2 電腦・網路

3 社交生活

4 日常生活

5 訊息・理解

6 想法・態度

7 情緒・狀況

8 行為舉止

9 時間地點・副詞片語

worry about

· worry that S+V
擔心…
· Don't worry about...
別擔心…
· have nothing to worry about
沒有要擔心的事

擔心… about 後面接要擔心的人或事物。

● This is dangerous. You've got to be careful.
● Don't **worry about** me.
　●這很危險，你得小心。　●別擔心我。

▶ You don't need to worry about that.
你不需要擔心那件事。
I'm not going to die that easy. Don't worry about that.
我不會那麼容易就死掉的，別擔心了。

be worried about

· be worried that[because]
擔心…〔因為…而擔心〕
· be worried about -ing
擔心…
· be angry about sb -ing
因為某人做…而生氣
» cf. I worry that = I'm worried that...
我擔心…

擔心… worry 當及物動詞時可以表示「使…擔心」，這裡是把它的被動態當成形容詞使用。

● I'm **worried** Pam won't come to the party.
● Why? Is she still angry with you?
　●我擔心 Pam 不會來派對。　●為什麼？她還在生你的氣嗎？

▶ I'm a little worried about my singing ability.
我有點擔心我的歌唱實力。
I'm worried you might be a little cold.
我擔心你可能有點冷。

be concerned about

· be concerned that S+V
擔心…
· be concerned with
和…有關

擔心… 把 concern（使…擔心）的被動態當形容詞用。about 可以換成 for，但如果換成 with 則是「與…有關」的意思。

● I'm **concerned about** my grades in school.
● You should be. They seem very low.
　●我擔心我的學校成績。　●你是該擔心。你成績看起來很低。

▶ I'm concerned about my math grade.
我擔心我的數學成績。
I'm concerned the earth will become more polluted.
我擔心地球會被汙染得更嚴重。

499

be anxious about

- be anxious about N/-ing
  擔心…
- be anxious for sth /to do
  渴望…

擔心… be anxious for 是「渴望…」，be anxious to do 是「渴望做…」的意思。

- You seem to be upset today.
- I'm **anxious about** the exam results.
  - 你今天看起來很心煩意亂。　● 我很擔心考試結果。

▶ Paula is anxious about her new schedule at work.
  Paula 在擔心她工作上的新行程。
  I'm so anxious to hear the decision.
  我真的很想聽到那個決定。

never mind

- Never mind A
  別在意 A
- not let A bother you
  不讓 A 害你煩心

沒關係，別在意 相當於 forget it，表示不必再去想某件事。

- My friend was saying that I'm ugly.
- **Never mind.** He's just teasing.
  - 我朋友說我很醜。　● 別在意，他只是在鬧著玩。

▶ Never mind that.
  別在意那件事。
  Does it bother you to go to the store every day?
  每天去那間店你會覺得麻煩嗎？

---

05 | 後悔 regret -ing

7-05.mp3

regret sth

- regret it later
  事後後悔
- regret sth for the rest of one's life
  往後的人生都在後悔某事
- regret the day S+V
  對於…的那天感到後悔

後悔某事 後面接事後感覺不該做的事。常接代名詞 it, that 等。

- Don't you **regret** anything about your past?
- No. If I had the chance, I'd do it all over again.
  - 對於你的過去，你沒有任何後悔嗎？
  - 沒有。如果有機會，我還是會重做一樣的事。

▶ I regret the day I met you.
  我後悔遇見你的那天。
  I'm sure he doesn't regret it that much.
  我確定他沒有那麼後悔。

1 職場・學校

2 電腦・網路

3 社交生活

4 日常生活

5 訊息・理解

6 想法・態度

7 情緒・狀況

8 行為舉止

9 時間地點・副詞片語

regret -ing

· regret to say/tell/inform
很遺憾地說…

· regret that S+V
後悔…，遺憾…

後悔做… -ing 改成 to do 的話，則是「遺憾」的意思。

● Do you like the new clothes you bought?

● I **regret** spending so much money on them.

●你喜歡你新買的衣服嗎？　●我後悔在那上面花了那麼多錢。

▶ I regret asking Suzie out the other day.
我後悔那天約了 Suzie 去約會。

I regret spending last night playing computer games.
我後悔把昨晚的時間花在玩電腦遊戲上。

have no regrets about

· with (no) regrets
（不）後悔地

· be full of regrets
滿是後悔

· feel remorse
後悔

對於…沒有後悔 regret 除了當動詞，也可以當名詞。

● Are you sorry that you dropped out of college?

● I **have no regrets about** quitting school.

●你對於大學輟學有遺憾嗎？　●我對於輟學一點也不後悔。

▶ They had no regrets about getting married.
他們不後悔結了婚。

I had no regrets about spending all of my money.
我不後悔花了我所有的錢。

should have + pp

· should not have+pp
真不該…的

· You shouldn't have.
（收到禮物時）不買禮物過來也沒關係的。

真該…的 用 should + 現在完成式表示與過去事實相反的句型。

● You **should have been** here hours ago.

● Sorry. I got held up at work.

●你幾個小時前就該到這裡的。　●抱歉，我被工作耽擱了。

▶ I should have gotten up early this morning.
我今天早上該早點起來的。

I shouldn't have bought this new car.
我不該買這台新車的。

you'll be sorry about

· You'll be sorry about -ing
你會後悔做…的

· You'll be sorry if S+V
如果…你會後悔的

你會後悔…的 請對方注意或者提出警告時用。

● You'll be sorry if you don't prepare for the test.

● Are you saying that I should study?

●你不準備考試的話，會後悔的。　●你是說我該讀書嗎？

▶ You'll be sorry about teasing me.
你會後悔開我玩笑的。

You'll be sorry if you don't obey your parents.
如果不聽你父母親的話，你會後悔的。

06 感謝
say thank you

7-06.mp3

---

thank you for

· thank you for N/-ing
  謝謝你的…／謝謝你做…
· thank you for the
  compliment
  謝謝你的誇獎

謝謝你… for 後面可以接名詞或動詞 -ing 形。

● **Thank you for** booking my ticket.
● If you need more tickets, call me anytime.
   ●謝謝你幫我訂了票。   ●如果你需要更多票，隨時打電話給我。

▶ Thank you for visiting me in the hospital.
  謝謝你來醫院探望我。
  I want to thank you for helping me.
  我想謝謝你幫了我的忙。

---

say thank you

· say hi
  打招呼
· say no
  拒絕

道謝 接 to sb 表示道謝的對象，接 for sth 表示道謝的理由。

● **Say thank you** to your grandfather.
● Grandpa, thanks for buying me a birthday gift.
   ●跟你的爺爺道謝。   ●爺爺，謝謝你買生日禮物給我。

▶ You must say thank you for his help.
  你一定要謝謝他幫你的忙。
  Say thank you for the new cell phone.
  為那支新手機（向某人）道謝吧。

It is nice of you to...

· be nice/kind of you to
  say...
  謝謝你說…
· be such a + 形容詞
  + 名詞
  真是個…

謝謝你做… 也就是 Thank you for doing something 的意思。

● You look beautiful tonight.
● Thanks. You're **such a kind person**.
   ●你今晚看起來好美。   ●謝謝，你人真好。

▶ You're such a good driver.
  你真是個好駕駛。
  I didn't know that our boss was such a partygoer.
  我都不知道我們老闆是個派對狂。

502

1 職場・學校

2 電腦・網路

3 社交生活

4 日常生活

5 訊息・理解

6 想法・態度

7 情緒・狀況

8 行為舉止

9 時間地點・副詞片語

appreciate one's support

· appreciate one's -ing
  感謝某人做…
· show one's appreciation
  表示某人的感謝
· appreciate one's hospitality
  感謝某人的招待

感謝某人的幫助 thank 的受詞是人，appreciate 的受詞則是值得感謝的行為。

● Don't worry. I'll get it done for you.
● I **appreciate your help**.
  ●別擔心，我會幫你做好。　●謝謝你的幫忙。

▶ The people here all appreciate your support.
  這裡的人們都很感謝你的幫助。
  I appreciate your support. You're a good friend.
  很感謝你的幫忙，你真是個好朋友。

be grateful to...

· be grateful to sb
  感謝某人
· be grateful to do
  感謝…（獲得幫助等）
· a token of thanks
  謝意的表示（指回禮或謝卡等等）

感謝… to sb 也可以改成 to do 或 that 子句。

● Why did George give his mom a necklace?
● He **is grateful to** her for raising him.
  ●George 為什麼送他媽媽項鍊？　●他很感謝母親撫養他長大。

▶ I am grateful to everyone who gave money.
  我感謝所有給錢的人。
  She was grateful to her school's English teacher.
  她感謝她學校的英文老師。

07 抱歉，遺憾
be sorry for

7-07.mp3

be sorry for

· I'm sorry about+N
  對於…我感到很抱歉
· feel sorry for...
  為…感到遺憾／難過

為…感到抱歉／遺憾 sorry 除了表示抱歉，也可以表示對別人的不幸感到遺憾。

● I **feel so sorry for** my mother. She's all alone.
● That must be difficult at her age.
  ●我為我母親感到遺憾，她隻身一人。
  ●以她的年紀而言，生活一定很不容易。

▶ I'm sorry for being late to work.
  我很抱歉上班遲到了。
  He is sorry for making everyone angry.
  他很抱歉讓每個人都生氣了。

be sorry to

· I'm sorry to say
(that)...
很抱歉得說…
· I'm sorry to trouble
you, but...
很抱歉打擾你,但…

很抱歉… 對現在的事表示抱歉。如果是過去的事,則說 be sorry
to have + pp。

● **I am sorry to** arrive late.
● **Where were you?**

  ●很抱歉我遲到了。　●你去哪裡了?

▶ I'm sorry to say we must break up.

  我很抱歉得這麼說,但我們一定得分手。

  I am sorry to have kept you waiting for so long.

  我很抱歉讓你等了那麼久。

I'm sorry that S+V

· I'm sorry, but...
很抱歉,但…

我很抱歉… I'm sorry, but... 則是委婉拒絕別人,並且說明理由的
句型。

● **I'm sorry** I'm late again. I got stuck in traffic.
● **You could have taken the subway.**

  ●抱歉我又遲到了,我遇到塞車了。　●你可以搭地鐵的。

▶ I'm sorry that I took the man's cell phone.

  很抱歉我拿了那個男人的手機。

  I'm sorry, but the answer is no.

  很抱歉,但答案是不行。

apologize for

· apologize to A for
N/-ing
為了…向 A 道歉

為…道歉 比 sorry 更慎重的道歉。apologize 後面接 to sb 表示對
象,for sth 表示要道歉的事情。

● **Ray is very angry at Jenny.**
● **It seems to me that she should apologize.**

  ●Ray 對 Jenny 非常生氣。　●我覺得她應該道歉。

▶ I must apologize for my colleague's behavior.

  我必須為我同事的行為道歉。

  You've got to apologize to me.

  你必須跟我道歉。

I'm afraid S+V

· I'm afraid so.
恐怕是的。
· I'm afraid not.
恐怕不是。

恐怕… 要提起不好或抱歉的事,或者事實和對方想的不一樣時,
可以這麼說。和表示害怕的 be afraid of 意義不同。

● **You always drink my kiwi juice.**
● **I'm afraid** I didn't do it this time.

  ●你總是喝我的奇異果汁。　●可是我這次沒喝。

▶ I'm afraid you have the wrong number.

  你恐怕打錯電話了。

  I'm afraid I've got some bad news.

  不好意思,我有些壞消息。

1 職場・學校

2 電腦・網路

3 社交生活

4 日常生活

5 訊息・理解

6 想法・態度

7 情緒・狀況

8 行為舉止

9 時間地點・副詞片語

08 尷尬，困惑
be embarrassed

7-08.mp3

be embarrassed

· be embarrassed at/ about/over
因為…覺得丟臉
· be embarrassed to do
做…很丟臉

尷尬，丟臉 be 也可以換成 get, look 等動詞。

● I heard you farted in front of your mother-in-law.
● That's true. I **was so embarrassed**.
● 我聽說你在你婆婆面前放屁。　● 是真的，我很尷尬。

▶ This is really embarrassing. I'm really embarrassed about that. 這真的很丟臉。我真的為那件事覺得很丟臉。
I was too embarrassed to tell you.
因為太丟臉了，我無法跟你說。

be confused

· be confused about
對…感到困惑
· get mixed up (over)
（因為…）感覺混亂
· get mixed up with...
和…鬼混
· get mixed up in...
牽連進（非法事件）

困惑 因為對方的話或碰上的狀況而感到混亂、無法理解。

● The menu has so many choices that I'**m confused**!
● I know, but nothing appeals to me today.
● 這菜單上有太多選擇，我覺得很混亂！
● 我知道，但今天沒有一樣菜吸引我。

▶ I was confused by the signs on the road.
路上的標誌讓我覺得很困惑。
She was confused when she visited Tokyo.
她去東京旅行時，覺得很困惑。

lose one's head

· be at a loss (for words)
不知所措（啞口無言）
· get tongue-tied
啞口無言

失去理智，驚慌失措 在緊迫的狀況下，失去了冷靜，不知所措的樣子。

● How did Jenny lose all of her money?
● She **lost her head** while gambling in a casino.
● Jenny 怎麼輸掉她所有錢的？　● 她在賭場賭博時，失去了理智。

▶ George lost his head when his wife left him.
當 George 的太太離開他時，他驚慌失措。
I lost my head when I saw the new sports car.
我看到那台新的跑車就興奮得昏頭了。

feel/get weird

· give A a weird look
奇怪地看了 A 一眼

覺得怪 感覺和正常的情況不太一樣。

● Ray, what's the matter with you?
● My stomach **feels weird**. I think I'm getting sick.

● Ray，你是怎麼了？　●我的胃怪怪的，我想我快生病了。

▶ It felt weird to leave school in the morning.
早上就離開學校感覺好怪。
Don't you think it's going to be weird?
你不覺得這樣會有點怪嗎？

be funny

· the funny thing
可笑的事，奇怪的事

奇怪 雖然 fun 是有趣的意思，但 funny 常常表示「奇怪」或「可笑」。

● The flavor of this food **is funny**.
● Maybe it needs to be thrown out.

● 這食物的味道怪怪的。　●也許這該扔掉了。

▶ Your new suit looks funny on you.
這套新西裝穿在你身上看起來很怪。
It smells funny in the kitchen today.
今天的廚房聞起來很怪。

---

09 | 不安，焦躁
be nervous

7-09.mp3

be nervous

· be nervous about
N/-ing
對…感到緊張
· get nervous
變得緊張
· seem/look nervous
看起來緊張

緊張 失去了平常心，覺得擔心或不安。

● He **seems nervous**. What's wrong?
● He's had a lot of stress lately.

● 他看起來很緊張。怎麼回事？　●他最近壓力很大。

▶ I got so nervous that I was not able to talk then.
我那時候太緊張，講不出話來。
I remember how nervous I was for my first interview.
我記得我第一次面試時有多緊張。

feel uneasy

覺得不安 因為 be anxious 或 nervous 而感覺不安。

- Is Jim prepared to go to South America?
- No. he **feels uneasy** about leaving his family and friends.
  - Jim 準備好要去南美洲了嗎?
  - 還沒，他對於要離開家人和朋友們覺得很不安。

▶ Everyone was uneasy when they heard the shouting.
  每個人聽到那個叫聲，都覺得很不安。
  The bad economy made many people uneasy.
  經濟不景氣讓許多人感到不安。

be on edge

擔心，不安 on edge 是指硬幣等薄型物體只靠邊緣豎立的樣子，用這種不安定的感覺來比喻精神上的不安。

- Gary **has been on edge** recently.
- I heard he's about to be fired.
  - Gary 最近很不安。 - 我聽說他快被炒魷魚了。

▶ My girlfriend's complaints put me on edge.
  我女朋友的抱怨讓我坐立不安。
  We have all felt on edge tonight.
  我們今晚都很焦躁。

pace around

- pace up and down
  踱來踱去
- pace the floor
  在室內踱來踱去

踱來踱去 很專心思考某件事時，走來走去繞圈子的樣子。

- Why **is** your mom **pacing around**?
- My sister is late coming home tonight.
  - 你媽媽為什麼走來走去的? - 我妹妹今天晚上晚回家。

▶ Jane started to pace around wondering what to do.
  Jane 開始來回踱步，思考該怎麼做。
  My father got nervous and got up to pace around.
  我父親感到緊張，開始起身踱步。

fret about

- begin to fret
  開始發愁
- Don't fret about...
  別為…發愁

為…發愁 無意義地不停擔心、不安的樣子。

- Do you think the students will like me?
- Don't **fret about** it. They'll love you.
  - 你覺得學生會喜歡我嗎? - 別為這種事苦惱。他們會很喜歡你的。

▶ Older people fret about small things.
  老人家們為小事發愁。
  The students fret about paying for school.
  學生們為了付學費而發愁。

1 職場・學校
2 電腦・網路
3 社交生活
4 日常生活
5 訊息・理解
6 想法・態度
7 情緒・狀況
8 行為舉止
9 時間地點・副詞片語

10 | 喜歡，討厭
like to

7-10.mp3

like to

· like+N
  喜歡…
· dislike+N
  不喜歡…

喜歡做… would like to 是當時想做的事，like to 則是長期維持不變的偏好。

● What do you do on Saturdays?
● I stay at home. I **like to** watch soccer games.
  ●你星期六都做些什麼？ ●我待在家裡。我喜歡看足球比賽。

▶ I like to jog in the morning. 我喜歡在早上慢跑。
  I like to get outdoors too. 我也喜歡到戶外。

be fond of

· be quite fond of
  N/-ing
  很喜歡…
· be one's favorite+N
  是某人最喜歡的…

喜歡… 非常喜歡，或是從很久前就一直喜歡到現在的東西。

● I'm **fond of** having a big breakfast.
● You should invite me over sometime.
  ●我喜歡吃豐盛的早餐。 ●你改天應該邀請我作客。

▶ Picasso was fond of visiting Paris. 畢卡索喜歡拜訪巴黎。
  This is my favorite place in the whole world.
  這裡是全世界我最喜歡的地方。

be a big fan of

· be such a fan of
  很喜歡…
· I'm not fan of
  我不喜歡…
· I've been fan of
  我一直很喜歡…

是熱愛…的人 fan 除了指歌迷、影迷以外，也可以指喜歡某種食物或事物的人。

● I'm **a big fan of** Justin Beiber.
● Really? I've never heard of him.
  ●我是 Justin Beiber 的忠實歌迷。 ●真的嗎？我從來沒聽過他。

▶ He's not a big fan of fried foods. 他不怎麼喜歡油炸食物。
  We are big fans of our local football team.
  我們是我們本地足球隊的超級球迷。

hate to

· hate N/-ing
  討厭…
· hate it when S+V
  討厭…
· hate A for N/-ing
  因為…討厭 A

討厭做… 比 do not like 或 dislike 更強烈的討厭。

● I **hate to** disturb you, but this is important.
● What seems to be the problem?
  ●我很不想打擾你，但這很重要。 ●發生什麼事了嗎？

▶ I hate you and that's why I'm leaving.
  我討厭你，所以我要離開了。
  I hate spending my time in the house.
  我討厭浪費時間待在家裡。

1 職場・學校
2 電腦・網路
3 社交生活
4 日常生活
5 訊息・理解
6 想法・態度
7 情緒・狀況
8 行為舉止
9 時間地點・副詞片語

prefer + N/-ing

· prefer to do
更喜歡做…

· prefer A to B
比起 B 更喜歡 A

· prefer A rather than B
比起 B 寧可選擇 A

更喜歡…，偏好… 就是 like...better 的意思。接比較對象的時候，要加上 to 或 rather than。

● Why are you always here in the library?
● I **prefer** studying **rather** than going out.
　●你為什麼總是在圖書館這裡？　●比起出門，我更喜歡讀書。

▶ I prefer indoor sports to outdoor ones.
比起戶外運動，我更喜歡室內運動。
I prefer to be alone. Please leave.
我想要一個人待著，請你離開。

---

11 | 驚訝
be surprised at

7-11.mp3

be surprised at

· be surprised that S+V
驚訝於…

· be surprised to see/
hear...
驚訝地看／聽到…

· It's (not) surprising
S+V
…（不）令人驚訝

驚訝於… surprised 是「感到驚訝的」，surprising 是「令人驚訝的」。

● Many people came to our rally today.
● Yeah, I'm **surprised by** how many are here.
　●今天有很多人來參加我們的集會。
　●是啊，我很驚訝這邊到底有多少人啊。

▶ He was surprised at Sarah's anger. 他被 Sarah 的怒氣嚇到了。
Don't be surprised by the strange costumes.
別被這些奇怪的裝扮嚇到了。

in/with surprise

· (much) to one's
surprise
使某人（非常）吃驚地

驚訝地 接在動詞後面作為修飾。這裡的 surprise 是名詞「驚訝」。

● What did you do when Brian showed up?
● I just looked at him **in surprise**.
　●Brian 出現的時候你做了什麼？　●我就驚訝地看著他。

▶ Jerry yelled in surprise when he saw the bear.
Jerry 看到熊的時候驚慌地大叫。
I dropped my package in surprise.
我嚇得掉了包裹。

take sb by surprise

- be taken by surprise
  吃驚，詫異
- have/get a surprise
  (for you)
  （為你）準備一場驚喜

嚇某人一跳 也有「向對方發動奇襲」或是「突然逮捕」的意思。take 可以換成 catch。

- So, did you know about the party?
- No, it **caught me by surprise**.
  - 所以，你知道派對的事嗎？　● 不知道，我很意外。

▶ The war caught many citizens by surprise.
  這場戰爭讓許多市民都很詫異。
  His marriage proposal caught Belinda by surprise.
  他的求婚讓 Belinda 嚇了一跳。

be shocked at/by

- be/look amazed at/by
  對…感到驚訝
- be astonished at/by
  對…感到非常驚訝

對…感到震驚 驚嚇的程度比 surprised 大得多。

- I **was shocked at** how much you ate.
- Well, I hadn't eaten all day.
  - 我被你的食量嚇壞了。　● 嗯，我一整天沒吃東西了嘛。

▶ In the 1960s, some people were shocked by mini skirts.
  在 60 年代，有些人對迷你裙感到震驚。
  My parents were shocked by my cell phone bill.
  我爸媽被我的手機帳單嚇了一大跳。

I can't believe

- It's hard to believe
  S+V
  很難相信…
- blow one's mind
  令某人震驚，令某人興奮

我不敢相信… 非常驚訝、很難接受是事實的意思。

- I **can't believe** they didn't give us a raise.
- I guess we'll all be on strike tomorrow.
  - 真不敢相信他們沒有加我們的薪。　● 我想明天我們都會去罷工。

▶ I can't believe Mom slapped me in the face.
  我不敢相信媽媽打了我一巴掌。
  I can't believe that she treated me that way.
  我不敢相信她竟然那樣對我。

1 職場・學校
2 電腦・網路
3 社交生活
4 日常生活
5 訊息・理解
6 想法・態度
7 情緒・狀況
8 行為舉止
9 時間地點・副詞片語

12 失望 let down

7-12.mp3

be disappointed in

- be disappointed about/at/with
  對…失望
- be disappointed to hear/see
  很失望聽到／看到…
- be disappointed that S+V
  失望於…

對…失望 除了 in 以外，介系詞也可以用 about, at 或 with。

- How would you like it if I decided to quit?
- Well, I'd **be very disappointed**.
  ●如果我決定辭職的話，你會覺得怎樣？　●嗯，我會非常失望。

▶ I was disappointed in the movie's ending.
  我對這部電影的結局失望。
  They were disappointed in their honeymoon.
  他們對蜜月旅行感到失望。

let sb down

- get sb down
  讓某人失望

讓某人失望 被動態則是 sb be let down，表示「失望」。

- Why are you so angry?
- You **let me down**. I thought I could trust you.
  ●你為什麼那麼生氣？　●你讓我失望了。我以為我可以相信你的。

▶ She let the group down when she was absent.
  她的缺席讓那個團體失望了。
  You have to work hard. Don't let me down.
  你得認真做，別讓我失望。

be a little down

- feel/seem a little down
  感覺／看起來有點沮喪

有點沮喪 be 也可以改成 feel 或 seem 等動詞。

- Why do you look so gloomy today?
- I've **been a little down** since summer ended.
  ●你今天看起來怎麼那麼憂鬱？　●夏天結束後我就一直有點沮喪。

▶ Shawn was a little down after losing the contest.
  Shawn 輸掉那場比賽後有點沮喪。
  The basketball team is a little down because they didn't win.
  那支籃球隊因為沒贏球而有點意志消沉。

511

be a shame to

· It's a shame to do/
  that...
  做…很可惜
· What a shame S+V
  …很可惜
· What a shame!
  太可惜了！

做…很可惜 Shame on you! 則是很嚴重地指責對方「你真可恥！」「不要臉！」的意思。

- Tony crashed her car and is in the hospital.
- **What a shame!**
  - Tony 撞壞了她的車，現在在醫院。　●太遺憾了！

▶ It's a shame to waste all of that food.
  浪費那些食物真是太可惜了。
  What a shame you got here too late.
  你太晚來了，真可惜。

lose heart

· be discouraged
  = lose heart
  灰心，沮喪

失去勇氣或自信 用 heart 比喻信心，表示開始不相信能成功。

- So Patty's marriage is going badly?
- Yeah, she's beginning to **lose heart** in it.
  - 所以 Patty 的婚姻狀況很差嗎？
  - 是啊，她開始對婚姻失去信心了。

▶ They lost heart in the project.
  他們對這個計畫失去了自信。
  I lost heart after hearing the bad news.
  聽了那個壞消息，我覺得很沮喪。

---

13 | 慰問，同情 take pity on

7-13.mp3

it's too bad that...

· That's too bad.
  真可惜。

真可惜… that 後面接 S+V。也可以只說 Too bad. 回應別人說的壞消息。

- We lost a lot of money last year.
- **That's too bad.** Did you buy stocks?
  - 我們去年損失了很多錢。　●太可惜了。你們買了股票嗎？

▶ It's too bad you lost the contest.
  真可惜你輸了比賽。
  It's too bad you didn't join us for dinner on Friday.
  星期五你沒跟我們一起吃晚餐，真是可惜。

take pity on

- It's a pity to do/that...
  …很可惜
- What/That's a pity!
  太可惜了！
- pity sb
  憐憫某人，同情某人

憐憫… on 後面接人。也可以說 feel pity for...。

- How did you get home from the party?
- Someone **took pity on** me and gave me a ride.

  ●你派對後怎麼回家的？　●有人可憐我，順道載我回家。

▶ I take pity on poor people in my neighborhood.
  我很同情我家附近的窮人。

  Take pity on the students who are failing.
  要同情不及格的學生。

have compassion for

- take/feel compassion for
  同情…
- show compassion
  表示同情
- be/feel compassionate for
  同情…

同情… compassion 的意義比較正面，形容詞 pathetic（可憐的）則經常會帶點瞧不起的感覺。

- You **have compassion for** animals.
- Yes, I try to help them when they are hurt.

  ●你對動物很有同情心。
  ●是啊，當牠們受傷時，我會努力幫助牠們。

▶ Mother Teresa had compassion for all people.
  德雷莎修女對所有人都抱持著同情心。

  Do you have compassion for the people you fight?
  你同情跟你打架的人嗎？

have sympathy for

- feel (a lot of) sympathy for
  （十分）同情…
- have no sympathy for
  不同情…
- convey/express one's sympathy for
  對…表示同情

同情… 表示對於別人的困境感同身受。

- I don't **have sympathy for** fat people.
- I know. They should go on a diet.

  ●我不同情胖子。　●我知道。他們應該減肥。

▶ She felt sympathy for her younger sister.
  她很同情她的妹妹。

  I feel sympathy for the newest students.
  我對新來的學生感到同情。

one's heart goes out to

- let one's heart go out to
  對…表示同情

對…心有戚戚焉 用 heart 比喻感情，好像能設身處地為他人著想一樣。

- There were many people killed in the flood.
- **My heart goes out to** the people that survived.

  ●許多人在這場洪水中去世。　●我很同情那些倖存者。

▶ Our heart goes out to you in this difficult time.
  在這困難的時期，我們很同情你們。

  My heart went out to my aunt after her accident.
  我對出了意外的姑姑深感同情。

1 職場・學校
2 電腦・網路
3 社交生活
4 日常生活
5 訊息・理解
6 想法・態度
7 情緒・狀況
8 行為舉止
9 時間地點・副詞片語

14 害怕
be afraid of

be afraid of

- be afraid of N/-ing
  害怕…
- be afraid to do
  害怕做…
- be afraid that...
  擔心…（在說不好的消息時，常常會說 I'm afraid...）

害怕… 因為有過不好的經驗，或者情況可能不利而感到害怕。
- I'm **afraid of** the dog in my neighbor's yard.
- It looks very big, and I think it's angry too.
  - 我怕我鄰居院子裡的那隻狗。
  - 牠看起來很大，而且我覺得牠好像在生氣。

▶ I'm afraid to be alone at night.
  我害怕晚上一個人獨處。
  Jim is afraid to ask her on a date.
  Jim 不敢約她去約會。

have a fear of

- be full of fear
  充滿恐懼
- one's fear of
  某人對…的恐懼
- fear that S+V
  害怕…，擔心…

害怕… 也可以用 fear 的形容詞形，說 be fearful of...。
- What is your greatest phobia?
- I guess it would **be my fear of** heights.
  - 你最害怕的是什麼？　● 我想是懼高症吧。

▶ Chris has a fear of large spiders.
  Chris 很怕大蜘蛛。
  I had a fear of speaking to large groups of people.
  我很怕在一大群人面前說話。

for fear of +N

- for fear that S+V
  因為害怕…
- in fear (of)
  因為害怕…
- without fear (of)
  不怕…

因為害怕… 也可以用 for fear that S+V 的句型。
- Why didn't you come out in the boat?
- I couldn't, **for fear of** the boat sinking.
  - 你為什麼不來船艙外面？　● 我沒辦法，因為怕船會沉。

▶ He wouldn't come outside for fear of insects biting him.
  因為怕蟲子會咬他，所以他不出來外面。
  She didn't bring money for fear of thieves stealing it.
  她沒帶錢，因為怕小偷會偷走。

dread -ing

· dread A -ing
  害怕 A 做…
· dread that S+V
  害怕…
· be dreadful
  害怕

懼怕…，擔心… 擔心好像會發生什麼事的樣子。dread 也可以接名詞當受詞。

● Are you coming on the skiing trip?
● No, I **dread** snow falling on me.
  ●你要來參加滑雪之旅嗎？　●不，我怕雪會把我給埋了。

▶ I'm beginning to dread teachers giving tests.
  我開始害怕老師要考試。
  She dreads her friends seeing her ugly clothes.
  她怕朋友們看到她醜陋的衣服。

be frightened of

· be frightened to do
  害怕做…
· be frightened that S+V
  害怕…

害怕… be frightened at 則是「受到…的驚嚇」。

● I **am frightened of** meeting new people.
● That makes it hard for you to travel.
  ●我害怕認識新的人。　●那你很難去旅行了。

▶ He was frightened by strange noises in the room.
  他被房間裡奇怪的噪音嚇到。
  Children are frightened of ghost stories.
  孩子們害怕鬼故事。

be/get scared of

· be scared to do/
  that S+V
  害怕做…／害怕…
· be scared to death
  怕得要死

害怕… 口語說法，把 scared 當成 afraid 來用。

● I **am scared of** gangsters.
● They can be very violent.
  ●我怕流氓。　●他們可能會很暴力。

▶ The baby is scared to sleep in the dark.
  這個嬰兒害怕在黑暗中睡覺。
  I am scared of flying on airplanes.
  我怕搭飛機。

scare the hell out of

· scare A into -ing
  嚇得 A 去做…
· scare A off/away
  把 A 嚇跑

把…嚇得要死 用 the hell 表示程度非常嚴重，是口語的說法。

● Did you hear the explosion yesterday?
● Yes! It **scared the hell out of** me.
  ●你昨天有聽到爆炸聲嗎？　●有！嚇死我了。

▶ Those soldiers scared the hell out of everyone.
  那些軍人把每個人都嚇壞了。
  The car accident scared the hell out of Sandra.
  那場車禍把 Sandra 嚇壞了。

1 職場・學校
2 電腦・網路
3 社交生活
4 日常生活
5 訊息・理解
6 想法・態度
7 情緒・狀況
8 行為舉止
9 時間地點・副詞片語

be terrified of

- be terrified to do/ that S+V
  非常害怕…
- be chicken = be afraid
  膽小
- be a chicken = be a person who is afraid
  是個膽小鬼
- in a panic
  驚慌（失去理智、驚慌失措的樣子）

非常害怕… of 後面可以接名詞或動詞 -ing 形。

- Why did your daughter start crying?
- She **was terrified of** large dogs.
  - 你女兒為什麼哭了起來？   她很怕大狗。

▶ My girlfriend is terrified of scary movies.
  我女朋友很怕恐怖片。
  People are terrified of losing their jobs.
  人們害怕丟掉工作。

be spooky

- It is spooky how S+V
  …很令人毛骨悚然
- a creepy ghost story
  令人毛骨悚然的鬼故事

好像有鬼，令人毛骨悚然 因為科學上無法解釋的情況或氣氛而感到害怕。

- Have you seen the old house in the neighborhood?
- It's on my street. Everyone thinks it**'s spooky**.
  - 你看過這附近那間老房子嗎？
  - 就在我那條街上。每個人都覺得那間房子令人毛骨悚然。

▶ The ghost story was very spooky.
  那則鬼故事很恐怖。
  The photos from a hundred years ago are spooky.
  那些一百年前的照片讓人毛骨悚然。

---

15 厭倦
be sick of

7-15.mp3

be sick of

- be tired/sick of N/-ing
  對…厭倦

厭倦…，受夠了… 這裡的 sick 不是生病的意思，而是對某個一直反覆、持續的事物感覺煩了。

- I'm **really getting sick of** winter.
- I don't like winter all that much myself.
  - 我真的受夠冬天了。   我自己也不是那麼喜歡冬天。

▶ You said you were sick of this. 你說你受夠這些了。
  I'm sick of her lies. 我受夠了她的謊言。

be fed up with

- be/get fed up with N/-ing
  受夠了…，對…厭煩
- be sick and tired of
  對…厭倦

受夠了… fed 是 feed 的過去分詞，字面上的意思就是「被餵飽了」。

- I'm **fed up with** the food in this cafeteria.
- It really needs to be improved.
  ● 我受夠這間自助餐廳的食物了。　● 這裡真的需要改進。

▶ Everyone is fed up with the freezing temperatures.
  每個人都受夠了寒冷的溫度。
  Lisa is fed up with her noisy neighbors.
  Lisa 受夠了她吵鬧的鄰居。

be/get bored

- be/get bored with
  對…感到厭煩／無聊
- be bored to death/ tears
  覺得無聊得要死
- be/seem/get boring to sb
  …對某人而言很無聊

覺得厭煩 bore 是及物動詞「使厭煩」，bored 就是「覺得厭煩的」，boring 則是「令人厭煩的」。bore 也可以解釋成「使人無聊」的意思。

- Why did Jason quit the chess club?
- He **was bored** with going to their meetings.
  ● Jason 為什麼退出西洋棋社了？
  ● 他對參加他們的會議感到厭煩了。

▶ I am bored of waiting for you to finish.
  我對於要等你完成覺得厭煩了。
  Kim got bored during the long bus ride.
  Kim 對漫長的公車車程感到無聊。

have had enough

- have had enough of
  受夠了…，無法再忍受…

受夠了，無法再忍受 討厭到簡直要發火，希望某個狀況快點結束的意思。

- I **have had enough** of that dog barking.
- Can someone make it be quiet?
  ● 我真的受夠那隻狗叫個不停了。　● 有人可以讓牠安靜點嗎？

▶ They have had enough of the high rent here.
  他們受夠了這裡昂貴的房租。
  We have had enough of this old computer.
  我們受夠這台老電腦了。

have had it with

- have had it up to here with
  真的已經受夠了…
- have had it
  忍無可忍，受夠了
- be in a rut
  處於一成不變的無聊情況

受夠了…，無法再忍受… 表示忍耐已經到了極限，拒絕再繼續下去了。

- Hey, John. I **have had it with** this job.
- Well, now is the time for you to change your career.
  ● 嘿，John，我真受夠這份工作了。　● 嗯，現在是你轉職的時機了。

▶ Everyone seems to have had it with you.
  每個人似乎都受夠你了。
  I have had it with this monotonous work.
  我受夠這份單調的工作了。

1 職場・學校
2 電腦・網路
3 社交生活
4 日常生活
5 訊息・理解
6 想法・態度
7 情緒・狀況
8 行為舉止
9 時間地點・副詞片語

16 害羞，丟臉
be ashamed of

7-16.mp3

be too shy to

- be shy of/about -ing
  因為有顧慮而不敢做…
- be shy of+N
  …不足

太害羞而無法做… 在某人面前感到害羞則是 be shy with sb。

● Is Melissa going to sing for the crowd?
● No, she **is too shy to** do that.
　●Melissa 會為大家唱歌嗎？　●不會，她太害羞不能唱。

▶ I was too shy to accept a date with him.
　我太害羞，沒辦法答應跟他約會。
　The children are too shy to talk to me.
　孩子們太害羞，不敢跟我說話。

be ashamed of

- be ashamed to do
  太羞愧而無法做…
- be ashamed of
  oneself for
  因為…感到難為情
- have nothing to be
  ashamed of
  沒有任何需要感到羞愧的
  事

對…感到羞愧 因為自己或別人的行為而感到羞愧、丟臉。

● You should **be ashamed of** cheating on your exam.
● What's the big deal? A lot of students do it.
　●你應該對考試作弊感到羞愧。
　●有什麼大不了的？很多學生都這麼做。

▶ You stole the money. I'm ashamed of you.
　你偷了錢。我真為你感到羞恥。
　I am ashamed of the problems I created.
　我對自己製造出來的問題感到羞愧。

be/feel humiliated

- humiliate A in front of
  在…的面前羞辱 A

被羞辱，丟臉 被別人侮辱，或遇上丟臉的狀況。

● So, your boyfriend was seeing other women?
● It's true. I **feel humiliated** now.
　●所以，你男朋友有跟其他女人見面？
　●是真的。我現在覺得好受辱。

▶ The team felt humiliated after losing the game.
　這個隊伍輸了比賽，覺得很丟臉。
　I felt humiliated that I failed the exam.
　我考試不及格，覺得很丟臉。

1 職場・學校

2 電腦・網路

3 社交生活

4 日常生活

5 訊息・理解

6 想法・態度

7 情緒・狀況

8 行為舉止

9 時間地點・副詞片語

lose face

· save face
保住顏面

失去面子，丟臉 反義的說法則是 keep one's face。

● I don't want to fight Frank.

● You have to, or else you'll **lose face**.

●我不想跟 Frank 爭吵。 ●你必須這麼做，不然你會丟臉的。

▶ It's bad to lose face in front of friends.
在朋友面前丟了面子很糟。
She lost face when she couldn't pay the money she owed. 她因為還不出她欠的錢而丟了面子。

shame on

· For shame!
真可恥！不要臉！

⋯真可恥 表示某人的行為很可恥、很不要臉。

● I stole this paper from the school.

● **Shame on** you! You know it's wrong to steal.

●我從學校偷了這張考卷。 ●你真可恥！你知道偷東西是不對的。

▶ Shame on everyone for not helping the blind girl!
每個沒幫忙那位盲女的人，都太可恥了！
Shame on you! You shouldn't be taking things from children. 你真不要臉！你不應該拿走小孩子的東西。

17 尊敬
think highly of

7-17.mp3

respect sb for

· be (well) respected (+N)
是（很）受尊敬的（⋯）
· show sb some respect
對某人表示尊敬
· have respect for
尊敬⋯

因為⋯而尊敬某人 for 後面接名詞或動詞 -ing 形。

● What do the employees think of the new boss?

● They **respect** him and are always working hard.

●職員對那位新老闆有什麼想法？
●他們很尊敬他，而且他們總是認真工作。

▶ People respect Marines for being so tough.
人們尊敬 Marines 的不屈不撓。
I respect him for being so smart.
我尊敬他，因為他很聰明。

admire sb for

- be admired for N/-ing
因為…受到敬佩
- be an admirer of...
敬佩…
- be revered
受尊崇

因為…而敬佩某人 對某人優秀的行為懷抱敬意。

- They plan to go bungee jumping.
- I **admire them for** their courage.

  ●他們打算去玩高空彈跳。　●我敬佩他們的勇氣。

▶ People admire Bill Gates for donating so much money.
人們很敬佩比爾・蓋茲，因為他捐贈了許多錢。
I admire my dad for working so hard.
我尊敬父親這麼賣力工作。

look up to

- look up to sb for
因為…而尊敬某人
- look down on
輕視…

尊敬… 用向上看的動作比喻很景仰某人。

- Did you talk with your grandfather?
- I did. I **look up to** him for advice.

  ●你跟你爺爺談過了嗎？　●有，我尊敬地向他請教。

▶ She looks up to her older sister.
她尊敬她的姊姊。
Tim looks up to his teachers at school.
Tim 尊敬學校的老師。

think highly of

- think a lot of A
看重 A

重視…，推崇… highly 前面可以加 so, very 等副詞來強調。

- Richard seems to be very popular here.
- Everyone **thinks highly of** him.

  ●Richard 在這裡似乎很受歡迎。　●每個人都很推崇他。

▶ The chef thinks highly of chocolate cake.
主廚很重視巧克力蛋糕。
I think highly of BMW motorcycles.
我很推崇 BMW 的摩托車。

hold A in high esteem

- be held in high
esteem
很受到尊敬
- have low self-esteem
自尊心低

很尊敬 A 是比較 formal 的說法。esteem 是名詞「尊重，尊敬」。

- Why was Barrack Obama elected the President?
- Many people **hold him in very high esteem**.

  ●歐巴馬為什麼當選了總統？　●很多人非常尊敬他。

▶ The citizens held the war hero in very high esteem.
市民們都十分尊敬那位戰爭英雄。
My friends hold me in very high esteem.
我朋友們都很尊重我。

18 引以為傲
be proud of

7-18.mp3

be proud of

- be proud to do
  做…感覺很驕傲

以…為傲 如果要說對某件事感到驕傲，可以說 be proud that S+V。

- I got the highest score in the class!
- Way to go! I'm so proud of you.
  - 我在班上考了最高分！ ● 做得好！我真為你感到驕傲。

▶ I'm so proud of your recent promotion. Here's to you!
  你最近升職，讓我引以為傲。這杯敬你！
  I'm proud of you all. You make me proud.
  我為你們所有人感到驕傲。你們讓我覺得很自豪。

take pride in

- pride oneself on N/-ing
  以…為傲
- be the pride of
  是…之光／…之寶

以…為傲 = feel proud of。pride（驕傲）是 proud（驕傲的）的名詞形。

- Wow, your house is really beautiful.
- I take pride in decorating it nicely.
  - 哇，你的房子真的很美。 ● 我很自豪把房子布置得那麼好。

▶ Cecil took pride in painting the picture.
  Cecil 很自豪畫了那幅畫。
  We pride ourselves on customer satisfaction here at Bloomingdale's.
  我們 Bloomingdale 百貨公司對於自己的高顧客滿意度很自豪。

have some pride

- have a lot of pride
  很驕傲
- have a sense of pride in
  對…感到驕傲

有點自尊 這裡的 pride 是自尊心的意思。用在不做某事以免自尊受損的情況。

- Why don't you just call her?
- I can't call her, I left a message! I have some pride.
  - 你為什麼不乾脆打電話給她呢？
  - 我不能打給她，我留了言！我也有點自尊的。

▶ She can't ask him out. She has some pride.
  她不能約他出去。她是有自尊的。
  I won't apologize again. I have some pride.
  我不會再道歉。我也有自尊。

1 職場・學校

2 電腦・網路

3 社交生活

4 日常生活

5 訊息・理解

6 想法・態度

7 情緒・狀況

8 行為舉止

9 時間地點・副詞片語

521

show A off

- make a boast of
  吹噓…
- boast about/of/that...
  吹噓…
- brag about/that...
  吹噓…
- talk big
  吹牛，說大話

炫耀 A 要表示「吹噓」的話，可以說 boast/brag about，請一併熟記。

- Where is Anna tonight?
- She went out to **show** her new car **off**.
  - Anna 今晚去哪裡了？　　● 她出去炫耀她的新車了。

▶ I wanted to show my high grades off.
  我想炫耀我的好成績。
  Did you show your diamond ring off?
  你炫耀你的鑽戒了嗎？（你戴鑽戒給大家看了嗎？）

---

19 被感動
be impressed by

7-19.mp3

be impressed by

- be impressed by/with
  對…印象深刻
- make a deep
  impression on
  使…深深感動
- impressive+N
  令人印象深刻的…

對…印象深刻 impress A with B 則是「用 B 使 A 印象深刻」。

- I'm **impressed with** your hard work.
- Really? Do you think I'm ready for a promotion?
  - 我對你的努力印象深刻。　　● 真的嗎？你覺得我有資格升職了嗎？

▶ I'm impressed with the amount of money you made.
  我對你所賺的金額印象深刻。
  You did a good job! I was very impressed.
  你做得真好！我印象非常深刻。

make an impression upon

- leave an impression of
  給人…的印象
- be under the
  impression (that)
  原以為…

在…心中留下印象 impression 前面可以加上 deep, good, bad 等形容詞修飾。

- Who is your role model as a Christian?
- Mother Teresa **left a lasting impression on** all the Christians.
  - 身為基督教徒，誰是你的模範？
  - 德雷莎修女在所有基督教徒的心中留下了長久的印象。

▶ It was a performance that is sure to make an impression on the judges. 那是個絕對會讓評審們留下印象的表演。
  I was under the impression you had been here before.
  我還以為你來過這裡。

be moved at/by

· move A to tears
  使 A 感動得流下眼淚

被…感動 也可以說 be deeply moved 強調非常感動。

● Did you listen to the president speaking?

● We **were all moved by** what he said.

　●你聽過總裁演說了嗎？　●我們都被他所說的感動了。

▶ Tim was moved by the sad little girl.
　Tim 為那位傷心的小女孩動容。
　I was moved by the ending of the movie.
　我為電影的結局而感動。

be touched by

· be touched that S+V
  因為…而感動
· touching+N
  令人感動的…

被…感動 跟 moved 比起來，touched 帶有「細微地觸動感情」的感性語調。

● Everyone **was touched by** the poem.

● It was so beautifully written.

　●每個人都被那首詩感動了。　●那真的寫得很美。

▶ She was touched by the starving people in Africa.
　她對非洲飢餓的人們充滿了感觸。
　Young people are often touched by Michael Jackson's songs. 年輕人們常為麥可‧傑克森的歌感動。

be affected by

· be affected by the heat
  中暑

被…影響，被…感動，被…感染 affect 除了「影響」以外，也有「使感動」的意思。affection 是「感情」的意思。

● I heard your kids are all at home today.

● They **were affected by** the flu this week.

　●我聽說你孩子今天都在家裡。　●他們這星期得了流感。

▶ My job was affected by the economy.
　我的工作被經濟狀況影響了。
　I was affected by my boss's angry mood.
　我被老闆生氣的情緒給影響了。

1 職場‧學校
2 電腦‧網路
3 社交生活
4 日常生活
5 訊息‧理解
6 想法‧態度
7 情緒‧狀況
8 行為舉止
9 時間地點‧副詞片語

20 瘋了，失去理智
be out of one's mind

7-20.mp3

---

be out of one's mind

- go out of one's mind
  發瘋，精神失常
- lose one's mind
  失去理智，驚慌失措
- » cf. lose one's head
  發瘋（「變得瘋了」的意思，be out of one's mind 則是瘋了的狀態）

瘋了，失去理智 Are you out of your mind? 這句話在日常生活中特別常用。

- John is wearing a T-shirt in the snowstorm.
- I can't believe it. He must **be out of his mind**.
  - John 在暴風雪中只穿一件 T 恤。　●真不敢相信，他一定是瘋了。

▶ You are out of your mind to date her.
  你跟她約會真是瘋了。
  The customer was out of her mind to pay such a high price. 那位客人付那麼多錢真是瘋了。

---

be crazy/mad

- be crazy to do
  瘋了去做…
- drive sb crazy
  讓某人發瘋
- be crazy about
  為…瘋狂（非常喜愛的意思）

瘋狂 go crazy 是「發瘋」的意思。至於 go mad，雖然也可以指發瘋，但通常是「發怒」的意思。

- The World Cup fans spent thousands of dollars to attend.
- They **are crazy** to spend that much money.
  - 世界盃球迷花了上千美元去看比賽。　●他們花那麼多錢真是瘋狂。

▶ The old woman down the street was crazy.
  街尾那位老太太是個瘋子。
  You're crazy if you don't plan your future.
  你如果不為未來做計畫就是瘋了。

---

be nuts

- drive sb nuts
  讓…發瘋
- be nuts about/over
  為…瘋狂
- nuthouse
  精神病院（帶貶意的口語說法）

瘋狂 go nuts 跟 go crazy 一樣，是「發瘋」（變得瘋狂）的意思。

- Doesn't Rick **drive you nuts**?
- Sometimes he can be a little annoying.
  - Rick 不會讓你發火嗎？　●他有時候有點煩人。

▶ Carla is nuts for turning down the job.
  Carla 拒絕那份工作真是瘋了。
  The politicians in this country are nuts.
  這個國家的政客都是瘋子。

1 職場・學校

2 電腦・網路

3 社交生活

4 日常生活

5 訊息・理解

6 想法・態度

7 情緒・狀況

8 行為舉止

9 時間地點・副詞片語

be not oneself

· be not all there
精神不太正常

· I'm not myself today.
我今天狀況不好。

身體／心理狀況失常 用「不是自己」比喻狀況不好、感覺不正常。

● You have been very quiet this morning.

● I don't feel good. I'm **not myself**.

●你今天整個早上都好安靜。　●我不太舒服，我狀況不太好。

▶ Jim is not himself since coming back from the hospital.
Jim 從醫院回來之後，狀況一直不好。

I was drinking all night, and I'm not myself today.
我喝了一晚的酒，今天狀況不好。

be insane

精神錯亂 比 crazy 更嚴重，可能會發生危險的程度。

● After September 11, 2001, the world **went insane**.

● Yeah, there was too much fighting.

●911 事件之後，整個世界都失控了。　●是啊，發生太多鬥爭了。

▶ All of this work will make me go insane.
這全部的工作會讓我發瘋。

She will be insane if she doesn't take some time off.
她如果不休息一下，會發瘋的。

---

21 壓力
have a lot of stress

7-21.mp3

have a lot of stress

· have too much stress
about
在…方面壓力太大

· get too much stress
得到太多壓力

壓力很大 也可以把 a lot of 換成 much。

● It's not fun to hang around with Barry.

● He **has a lot of stress** these days.

●跟 Barry 出去晃一點也不好玩。　●他最近壓力很大。

▶ She has a lot of stress in her classes.
她課堂上的壓力很大。

The soldiers at the border have a lot of stress.
國界上的士兵們壓力很大。

be under a lot of stress

· give sb stress
  給某人壓力
· die from too much stress
  因為壓力太大而過世

壓力很大 用介系詞 under「處在…的情況下」表示面臨壓力。

● Craig died when he was 49 years old.
● He **was always under a lot of stress**.
　●Craig 49 歲過世。　●他的壓力一直很大。

▶ I think you were just under a lot of stress this past month. 我想你過去這個月只是壓力太大了。
　She's been under a great deal of stress.
　她一直壓力很大。

cause too much stress

· caused by stress
  因為壓力引起的

引起太多壓力 後面可以加上 on 接承受壓力的人。

● I heard it's bad to live near an airport.
● The sound of jets **causes too much stress**.
　●我聽說住在機場附近不好。　●噴射機的聲音會引起過多的壓力。

▶ Working late every night causes too much stress.
　每天工作到很晚會引起過多壓力。
　The couple's fighting caused too much stress.
　那對夫妻吵架引起了很多壓力。

be/feel stressed about...

· get stressed
  變得有壓力
· look stressed
  看起來有壓力

對…感覺有壓力 about 後面接引起壓力的原因。

● Why does Tom **look so stressed**?
● He is afraid of ghosts and he thinks a ghost is here.
　●Tom 為什麼看起來壓力那麼大？　●他怕鬼,而且他覺得這邊有鬼。

▶ She is stressed about the blind date.
　她對聯誼感覺壓力很大。
　I am feeling so stressed these days.
　我最近覺得壓力很大。

be stressed out

· burnout
  因長期壓力造成的倦怠

壓力大到快受不了 口語中用 out 表示「完全」的意思,例如 burn out「燒光」、wipe out「消滅」、wash out「洗掉」等等。

● You **look stressed out**. What's wrong?
● I've got so much to do and I have to go now.
　●你看起來壓力很大。怎麼了？　●我有很多事要做,我該走了。

▶ Jill is stressed out from the conference.
　Jill 因為會議,壓力非常大。
　I guess you're a little stressed out right now.
　我想你現在壓力有點大。

have a stressful day

· get/be too stressful
變得太有壓力

· have been stressful
一直壓力很大

過了壓力很大的一天 也可以說「It's been a long day」表示因為很辛苦而感覺特別漫長。

- You look gloomy. Cheer up!
- I **had a really stressful day** at work.
  - 你看起來很陰沉，打起精神來！
  - 我今天一整天的工作壓力真的很大。

▶ It's been a really stressful day. I need to relax.
今天真的壓力好大，我需要放鬆。

Things have been getting too stressful.
狀況變得越來越緊張了。

reduce stress

· stress-related (+N)
與壓力相關的（…）

減少壓力 動詞 reduce 也可以換成 relieve（減緩）。

- What do you do to **reduce stress**?
- I like to exercise or practice yoga.
  - 你做什麼來消除壓力？ 我喜歡做運動或練瑜伽。

▶ It's important to find a way to reduce stress.
找到一個消除壓力的方法很重要。

My lifestyle is unhealthy and I need to reduce my stress.
我的生活方式很不健康，我需要消除壓力。

put pressure on

· be under (a lot of) pressure
受到（很大的）壓力

· have a lot of pressure at work
在工作上有很多壓力

給…壓力 用 under pressure「在壓力之下」的比喻來說，施加壓力的人就是把壓力「放在某人上面」。

- Tina **has a lot of pressure** at work.
- She seems so unhappy because of it.
  - Tina 在工作上有很多壓力。 因為這樣，她看起來很不快樂。

▶ Are your parents putting pressure on you to find a good job? 你的父母有給你壓力，要你去找個好工作嗎？

She works hard when she's under pressure.
她處於壓力下的時候，會努力工作。

place a strain on

· stresses and strains
壓力與緊張

· strain
身心的負擔或緊張狀態

給…負擔 strain 意為負擔、緊張。place 也可以換成 put。

- The kids **are putting a strain on** my money.
- Schools cost a lot of money to attend.
  - 孩子們造成我金錢上的負擔。 上學要花很多錢。

▶ The storm will put a strain on travelers.
暴風雪會造成旅行者的負擔。

The new rules put a strain on the workers.
新的規定造成了員工的負擔。

1 職場・學校
2 電腦・網路
3 社交生活
4 日常生活
5 訊息・理解
6 想法・態度
7 情緒・狀況
8 行為舉止
9 時間地點・副詞片語

22 沉著，冷靜
take it easy

7-22.mp3

keep cool

- stay/keep cool/calm
  保持冷靜
- keep a cool head
  保持冷靜

保持冷靜 不被興奮、焦躁等情感所影響的安定狀態。keep 可以換成 stay 或 be。

- Randy is always making me angry.
- **Keep cool.** Don't let him bother you.

　●Randy 總是讓我生氣。　●冷靜，別為他心煩。

▶ It's best to keep cool when you're in trouble.
　遇到困難時，最好的應對方式就是保持沉著。
　I kept cool when my boss visited my office.
　老闆來我辦公室的時候，我保持了冷靜。

calm down

- calm oneself down
  使情緒鎮定下來

鎮定，使鎮定 發脾氣後鎮定下來，或是使別人的情緒鎮定下來的意思。

- Some of my friends got really angry today.
- How long did it take them to **calm down**?

　●我有一些朋友今天非常生氣。　●他們花了多久的時間才冷靜下來？

▶ It was raining hard, but now it has calmed down.
　雨原本下得很大，現在已經停了。
　Look guys, try to calm down. OK?
　嘿，大家，試著冷靜點，好嗎？

take it easy

- take it easy = take
  things easy
- Easy does it
  慢慢來！小心！

別緊張，放輕鬆 在美國的口語中，也有「再見」的意思。

- I'm looking forward to getting to know you.
- **Take it easy.** We have a lot of time.

　●我期待可以更加認識你。　●別緊張，我們有很多時間。

▶ Take it easy when you're driving on the highway.
　在高速公路上開車時要放輕鬆。
　Just take it easy and try to relax.
　別緊張，試著放鬆。

1 職場・學校

2 電腦・網路

3 社交生活

4 日常生活

5 訊息・理解

6 想法・態度

7 情緒・狀況

8 行為舉止

9 時間地點・副詞片語

relax

· relax on the sofa
  在沙發上休息
· sit down and relax
  坐下休息
· lay on the bed and relax
  躺在床上休息

放鬆 也可以當及物動詞，表示「使某人放鬆」。

● What do you plan to do this weekend?
● I'm just planning to **relax**.

 ●你這週末打算做什麼？ ●我打算就放鬆休息。

▶ Relax while I put on some music.
  我放音樂時，放鬆休息一下吧。
  Please, come into the living room and relax.
  請進客廳休息一下。

be relieved

· be relieved to see/know
  看到／知道…很安心
· be relieved that S+V
  對…感到安心
· relieve one's pain
  減輕痛苦

放心了 沒有擔憂的輕鬆狀態。

● The test was postponed until next week.
● The students **were relieved** they don't have to study.

 ●考試延到下星期了。 ●學生們因為不用念書，鬆了一口氣。

▶ She was relieved that she didn't have cancer.
  知道自己沒有得癌症，她放心了。
  I'm relieved that I don't have to fly to LA.
  不用飛洛杉磯，讓我鬆了一口氣。

23 有同感 feel the same way

7-23.mp3

feel the same way

· feel the same way about sb/sth
  對於…有同感

有同感 要表明和誰有同感，可以在後面加上 as sb do。

● You're my best friend and I love you.
● I **feel the same way** about you, too.

 ●你是我最好的朋友，我愛你。 ●我對你也是這麼想。

▶ I hope that you feel the same way about me.
  我希望你也是這麼想我的。
  I'm sorry, I don't feel the same way about that.
  不好意思，我對那件事有不同感想。

likewise

同樣地 除了一般的副詞用法，在口語中也可以表示同意對方所說的話。

- I really enjoy walking in the park.
- **Likewise.** It's very relaxing here.

  ●我真的很喜歡在這座公園裡散步。　●我也是。這裡很令人放鬆。

▶ Shelly told me that she didn't feel likewise.

　Shelly 跟我說她沒有同感。

　Likewise, we also enjoy eating pizza.

　我們也一樣喜歡吃披薩。

be sympathetic to

· look sympathetic
  看起來同情

同情… 有「能夠理解對方陷於困境中的心情」的意思。

- Tim is back in the hospital.
- I **am sympathetic to** his situation.

  ●Tim 回到醫院了。　●我很同情他的處境。

▶ My brother looked sympathetic when I fell down.

　我跌倒時，我哥哥看起來很同情我。

　We were sympathetic to Glen's condition.

　我們很同情 Glen 的狀況。

feel for

· I feel for you
  我同情你
· feel one's pain
  感受到某人的痛苦

同情… for 後面接同情的對象。

- I **feel for** Stephanie.
- She can't find a good boyfriend.

  ●我同情 Stephanie。　●她找不到好的男朋友。

▶ That is too bad. I feel for you.

　真是太糟了，我很同情你。

　The president said he feels our pain.

　總裁說他能感受到我們的痛苦。

that makes two of us

· So do I.
  我也是。
· Me too.
  我也是。
· Neither can I.
  我也不能。

我也是 附和對方，表示自己的情況或想法也一樣。

- I'm tired and I want to go home.
- Yeah, **that makes two of us.**

  ●我累了，我想回家。　●嗯，我也是。

▶ You like this music? So do I.

　你喜歡這個音樂？我也是。

　I heard he collects stamps. Me too.

　我聽說他有在集郵。我也是。

24 沒問題，OK
be all right

7-24.mp3

be all right

· be all right with/by/for/to
  對於⋯是可以接受的
· It's all right.
  別擔心。沒關係的。
· That's/It's all right.
  沒關係。（對於別人的道謝或道歉的回應）

沒問題，好的　不可以和表示「對，正確」的 be right 混淆。
- Honey, everything's going to **be all right**.
- What do you know?
  ●親愛的，所有事都會沒問題的。　●你怎麼知道？
- ▶ It's all right with me. 我沒關係。
  It's going to be all right. 會變好的。

go all right

· feel all right
  感覺還不錯
· sound all right
  聽起來不錯
· turn all right
  （情況）變好

順利進行　all right 也可以當副詞用，表示「順利」的意思。
- Is everything set up for the meeting?
- Yes. I'm sure it's going to **go all right**.
  ●會議的準備都完成了嗎？　●是的，我相信會進行得很順利的。
- ▶ My first day on the job went all right. 我上班第一天很順利。
  I hope our trip to Vietnam will go all right.
  我希望我們的越南旅行會很順利。

be fine

· look/seem fine
  看起來不錯
· feel fine
  感覺健康
· That's fine by/with me.
  我沒意見。

不錯，適合　除此之外，也可以表示健康狀況良好。
- Does this suit look OK on me?
- It's fine. Let's buy it so we can leave.
  ●這套西裝我穿起來還可以嗎？　●還不錯啊。買了它我們就離開吧。
- ▶ This soup will be fine for dinner. 這道湯很適合晚餐。
  The computer is fine for typing the report.
  這台電腦拿來打報告沒問題。

be/feel okay

· look OK
  看起來還可以
· be okay with/by sb
  某人可以接受
· It's okay for A to do...
  A 可以去做⋯沒關係

好，可以，不錯　okay 常常簡寫成 OK。
- Look, Charlie, it's going to **be okay**.
- That's easy for you to say.
  ●嘿，Charlie，會沒事的。　●你說來可容易。
- ▶ All of the people in the accident are okay.
  所有遭受意外的人都沒事。
  It is okay for you to go out with my sister.
  你可以跟我妹妹出去。

1 職場‧學校
2 電腦‧網路
3 社交生活
4 日常生活
5 訊息‧理解
6 想法‧態度
7 情緒‧狀況
8 行為舉止
9 時間地點‧副詞片語

531

if it's okay with you

· if you don't mind
你不介意的話

你沒問題的話 向對方提出請求或提議，並且請求對方諒解。

- **If it's okay with you** I'll take tomorrow off.
- Let me check the schedule.

　　●你沒問題的話，我明天想休息。　　●讓我確認一下時間表。

▶ I'll come at eleven thirty if that's okay with you.
你沒問題的話，我會在 11 點半過來。
If it's okay with you, I'll take tomorrow off instead of Monday. 你沒問題的話，我要把禮拜一的休假改成明天。

be not that bad

· be not too/so bad
雖然還是不好，但比想像
中好

沒那麼糟 雖然也不能說很好，但至少沒有想像中那麼差。

- Many people said they don't like McDonald's food.
- It's **not that bad**. You should try it.

　　●很多人說他們不喜歡麥當勞的食物。　　●沒那麼糟。你應該試試看。

▶ Studying English is not that bad.
學英文沒那麼難。
This old movie is not that bad.
這部老電影沒那麼糟。

suit sb fine

很適合某人 主詞是事物。這裡的 fine 是副詞，相當於 well。

- Do you like working at the post office?
- Sure. It **suits me just fine**.

　　●你喜歡在郵局工作嗎？　　●當然，那很適合我。

▶ Eating out every night suits Tara fine.
Tara 習慣每天晚上在外面吃飯。
The artwork suits the new owner fine.
這件藝術品很適合這位新的收藏家。

have no problem with...

· No problem.
沒問題。沒關係。（除了
用來回應請求，也可以作
為對於道謝或道歉的回
答。「No sweat」的用法
也一樣。）

覺得…沒關係／可以接受 with 後面可以接人或事物，表示「沒什麼不好」的感覺。

- Is it OK if I come to work ten minutes late?
- Sure. I **have no problem with** that.

　　●我上班如果遲到十分鐘可以嗎？　　●可以，我沒什麼關係。

▶ I have no problem with people who have different religions. 我可以接受擁有不同宗教信仰的人。
We have no problem with waiting for you.
我們可以等你沒關係。

will do

- will do for sb
  對某人足夠
- It won't do to...
  …是不行的

足夠 這裡的 do 是 be enough 的意思。

- Hi honey. Are you hungry tonight?
- No. Just a small meal **will do** for me.
  ●嘿，親愛的。你今晚餓嗎？　●不餓，我吃一點點就夠了。

▶ This old car will do as a means of transportation.
  這台舊車當作交通工具夠用了。
  A small cake will do for the party.
  派對上有小蛋糕就夠了。

---

 all right 與 right

　　雖然只差一個 all，但意義大有不同。首先，right 表示「正確的」、「對的」。如果說 You're right，表示同意對方所說的話。That's right 同樣表示「沒錯」，代表同意對方的意見。但 all right 呢？I'm all right 的意思是「我沒關係」、「我沒問題」，而 That's all right 隨著情境的不同，會有「沒關係」、「別擔心」等意義，甚至可以表示對方說的完全正確。單獨說 All right 時，表示「Yes」或「OK」，可以用來贊同某個提議。

---

25 必須做… have to

7-25.mp3

have to

- have got to do
  必須做…
- don't have to do
  不必做…

必須做… had to 表示過去必須做，will have to 則是未來必須做。口語中則常常會說 have got to do。

- I **have to** leave right away for the meeting.
- I'll catch up with you later.
  ●我現在要馬上離開去開會了。　●我稍後會聯絡你。

▶ Do you have to work this weekend?
  你這個週末需要工作嗎？
  I don't have to pay him any money.
  我不必付他任何錢。

1 職場・學校
2 電腦・網路
3 社交生活
4 日常生活
5 訊息・理解
6 想法・態度
7 情緒・狀況
8 行為舉止
9 時間地點・副詞片語

must

必須 表示有強烈的義務要去做，和 have to 相似。

- I can't find a good job.
- Never say die. You **must** keep trying.
  - 我找不到好工作。　●別氣餒，你必須再接再厲。

▶ You must do the laundry tonight.
　你今晚一定要洗衣服。
　Each student must do extra homework.
　每位學生都必須做額外的作業。

should

· ought to do
　應該做…

應該 強度比 must 弱，通常用來勸別人做某件該做的事。

- You **shouldn't** put off that work for much longer.
- I'll try and finish it before I go.
  - 你不應該再把那件工作拖延下去了。　●我會努力在下班前完成它。

▶ You should put on a sweater. It's cold outside.
　你應該穿上毛衣。外面很冷。
　You should be more careful.
　你該更謹慎點。

had better

· (You) Better do
　（你）最好做…
· had better not do
　最好不要做…

最好… 對朋友或晚輩使用，勸對方聽從自己的建議。

- We **had better** do the dishes tonight.
- Yeah, otherwise the kitchen will be dirty.
  - 我們今晚最好洗碗盤。　●是啊，不然廚房會很髒。

▶ You had better finish the report soon.
　你最好快點完成報告。
　They had better pay me my money.
　他們最好把我的錢付給我。

---

 have to

　　must, have to, should, ought to 雖然意思相似，但 should 和 ought to 的用法比較接近，而 must 則和 have to 相似。當帶有強烈自信，可以斷定「一定得這麼做」時，會用 must 或 have to，但口語中比較常說 have to。想表達「最好去做」某件事時，則會用 should 或 ought to。舉例來說，想勸告朋友禁煙時，可以說 You should quit smoking.。但如果是醫生勸告戒煙的時候，就會說 You must quit smoking.。

1 職場・學校

2 電腦・網路

3 社交生活

4 日常生活

5 訊息・理解

6 想法・態度

7 情緒・狀況

8 行為舉止

9 時間地點・副詞片語

26 無法不做…
can't help -ing

7-26.mp3

can't help -ing

· can't help it
忍不住
· can't help feeling/
thinking...
忍不住覺得…

忍不住… 忍不住做某事，無法控制自己。這裡的 help 是 stop 的意思。

● Just forget about your ex-girlfriend.
● I tried, but I **can't help** thinking about her.
　●就把你前女友給忘了吧。　●我試了，但我就是忍不住想她。

▶ She can't help drinking so much alcohol.
　她無法不喝那麼多酒。
　I can't help being cautious. 我不得不謹慎。

can't help but

· can't help oneself
無法克制自己
· It can't be helped.
那是沒辦法的。

忍不住… 請注意 but 後面接動詞原形。

● I **can't help but** watch TV when I'm bored.
● Maybe you need to find a hobby.
　●當我無聊的時候，我會忍不住看電視。　●也許你需要找個嗜好。

▶ I can't help but think that he's a loser.
　我無法不覺得他是個輸家。
　I can't help but think about Jessica. 我無法不想 Jessica。

have no choice but to...

· cannot but do
不得不做…

除了做…以外別無選擇 也可以說 cannot choose but to...。

● I **have no choice but to** buy her a fur coat.
● It's going to be really expensive.
　●我別無選擇，只能買毛皮大衣給她。　●那真的會很貴的。

▶ I had no choice but to get divorced.
　我除了離婚以外別無選擇。
　I have no choice but to do that. 我除了那麼做以外別無選擇。

be forced to

· force A to do
強迫 A 做…

被迫做… 因為被強制要求，就算不想做也得做。

● What happened when you didn't get a visa?
● I **was forced to** leave the country right away.
　●你沒拿到簽證之後怎麼了？　●我立刻被強制出境。

▶ He was forced to listen to the music. 他被迫聽那個音樂。
　They were forced to help with the crime.
　他們被迫幫助犯罪。

535

can't stop -ing

· stop oneself from -ing
停止做…

無法不做… 也就是 be unable to stop a habit or activity 的意思。

● Could you just shut up for a little while?
● I **can't stop** singing to myself.

　●你能閉嘴一下嗎？　●我無法不哼歌。

▶ John can't stop eating junk food.

　John 無法不吃垃圾食物。

　My son can't stop playing video games.

　我兒子無法不打電動。

---

27 變好，變壞
get worse

7-27.mp3

---

go bad

· go badly for sb
對某人而言不順利

變壞，腐壞 指食物壞掉或情況變差。

● So, how was the dance party?
● Terrible. Everything **went bad** last night.

　●舞會怎麼樣呢？　●糟透了。昨晚每件事都出了錯。

▶ I will just leave if things go bad.

　如果狀況變差，我就會離開。

　Things went bad when I interviewed for the job.

　我接受這份工作的面試時情況很糟。

get worse

· be getting worse
正逐漸變差
· get worse and worse
變得越來越差

變得更差 狀況惡化。常以進行式 be getting worse 的型態出現。

● The air in this city is so polluted.
● It's going to **get worse** in the future.

　●這個城市的空氣污染很嚴重。　●未來會變得更差。

▶ Did things get worse after you left?

　你離開之後，情況惡化了嗎？

　The problem got worse when it wasn't fixed.

　這個問題沒有解決，於是更加惡化。

get better

· be getting better
  正逐漸變好

變好，好起來 表示情況、能力變好，也經常指身體狀況變好。

● Some days I just feel like giving up.
● Be strong. Things will **get better** soon.

　●有時候我只想要放棄。　●堅強點，情況很快會變好的。

▶ There's a chance he can get better.
　他的健康有機會好轉。
　I'd like to get better at speaking English.
　我希望自己的英文會話能力變好。

go from bad to worse

每況愈下 從 bad 變得更 bad，表示狀況越來越差。

● How are things at your office?
● They seem to **be going from bad to worse**.

　●你辦公室的狀況怎樣？　●似乎每況愈下。

▶ The government programs have gone from bad to
　worse. 政府計畫的狀況每況愈下。
　My economic situation went from bad to worse.
　我的經濟狀況每況愈下。

make sth worse

· make things/it worse
  使狀況惡化
· to make matters
  worse
  使狀況惡化

使某事物更差 使役動詞 make + 受詞 + 受詞補語的句型。

● Did the gift make Sandra happy?
● No, it just **made her mood worse**.

　●那份禮物有讓 Sandra 開心嗎？　●沒有，只是讓她的情緒更糟而已。

▶ The virus made the computer worse.
　病毒讓電腦的狀況變得更差。
　The stock market has made the economy worse.
　股市讓經濟變得更糟。

have improved

· improve something
  改善某事物
· need to be improved
  需要被改善
· be an improvement
  …是一項進步

改善了 用現在完成式，表示現在的狀況已經比過去好了。

● I think the Korean team **has improved** significantly.
● I know. I hope we can make it to the second round.

　●我覺得韓國隊有很顯著的進步。
　●是啊，希望我們能進入第二輪的比賽。

▶ The store has improved its items.
　那家店改善了商品的品質。
　I need to improve my English to travel overseas.
　為了出國旅行，我需要加強英文。

1 職場・學校

2 電腦・網路

3 社交生活

4 日常生活

5 訊息・理解

6 想法・態度

7 情緒・狀況

8 行為舉止

9 時間地點・副詞片語

fall apart

· hit bottom
　跌落谷底

破碎，完全失敗 原意是「摔碎」，比喻變糟、失敗、搞砸等情況。

● I think I need to buy a new car.

● Why? Is your old car going to **fall apart**?

　●我想我需要買輛新車。　　●為什麼？你的舊車要壞了嗎？

▶ Christian fell apart after losing his job.
　Christian 丟掉工作後，變得一蹶不振。

　Some people fall apart during difficult times.
　有些人在困境中會一蹶不振。

pick up

· be getting better
　正在變好

好轉 表示情況逐漸好轉，意義與 improve 相近。

● Has your daughter gotten better grades?

● Yes, they are starting to **pick up** this year.

　●你女兒有得到比較好的成績？　　●有，今年開始變好了。

▶ The sales of the company picked up this month.
　公司這個月的銷售額變好了。

　I hope the economy will pick up soon.
　我希望經濟很快能好轉。

 有多種意義的 pick up

　　說到 pick up，除了「撿起來」以外，最常用的意義是「開車接某人」。其他用法還有像是去商店 pick up 某個東西，表示「買」或者「得到」、「領取」某個東西。這一節介紹的用法或許大家不太熟悉，是以 economy, things 或 life 等與狀況有關的詞彙為主詞，表示狀況「變好」，也就是 improve 的意思。I forgot to pick up my dry cleaning 表示「忘了去拿乾洗的衣服」，I picked this up at a flea market 是「我在跳蚤市場買到這樣東西」，Let me pick you up in the morning 則是「我早上開車去接你」的意思。

28 狀況，處境
get caught in

1 職場・學校

2 電腦・網路

3 社交生活

4 日常生活

5 訊息・理解

6 想法・態度

7 情緒・狀況

8 行為舉止

9 時間地點・副詞片語

be in good condition

· be in excellent condition
狀況優良
· be in bad condition
狀況不好

狀況好 特別常表示物體或身體的狀況。

● Are you selling your apartment?
● I am. It's **in good condition**.
　●你要賣掉你的公寓嗎？　●要，房子的狀況很好。

▶ The computer is still in good condition.
　電腦的狀況依然很好。
　The items in the shop are in good condition.
　這間店裡的商品狀況良好。

under...condition

· under one condition
在一個條件下
· (on) one condition
有一個條件
· under similar condition
在相似的條件下

在…的狀況下 condition 除了表示整體情況以外，也有「條件」的意思。

● Can you help me with this homework?
● I'll help you **under one condition**.
　●你可以幫我做這份作業嗎？　●我可以幫你，但有個條件。

▶ You're going to have to work under different conditions.
　你將需要在不同情況下工作。
　I can't stay here under these conditions.
　在這些（惡劣的）狀況下，我無法待在這裡。

be in the same situation

· be in a more favorable situation
處於更有利的狀況
· be in the same boat
在同一條船上
→處於一樣困難的處境

處境相同 也可以說 in difficult/serious condition 表示處境艱困。

● It's been very difficult for me this year.
● I know. I **am in the same situation**.
　●今年對我而言很辛苦。　●我知道，我也是同樣的狀況。

▶ She is in the same situation as her sister.
　她跟她姐姐處境相同。
　Everyone in the class is in the same situation.
　班上每個人都處於相同的狀況。

be a different story

- be a totally different situation
  是完全不同的狀況
- be another story
  是另一回事

是另一回事 different 可以加上 whole 或 totally 強調「完全是另一回事」。

- I heard you got in trouble yesterday.
- It's true, but that's a different story.
  - 我聽說你昨天碰上麻煩。　● 是啊，但那是另一回事了。

▶ Someone stole my bike, but that's a different story.
  有人偷了我的腳踏車，但那是另一回事了。
  We were supposed to go on vacation, but that's a different story. 我們原本應該去度假的，但那是另一回事了。

get/be caught in

- be stuck with
  被…纏住

碰上困難的狀況 也常說 get into trouble。get caught in the rain 則是被雨淋到的意思。

- My gosh! You are really soaked.
- Yes, I am. I was caught in a shower.
  - 我的天啊！你完全濕透了。　● 是啊。我被陣雨淋到了。

▶ I got caught in a shower on my way home.
  我在回家的路上被陣雨淋到了。
  She got caught in bed with his neighbor's husband.
  她和鄰居的先生被捉姦在床。

that depends on...

- That/It all depends on...
  那完全取決於…
- depending on
  依…而定

取決於… 如果簡單地說 That depends.，就是「那要看情況」的意思。

- Are you coming on the class trip?
- That depends on whether my parents allow it.
  - 你會來班遊嗎？　● 那要看我爸媽同不同意。

▶ That depends on which person you talk to.
  那取決於你是和誰談的。
  That depends on the route you take on the subway.
  那取決於你搭乘的地鐵路線。

if I were you

- if I were in your shoes
  如果我身在你的處境
- if I were in your place/situation
  如果我站在你的立場上
- be in another person's position
  站在另一個人的立場上

如果我是你 用與現在事實相反的假設語氣（因為我不可能是你），向對方提出建議或忠告。

- If I were in your shoes, I wouldn't sell it yet.
- Do you think the stock will bounce back?
  - 如果我處在你的立場，我還不會賣掉。
  - 你覺得這支股票會回漲嗎？

▶ If I were you, I would go to see a doctor.
  如果我是你，我會去看醫生。
  What would you do if you were in her situation?
  如果你處於她的情況下，你會怎麼做？

1 職場・學校

2 電腦・網路

3 社交生活

4 日常生活

5 訊息・理解

6 想法・態度

7 情緒・狀況

8 行為舉止

9 時間地點・副詞片語

put oneself in one's place

· put oneself in one's shoes
站在某人的處境設想

設身處地為某人想 意思跟 put oneself in one's shoes 一樣。

● Yousef was very rude to me today.

● He's stressed. **Put yourself in his place**.

　●Yousef 今天對我很沒禮貌。　●他壓力很大。設身處地為他著想吧。

▶ Put yourself in a poor person's place.
站在窮人的立場想一想。

You should put yourself in Dave's place.
你應該設身處地為 Dave 著想。

---

29 處於困境
get in trouble

7-29.mp3

get/be in trouble

· get/be in trouble for (not) -ing
因為（沒）做…而陷入困境

· get A in trouble
讓 A 陷入困境

· get oneself into trouble
讓自己陷入困境

陷入困境 碰上問題或事故。in 也可以改成 into。

● You're in trouble. The boss wants to see you.

● Really? What did I do?

　●你有麻煩了，老闆想見你。　●真的嗎？我做了什麼？

▶ You will get in trouble if you do that.
你那麼做的話會有麻煩的。

I'm not here to get you in trouble.
我不是來害你陷入困境的。

have trouble with

· have problems/difficulty with/-ing
在…方面有困難

· have no trouble -ing
做…沒有困難

在…方面有困難 trouble 也可以改成 problem 或 difficulty。

● I **have trouble with** studying here.

● It's noisy. Let's go to the library.

　●我沒辦法在這裡讀書。　●這裡很吵。我們去圖書館吧。

▶ She had trouble with making a living.
她在維持生計方面有困難。

They have trouble with playing their instruments.
他們在演奏樂器上碰上問題。

cause trouble

· not cause any trouble
  不引起任何問題
· make trouble for A
  給 A 惹麻煩
· make things difficult
  把狀況變得困難／複雜

引起問題 也可以說 make trouble。專惹麻煩的人叫 troublemaker。

● Some of the students **cause trouble** in class.
● They may be asked to leave the school.
  ●有些學生在課堂上引起問題。　●他們可能會被要求退學。

▶ The software caused trouble in my computer.
  那個軟體在我的電腦上引起了問題。
  Jack causes trouble when he drinks alcohol.
  Jack 喝酒就會惹麻煩。

it's difficult when...

· It was difficult when
  S+V
  …時情況很困難

…時情況很困難 when 後面接 S+V。it 指的是「情況」。

● **It was difficult when** the storm cut our electricity.
● Thankfully, everything was fixed quickly.
  ●當暴風雪切斷了我們的電力時，情況很困難。
  ●令人感謝的是，一切都很快修復了。

▶ It was really difficult when my father lost his job.
  我父親失去工作時，狀況很艱難。
  It's difficult when you are too sleepy to study.
  睏到無法讀書時很辛苦。

have a hard time -ing

· have an awful time in
  this place
  很難待在這個地方
· go through a hard
  time
  度過困難

做…有困難 time 後面本來有介系詞 in，口語中通常省略。

● I'm still **having a hard time** accepting the decision.
● I'm sure you'll be fine in a few days.
  ●我還是很難接受這個決定。　●我相信過幾天你就會覺得好多了。

▶ Holly has a hard time making new friends.
  Holly 很難結交新朋友。
  I have a hard time following the highway signs to the
  airport. 我無法跟著高速公路上的指示牌前往機場。

give...a hard time

找…麻煩，訓斥… 例如公司主管的斥責、刁難等等。

● Why is Kevin so unhappy these days?
● His science teacher **gives him a hard time** in class.
  ●Kevin 最近為什麼那麼不開心？　●他的科學老師在課堂上刁難他。

▶ I gave the girls a hard time for they wore too much
  make-up. 那些女孩子畫的妝太濃，所以我訓斥了她們。
  The coach gave the player a hard time because he was
  lazy. 因為那位球員太懶惰，所以教練訓斥了他。

be harder than one thinks

- be harder than one thought
  比某人過去以為的還難
- be harder than it looks/sounds
  比看起來／聽起來還難

比某人想像中難　be harder than it seems 則是「比看起來還難」。

- I could probably write a romance novel.
- No way. It **is harder than you think**.

  ●我可能可以寫一本言情小說。　●不可能。那比你想像的還難。

▶ Joining the military was harder than Brian thought it would be. 從軍比 Brian 想像中困難。

Becoming a millionaire is harder than most people think.
成為百萬富翁比大多數人想像的還難。

suffer from

- be suffering from a lot of stress
  苦於巨大的壓力

苦於…，得（病）　遭遇困難、不幸的狀況，或是因病受苦。

- Do you **suffer from** back pain?
- Only if I lift heavy objects.

  ●你有背痛嗎？　●抬重物的時候才會。

▶ Some men are also suffering from sexual harassment.
有些男性也遭受性騷擾。

Do you suffer from insomnia?
你會失眠嗎？

if worst comes to worst

如果發生最壞的情況　用兩個最高級強調情況糟到不能再糟。

- Our computer is broken and can't be fixed.
- **If worst comes to worst**, we'll borrow another one.

  ●我們的電腦已經壞了，也沒辦法修。
  ●實在不行的話，我們就借一台。

▶ If worst comes to worst, we won't have enough food.
在最壞的情況下，我們食物會不夠。

If worst comes to worst, the nations will go to war.
如果情勢壞到極點，這些國家會開戰。

---

 get in trouble

　　表達遭受困難時，最常用的三種說法是 problem、hard time 和 trouble。但就像我們在這一節看到的，get/be in trouble、have trouble、cause trouble、make trouble 裡的 trouble 都不加冠詞 a，也不用複數形。

I'm having a trouble with checking my email. (X)
I'm having troubles with checking my email. (X)
I'm having trouble with checking my email. (O)

1 職場・學校

2 電腦・網路

3 社交生活

4 日常生活

5 訊息・理解

6 想法・態度

7 情緒・狀況

8 行為舉止

9 時間地點・副詞片語

30 有／沒有問題
have a problem

have a problem with

· have a big / a lot of problem
有很大的／很多的問題
· have a problem -ing
做⋯有問題
· have heart problem
有心臟問題

在⋯方面有問題 後面通常接事物。接人的時候表示「很難相處」。

● How long **have** you **had a problem with** indigestion?
● Ever since I started my new job.
●你消化不良多久了？　　●從我開始新工作開始。

▶ I have a problem with people who are rude.
我很難跟粗魯的人相處。
Do you have a problem with that?
你做那件事有困難嗎？

have a problem because...

· have a lot of problems because S+V
因為⋯而有很多問題
· have a lot of problems at one's workplace
在職場有很多問題

因為⋯而有問題 後面接 S+V 說明問題發生的理由。

● We **have a problem because** we finished too late.
● Do you think we are going to get in trouble?
●因為我們太晚完成，所以造成了問題。　　●你覺得我們會有麻煩嗎？

▶ You have a problem because your visa expired.
你的簽證過期了，所以會有問題。
Belinda has a problem because she upset all of her friends.
Belinda 因為讓所有朋友都不高興而陷入困境。

have the same problem

有相同的問題 常用來附和別人，表示自己也有親身體驗。

● My stomach has been hurting since we ate lunch.
● I **have the same problem.** Was the food bad?
●我們吃了午餐以後，我的胃就一直在痛。
●我也是。是食物壞了嗎？

▶ The worst students have the same problem every year.
最糟糕的學生們每年都有一樣的問題。
My best friend had the same problem as I did.
我最好的朋友和我有一樣的問題。

have money problems

- have personal problems
  有個人問題
- have financial problems
  有財務問題

有金錢問題 也可以說 have financial（財務的）problem。

- Why don't you just buy a house?
- I can't. I **have money problems**.
  - 你為什麼不乾脆買間房子呢？　●我沒辦法，我金錢上有困難。

▶ The couple divorced because they had money problems.
  這對夫妻因為有金錢問題而離了婚。
  I quit school because I have money problems.
  因為金錢方面的問題，我休學了。

the problem is that...

- There's a problem with...
  …有問題

問題是… 跟 the point is that...（重點是…）相似的句型，用來強調問題癥結在哪裡。

- Should Jason practice on the piano every night?
- **The problem is that** he has no talent.
  - Jason 應該每晚練習鋼琴嗎？　●問題是他沒天分。

▶ The problem is that it can't be fixed.
  問題是那修不好。
  The problem is that we can't find the keys.
  問題是我們找不到鑰匙。

have you had any problems...?

- have a big / a lot of problem
  有很大的／很多的問題
- have a problem -ing
  做…有問題
- have heart problem
  有心臟問題

你做…有任何問題嗎？ 後面接動詞 -ing 形。這裡用的是現在完成式，所以是問之前有過什麼問題。

- **Have you had any problems** using the Internet?
- Yes. My Internet service hasn't worked all day.
  - 你在使用網路上有碰到任何問題嗎？
  - 有，我的網路整天都連不上。

▶ Have you had any problems cooking the food?
  你煮菜的時候有碰到任何問題嗎？
  Have you had any problems finishing your homework?
  你做功課的時候有任何問題嗎？

have no problem -ing

- have no problem with...
  在…方面沒有問題

做…沒有問題 -ing 也可以換成 with sth。

- Can you take Logan on a tour of the building?
- Sure. I **have no problem** showing him around.
  - 你可以帶 Logan 參觀這棟大樓嗎？　●當然。我可以帶他到處看看。

▶ She has no problem working late at night.
  她可以工作到深夜沒問題。
  They have no problem donating money to the charity.
  他們可以捐錢給慈善機構沒問題。

1 職場・學校

2 電腦・網路

3 社交生活

4 日常生活

5 訊息・理解

6 想法・態度

7 情緒・狀況

8 行為舉止

9 時間地點・副詞片語

be nothing wrong with

…沒什麼不對 表示行為沒錯，或者人事物沒什麼問題（很正常）。

- You shouldn't complain so much.
- There **is nothing wrong with** talking about how I feel.

  ●你不該抱怨這麼多。　●我說出自己的感受沒什麼不對。

▶ There is nothing wrong with your clothing.
  你的穿著沒什麼問題。
  There is nothing wrong with the car you want to buy.
  你想買的車沒有什麼問題。

cause problem for sb

- cause problems at...
  在…造成問題
- cause trouble around here
  給這邊帶來問題
- cause trouble for sb
  給某人帶來問題

對某人造成問題 也可以改成前一節學過的 cause trouble。

- Carla and Bill broke up a week ago.
- She thinks Bill will **cause problems for** her.

  ●Carla 和 Bill 一個星期前分手了。　●她認為 Bill 會給她帶來問題。

▶ Don't cause problems for the people here.
  別給這邊的人惹麻煩。
  The extra work caused problems for all of us.
  額外的工作對我們所有人都造成了問題。

pose a problem

- create trouble/ difficulty
  造成問題

引起問題 pose 在這邊是造成、引起的意思，它通常接 danger, risk 等名詞當受詞。

- Was anyone hurt in the big traffic accident?
- No, but it will **pose a problem** during rush hour.

  ●有任何人在這場重大車禍中受傷嗎？
  ●沒有，但車禍會對尖峰時間造成問題。

▶ The snowstorm posed a problem for travelers.
  暴風雪對旅客造成了問題。
  Ken's lost passport posed a problem for him.
  Ken 弄丟護照，對他造成了問題。
  （直譯：Ken 弄丟的護照對他造成了問題。）

1 職場・學校
2 電腦・網路
3 社交生活
4 日常生活
5 訊息・理解
6 想法・態度
7 情緒・狀況
8 行為舉止
9 時間地點・副詞片語

31 運氣好／壞 have luck

7-31.mp3

be lucky

- be lucky to do / if...
  做…很幸運／如果…很幸運
- be lucky with something
  在…方面很幸運

幸運 後面接 if 子句、to do、with + 名詞等句型。

- Your new girlfriend is just gorgeous.
- I know. I'**m lucky to** have met her.
  - 你的新女友真的很美。　● 我知道，我真的很幸運能遇見她。

▶ I guess I'm lucky to have a friend like you.
  我想，我很幸運能有個像你這樣的朋友。
  I'm really lucky to be working for a big company.
  我真的很幸運能在大公司工作。

be out of luck

- be in luck
  運氣好

運氣不好 缺乏（out of）運氣（luck）的情況。

- I want to buy a TV that is on sale.
- You'**re out of luck**. We sold the last one.
  - 我想買一台在特價的電視。　● 你運氣不好，我們賣掉最後一台了。

▶ He was out of luck after missing the last bus.
  他運氣不好，錯過了最後一班公車。
  The stores are closed, so we're out of luck.
  店家都關了，看來我們運氣不好。

have luck

- have much luck with...
  在…方面運氣好
- have bad luck
  運氣不好
- have luck -ing
  在…方面運氣好

運氣好 have no luck 是沒有運氣，have bad luck 是運氣很差。

- Did you **have any luck** finding your necklace?
- No. I'm not sure where I lost it.
  - 你有幸運找到你的項鍊嗎？　● 沒有，我不確定我在哪裡弄丟了。

▶ You should have some luck finding a job.
  你在找工作方面應該是有點運氣的。
  He had luck in reaching his sister on the phone.
  他幸運地用電話聯絡上他妹妹。

have the fortune to...

· be fortune
是好運的事

· Fortunately
幸運地

· Unfortunately
不幸地

做…運氣很好 fortune 在這裡是「好運」的意思。fortune 也可以指財富。

● How did Donald get to be so rich?

● He **had the good fortune to** have wealthy parents.

●Donald 為什麼變得那麼有錢？　●他運氣好，有富有的爸媽。

▶ We had the good fortune to meet President Obama.

我們運氣好，見到了歐巴馬總統。

I had the good fortune to be invited to her house.

我很幸運受邀到她家。

good luck to...

· Good luck on/in...
祝…能順利進行

祝…好運 後面接人，希望他能有好運。

● **Good luck to** everyone in the marathon.

● It's going to be a difficult race to compete in.

●祝每個參加馬拉松的人都有好運。　●這將會是場困難的競賽。

▶ Good luck to the students who are graduating.

祝所有的畢業生好運。

Good luck to the people who entered the contest.

祝參與競賽的人能有好運。

wish sb luck

· wish sb luck in...
希望某人在…方面有好運

祝某人好運 wish sb sth 的句型，表示希望某人擁有某事物。

● I'm going for an interview. **Wish me luck.**

● I know you'll do very well in it.

●我要去參加一場面試。祝我好運吧。　●我相信你會表現得很好。

▶ Wish Sam luck before he leaves.

Sam 離開之前，祝他好運吧。

Wish the mountain climbers luck before they start.

在登山者出發前，祝他們好運。

try one's luck

· try one's luck -ing
碰碰運氣做…

· Any luck?
進行得順利嗎？

試試運氣 即使看起來沒什麼希望，但還是想試試運氣如何。

● We're going to **try our luck** at the casino.

● I think you'll lose all of your money.

●我們要去賭場試手氣。　●我覺得你們會把錢輸光。

▶ Have you tried your luck at other jobs?

你試過其他工作了嗎？

I'll try my luck at finding a girlfriend.

我會碰碰運氣，找個女朋友。

push one's luck | **心存僥倖去冒險** 太過相信自己的好運，想要得寸進尺。也就是 go too far。
- Someday I'm going to go skydiving.
- That's very dangerous. Don't **push your luck**.
  ● 總有一天我要去玩高空跳傘。　● 那很危險，不要心存僥倖。

▶ She pushed her luck by investing too much.
她得寸進尺，投資了太多錢。
I'll stop because I don't want to push my luck.
我要收手了，因為我不想越賭越大。

---

have it good
- cause problems at...
  在…造成問題
- cause trouble around here
  在這邊造成問題
- cause trouble for sb
  造成某人的問題

幸運，有能耐 be in luck 也是「運氣好」的意思。
- So many people are starving in Africa.
- I know. We really **have it good** here.
  ● 非洲有許多人處於飢餓中。　● 我知道，我們在這裡真的很幸運。

▶ Employees at Google have it good.
Google 的員工很有福氣。
Pop musicians really seem to have it good.
流行歌手們看起來真的很有兩下子。

---

32 日子好／壞
have a bad day

7-32.mp3

---

be not one's day
- think of
  想到／考慮…
- think about sb/sth
  思考…

某人整天諸事不順 用「不是某人的日子」比喻這一整天運氣不好。
- Albert said you were two hours late to work.
- I overslept. It's **just not my day**.
  ● Albert 說你上班遲到了兩個小時。　● 我睡過頭了。今天運氣真差。

▶ It wasn't Page's day because she had many problems.
Page 今天諸事不順，碰上了很多問題。
The teacher just punished me. It isn't my day.
老師剛才處罰我。我今天運氣真差。

1 職場・學校
2 電腦・網路
3 社交生活
4 日常生活
5 訊息・理解
6 想法・態度
7 情緒・狀況
8 行為舉止
9 時間地點・副詞片語

have a bad day

· have a bad day at work
  在工作場合過得不好

一整天過得很不好 bad 也可以換成 rough。

● What is the matter with Laura?

● She's **having a bad day**. She feels upset.

  ●Laura 怎麼了？　●她今天過得很不好，覺得很煩惱。

▶ I had a bad day on Monday.
  我星期一過得很不好。
  You look like you had a bad day.
  你看起來過了不太好的一天。

have a rough day

· have a really rough day
  一整天過得非常辛苦

一整天過得很辛苦 rough 在口語中有「辛苦」的意思。原意是「粗糙」，也有「粗略」的意思。

● You look very tired tonight.

● I **had a rough day** on the job.

  ●你今晚看起來很累。　●我今天工作很辛苦。

▶ This extra work means we'll have a rough week.
  這份額外的工作意謂著我們會度過辛苦的一週。
  Did you have a rough day at your school?
  你今天在學校過得很辛苦嗎？

be a long day

· It's been a long day
  真是漫長的一天
· I've had a long day at work
  我在工作上度過了漫長的一天
· after a long day at work
  在一整天漫長的工作之後

是漫長的一天 既辛苦又無趣，感覺時間過得很慢。

● We need to have this report finished by tonight.

● Oh no! It's going to **be a long day**.

  ●我們得在今晚之前完成這份報告。　●噢不！今天會是漫長的一天。

▶ Everyone is unhappy and it's going to be a long day.
  每個人都不開心，今天會是漫長的一天。
  It has been a long day.
  真是漫長的一天。

be one's lucky day

· not be a lucky day for A
  不是 A 的幸運日

是某人的幸運日 和前面的說法相反，表示一整天很幸運。

● It looks like you just won some money.

● Great! It must **be my lucky day**.

  ●看來你剛贏了一點錢。　●太棒了！今天一定是我的幸運日。

▶ When she met Charlie, it was her lucky day.
  她遇見 Charlie 那天是她的幸運日。
  I think today will be my lucky day.
  我覺得今天會是我的幸運日。

33 有／沒有機會或可能性
get a chance

7-33.mp3

1 職場・學校

2 電腦・網路

3 社交生活

4 日常生活

5 訊息・理解

6 想法・態度

7 情緒・狀況

8 行為舉止

9 時間地點・副詞片語

have/get a chance

· have/get a chance to do
有機會做…

· when you get a chance
當你有機會時

有機會 chance 有機會（opportunity）和可能性（possibility）兩個意思。這裡用的是「機會」的意思。

● Come and see my new apartment when you **have a chance**.

● Can I come over on Wednesday night?

●有機會的話，來看看我的新公寓吧。　●我星期三晚上過去可以嗎？

▶ Did you have a chance to check it?
你有機會能確認嗎？
I am glad that we finally had a chance to talk.
我很高興我們終於有機會談談。

chances are S+V

· have a good chance of...
…有很大的可能性

· have a better chance at
在…方面更有機會

· have no chance of
沒有…的機會

很有可能… 這裡的 chance 是可能性（possibility）的意思。

● Have you seen Raul around?

● **Chances are** he is working in his office.

●你有在附近看到 Raul 嗎？　●他很有可能在辦公室工作。

▶ Chances are she will visit us tomorrow.
她明天很有可能來拜訪我們。
Chances are you will find a job.
你很有可能會找到工作。

stand a chance

· stand a chance of -ing
有可能…

· stand good/excellent chance
很有可能

· not stand much chance
不太可能

有可能／有希望（成功） 可以說 a better chance 表示更有可能，或者說 a much better chance 強調可能性高出許多。

● Do you think he is going to win the election?

● He **stands a chance** of being the winner.

●你覺得他會贏得選舉嗎？　●他有可能會是贏家。

▶ Jill doesn't stand a chance of finishing on time.
Jill 不可能準時完成。
Dan stands a good chance of receiving a bonus.
Dan 很有可能會得到獎金。

have the opportunity

- have the opportunity to do
  有做…的機會
- take the opportunity to do
  利用機會去做…

有機會 have little opportunity 則是「沒什麼機會」。

- Do you think I'll be able to meet a movie star?
- You may **have the opportunity to** do that.
  ●你覺得我能遇見電影明星嗎？　●可能有機會。

▶ We had the opportunity to visit Los Angeles.
  我們得到了機會去洛杉磯。
  You'll have the opportunity to become famous.
  你有機會出名。

there's a possibility that...

- There's no possibility of
  沒有…的可能
- There is a/little chance of
  有／幾乎沒有…的可能
- have the possibility of...
  有…的可能性

有可能… slight possibility 是「微薄的可能性」，中文裡的「沒有一絲可能」則是 there is not the slightest possibility。

- Why do you like to gamble?
- **There's a chance** I will win a lot of money.
  ●你為什麼喜歡賭博？　●因為我有機會贏大錢。

▶ There is a possibility that the bus will be late.
  公車有可能會晚到。
  There's a good chance that it will rain today.
  今天很有可能會下雨。

---

34 | 給予／錯過機會
take the chance

7-34.mp3

give sb a chance

- give sb a chance to do
  給某人機會做…
- provide an opportunity for
  提供…的機會
- offer sb a chance
  提供某人機會

給某人機會 give 也可以換成 offer, provide 等有「提供」意義的動詞。

- I don't like the new student in our class.
- **Give her a chance to** become your friend.
  ●我不喜歡我們班上的新學生。　●給她一個成為你朋友的機會。

▶ Give them a chance to finish the project.
  給他們一個機會完成企畫案。
  Give Susan a chance to do her job.
  給 Susan 一個做她份內工作的機會。

1 職場・學校

2 電腦・網路

3 社交生活

4 日常生活

5 訊息・理解

6 想法・態度

7 情緒・狀況

8 行為舉止

9 時間地點・副詞片語

take the chance

· grab the chance
抓住機會

· jump at (the chance)
迅速抓住機會（seize an opportunity）

利用機會 take a chance 則是「冒險看看」的意思。

● I'm not sure if I should attend Harvard University or not.

● You should **take the chance**. It's a great school.

　●我不確定我應不應該去哈佛大學。

　●你應該把握機會，這是間好學校。

▶ Take the chance to get to know some new people.
利用機會去認識一些新的人。

I'll take the chance of investing in the stock market.
我要利用機會投資股票市場。

give a break

· give sb a break
通融某人，放某人一馬

· Give me a break!
通融一下嘛！放我一馬！

通融一下，放人一馬 依照狀況的不同，有破例給予機會的意思，也有不要再苛責或刁難某人的意思。

● I can't give you a discount on this.

● Come on, **give me a break** on the price.

　●這個我不能給你折扣。　　●拜託，通融一下。

▶ Give him a break. It's his first day working here.
放他一馬吧，這是他第一天在這裡工作。

They don't speak English well, so give them a break.
他們英文說得不好，放他們一馬吧。

miss out on

· lose a chance/ opportunity
喪失機會

· pass up one's chance
放過某人的機會

錯過（好機會） on 後面可以接 holiday, experience, chance 等名詞。

● Are you going shopping tomorrow?

● Yes. I don't want to **miss out on** some bargains.

　●你明天要去逛街嗎？　　●要，我不想錯過一些特價。

▶ Brian missed out on the class party.
Brian 錯過了班上的派對。

She won't miss out on the award ceremony.
她不會錯過頒獎典禮。

---

take the chance vs. take a chance

　　雖然只是 the 和 a 的差異，但意思完全不同。使用定冠詞 the 的 take the chance 意為「抓住某個特定的機會」，也就是「利用機會」（use the opportunity）。至於不定冠詞 a 的 take a chance，則是「即使有危險還是去做」的意思。

35 有／沒有差別
be different from

7-35.mp3

---

be different from

- differ from
  和…不同
- There's no difference between...
  …之間沒有差別
- What's the difference between...?
  …之間的不同點是什麼？

和…不同 如果要表示「有很大的不同」，則在 different 前面加上 quite, very 等副詞。

- Is that coat made by Burberry?
- No, it **is different from** Burberry coats.
  - ●那是 Burberry 的大衣嗎？　●不是，這和 Burberry 的大衣不一樣。

▶ This food is different from the type I normally eat.
這份食物和我平常吃的種類不同。
My computer is different from Tim's.
我的電腦和 Tim 的不一樣。

---

make no difference

- It makes no difference to sb
  對某人沒差／不重要
- make a/the difference
  有差，重要

沒差，不重要 後面可以加 to 接對象，表示對誰而言沒差。

- What kind of ice cream do you want?
- Oh, it **makes no difference to** me.
  - ●你想要哪種冰淇淋？　●噢，我都沒差。

▶ The type of music makes no difference to us.
音樂的類型對我們來說不重要。
My girlfriend's friends make no difference to me.
我女朋友交的朋友對我來說不重要。

---

tell A from B

- tell A apart
  分辨 A（兩個以上的人事物）
- tell the difference between
  分辨…之間的差異

分辨 A 和 B 辨識雙方的差異點並且作出區分。know sth apart（sth 是兩個以上的人事物）也有分辨的意思。

- Are these your eye glasses?
- I can't **tell** my glasses **from** someone else's.
  - ●這是你的眼鏡嗎？　●我分不出自己和別人的眼鏡。

▶ She can't tell one pop star from another.
她分不出流行歌手之間的差別。
Tom can't tell his car from his brother's car.
Tom 無法區分他自己的車和他弟弟的車。

1 職場・學校

2 電腦・網路

3 社交生活

4 日常生活

5 訊息・理解

6 想法・態度

7 情緒・狀況

8 行為舉止

9 時間地點・副詞片語

distinguish A from B

· distinguish between
  區分…兩者
· be a far cry from
  和…大相逕庭
· vary with
  隨…而變化

區分 A 和 B 確認兩者之間的差異。

● Can you **distinguish** summer **from** winter?

● Of course. Summer is hot and winter is cold.

  ●你能區分夏天和冬天嗎？　●當然。夏天很熱，冬天很冷。

▶ I need to distinguish smog from pollution.
  我需要把煙霧和污染區分開來。
  It's hard to distinguish Germans from Austrians.
  德國人和奧地利人很難區分。

be not the same as

· be not the same with
  跟…的情況不同

和…不同　It is not the same with... 則是「和…的情況不一樣」的意思。

● I read many newspapers and comic books.

● Newspapers **are not the same as** comic books.

  ●我讀很多報紙和漫畫書。　●報紙跟漫畫書不同吧。

▶ Japanese people are not the same as Koreans.
  日本人和韓國人不同。
  This restaurant is not the same as the one in my neighborhood.
  這間餐廳和我家附近那間不同。

36 像，相似
be similar to

7-36.mp3

be similar to

· N + similar to
  和…類似的 N

和…類似　雖然不是 100% 相同，但很相似。注意介系詞是 to。

● Are you carrying a Louis Vuitton suitcase?

● No, but it **is similar to** a Louis Vuitton suitcase.

  ●你帶的是 LV 的行李箱嗎？　●不是，但它跟 LV 的行李箱很像。

▶ Cheju Island is similar to the Hawaiian Islands.
  濟州島跟夏威夷群島很像。
  In what ways is it similar?
  這在哪方面是類似的？

be alike

- be alike in many ways
  在許多方面很像
- look alike
  看起來相像
- think alike
  想法相近

相像 主詞是兩個以上的人事物。可以說 very much / a little bit alike 表示相像的程度。

- Brad and his brother **are very alike**.
- Yes. I think they look like twins.

  ●Brad 和他弟弟長得很像。　●是啊，我覺得他們看起來像雙胞胎。

▶ These apartment buildings are alike in many ways.

  這些公寓大樓在很多方面都很相似。

  The gifts we gave at the wedding are alike.

  我們在婚禮上給的禮物很像。

look like

- What be...look like?
  …看起來怎麼樣？
- What be+N+like?
  …怎麼樣？（個性或性質）

看起來像… 形容外貌或外觀。除了接名詞以外，也可以接 S+V。

- What does your uncle look like?
- I think he **looks like** Tom Cruise.

  ●你叔叔長得怎麼樣？　●我覺得他長得像湯姆‧克魯斯。

▶ This food looks like it is spoiled.

  這食物看起來像是壞了。

  You look like you stayed up late.

  你看起來像是熬夜到很晚。

take after

像… 和家族裡的某個長輩很像，像是遺傳的一樣。

- Your daughter seems very smart.
- Well, she **takes after** her grandmother.

  ●你女兒看起來很聰明。　●嗯，她就像她奶奶一樣。

▶ Mike takes after his father's side of the family.

  Mike 跟他爸爸那邊的人很像。

  She takes after her great aunt.

  她和她姑婆很像。

be equal to

- be equivalent
  相同／相等
- be no better than
  不比…好
» cf. be second to none
  首屈一指

等於… 基本的意思是數量上的相等。

- This money **is equal to** one month's salary.
- You should be very careful with it.

  ●這些錢等於一個月的薪水。　●你應該非常小心保管。

▶ Each calendar is equal to one year's time.

  每份月曆都等於一年的時間。

  The money you have now is equal to my life savings.

  你現在擁有的錢，跟我這輩子的積蓄一樣多。

something like that

像那樣的事　...and the like 則是「…等等（諸如此類的事物）」。

- How could you do **something like that**?
- I promise I won't let it happen again.

　●你怎麼可以做出那樣的事？　●我發誓不會再讓它發生了。

▶ I didn't think something like that would happen.
　我以為那樣的事不會發生。
　Brenda always does something like that.
　Brenda 總是做那樣的事。

be the same as...

- be the same as S+V
  和…相同
- be the same with
  和…的情況一樣

和…相同　as 後面接名詞或 S+V。

- Take a look at my diamond earrings.
- They **are the same as** the pair my aunt has.

　●看看我的鑽石耳環。　●這跟我阿姨那副一樣。

▶ The temperature is the same as it was yesterday.
　今天的氣溫和昨天相同。
　This TV show is the same as most other game shows.
　這個電視節目和大多數的遊戲節目一樣。

have the same...

- have the same + N as
  + 比較對象
  和…有相同的 N

擁有相同的…　表示在某部分、某方面相同。

- Pat **has the same** last name as you.
- That is because he is my cousin.

　●Pat 的姓和你一樣。　●因為他是我的堂弟。

▶ I have the same goals in life as you do.
　我和你有相同的人生目標。
　She has the same dress as I do.
　她有跟我一樣的洋裝。

look as if S+V

- as if S+V
  好像…的樣子

看起來好像…　也可以說 seem as if S+V。

- It **looks as if** Henry is going home.
- He told me he was feeling sick today.

　●Henry 看來像是要回家了。　●他跟我說他今天覺得不舒服。

▶ It looks as if I need a better job.
　看來我需要一份更好的工作。
　It looks as if we'll be leaving tomorrow.
　看來我們明天要離開了。

1 職場・學校
2 電腦・網路
3 社交生活
4 日常生活
5 訊息・理解
6 想法・態度
7 情緒・狀況
8 行為舉止
9 時間地點・副詞片語

run in the family

- think of sb/sth
  想到，考慮…
- think about sb/sth
  思考…

在家族中遺傳 疾病或特徵在家族內代代相傳的情況。

- ● Fred's mom and two of her brothers had cancer.
- ● That's too bad. It must **run in the family**.
  - ● Fred 的媽媽和她的兩位兄弟都有癌症。
  - ● 真是太糟了。這應該是家族遺傳吧。

▶ Being short runs in Melissa's family.
  Melissa 家族裡的人都是矮個子。
  Does intelligence run in your family?
  你們家族的人都很聰明嗎？

---

37 | 適應，變得熟悉
get used to

7-37.mp3

---

get/be used to

- get accustomed to
  N/-ing
  變得習慣於…

習慣… 後面接名詞或動詞 -ing 形。used to（前面沒有 get/be）則是接原形動詞，表示過去規律的行為或狀態，請分辨清楚。

- ● Did you **get used to** the weather in Canada?
- ● Yes, but it is awfully cold in the winter.
  - ● 你習慣加拿大的天氣了嗎？　● 習慣了，但冬天實在冷得要命。

▶ You need to get used to eating different foods.
  你需要習慣吃不同的食物。
  You'd better get used to it. 你最好習慣。
  Did you get used to driving in the rain?
  你習慣在雨中開車了嗎？

be familiar with

- be familiar with sth
  熟悉某事
- be familiar to sb
  對某人而言很熟悉

熟悉… with sth 意為「熟悉某事」，to sb 則是「對某人而言很熟悉」。

- ● This music was composed by Chopin.
- ● I **am not familiar with** his music.
  - ● 這音樂是蕭邦作曲的。　● 我跟他的音樂不熟。

▶ Sherry was not familiar with the school's classrooms.
  Sherry 不熟悉學校的教室。
  Are you familiar with using computers? 你用電腦熟練嗎？
  Does she seem familiar to you? 你覺得她面熟嗎？

1 職場・學校

2 電腦・網路

3 社交生活

4 日常生活

5 訊息・理解

6 想法・態度

7 情緒・狀況

8 行為舉止

9 時間地點・副詞片語

be experienced in

· be well qualified for
很有資格擔任…
· seasoned
經驗豐富的

在…方面有經驗 experienced 是由 experience 的動詞用法「經歷，體驗」衍生出的形容詞。

● Tell me why you want to be a teacher.

● I **am experienced at** helping students with their work.

●告訴我你為什麼想當老師。　●我對於幫助學生的課業很有經驗。

▶ He was experienced in repairing TVs.
他修理電視很有經驗。
Steven is experienced in creating web pages.
Steven 在製作網頁方面很有經驗。

get the hang of

· get the knack of
掌握…的要領

掌握…的訣竅 the hang 在這裡是「訣竅」的意思。

● Have you learned how to salsa dance yet?

● Well, I'm starting to **get the hang of** it.

●你學會怎麼跳 salsa 舞了嗎？　●這個嘛，我開始掌握到訣竅了。

▶ Sam couldn't get the hang of using chopsticks.
Sam 無法掌握使用筷子的訣竅。
You'll get the hang of using your new cell phone.
你會熟悉新手機的使用方法的。

---

38 | 像，相似
be hard to

7-38.mp3

be easy to

· It's easy to do
做…簡單
· It's not easy to do
做…不簡單

做…簡單 通常以 It's easy to do... 的形態呈現。

● It's **easy to** talk to my girlfriend.

● You have a good relationship with her.

●跟我女朋友說話很輕鬆。　●你跟她的關係真好。

▶ It is easy to fix this problem.
修正這個問題很簡單。
They are easy to work with.
和他們共事很輕鬆。

be hard to

做…困難 to 前面加上 for sb 可以表示對誰而言困難。

- These apartment buildings are so ugly.
- **It is hard to** design attractive apartment buildings.
  - 這些公寓大樓真醜。　●設計吸引人的公寓大樓很難。

▶ It is hard to teach the new students.
　教新學生很難。
　It is hard to find a good bargain.
　便宜實惠的東西很難找。

be difficult to

做…困難 hard 是口語中比較常用的說法，difficult 的語氣稍微鄭重一點，常常表示需要一定程度的技術才能做到。

- I don't like the notebook computer I have.
- **It is not difficult to** buy a different model.
  - 我不喜歡我的筆記型電腦。　●買一台不同的機種並不難。

▶ It is not difficult to see the ocean from here.
　從這邊不難看到海。
　It is not difficult to cook this food.
　煮這種食物並不難。

make sth easy

· make things easier
　讓事情變得簡單些
· make it easy (for sb)
　to do
　使（某人）做…變簡單

使某事簡單 使役動詞 make + N + Adj「使某個人事物變得…」的句型。

- I just can't understand this homework.
- I'll help you **make** finishing it **easy**.
  - 我就是搞不懂這份作業。　●我會幫你把完成這份作業變得簡單。

▶ Can you make painting pictures easy?
　你能夠讓作畫變得簡單嗎？
　Let me make it easy for you to get it.
　讓我簡單說明一下，好讓你能了解。

make sth hard

· make it hard/difficult
　to do
　使做…變困難

使某事困難 類似的說法還有 make sth complex「把某事變複雜」。

- Why don't you like your teacher?
- She **made** our class **hard**.
  - 你為什麼不喜歡你的老師？　●她把課變得很難。

▶ The snow made it hard to travel.
　雪使得旅行變困難。
　The darkness made seeing her hard.
　因為黑暗，所以很難看見她。

1 職場・學校
2 電腦・網路
3 社交生活
4 日常生活
5 訊息・理解
6 想法・態度
7 情緒・狀況
8 行為舉止
9 時間地點・副詞片語

39 過得好
be doing okay

7-39.mp3

be doing okay

· be doing (just) fine
  過得不錯
· be okay
  還可以，過得去

過得還可以 okay 也可以換成 good 或 great。

- I haven't seen your parents in a while.
- My dad and mom **are doing okay**.
  - 我好一陣子沒見到你父母親了。　● 我爸媽過得還可以。

▶ I'm glad to see you're doing okay.
  我很高興看到你過得還不錯。
  You're doing great. 你做得很好。

be cool

· be fine/okay
  不錯

很酷，很棒，冷靜 cool 在口語裡相當於 great 的意思。「很棒」還有 wonderful, fantastic, terrific 等說法。

- How are things going in your school?
- My classes **are cool**. I really like my teachers.
  - 在學校過得怎樣？　● 我的課都很棒，我真的很喜歡我的老師們。

▶ Be cool and try not to get so stressed.
  冷靜點，試著不要有那麼多壓力。
  The art class is cool and a lot of fun. 美術課很棒而且很有趣。

be not bad

· be not that bad
  沒那麼差

還不錯 對於「…怎麼樣？」的問題，可以直接回答 Not bad.。

- What is it like living in Australia?
- It **is not bad**. Sydney is an interesting city.
  - 在澳洲的生活怎麼樣？　● 還不錯，雪梨是個有趣的城市。

▶ This fish soup is not bad. 這魚湯還不錯。
  Your athletic ability is not bad. 你的運動才能不差。

couldn't be better

再好不過了 「不可能更好了」，表示「是最好的狀態」。

- How are things going around here?
- They **couldn't be better**.
  - 這邊一切都還好嗎？　● 再好不過了。

▶ The weather today just couldn't be better.
  今天的天氣再好不過了。
  The taste of chocolate couldn't be better.
  巧克力的味道真是再好不過了。

could be better

· could be worse
  不算太糟

不怎麼好，還可以更好　還能比現在更好，表示對現在的狀況不太滿意。雖然有 better，卻不是正面的意思。

● How have you been feeling lately?
● I **could be better**. I'm still sick.

　● 你最近覺得怎樣？　● 不怎麼好，我還是在生病。

▶ Your test scores could be better. 你的測驗成績可以更好的。
　This vacation tour could be better. 這趟假期旅行不怎麼好玩。

can't complain

還可以，還算滿意　沒什麼好抱怨的，表示大致上還可以。

● Are you enjoying being married to Ben?
● I **can't complain**. He's a good man.

　● 你嫁給 Ben 開心嗎？　● 還可以，他是個好男人。

▶ Harriet can't complain about her new boots.
　Harriet 對她新買的靴子還算滿意。
　I can't complain about the food here.
　我對這裡的食物還算滿意。

nothing much

· Not very well.
  （過得）不是很好。

沒什麼事　通常用來回答「What's up?」這個問題。

● What's up, Chris?
● **Nothing much**... How are you doing?

　● Chris，過得還好嗎？　● 沒什麼啊…你過得怎樣？

▶ Nothing much is going on today. 今天沒發生什麼事。
　Nothing much. What's going on with you?
　沒什麼事。你過得怎樣？

get along

· get along with sb
  和某人相處融洽

相處融洽　後面接 with sb。

● Did he **get along** well with your parents?
● Yes, they loved him.

　● 他和你父母親處得好嗎？　● 嗯，他們很喜歡他。

▶ We got along with everyone in the club.
　我們和社團中的每個人都相處融洽。
　Do you get along with your mother? 你和你母親處得好嗎？

go on with

· go on with sb
  和某人繼續合作／在一起
· go on with sth
  繼續某事

繼續…，和…繼續合作／在一起　也可以只說 go on，單純表示「繼續下去」的意思。

● Do you plan to **go on with** your current secretary?
● No, I need to hire a better person.

　● 你打算繼續用你現在這位秘書嗎？　● 不，我需要找個更好的人。

▶ I can't go on with my story. 我無法繼續說我的故事。
　I'm just going to go on with the tour group.
　我打算就跟旅行團繼續走下去。

Various Actions

日常生活中各種行為舉止的慣用語

CHAPTER 8

01 選擇，挑選
choose to

8-01.mp3

choose to

- choose sth/sb
  選擇…
- choose A to do
  選擇 A 去做…
- get/be chosen for
  被選為…

選擇做… 和 decide to 比起來，choose to 更強調從許多可能性中選出一個的意思。

- What is Ken going to do tomorrow?
- I think he'll **choose to** go to the park.
  - Ken 明天要做什麼？　●我想他會選擇去公園。

▶ We can choose to do what is right.
  我們可以選擇去做對的事。
  Tell me why you chose to pursue a career in engineering.
  告訴我你為什麼選擇以工程師為職業。

have a choice

- have a choice to do
  有做…的選擇
- make a choice (of)
  做（…的）選擇
- make a bad choice
  做出壞選擇

有選擇 表示不是非得怎樣做才行。have no choice 意為「沒有選擇」。

- You should skip school tomorrow.
- I don't **have a choice** about going to school.
  - 你明天應該蹺課。　●對於去上學這件事，我沒有選擇。

▶ You don't have a choice right now.
  你現在沒有任何選擇。
  I just need to make a choice and get it over with.
  我只需要做個選擇，把事情了結。

give sb a choice

- give sb a choice in this matter
  在這件事上給某人選擇的權力
- give sb no choice
  不給某人選擇的權力

給某人選擇的權力 give sb no choice 則是不給某人選擇。

- I **gave** Kelly **a choice of** what to do.
- Has she made a decision yet?
  - 我讓 Kelly 選擇要怎麼做。　●她下決定了嗎？

▶ You need to give the students a choice in this matter.
  在這件事上，你需要給學生們選擇。
  Dad gave me a choice of birthday presents.
  爸爸讓我選生日禮物。

pick out

- pick sth
  挑選某物
- single out
  單獨挑出…（作為表揚或告誡）

挑出… 在許多選項中，選出符合某種特定目的人或事物。

- Can you help me **pick out** a wedding ring?
- I'd be happy to help you.
  ●你可以幫我選婚戒嗎？　●我很樂意幫忙。

▶ I'm going to pick out some new clothes.
  我要去挑些新衣服。
  Feel free to pick out whatever you need.
  隨意挑選你需要的任何東西。

take one's pick

- take one's pick of...
  選擇…

（依照個人喜好）選擇 take 也可以換成 have。

- Can I have a piece of your candy?
- Sure, you can **take your pick**.
  ●我可以吃顆你的糖嗎？　●當然，選顆你喜歡的吧。

▶ I took my pick of the books to read.
  我選了我要讀的書。
  They took their pick of the DVDs.
  他們選了喜歡的 DVD。

take sth

- I'll take sth
  我要（買）某個東西
- take it or leave it
  要不要隨你
- It's now or never.
  現在不做就沒機會了。

取得／接受某事物 視情況不同，take 有時候會帶點「選擇…」的意思。

- I'll **take** this one.
- Do you want me to wrap it up for you?
  ●我要買這個。　●需要我幫你包裝嗎？

▶ That's my offer, take it or leave it.
  這是我的提案，接不接受隨你。
  You need to decide. It's now or never.
  你需要下決定，現在不做就沒機會了。

go with

隨著…而去，選擇… 隨著情況的不同，意思也會不一樣，其中一個意思是「選擇／要某個東西」。

- Which ring do you prefer?
- I'm going to **go with** the silver one.
  ●你比較喜歡哪個戒指？　●我會選銀製的那個。

▶ You should go with the newest computer.
  你應該選最新的電腦。
  I decided not to go with the LG phone.
  我決定不要選 LG 的手機。

1 職場・學校
2 電腦・網路
3 社交生活
4 日常生活
5 訊息・理解
6 想法・態度
7 情緒・狀況
8 行為舉止
9 時間地點・副詞片語

opt for

- opt for the name brand
  選擇名牌
- opt to do
  選擇做…

選擇… option（選項）就是動詞 opt 的名詞形。
- What would you like for lunch?
- I'm going to **opt for** the pizza.
  - 你午餐想吃什麼？ ● 我要選披薩。

▶ She opted for a college in her hometown.
  她選擇了在家鄉的大學。
  They opted for an action movie.
  他們選擇了動作片。

prefer to

偏好做…，寧可做… prefer 就是 like better 的意思，表示以個人喜好加以比較。
- We should stop and take a break.
- I **prefer to** work until we finish.
  - 我們應該停下來休息一下。 ● 我寧可工作到完成為止。

▶ Most kids prefer to enjoy free time rather than study.
  比起讀書，大多數的孩子更喜歡享受空閒時間。
  She prefers to be alone all the time.
  她比較喜歡隨時都單獨行動。

---

02 改變，替換
change one's mind

8-02.mp3

change one's mind

- change one's mind about...
  對於…改變心意

改變心意 對已經做了決定或選擇的事改變心意。
- I thought you were going to go on leave.
- I was thinking about that, but I **changed my mind**.
  - 我以為你要休假。 ● 我有在考慮，但我改變主意了。

▶ I changed my mind. I'll have dinner with you.
  我改變心意了，我會跟你一起吃晚餐。
  I had to change my plans for the summer.
  我必須變更我的夏季計畫。

make a change

· change sth
  改變某事物
» cf. get/be changed
  換衣服
· make change
  找零錢

做出改變 make a lot of changes 意為「做出很多改變」。去掉冠詞「a」的 make change 則是「找零錢」的意思。

● Why did you decide to move away?
● I needed to **make a change** in my life.
  ●你為什麼決定搬走？　●我需要在人生中做出改變。

▶ Doris decided to change her hairstyle.
  Doris 決定改變她的髮型。
  Excuse me. I need a minute to get changed.
  不好意思，我需要一點時間換衣服。

have changed

· have a change of
  heart
  改變心意
· Things/Times have
  changed.
  狀況改變了。

改變了 和過去式 changed 比起來，現在完成式 have changed 更強調「和過去不同了」的意思。

● Sharon is acting strange these days.
● Yeah, she **has changed** a lot.
  ●Sharon 最近行為舉止很奇怪。　●是啊，她變了很多。

▶ I was going to leave, but I had a change of heart.
  我原本要離開了，但我改變了心意。
  Things have changed since we last met.
  我們上次見過面後，事態改變了。

remain unchanged

· stay the same
  保持一樣

保持不變 remain + 形容詞的句型。changed 是「被改變的」，加上字首 un- 就是「沒變的」。

● Is your hometown any different these days?
● No, it's pretty much **remained unchanged**.
  ●你的家鄉最近有任何不同嗎？　●沒有，幾乎沒什麼變化。

▶ This restaurant always stays the same.
  這間餐廳總是維持原樣。
  My best friend remains unchanged from high school.
  我最好的朋友從高中開始就一直沒有改變。

get one's ID renewed

· renew sth
  更新某物

更新身分證 get A pp 的句型，表示使 A 獲得某種處理。

● Why are you going to the government office?
● I need to **get my ID renewed**.
  ●你為什麼要去政府辦公室？　●我需要更新我的身分證。

▶ Did you renew your driver's license?
  你更新你的駕照了嗎？
  This office is for the renewal of your passport.
  這間辦公室可以更新你的護照。

1 職場・學校
2 電腦・網路
3 社交生活
4 日常生活
5 訊息・理解
6 想法・態度
7 情緒・狀況
8 行為舉止
9 時間地點・副詞片語

take it back

拿回來，拿回去 歸還或拿回某個東西。take back 也可以表示「收回」說過的話。

- I heard that Chip gave you his i-Pod.
- No, he came and **took it back**.
  - ●聽說 Chip 把他的 i-Pod 給你了。 ●沒有，他來把它拿回去了。

▶ The TV doesn't work and I'll take it back to the store.
這電視不能用，我要把它退回店裡。
If you don't like the ring, take it back.
如果你不喜歡那個戒指，就還來。

replace A with B

· need replacing
需要更換

將 A 更換為 B 被動句型的說法則是 A is replaced by B。

- That is a very old notebook.
- I know. I'll **replace** it **with** a newer one.
  - ●那本筆記本很舊。 ●我知道，我會去換一本比較新的。

▶ The tires on my car need replacing.
我車子的輪胎需要更換。
Can you replace this stove with another one?
你可以把這暖爐換成另一個嗎？

substitute A for B

· be substituted with
被替換為…
· a substitute
代替物，替補球員

用 A 代替 B 用某種類似的代替物，扮演原有物品的角色。

- We ran out of the cake.
- Well, you can **substitute** pie **for** cake.
  - ●我們的蛋糕吃完了。 ●嗯，你可以用派來替換蛋糕。

▶ This is a substitute for what you ordered.
這是你訂購物品的替代品。
I'm going to substitute water for Coke.
我要用水來代替可樂。

in place of

· in place of my boss
接替我的老闆

代替… 意思和 instead of 一樣。

- Why is Beth teaching your class?
- She's here **in place of** our science teacher.
  - ●Beth 為什麼在教你們班？ ●她接任我們的科學老師。

▶ New manager was put in place of my boss.
新的主管替補了我的上司。
We ate ice cream in place of yogurt.
我們吃冰淇淋來代替優格。

change the baby

　　有一位由於先生職務之故，跟著到美國生活的台灣妻子，跟附近的美國媽媽推著各自的嬰兒車，一起走到公園，坐在長椅上享受秋高氣爽的天氣。過了一會兒，美國媽媽突然說「It's time to change the baby.」。這位台灣媽媽聽了，大驚失色地說：「真的能這樣嗎？我是聽說過換妻（wife swapping），但怎麼可以連孩子都…」，就黯然離開了。這個悲情的故事在美國移民之間流傳了好一陣子呢。這邊的 change the baby 並不是交換孩子的意思，而是指更換小孩穿的尿布。

03

決定，決心
make a decision

8-03.mp3

---

decide to

· decide that S+V
  決定…

決定做… 考慮過利弊得失之後，決定去做某事。

● I **decided to** leave early in the morning.
● You should get a good night's sleep.

　　●我決定早上早點離開。　　●你晚上應該好好睡一覺。

▶ I decided I wanted to come to your party.
　　我決定要來參加你的派對。
　　What made you decide to quit your job?
　　你為什麼決定辭掉工作？

---

make a decision

· make a huge decision
  下重大決定
· make decisions about...
  做出關於…的決定
· make wise decisions
  做出有智慧的決定

下決定 後面可以接 on/about sth 表示是關於什麼的決定。

● I don't know if I want to marry Jen.
● You need to **make a decision** about that.

　　●我不知道我是否想娶 Jen。　　●你需要對這件事下決定。

▶ When will you make a decision?
　　你什麼時候會下決定？
　　We need to make a decision on who's going to be fired.
　　我們需要決定誰要被解雇。

569

右側書側標籤：
1 職場・學校
2 電腦・網路
3 社交生活
4 日常生活
5 訊息・理解
6 想法・態度
7 情緒・狀況
8 行為舉止
9 時間地點・副詞片語

come to a decision

· reach a decision
  做出決定

做出決定 decision 是 decide 的名詞形。come to 也可以換成 reach。

- I need to know what you are going to do.
- I haven't **come to a decision** yet.
  - 我需要知道你要怎麼做。　●我還沒有做出決定。

▶ The board will reach a decision this afternoon.
　董事會會在今天下午做出決定。
　Have you come to a decision about it?
　你對那件事做出決定了嗎？

make up one's mind

· make up one's mind
  to do
  下定決心去做…
· make up one's mind
  about...
  對於…下定決心
· make up one's mind
  that...
  下定決心要…

下定決心 特別指猶豫了一陣子之後終於做出決定的情況。

- Hurry up and **make up your mind**.
- It's not easy. Give me more time.
  - 趕快下定決心。　●這並不容易。給我更多時間。

▶ Make up your mind. What time is okay for you?
　快決定。你幾點方便？
　You have to make up your mind pretty quick.
　你必須迅速下定決心。

draw a conclusion

· draw a conclusion
  that S+V
  得出…的結論
· bring A to a
  conclusion
  將 A 作結
· conclude sth/that...
  結束…，斷定…

得出結論 jump to conclusions 意為「貿然下結論」。

- I like to sleep all day.
- People will **draw a conclusion** you're lazy.
  - 我喜歡睡一整天。　●人們會下結論說你很懶惰。

▶ It's time to bring the meeting to a conclusion.
　該是把會議作結的時候了。
　We concluded the festival on Sunday evening.
　我們在星期天傍晚結束了慶典。

call the shots

當家作主，做決定，負責 表示處於決策階層，下達命令。

- Are you in charge today?
- That's right. I'll **call the shots**.
  - 今天是由你負責嗎？　●是的，我會做決定。

▶ Ken calls the shots on the football team.
　Ken 在足球隊中發號施令。
　My boss calls the shots at work.
　在工作上，是我老闆當家作主。

make a resolution

· make a resolution to do
  決定做⋯
· The ball's in your court.
  現在球在你的場上
  →輪到你採取行動了。

下決心　resolution 是指「要達到某個目標」的決心或決定。

● How are things with your boyfriend?
● We **made a resolution** not to argue.

　●妳和妳男朋友情況怎樣？　●我們下定決心不要吵架。

▶ The ball's in your court if you want to do something.
　如果你想做些什麼，你該採取行動了。
　Let's make a resolution to meet next year.
　讓我們約定明年見吧。

have one's heart set on sth

決心做某事　heart 也可以換成 mind，意思一樣。

● My son **has his heart set on** going to Africa.
● That will be an expensive trip to make.

　●我兒子下了決心要去非洲。　●那會是趟昂貴的旅行。

▶ I have my heart set on marrying her.
　我決心要跟她結婚。
　They had their heart set on a big party.
　他們下了決心要辦一場盛大的派對。

 ### shot 的各種使用方式

　　call the shots 原本是指在射擊獵物之前先預告自己的目標，後來引申出「做決定」（make a decision）和「處於下達命令的地位」（be in a position to give orders）的意思。打撞球的人也會說 call the shots，這時候則是預告要把哪顆球打進哪個球袋的意思，shot 在撞球中剛好是指「擊球」的動作。跟 call the shots 意思相同的慣用語還有 call the tune，原本的意思是付錢向吹笛子的人點歌。

　　shot 在口語中也有「嘗試」（attempt）的意思，be a long shot 則是指「即使再怎麼試，可能性也很小」。a shot in the dark 就像字面上的意思一樣，用「在黑暗中射擊」比喻「胡亂嘗試」或「瞎猜」。a big shot 則是指業界的「大人物」。

1 職場 · 學校

2 電腦 · 網路

3 社交生活

4 日常生活

5 訊息 · 理解

6 想法 · 態度

7 情緒 · 狀況

8 行為舉止

9 時間地點 · 副詞片語

have things one's way

· have everything one's own way
所有事情都照某人自己的意思來做

照某人的意思做 have 可以換成 get，意思一樣。

● Why do you act so selfish all the time?
● I need to **have things my way**.
　●你為什麼行為總是那麼自私？　●我需要照我的意思來做事。

▶ Lucy demands to have everything her way.
　Lucy 要求所有事都照她的意思來。
　It's nice to have things my way here.
　這裡能照我的意思來做事，真的很好。

get one's own way

· have/get one's own way
前面的 have things one's own way 意為「想照自己的方式去做某件事」，而 have one's own way 則是「即使別人反對也不在乎，仍然照著自己想做的去做」。

照某人自己的意思做 即使別人反對也不在乎，只照自己想做的去做。

● My girlfriend decided not to come.
● She always has to **have her own way**.
　●我女朋友決定不要來。　●她總是想怎樣就怎樣。

▶ I want to have my own way when I travel.
　旅行的時候，我想要照自己的意思來。
　You always get your own way.
　你總是照自己的意思做事。

suit oneself

照自己的心意去做 與善惡對錯無關，就照自己的意思去做也可以。常用在祈使句。

● I'm tired and going home.
● **Suit yourself**, but you'll be sorry later.
　●我累了，要回家。　●隨你便，但你之後會後悔的。

▶ I decorated the apartment to suit myself.
　我照我的喜好布置了公寓。
　I don't agree, but you can suit yourself.
　我不同意，但你可以隨你的心意去做。

do as one pleases

· the right to do as one pleases
照自己想要的去做的權利

照某人想要的去做 pleases 也可以換成 likes，意思一樣。

● Maria says she will take the job she was offered.
● Well, she can **do as she pleases**.
  ● Maria 說她會接受她獲得的工作機會。
  ● 嗯，她可以照她想要的去做。

▶ All people have the right to do as they please.
  每個人都有權利照自己想要的去做。
  Please do just as you please.
  請就照你想要的去做。

follow one's heart

跟隨某人的心意 follow one's voice 則是指順從內心深處的指示去做。

● What has Sam decided to do?
● He's going to **follow his heart** and study music.
  ● Sam 決定做什麼？　● 他決定跟隨自己的心去學音樂。

▶ Follow your heart rather than following money.
  順從你的心，不要向錢看。
  If you want a happy life, follow your heart.
  如果你想要快樂的人生，就順從你的心吧。

---

05 固守，執著
hold on to

8-05.mp3

stick to sth

固守／忠於某事物 即使有困難，仍然繼續做某事。或者指繼續選擇某個商品、合作對象等等。

● Do you think I'll be successful?
● **Stick to** your plans and you'll be OK.
  ● 你覺得我會成功嗎？　● 堅持你的計畫，就沒問題了。

▶ We decided to stick to our schedule.
  我們決定維持我們的行程。
  You have to stick to your diet.
  你必須堅持減肥。

1 職場・學校

2 電腦・網路

3 社交生活

4 日常生活

5 訊息・理解

6 想法・態度

7 情緒・狀況

8 行為舉止

9 時間地點・副詞片語

hold on to

· hold on to the belief
保持信念

保有⋯，守住⋯ 原意是「緊握」。hold fast to 也是一樣的意思
（這裡的 fast 是「緊」的意思）。

- Wow, it is so windy outside today.
- Yeah, it's difficult to **hold on to** my umbrella.

　●哇，今天外面風好大。　　●是啊，很難抓緊我的傘。

▶ Jane held on to the belief that he was innocent.
Jane 堅持相信他是清白的。
You should hold on to that jewelry.
你應該看好那件珠寶。

be hung up on sth

· be/get hung up on the issue
執著／埋首於問題

為某事心神不寧 一直掛念著，無法專心的意思。

- Jack **is really hung up on** that actress.
- Well, she is quite beautiful.

　●Jack 真的對那位女演員很著迷。　　●嗯，她很美。

▶ The committee got hung up on an issue.
委員會埋首於一個問題。
Don't get hung up on that report.
別為了那份報告心神不寧。

be obsessed with

· obsessed fan
狂熱的支持者
· be obsessed with
one's looks
太過在意某人的外表

被⋯迷住，太在意⋯ 心思完全被佔據。with 也可以換成 by。

- Some teens **are obsessed with** Justin Beiber.
- He's giving a concert tomorrow night.

　●有些青少年很迷 Justin Beiber。　　●他明天晚上要開演唱會。

▶ The obsessed fans waited outside the hotel.
狂熱的歌迷們在飯店外等候。
Gina is just too obsessed with her looks.
Gina 太在意她的外表了。

follow suit

· follow one's example
跟隨某人為榜樣

跟隨前例 源於紙牌遊戲，跟著出同樣花色的意思。

- I will **follow my father's example**.
- He seems to know the secret of success.

　●我會跟隨我父親這個榜樣。　　●他看起來好像知道成功的祕訣。

▶ I'm confused, so don't follow my example.
我很困惑，所以別跟從我的例子。
The students followed their teacher's example.
學生們跟隨他們老師為榜樣。

1 職場・學校

2 電腦・網路

3 社交生活

4 日常生活

5 訊息・理解

6 想法・態度

7 情緒・狀況

8 行為舉止

9 時間地點・副詞片語

06 招來，引起
cause trouble

8-06.mp3

cause trouble

- cause A for B
  對 B 引起 A
- cause (sb) sth
  （對某人）引起某事
- cause sb
  embarrassment
  使某人難堪

引起問題 cause 通常是指引起不好的結果。

- Will the storm **cause trouble** for us?
- No, I think everything will be OK.
  - 暴風雨會對我們造成問題嗎？　● 不會，我想一切都會沒問題的。

▶ The broken train caused a delay.
　故障的列車造成了誤點。
　Our dirty house caused us embarrassment.
　我們骯髒的房子讓我們很難堪。

lead to

- lead to failure
  導致失敗

導向…，導致… lead 是引導的意思。這裡是指把事情引導到某個結果。

- I decided to study harder in school.
- That will **lead to** better grades.
  - 我決定在學校更認真學習。　● 那樣會讓你成績更好。

▶ Poor planning leads to failure.
　不完善的計畫會導致失敗。
　Ted and Betty's friendship led to romance.
　Ted 和 Betty 的友情轉變為愛情。

have an effect on

- have a positive
  effect on
  對…有正面影響
- have a negative
  effect on
  對…有負面影響

對…有影響 effect 前面可以加上 positive 或 negative 表示是正面或負面的影響。

- Everyone is in a good mood today.
- The nice weather **has an effect on** us all.
  - 每個人今天心情都很好。　● 好天氣影響了我們所有人。

▶ The new computer has a positive effect on my work.
　這台新電腦對我的工作有正面的影響。
　My lazy brother had a negative effect on me.
　我懶惰的弟弟對我有負面影響。

result in

- result from
  起因於…
- result in bloodshed
  造成流血事件
- as a result of war
  由於戰爭而造成…的結果

造成…的結果 主詞是原因，in 的後面是結果。result from 則相反，主詞是結果，from 之後是原因。

- Tad graduated at the top of his class.
- That should **result in** a good job for him.
  - Tad 在班上以第一名畢業。 ● 那應該會讓他得到一份好工作。

▶ Many injuries resulted from the accident.
  那場事故造成許多人受傷。
  The fight resulted in bloodshed.
  那場爭吵造成流血事件。

turn out

- turn out well/badly
  結果好／不好
- turn out alright
  結果還不錯
- turn out to be...
  結果變成…
- turn out that S+V
  結果是…

結果… 通常表示結果和最初的預期不一樣。後面可以接副詞或 to be...，或者用 It turns out that...（結果是…）的句型。

- How did your blind date **turn out**?
- It was terrible. I never want to see her again.
  - 你的聯誼結果怎樣？ ● 很糟，我永遠都不想再見到她。

▶ Everything turned out alright at the office.
  辦公室裡的每件事結果都不錯。
  We'll wait to see how the meeting turns out.
  我們等著看會議結果會怎樣。

grow out of

從…發展出來 表示事情是由另一件比較小的事發展形成的。或者從字面的意義解釋，表示小孩長大了，超過舊衣服的尺寸，或是擺脫了小時候的習慣。

- My daughter **grew out of** her clothes.
- You'd better buy her some new ones.
  - 我的女兒長大了，穿不下舊衣服。 ● 你最好買點新衣服給她。

▶ Most kids grow out of playing with toys.
  大多數的孩子長大後就不玩玩具了。
  I hope she'll grow out of sucking her thumb.
  我希望她長大後會戒掉吸大姆指的習慣。

end up -ing

- end up spending the
  night in the airport
  結果在機場過夜

結果… 表示最後的結果是在做某事。end up 後面也可以接介系詞片語，表示最後到了哪裡。

- What happened to Bob at his workplace?
- He **ended up** getting fired by his boss.
  - Bob 在工作的地方發生什麼事了？ ● 他最後被老闆開除了。

▶ We ended up spending the night in the Paris airport.
  結果我們在巴黎機場過夜。
  Michelle ended up missing the bus.
  結果 Michelle 錯過了公車。

1 職場・學校
2 電腦・網路
3 社交生活
4 日常生活
5 訊息・理解
6 想法・態度
7 情緒・狀況
8 行為舉止
9 時間地點・副詞片語

bring about sth

· bring about a change in the law
造成法律的修訂

帶來…的結果 主要用在帶來某種改變的情況。

● The economy has been terrible this year.

● It should **bring about** some new government programs.

　● 今年經濟狀況很差。　● 這應該會促成一些新的政府計畫。

▶ The crime brought about a change in the law.
那件犯罪行為促成了法律的修訂。

The party brought about some new friendships.
那場派對帶來了一些新的友誼→讓某人結交了一些新朋友。

had it coming

· You had it coming.
你自找的。

…自找的 用使役動詞 have，說主詞讓 it「coming」，表示這個結果是他自己招來的。這個慣用語固定用過去式。

● Brooke broke up with Jack today.

● Jack **had it coming**. He's no good.

　● Brooke 今天和 Jack 分手了。　● Jack 自找的。他沒什麼好的。

▶ You failed the test, but you had it coming.
你考試不及格，但這是你自找的。

You had it coming after you made her angry.
你讓她生氣是你自找的。

---

07 支持，保護 back sb up

8-07.mp3

give support to

· provide support to
提供支援給…

· support sb/sth
支援…

· support the idea that S+V
支持…的想法

支援… support 當名詞用。to 後面接「接受幫助的人」。

● Are you giving that food to poor people?

● Yes, we've got to **give support to** them.

　● 你要把那個食物給窮人嗎？　● 是啊，我們必須幫助他們。

▶ I provided support to the workers.
我為勞工提供支援。

She supported her husband when he went to school.
她先生上學的時候，她為他提供了金援。

be supportive of

· be in support of
  支援⋯

支援⋯ 對處於困難狀態的人提供援助。

● They are having a very hard time.
● Let's try to **be supportive of** them.
  ●他們過得很辛苦。　●我們試著幫助他們吧。

▶ The demonstration was in support of factory workers.
  那場示威是為了支援工廠的工人。
  Thank you for being so supportive.
  謝謝你這麼支持。

back sb up

· back up the story
  增加故事的說服力
· get/have sb's back
  （困難的時候）幫忙某人

支援某人 如同字面的意思，表示在後方給予依靠。

● Did you help Ryan out?
● Yeah, we all **backed him up**.
  ●你們有幫 Ryan 克服困難嗎？　●有，我們都支援了他。

▶ I had to back up the story with pictures.
  我必須用圖片來增加故事的說服力。
  Don't worry. I've got your back.
  別擔心，我會幫你的。

stand up for

· stand up for what you
  believe in
  維護你所相信的事物
· stand up for oneself
  自立
· stand by sb
  支持某人，對某人不離不
  棄

支持⋯，維護⋯ 可以想成是「為某人站出來」的意思。

● I **stood up for** my little brother.
● Good. Some other kids were bothering him.
  ●我保護了我的弟弟。　●做得好，有些孩子在找他麻煩。

▶ You need to stand up for what you believe in.
  你必須維護你所相信的事物。
  She stood by her husband even when he was in prison.
  即使她的先生坐了牢，她還是支持他。

protect sb from

· protect sb against
  保護某人免於⋯
· protect oneself
  against
  保護自己免於⋯

保護某人免於⋯ 介系詞 from 在這裡是「離開」、「避免」的
意思。

● It's been raining hard all day.
● Your umbrella will **protect you from** getting wet.
  ●大雨下了一整天。　●你的傘會保護你不被淋濕。

▶ The medicine protected me against getting sick.
  藥物讓我不生病。
  Protect yourself against being robbed.
  保護你自己，以免被搶劫。

08 容許，許可
allow sb to

8-08.mp3

1 職場・學校
2 電腦・網路
3 社交生活
4 日常生活
5 訊息・理解
6 想法・態度
7 情緒・狀況
8 行為舉止
9 時間地點・副詞片語

allow sb to

· be allowed to do
  被允許做…
· be permitted to do
  被允許做…

允許某人做… 常用被動態 (not) be allowed to 表示「（不）可以做…」。

● Where did Cheryl stay last night?
● We **allowed her to** sleep at our place.
　● Cheryl 昨晚在哪裡過夜？　　● 我們讓她在我們家睡。

▶ You're not allowed to talk in class.
  你在課堂上不可以說話。
  I'm not allowed to watch TV tonight.
  我今晚不被允許看電視。

give permission to

· without one's
  permission
  沒有某人的同意
· get special permission
  得到特別許可
· ask for one's
  permission
  尋求某人的許可

給予做…的許可 give sb permission to 意為「給某人許可去做…」。

● Why didn't you come to class today?
● My teacher **gave me permission to** stay home.
　● 你今天為什麼沒來上課？　　● 我的老師准許我待在家裡。

▶ You can't stay here without my permission.
  沒有我的同意，你不能待在這裡。
  Paul got special permission to come with us.
  Paul 得到特別許可，能跟我們一起來。

be authorized to

· be authorized to carry
  a gun
  被授權可以持有槍械
· be admitted to
  獲准進入…

獲得授權去做… authorize 表示正式給予許可。

● Did the plumber repair your sink?
● Yes, he **was authorized to** fix it.
　● 那位水管工修了你的水槽嗎？　　● 嗯，他被允許可以去修。

▶ The policeman was authorized to carry a gun.
  警察被授權可以持有槍械。
  The old man was admitted to the hospital yesterday.
  這位老先生昨天獲准入院了。

579

enable sb to

· enable users to video chat live
讓使用者能即時影音聊天

使某人能夠做… 主詞讓某人有能力做某事。

● Do you like your notebook computer?
● Yes, it **enables me to** work anywhere.
　● 你喜歡你的筆記型電腦？　● 喜歡，它讓我能在任何地方工作。

▶ These cameras enable users to video chat live.
這些攝影機讓使用者能即時影音聊天。
The winter coats enabled us to stay outside.
這些冬天的大衣讓我們能待在外頭。

you may

· Be my guest.
（回應請求）請便。

你可以… 除了表示允許以外，也可以表示可能性，翻譯成「你可能…」。

● Mr. Smith, I finished all of my class work.
● Good job. **You may** go now.
　● Smith 老師，我把所有課堂作業都做完了。
　● 做得很好。你現在可以走了。

▶ You may talk to the other students.
你可以跟其他學生談話。
You may take your sister to the store.
你可以帶你妹妹去那間店。

---

09 | 祝賀，稱讚 credit A with B

8-09.mp3

congratulate sb on...

· congratulate one another
互相祝賀
· congratulate sb on sth
因為某事恭喜某人
· Congratulations on sth
恭喜…

恭喜某人… 當面恭喜某人時，則會說 Congratulations on...!

● **Congratulations on** your graduation!
● I'm so happy to be finished with school.
　● 恭喜你畢業！　● 能夠畢業，我真是太開心了。

▶ I never had a chance to congratulate you on the baby.
我一直沒有機會恭喜你有了孩子。
Peter, I just came here to congratulate you.
Peter，我是來恭喜你的。

be honored for

· be flattered
  榮幸，受寵若驚
· be recognized for
  因為…而受肯定

因為…得到表揚 honor 當動詞用。介系詞 for 是用來說明事情的理由。

● Is your father going to be retiring soon?
● Yes, he'll **be honored for** the years he worked.
  ● 你父親快要退休了嗎？
  ● 嗯，由於他長年的服務，他將會得到表揚。

▶ I am flattered that you remember me.
  我很榮幸你還記得我。
  All mothers are recognized for their hard work.
  所有母親都因為努力而受肯定。

speak well of

· say nice things about...
  說…的好話
· speak ill of
  說…的壞話

稱讚… well 也可以改成 highly。speak ill of 則是說壞話的意思。

● Is Lisa a popular student?
● Sure. Everyone **speaks well of** her.
  ● Lisa 是個受歡迎的學生嗎？　● 當然，每個人都稱讚她。

▶ Kevin says nice things about our president.
  Kevin 都會說關於我們總裁的好話。
  Don't speak ill of people who have died.
  別詆毀那些已經過世的人。

credit A with B

· give sb credit
  認可某人，稱讚某人有功勞
· take credit for
  對…居功

將 B 歸功於 A 通常用來稱讚 A 是 B 的重要功臣。

● You look really healthy these days.
● I **credit** my doctor **with** making me better.
  ● 你最近看起來真的很健康。　● 多虧我醫生讓我變得健康。

▶ I give Bart credit for finishing dental school.
  我讚揚 Bart 完成了牙醫系的學業。
  Tanya took credit for our group's success.
  Tanya 把我們這組成功的功勞攬在自己身上

applaud sb

· applaud sb for -ing
  稱讚某人做了…
· praise sb
  稱讚某人
· give sb a big hand
  給某人熱烈的鼓掌

稱讚某人 原意是「拍手」或「喝采」，也可以引申為「稱讚」的意思。

● I have been working on this for years.
● We **applaud** you for doing so much work.
  ● 我為這件事努力好幾年了。　● 對於你做了這麼多，我們為你喝采。

▶ Frank's dad praised his good grades.
  Frank 的爸爸稱讚他的好成績。
  The audience gave the singer a big hand.
  聽眾們給那位歌手熱烈的鼓掌。

1 職場・學校
2 電腦・網路
3 社交生活
4 日常生活
5 訊息・理解
6 想法・態度
7 情緒・狀況
8 行為舉止
9 時間地點・副詞片語

10 鼓勵，說服
talk sb into -ing

talk sb into -ing

- talk sb in(to) sth/-ing
  說服某人做…
- talk me into
  marrying her
  說服我跟她結婚
- persuade sb to do
  說服某人去做…

說服某人去做… 說到說服，可能會有人馬上想到 persuade，但口語裡還是說 talk into 比較自然。

- I want to play a computer game.
- I'll try to **talk** Sarah **into** bringing some over.
  - 我想玩電腦遊戲。　● 我會試著說服 Sarah 帶一些過來。

▶ There's no way you're going to talk me into this.
　你絕無可能說服我做這件事。
　My mom talked me in coming with her.
　我媽媽說服我跟她一起來。

talk sb out of -ing

說服某人不要做… 把上一個慣用語的 into 改成 out of，就變成相反的意思。

- Did Rick go to Thailand?
- No, we **talked** him **out of** leaving.
  - Rick 去泰國了嗎？　● 沒有，我們說服他不要去。

▶ They talked me out of drinking whiskey.
　他們說服我不要喝威士忌。
　Please talk her out of dating Brandon.
　請說服她，不要跟 Brandon 約會。

encourage sb to

- be encouraged to do
  被鼓勵去做…
- encourage sb
  鼓勵某人

鼓勵某人做… 「讓某人打消…的主意」則是 discourage sb from...。

- Your daughter is a talented piano player.
- We'**ve encouraged** her **to** take more piano lessons.
  - 你女兒是位很有天分的鋼琴演奏者。
  - 我們已經鼓勵她上更多鋼琴課了。

▶ James was encouraged to cook her some dinner.
　James 被鼓勵去煮些晚餐給她。
　I encouraged him to go and take the exam.
　我鼓勵他去考試。

convince A of B

- convince A to do
  說服 A 去做⋯
- remain convinced of
  her innocence
  依然確信她的清白

說服 A 相信 B　被動態 be convinced that 的意思是「確信⋯」。

- Jeff **convinced** everyone **of** his honesty.
- We all believe in him.
  - ●Jeff 說服每個人相信他是誠實的。　●我們都相信他。

▶ She convinced Jay to help with the homework.
  她說服 Jay 幫忙做作業。
  The family remained convinced of her innocence.
  這家人依然確信她是清白的。

cheer sb up

- give a pep talk
  給予精神喊話

使某人振作起來　鼓勵某人時可以說 Cheer up!，喝酒乾杯時則說 Cheers.。

- You'll have a good job interview. **Cheer up.**
- Thanks. I'll do my best.
  - ●你工作面試會表現得很好的。加油。　●謝謝。我會盡我所能。

▶ Cheer up! You look so gloomy.
  開心點！你看起來好憂鬱。
  Do you know what might really cheer me up?
  你知道什麼可以真的讓我開心起來嗎？

11 | 忠告
give some advice

8-11.mp3

advise sb to

- be advised to do
  被勸告做⋯
- Please be advised
  that S+V
  請知悉⋯，請注意⋯

建議某人做⋯　被動態 be advised to 的意思是「被勸告做⋯」。

- I **advised** Bill **to** change jobs.
- He's very unhappy at his work.
  - ●我建議 Bill 換工作。　●他在工作上很不開心。

▶ She should be advised to stay home.
  她應該被建議待在家。
  Please be advised that I'm leaving now.
  我現在要離開了，請知悉。

1 職場・學校
2 電腦・網路
3 社交生活
4 日常生活
5 訊息・理解
6 想法・態度
7 情緒・狀況
8 行為舉止
9 時間地點・副詞片語

give sb some advice

· give sb advice about how to do
建議某人該怎麼做⋯

· ask sb for some advice
向某人尋求建議

給某人一點建議 後面加上 about how to do... 表示「建議怎麼做⋯」。

● **Give Bob some advice about** his future.

● Is he confused about what he will do?

●給 Bob 一點關於他未來的建議。　●他對於要做什麼很迷惘嗎？

▶ Heather gave me advice about how to fix the computer.
Heather 建議我該怎麼修電腦。

Do you need me to give you some advice?
你需要我給你一點建議嗎？

take the/one's advice

· want some advice
想要一點建議

· listen to sb's advice
聽某人的建議

· have advice for
有建議要給⋯

接受建議 可以用動詞 take 或 follow 表示接受建議。

● My friend told me to buy a car.

● You should **take the advice** he gave.

●我朋友叫我買台車。　●你應該接受他的建議。

▶ I want some advice about the future.
我想要一點關於未來的建議。

My grandfather has advice for you.
我爺爺有建議要給你。

recommend that S+V

· recommend -ing
建議做⋯

· strongly recommend that...
強烈建議⋯

建議⋯ recommend 可以表示建議做某件事，或者推薦某個東西。

● This cold medicine is really strong.

● Doctors **recommend that** you don't drive when using it.

●這感冒藥的藥效很強。　●醫生建議使用時不要開車。

▶ I strongly recommend that you start exercising.
我強烈建議你開始運動。

The hotel recommends booking early.
旅館建議提早訂房。

counsel sb to do

· be counseled to do
被勸告去做⋯

· counsel sb
勸告某人，給某人忠告

勸告某人去做⋯ 用在比較正式的情況下。

● What did your dad say to you?

● He **counseled me to** marry my girlfriend.

●你爸爸跟你說了什麼？　●他勸我跟我女朋友結婚。

▶ Jane counsels rape victims downtown.
Jane 在市中心輔導強暴受害者。

The two countries were counseled to end the war.
這兩個國家被勸告停止戰爭。

1 職場・學校
2 電腦・網路
3 社交生活
4 日常生活
5 訊息・理解
6 想法・態度
7 情緒・狀況
8 行為舉止
9 時間地點・副詞片語

12 警告，告誡
warn sb about

8-12.mp3

warn sb about

- warn sb
  警告某人
- warn sb about/on/of
  警告某人關於…
- warn sb not to do
  警告某人不要做…

警告某人關於… 介系詞 about 也可以換成 of 或 on。

● Mickey broke my heart.
● I **warned you about** dating him.

●Mickey 傷了我的心。　●你要跟他約會時，我就警告過你了。

▶ I'm not going to warn you about that again.
關於那件事，我不會再警告你。
Didn't I warn you about calling me names?
我沒警告過你不要侮辱我嗎？

warn that S+V

- warn sb that S+V
  警告某人…

警告… 要用一個句子表示警告的內容時，可以在 warn 後面接 that S+V。

● Rhoda just threw a glass at me!
● I **warned you** she felt angry.

●Rhoda 剛才對我丟了個玻璃杯！　●我警告過你她在生氣了。

▶ He warned me that the computer was broken.
他提醒我那台電腦壞了。
You should warn people there's no elevator.
你應該提醒人們沒有電梯的事。

give sb a warning to

- give sb a warning of...
  警告某人關於…

警告某人去做… 表示不做某事可能會有不好的結果，或者發生危險。

● The ranger **gave us a warning to** put out the campfire.
● We'd better do what he says.

●國家公園管理員警告我們把營火熄掉。　●我們最好照他說的做。

▶ I suppose I could give him a warning.
我想我可以給他個警告。
I just can't believe that Mike didn't give me any warning.
我真不敢相信 Mike 沒有給我任何警告。

without warning

無預警地 沒有任何事先預告，突然發生某事。

● Did you know Ellen was leaving?
● No, she just left **without warning**.

●你知道 Ellen 要離開嗎？　●沒有，她沒有任何預告就走了。

▶ The snow began to fall without warning.
雪忽然下了起來。
Peter often shows up without warning.
Peter 常常無預警地現身。

caution sb to

· caution sb against
　-ing
　告誡／警告某人不要做…

告誡／警告某人做… caution 在這裡是動詞。caution 當名詞時可以這麼說：give caution to sb（給某人警告）。

● Did you hear that Brady had an accident?
● I **cautioned him against** driving home.

●你有聽說 Brady 出車禍了嗎？　●我告誡過他不要開車回家了。

▶ The teacher cautioned the students against drug abuse.
老師告誡學生們不要濫用毒品。
The policeman cautioned her to slow down.
警察告誡她放慢速度。

---

13 | 要求
tell sb to

8-13.mp3

---

tell sb to

· be told to do
　被指示／要求做…
· do as one is told
　依照被要求的去做

叫某人做… 指示某人去做某事，但沒有 order sb to（命令某人做…）那麼強烈。

● **Tell Katie to** bring me a drink.
● I think she's busy right now.

●叫 Katie 帶點喝的給我。　●我想她現在很忙。

▶ Erica was told to go to bed early.
Erica 被説要早點睡覺。
He told me to cut down on my intake of fast food.
他要我減少速食的攝取量。

call for

· call for prompt action
　需要迅速行動

需要…，要求… 另外，「call for sb」是接某人的意思。

● I just got a big raise at work.
● Great! That **calls for** a celebration.
　● 我在工作上剛獲得一大筆加薪。　● 太棒了！這需要慶祝一下。

▶ The software problem calls for prompt action.
　這個軟體問題需要迅速處理。
　The illness called for some medicine.
　這個疾病需要藥物治療。

at the request of

· at one's request
　依照某人的要求
· as requested
　依照被要求的

依…的要求 這個說法帶有一點正式用語的色彩。

● I'm working this weekend **at the request of** my boss.
● You're going to be really tired on Monday.
　● 因為我老闆要求，所以我這週末要工作。　● 你星期一會很累的。

▶ Hank brought the file as requested.
　Hank 依照要求把檔案帶來了。
　I bought some beer at the request of my friend.
　依照朋友的要求，我買了點啤酒來。

be required to

· require sth
　要求某事物
· require sb to do
　要求某人做…

被要求做…，必須做… 意思和 must... 或 need to... 相近。

● Did you go jogging this afternoon?
● No, I **was required to** stay at home.
　● 你今天下午有去慢跑嗎？　● 沒有，我必須待在家。

▶ The party requires a cake and drinks.
　派對需要蛋糕和飲料。
　They required us to arrive early.
　他們要求我們早點抵達。

demand to

· demand sth
　要求某事物
· demand that S+V
　要求…

要求做… 表示比較有強制性的要求。

● I **demand to** talk to your manager!
● I'm sorry, but he's not here right now.
　● 我要求跟你們主管說話！　● 不好意思，但他現在不在。

▶ The diner demanded a free meal.
　用餐的客人要求餐點免費。
　Tim demanded that the TV be turned off.
　Tim 要求把電視關掉。

1 職場・學校
2 電腦・網路
3 社交生活
4 日常生活
5 訊息・理解
6 想法・態度
7 情緒・狀況
8 行為舉止
9 時間地點・副詞片語

14 請託 ask sb to

8-14.mp3

ask sb to

- ask sb for help
  請某人幫忙
- ask a favor of sb
  請某人幫忙
- have a favor to ask
  有事相求

要求某人做⋯ 和 tell sb to... 不同，這裡強調的是拜託對方去做某事。

- Dana **asked me to** find a nice hotel.
- Why don't you check the Internet?

  ●Dana 拜託我找一間好飯店。　●你何不上網找找呢？

▶ Ambrosia asked another student for help.
  Ambrosia 請求另一位學生幫忙。
  We have a favor to ask of you.
  我們有事要請你幫忙。

do sb a favor

- Could you do me a favor and do...
  你可以幫我⋯嗎？

幫某人的忙 簡單地說，就是 do something for someone 的意思。

- What is this thank you card for?
- I **did Pam a favor** last week.

  ●這張感謝卡是做什麼的？　●我上星期幫了 Pam 的忙。

▶ Could you do me a favor and get me a snack?
  你可以幫我拿點零食來嗎？
  Do Ryan a favor and call his mom.
  幫 Ryan 打電話給他媽媽。

be just wondering (if S+V)

- be just wondering if you could help me
  不知道你能不能幫我

不知道是否⋯ 看起來是在詢問，但實際上是請求。

- I **was wondering if** I could leave this with you.
- Sure, I'll put it behind the desk.

  ●不知道我能不能把這個託你保管。
  ●當然，我會把它放在桌子後面。

▶ I was just wondering if you want to come.
  不知道你想不想來？
  I was wondering if I could speak to a manager.
  不知道我能不能跟經理說話？

1 職場・學校

2 電腦・網路

3 社交生活

4 日常生活

5 訊息・理解

6 想法・態度

7 情緒・狀況

8 行為舉止

9 時間地點・副詞片語

would appreciate it if you

· would appreciate it if you could do...
如果你能…的話，就太感謝了

· would appreciate any information
歡迎提供任何資訊

如果你…就太感謝了 看起來是感謝，但實際上是請求。

● I'd **appreciate it if you could** bring an appetizer.
● Is there anything else you need?

● 如果你可以拿開胃菜來，我會很感謝的。　● 還有其他需要的嗎？

▶ I'd appreciate it if you kept it secret.
如果你可以保守祕密的話，我會很感謝的。

I'd appreciate it if you would let me know.
如果你可以告訴我的話，我會很感謝的。

beg for

· beg to do
懇求能做…

· beg sb to do
懇求某人做…

懇求… beg 的原意是乞討，在這裡表示放低姿態、急切地懇求。

● Jerry **begged for** a higher salary.
● Did the boss give it to him?

● Jerry 懇求加薪。　● 老闆有答應他嗎？

▶ She pleaded with us to buy her a car.
她懇求我們買台車給她。

Paula begged me for a pearl necklace.
Paula 懇求我買條珍珠項鍊給她。

15 提供／接受幫助 help sb do

8-15.mp3

help sb do...

· help to do
幫忙做…

幫某人做… help 的基本句型。請注意 help sb 後面不用加 to，直接接動詞原形。

● I have difficulty turning this knob.
● Let me **help you do** that.

● 我轉不動這個門把。　● 讓我來幫你。

▶ You should help move that desk.
你應該幫忙移動那張桌子。

Can you help me finish this work?
你可以幫我完成這個工作嗎？

help A with B

幫 A 做 B　B 的部分是用名詞表示幫忙做的事。

- I can **help you with** cooking the food.
- Thanks. It's difficult to do this alone.

    ●我可以幫你煮菜。　●謝謝。這很難一個人做。

▶ Joe helped the lady with her flat tire.

   Joe 幫那位女士換漏氣的輪胎。

   I need you to help me with my homework.

   我需要你幫忙做我的功課。

help sb a lot

幫某人很大的忙，對某人很有幫助　這裡的 a lot 當副詞用，表示程度。

- The i-Pad is a very useful device.
- Yeah, it has **helped me out a lot**.

    ●i-Pad 是很有用的設備。　●是啊，它對我很有幫助。

▶ Morty helps his friends out a lot.

   Morty 對他朋友很有幫助。

   The tutor helped the student a lot.

   那位家教幫了學生很大的忙。

help sb out

· help sb out with
  幫忙某人解決…的問題
· help each other
  幫助彼此

幫忙某人（解決問題）　在對方很忙碌或遇到問題時提供幫助。out 可以理解成 out of trouble（脫離困境）的意思。

- Can you **help me out with** some money?
- Sorry, but I've got no money for you.

    ●你可以借錢讓我度過難關嗎？　●抱歉，但我沒有錢可以借你。

▶ Are you sure you don't want to help me out?

   你真的不想幫我解決嗎？

   Can you help me out here?

   你可以幫我一下嗎？

give sb a hand

· give sb a hand with
  幫忙某人做…
· give sb a hand -ing
  幫忙某人做…

幫某人一個忙　也可以說 give sb a helping hand，明確表示「伸出支援之手」。

- Would you mind **giving me a hand**?
- Sorry, but I'm really busy at the moment.

    ●你介意幫我個忙嗎？　●抱歉，但我現在真的很忙。

▶ Why don't you give me a hand?

   你為什麼不幫我個忙呢？

   Could you give me a hand watering the flower?

   你可以幫我澆花嗎？

get help

- get help -ing
  取得幫助做…
- get some help
  取得一點幫助

取得幫助 這裡的 help 是名詞。help 當名詞時還有 need help、ask for help 等各種用法。

- I need to **get help** carrying these boxes.
- Some of my friends will help you out.
  - ●我需要有人幫我搬這些箱子。　●我的幾個朋友會幫你的忙。

▶ Can you get help for the old woman?
你可以幫這位老太太取得幫助嗎？
The workers got help in the doctor's office.
這些員工在診療室得到了幫助。

be a great help to

- be a little help to sb
  對某人有一點幫助
- be of help
  幫上忙
- try to be of help to you
  努力想幫上你的忙

對於做…有很大的幫助（to do），對於…有很大的幫助（to sb） to 後面接動詞或人。

- Did you finish your report?
- Yes. Wikipedia **was a great help to** write it.
  - ●你完成報告了嗎？　●嗯，維基百科在寫報告上提供了很大的幫助。

▶ The medicine was a great help to the patient.
這種藥對患者提供了很大的幫助。
I try to be of help to my grandparents.
我努力想為祖父母幫上忙。

be helpful

- be helpful in -ing
  在做…方面有幫助

有幫助，幫上忙 意思和 be supportive 相近。

- I'm not sure what I should study in school.
- I can **be helpful** in giving you advice.
  - ●我不確定該在學校學什麼。　●我可以幫忙給你建議。

▶ The money you gave us was helpful.
你給我們的錢幫上了忙。
They were supportive when Fred had problems.
Fred 碰上問題時，他們幫上了忙。

with the help of

- with the help of sb
  藉著某人的幫助（with sb's help）
- with the help of sth
  藉著某事物的幫助

藉著…的幫助 of 後面可以接人或事物。如果提供幫助的是人，還可以說 with sb's help。

- I painted my apartment **with the help of** friends.
- Well, it really looks nice in here.
  - ●我藉著朋友們的幫助粉刷了公寓。　●嗯，這裡看起來真的不錯。

▶ The church operates with the help of its members.
這間教會是憑藉著成員的幫助營運的。
The building was built with the help of workers.
這棟大樓是憑藉工人們的幫助而完成的。

1 職場・學校
2 電腦・網路
3 社交生活
4 日常生活
5 訊息・理解
6 想法・態度
7 情緒・狀況
8 行為舉止
9 時間地點・副詞片語

call for help

要求幫助 想要 get help 的話，就需要 call for help。

- What did you do when the fight started?
- I **called for help** right away.

  ●開始打架的時候你做了什麼？　　●我馬上找人幫忙。

▶ Call for help if there is trouble. 如果有問題的話，找人幫忙。
  I didn't hear his call for help. 我沒聽到他的求助。

need some help

- need some (more)
  help with
  在…方面需要（更多）一
  些幫助
- need some (more)
  help -ing
  需要（更多）一些幫助
  做…
- in need
  在困難中，在窮困中

需要一些幫助 need 也可以當名詞用，in need 就是「在困難中（有需要）」的意思。

- Do you **need some help** with this work?
- No, I've got it all taken care of.

  ●你這件工作需要幫忙嗎？　　●不用，我一切的事都打理好了。

▶ We need some more help fixing this.
  我們需要更多幫助來修這個。
  I'll let you know if I need help.
  如果我需要幫助，我會讓你知道。

be there for

去幫忙…，去參加… 比喻性的表達方式，用「為了某人到那裡」表示「到某人身邊提供幫助」的意思。

- I'll **be there for** you if you have problems.
- Thanks. I appreciate your friendship.

  ●有問題的話，我會幫你的。　　●謝謝，我很感謝你的友情。

▶ They'll be there for your race. 他們會去你的比賽現場支持你。
  She'll be there for Josh's graduation.
  她會去參加 Josh 的畢業典禮。

back sb up on

支持某人的… 提供或表示支持的意思。

- Did Josh really meet Brad Pitt?
- I was there. I can **back him up on** that.

  ●Josh 真的見到布萊德·彼特了嗎？　　●我也在場。我可以幫他作證。

▶ Back me up on what I said. 請支持我所說的話。
  She backed Tim up on his statement. 她支持了 Tim 的說法。

be useful to

- be useful to know that
  知道那件事很有幫助
- be useful for picnics
  對野餐有幫助→適合野餐

做…有幫助 be useful for 意為「對…有幫助」。

- Do you use the Internet a lot?
- Yes. It'**s useful to** find information.

  ●你很常上網嗎？　　●是啊，尋找資訊是很有幫助的。

▶ It's useful to know that there is a hospital close by.
  知道這附近有間醫院，很有幫助。
  This park is useful for picnics. 這座公園很適合野餐。

1 職場・學校
2 電腦・網路
3 社交生活
4 日常生活
5 訊息・理解
6 想法・態度
7 情緒・狀況
8 行為舉止
9 時間地點・副詞片語

16 教導，學習
teach sb to

8-16.mp3

teach sb to

· teach sb about
  教某人關於…
· teach at a college
  在大學教書
· teach sb a lesson
  給某人上課，教訓某人

教某人做… 表示教某人如何做某事（teach sb how to...），或者應該做某事（teach sb that he/she should...）。

● Sharon **taught us to** cook Italian food.
● You can make a meal for me then.

●Sharon 教我們做義大利料理。　●那你可以煮東西給我吃囉。

▶ Walter taught us about camping.

Walter 教我們露營。

I hope to teach at a college in a few years.

我希望幾年後能在大學教書。

be taught that S+V

· teach sb that S+V
  教導某人…

被教導… 雖然跟 learn that 一樣有「學到」的意思，但更強調「被某個人事物教導」的層面。

● I **was taught that** science helps everyone.
● Yes, scientists invented many things.

●我學到科學能幫助每個人。　●是啊，科學家發明了許多東西。

▶ He was taught that cigarettes cause cancer.

他被教導香菸會引發癌症。

We are taught that there are seven deadly sins.

我們被教導世上有七大原罪。

learn to

· learn sth by heart
  記憶／背誦某事

學習做… 一樣可以理解為學習如何做（learn how to...）或學到應該做（learn that one should...）的意思。

● I am broke again this week.
● You should **learn to** manage your money.

●我這禮拜又破產了。　●你應該學習去管理自己的錢。

▶ Gina learned the song by heart.

Gina 記住了這首歌。

Lenny learned to fly an airplane.

Lenny 學習駕駛飛機。

593

learn about

- learn A from B
  從 B 那裡學到 A
- give a lesson
  教課，教訓
- learn a lesson
  得到教訓

學習關於… 「學習更多」則是 learn more about...。

- What did you **learn about** today?
- The teacher taught us about European history.
  - 你今天學了些關於什麼的東西？
  - 老師教了我們關於歐洲歷史的事情。

▶ Ms. Thompson gave a lesson to the elementary students. Thompson 老師給小學生們上了一課。
I spent a lot of time learning about fashion.
我花了很多時間學習流行時尚。

instruct sb to

- instruct (sb) that S+V
  指示（某人）…
- be instructed in sign language
  接受手語教育
- train sb for sth
  為了某事而訓練某人（從事特別的職業或運動）

指示／教導某人做… 表示比較正式的指示或教導。

- What did the policeman say?
- He **instructed** everyone **to** stay inside.
  - 警察說了什麼？　●他指示所有人待在室內。

▶ We were instructed in sign language at school.
我們在學校學了手語。
The country trained soldiers for the war.
這個國家為了應備戰爭而訓練軍人。

17 原諒 excuse sb for

8-17.mp3

excuse sb for...

- Excuse us for leaving so early.
  請原諒我們這麼早離開。

原諒某人… for 後面接名詞或動詞 -ing 形。

- Please **excuse me for** being rude.
- You'd better try to be nicer.
  - 請原諒我的無禮。　●你最好試著更有教養一點。

▶ Excuse me for being so late.
請原諒我遲到這麼久。
Excuse her for acting so rude.
請原諒她行為如此無禮。

if you'll excuse me

不好意思，可以的話 有事需要暫時離開或告別的狀況。

- **If you'll excuse me**, I need to go.
- I'll see you again tomorrow.

    ●可以的話，我得走了。 ●明天再見。

▶ If you'll excuse me, my phone is ringing.

  不好意思，我的手機在響。

  If you'll excuse me, I have a meeting to go to.

  不好意思，我有個會議要去參加。

forgive sb for

- forgive sb for sth/-ing
  原諒某人的某事
- forgive and forget
  原諒並遺忘

原諒某人… 指「原諒」時，excuse 通常接 me 當受詞，forgive 就沒有這種習慣。

- Jan and Mike are staying together.
- Did she **forgive him for** dating other women?

    ●Jan 和 Mike 在一起。 ●她原諒他和其他女人約會的事了嗎？

▶ Do you want me to forgive you? Why should I?

  你想要我原諒你嗎？我為什麼要這麼做？

  You're going to forgive me for not going to school?

  你會原諒我沒去學校嗎？

be forgiven

- seek forgiveness
  尋求原諒

被原諒 You're forgiven 是口語說法，用在已經消了氣、原諒對方的時候。

- I heard that Thad caused problems for his parents.
- Yes, but he **was forgiven** by them.

    ●我聽說 Thad 給他父母惹了麻煩。 ●是啊，但他們原諒他了。

▶ Kari sought forgiveness from her friends.

  Kari 尋求朋友們的原諒。

  I was forgiven for hurting him.

  他原諒了我傷害他的事。

pardon sb for

- pardon me for
  interrupting you
  請原諒我打斷你（的話）
- condone sb/sth
  寬恕…

原諒／饒恕某人… 意思跟 excuse 一樣，用法也相同（通常只說 pardon me），但感覺更正式。

- **Pardon me for** smoking here.
- Don't worry, it's fine with me.

    ●請原諒我在這裡抽菸。 ●別擔心，我沒關係。

▶ Pardon me for interrupting you, but I must say something. 請原諒我打斷你，但我一定要說些話。

  Pardon me for not showing up in the morning meeting.

  請原諒我沒有參加早上的會議。

1 職場・學校

2 電腦・網路

3 社交生活

4 日常生活

5 訊息・理解

6 想法・態度

7 情緒・狀況

8 行為舉止

9 時間地點・副詞片語

18 接待，對待
wait on

8-18.mp3

treat sb to

· serve tea to sb
  招待某人用茶
· be one's treat
  …是某人請客

招待某人⋯ 請別人吃飯或享受某種東西，後面接名詞。

● Is anyone else feeling hungry?
● I can **treat you to** lunch.
    ●有人也餓了嗎？　●我可以請你吃午飯。

▶ My aunt served tea to the group.
    我的阿姨招待了這個團體用茶。
    The ice cream is my father's treat.
    冰淇淋是我爸爸請的。

---

treat sb like

· treat me like a brother
  待我像兄弟一樣
· treat me like dirt
  待我如塵土→把我看得一文不值

對待某人像⋯一樣 like 也可以換成 as。

● Is your boss tough to work for?
● Yes, he **treats** his workers **like** slaves.
    ●你的老闆很難共事嗎？　●是啊，他對員工就像對待奴隸一樣。

▶ Dave treated me like a brother.
    Dave 待我像兄弟一樣。
    You shouldn't treat me like this.
    你不該這樣對我。

---

treat sb very well

· treat sb so unfairly
  對某人很不公平
· treat sb that way
  那樣對待某人

對某人非常好 treat sb 後面接副詞表示是怎樣對待某人的。

● Tim and Lulu seem like good parents.
● They **treat** their children **very well**.
    ●Tim 跟 Lulu 看起來是對好父母。　●他們對他們的孩子非常好。

▶ The teacher treated Katie so unfairly. 老師對 Katie 很不公平。
    Don't treat your pets that way. 別那樣對待你的寵物。

---

wait on

· wait on sb hand and foot
  無微不至地服侍某人

接待／伺候某人 常指商店或餐廳的人員對顧客的服務。

● Is this restaurant even open?
● Someone will **wait on** us soon.
    ●這間餐廳真的在營業嗎？　●很快就會有人來招呼我們了。

▶ Sarah had to wait on her mother-in-law hand and foot.
    Sarah 必須無微不至地服侍她的婆婆。
    I won't wait on you even if you are sick.
    即使你病了，我也不會伺候你。

1 職場・學校

2 電腦・網路

3 社交生活

4 日常生活

5 訊息・理解

6 想法・態度

7 情緒・狀況

8 行為舉止

9 時間地點・副詞片語

entertain sb

讓某人開心，娛樂某人 給予飲食以外的娛樂或招待，使某人開心。

- It is difficult to **entertain** children.
- Why don't you buy them some toys?

●要讓孩子們開心很難。 ●你何不買些玩具給他們？

▶ The magician entertained us with tricks.

魔術師用魔術娛樂了我們。

A businessman needs to entertain his clients.

商人需要讓他的客戶開心。

---

19 約定 keep one's word

8-19.mp3

promise to

· promise oneself that S+V
向自己保證…

· like you promised
(= as promised)
照你答應/保證的

· make a promise
(to do)
保證（做…）

答應/保證做… 跟 agree to（同意做…）相比，更有「保證會做到」的意思。

- I **promise to** make you a happy woman.
- Well, then I will be glad to marry you.

●我保證會讓你成為幸福的女人。 ●那麼，我很樂意嫁給你。

▶ I promised myself that I will exercise more.

我向自己保證會做更多運動。

You need to give me the money like you promised.

你需要照你答應的把錢給我。

keep one's word

· honor one's promise
遵守諾言

· fulfill a promise
實踐諾言

遵守諾言 守住自己說過的話，就是遵守諾言的意思。

- Are you still coming to my party?
- Sure. I always **keep my word.**

●你還是會來參加我的派對嗎？ ●當然，我總是遵守諾言。

▶ You'd better honor your promise to our kids.

你最好對我們的孩子守約。

She had to go to her hometown to fulfill a promise.

為了實踐諾言，她必須回老家一趟。

give (sb) one's word that...

（對某人）保證… that 後面接 S+V 說明承諾的內容。
- Can we trust Tom to keep quiet?
- He **gave his word that** he won't tell our secret.
  - 我們可以相信 Tom 不會說出去嗎？　●他保證不會說出我們的祕密。

▶ Mindy gave her word that she would pay for it.
  Mindy 保證她會付錢。
  I give my word that I'll come back tomorrow.
  我保證我明天會回來。

take one's word for it

- have one's word (for it)
  （關於這件事）相信某人的話
- You have my word (on sth)
  我向你保證（某事）

相信某人的話準沒錯 take 可以換成 have，意思一樣。
- **Take my word for it**. He's really violent.
- I'll keep that in mind.
  - 相信我的話準沒錯。他真的很暴力。　●我會記住的。

▶ Take my word for it, he's the best in the business.
  相信我的話準沒錯。他在這業界是最棒的。
  Take my word for it. He's found another girl.
  相信我的話準沒錯。他愛上了另一個女孩子。

break one's word

- break one's word to sb
  對某人食言
- break one's word on sth
  對某事食言

食言，失信 break 自己的諾言，就是 not keep one's word。
- Did Darlene pay you the money?
- No, she **broke her word** on that.
  - Darlene 有付你錢嗎？　●沒有，她食言了。

▶ I never break my word to my friends.
  我從來不對朋友食言。
  The auto salesman broke his word to us.
  這個汽車業務沒遵守對我們的承諾。

pledge to

- pledge support
  保證提供幫助
- pledge to support
  保證幫助
- pledge that S+V
  保證…

保證／發誓做… 正式且公開地保證會做某事。
- Are the parents going to assist the students?
- They **pledged to** help the school.
  - 這些父母會幫助學生嗎？　●他們保證會協助學校。

▶ I pledge to love you forever.
  我發誓會永遠愛你。
  Jane pledged to set up the picnic.
  Jane 保證會準備野餐的事。

1 職場・學校

2 電腦・網路

3 社交生活

4 日常生活

5 訊息・理解

6 想法・態度

7 情緒・狀況

8 行為舉止

9 時間地點・副詞片語

swear to

· swear that S+V
發誓…

· I swear to God.
我對神發誓。

發誓做… 可能有點令人意外，但 swear 當不及物動詞時也有「辱罵」的意思，請注意。

● Are you going to win the race?

● I **swear to** run as fast as I can.

　●你會贏得這場賽跑嗎？　　●我發誓會用最快的速度去跑。

▶ The soldiers swore allegiance to each other.
　士兵們發誓對彼此忠誠。

　The ex-president swore to stay out of politics.
　那位前總統發誓要遠離政治。

---

promise vs. agree

　　這兩個單字在中文裡都可以翻譯成「答應」，但 promise 比 agree 更強烈地表示「承諾一定會做某事」，agree 則只是表示「會去做某事」。另外，agree 有「同意」的意思，promise 則沒有。

　　例句：

　　I promise to love you forever.（承諾）

　　I agree that fast food is bad for health.（同意）

---

20 準備
prepare for

8-20.mp3

prepare for

· prepare to do
準備做…

· prepare sth for sb
為某人準備某物

· prepare oneself for
為…做好準備

準備… 為了將來要做的某件事預先計畫並準備。

● What is taking you so long?

● I'm **preparing for** my interview tomorrow.

　●什麼事耽擱你那麼久？　　●我在準備明天的面試。

▶ My sister prepared to make some food.
　我妹妹準備要做點菜。

　It will take time for us to prepare for the speech.
　準備演講會花我們一點時間。

be prepared to

- make preparations for
  為…做準備
- have/get sth prepared
  使某物準備好

準備好做… 後面接動詞原形。以被動態表示已經準備好了，這裡的 prepared 可以看成形容詞「有準備的」。

- We may have to travel to Busan.
- I **am prepared to** leave at any time.

  ●我們可能得去釜山一趟。 ●我準備好了，隨時都可以出發。

▶ The family made preparations for the reunion.

  這個家庭為團聚做了準備。

Are you prepared to face the challenges ahead?

  你準備好要面對面前的挑戰了嗎？

get ready for

- get ready to do
  準備好做…
- get sth ready to do
  準備好某物去做…

為…做好準備 for 可以換成 to do，get 也可以換成 be。

- **Get ready for** the snow storm.
- It is supposed to be a very big storm.

  ●要為暴風雪做好準備。 ●這應該會是場很大的暴風雪。

▶ I came here to see if you were ready.

  我來看你是否準備好了。

Let me make sure Mom is ready to leave.

  讓我確認媽媽是不是準備好離開了。

be (all) set to

- be all set for sth
  對某事做好了萬全準備
- be all set to go on a vacation
  完全準備好要去度假了

完全準備好去做… 表示一切都準備到位了。要表示自己都準備好了，可以說「(I'm) all set.」

- **Are** you **all set for** your trip?
- I have a few more things to get and then I'll be ready.

  ●旅行的準備都完成了嗎？

  ●我還有幾樣東西要買，然後就沒問題了。

▶ I'm packed and all set to go on vacation.

  我已經打包好，完全準備好要去度假了。

Are you all set for your vacation?

  你完全準備好要去度假了嗎？

arrange to

- arrange for sth
  為某事安排
- arrange a meeting
  安排會議
- arrange for sb to do sth
  安排某人做某事

安排做… 也可以用 arrange 的名詞形，以 make some arrangement for sth 來表達。

- Are you traveling to your hometown?
- Yeah, I**'ve arranged to** meet some of my old teachers.

  ●你要回老家嗎？ ●是啊，我安排了跟幾位以前的老師見面。

▶ We arranged for a place to stay. 我們安排了住宿的地方。

The company arranged a meeting for tomorrow.

  公司在明天安排了會議。

21 由來
date back

8-21.mp3

1 職場・學校

2 電腦・網路

3 社交生活

4 日常生活

5 訊息・理解

6 想法・態度

7 情緒・狀況

8 行為舉止

9 時間地點・副詞片語

come from
· come/be from + 地名
　出生於…

來自… 也可以說 be from。這兩個說法也可以表示「出生於…」的意思。

● Where **is** this vase **from**?
● I bought it when I was in Israel.
　●這花瓶是哪裡來的？　●我在以色列的時候買的。

▶ The groceries came from the corner store.
　這些食品雜貨是從轉角的那間店買來的。
　Where did this pair of socks come from?
　這雙襪子是哪裡來的？

date back to

可以追溯到…，製造於… 後面接 a particular time in the past（過去某個特定的時代）。

● This is a very old coin.
● It **dates back to** Roman times.
　●這是個很舊的硬幣。　●它製造於羅馬時代。

▶ The Chinese furniture dates back to the last century.
　這件中國家具是上個世紀製作的。
　This mummy dates back to ancient Egypt.
　這具木乃伊可以追溯到古埃及時期。

be the source
· find the source
　找到源頭

是源頭／產地 後面可以接 of sth，表示是某物的源頭或產地。

● What **is the source of** this clothing?
● I'm pretty sure it was made in Italy.
　●這件衣服的產地是哪裡？　●我很確定是在義大利製造的。

▶ It was difficult to find the source of the problem.
　要找到這個問題的源頭很難。
　Jerry was the source of our inspiration.
　Jerry 是我們靈感的源頭。

601

originate from

- originate with sb
  源自某人

源自… from 後面可以接地名或人。改成 in 的話，後面接發源地。改成 with 的話，則接發明／引領風潮的人。

- Who invented cigarettes?
- They **originated from** South America.
  - 誰發明了香菸？　●香菸源自南美洲。

▶ That style originated with a pop star.
  那種造型源自一位流行歌手。
  Pizza originated from the Italians.
  披薩是義大利人發明的。

be derived from

- derive from
  起源於…
- fear derived from superstition
  源於迷信的恐懼

起源於… 特別的是，被動態的 be derived from 和主動態的 derive from 意思相同。

- The Bible **derives from** ancient writings.
- Many people consider it the holiest book.
  - 聖經起源於古代文書。　●許多人認為它是最神聖的書。

▶ The test was derived from our textbook.
  測驗是從我們的課本中出題的。
  The villagers' fear was derived from superstition.
  村民們的恐懼源於迷信。

---

22 | 帶來 get sth from

8-22.mp3

get sth from

- get A B (= get B for A)
  拿 B 給 A
- get sth as a present for sb
  買某物當作給某人的禮物

從…拿／得到某物 隨著句義的不同，get 會有「從某人那邊拿到」，或是「在特賣會上買到」等意義。

- Did you have a good holiday?
- Sure. I **got a ring from** my boyfriend.
  - 休假過得好嗎？　●當然。我從我男朋友那邊收到一只戒指。

▶ Get a chair for her to sit in.
  拿張椅子來給她坐。
  Get a new shirt for him to wear.
  買件新襯衫來給他穿。

have got sth for sb

· Here is sth for sb
  這裡有某物要給某人

有某物要給某人　請記住口語裡的 have got 就是 have 的意思。介系詞 for 則是「為⋯準備」、「給⋯」的意思。

● **Here is something for** you to eat.
● Thanks. I don't mean to cause extra work.

　　●我這裡有一點東西要請你吃。　　●謝謝，我沒打算麻煩你的。

▶ We have got a present for our teacher.
  我們有個禮物要給老師。
  Here is a DVD for you to watch.
  這邊有一片 DVD 要給你看。

bring sb sth

帶來某物給某人　sb 和 sth 如果互換位置，要加上介系詞：bring sth to sb。

● Could you let me know the total cost?
● I'll **bring** you the bill.

　　●可以告訴我總金額嗎？　　●我把帳單拿給你。

▶ Don't forget to bring your girlfriend to the party.
  別忘了帶你女朋友來派對。
  Bring me a coffee on your way back.
  在你回程的路上買杯咖啡給我。

take sth from

從⋯拿某物　相反的，take sth to 就是「把某物拿到⋯」的意思。

● Where did you get something to read?
● I **took** a magazine **from** the rack.

　　●你從哪裡拿到東西讀的？　　●我從架子上拿了雜誌。

▶ He took a beer from the fridge.
  他從冰箱拿了一罐啤酒。
  Take some food from my plate.
  從我的盤子裡拿點食物吧。

hand over

· provide A with B
  提供 B 給 A
· present A with B
  贈與 B 給 A
· pass sb sth
  遞某物給某人

交出⋯　這裡的 hand 是當動詞用，表示用手拿東西給別人。

● Are you finished moving your things?
● Yeah, but I need to **hand over** my apartment key.

　　●你搬完你的東西了嗎？　　●嗯，但我需要交出我的公寓鑰匙。

▶ The teacher provided the students with exams.
  老師給學生們考試。
  The manager presented one of his workers with an
  award. 主管頒獎給一位員工。

1 職場・學校
2 電腦・網路
3 社交生活
4 日常生活
5 訊息・理解
6 想法・態度
7 情緒・狀況
8 行為舉止
9 時間地點・副詞片語

want sth back

· would like sth back
　想要回某物（比 want 更
　禮貌的說法）

想要回某物　用「希望某物回來」簡單地表示希望拿回某個東西。如果受詞是人，則是希望他回到身邊。

● I **want** my old boyfriend **back**.
● But you broke up with him a year ago.
　●我想要我的前男友回來。　●但你一年前就跟他分手了。

▶ Larry would like his i-Pod back.
　Larry 想要回他的 i-Pod。
　She said she wants her necklace back.
　她說她想要回她的項鍊。

bring sth back
to + 地點

· bring back books to
　the library
　把書還給圖書館
· bring sb back
　帶某人回來

把某物帶回某地　有個例外是 bring sth back home，請注意 home 前面不加 to 就能表示「到家」的意思。

● This shirt is too small.
● **Bring it back to** the store.
　●這襯衫太小了。　●把它拿回店裡吧。

▶ I must bring back some books to the library.
　我得還圖書館一些書。
　Bring some of your money back to your parents.
　還給你父母一些錢。

take (sth) back

· take sth back to
　+ 地點／人
　把某物歸還給⋯
· take a defective item
　back
　退回不良品

歸還（某物）　除了「歸還」以外，也可以表示「拿回來」。take back one's words 則是「收回自己說過的話」。

● Peter had many problems with his new car.
● He said he wants to **take it back**.
　●Peter 的新車有很多問題。　●他說他想把車退回去。

▶ Take this paperwork back to Mary.
　把這份文件拿回去給 Mary。
　We need to take the defective items back to the store.
　我們需要把不良品退回店裡。

give back sth to sb

- give back sth by
  + 時間
  在某個時間前歸還某物
- Here is sth back
  這是我還你的某物
- hand back
  歸還
- turn back
  歸還

將某物歸還給某人 give back 和 return 同義。give 也可以換成 hand 或 turn。

- Henry has borrowed a lot from his parents.
- He **is giving back** the money **to** his mother.
  ●Henry 向他父母借了很多錢。 ●他在還錢給他母親。

▶ Here is your dictionary back.
  這是我還你的字典。
  Mr. Lewis will hand back the exams today.
  Lewis 老師今天會發還測驗卷。

get (sth) back

拿回（某物） 也可以說 get back sth，但請記住 sth 是代名詞時必須放在介系詞 back 前面。

- Why do you need to talk to Don?
- I want to **get** my computer games **back**.
  ●你為什麼需要跟 Don 談？ ●我想把我的電腦遊戲拿回來。

▶ Can you get the cell phone back?
  你能把手機拿回來嗎？
  I need to get my money back.
  我需要把我的錢拿回來。

---

24 繼承，流傳
hand sth down

8-24.mp3

inherit sth from sb

- inherit sth
  繼承某物
- inherit a fortune from
  one's parents
  繼承雙親的大筆財產

從某人繼承某物 從長輩那邊繼承財產的意思。

- Kathy is taking a trip to Europe.
- I heard she **inherited** money **from** her grandmother.
  ●Kathy 要去歐洲旅行。 ●我聽說她繼承了她祖母的錢。

▶ You'll inherit my house when I die.
  我死了以後，你會繼承我的房子。
  The young man inherited a fortune from his parents.
  這位年輕人繼承了他雙親的大筆財產。

1 職場・學校
2 電腦・網路
3 社交生活
4 日常生活
5 訊息・理解
6 想法・態度
7 情緒・狀況
8 行為舉止
9 時間地點・副詞片語

hand sth down (to sb)

· be handed down to
  被傳給…

流傳某事物（給某人）　除了財產以外，也可以指流傳物品、技術、習俗等等。

- This is a nice antique chair.
- My grandfather **handed** the chair **down to** me.
  - ●這是張很棒的古董椅。　●我外公把這張椅子傳給我的。

▶ The money was handed down to the children.
  這筆錢傳給了孩子們。
  Uncle John plans to hand his business down to his kids.
  John 叔叔打算把他的事業傳給他的孩子們。

leave a small inheritance for

· leave a small
  inheritance for sb
  留一小筆遺產給某人

留給…一小筆遺產　inheritance（遺產）是 inherit 的名詞形。

- You seem to live very comfortably.
- Mom and dad **left a small inheritance for** me.
  - ●你看起來過得很舒服。　●爸媽留了一小筆遺產給我。

▶ I will leave a small inheritance for my relatives.
  我會留一小筆遺產給我的親戚們。
  The couple left a small inheritance for their daughter.
  這對夫婦留了一小筆遺產給他們的女兒。

leave a legacy of

· be left with a legacy of
  pollution
  留下了污染
· leave an estate of
  留下…的財產

留下…的遺產　legacy 除了指財物以外，也可以指文化、精神層面的傳統。

- Stan was a very unkind old man.
- He **left a legacy of** sadness for his kids.
  - ●Stan 是一位很不親切的老人。　●他留下了悲傷給他的孩子們。

▶ The factory town was left with a legacy of pollution.
  這個工業城留下了污染。
  Simon left a legacy of broken hearts behind him.
  Simon 留下了許多破碎的心（→傷了許多人的心）。

25 贈與，捐贈
make a donation

8-25.mp3

1 職場・學校

2 電腦・網路

3 社交生活

4 日常生活

5 訊息・理解

6 想法・態度

7 情緒・狀況

8 行為舉止

9 時間地點・副詞片語

donate sth to

· donate money to charity
捐錢給慈善團體
· donate one's organ
捐贈器官
· donate blood
捐血

捐贈某物給… 除了捐錢、捐物資以外，捐血、捐器官也是說 donate。

● What can we do with this piano?
● Let's **donate** it **to** our church.
  ●我們可以怎麼處理這架鋼琴呢？ ●我們把它捐給我們的教會吧。

▶ Cindy donates money to charity every Christmas.
Cindy 每年耶誕節都會捐錢給慈善團體。
Many students decided to donate blood.
許多學生決定要捐血。

make a donation

· make a donation to...
捐獻給…
· anonymous donation
匿名捐贈
· organ donation
器官捐贈

捐獻 使用 donate 的名詞形 donation。後面可以加上 to 接對象。

● I am going to **make a donation** to the Red Cross.
● That is a good way to use your money.
  ●我要捐錢給紅十字會。 ●那是個使用金錢的好方法。

▶ Jim made an anonymous donation to the group.
Jim 匿名捐獻給這個團體。
Organ donations help save many lives.
器官捐贈能幫助拯救許多生命。

contribute sth to...

· contribute money to...
捐贈金錢給…

捐贈／貢獻某物給… sth 可以是金錢、幫助、時間等等有助於他人的東西。

● The flood really created a mess.
● I will **contribute** money **to** the clean up.
  ●這場洪水真的造成了很大的混亂。 ●我會捐錢幫助後續清理。

▶ Can you contribute some money to our school?
你能捐點錢給我們學校嗎？
Mom contributed food to the party.
媽媽提供食物給這個派對。

make a contribution

· make a contribution to
  捐獻給…

捐獻 使用 contribute 的名詞形 contribution。

● I **made a contribution** to the Red Cross.

● How much money did you give?

　● 我捐獻給紅十字會。　● 你捐了多少錢？

▶ Every member is expected to make a contribution.

　每位成員都被期望能捐獻。

　Make a contribution to the community's church.

　請捐獻給社區教會。

give sth to charity

· give clothes to charity
  捐衣服給慈善團體
· leave sth to charity
  捐某物給慈善團體

捐某物給慈善團體 如果是指特定的慈善團體，charity 也可以加上冠詞，或者用複數表示很多慈善團體，但平常經常只說 charity 泛指一般的慈善團體。

● Do you plan to **give anything to charity**?

● I have no extra money right now.

　● 你打算要捐什麼給慈善團體嗎？　● 我現在沒有多的錢。

▶ Sharon gave her old clothes to charity.

　Sharon 把她的舊衣服捐給慈善團體。

　My family give money to charity every year.

　我家的人每年都會捐錢給慈善團體。

26 分開，分類
sort out

8-26.mp3

separate A from B

· be separated from
  和…分開
· separate politics from
  religion
  把政治和宗教分離

把 A 跟 B 分開 使兩者分離，或者劃清兩者之間的界線。

● My boss and I went out drinking twice this week.

● You should **separate** your private life **from** work.

　● 我老闆跟我這星期出去喝了兩次酒。

　● 你應該把你的私生活跟工作分開。

▶ The student was separated from his parents for a year.

　這位學生和他的雙親分開了一年。

　The law separates politics from religion.

　法律把政治和宗教分離。

keep A off B

· take A apart
拆開 A

使 A 遠離 B 如果沒有受詞 A 的話，就是表示「主詞遠離 B」。

● **Keep** your dogs **off** my lawn.

● I'm sorry, I'll move them.

　●別讓你的狗到我的草地上。　●抱歉，我會帶走牠們。

▶ We have to take your watch apart to fix it.
　我們得把你的手錶拆開好修理它。
　Keep your feet off the coffee table.
　把你的腳從咖啡桌移開。

sort sth out (from sth)

· sort out faulty goods
挑出不良品

（從某物中）區分出某物 如果只說 sort sth out，也可以表示「整理某物」。

● This bedroom is a real mess.

● It will take time to **sort it out**.

　●這臥室真是亂七八糟。　●這需要花時間整理。

▶ The factory had to sort out its faulty goods.
　工廠必須挑出不良品。
　Let's sort the report out together.
　我們一起來整理報告吧。

divide A into B

· divide the class into three groups
把全班分成三組

· his property was divided among his children
他的財產分給孩子們了

把 A 分成 B 跟 separate 意思相似，是指把東西分成兩個以上的部分。

● This is a large pizza.

● We should **divide it into** five pieces.

　●這是個很大的披薩。　●我們應該把它分成五塊。

▶ Our instructor divided the class into three groups.
　我們的講師把全班分成三組。
　The old man's property was divided among his children.
　這位老先生的財產分給他的孩子們了。

classify A as B

· classified ads
分類廣告

· be classified according to subjects
依主題被分類

把 A 分類為 B 依照特徵給予某個分類。

● Jim didn't show up at school today.

● He will **be classified as** absent.

　●Jim 今天沒有上學。　●他會被以曠課處理。

▶ We advertised the car in a classified ad.
　我們在分類廣告欄裡宣傳了這台車。
　The courses were classified according to subjects.
　課程是依主題分類。

1 職場·學校
2 電腦·網路
3 社交生活
4 日常生活
5 訊息·理解
6 想法·態度
7 情緒·狀況
8 行為舉止
9 時間地點·副詞片語

27 | 經驗
go through

8-27.mp3

have a lot of experience

· have more experience with
對於…有更多經驗

· have a bad experience with
對於…有不好的經驗

有許多經驗 experience 後面可以接 of, in, with 等介系詞說明是怎樣的經驗。

● Have you worked in an office before?

● Yes, I **have a lot of experience** with businesses.

　　● 你之前在辦公室工作過嗎？　　● 是的，我有許多業界經驗。

▶ The computer repairman had more experience with IBM.
這位電腦維修員對於 IBM 更有經驗。

We had a bad experience with that company.
我們和那間公司有過不好的經驗。

learn from experience

· speak from a personal experience
根據個人的經驗來說

· be a good experience for sb
對某人而言是好經驗

· experience sth
經歷某事

從經驗中學習 從經驗中得到知識，所以介系詞是 from。

● It's too cold outside today.

● I **learned from experience** cold weather makes me sick.

　　● 今天外面太冷了。　　● 我從經驗中學到，冷天氣會讓我生病。

▶ The old woman spoke from personal experience.
這位老太太是根據個人經驗說的。

The trip to Japan was a good experience for everyone.
那趟日本旅行對每個人而言都是好的經驗。

judging from one's experience

· in one's experience
在某人的經驗裡

· from one's experience
從某人的經驗來看

從某人的經驗判斷 judging 也可以換成 speaking 來用。

● I just can't trust my boyfriend.

● He's a bad guy, **judging from your experience**.

　　● 我就是不能相信我男朋友。　　● 從你的經驗來看，他是個壞男人。

▶ In my experience, it's good to eat a lot of fruit.
依我的經驗，多吃水果很好。

From my experience, the cars from this maker are of good quality. 依我的經驗，這家廠商的車品質很好。

go through

· undergo
經歷…

經歷… 特別指經歷某些困難或不好的事。

● We had to **go through** three months of training.
● Was it difficult being in the military?

●我們必須經歷三個月的訓練。　●在軍隊裡很辛苦嗎？

▶ Our economy has gone through some very hard times.
我們的經濟經歷過一些很困難的時刻。
I don't want to go through that.
我不想經歷那種事。

have been there

· Been there, done that
經歷過，也做過（全都經歷過的意思）

經歷過了 用現在完成式表示經驗。there 不是指地點，而是抽象地表示「經驗」。

● I'm having trouble finding a job.
● I understand. I**'ve been there** myself.

●我找工作碰到了困難。　●我懂。我自己也經歷過。

▶ Don't drink too much. Been there, done that.
別喝太多。這方面我都經歷過了。
You're right. We have all been there.
你是對的。我們都經歷過。

---

28 報告，申報
report sth to

8-28.mp3

report sth to sb

· report sth/-ing
報告或告發某事
· report it to the authorities
向當局告發那件事
· file a report
報案

向某人報告某事 就像中文一樣，可以指學術性的報告，或者向上位者告知情況的報告。

● Did you tell Mason about the problem?
● Someone **reported the problem to** him.

●你跟 Mason 說這個問題了嗎？　●有人跟他報告這個問題了。

▶ You should report the cheating to your teacher.
你應該跟老師報告作弊的事。
Leo reported the theft to the authorities.
Leo 向當局告發了偷竊行為。

1 職場·學校
2 電腦·網路
3 社交生活
4 日常生活
5 訊息·理解
6 想法·態度
7 情緒·狀況
8 行為舉止
9 時間地點·副詞片語

declare sth

- declare that S+V
  宣稱…
- declare bankruptcy
  宣告破產

申報某物 正式的申報，可以用在稅務申報、海關申報等情況。

- You've got to **declare** your income every year.
- I really hate paying taxes.
  - 你每年都必須申報所得。　● 我真的很討厭繳稅。

▶ Phil declared his birthplace as Toronto.
  Phil 宣稱自己的出生地是多倫多。
  The fourth of July was declared a holiday.
  七月四號被宣布為假日。

register sth

- register a marriage/
  birth/death
  登記結婚／出生／死亡
- registered mail
  掛號信

登記某事 主要用在出生、死亡等登記上，或者指給郵件「掛號」。

- Why did you come to this office?
- I need to **register** as a foreign citizen.
  - 你為什麼來辦公室？　● 我需要登記為外國公民。

▶ People register marriages at the courthouse.
  人們在法院登記結婚。
  The letter arrived via registered mail.
  這封信是用掛號寄達的。

brief sb on

- be briefed on the plan
  聽取了關於計畫的簡報

向某人做關於…的簡報 主要指內容正式的 briefing（brief 的名詞形）。

- You'd better **brief** the president **on** the situation.
- He is very worried about it.
  - 你最好向總裁簡單報告狀況。　● 他很擔心這件事。

▶ The whole committee was briefed on the plan.
  委員會全體人員都聽取了計畫的簡報。
  I'll brief you on what happened in the meeting.
  我會向你簡單報告會議裡發生了什麼事。

tell on sb

- threaten to tell on sb
  威脅要告發某人

告發某人 就是 inform 另一個人，說某人做了不好的行為。

- Bart **told on** his little sister to his parents.
- He should respect her privacy.
  - Bart 向他父母打妹妹的小報告。　● 他應該尊重她的隱私。

▶ Another student threatened to tell on me.
  別的學生威脅要告發我。
  You should tell on the cheater in your class.
  你應該告發班上作弊的人。

29 利用
make use of

8-29.mp3

1 職場・學校
2 電腦・網路
3 社交生活
4 日常生活
5 訊息・理解
6 想法・態度
7 情緒・狀況
8 行為舉止
9 時間地點・副詞片語

use sth for

· use sth as
把某物用作…
· be used for
被用來…
· be used to do
被用來做…

把某物用來… 接名詞表示當成什麼來用，接動詞 -ing 形表示用途。

● Brian gave me a lot of books.
●**Use** my bag **for** taking them home.
　●Brian 給了我很多書。　●用我的袋子把它們帶回家吧。

▶ We used the room as a place to meet.
我們把這間房間用來聚會。
This car was used for a taxi.
這台車被當成計程車使用。

take advantage of

· have the advantage of
有…的優點

利用… 為了達到自己的目的，利用某個人或事物。

● Let's go shopping today.
● We can **take advantage of** some sales.
　●我們今天去逛街吧。　●我們可以利用一些特賣的機會。

▶ We went outside to take advantage of the warm weather.
我們趁著溫暖的天氣去了戶外。
I took advantage of the low cost of rent.
我利用了租金低的優點。

make use of

· make good use of...
善用…
· put sth to use
利用某物

利用… 表示使某個東西變得有用。

● Can you **make use of** these clothes?
● Sure, I'll give them to my brother.
　●你能夠利用這些衣服嗎？　●當然，我會把它們給我弟弟。

▶ The diners made good use of the extra food.
這些小餐廳善用了多餘的食物。
Cathy put the old car to use.
Cathy 利用了那台舊車。

get the most out of

- get the most out of life
  充分享受人生
- make the most out of sth
  充分利用某物

充分利用／享受… 從某物中「得到最多的東西」，就是盡量利用的意思。

- You've worn that old coat for years.
- I like to **get the most out of** things I own.
  ●你穿那件舊大衣穿了好多年。　●我喜歡充分利用我的東西。

▶ My wife and I get the most out of life.
  我太太和我充分享受人生。
  Who got the most out of that class?
  誰最充分利用了那堂課？

cash in on

- cash in on one's daughter's fame
  用某人女兒的名聲賺錢

靠…獲利 利用某個事物或機會取得金錢上的利益。

- The value of these stocks has really gone up.
- Maybe it's time to **cash in on** them.
  ●這些股票的價格真的都漲了。　●也許是靠這些股票獲利的時候了。

▶ Pam decided to cash in on her daughter's fame.
  Pam 決定要用他女兒的名聲賺錢。
  The old couple cashed in on the value of their house.
  這對老夫婦靠他們房子的價值而獲利。

30 解決
solve a problem

8-30.mp3

solve a problem

- solve a math problem
  解數學題
- solve a puzzle
  解謎
- fix a problem
  解決／修復問題

解決問題 動詞 solve 也可以換成 fix。

- I heard you spent a lot fixing your car.
- Yeah, but it didn't **solve the problem** I was having.
  ●我聽說你花很多錢修車。　●是啊，但並沒有解決我的問題。

▶ It takes time to solve a math problem.
  解數學問題要花時間。
  I have to fix a problem with this computer.
  我必須解決這台電腦的問題。

find a/the solution to

- find a way (for sb) to do
  （幫某人）找到做⋯的方法／路
- find a solution to one's problem
  找到某人問題的解決方法

找出⋯的解決方法 類似的慣用語還有 find the answer to（找到⋯的答案）。

- Did you **find the solution to** the mystery?
- No, we still don't understand what happened.
  - 你找到這個謎團的解決方法了嗎？
  - 還沒，我們還是不了解發生了什麼事。

▶ She couldn't find a way to go home.
  她找不到回家的路。
  We need to find a solution to our problem.
  對於我們的問題，我們需要找出解決的方法。

settle the problem

- settle the problem with...
  解決和⋯的問題
- settle a civil complaint
  解決民事訴訟
- That settles it.
  終於搞定了。

解決問題 settle 主要接爭論、爭吵、糾紛、訴訟等受詞，指解決或達成協議。

- I **settled the problem** with my neighbor.
- So, are you both getting along?
  - 我跟鄰居的問題解決了。　● 那你們現在處得好嗎？

▶ They went to court to settle a civil complaint.
  他們去法院解決一項民事訴訟。
  That settles it. I'm finished working here.
  終於搞定了。我在這邊的工作完成了。

resolve a conflict

- resolve sth
  解決某事
- get sth resolved
  使某事獲得解決

解決糾紛 resolve 和 settle 都有解決的意思。resolve 是指找出解決問題或處理狀況的方法。

- I want to punch Frank in the nose.
- Fighting is the wrong way to **resolve a conflict**.
  - 我想在 Frank 的鼻子上揍一拳。　● 打架是解決糾紛的錯誤方法。

▶ It took an hour to resolve the argument.
  解決爭執花了一小時。
  Let's try to get this resolved.
  我們試著解決這件事吧。

work itself out

- problem works itself out
  問題自然解決

⋯自然解決 沒做什麼特別的處理，問題就自己解決，意思和「船到橋到自然直」相近。主詞是表示問題的名詞。

- My washing machine is very loud.
- Maybe the noise will **work itself out**.
  - 我的洗衣機很吵。　● 或許那噪音會自然消失。

▶ The problem between them worked itself out.
  他們之間的問題自然解決了。
  Your trouble will work itself out soon.
  你的問題很快會自然解決的。

1 職場・學校
2 電腦・網路
3 社交生活
4 日常生活
5 訊息・理解
6 想法・態度
7 情緒・狀況
8 行為舉止
9 時間地點・副詞片語

615

31 指責，起訴
find fault with

8-31.mp3

accuse A of B

- accuse sb of sth/-ing
  控告某人做了某事
- be accused of
  被控告做了…
- charge A with B
  控告／起訴 A 做了 B

控告 A 做了 B 常見的法律用語。指責、起訴之意。B 是名詞或動名詞（-ing）。

- Jenny **accused** her husband **of** hitting her.
- Her husband has a bad temper.
  - Jenny 控告她丈夫毆打她。　● 她先生的脾氣很差。

▶ The man was accused of stealing a gold ring.
  這個男人被控告偷竊黃金戒指。
  Police charged Tom with causing an accident.
  警察起訴 Tom 肇事。

find fault with

- find fault with one's boss
  挑某人老闆的毛病

挑…的毛病 通常指 intentionally（故意）找出對方的錯誤，藉以指責對方。

- My parents always **find fault with** my schoolwork.
- But you get really good grades.
  - 我的父母總是挑我學校作業的毛病。　● 但你的成績真的很好啊。

▶ All of the workers found fault with their boss.
  所有員工都挑他們老闆的毛病。
  It was easy to find fault with the old computer.
  挑這台舊電腦的毛病很容易。

criticize sb for...

- criticize sb for sth/-ing
  批評某人做了某事
- be/get criticized for
  因為…被批評

批評某人… for 後面以名詞或動名詞表示被批評的事。

- Did you enjoy the tour of the city?
- No. The guide **criticized me for** being late.
  - 市區觀光玩得開心嗎？　● 不開心。導遊罵我遲到。

▶ We criticized Roger for his laziness.
  我們批評了 Roger 的懶惰。
  Several students were criticized for poor spelling.
  幾位學生因為糟糕的拼字錯誤而被指責。

1 職場・學校
2 電腦・網路
3 社交生活
4 日常生活
5 訊息・理解
6 想法・態度
7 情緒・狀況
8 行為舉止
9 時間地點・副詞片語

blame A for B

- be to blame for sth
  對於某事要負責任
- take the blame for sth
  承擔某事的責任
- lay the blame on
  怪罪…

把 B 怪罪到 A 的頭上 指責 A 對於造成 B 的結果有責任。

- An old stove **was blamed for** the house fire.
- Wow, it burned everything to the ground.
  - 老舊的暖爐被認為是房屋起火的原因。
  - 哇，它把所有東西都燒光了。

▶ Karen was to blame for ending the marriage.
結束婚姻是 Karen 的錯。
The coach lay the blame on one of the team members.
教練怪罪其中一位隊員。

file a complaint against

- file a complaint against A for -ing
  投訴 A 做了…
- file a complaint against the store
  對商店提出客訴

投訴… against 後面接人或機關等不滿的對象。

- The new neighbor has his music on all night.
- Why don't you **file a complaint against** him?
  - 新來的鄰居音樂放了一整夜。　● 你為什麼不投訴他呢？

▶ Madge filed a complaint against the store for poor service.
Madge 對於這間店糟糕的服務提出了客訴。
He filed a complaint against Sam for damaging his car.
他投訴 Sam 損壞了他的車。

32 | 說笑，開玩笑 make fun of

8-32.mp3

joke about

- joke with sb
  和某人開玩笑
- make jokes about
  開關於…的玩笑

開關於…的玩笑 可以接事物或人當受詞。

- What did you do with your high school friends?
- We **joked about** things we had done.
  - 你跟高中時期的朋友們做了什麼？
  - 我們開了以前做過的事的玩笑。

▶ Our teacher jokes with us a lot.
我們老師常跟我們開玩笑。
We made jokes about our strange classmate.
我們開了關於我們奇怪同學的玩笑。

play a joke

· play a joke on...
  捉弄…
· play a trick on...
  捉弄…

開玩笑，捉弄，惡作劇 後面可以加 on 接被捉弄的對象。

● Why are you all hiding?
● We**'re playing a joke** on your sister.

●你們為什麼都躲著？ ●我們在跟你妹妹鬧著玩。

▶ On April 1st, people play jokes on their friends.
  四月一號的時候，人們會捉弄自己的朋友們。
  Did you play a trick on me?
  你是在耍我嗎？

make fun of

· make a fool of
  愚弄…

取笑… 帶著輕蔑或惡意去嘲笑某人。

● Many people **make fun of** beggars.
● That seems very unkind.

●很多人會取笑乞丐。 ●那樣似乎很不友善。

▶ My ex-boyfriend made a fool of me.
  我前男友愚弄了我。
  Don't make fun of disabled people.
  不要取笑殘障人士。

pull one's leg

跟某人開玩笑 請注意這不是指中文的「扯某人後腿」（be a drag on someone）。

● Did you really win a beauty contest?
● No, I **was just pulling your leg**.

●你真的贏了選美比賽嗎？ ●沒有。我只是在跟你開玩笑。

▶ Uncle Bob likes to pull my leg.
  Bob 叔叔喜歡跟我開玩笑。
  You must be pulling his leg.
  你一定是在跟他開玩笑。

tease sb about

· kid sb
  取笑某人

取笑某人的… 針對某個人事物取笑某人，惹對方不高興。

● What made Jason so angry?
● Someone **teased him about** his hairstyle.

●什麼事讓 Jason 那麼生氣？ ●有人取笑了他的髮型。

▶ We kidded Lotta about her new boyfriend.
  我們取笑了 Lotta 的新男友。
  The children teased Mary about her orange dress.
  孩子們取笑了 Mary 穿的橘色洋裝。

1 職場·學校
2 電腦·網路
3 社交生活
4 日常生活
5 訊息·理解
6 想法·態度
7 情緒·狀況
8 行為舉止
9 時間地點·副詞片語

33 折磨
be hard on

8-33.mp3

be hard on

· sb be hard on sb
  某人對某人嚴格
· sth be hard on sb
  某事對某人很勉強
· be hard on the body
  對身體很勉強

嚴格對待… 故意給對方很多工作、要求，或者用其他方法使他覺得沉重、辛苦。

● Our new manager really doesn't like you.
● Yes, she **has been very hard on** me.
  ●我們的新主管真的很不喜歡你。　●嗯，她對我非常嚴苛。

▶ Too much running is hard on the body.
  跑太多步對身體很勉強。
  The busy schedule was hard on everyone.
  忙碌的行程對每個人都很勉強。

give sb a hard time

讓某人不好過 特別指責備某人，或者用其他方法讓他有壓力。

● Andrea has made many mistakes.
● She's new. Don't **give her a hard time**.
  ●Andrea 犯了很多錯誤。　●她是新來的，別給她壓力。

▶ The policeman gave me a hard time. 警察對我態度很兇。
  He gave Cecil a hard time until he quit.
  他一直到 Cecil 辭職為止都讓他很不好過。

pick on

找…的碴，指責… 特別指很不公平地專找某人麻煩。

● Beth has a very big nose.
● It's not nice to **pick on** people.
  ●Beth 的鼻子很大。　●這樣挑人毛病不好。

▶ Some people pick on my little brother.
  有些人找我弟弟的麻煩。
  Why are you picking on me? 你為什麼要找我的碴？

get on one's nerves

· get off one's back
  不再煩某人

惹毛某人 某件煩人的事一直持續，終於把人惹得生氣的意思。

● Do you like being around Levi?
● No, he really **gets on my nerves**.
  ●你喜歡跟 Levi 在一起嗎？　●不喜歡，他真的很會惹毛我。

▶ Get off my back about paying the bills!
  不要再跟我嘮叨付帳單的事了！
  That noise gets on our nerves. 那噪音惹毛了我們。

bother A with B

- sorry to bother you
  抱歉打擾你
- harass sb
  騷擾某人
- nag
  使…心煩

用 B 打擾 A 用 with B 來說明是用什麼事物使 A 心煩。

- Would you like to buy a vacuum cleaner?
- Don't **bother me with** that right now.
  - 你想買台吸塵器嗎？　● 現在別用那件事煩我。

▶ Sorry to bother you, but your mom is calling.
  抱歉打擾你，但你媽媽打電話來了。
  John harassed the girl until she left.
  John 一直騷擾那個女生到她離開為止。

---

34 欺騙，詐欺
cheat sb out of

8-34.mp3

---

trick sb into -ing

- be/get tricked into
  -ing
  被騙去做…
- trick sb out of sth
  騙走某人的某物

騙某人做… trick 常常帶有藉由欺騙獲得某些利益的意思。

- There is a big scam on the Internet.
- Olivia **was tricked into** sending money to it.
  - 網路上發生了很大的詐騙事件。　● Olivia 被騙了，匯了錢過去。

▶ We were tricked into working today.
  我們今天被騙來工作。
  Patty was tricked into marrying Sal.
  Patty 被騙而嫁給了 Sal。

cheat sb out of

騙走某人的… cheat 除了作弊和感情出軌的意思以外，也有騙走財物的意思。

- The lawyer **cheated Terry out of** her money.
- I hope she can get some back.
  - 那位律師騙走了 Terry 的錢。　● 我希望她能拿回一些錢。

▶ Harry cheated her out of the rent money.
  Harry 騙走了她的房租。
  They cheated me out of a prize!
  他們把我的獎品騙走了！

con sb out of

· con sb into...
  騙某人做（某事）

騙走某人的（財物） con artist 是「騙子」的意思。

- Jerry was never honest with us.
- He **conned everyone out of** their paychecks.

　●Jerry 從來沒對我們誠實。　●他騙走了每個人的薪水。

▶ The criminal conned his family out of their savings.
　那個犯人把他家人的存款騙走了。
　The businessman was conned into paying more money.
　那位商人被騙而付了更多錢。

fall for a trick

· fall for the same trick
  被相同的伎倆給騙了

上當 fall for sb 則是「深深愛上某人」的意思。

- You can trust me with your money.
- No I can't. I **fell for that trick** before.

　●你可以安心把錢交給我。　●我沒辦法。我之前就上過這個當。

▶ My brother fell for the same trick.
　我哥哥被相同的伎倆給騙了。
　Don't fall for Paul's tricks.
　別上了 Paul 的當。

be arrested for fraud

· through/by fraud
  透過詐騙

· do a number on sb
  欺騙／傷害某人

· commit a fraud
  犯下詐騙行為

因詐騙被逮捕 fraud 是名詞，通常指財物方面的詐騙。

- The bank manager **was arrested for fraud**.
- What problems did he cause?

　●那位銀行經理因為詐騙而被逮捕了。　●他引發了怎樣的問題？

▶ Most of the money was stolen through fraud.
　大部分的錢都因為詐騙而被偷走了。
　That stockbroker really did a number on us.
　那個股票經紀人真是太欺負我們了。

1 職場・學校
2 電腦・網路
3 社交生活
4 日常生活
5 訊息・理解
6 想法・態度
7 情緒・狀況
8 行為舉止
9 時間地點・副詞片語

35 偷竊，搶奪
rob A of B

8-35.mp3

steal sth

- steal A from B
  偷走 B 的 A
- be caught stealing sth
  被抓到偷某物

偷竊某物 steal 後面接偷竊的東西。rob 後面則是接搶劫的對象或地點。

- Why are the policemen outside?
- Someone **stole** my new car.

  ●警察為什麼在外面？　●有人偷了我的新車。

▶ He stole some money from the old woman.

他偷了那位老婦人一些錢。

Danny got caught stealing a purse from the store.

Danny 被抓到偷了那間店的皮包。

be stolen from

- have sth stolen
  有某物被偷

從…被偷走 如果用被偷東西的人當主詞，可以說 have sth stolen。

- A television **was stolen from** Wendy's apartment.
- Was it expensive to replace?

  ●有一台電視從 Wendy 的公寓被偷走了。　●重買一台很貴嗎？

▶ The jewelry store had many diamonds stolen from it.

那間珠寶店被偷了很多鑽石。

I had my watch stolen.

我的手錶被偷了。

rob A of B

- rob a bank downtown
  搶市區的銀行
- be robbed of one's money
  被搶走某人的錢

搶走 A 的 B 注意 rob 後面接搶劫的對象，而不是搶走的財物。

- The thief **robbed us of** our Christmas presents.
- Wow, that's a terrible thing to do.

  ●小偷搶走了我們的耶誕禮物。　●哇，他那樣做真是糟糕。

▶ Someone robbed a bank downtown.

有人搶了市區的銀行。

The tourists were robbed of their money.

觀光客們的錢被搶了。

1 職場‧學校

2 電腦‧網路

3 社交生活

4 日常生活

5 訊息‧理解

6 想法‧態度

7 情緒‧狀況

8 行為舉止

9 時間地點‧副詞片語

hold up sth

· hold up the store
  搶劫商店
· holdup
  持槍搶劫（名詞）

搶劫某處 主要表示帶著 gun 等 deadly weapon 進行的搶劫。

● The robber **held up** the bank.
● I hope the police will catch him.

● 這個強盜搶劫了銀行。　● 我希望警察會抓到他。

▶ He ran out after he held up the store.
他搶劫商店之後跑了出去。
Tim was caught after he held up the McDonald's.
Tim 搶了麥當勞之後被抓到了。

be deprived of

· be deprived of one's
  freedom
  被剝奪自由
· deprive sb of sth
  剝奪某人的某物

被剝奪… 表示本來理所當然的事物被奪走。

● Was it difficult to stay in jail?
● We **were deprived of** food and water for a while.

● 待在監獄裡很苦嗎？　● 我們有陣子連食物跟水都被剝奪了。

▶ Linda was deprived of freedom after being arrested.
Linda 被逮捕後，被剝奪了自由。
The people were deprived of sunlight during the rainy
days. 雨季期間，人們失去了陽光。

---

36 爭吵，打架
have words with

8-36.mp3

argue about

· argue with sb
  about sth
  跟某人吵某事
· argue it out
  把事情辯個清楚

爭吵／爭論關於…的事 about 也可以換成 over。

● My car is much nicer than yours.
● I don't want to **argue about** it.

● 我的車比你的好得多。　● 我不想吵這個。

▶ Can we argue about this later?
我們可以晚一點再爭這件事嗎？
You really want to argue with me about this?
你真的想跟我吵這件事嗎？

have words with

- have a few words with sb
  和某人說些話
- be at odds with
  和⋯的意見不合

和⋯吵架 have a word with 則是「私下和⋯談」的意思。

- Were Jimmy and Bill really fighting?
- No, but they **had words about** something.
  - Jimmy 和 Bill 真的打了架嗎？　●沒有，但他們在吵某件事。

▶ I need to have a few words with you right now.
  我現在需要跟你說幾句話。
  Some of the students were at odds with the teacher.
  有些學生和老師的意見不合。

have a fight

- start a fight with sb
  和某人開始打架
- fight a lot with sb
  常和某人打架

打架，吵架 fight 可以指肢體上的衝突或口頭上的爭執（quarrel）。

- What happened to Sylvester?
- I think he **got into a fight**.
  - Sylvester 怎麼了？　●我想他打架了吧。

▶ Tom and I had a really big fight.
  Tom 跟我大打了一架。
  My parents got into a big fight and got divorced.
  我的父母大吵了一架，然後離婚了。

call sb names

- insult sb
  侮辱某人
- shout/yell at sb
  對某人大吼

辱罵某人 不是叫某人的名字，而是用難聽的稱呼叫他。請注意 sb 是受格而不是所有格。

- Jethro is just a dummy.
- Come on, don't **call him names**.
  - Jethro 就是個笨蛋。　●幹嘛這樣，不要罵他。

▶ The fight started after he insulted my girlfriend.
  他侮辱我的女朋友之後，我們就開始打架。
  She got so angry that she began to shout at everyone.
  她太生氣了，開始對每個人大吼。

bring it on

放馬過來 主要用於祈使句，表示已經準備好和對方打架或者接受挑戰。

- I can beat you up any time.
- When you're ready to fight, **bring it on**.
  - 我隨時都可以痛扁你。　●你準備好要打架的話，就放馬過來。

▶ If you're tough enough, bring it on!
  你夠猛的話，就放馬過來！
  We can handle it. Bring it on.
  我們可以應付的。放馬過來吧。

1 職場・學校
2 電腦・網路
3 社交生活
4 日常生活
5 訊息・理解
6 想法・態度
7 情緒・狀況
8 行為舉止
9 時間地點・副詞片語

37 | 毆打 beat up

8-37.mp3

hit sb hard

· be hit by a car
  被車撞
· hit sb in the face
  打某人的臉
· punch sb in the nose
  揍某人的鼻子

重擊某人 也可以指在財務、心理等各種層面造成重大打擊。打某個身體部位則是「hit sb in the + 身體部位」。

● How did Pat get hurt?

● Another guy **hit him hard**.

　●Pat 怎麼受傷的？　●有個男的用力打了他。

▶ The bicyclist was hit by a car. 那位腳踏車騎士被車子撞了。
　The baseball hit Tara in the face. 棒球砸中 Tara 的臉。

beat sb up

· beat sb up in a fight
  在打架中痛毆某人

痛毆某人 up 搭配動詞時，有「徹底」的意思，例如 eat/drink sth up（吃／喝光某物），而在這裡是「徹底打一頓」的意思。

● Several people **beat Jason up**.

● How did he make them angry?

　●有幾個人痛扁了 Jason。　●他怎麼惹他們生氣的？

▶ Todd beat him up in a fight. Todd 在打架中痛扁了他一頓。
　I am going to beat him up. 我要好好揍他一頓。

slap sb in the face

· spank sb
  打某人屁股

甩某人一巴掌 slap 也可以當名詞，說法是 give sb a slap。

● What happened when you tried to kiss Sue?

● She **slapped me in the face**.

　●你試著要親 Sue 的時候，發生了什麼事？　●她甩了我一巴掌。

▶ The angry woman slapped her boyfriend in the face.
　那位生氣的女人打了她男朋友一巴掌。
　I almost slapped you in the face. 我差點就要甩你一巴掌。

smack sb

打某人 多半表示為了處罰或教訓，而用手掌用力打。

● What did Sandra do when her husband dated other women?

● She **smacked** him across his face.

　●Sandra 的老公跑去跟別的女人約會時，她怎麼做的？
　●她甩了他一巴掌。

▶ I am going to smack you if you don't shut up.
　你不閉嘴的話，我會打你。
　Dave smacked his little brother. Dave 打了他的弟弟。

knock...down

- knock down the wall
  拆毀牆壁
- be knocked down by storm
  被暴風雨吹倒

擊倒，弄倒 knock out 是把人打得倒地不起，也是拳擊用語，縮寫就是我們常說的 K.O.。

- The old woman just **knocked me down**.
- Well, she really wanted to get on the bus.
  - ●那位老太太剛才把我撞倒了。　●嗯，她真的很想搭上公車。

▶ We'll knock down the wall before starting construction.
  建設工程開始前，我們會把這座牆拆掉。
  The big tree was knocked down by the storm.
  這棵大樹被暴風雨吹倒了。

---

38 | 報仇，報復
get even with

8-38.mp3

---

get even with

- get even with sb one day
  有一天會向某人報仇

報復… 把過去遭受的 trouble 或 harm 原封不動地還給對方，讓兩人之間扯平（even 是「對等」的意思）。

- Brad decided to **get even with** his ex-girlfriend.
- What is he going to do?
  - ●Brad 決定要報復他的前女友。　●他要怎麼做？

▶ I'll get even with my enemies some day.
  我總有一天會向我的敵人們報仇。
  I will get even with my boss for firing me.
  我會向我老闆報炒我魷魚的仇。

get back at

- get back at sb for -ing
  報某人做某事的仇

向…報復 把自己的不幸還給對方的意思。

- Why did Mark break your window?
- He was trying to **get back at** me.
  - ●Mark 為什麼打破你的窗戶？　●他想要向我報仇。

▶ I'll get back at Carol for saying bad things about me.
  我會向 Carol 報說我壞話的仇。
  Don't try to get back at him.
  不要試圖報復他。

pay back

- pay sb sth back
  把某物償還給某人
- pay sb back for sth
  為某事報復某人

報仇，償還 本來是償還的意思，引申為向對方報仇。

- ● Why did you cut up my clothes?
- ● It was **pay-back** for you cheating on me.
  - ●你為什麼剪碎我的衣服？　●這是報你背著我偷吃的仇。

▶ You must pay back the money within a week.
  你一定要在一星期內還錢。
  Sarah got pay back by breaking his cell phone.
  Sarah 砸爛他的手機來報仇。

get revenge on

- get some revenge
  for...
  報…的仇
- take revenge on sb
  對某人報仇

對…報仇 on 後面接報仇的對象。可以再加 for 接報仇的理由。

- ● I heard Paul stole your girlfriend.
- ● Yeah, I'll **get revenge on** him for that.
  - ●我聽說 Paul 搶走了你的女朋友。　●嗯，我會為此向他復仇的。

▶ Paula got revenge for being insulted.
  Paula 報了被侮辱的仇。
  My uncle took revenge on his enemies.
  我的叔叔對他的敵人們報了仇。

seek revenge

- look for revenge
  尋找復仇的方法

尋求復仇的機會 seek 可以換成意思相同的 look for。

- ● I'm going to **seek revenge** for what he did.
- ● Don't do anything that will get you in trouble.
  - ●對於他所做的事，我要找報仇的機會。
  - ●別做任何會讓你惹上麻煩的事。

▶ Some people look for revenge on the Internet.
  有些人在網路上尋求復仇的方法。
  He waited for ten years to seek revenge.
  為了報仇的機會，他等了十年。

1 職場・學校

2 電腦・網路

3 社交生活

4 日常生活

5 訊息・理解

6 想法・態度

7 情緒・狀況

8 行為舉止

9 時間地點・副詞片語

39 | 和好
make up with

make up with

· make up with sb
和某人和好

和…和好 打架、爭吵後消了氣，恢復過往的關係。

- Polly and her boyfriend **made up with** each other.
- So they are not fighting any more?
  - ●Polly 和她男朋友和好了。　●所以他們已經沒在吵架了？

▶ You should make up with your brothers and sisters.
　你應該跟你的兄弟姊妹和好。
　I couldn't make up with my worst enemy.
　我沒辦法跟我最壞的敵人和好。

patch things up with

和…重修舊好 patch up 是修補的意思，比喻修補破碎的關係。

- Why did you meet with Ron?
- I wanted to **patch things up** after our argument.
  - ●你為什麼跟 Ron 見面？　●吵完架後，我想跟他重修舊好。

▶ Try to patch things up with your family.
　試著和你的家人們重修舊好。
　We'll patch things up when we get together.
　我們會在見面時重修舊好。

resolve one's differences

· settle one's differences
解決某些人的歧見

消除某些人的歧見 這裡的 difference 是指意見不同。

- I heard Mike and Eric stopped fighting.
- It took several hours to **resolve their differences**.
  - ●我聽說 Mike 和 Eric 不再爭吵了。　●他們花了幾個小時消除歧見。

▶ Let's settle our differences like real men.
　我們像男子漢一樣來解決歧見吧。
　We can resolve our differences another time.
　我們可以改天再消除我們的歧見。

1 職場・學校

2 電腦・網路

3 社交生活

4 日常生活

5 訊息・理解

6 想法・態度

7 情緒・狀況

8 行為舉止

9 時間地點・副詞片語

reach a settlement

達成和解，達成協議 settlement 是「解決」的意思，但在這個用法裡通常表示和解或協議。

- How is your court case going?
- I finally **reached a settlement**.
  - 你的訴訟案怎麼樣了？ ●我終於達成了和解。

▶ Joan reached a settlement with the insurance company.
Joan 和保險公司達成了協議。
Will you ever reach a settlement with her?
你和她真的有可能和解嗎？

iron out

解決 原意是用熨斗去除皺摺，比喻消除歧見、解決問題。

- Is Stan still upset with you?
- No, we **ironed out** the problem.
  - Stan 還是對你很火大嗎？ ●不，我們把問題解決了。

▶ It will take time to iron out these issues.
解決這些問題會花點時間。
Have you ironed out the computer problem?
你解決電腦問題了嗎？

40 背叛 turn against

8-40.mp3

go behind one's back

在某人背後搞鬼 turn against sb 也是類似的意思。

- Should I tell someone about the problem?
- Don't **go behind your teacher's back**.
  - 我該告訴誰這個問題嗎？ ●別在你的老師背後搞鬼。

▶ She went behind my back to the boss.
她背著我對老闆說我壞話。
I went behind my wife's back to buy the computer.
我背著我太太買了電腦。

betray one's friend

· betray one's trust
背叛某人的信賴

背叛某人的朋友 betray 的受詞是遭到背叛的人。如果接事物當受詞，也有「洩漏」的意思。

● Ashley always **betrays her friends**.
● That's why no one trusts her.

　●Ashley 總是背叛她的朋友們。　●所以才沒有人相信她。

▶ The man betrayed all of his friends.
　那個男人背叛了他所有朋友。
　She betrayed her friends while in high school.
　她在高中時背叛了朋友。

stab sb in the back

在背後捅某人一刀，誹謗某人 被信賴的人從後面刺一刀，最有名的例子就是被 Brutus 刺殺，說出「You too, Brutus?」的凱薩（Caesar）大帝。

● Businessmen **stab** each other **in the back** all the time.
● Yeah, it's tough to have a job like that.

　●商人們總是在暗地裡中傷彼此。
　●是啊，要做那樣的工作很不容易。

▶ My best friend stabbed me in the back.
　我最好的朋友在背後捅我一刀。
　I can't believe you stabbed me in the back!
　我不敢相信你在暗地裡中傷我！

blow the whistle on

告發… 把不正當、不合理的事情讓外界知道的良心行為。

● Hank **blew the whistle on** his boss.
● That's why he was just fired.

　●Hank 告發了他的老闆。　●所以他剛才被炒魷魚了。

▶ It's difficult to blow the whistle on wrongdoing.
　告發不當行為很困難。
　She never blew the whistle on the illegal operation.
　她從來沒告發過非法營業。

turn against

背棄…，轉而反對… 「轉身背對某人」，表示從支持某人轉為反對某人。

● Courtney **turned against** her friends.
● She spends a lot of time alone now.

　●Courtney 背棄了她的朋友們。　●她現在常常自己一個人過。

▶ The voters turned against the President. 選民們背棄了總統。
　We turned against our strict teacher.
　我們反對我們嚴厲的老師。

41 | 給予教訓，訓誡
teach a lesson

8-41.mp3

1 職場・學校

2 電腦・網路

3 社交生活

4 日常生活

5 訊息・理解

6 想法・態度

7 情緒・狀況

8 行為舉止

9 時間地點・副詞片語

punish sb for

- punish sb for sth/-ing
  處罰某人做某事的行為
- punish sb by -ing
  做…來處罰某人
- get/be punished
  被處罰

因為…處罰某人 for 後面接名詞或動詞 -ing 形表示處罰的理由。

- Why is your son sitting over there?
- I **punished him for** hitting his older brother.

  ●你兒子為什麼坐在那邊？ ●因為他打了哥哥，所以我處罰他。

▶ The government should punish them for stealing money.
政府應該處罰他們偷錢的行為。
We punished them for skipping school.
我們懲罰了他們的蹺課行為。

teach sb a lesson

- teach sb manners
  教導某人規矩
- lesson learned
  學到的教訓

給某人一個教訓 也就是 let sb learn a lesson（讓某人學到一個教訓）。

- Did Harry get sent to jail?
- Yes. I hope it **teaches him a lesson**.

  ●Harry 被送去監獄了嗎？ ●嗯，希望這會給他一個教訓。

▶ These problems really taught me a lesson.
這些問題真的給了我一個教訓。
I'll teach you a lesson about disrespecting me!
我會讓你知道不尊重我的後果是什麼！

kick one's ass

- get one's ass kicked
  被教訓
- kick one's ass out of
  把某人踢出…

教訓… 口語說法，用「踢屁股」比喻教訓。如果只說 …kick ass，就是很強、非常厲害的意思。

- Brett says he's going to **kick your ass**.
- No way. I'm much tougher than he is.

  ●Brett 說他要教訓你。 ●想得美。我比他強壯多了。

▶ The boxer got his ass kicked in this fight.
這位拳擊手在打鬥中被教訓了一頓。
I'll kick your ass right out of my house.
我會把你踢出我家。

scold sb for

- scold sb for sth/-ing
  罵某人做了某事
- get a scolding from
  被…責罵

因為…罵某人 例如小孩子做錯事時責罵他們的情況。
- Mom **scolded Sally for** talking too much.
- Sally should learn to be quieter.
  - ●媽媽罵 Sally 太愛講話。 ●Sally 應該學著安靜一點。

▶ Busby got a scolding from his teacher.
  Busby 被他的老師罵了一番。
  I had to scold Jill for not paying me.
  Jill 不還我錢，所以我不得不罵她。

get away with

- get away with murder
  殺了人卻逃過懲罰

做了…而沒受罰 也就是 avoid punishment for。
- Did you watch the trial?
- Yes. The man **got away with** robbing the bank.
  - ●你看了審判了嗎？ ●看了。那個男的搶了銀行，卻沒被懲罰。

▶ I think Helen got away with murder.
  我想 Helen 逃過了謀殺的懲罰。
  She got away with stealing something from the store.
  她從店裡偷了東西，卻沒被懲罰。

42 放棄
give up

8-42.mp3

stop -ing

- stop a bad habit
  戒掉壞習慣
- kick the habit
  戒掉習慣

停止做… stop to do 則是停下手邊的事情去做某事。
- Let's **stop** working and finish this tomorrow.
- That's a good idea. I'm tired.
  - ●我們停止工作，明天再完成這件事吧。 ●這是個好主意。我累了。

▶ I have tried every year since 2005 to stop smoking.
  我從 2005 年開始，每年都試圖戒菸。
  Stop complaining and get back to work.
  別抱怨了，回去工作吧。

quit -ing

· quit school
  休學

· quit drinking
  戒酒

中斷⋯，戒掉⋯ 中斷學業或工作，或戒掉不好的習慣。

● What made you **quit your job**?

● I really hated to wake up early.

　●什麼原因讓你辭了職？　●我真的很討厭早起。

▶ Bill quit school last year.
　Bill 去年休學了。
　Didn't you quit smoking last year?
　你去年不是戒菸了嗎？

give up

· give up work
  放棄工作

· Don't give up.
  別放棄。

放棄⋯，不再做⋯ 除了指放棄事物，也可以表示不再繼續某個習慣。

● Why did you **give up** drinking?

● It was making me very unhealthy.

　●你為什麼不喝酒了？　●那讓我變得很不健康。

▶ Jean gave up working daily.
　Jean 放棄每天工作.
　Don't give up. Things will get better.
　別放棄。狀況會好起來的。

knock it off

· knock off early
  早點結束

· Come off it!
  別再說了！別再做了！

· Cut it out!
  別再說了！別再做了！

停止 要別人停止做某事時使用。cut it out, come off it 都是類似的表達方式。

● It's too cold. Turn up the heat!

● **Knock it off**. The temperature is fine.

　●太冷了。把暖氣打開吧！　●別這麼做。溫度剛剛好啊。

▶ Let's knock off early and grab a beer.
　我們早點結束，然後去喝杯啤酒吧。
　Come off it! You don't have that many problems.
　別再說了！你沒有那麼多問題。

break off

· leave off
  停止

中斷（談話或行為） 話講到一半，或者事情做到一半突然停止。

● I will have to **break off** right now.

● Do you have other plans?

　●我得馬上停止了。　●你還有其他計畫嗎？

▶ The speaker broke off in mid-sentence.
　那位演講者一句話講到一半突然停下來。
　We left off on page number eighty one.
　我們在第 81 頁停下來了。

1 職場・學校

2 電腦・網路

3 社交生活

4 日常生活

5 訊息・理解

6 想法・態度

7 情緒・狀況

8 行為舉止

9 時間地點・副詞片語

stop sb from -ing

阻止某人做⋯ stop 也可以換成 keep 或 prevent，不過 prevent 比較強調「預防」的意思。

- We **stopped Gary from** fighting with Tom.
- Good. Those guys don't like each other.
  - 我們阻止了 Gary 跟 Tom 打架。　● 很好。他們倆都不喜歡對方。

▶ The police prevented the thief from stealing money.
　警察預先阻止了小偷偷錢。
　The airport stopped people from getting on the plane.
　機場停止讓旅客們登機。

keep sb from -ing

- keep sb from sth
  使某人遠離某事物
- keep sth from sb
  不讓某人知道某事
- keep oneself from -ing
  克制自己不做⋯

防止某人做⋯，保護某人免於⋯ 這裡的 keep 有防止、禁止的意思。

- Do these vitamins really work?
- They **kept me from** getting sick.
  - 這些維他命真的有效嗎？　● 它們保護我不生病。

▶ Keep the TV from playing too loud.
　不要把電視開得太大聲。
　I can't keep him from drinking.
　我阻止不了他喝酒。

get in the way

- be in the way
  造成妨礙
- get out of the way
  讓開，躲開
- keep out of one's way
  避開某人

擋路，妨礙 get 也可以換成 stand，意思一樣。

- Don is the worst member of our group.
- He always **gets in the way** when we do things.
  - Don 是我們團隊中最糟糕的團員。
  - 我們在做事時，他總是妨礙我們。

▶ The table is in the way of the door.
　這張桌子擋到門了。
　The tree is falling. Get out of the way!
　樹要倒了，快躲開！

disturb sb/sth

· sorry to disturb you
  抱歉打擾你
· disturb one's sleep
  打擾某人的睡眠
· interrupt sb
  打斷某人(的話或工作)

打擾··· 使人心煩，或者干擾事物的和諧狀態。

● Did you hear all the yelling last night?
● Yes, it **disturbed** everyone in my apartment building.

●你昨晚有聽到吼叫聲嗎？　●有，那聲音打擾到我公寓裡的每個人。

▶ Be careful not to disturb the sleeping baby.
  小心不要吵醒正在睡覺的嬰兒。
  The speech continued without interruption.
  這場演説未受干擾地持續著。

block one's way

· block sth
  阻擋某物
· set back
  阻止，阻擋

擋住某人的路 block 當名詞是指方塊狀的物體，當動詞則是阻擋的意思。

● Why was the bus late getting here?
● There was an accident that **blocked its way**.

●公車為什麼晚來了？　●有一場事故擋住了公車的路。

▶ Tim blocked Jena from leaving his room.
  Tim 擋住了 Jena，不讓她離開他房間。
  My boss tried to set back my plan for vacation.
  我老闆試圖阻撓我的休假計畫。

---

44 | 遠離，擺脫 keep away from

8-44.mp3

keep away from

· keep sb away from
  使某人遠離···

遠離··· 也就是 keep oneself away from sb/sth 的意思。

● **Keep away from** the boss. He's in a bad mood.
● I saw that he looked upset.

●離老闆遠一點。他心情不好。　●我看到他好像很煩。

▶ Keep away from that old house.
  離那間舊房子遠一點。
  Keep away from the sharp knives.
  離那些鋒利的刀遠一點。

1 職場·學校
2 電腦·網路
3 社交生活
4 日常生活
5 訊息·理解
6 想法·態度
7 情緒·狀況
8 行為舉止
9 時間地點·副詞片語

stay away from

遠離… 除了指具體的「遠離」，也可以表示抽象的「不牽扯進某件事」。

- Have you been to this neighborhood?
- **Stay away from** there. It's dangerous.

  ●你去過這附近嗎？　●離那邊遠遠一點。那裡很危險。

▶ Stay away from dishonest people.

要遠離不誠實的人。

Stay away from my wallet.

離我的皮夾遠一點。

keep off

不接近…，避開… 草坪上常會看到 keep off the grass。

- **Keep off** the sidewalk.
- I see it is being repaired.

  ●離人行道遠一點。　●我看到它正在整修中。

▶ You'd better keep off my lawn.

你最好離我的草坪遠一點。

She said to keep off the new furniture.

她說不要靠近新買的家具。

get out of

· get out of sth/-ing
　逃避某事

逃避（不想做的事） 也就是 succeed in not doing something what one doesn't want to do 的意思。

- We have to work all day Sunday.
- Is there any way to **get out of** it?

  ●我們星期天得工作一整天。　●有任何可以逃掉的方法嗎？

▶ I got out of going on that blind date.

我避開了那場聯誼。

You need to get out of the schedule you have.

你需要推掉你的行程。

sneak out of

· sneak out of work/
　school
　從公司／學校悄悄溜出去

從…悄悄溜出去 senak 是指悄悄地、不被發覺地走。

- Are you sure you can meet me today?
- Sure. I'll **sneak out of** our office meeting.

  ●你確定你今天能跟我見面嗎？

  ●當然，我會從公司會議裡偷溜出去。

▶ Don't sneak out of work on Friday.

星期五不要從公司溜走。

Three students sneaked out of school.

三名學生悄悄從學校溜了出去。

45 釋放，使自由
set free

1 職場・學校

2 電腦・網路

3 社交生活

4 日常生活

5 訊息・理解

6 想法・態度

7 情緒・狀況

8 行為舉止

9 時間地點・副詞片語

set sb free

- be set free
  被釋放
- become/get free/loose
  變自由

使某人自由，釋放某人 allow sb to be free 的意思。

- What will happen to the animals in this zoo?
- They will **be set free** in the future.
  ● 這間動物園的動物們會怎麼樣？ ● 將來牠們會被放生。

▶ The court set the prisoner free.
法院釋放了那名囚犯。
The boat was lost when it got free of the dock.
那艘船從碼頭鬆開後就不見了。

be released from

- release a hostage
  釋放人質
- be released from a cage
  從籠子裡被放出來

從…被釋放出來 release 是「把抓住的人或動物釋放」的意思。

- My brother **was just released from** jail.
- Really? Why was he in jail?
  ● 我哥哥剛從監獄被釋放出來。 ● 真的嗎？他為什麼坐牢？

▶ The terrorists agreed to release a hostage.
恐怖份子同意釋放一名人質。
The animals were released from their cage.
動物從籠子裡被釋放出來。

let out

- let the dog out
  把狗放出來

讓…出去／出來 使困在裡面的東西得以釋放。

- I think someone locked the door.
- I'll **let out** the people who are inside.
  ● 我想有人把門鎖住了。 ● 我會把裡面的人弄出來。

▶ Gwen must go home and let the dog out.
Gwen 一定要回家把狗放出來。
Open the window and let out the smoke.
把窗戶打開，讓煙飄出去。

turn sb loose

· set/let sb loose
  釋放某人

釋放··· turn 也可以換成 set 或 let，意思一樣。

● I heard Brandon was detained at the airport.
● Yes, but they **turned him loose** after a few hours.

　● 我聽說 Brandon 被拘留在機場。
　● 嗯，但幾小時之後，他們就釋放他了。

▶ The vampire was turned loose in a dark place.
　吸血鬼從黑暗的地方被釋放出來。
　I hope they never turn him loose.
　我希望他們永遠都不要釋放他。

get out of prison

· put sb in prison
  押某人入獄

出獄 入獄則是 go to prison。

● What happened to the bank robber?
● He **got out of the prison** after completing his term.

　● 那個銀行強盜怎麼樣了？　● 服刑結束後，他就出獄了。

▶ After getting out of the prison, he became a Christian.
　出獄之後，他成為了基督徒。
　Try to visualize the moment when you get out of prison.
　試著想像你出獄的瞬間。

46 | 行動，舉止
take action

8-46.mp3

act like + N

· act like a fool
  表現得像個傻子
· act like / as if S+V
  表現得好像···

表現得像··· act like 後面也可以接 S+V 句型。

● You're married. Don't **act like** a single guy.
● I'm not. I was just talking to these girls.

　● 你已經結婚了。別裝得像是單身漢一樣。
　● 我沒有。我只是跟這些女孩子說話而已。

▶ Gina just acted like she didn't know me.
　Gina 剛才表現得像是不認識我。
　Tony acts like he has a lot of money.
　Tony 表現得好像他很有錢的樣子。

act + 副詞

- act strangely
  行為舉止很奇怪
- act so badly
  行為舉止很不好

行為… 用副詞說明行為是什麼樣子。

- Kari **was acting strangely** today.
- What was wrong with her?
  - ●Kari 今天的行為舉止很奇怪。　●她怎麼回事？

▶ Act quickly before it is too late.
  在變得太遲之前，快點行動。
  I always act friendly to people I don't know.
  我總是對不認識的人很友善。

act + 形容詞

- act cruel
  行為舉止很殘忍
- act strange all day
  整天行為舉止都很奇怪
- act very crazy
  行為舉止很瘋狂
- act the fool
  裝傻

行為… 在口語中，act 也可以直接接形容詞表示行為舉止如何。
act 接名詞則是「裝作／扮演…」的意思

- Why were you and Gerald fighting?
- He **acted very cruel** towards me.
  - ●你為什麼跟 Gerald 吵架？　●他對我非常殘忍。

▶ Brandon acts crazy when he has been drinking.
  Brandon 喝醉時，他的行為舉止會很瘋狂。
  Our new teacher acts funny.
  我們的新老師行為舉止很奇怪。

take action

- take (some) steps
  採取步驟

採取行動 action 也可以換成 measures（措施）或 steps（步驟）。

- I owe more money every day.
- You should **take action** and pay your debts.
  - ●我每天都會欠更多錢。　●你應該採取行動去還債。

▶ They took action to stop the thief.
  他們採取行動來阻止小偷。
  Melinda took action to lose weight.
  Melinda 採取行動來減肥。

behave like + N

- behave as if S+V
  表現得好像…
- behave strangely
  表現得很奇怪

表現得像… behave 是指在禮儀方面的表現，或者表現得像某種
身分。「Behave yourself.」是要小孩子守規矩時會說的話。

- The kids acted badly on the subway.
- I agree. They **behaved like** little monkeys.
  - ●這些孩子們在地鐵上很不守規矩。
  - ●我同意。他們表現得像小猴子一樣。

▶ The businessmen behaved like gangsters.
  這些商人表現得像流氓一樣。
  The man and woman behaved like lovers.
  這對男女的舉止看起來像是一對戀人。

1 職場・學校
2 電腦・網路
3 社交生活
4 日常生活
5 訊息・理解
6 想法・態度
7 情緒・狀況
8 行為舉止
9 時間地點・副詞片語

make a move

· make a move to do
採取行動去做…

» cf. make a move
on sb
勾引某人

採取行動 為了解決問題或達成目標去行動。請注意這裡的 move 是名詞。

● I'm worried that I will lose all my money.
● You should **make a move** to protect it.
　●我擔心我會失去所有的錢。　●你應該採取行動來保護你的錢。

▶ Rick made a move to find a better job.
　Rick 採取了行動去找更好的工作。
　The students made a move to join another class.
　學生們採取行動，換到另一班上課。

meet a challenge

迎接挑戰 對於困難的事情不逃避，而是迎頭面對。

● Our basketball team is pretty talented.
● They can **meet a challenge** from any other team.
　●我們的籃球隊很有打球的天分。　●他們能迎接任何隊伍的挑戰。

▶ Are you ready to meet a challenge from someone else?
　你準備好要迎接其他人的挑戰了嗎？
　We can meet a challenge from another company.
　我們能夠應付其他公司的挑戰。

cope with

處理／應付事情 妥善處理問題或狀況。

● Darian's parents both died this year.
● It must be difficult for her to **cope with** that.
　●Darian 的雙親今年都去世了。　●這對她而言一定很難克服。

▶ I can't cope with all the work I have to do.
　我無法處理所有我必須做的工作。
　How did you cope with getting fired?
　你是怎麼克服被解雇這件事的？

1 職場·學校

2 電腦·網路

3 社交生活

4 日常生活

5 訊息·理解

6 想法·態度

7 情緒·狀況

8 行為舉止

9 時間地點·副詞片語

47 冒險 take a chance

8-47.mp3

take a chance

- take one's chance
  冒險，碰運氣
- take chances
  冒險
- take a chance on...
  在…上冒險
- » cf. take the chance
  抓住機會

冒險，碰運氣 即使有風險也不在意，要試一次看看。

- Do you think I should get this leather coat?
- It may be bad quality. You'd **be taking a chance on** it.
  - 你覺得我該買這件皮大衣嗎？
  - 品質可能不好，買這件很冒險。

▶ Take a chance and do something new.
冒點險，去做點新的事情。
Pam took a chance and tried Internet dating.
Pam 抱著碰運氣的心態嘗試網路交友。

run a risk

- run/take the risk of -ing
  冒著…的危險
- take some risk
  冒著一點危險

冒著危險 run 也可以換成 take。後面接 of -ing 表示可能發生的危險。

- We are going to break into the school tonight.
- You **run a risk of** being caught by the police.
  - 我們今晚要闖入學校。　● 你們會有被警察抓的危險。

▶ Every soldier runs a risk of being shot.
每位士兵都有會被射殺的危險。
I didn't study and run a risk of failing the exam.
我沒有讀書，有考試被當的危險。

risk -ing

- risk it
  豁出去，冒險
- risk one's life/fortune
  賭上性命／財產

冒…的險 risk 當動詞用，後面接名詞或動詞 -ing 形。

- Lucy brought all of her money to the casino.
- Is she going to **risk** losing it all?
  - Lucy 把她所有錢都帶去賭場了。　● 她要冒把錢輸光的風險嗎？

▶ He risked falling off the side of the cliff.
他冒著會從懸崖邊掉下去的危險。
You risk hurting someone with that knife.
你冒著會用那把刀傷到人的危險。（→你那把刀可能會傷到人）

at the risk of -ing

- There is a risk of...
  有…的危險
- be worth the risk
  值得冒險
- at all risks
  無論冒什麼危險，一定

冒著…的危險 表示可能有某種危險。如果沒有 the，說 at risk of 的話，就是表示已經瀕臨某種危險。

- Gee, why is Hattie making so much noise?
- I don't know, but she is **at risk of** making people angry.
  - 媽呀，為什麼 Hattie 那麼吵？
  - 我不知道，但她恐怕會把其他人惹毛。

▶ Smokers are at risk of getting cancer.
吸菸者有得到癌症的危險。
Fast drivers are at risk of getting stopped by police.
開快車的駕駛有被警察攔下來的危險。

be in danger

- be in danger of -ing
  處於…的危險
- put sb in danger/
  at risk
  使某人陷入危險

處於危險 後面可以接 of -ing 說明是怎樣的危險。

- You **are in danger of** getting fired.
- Is there anything I can do to save my job?
  - 你有被解雇的危險。 ● 有什麼能保住我工作的方法嗎？

▶ The city's water is in danger of being polluted.
這個城市的水處於被汙染的危險中。
Joe is in danger of failing math class.
Joe 有數學課不及格的危險。

---

48 申請，登記
register for

8-48.mp3

register for

- register for a course
  登記選課
- register for a dance
  class
  報名舞蹈課
- » cf. register sth
  登記／申報某事物

登記…，報名… 表示出生、死亡、婚姻的登記，或課程、活動的報名。

- Why are there so many students here?
- They **are registering for** their classes.
  - 為什麼這裡有這麼多學生？ ● 他們在登記選課。

▶ Robert registered for a cooking class.
Robert 報名了一堂烹飪課。
I have registered to take the written test for a driver's license. 我已經報名參加駕照筆試。

enroll in

- enroll in an advanced class
  報名進階班
- enroll in the course
  報名課程

註冊…，報名… enroll sb on the list of... 意為「將某人的名字記入…的名冊」。

- I hope to **enroll in** a course this summer.
- Any course in particular?

  ●今年夏天我希望能報名一門課。　●有特別想上的課嗎？

▶ Laura wants to enroll in Princeton University.
  Laura 想要註冊進入普林斯頓大學。
  Did you enroll in my English class?
  你有報名我的英文課嗎？

hand in

- hand out
  分發…
- hand-out
  （上課時發給學生的）講義

繳交…，提出… turn in 和 give in 的意思也類似。用一個字來說，就是 submit。

- Before I go any further, Bill has something to say.
- I **handed in** my resignation this morning.

  ●在我繼續說下去之前，Bill 有句話要說。
  ●我今天早上提出我的辭呈了。

▶ I got him to turn in the report.
  我讓他交出了報告。
  Make sure that you turn in your keys at the end of the day.
  在一天結束的時候要記得交出鑰匙。

fill out

- fill in
  填寫（空格等）
- complete a form
  完成表格

填好（表格） 把整張表格填完。fill in 則是一般的「填寫」，例如填空格等。

- Don't forget to **fill out** those forms before you go.
- I'll leave them on your desk before I go.

  ●在你離開之前，別忘了把那些表格填好。
  ●我離開前會把表格放在你桌上。

▶ Would you fill out this form, please?
  可以請您填寫這張表嗎？
  I'd like you to fill out this questionnaire for me.
  我希望你能幫我填寫這份問卷。

1 職場・學校
2 電腦・網路
3 社交生活
4 日常生活
5 訊息・理解
6 想法・態度
7 情緒・狀況
8 行為舉止
9 時間地點・副詞片語

Time, Place & etc.

各種副詞片語與時間地點的慣用語

CHAPTER 9

01 | 軍隊
in the service

be in the service

· enter the service
  入伍
· do one's military
  service
  服兵役

服役中 be in the service of... 是「服務…」的意思，只說 in the service 的話就是指服役。

● When **were** you **in the service**?
● In the '90s.
  ●你是什麼時候當兵的？ ●90 年代的時候。

▶ I entered the service just after my 18th birthday.
   我過了 18 歲生日之後，馬上就入伍了。
   Several men are away doing their military service.
   幾名男子離開去服役。

serve in the army

· serve in the military
  服兵役

服兵役 army 也可以換成 military，或更精確的 air force（空軍）、navy（海軍）。army 可以泛指軍隊或指陸軍。

● All citizens of Israel must **serve in the military**.
● Does that include women too?
  ●所有以色列的公民都必須服兵役。 ●也包含女性嗎？

▶ I served in the army about twenty years ago.
   我大約 20 年前當了兵。
   Kevin chose not to serve in the military.
   Kevin 選擇不去當兵。

join the army

· enlist in the army
  加入軍隊
· go into the army
  加入軍隊

入伍 join 也可以換成 go into 或 enlist in。

● What made you **join the army**?
● I wanted to have a career as a soldier.
  ●你為什麼加入軍隊？ ●我想要以軍人為職業。

▶ He decided to go enlist in the army.
   他決定加入軍隊。
   The young men went into the army last year.
   那些年輕人去年入伍了。

1 職場・學校
2 電腦・網路
3 社交生活
4 日常生活
5 訊息・理解
6 想法・態度
7 情緒・狀況
8 行為舉止
9 時間地點・副詞片語

volunteer for military service

自願服役 volunteer for 是「自願做…」的意思。

● Do you plan to **volunteer for military service**?
● Yes, I will as soon as I finish high school.
　●你打算服志願役嗎？　　●嗯，我高中一畢業，就會這麼做。

▶ In the US and Canada, people can volunteer for military service.
　在美國和加拿大，人們可以自願加入軍隊。
　John volunteered for military service during the war.
　在戰爭期間，John 自願加入軍隊。

be discharged from the army

· leave the army
　退伍
· honorary discharge
　榮譽退伍（名詞片語）

退伍 discharge 可以表示軍隊或醫院「允許…離開」。

● What is the happiest day you can remember?
● It was when I **was discharged from the army**.
　●你記憶中最開心的一天是什麼時候？　●是我退伍的時候。

▶ Mark left the army after being injured.
　Mark 受傷後就退伍了。
　The older students are finished with their military service.
　較年長的學生們已經服完役了。

02 | 犯法 break the law

9-02.mp3

break the law

· feel guilty
　有罪惡感
· go into effect
　（法律等）生效

違反法律 反義的說法是 keep the law（遵守法律）。

● It is illegal to throw garbage in the street.
● I think we shouldn't **break the law**.
　●把垃圾丟在街上是違法的。　　●我想我們不該違反法律。

▶ The little boy felt guilty about stealing candy.
　那個小男孩因為偷了糖果而有罪惡感。
　New traffic laws go into effect this year.
　新的交通法規今年開始生效。

get caught -ing

- catch sb -ing
  抓到某人做某事
- catch sb with the
  security camera
  用監視攝影機抓到某人

被抓到在做… 做違法或不好的行為時，被當場逮到。

- I read in the paper that the police **caught** a thief.
- Good. I feel safer hearing that.
  - ●我在報紙上看到警察抓了一個小偷。
  - ●太好了，聽到這個消息我覺得安心了點。

▶ Jerry got caught stealing a watch.
  Jerry 偷錶被抓到。
  I caught him looking in my windows.
  我逮到他從窗戶偷窺我房間。

get arrested for

- be under arrest for
  因為…被逮捕了
- call the police
  打電話叫警察

因為…被逮捕 由於違法的行為被警察逮捕到案。

- Why is Teresa in jail?
- She **got arrested for** stealing a pair of shoes.
  - ●Teresa 為什麼在坐牢？　●她因為偷了一雙鞋被逮捕。

▶ Several people are under arrest for breaking windows.
  有幾個人因為打破窗戶被逮捕。
  This is dangerous. Let's call the police.
  這很危險。我們打電話叫警察吧。

go on trial

- file a lawsuit against
  向…提起訴訟
- win[lose] a lawsuit/
  case
  贏〔輸〕了訴訟
- reach a verdict
  做出裁決

接受審判 under trial 意為「審理中」，without trial 則是「不經審判」的意思。

- What happened after Carl was arrested?
- He's **going on trial** in a few weeks.
  - ●Carl 被逮捕後怎麼樣了？　●他幾週後要接受審判。

▶ I had to file a lawsuit against the company.
  我必須對這間公司提起訴訟。
  The old man won a lawsuit against LG.
  這位老先生贏了跟 LG 的訴訟。

put sb in jail

- go to jail
  入獄

使某人入獄 in jail 是在坐牢、服刑中的意思。

- Was Lisa arrested last night?
- Yeah, the police **put her in jail.**
  - ●Lisa 昨晚被逮捕了嗎？　●嗯，警察把她送進監獄了。

▶ You'll go to prison if you are caught.
  如果你被抓的話，會進監獄的。
  After the riot, police put many people in jail.
  那場暴動後，警察把很多人送進了監獄。

1 職場・學校
2 電腦・網路
3 社交生活
4 日常生活
5 訊息・理解
6 想法・態度
7 情緒・狀況
8 行為舉止
9 時間地點・副詞片語

03 | 保險 buy insurance

9-03.mp3

be insured for + 錢

· be insured for sth
  有保⋯的險

已經投保了多少金額 主詞是被保險的人或物。

● Your car was damaged in the accident.
● Yeah, but I **was insured for** traffic accidents.
  ●你的車在車禍中受損了。　●嗯，但我有保交通意外險。

▶ The large diamond was insured for a million dollars.
  那顆大鑽石投保了一百萬美元。
  Our home is insured for floods and fires.
  我們家有保洪水和火災險。

buy insurance

· buy insurance for
  one's house
  幫某人的房屋買保險
· purchase life
  insurance
  購買壽險
· take out insurance
  加入保險
· sell insurance to sb
  賣保險給某人

買保險 sell insurance to sb 當然就是賣保險給某人。

● I was wondering if you **sold travel insurance**.
● I'm sorry we don't, but our sister company does.
  ●我想知道你們有沒有賣旅遊險。
  ●很抱歉我們沒有，但我們的姊妹公司有賣。

▶ I must buy insurance for my house.
  我必須幫我的房屋買保險。
  I'm not interested in purchasing life insurance.
  我沒興趣買壽險。

have insurance for/on

· have health insurance
  有健康保險
· have insurance on
  one's house
  某人的房子有保險

有⋯的保險 for 或 on 後面接保險項目。或者不使用介系詞，在 insurance 前面說明保險種類。

● Do you **have health insurance**?
● No, it's too expensive to purchase.
  ●你有健康保險嗎？　●沒有，那太貴了。

▶ Paul had health insurance when he got sick.
  Paul 生病時有健康保險。
  Do you have any life insurance at the moment?
  你目前有任何壽險嗎？

(insurance) covers…

· A be covered by the insurance
  A 在保險範圍內

（保險）範圍涵蓋… 名詞片語 insurance coverage 是「保險涵蓋範圍」。

● The tree fell right on my house.
● I hope my insurance **covers that damage**.
　●樹正好倒在我房屋上。　　●希望那在我的保險範圍內。

▶ Jackie's operation was covered by her insurance.
　Jackie 的手術在她的保險理賠範圍內。
　His insurance covers that property.
　他的保險範圍涵蓋那棟房產。

file an insurance claim

· commit insurance fraud
  犯保險詐欺罪
  →詐領保險金

申請保險理賠 向保險公司提出相關資料申請理賠。

● Wow, the flood destroyed your house.
● I have to **file an insurance claim** to rebuild it.
　●哇，那場洪水毀了你的屋子。　●我得申請保險理賠來重建。

▶ Jim was arrested after committing insurance fraud.
　Jim 詐領保險金後被逮捕了。
　They filed an insurance claim to replace their car.
　他們申請保險理賠來換車。

---

04 受害，受益
do damage to

9-04.mp3

do damage to

· do some serious damage
  造成嚴重的損害
· cause damage to
  對…造成損害

對…造成損害 damage is done 則是「傷害已經造成」的意思。

● Was anyone hurt in the accident?
● No, but it **did damage to** the car.
　●有任何人在車禍中受傷嗎？　●沒有，但是車子受損了。

▶ This software can cause damage to your computer.
　這個軟體會傷害你的電腦。
　It could do some serious damage to our firm's image.
　這可能對我們公司的形象造成嚴重的傷害。

no harm done

沒什麼大礙，沒有人受傷 表示「沒有關係」或「事故中沒有人受傷」。

- I'm sorry I spilled juice on your sofa.
- **No harm done**. I'll have it cleaned.

  ●很抱歉我把果汁灑在你沙發上了。
  ●沒什麼大礙。我會把它清理乾淨。

▶ No damage. It's an easy problem to fix.

　沒什麼大礙。這是個很容易解決的問題。

　Don't worry about it. No harm done.

　別擔心，沒什麼大礙的。

do sb good

· do sb harm
  對某人造成傷害
· be doing good in
  business
  事業興隆（有獲利）

對某人有好處 do sb bad 就是「對某人不好」。

- Harold looks much healthier now.
- His long vacation **did him good**.

  ●Harold 現在看起來健康許多。　●他休的長假對他很有益。

▶ The economic problems have done us harm.

　經濟問題對我們造成了傷害。

　Your uncle is doing good in his business.

　你叔叔的事業很順利。

make a profit

獲利 動詞 make 也可以換成 turn 或 earn。

- How is your company doing?
- It's fine. We**'re making a profit**.

  ●你公司的狀況怎麼樣？　●還不錯，我們有獲利。

▶ You can't make a profit selling vitamins.

　你無法靠販賣維他命獲利。

　I need to make a profit this month.

　我這個月需要獲利。

suffer a loss

· make a loss of...
  損失，虧損（多少錢）

遭受損失，虧損 也可以說 make a loss。make a loss 不是「造成損失」的意思，而是 make a profit 的反義語。

- Jill seems very unhappy.
- She **suffered a loss** on her investments.

  ●Jill 看起來很不開心。　●她投資虧錢了。

▶ The firm suffered a loss last year.

　這間公司去年虧損了。

　Many people on Wall Street suffered a loss.

　華爾街有許多人虧了錢。

1 職場・學校
2 電腦・網路
3 社交生活
4 日常生活
5 訊息・理解
6 想法・態度
7 情緒・狀況
8 行為舉止
9 時間地點・副詞片語

05 補償
make up for

9-05.mp3

make up for

- make up (to sb) for sth
  （對某人）補償某事
- make up for lost time
  彌補失去的時光

補償… for 後面接損失或錯誤的行為。

● I can't believe you didn't remember our date.
● I'll **make up for** it tomorrow, I promise.
 ●我不敢相信你忘了我們的約會。　●我明天會補償你的，我保證。

▶ We talked for hours, making up for lost time.
 我們說了好幾個小時的話來彌補失去的時光。
 Is this your first step to make up for it?
 這是你補償錯誤的第一步嗎？

make it up to

- make it up
  補償
- make it up to sb
  補償某人

補償… to 後面接要補償的對象。

● He'll have to make up for the time he's been away.
● He said he'll **make it up** this weekend.
 ●他必須把他沒來的工作時數補足。　●他說他這週末會補足。

▶ I'll make it up to you later.
 我之後會補償你。
 There is no way to make it up to me.
 沒有任何可以補償我的方法。

get/be rewarded

- pay back
  償還，報答，報復

得到獎賞／報答 後面可以加上 for，接 sth 或動詞 -ing 形來說明原因。

● Kelly **was rewarded for** being the top salesperson.
● I heard she was given a new car.
 ●Kelly 因為是業績第一名的業務而獲得獎賞。
 ●我聽說她得到了一台新車。

▶ When do you plan to pay back my money?
 你打算什麼時候償還我錢？
 Melvin was rewarded for good behavior.
 Melvin 因為品行優良而得到獎賞。

1 職場‧學校

2 電腦‧網路

3 社交生活

4 日常生活

5 訊息‧理解

6 想法‧態度

7 情緒‧狀況

8 行為舉止

9 時間地點‧副詞片語

pay for all the damage

賠償所有的損害 pay for 除了表示付錢買東西，也可以表示賠償的意思。

- The item inside the package was broken.
- Well, the shipper should **pay for all the damage**.

　●包裹裡的物品損壞了。　　●嗯，貨運公司應該賠償所有損失。

▶ I'll pay for all the damage to your house.
　我會賠償你屋子的所有損壞。
　She paid for all the damage she caused.
　她賠償了她造成的所有損失。

seek compensation for

- as compensation
  作為賠償
- monetary
  compensation
  金錢賠償

尋求對⋯的賠償 動詞 seek 也可以換成 demand 或 claim。

- Why is she hiring a lawyer?
- She's **seeking compensation for** getting hurt.

　●她為什麼要雇用律師？　　●她想要獲得受傷的賠償。

▶ A large amount of money was given as compensation.
　有一大筆款項被付出作為賠償。
　I need monetary compensation for my property.
　對於我的房產，我需要金錢賠償。

06 屬於，擁有 belong to

9-06.mp3

belong to

- belong to nobody
  不屬於任何人
- belong here
  屬於這裡
- belongings
  隨身物品

屬於⋯ 表示「是⋯所擁有的」，是很基本的說法。

- Is this your suitcase?
- No, it **belongs to** my brother.

　●這是你的行李箱嗎？　　●不是，那是我弟弟的。

▶ She gathered her belongings and left.
　她收拾了她的隨身物品就離開了。
　These pencils belong to my students.
　這些鉛筆是我學生的。

own a car

- first owner
  （車輛的）第一手主人
- call sth one's own
  稱某物是自己的

有車 租車是 lease/rent a car，但 lease 是指簽了長期合約的租用，rent 則是短期租用（到期可自動續約）。不過，在口語中 lease 和 rent 常有混用的現象。

- Do you **own a car**?
- Yes. I drive to work every day.
  - ●你有車嗎？　●有，我每天開車上班。

▶ They called the little house their own.
  他們說這間小屋子是他們的。
  I'll own a car when I finish college.
  我大學畢業後，會擁有一台車。

be in possession of

擁有⋯，持有⋯ 後面接擁有的物品。但 sth is the possession of mine/yours/his/hers 則是以物品為主詞，後面接所有代名詞，表示「某物是我／你／他／她的」。

- I **am in possession of** some gold coins.
- Make sure no one steals them.
  - ●我有一些金幣。　●小心不要讓人偷走。

▶ Tammy was in possession of a new coat.
  Tammy 有一件新大衣。
  Mike was in possession of three dictionaries.
  Mike 有三本字典。

share sth with

和⋯分享某物 除了分享物品以外，也可以表示分享感情或有同感，例如 share happiness/sadness。

- I forgot to bring my lunch today.
- I could **share** my food **with** you.
  - ●我今天忘了帶午餐來。　●我可以把我的食物分你。

▶ She shared her textbook with her friend.
  她把課本分給朋友一起看。
  Do you want to share this taxi with me?
  你想跟我合搭這台計程車嗎？

be on sth

- be on the management committee
  隸屬於管理委員會
- Whose team are you on?
  你是誰隊上的？

隸屬於⋯ on 後面如果接運動隊伍或委員會等為了特定目的組成的團體，可以表示隸屬、參與的意思。

- Christy **is on** the student council.
- Good, she's a very smart girl.
  - ●Christy 隸屬於學生會。　●很好。她是個很聰明的女孩。

▶ They were on the baseball team. 他們隸屬於棒球隊。
  Is Frank on our chess team? Frank 是我們西洋棋隊伍的人嗎？

1 職場・學校

2 電腦・網路

3 社交生活

4 日常生活

5 訊息・理解

6 想法・態度

7 情緒・狀況

8 行為舉止

9 時間地點・副詞片語

07 屬於，擁有 deserve to

9-07.mp3

deserve + N

- deserve a day off
  應該得到一天休假
- deserve more money
  應該得到更多錢

值得／應該得到… deserve more than + N 則是「應該得到比…更多／更好的東西」。

- Everyone in the office has been working very hard.
- They **deserve** time to relax and enjoy themselves.
  - 辦公室每個人都工作得很認真。
  - 他們應該得到放鬆和玩樂的時間。

▶ You deserve a reward for helping me.
你幫助了我，應該得到報答。
She deserves a good grade in English class.
她在英文課值得拿到好成績。

deserve to

值得／應該做… 後面接動詞原形。deserve + N 和 deserve to 都可以用在應該得到獎賞或處罰的狀況。

- Kevin works very hard in class.
- He **deserves to** get the highest grade.
  - Kevin 在班上非常努力。　● 他值得拿到最高的成績。

▶ I deserve to have a day off.
我值得休一天假。
The children deserve to get ice cream.
孩子們值得得到冰淇淋。

be qualified for/to

- qualify for
  取得…的資格
- qualify as (a lawyer)
  取得擔任（律師）的資格
- qualify A for sth/to do
  使 A 有資格得到某事物／做某事

有資格得到／做… for 後面接名詞，表示「有資格得到…」；to 後面接動詞原形，表示「有資格做…」。

- Bart talks like he is a lawyer.
- He **is qualified to** practice law in New York.
  - Bart 講話的方式彷彿是個律師。　● 他有資格在紐約當律師。

▶ I am qualified to teach in high schools.
我有在高中教書的資格。
She isn't qualified to write that exam.
她沒有資格參加那個測驗。

655

be eligible for/to

· be entitled to do
  有權力做…

有資格得到／做… 雖然句型和 qualified 相同，但 qualified 通常指符合能力上的資格，eligible 則是符合比較客觀的資格條件。

● Mark has worked the hardest of anyone.

● He **is eligible for** a bonus at work.
  ●Mark 是所有人裡面最認真工作的。
  ●他在工作上有資格得到獎金。

▶ The soldiers are eligible for a vacation.
  這些士兵有資格獲得休假。
  Older people are eligible for discounts.
  年長者可以得到折扣。

be cut out for

· not be cut out for
  sth/-ing
  不是當…／做…的料
· not be cut out to
  be sth
  不是當…的料

天生適合… have the necessary skills or talent for（擁有對…必要的技能或天分）的意思。for 後面接表示活動或工作內容的名詞或動名詞（-ing）。

● You can't run very fast, John.

● I'm **not cut out for** being in a race.
  ●John，你沒辦法跑得很快耶。　●我不適合參加賽跑。

▶ Most people aren't cut out for being politicians.
  大部分的人都不適合當政治家。
  He was cut out for working as an actor.
  他是當演員的料。

earn sth

· earn a living
  賺取生活費
· earn a reputation for
  贏得…的名聲
· You've earned it.
  你應得的。

賺到／贏得某物 除了表示賺取財物以外，也有因為良好的表現而獲得回報的意思。

● I want a higher grade than a B.

● You need to **earn** an A in this class.
  ●我想得到高於 B 的成績。　●你需要在這門課得到 A。

▶ She earned a lot of money at her job.
  她在工作上賺了很多錢。
  Daniel's artwork earns praise from critics.
  Daniel 的藝術作品贏得評論家的讚賞。

serve (sb) right

· It serves sb right to do
  …是某人活該

…是（某人）應得的 It serves you right 意為「（有那種結果是）你活該」。用在因為不好的行為遭到報應的情況。

● Aurora got thrown out of her apartment.

● It **serves her right**. She never paid her rent.
  ●Aurora 從她的公寓被趕出來了。　●她應得的。她從來不付房租。

▶ It serves criminals right to be sent to jail.
  犯人被送到監獄是罪有應得。
  It serves him right to fail the class. 他這堂課被當掉活該。

I'm not cut out for that job

　　句意為「我不適合那個工作」。量身訂做衣服的時候，會把衣料裁剪（cut out）得合身，所以 be cut out for 就是用衣服比喻一個人適合做某件事（be well suited for...），具有那方面的天分（have a talent for...）。除了 be cut out for＋N 以外，也可以用 be cut out to do 的句型。

08 變成…，…化
go digital

9-08.mp3

go digital

· go green
環保化

· go global
國際化

數位化 在口語中，go 後面接形容詞是「變得…」的意思。

● It's so easy to use the Internet here.

● Korea was very quick to **go digital**.

　●這邊使用網路真簡單。　●韓國數位化得非常迅速。

▶ My cousin decided to see the green this summer.
我堂弟決定這個夏天要去森林看綠樹。

This firm went global about 30 years ago.
這間企業大約 30 年前開始國際化。

get old

· get cold
變冷

變老 雖然也可以說 become...，但口語中最常用 get 表示「變得…」。

● My grandmother is always complaining.

● Well, she's probably unhappy about **getting old**.

　●我奶奶總是在抱怨。　●嗯，她可能對於變老感覺不開心吧。

▶ Our car got old over the years.
經年累月後，我們的車變舊了。

Are you aware of prices getting higher?
你有察覺到物價正在上漲嗎？

1 職場・學校

2 電腦・網路

3 社交生活

4 日常生活

5 訊息・理解

6 想法・態度

7 情緒・狀況

8 行為舉止

9 時間地點・副詞片語

turn gray

- turn white
  變白
- turn cold
  變冷
- turn violent
  變暴力

變灰，（頭髮）變白 同樣接形容詞，turn 比 get 更有「轉變成不同性質」的含意。

- The skies often **turn gray** in January.
- It's the most gloomy time of the year.
  - 一月的時候，天空常常變得灰濛濛的。
  - 那是一年裡最陰沉的時候。

▶ This letter turned out to be very important.
  這封信結果變得很重要。
  I thought you said the weather turned cold.
  我以為你說天氣變冷了。

grow to be...

- grow old
  變老
- grow to be successful
  長大變成功，逐漸變得成功

長成⋯，逐漸變得⋯ 可以指生理上的成長，或者比喻逐漸變成某種狀態。

- I remember Greg when he was a kid.
- He **grew to be** quite successful.
  - 我記得 Greg 還是小孩子的時候。　● 他長大後變得相當成功。

▶ My grandparents plan to grow old in Florida.
  我的祖父母打算在佛羅里達度過老年。
  The little tree grew to be quite tall.
  那棵小樹變得很高。

09 任何事物
whatever you want

9-09.mp3

whatever you want

- whatever you do
  不論你做什麼
- whatever you ask
  不論你要求什麼

不論你想要什麼 whatever（不管什麼）稱為「複合關係代名詞」，相當於 no matter what 或 anything that。

- Good enough! Let's work on the rest tomorrow.
- **Whatever you say**, boss.
  - 這樣就夠了！剩下的我們明天再做吧。　● 就聽你的，老闆。

▶ We can do whatever you want tonight.
  今晚我們可以做你想做的任何事。
  OK, I will do whatever you ask.
  好，不論你有什麼要求，我都會去做。

do anything for

· (would) do anything
to do
（會）為了做…而做任何
事

· give anything to do
為了做…什麼都願意給

為…做任何事　do anything to do 則是「為了做…而做任何事」。

● So, it looks like you have a pretty good friend there.
● Yeah. He'll **do anything for** me.
　●看來你有個很好的朋友。　　●是啊，他會為我做任何事。

▶ I would do anything to avoid studying.
　只要能夠不用讀書，我願意做任何事。
　She is willing to do anything for money.
　她願意為了錢做任何事。

anything else

其他任何東西　用在疑問句或否定句。something else（其他某個
東西）則用在肯定句或疑問句。

● Could you do me a favor and lift this box?
● Sure. I can help you with that. **Anything else**?
　●你可以幫我個忙，把這個箱子抬起來嗎？
　●當然，我可以幫你這個忙。還有其他要幫的嗎？

▶ Is there anything else you need?
　你還需要其他任何東西嗎？
　Well, do you want to eat something else?
　嗯，你還想吃什麼別的嗎？

or whatever

· or something
…或什麼的

或者任何東西　有「不論什麼都沒差」的意思。

● We can do what I want **or whatever** you want.
● Thanks. Let's do the things I want to do.
　●我們可以我想做或任何你想做的事。　　●謝謝，來做我想做的事吧。

▶ We'll go to a nightclub or whatever bar is open.
　我們會去夜店，或是隨便任何一間開著的酒吧。
　I need to buy her a necklace or something.
　我需要買條項鍊或什麼的給她。

anything but

…以外的任何東西　這邊的 but 是 except 的意思。

● I thought I'd make hamburgers for dinner.
● No, **anything but** burgers. I hate them!
　●我想我要做漢堡來當晚餐。
　●不要，除了漢堡以外什麼都好。我討厭漢堡！

▶ You can watch anything but sports with me.
　除了體育以外，你什麼都可以跟我一起看。
　Dan will eat anything but apples.
　Dan 除了蘋果以外什麼都會吃。

1 職場·學校
2 電腦·網路
3 社交生活
4 日常生活
5 訊息·理解
6 想法·態度
7 情緒·狀況
8 行為舉止
9 時間地點·副詞片語

10 | 當然，不用説
let alone

let alone

何況是… 使用在否定句之後。隨著比較對象的不同，可與多種詞性連接。

- Did you pay Brian the money you owe him?
- I can't pay my bills, **let alone** Brian's money.
  - 你把欠 Brian 的錢還他了嗎？
  - 我連我自己的帳單都付不起，何況 Brian 的錢。

▶ We couldn't pay the interest, let alone the full amount.
  我們連利息都付不出來了，何況是本金。
  They didn't fly overseas, let alone to Europe.
  他們根本沒出過國，也不可能到過歐洲。

to say nothing of

· not to mention
　更不用説…
· not to speak of
　更不用説…，不提到…

更不用説… 與 not to speak of、not to mention 同義。

- How has Kendra been doing in your class?
- She's a great student, **to say nothing of** her exam scores.
  - Kendra 在你班上表現得怎麼樣？
  - 她是個很棒的學生，更不用説考試成績了。

▶ It's very cold, not to mention the snow that is falling.
  真的好冷，更不用説還在下雪。
  She told us not to speak of her ex-husband.
  她叫我們別提到她的前夫。

It goes without saying that

· needless to say
　不用説

不用説…，…是不言而喻的 不需要説也應該知道的意思。

- Are we going to be working on Sunday?
- **It goes without saying that** we'll be off on Sunday.
  - 我們星期天要工作嗎？　● 那還用説，我們星期天當然是放假啊。

▶ Needless to say, we need to make more money.
  不用説，我們需要賺更多錢。
  It goes without saying that our partnership is finished.
  不用説，我們的合作關係結束了。

no wonder

· it is natural for sb to do
  某人做某事是很自然的

難怪，怪不得 知道了某個原因，才知道某件事其實很合理，並不奇怪。

● The Smiths just got back from vacation.
● **No wonder** they're so tanned.

　●Smith 全家剛度假回來。　●難怪他們曬得那麼黑。

▶ No wonder that movie is so popular.
　難怪那部電影那麼受歡迎。
　It's natural for girls to like you.
　女孩子喜歡你是很自然的。

be no surprise that...

· not surprisingly
  不令人驚訝地，不意外地

…不令人驚訝 no surprise 也可以換成 not surprising。

● My best friend was sad when I moved away.
● It **was no surprise** she came to visit.

　●當我搬走時，我最好的朋友很難過。
　●那她之前來看你也不意外了。

▶ Not surprisingly, the new shop failed.
　毫不意外地，那間新開的店倒閉了。
　It is no surprise that the book was published.
　那本書的出版並不令人驚訝。

---

11 用…的方式 in the way that...

9-11.mp3

be the only way to

· be the best way to do
  是做…最好的方法

是做…唯一的方法 only 可以改成 best，表示「最好的方法」。

● I think you are working too hard.
● It's **the only way** for me to make extra money.

　●我覺得你工作得太辛苦了。　●這是我賺更多錢的唯一方法。

▶ This is the best way to go.
　這是最好的方法。
　Excuse me. Is this the way to the airport?
　不好意思，這是往機場的路嗎？

1 職場・學校
2 電腦・網路
3 社交生活
4 日常生活
5 訊息・理解
6 想法・態度
7 情緒・狀況
8 行為舉止
9 時間地點・副詞片語

be the way that S+V

· Is there any way that S+V?
有任何…的方法嗎？

是…的方式 that 後面接 S+V 說明是誰做什麼事情的方式。

● Why are you eating with your hands?
● This **is the way that** everyone eats food here.
　●你為什麼在用你的手吃飯？　●這邊每個人都是這樣吃東西的。

▶ Is this the way your mom cleans the house?
這是你媽媽打掃房屋的方式嗎？
This is the way that the system works.
這是這個系統運作的方式。

in the way that S+V

· from the way that S+V
從…的方式裡

在…的方式中 通常用在「從…的方式中觀察到某一點」的情況。

● Cathy is in love with her boyfriend.
● I saw it **in the way that** she looks at him.
　●Cathy 很愛她的男朋友。　●我從她看他的樣子看出來了。

▶ There's something special in the way this cake was baked. 這塊蛋糕烘焙的方式有些特別的地方。
The sky is more beautiful in the way the stars are shining. 當星星在閃爍時，天空更漂亮。

like the way S+V

喜歡…的方式 這裡的 way 後面省略了 that。

● I **like the way** you talk to me.
● Perhaps we should go on a date.
　●我喜歡你跟我說話的樣子。　●也許我們應該去約會。

▶ Students like the way he teaches his classes.
學生們喜歡他教課的方式。
Do you like the way the food is cooked?
你喜歡那種食物烹調的方式嗎？

that way

· put it the other way
用另一種方式來說
→換句話說

那樣子，用那種方法 意思相當於 in that way。the other way 也可以不加介系詞，直接當副詞使用，表示「用另一種方法」。

● It's like something's changed.
● What makes you feel **that way**?
　●好像有什麼變了。　●你為什麼會那樣覺得？

▶ Don't act that way.
不要那個樣子。
I never thought of it that way before.
我以前從來沒那麼想過。

1 職場・學校

2 電腦・網路

3 社交生活

4 日常生活

5 訊息・理解

6 想法・態度

7 情緒・狀況

8 行為舉止

9 時間地點・副詞片語

12 最…的
be the first to

9-12.mp3

be the first to

· be the first to ask
  當最先發問的人

當第一個做…的人 the first 後面省略了 person。

● Why does Nadine study so hard?
● She wants to **be the first to** score 100 percent.

　●Nadine 為什麼那麼用功？　●她想當第一個拿到一百分的學生。

▶ I was the first to enter the school.
　我是第一個進學校的人。
　Every boy wants to be the first to kiss Vera.
　每個男孩都想當第一個親吻 Vera 的人。

be the last thing I want to...

· be the last thing I
  think of
  是我最想不到的事
· be the last thing I
  expect
  是我意料之外的事

是我最不想…的事 「是我最後才想做的事」，表示很不願意做的意思。

● Wouldn't it be great if all of our friends came to visit us?
● No, that's **the last thing I want to** see.

　●如果所有朋友都來看我們，那不是很棒嗎？
　●不，那是我最不希望看到的事。

▶ Jail is the last place I want to visit.
　監獄是我最不想去的地方。
　Math is the last subject I want to study.
　數學是我最不想學習的科目。

the best...I've ever seen

· the best...I've ever
  heard
  我聽過最好的…
· the best...I've ever
  thought
  我想過最好的…

我看過最好的… seen 也可以換成其他表示經驗的過去分詞。

● Dan is **the best** athlete **I have ever seen**.
● He prefers exercising rather than staying at home.

　●Dan 是我看過最棒的運動選手。　●比起待在家哩，他寧可去運動。

▶ The concert had the best music I've ever heard.
　那場音樂會表演了我聽過最棒的音樂。
　That was the best zoo I've ever visited.
　那是我參觀過最棒的動物園。

比較級 + than ever before

- study harder than ever before
  比以前任何時候都更用功讀書
- less than before
  比以前更少

比以前都還要… ever before 是指過去任何時候，所以這個句型其實有最高級的意思。

- Wow, it's raining harder **than ever before**.
- I think the river is going to overflow.

  ●哇，這雨下得比以前都還要大。　●我想河水要泛濫了。

▶ You need to study harder than ever before.

  你需要比以前任何時候都更用功讀書。

  My doctor told me to drink less than before.

  我的醫生要我喝酒喝得比以前少。

be one of the 最高級 + 名詞

- be one of the best athletes
  是最好的運動員之一
- best of the best
  頂尖中的頂尖

是最…的…之一 不敢說是程度最高的，但起碼屬於程度最高的那一群。

- What do you think about Hitler?
- He's **one of the** most shameless men that ever lived.

  ●你覺得希特勒怎麼樣？　●他是曾經活在世界上最無恥的人類之一。

▶ He's one of the best painters I've ever seen.

  他是我所見過最好的畫家之一。

  I heard he was one of the best athletes in the game.

  我聽說他是那場比賽裡表現最好的運動員之一。

think it is best to

- think it would be best if S+V
  覺得…的話會是最好的

覺得做…是最好的 think it better to do 則是「覺得做…比較好」的意思。

- Should we stay for another drink?
- I **think it is best to** go home now.

  ●我們應該留下來再喝一杯嗎？　●我想現在回家是最好的。

▶ I think it would be best if he retires.

  我想他退休會是最好的。

  The owner thinks it is best to close his business.

  這位業主覺得結束他的事業是最好的。

the best part is

- the best part is the ending
  最棒的部分是結尾

最棒的是… 常用在說了一些優點以後，強調最棒的部分是什麼的情況。

- So you got a new job?
- Yes, and **the best part is** it pays a lot of money.

  ●所以你有新工作了？　●嗯，而且最棒的是薪水很多。

▶ The hard part is to stay awake at night.

  困難之處在於要在晚上醒著。

  The best part is the ending of the movie.

  最棒的部分是電影的結尾。

second to none

· second to none in sth
  在某方面是首屈一指的
· the wine is second to
  none
  這葡萄酒是最棒的

首屈一指 不會落居其他任何事物的第二，表示絕對是第一名。

● This is a very nice jacket.

● The company that made it is **second to none**.

  ● 這是件很不錯的外套。　 ● 做這件外套的公司是首屈一指的。

▶ Sandra is second to none in her science class.
  Sandra 在科學課的表現是首屈一指的。

  The wine at this restaurant is second to none.
  這間餐廳的葡萄酒是首屈一指的。

never have it so good

· there's no such
  thing as
  沒有像…的事

從來沒過得這麼好 也就是 be in a better situation now than before。

● Stop complaining. You**'ve never had it so good**.

● But I always want things to get better.

  ● 別再抱怨了，你的生活從來沒這麼好過。

  ● 但我總是希望一切能變得更好。

▶ The kids have never had it so good.
  孩子們從來沒有過得這麼好過。

  There's no such thing as a free lunch.
  天下沒有白吃的午餐。

be nothing like that

完全不是那樣，沒有像那樣的東西 有兩個意思，一個相當於 be not like that at all，另一個則是用在 there is... 的句型，表示沒有什麼比得上那個東西。

● Is it true that Sally is unkind to her family?

● No, Sally **is nothing like that**.

  ● Sally 真的對她的家人很不好嗎？　 ● 不是的，Sally 絕不是那樣的人。

▶ There's nothing like that in the world.
  那是天下極品啊。

  There's nothing like sleeping in on a Sunday.
  沒有什麼事比得上在星期天睡懶覺。

1 職場·學校
2 電腦·網路
3 社交生活
4 日常生活
5 訊息·理解
6 想法·態度
7 情緒·狀況
8 行為舉止
9 時間地點·副詞片語

13 有做…的權利
have the right to

9-13.mp3

have the power to

· have the power to perform miracles
有展現奇蹟的能力

有做…的能力 表示自身的能力，或者對於其他人事物的權力。

● I **have the power to** stop everyone from working.

● You must be happy to be the company manager.

　● 我有打斷任何人工作的權力。　● 你當公司主管一定很開心。

▶ They say Jesus had the power to perform miracles.
傳說耶穌有展現奇蹟的能力。
He has the power to make laws in his country.
他在他的國家有立法的權力。

have the right to

· have every right to complain
充分擁有抱怨的權利
· have no right to do
沒有做…的權利

有做…的權利 the 可以改成 every，強調「充分擁有做…的權利」。

● I hate working at this factory.

● You **have the right to** quit your job.

　● 我討厭在這間工廠工作。　● 你有權利辭職。

▶ None of you have the right to complain.
你們沒有人有權利抱怨。
You have no right to talk bad about me.
你沒有權利說我的不是。

have the authority to...

· have absolute authority over sth
對某事物有絕對的權力
· be legally authorized to do
經法律授權能做…

有做…的權限 authority 除了指權限，也可以指擁有權限的「當局」、「政府機關」。

● What makes you think you can do this?

● I **have the authority to** do whatever I want.

　● 你為什麼覺得你能做這件事？　● 我有權做任何我想做的事。

▶ The dictator has absolute authority over the citizens.
獨裁者對國民有絕對的權力。
The policeman has the authority to stop traffic.
警察有管制交通的職權。

give sb full authority

· beyond one's authority
  在某人的權限之外
· be given with full authority
  被賦予所有權限

給某人所有權限 後面可以加上 to do 說明是做什麼的權限。

● You can't take my computer.
● Our boss **gave me full authority** to take it.

● 你不能拿走我的電腦。　● 老闆給了我權限這麼做。

▶ Making new rules is beyond my authority.
　制定新規定不在我的權限內。
　They gave Jen full authority to fire people.
　他們賦予 Jen 所有權限去解雇人們。

be in a position

· be in a position to do
  處於能做…的地位

處於某個地位 後面加上 to do，表示因為處於某個位階或情況而能做某事。

● You've got to give me some more money.
● I **am not in a position** to give you a raise.

● 你必須多給我一點錢。　● 我的職位沒辦法幫你加薪。

▶ Harry is in a position to help Callie.
　Harry 可以扮演幫助 Callie 的角色。
　Are you in a position to talk to the owner?
　你的位階能和業主說話嗎？

---

14 差一點就…，險些…
come close to

9-14.mp3

almost got

· almost got hit by a car
  差點被車撞

差點就得到… almost 也可以換成 nearly。

● I **almost got** an apartment in Manhattan.
● What stopped you from signing the lease?

● 我差點就在曼哈頓租公寓了。　● 什麼原因讓你不簽租約了呢？

▶ The group almost got left behind.
　這個團體差點被甩在後頭。
　Mom almost got a new oven for the kitchen.
　媽媽差點就要幫廚房添購新的烤箱。

1 職場·學校
2 電腦·網路
3 社交生活
4 日常生活
5 訊息·理解
6 想法·態度
7 情緒·狀況
8 行為舉止
9 時間地點·副詞片語

come close to

- come close to sth/-ing
  差一點就…
- come close to death
  差點就喪命

差一點就… to 後面接名詞或動名詞（-ing）。

● Did you visit the Hawaiian Islands?
● No, but we **came close to** sailing there.
　●你們有去夏威夷群島嗎？　●沒有，但我們差一點就航行到那裡了。

▶ The soldiers came close to death in the battle.
　士兵們差點就在戰場上喪命。
　The couple came close to meeting a movie star.
　這對情侶差點就碰到電影明星。

come near -ing

- come/go near -ing
  差一點就…
- come near being drowned
  差點就被淹死

差一點就… 這裡的 come 可以換成 go，意思一樣。

● The rain came down hard this weekend.
● We **came near** going home instead of hiking.
　●這週末雨下得很大。　●我們差點就要放棄健行回家了。

▶ The swimmer came near being drowned in the river.
　游泳的人差點就被淹死在河裡。
　I came near asking my boss for time off.
　我差點就要去跟老闆要求休息。

stop short of

- stop short of sth/-ing
  （在最後關頭）
  決定不做…
- stop short of one's desire
  放棄追求想要的事物

（在最後關頭）決定不做… of 的後面要接名詞或動名詞（-ing）。

● Did Ray ask his girlfriend to marry him?
● No, he **stopped short of** popping the question.
　●Ray 有跟他女朋友求婚嗎？　●沒有，他在問題說出口之前打住了。

▶ Too many people stop short of their desires.
　有太多人放棄追求想要的東西。
　I had some wine but stopped short of drinking it.
　我有些酒，但最後決定不喝。

be shy of -ing

- be too shy to say sth
  太害羞以至於無法說某事
- be shy around strangers
  對陌生人很怕生

還差一點就… be shy to do... 是「因為害羞而不做…」，be shy of N 則是「…不足」。

● How old is your grandmother?
● She **is just shy of** turning 70.
　●你外婆多大了？　●她就要 70 歲了。

▶ He was too shy to ask Melissa to dance.
　他太害羞，沒辦法邀 Melissa 跳舞。
　Her daughter is very shy around strangers.
　她的女兒對陌生人很怕生。

15 舉例
such as

9-15.mp3

for example

· for instance
舉例來說

· be an example to sb
是某人的榜樣

舉例來說 為了使自己的意思更具體而舉例。

● Why do you think I'm not clean?

● **For example**, you never wash your clothes.

　●你為什麼覺得我不乾淨？　　●舉例來說，你從來不洗衣服。

▶ Jim was an example to the younger kids.

　Jim 是年輕孩子們的榜樣。

　For example, this plant needs to be watered.

　舉例來說，這株植物需要澆水。

such as

例如… 跟 for example 意思相近，但 for example 可以放在句首、句中或句尾，such as 則出現在句中。

● How can we improve our house?

● We can do many things, **such as** paint it.

　●我們可以怎樣改善我們的房子？　　●我們可以做很多事，例如粉刷。

▶ You do good work, such as in this report.

　你做事做得很好，就像在這份報告裡一樣。

　He sleeps too long, such as on the weekends.

　他睡得太久了，例如在週末的時候。

...or something like that

· things like that
那之類的事情

· like/as in
像…裡一樣

…之類的 還想舉些別的例子，又想不出什麼的時候，會這樣說。

● What should I cook for dinner?

● Make spaghetti, **or something like that**.

　●我晚餐該煮什麼？　　●做義大利麵之類的。

▶ You can wash the dishes, and things like that.

　你可以洗碗之類的。

　Paris was romantic, like in the movies.

　巴黎很浪漫，就像電影裡一樣。

1 職場・學校

2 電腦・網路

3 社交生活

4 日常生活

5 訊息・理解

6 想法・態度

7 情緒・狀況

8 行為舉止

9 時間地點・副詞片語

and so on

· and so forth
  …等等
· and the like
  …等等

…等等 and so forth、and the like、et cetera (etc.) 都是表示一樣的意思。

● Who do you spend your free time with?
● I have many friends, Jill, Rick, Simon, **and so on**.
  ●你都跟誰度過空閒時間？
  ●我有很多朋友，有 Jill、Rick、Simon 等等。

▶ The healthy foods are apples, grapes, tomatoes and so on. 健康的食物有蘋果、葡萄、番茄等等。
  We'll go out to eat, go dancing, and so on.
  我們會出去吃飯、跳舞等等。

to name a few

· to name but a few
  只舉幾個例子來說的話
· you name it
  只要你說得出來的都有

只舉幾個例子來說的話 用於句尾，表示以上只是幾個例子，其他還有很多，意思和「族繁不及備載」相近。

● What is your favorite drink?
● Well, I like wine, juice, and cider, **to name a few**.
  ●你最喜歡的飲料是什麼？
  ●嗯，我喜歡葡萄酒、果汁、蘋果汁，太多了說不完。

▶ I want a necklace, a ring, and a dress, to name a few gifts. 我想要項鍊、戒指和洋裝等等禮物，族繁不及備載。
  The nightclubs are Ringo's, Salsa Time, and Club 59, to name a few.
  那些夜店，只舉其中幾個例子來說的話，有 Ringo's、Salsa Time、Club 59。

16 第一次 never happened

9-16.mp3

be the first time that...

· be one's first time skiing
  是某人第一次滑雪

是第一次… 後面接 S+V 子句，that 也可以省略。也可以說 be one's first time to do...（是某人第一次做…）。

● Is this **your first time to** visit England?
● Yes, and I'm having a great time.
  ●這是你第一次來英國嗎？ ●是的，而且我玩得很開心。

▶ This is my first time to come here. 這是我第一次來。
  That was the first time you said that. 那是你第一次那麼說。

never happened to sb before

從來沒發生在某人身上 強調以前從來沒遇過類似的事。

- Have you won any money gambling?
- No, that **never happened to me before**.

  ●你賭博有贏過錢嗎？ ●沒有，從來沒發生在我身上。

▶ This feeling has never happened to me before.

  我以前從來沒有這種感覺。

  A car accident has never happened to me before.

  這是我第一次碰上車禍。

never heard of such a thing

· never heard of such a
  thing as sth
  從來沒聽過像某事的事

從來沒聽過這種事 句尾也可以加上 until now，意為「直到現在才第一次聽到」。

- A monkey was climbing the side of my apartment building.
- No way! I **never heard of such a thing**.

  ●有隻猴子在我公寓外牆爬。 ●哪有可能！這種事我聽都沒聽過。

▶ He'd never heard of such a thing as a TV in a car.

  他從來沒聽過車裡裝電視這種事。

  Tim has never heard of my favorite singer.

  Tim 從來沒聽說過我最喜歡的歌手。

never seen anything like it

· never done anything
  like that
  從來沒做過那樣的事

從來沒看過像那樣的事 it 可以換成 this/that。最後面加上 before，可使意思更加明顯。

- Look at the high score of this game.
- Wow! I've **never seen anything like it**.

  ●看看這比賽的高分。 ●哇！我第一次看到這種分數。

▶ I've never seen anything like that before in my life.

  我這輩子從來沒看過那種事。

  Have you ever seen anything like that before?

  你以前看過那樣的事嗎？

can't remember the last time...

· remember the last
  time S+V
  記得最後一次／上次…

記不得最後一次／上次…是什麼時候 後面接 S+V。

- I **can't remember the last time** we met.
- It was at least ten years ago.

  ●我記不得我們最後一次見面是什麼時候了。 ●至少十年前。

▶ We can't remember the last time it snowed.

  我們記不得最後一次下雪是什麼時候了。

  I can't remember the last time I had a good meal.

  我記不得上次吃到好吃的食物是什麼時候了。

1 職場·學校
2 電腦·網路
3 社交生活
4 日常生活
5 訊息·理解
6 想法·態度
7 情緒·狀況
8 行為舉止
9 時間地點·副詞片語

17 充分，超過，不足
enough to

enough to

- have enough to do
  有足夠的資源能做⋯
- be enough to do
  足以做⋯

足以做⋯ be enough to do 的主詞是事物。如果要用人當主詞，表示擁有足夠的資源能做，則說 have enough to do。

- Will that be cash or charge?
- I think I have **enough to** pay cash.
  - 要付現還是刷卡？　● 我想我的錢夠付現金。

▶ He is old enough to know better.
他已經夠大，應該知道什麼事不該做。
Do you have enough to read on the airplane?
你有足夠的讀物能在飛機上讀嗎？

have enough + 名詞 + to...

有足夠的⋯能做⋯ 和 have enough to do 相比，更明確表示是什麼東西足夠。

- Would you like to go to the grocery store?
- No, we **have enough food to** eat for a few days.
  - 你想去雜貨店嗎？　● 不想，我們的食物夠吃幾天。

▶ They had enough work to stay busy all day.
他們有足夠的工作可以忙上一整天。
Do you have enough money to start up the company?
你有足夠的資金創業嗎？

go beyond

- go beyond oneself
  超越自己

超過⋯ 除了表示超過某個範圍，也可以表示比某人更優秀。

- You can be successful in your hometown.
- I'd like to **go beyond** my hometown.
  - 你可以在你的老家成功的。　● 我想要走出我的家鄉。

▶ This secret goes beyond you and I.
這個祕密被我們兩個以外的人知道了。
The bills went beyond the money they had.
帳單的金額比他們擁有的錢還多。

have gone too far

太離譜，太過分 go too far 是說行為超出合理的限度，這裡用完成式，表示已經做出的行為太過分。

- Look at all the ads in this newspaper.
- I think the advertisers **have gone too far**.

  ●看看這報紙裡的整堆廣告。　●我覺得這些廣告商太離譜了。

▶ Jason has gone too far and angered everyone.

  Jason 做得太過分，惹火了每個人。

  The fighting couple went too far and upset their parents.

  這對吵架的情侶做得太過火，把他們的父母惹惱了。

be full of

· be full of energy
  充滿活力
· be filled with
  充滿…

充滿… be full of 就是 be filled with 的意思。

- Lyman always talks about how strong he is.
- I don't believe it. He's **full of** hot air.

  ●Lyman 總是在説他有多強壯。　●我才不信。他滿口大話。

▶ I was full of energy after drinking some coffee.

  喝了點咖啡後，我充滿活力。

  The crowd was full of excitement as they waited.

  觀眾們滿懷興奮地等待。

fall short of

· fall short of sth/-ing
  缺少某物，不符合某事的標準
· be short of...
  …不足

缺少…，不符合…的標準 可以接缺乏的物質，或沒有達到的標準。

- Did you get admitted to Harvard?
- No, I **fell short of** getting in.

  ●你有被哈佛錄取嗎？　●沒有，我沒有達到入學的標準。

▶ He was short of money for the cab ride.

  他的錢不夠付計程車車資。

  Leona fell short of being the best student.

  Leona 不夠資格成為最優秀的學生。

run out of

用光… be out of sth 是表示用完了某物的狀態，這裡用動詞 run 表示把東西用完的行為。

- We **ran out of** paper for the copier.
- I'll get the secretary to get some more.

  ●我們用光影印紙了。　●我會請祕書再買一些。

▶ The store ran out of ice cream.

  這間店的冰淇淋賣光了。

  We're about to run out of gas.

  我們的汽油要用完了。

1 職場・學校
2 電腦・網路
3 社交生活
4 日常生活
5 訊息・理解
6 想法・態度
7 情緒・狀況
8 行為舉止
9 時間地點・副詞片語

run low on

…很少，…快用完了　這裡 run 的用法和 run out of 類似，都是「變得…」的意思。low 表示數量很少，即將用盡。

● Can I get anything for you?
● I'm beginning to **run low on** toilet paper.
　●要我幫你買點什麼嗎？　●我的衛生紙快用完了。

▶ My trainees ran low on energy this afternoon.
　我的受訓者們今天下午沒什麼精神。
　My father ran low on time before going to work.
　我爸爸去上班的時間不夠→我爸爸當時快趕不及上班了。

lack of

缺乏…　lack of 後面通常接名詞，但也可以接 -ing 表示「做…做得不夠」。

● Why did the business fail?
● There was a **lack of** planning for the future.
　●這間企業為什麼倒閉了？　●對未來的計畫不夠。

▶ The country had a lack of educated people.
　這個國家缺乏受過教育的人民。
　There was a lack of rain this summer.
　今年夏天的雨水不足。

---

18 立刻，馬上
in no time

9-18.mp3

pretty soon

· right now
　目前，現在馬上

不久之後，很快　和 at once、right away、immediately 的意思相近。

● I didn't order this!
● I'm sorry, I'll get you your food **right away**.
　●我沒點這個！　●抱歉，我馬上把您的餐點送來。

▶ I'm not saving any money right now.
　我目前完全沒在存錢。
　Let's not do our homework right now.
　我們現在不要做功課吧。

before you know it | **很快，瞬間** 直譯為「在你知道之前」，表示比對方能察覺的速度還要快，是一種誇飾法。
- We have to work for ten hours today.
- Let's work hard and **before you know it**, we'll be done.
  - 我們今天得工作十小時。　●我們努力做吧，一轉眼就能完成了。

▶ Before you know it, my birthday will be here.
  我生日馬上就要到了。
  It will be winter before you know it.
  冬天馬上就要來了。

before long | **不久之後，很快** 與 shortly 同義。
- Our class will graduate in June.
- **Before long**, we'll be looking for jobs.
  - 我們班會在六月畢業。　●沒多久我們就要找工作了。

▶ Dad will be home before long.
  爸爸很快就會到家了。
  It will be dark before long.
  天很快就要變黑了。

in no time
· in no time at all
  很快

很快 也就是 very quickly。後面也可以加 at all 增強語氣。
- Can you type up this paper?
- Sure, I'll have it done **in no time**.
  - 你可以打完這份報告嗎？　●當然，我很快就會完成。

▶ The house was cleaned in no time.
  房子很快就打掃好了。
  We arrived at the store in no time.
  我們很快就抵達商店了。

in a moment
· be back in a moment
  馬上回來

一下子，馬上 這裡的 in 是「（一段時間）之後」的意思，所以是表示不久後的未來。moment 也可以換成 minute 或 second。
- Could we get another pitcher of water?
- Sure, I'll bring it for you **in a minute**.
  - 我們可以再要一壺水嗎？　●當然，我馬上拿來給您。

▶ The shopkeeper will be back in a moment.
  店長馬上會回來。
  I can help you out in a minute.
  我馬上可以幫你。

1 職場・學校
2 電腦・網路
3 社交生活
4 日常生活
5 訊息・理解
6 想法・態度
7 情緒・狀況
8 行為舉止
9 時間地點・副詞片語

19 首先
to begin with

9-19.mp3

to begin with

首先 表示接下來要說的或剛才說的是第一點，或者最重要的一點。

● What do you want to talk about?
● **To begin with**, we need to discuss money.

●你想談什麼？ ●首先，我們需要討論錢的事。

▶ To begin with, I missed my train.
首先，我錯過了火車。
To begin with, I don't like her appearance.
首先，我不喜歡她的長相。

for a start

· firstly
  首先
· to start with
  首先

首先 跟 to begin with 一樣，可以放在句子開頭，或者在句子結束後補上。

● What problems have you been having?
● **For a start**, I've had a lot of headaches.

●你有什麼問題？ ●首先，我很常頭痛。

▶ Firstly, we can start on our homework.
首先，我們可以開始做功課。
To start with, he needs to leave my party.
首先，他得離開我的派對。

at first

· among other things
  除了別的以外，首先

一開始 at first sight 意為「第一眼就…」，at first hand 則是「第一手」→「直接」的意思。

● What did you think about my friend Mac?
● **At first**, I really didn't like him.

●你覺得我朋友 Mac 怎麼樣？ ●一開始，我真的不喜歡他。

▶ Among other things, you should shut off the computer.
首先，你應該把電腦關掉。
At first, I was very surprised to see Annie.
起先我很驚訝見到 Annie。

for the first time

- for the first time in years
  近年來第一次
- first thing in the morning
  一大早
- for the last time
  最後一次

第一次 如果後面加上 in one's life，表示「這輩子第一次」，是一種強調的說法。

- Has he ever been here before?
- No, he's coming here **for the first time**.
  - 他之前來過這裡嗎？ - 沒有，他是第一次來這裡。

▶ For the first time in years, I came home very late.
我這些年來第一次那麼晚回家。
I'll call him first thing in the morning.
我一大早就會打電話給他。

in the beginning

- in the beginning of
  在…的開始
- at the beginning of
  在…的開始
- from the beginning of
  從…的開始

一開始 beginning 當名詞用，表示「開始」、「最初」。

- How has their marriage been?
- **In the beginning**, it was very happy.
  - 他們的婚姻怎麼樣？ - 一開始是很開心的。

▶ In the beginning of the show, you'll see my sister.
在這場表演的開頭，你會看到我妹妹。
At the beginning of class, we practice English.
在課堂的開頭，我們練習英文。

---

20 時間先後
at the same time

9-20.mp3

in a few years

- in less than a year
  在少於一年的時間之後
  →一年內
- in about an hour or so
  大約一小時之後
- in a few moments
  一下下

幾年後 in 後面接特定的期間，表示「在…」；接非特定的期間，則表示「…之後」。

- This is a small apartment.
- **In a few years**, I'll move elsewhere.
  - 這是間小公寓。 - 幾年後，我會搬到別的地方。

▶ In less than a year, she'll come back from America.
一年內，她會從美國回來。
I'll just come back in a few minutes.
我幾分鐘後會回來。

1 職場・學校
2 電腦・網路
3 社交生活
4 日常生活
5 訊息・理解
6 想法・態度
7 情緒・狀況
8 行為舉止
9 時間地點・副詞片語

before -ing

- before dark
  天色變暗之前
- before I leave
  我離開之前
- the night before
  前晚（= the previous night）

做⋯之前 before 除了當連接詞以外，也可以當介系詞，後面接名詞或動名詞（-ing）。

- Have some dinner **before** you go out.
- Mom, I'm not hungry right now.
  - 出去前吃點晚餐吧。　● 媽，我現在不餓。

▶ We'll wait for you to get back before starting.
  我們開始之前，會先等你回來。
  Would you like a glass of wine before dinner?
  晚餐前你想來杯葡萄酒嗎？

after -ing

- after the accident
  事故後
- after a while
  過一會兒

做⋯之後 同樣的，after 也可以當連接詞或介系詞使用。

- **After** unpacking, I went downstairs for dinner.
- How was the food in the hotel's restaurant?
  - 打開行李拿出東西之後，我下樓去吃晚餐。
  - 飯店餐廳的食物怎麼樣？

▶ Do they play sports after school?
  他們放學後會打球嗎？
  Do you want to go to a new bar after work?
  你下班後想去一間新的酒吧嗎？

from now on

- be safe from now on
  從現在開始保持安全

從現在開始 也就是 starting from now 的意思。

- **From now on**, we're going to exercise more.
- Shall we go jogging together?
  - 從現在開始，我們要更常運動。　● 我們要一起去慢跑？

▶ Look around, and be safe from now on.
  從現在開始注意四周，保持安全。
  From now on, you need to ask me first.
  從現在開始，你得先問我。

in advance

- thank you in advance
  先謝謝你
- 時間 + in advance
  多少時間之前
- a year in advance
  在一年之前

預先，事前 意思相同的說法還有 beforehand、ahead of time。

- When is the meeting scheduled for?
- They will tell us **in advance** of it.
  - 會議定在哪時候？　● 他們會事先告訴我們。

▶ Thank you in advance for all your help.
  先謝謝你的一切幫助。
  We ordered the new i-Pod in advance.
  我們預訂了新的 i-Pod。

678

a few days ago

- a month ago
  一個月前
- a long time ago
  很久以前
- some time ago
  一陣子之前

幾天前 ago 是副詞，前面接表示時間長度的名詞片語。

- When was the last time you went traveling?
- I went to Japan **five years ago**.
  ●你上次去旅行是什麼時候？　●我五年前去了日本。

▶ I graduated from a university about ten years ago.
  我大約十年前從大學畢業。
  It's hard to believe that was six years ago.
  真難相信那是六年前的事了。

once S+V, ...

一旦⋯就⋯ 這裡的 once 是連接詞，後面接表示條件的子句。

- I heard your girlfriend had a lot of homework.
- **Once** she finished, we went out.
  ●我聽說你女朋友有很多作業。　●她一做完，我們就出門了。

▶ Once I get rich, I'll buy a big car.
  只要我變有錢，我就會買一台大車。
  Once you eat this, you'll feel better.
  你只要吃這個，就會覺得舒服些。

ahead of time

提前，提早 比平常的時間或預期的時間還要早。

- The concert tonight is sold out.
- We bought our tickets **ahead of time**.
  ●今晚的演唱會門票已經賣光了。　●我們提早買了票。

▶ The bookwork was done ahead of time.
  書籍的研讀提前完成了。
  The building was completed ahead of time.
  這棟建築物提前完工了。

on time

- in time
  及時
- in the nick of time
  在最後關頭，及時

準時 at the exact time 的意思。至於 in time，則表示「沒有遲到」、「及時」的意思，相當於 early/soon enough。

- Has the meeting started? Am I late?
- No, you're just **on time**.
  ●會議開始了嗎？我遲到了嗎？　●沒有，你剛好準時。

▶ I got there on time.
  我準時抵達了那裡。
  You'd better be on time tomorrow.
  你明天最好準時。

1 職場・學校
2 電腦・網路
3 社交生活
4 日常生活
5 訊息・理解
6 想法・態度
7 情緒・狀況
8 行為舉止
9 時間地點・副詞片語

at the same time

· one at a time
一次一個，一個一個來

同時 可以用一個副詞 simultaneously（同時地）來表達。

● We got here **at the same time**.
● Did you take the subway from Yaksu?

●我們同時抵達這邊。　●你是從 Yaksu 站搭地下鐵的嗎？

▶ We'll meet here tomorrow at the same time.

我們明天同一個時間在這邊見。

We can travel and make money at the same time!

我們可以一邊旅行一邊賺錢！

---

21 現在，最近
at the moment

9-21.mp3

---

at the moment

· at this point
這一刻，目前
· at that moment (in time)
在那一刻
· at this (very) moment
（就）在此刻

現在，此刻 也就是 at this point (of time)，或者直接說 now。

● Is Veronica in?
● She is not in **at the moment**.

●Veronica 在嗎？　●她現在不在。

▶ I'm not available at the moment.

我現在沒空。

I'm sorry, he's on another line at the moment.

不好意思，他現在正在講另一通電話。

as of + 時間點

· as of September 10th
在 9 月 10 日，自 9 月
10 日起

就在⋯ 意思是「在⋯這一刻」，但實際上常常表示狀態改變的時刻，所以也帶有「自⋯起」的意思。

● Are classes going to begin soon?
● No, they were canceled **as of** 9 am.

●馬上要開始上課了嗎？　●不，九點之後的課都取消了。

▶ You're fired, as of right now.

你被解雇了，從此時此刻開始。

We'll be leaving, as of midnight tonight.

我們會在今天半夜離開。

for now

· for the moment
目前（未來會改變）

目前，暫時 表示「目前暫時…」或者「在狀況改變之前暫時…」。

● What're you going to do next?
● I don't have any plans **for now**.

　　●你接下來要做什麼？　　●我目前沒有任何計畫。

▶ We'll rent this house, for now.
我們會暫時租這間房子。
At this point, no one has canceled the meeting.
目前沒有人取消會議。

these days

最近，近來，這陣子 也可以說 of late 或 lately。

● You don't look good **these days**.
● Yeah, I've been sick a lot.

　　●你最近看來不太好。　　●嗯，我生了大病。

▶ Why do you get up so early these days?
你最近為什麼那麼早起？
Why are you working so late these days?
你最近為什麼工作到那麼晚？

recently

最近 quite recently 則是「最近不久」的意思。

● How are things going with you **recently**?
● I've been doing the same old thing - a lot of work, as usual.

　　●最近你過得怎麼樣？　　●我還是老樣子——一堆工作，跟平常一樣。

▶ You seem to be working really slowly recently.
你最近看起來工作得很慢。
Did you see any movies recently?
你最近有看什麼電影嗎？

1 職場・學校

2 電腦・網路

3 社交生活

4 日常生活

5 訊息・理解

6 想法・態度

7 情緒・狀況

8 行為舉止

9 時間地點・副詞片語

22 | 直到⋯ to date

until next year

- until + N/S+V
  到⋯為止
- until now
  到現在為止
- until next year
  到明年為止
- until everything is finished
  到每件事都完成為止

到明年為止 until 表示動作或狀態持續到某個時間點為止。

- I put Bill in charge **until** I return.
- Are you sure that's a good idea?

  ●直到我回來前，我讓 Bill 負責管事。　●你確定那是個好主意嗎？

▶ You may play music until 10 pm.

你可以放音樂到十點為止。

I'm going to keep asking her until she says yes.

我會一直問她，直到她說好為止。

by then

- by + N
  不晚於⋯
- by now
  到了現在
- by the end of next week
  在下週末，在下週末前

到時候 by 可以表示「到了⋯的時候」，或者表示期限：「不晚於⋯」。

- Will the stage be ready by Friday?
- They should be able to get it ready **by then**.

  ●舞台星期五會完成嗎？　●他們應該可以在那之前準備好。

▶ I think our meal should be ready by now.

我想我們的餐點現在應該好了。

The movie will be in theaters by the end of next week.

這部電影會在下週末上映。

up to now

到目前為止 up to 是「直到⋯」的意思。up to you 則是「隨你」、「由你決定」。

- How are you enjoying summer camp?
- I've loved it **up to now**.

  ●你的夏令營玩得開心嗎？　●到目前為止我都很享受。

▶ Up to now, we've been disappointed in our classes.

到目前為止，我們對課堂很失望。

Everyone has had a good time, up to now.

到目前為止，每個人都玩得很開心。

so far

· so far, so good
  到目前為止還不錯

到目前為止 也可以說 thus far，但屬於比較正式的說法。

● Does your son like going to university?
● **So far**, he thinks it is great.
  ●你兒子喜歡上大學嗎？　●到目前為止，他都覺得大學很棒。

▶ It is going well. So far, so good.
  進展順利。到目前為止都還不錯。
  We haven't seen any of our friends so far.
  我們到目前為止沒見到任何朋友。

to date

迄今 雖然看起來有點不同，但意思和前面的 up to now 一樣。

● Has Alicia come to see you?
● **To date**, she hasn't been here.
  ●Alicia 有來看你嗎？　●至今都還沒有。

▶ To date, nothing special has happened.
  至今都還沒有什麼特別的事發生。
  To date, the business has been doing fine.
  事業迄今都很順利。

23 期間 for a while

9-23.mp3

for a while

· for a couple of days
  幾天

一會兒 while 表示一段不是太長的時間。

● I hope you'll come back soon.
● I'm only going out **for a while**.
  ●我希望你很快會回來。　●我只是出去一會兒。

▶ You've been in the bathroom for an hour.
  你已經在廁所裡一小時了。
  I need you to be quiet for a while.
  我需要你安靜一會兒。

1 職場・學校
2 電腦・網路
3 社交生活
4 日常生活
5 訊息・理解
6 想法・態度
7 情緒・狀況
8 行為舉止
9 時間地點・副詞片語

for a moment

· for a minute
一下
· for a second
一下（想強調真的很短暫的說法）

一下 表示時間很短暫。請不要和表示「目前」的 for the moment 搞混。

● Do you mind if I sit here **for a second**?
● Yeah, sure thing!

●你介意我在這裡坐一下嗎？　●你當然可以坐。（口語說法）

▶ Would you please excuse me for a moment?
我可以暫時離開一下嗎？
I was wondering if I could talk to you for a sec.
我想知道能不能跟你說一下話。

for the time being

暫時 表示目前暫時的狀態或權宜之計。

● Can you move this piano out of here?
● It has to stay **for the time being**.

●你可以把鋼琴從這邊搬走嗎？　●它得暫時放在這裡。

▶ I will wait for her for the time being.
我暫時會等她。
For the time being, let's eat dinner.
我們現在先吃晚餐吧。

for a long time

· for so long
很久
· for ages = in ages
很久
· for some time
有一陣子

很長一段時間 for 後面接表示時間長度的名詞片語，表示動作或狀態的持續期間。

● She's been in school **for a long time**.
● She must be a very good student.

●她在學校待好久了。　●她一定是位很好的學生。

▶ This handbag will not last for a long time.
這手提包沒辦法用很久。
Our friendship will last for a long time to come.
我們的友誼以後會長長久久。

over the years

· over the next month
下個月
· over the past week
上星期

多年來 over 後面接一段時間，表示 during 的意思，但也有可能是「超過」的意思。

● When was the company started?
● It was founded **over a hundred years ago**.

●這公司是什麼時候開業的？　●是一百多年前創立的。

▶ We've been great friends over the years.
我們是多年的好朋友。
The schedule will be changed over the next month.
下個月行程會改變。

during the vacation

· during one's vacation
在某人的假期中
· during this summer
在這個夏天
· during the meeting
在會議中

在假期中 during 通常接一段比較長的時間。

● Let's go to New York **during summer vacation**.
● That would be a lot of fun.
　●我們暑假時去紐約吧。　●應該會很好玩。

▶ Our high school will be closed during the vacation.
　我們的高中在放假期間會關閉。
　What will you do during your vacation?
　你在假期中要做什麼？

all the time

· all year
一整年
· all night
整晚

一直 即 always。另外，也可以表示「一直持續」的意思。

● Hey Joe, you sound tired.
● I know. I've been awake **all night**.
　●嘿 Joe，你（的聲音）聽起來好累。　●我知道，我整晚都醒著。

▶ We used to play together all the time.
　我們曾經一直玩在一起。
　I'm so tired. I've been studying all night.
　我好累。我讀了一整晚的書。

all day long

一整天 與 all day 同義。同樣的，一整晚就是 all night long。

● How long have you been working on that project?
● I have been working on it **all day long**.
　●你做那個案子多久了？　●我一整天都在處理它。

▶ Our festival will last all day long.
　我們的慶典會持續一整天。
　Where has Jessica been all day?
　Jessica 整天都去哪了？

in the meantime

在這段期間 表示在某件事之前，或者與某件事同時。

● I think mom and dad will be here soon.
● **In the meantime**, let's play a game.
　●我想爸媽很快會到這裡。　●在這段期間，我們來玩遊戲吧。

▶ In the meantime, they began talking.
　在這段期間，他們開始談話。
　They plan to keep working in the meantime.
　他們打算在這段期間繼續工作。

1 職場·學校
2 電腦·網路
3 社交生活
4 日常生活
5 訊息·理解
6 想法·態度
7 情緒·狀況
8 行為舉止
9 時間地點·副詞片語

24 重複與頻率
on a daily basis

9-24.mp3

three times a week

· once a week
一週一次
· twice a month
一個月兩次
· once in a blue moon
很少（一個月裡出現兩次
滿月時才發生，比喻 very
rarely）
· many times
很多次

一週三次 「...times + 期間名詞」表示頻率。一次則說 once，兩次則是 twice。

● Is this your first time to meet a movie star?
● No, I've met famous people **many times**.

●這是你第一次碰到電影明星嗎？　●不是，我碰過名人好多次了。

▶ My favorite show is on once a week.
我最愛的表演每週上演一次。
We'll meet up at least twice a month.
我們一個月至少會見兩次。

over and over (again)

· time after time
一再
· again and again
一再
· go on and on
一直持續

一再，再三 後面加上 again 可以更加強調語氣。

● Is your girlfriend angry at you again?
● Yes. This has happened **over and over again**.

●你女朋友又在生你的氣了嗎？　●是啊，這總是一再發生。

▶ He has called my phone again and again.
他一直打我的電話。
The snowstorm seemed to go on and on.
這暴風雪看來會一直持續下去。

on a daily basis

· on a weekly basis
每週，以週為單位
· on a bi-monthly basis
兩個月一次，一個月兩次
（為了避免混淆，可以用
semi-monthly 表示「半個
月一次」）

每天，按日 表示每天做一次，或者以每天為一個單位計算。

● Do you brush your teeth often?
● Sure, I brush them **on a daily basis**.

●你常刷牙嗎？　●當然，我每天刷。

▶ Mom goes shopping on a weekly basis.
我媽媽每週逛一次街。
He goes to meetings on a bi-monthly basis.
他每兩個月出席一次會議

every day

- every month
  每個月
- every night
  每晚
- every other day
  兩天一次

每天 連成一個字的 everyday 則是形容詞，意思是「日常的」。

- ● Are you still jogging **every day**?
- ● Yes, I run about thirty miles per week.
  - ● 你還會每天慢跑嗎？　● 會，我一個星期大約跑 30 英里。

- ▶ How much TV do you watch every day?
  你每天看多少電視？
  I watch the news every morning.
  我每天早上都看新聞。

every + N + that I have

- every opportunity that I have
  我一有機會

我擁有的每個… 用 every 強調每一個都是同樣的情況。

- ● **Every machine that** I have has broken.
- ● Maybe you should take better care of them.
  - ● 我的每台機器都壞了。　● 也許你應該更用心保養它們。

- ▶ I will meet her every opportunity that I have.
  我一有機會就會見她。
  Jean gave away every piece of furniture she had.
  Jean 把她每一件家具都送給別人了。

day in and day out

- year after year
  年復一年

每天，日復一日 與 day after day 同義，表示長時間持續的習慣。

- ● Your dad is a very hard worker.
- ● Yeah, he's on the job **day in and day out**.
  - ● 你爸爸是個很勤奮的員工。　● 嗯，他每天都上班。

- ▶ The company keeps growing, year after year.
  這間公司年復一年持續成長。
  She is always nice, time after time.
  她總是很親切，每次都一樣。

in a row

- stand in a row
  站成一排
- fifth win in a row
  連續第五勝

…成一排，連續的… 除了表示具體地形成一個 row，也可以表示連續發生同樣的事情。

- ● It's time to start exercising.
- ● OK, everyone line up **in a row**.
  - ● 是開始運動的時間了。　● OK，所有人排成一排。

- ▶ The soldiers stood in a row for an hour.
  士兵們成排站了一小時。
  This is our team's fifth win in a row.
  這是我們隊伍的連續第五勝。

1 職場・學校

2 電腦・網路

3 社交生活

4 日常生活

5 訊息・理解

6 想法・態度

7 情緒・狀況

8 行為舉止

9 時間地點・副詞片語

all over again

- start all over again
  重新開始

重新，從頭再來 也就是 starting form the beginning 的意思。
- Look, there is a big problem here.
- We'll have to do it **all over again**.
  - 看，這邊有個大問題。　- 我們得從頭再做一次了。

▶ He started all over again after he failed the exam.
  他考試不及格後，就從頭重新開始。
  I don't want to begin all over again.
  我不想從頭再來一次。

---

 every day vs. everyday

　　every day 是副詞片語，和 every week（每星期）、every year（每年）、every month（每個月）的結構相同。但如果把 every 和 day 連成 everyday，就變成形容詞，意思是「日常的」、「平常的」，會放在名詞前面做修飾。類似的例子還有 some time、sometime、sometimes。some time 是「（不短的）一些時間」（a considerable amount of time; quite a lot of time），sometime 則是不明確的「（將來的）某個時間」。加了 s 的 sometimes，則是表示「有時候」（on some occasions）的頻率副詞。

---

25 有時，多次
from time to time

9-25.mp3

from time to time

- think of sb from time to time
  不時想起某人
- sometimes
  有時候
- » cf. sometime
  某個時候，改天
- some time
  一些時間

有時，不時 sometimes, but not often 的意思。
- Your clock on the wall stopped working.
- **From time to time** the battery goes dead.
  - 你牆上的鐘不動了。　- 電池不時會沒電。

▶ I think of my ex-girlfriend from time to time.
  我不時會想起我前女友。
  From time to time you'll have to use this computer.
  你不時會需要用這台電腦。

(every) now and then

有時，偶爾 sometimes, but not regularly 的意思。

● Do you go out to eat often?
● Well, we go out to restaurants **every now and then**.
　　●你們常出去吃飯嗎？　　●嗯，我們偶爾會去餐廳吃飯。

▶ Now and then I get to see Rob.
　我偶爾會見到 Rob。
　Every now and then a train goes by the house.
　有時會有火車駛過房屋旁。

more often

· every so often
　不時，偶爾（sometimes, but not frequently）

更常 more often than not 則是 in most occasions（往往，通常）的意思。

● We have to come here **more often**.
● That's fine with me as long as you pay!
　　●我們得更常來這裡。　　●只要你付錢，我沒有意見！

▶ It happens more often than we think.
　這發生得比我們所想的還頻繁。
　What an amazing dinner! We should come here more often. 多棒的一頓晚餐呀！我們應該更常來。

once in a while

有時 也可以說 every once in a while。

● **Once in a while** I paint a picture.
● Your paintings look really great.
　　●我有時會畫畫。　　●你的畫看起來真的很棒。

▶ I water the plants every once in a while.
　我有時會給植物澆水。
　Once in a while my father gets angry.
　我爸爸有時會生氣。

at times

有時 at the time 則是「那時候」的意思，請注意定冠詞有無的差別。

● Do you travel to other countries?
● I've traveled overseas **at times**.
　　●你會去別的國家旅行嗎？　　●我有時會去國外旅行。

▶ I come to this restaurant at times.
　我有時會來這間餐廳。
　I have to work overtime sometimes.
　我有時得加班。

1 職場·學校

2 電腦·網路

3 社交生活

4 日常生活

5 訊息·理解

6 想法·態度

7 情緒·狀況

8 行為舉止

9 時間地點·副詞片語

689

26 趕緊
as soon as

9-26.mp3

as quickly as possible

» cf. as much as possible
盡可能多

盡快 在能力或情況許可的範圍內，用最快的速度進行。

● When do you want this finished?
● It must be done **as quickly as possible**.

●你希望這什麼時候完成？　●這必須盡快完成。

▶ Come to my office as quickly as possible.
盡快來我辦公室。
Joseph started to work as quickly as possible.
Joseph 盡快開始了工作。

as soon as possible

· reply ASAP
盡早回覆（信件用語）
· as soon as one can
盡早

盡早 也會縮寫成 ASAP。感覺和 as quickly as possible 很像，但 soon 著重於時間點的早晚，quickly 則是指進行速度的快慢。

● He always wants us to finish **as soon as possible**.
● Your boss is a tough guy to work for.

●他總是希望我們盡早完成。　●你的老闆是個很難共事的人。

▶ Please have her return my call as soon as possible.
請她盡早回我電話。
I'll try and get there as soon as possible.
我會試著盡早抵達那裡。

as soon as S+V,

一···就 這裡的 as soon as 用法和連接詞相似。相當於 right after S+V。

● When are you going to take your driving test?
● **As soon as** I get used to driving in the rain.

●你什麼時候要考駕照？　●等我習慣在雨中開車以後就去。

▶ Could you ask him to call me back as soon as he gets in?
可以請他一進公司就回我電話嗎？
As soon as you exit the station, you'll see Bloomingdale's.
你一走出車站，就會看到 Bloomingdale's 百貨公司。

690

1 職場‧學校

2 電腦‧網路

3 社交生活

4 日常生活

5 訊息‧理解

6 想法‧態度

7 情緒‧狀況

8 行為舉止

9 時間地點‧副詞片語

any time now

· at any time
在任何時候，隨時

很快，馬上 雖然不知道確切的時間，但 very soon 的意思。

● Has the mailman come yet?
● No, but he'll probably come **any time now**.

　●郵差來了嗎？　●還沒，但他可能馬上就會來了。

▶ It may start to rain at any time.
可能很快會下雨。
Susan is due to arrive any time now.
Susan 預計很快抵達。

sooner than expected

· arrive home sooner than expected
比預期的還早到了家

比預期的早 sooner than you think 的意思也相近。

● I thought you were still working.
● We finished **sooner than expected**.

　●我以為你們還在工作。　●我們比預期的還要早完成了。

▶ The students arrived home sooner than expected.
學生們比預期的還要早到了家。
My package came sooner than expected.
我的包裹比預期的還要早來。

---

27 | 特定時間 later this week

9-27.mp3

this year

· this morning
今天早上
· this time
這次
· this week
這星期
· this time of year
一年裡的這個時候

今年 this time of year 則是「一年裡的這個時候」。

● Your son has grown quite a lot.
● He's a junior in high school **this year**.

　●你兒子長大了很多。　●他今年高三。

▶ Are you going to the beach this summer?
你今年夏天會去海邊嗎？
Are you aware of Jen graduating this year?
你知道 Jen 今年畢業嗎？

on Friday

· on the weekend
　在週末
· on weekends
　每週末

在星期五 跟日期一樣，星期的前面加 on 表示在哪一天。

● Are you going to be here **on the weekend**?
● Yes, I will. I have no plans yet.
　●你週末會來這裡嗎？　●會。我（當天）還沒有任何計畫。

▶ I'm not sure what to do on Saturday.
　我不確定星期六要做什麼。
　I made it a rule to play golf on the weekends.
　我習慣每週末打高爾夫球。

last year

· last month
　上個月
· last night
　昨晚
· last week
　上星期

去年 last, next, this 後面加時間名詞的組合，前面不用加介系詞。

● I stayed out drinking beer **last night**.
● That's not smart. Your wife will be angry.
　●我昨晚待在外面喝啤酒。
　●那不是個明智的舉動。你太太會生氣的。

▶ I saved five times as much as I did last year.
　我存了去年五倍的錢。
　I had a really hard time last month.
　我上個月過得真的很辛苦。

next month

· next Monday
　下星期一

下個月 next 後面也可以接 year, week, day 等時間名詞。

● Have you had your wisdom teeth pulled out?
● No, but I'm planning to have them extracted **next month**.
　●你拔掉你的智齒了嗎？　●還沒，但我打算下個月去拔。

▶ I've got a job interview next Monday.
　我下星期一有個工作面試。
　I heard about you getting married next month.
　我聽說你下個月要結婚了。

later this week

· later this year
　今年下半年

這星期稍晚 表示在這個星期的後半。

● When will your brother arrive?
● He's coming **later this week**.
　●你哥哥什麼時候會抵達？　●他這星期稍晚會來。

▶ I'll plant a garden later this year.
　我今年下半年會栽種花園。
　Your books will be here later this week.
　你的書這星期稍晚會到。

in the upcoming year

· in the coming years
  在未來幾年

明年 upcoming 的意思是「即將來臨的」，當形容詞用。

● **In the upcoming year**, I'll start university.
● I hope you enjoy studying there.

●明年我就會開始上大學了。　●我希望你會喜歡在那裡讀書。

▶ My family is moving in the upcoming year.
  我們家明年會搬家。
  The economy will improve in the upcoming year.
  經濟明年會變好。

at the end of the day

在一天的結尾 at the end 也可以表示「結果⋯」或「最重要的是⋯」。

● When do you play World of Warcraft?
● I usually start to play **at the end of the day**.

●你什麼時候打「魔獸世界」？
●我通常會在一天結束的時候開始玩。

▶ We take long walks at the end of the day.
  我們在一天結束時會散步到遠處。
  At the end of the day they will be in New Zealand.
  在那天結束的時候，他們會在紐西蘭。

some day

· maybe some other
  time
  或許在其他時間

（將來）有一天 要表示將來某個不特定的時間，some day 和 someday 可以互換，但如果要表示特定的日子，則必須用 some day。one day 是「過去的某一天」。

● When are you going to make a trip to Finland?
● **Some day**, I will make sure to visit Helsinki.

●你什麼時候要去芬蘭旅行？
●總有一天，我一定會去拜訪赫爾辛基。

▶ Some day I'll have a lot of money.
  總有一天，我會很有錢。
  Maybe some other time we can get together.
  或許我們可以在其他時間見面。

in the future

· in the near future
  在不遠的未來

未來 in the near future 則是「在不遠的未來」。

● I don't care what happens **in the future**.
● How can you not care about your future?

●我不在乎未來會發生什麼。　●你怎麼可以不在意你的未來呢？

▶ We'll have tiny cell phones in the near future.
  在不遠的將來，我們會有很小的手機。
  She is going to become a president in the future.
  她將來會當上總統。

1 職場・學校

2 電腦・網路

3 社交生活

4 日常生活

5 訊息・理解

6 想法・態度

7 情緒・狀況

8 行為舉止

9 時間地點・副詞片語

28 突然，瞬間
on such short notice

9-28.mp3

all of a sudden

· stop all of a sudden
  突然停止
· sudden death
  猝死（名詞）

突然地 類似的說法還有 all at once、suddenly、unexpectedly 等等。

● What happened when you were driving?
● **All of a sudden**, I saw a policeman.

  ●你開車時發生了什麼事？　●我突然看到警察。

▶ The train stopped all of a sudden.
　火車突然停了下來。
　They are still shocked by the sudden death of Bill.
　他們仍然因為 Bill 的猝死而震驚。

in the blink of an eye

一眨眼間，瞬間 blink 也可以換成 twinkling，意思一樣。

● I hear that Paul has no money now.
● Yeah, he lost it all **in the blink of an eye**.

  ●我聽說 Paul 現在沒錢了。
  ●是啊，他一眨眼的工夫就把錢輸光了。

▶ We finished the work in the blink of an eye.
　我們瞬間就把工作完成了。
　The robber was gone in the blink of an eye.
　強盜一眨眼間就不見了。

on such short notice

· be short notice
  （通知）很突然
· without notice
  沒事先通知

這麼突然地（通知） 毫無預警地告知，令人措手不及。

● Can we have a party tonight?
● It will be difficult **on such short notice**.

  ●我們今晚可以開派對嗎？　●這麼突然的話，會很困難。

▶ There was short notice before the meeting was held.
　突然有通知說要開會。
　My favorite store closed without notice.
　我最喜歡的店沒事先通知就關了。

out of the blue | **突如其來地** 就像晴朗的藍天忽然下起大雨般地突然。
- ●Did you know she was coming to town?
- ●No, she arrived here **out of the blue**.
  - ●你知道她要到市區來嗎？　●不知道，她是突然來這裡的。
- ▶ Linda got chosen out of the blue. Linda 突然被選中了。
  The manager was fired out of the blue. 主管突然被解雇了。

---

29 | 最後，終於
in the end

9-29.mp3

1 職場・學校
2 電腦・網路
3 社交生活
4 日常生活
5 訊息・理解
6 想法・態度
7 情緒・狀況
8 行為舉止
9 時間地點・副詞片語

---

at last

・at length
　終於，詳細地

最後，終於 也可以說 after all 或 finally。
- ●The letter from my boyfriend came **at last**.
- ●Why did it take so long to arrive?
  - ●我男朋友寫的信終於來了。　●為什麼那麼久才寄到？
- ▶ We are getting married, at long last. 我們終於要結婚了。
  The professor talked at length about our project.
  教授詳細地談論了我們的計畫。

in the long run

最終 長期的、不能從一時的情況論斷的結果。相當於 eventually。
- ●I heard you succeeded in getting a job.
- ●Yeah, everything was fine **in the long run**.
  - ●我聽說你成功找到工作了。　●嗯，最後一切都順利了。
- ▶ Honesty will win in the long run. 誠實最終將會贏得勝利。
  Just keep on trying and eventually you'll succeed.
  持續嘗試，最終你會成功的。

in the end

最後，終究 口語中常用的說法，相當於 finally。
- ●So, you aren't trying to date Renee anymore?
- ●No, **in the end** I just gave up.
  - ●所以你不會再嘗試找 Renee 約會了？　●不會，我最後放棄了。
- ▶ Everything was fixed, in the end. 最後所有事都解決了。
  In the end, we decided not to buy it. 最後我們決定不要買它。

once and for all

· end sth once and for all
  徹底結束某事

一勞永逸地，徹底，永遠 做了這次就不用再做，completely and finally 的意思。

● Barney and his girlfriend always argue.
● They should just break up **once and for all**.

　●Barney 和他女朋友總是吵架。　　●他們應該徹底分手算了。

▶ We had to end our relationship once and for all.
　我們必須徹底結束我們的關係。
　The TV show concluded, once and for all.
　這個電視節目永遠結束了。

sooner or later

· be fired sooner or later
  遲早被解雇

早晚，遲早 也可以說 early or late。

● I never learned how to drive.
● **Sooner or later** you'll need to buy a car.

　●我從來沒學過開車。　　●你遲早會需要買台車。

▶ Gary is going to be fired sooner or later.
　Gary 遲早會被解雇。
　She's going to get in trouble sooner or later.
　她早晚會捲入麻煩中。

---

30 | 追加，強調
in addition to

9-30.mp3

---

above all else

· most of all
  尤其是，最重要的是

勝過一切，最重要 above all 也是「最重要」的意思，常常放在句首，帶出要說的重點。

● You need to make money **above all else**.
● But I want to find a job I enjoy too.

　●比起所有事情，你最需要賺錢。
　●但我也想找個我會享受其中的工作。

▶ Felicia liked my present most of all.
　在所有禮物裡，Felicia 最喜歡我的。
　Health is above all else.
　健康是最重要的。

to top it (all) off

· on top of it
此外
· what is more
此外

最棒／最糟的是 表示接下來要說的比之前提過的每件事都還好／還糟。

● Your brother was very rude at the party.

● **To top it all off**, he got drunk.

　　●你哥哥在派對上很粗魯。　●最糟的是，他還喝醉了。

▶ To top it off, we're going to Switzerland.
　　最棒的是，我們要去瑞士。
　　To top it all off, she left me with huge debts.
　　最糟的是，她留下一屁股債給我。

in addition to

· in addition
此外

除了…以外 to 後面接名詞，強調除此以外還有更多。相當於 besides sth。

● So, people say you like to go jogging.

● **In addition to** jogging, I also do aerobics.

　　●大家都說你喜歡慢跑。　●除了慢跑，我也做有氧運動。

▶ Besides working, he likes fishing in his free time.
　　除了工作，他也喜歡在空閒時去釣魚。
　　She's a wonderful friend, in addition to being a
　　wonderful mother. 她不只是個很好的母親，也是很好的朋友。

not only A but also B

· B as well as A
不只 A 還有 B

不僅 A 而且 B 強調的重點在於 B。

● Which one of these phones do you want to buy?

● I'll take the silver one, **as well as** the black one.

　　●你想要買這裡面的哪隻手機？　●除了黑的以外，我還要買銀的。

▶ We're not only tired, but also hungry.
　　我們不只很累，還很餓。
　　Jill has a good education, as well as being pretty.
　　Jill 不只漂亮，還受了很好的教育。

by far

· What in the world/
on earth...
到底…什麼

顯然 通常接在形容詞或副詞最高級前面，是強調用的副詞片語。

● This is **by far** my favorite TV show.

● Me too. I love the main actor.

　　●這絕對是我最喜歡的電視節目。　●我也是。我好喜歡那個男主角。

▶ What in the world is Neil doing?
　　Neil 到底在做什麼？
　　You are by far the most handsome student.
　　你絕對是長得最帥的學生。

1 職場・學校
2 電腦・網路
3 社交生活
4 日常生活
5 訊息・理解
6 想法・態度
7 情緒・狀況
8 行為舉止
9 時間地點・副詞片語

31 不管⋯，另一方面
on the other hand

9-31.mp3

in spite of

· in spite of one's age
  就算是某人那樣的年紀

不管⋯，儘管⋯ 後面接名詞或動名詞（-ing）。也可以說 despite sth。

- I can't believe you went jogging this morning.
- **In spite of** being tired, I decided to exercise.
  - 我不敢相信你今天早上去慢跑了。
  - 就算很累，我還是決定要運動。

▶ My parents are healthy, in spite of their age.
就算已經那把年紀了，我父母還是很健康。
We arrived in time, despite the traffic jam.
儘管塞車，我們還是及時抵達了。

even though S+V

· even though it is true
  即使這是事實

即使⋯ S+V 是目前的或已經發生的事實。even if S+V 雖然也翻譯成「即使⋯」，但 even if 後面的 S+V 是假設的情況。

- Do you want to get something to eat?
- I'm still hungry, **even though** I had dinner.
  - 你想要買點東西吃嗎？　● 我還是餓，雖然我有吃晚餐。

▶ Don't tell anyone, even though it is true.
即使這是事實，也不要跟任何人說。
Even though he left, I still miss him.
即使他離開了，我還是想念他。

even so

即便如此 這是從 even if it were so 簡化而成的說法。

- Darryl is a very cruel man.
- **Even so**, we can't change his character.
  - Darryl 是個很殘酷的男人。
  - 即便如此，我們也無法改變他的個性。

▶ Even so, they must follow the rules.
即便如此，他們也必須遵守規定。
Even so, Jerry can't stay here.
即便如此，Jerry 也不能待在這裡。

on the other hand

· instead of
　代替…，而非…

另一方面，相反地 用人的兩隻手比喻事情的兩方面，句型是「(On one hand,) ...; on the other hand, ...」（一方面…，另一方面…）。

● We can go camping this summer.
● **On the other hand**, we can stay in a hotel too.
　● 我們這個夏天可以去露營。　● 另一方面，我們也可以住在旅館。

▶ They chose cake instead of ice cream.
　他們選擇蛋糕，而非冰淇淋。
　I think I'll drive instead of walking.
　我想我會開車，而不會用走的。

but then S+V

然而…，但是… 在一項敘述之後，帶出一個不太一樣的觀點。

● Let's leave work early today.
● **But then** we might lose our jobs.
　● 我們今天早點下班吧。　● 但我們有可能會丟掉工作。

▶ But then she started to cry.
　然而她開始哭了起來。
　This is better, but then again it costs more.
　這比較好，但也比較貴。

---

1 職場·學校
2 電腦·網路
3 社交生活
4 日常生活
5 訊息·理解
6 想法·態度
7 情緒·狀況
8 行為舉止
9 時間地點·副詞片語

32 換句話說，簡而言之
in other words

9-32.mp3

so to speak

· as it were
　可以說

可以說 用一個說法來總結自己的話。

● I didn't know your wife liked sewing.
● It's one of her hobbies, **so to speak**.
　● 我不知道你太太喜歡縫紉。　● 這可以説是她的嗜好之一。

▶ This is the finest resort, so to speak.
　這裡可以説是最棒的度假村。
　Congressmen were back in school today, so to speak.
　國會議員們今天可以説是開學（開始會期）了。

in short

簡而言之，總之　相當於 in brief, in a word。

- How was your first day at work?
- **In short**, everything went wrong.
  - 你工作第一天狀況怎樣？　●總之，什麼都出了錯。

▶ In brief, she said we had to break up.
簡而言之，她說我們得分手。
In short, we don't have money.
簡而言之，我們沒有錢。

in a nutshell

概括地說，總之　nutshell 是堅果的外殼，比喻簡短地概述整體情況或下結論。

- So, we must move to another department?
- Yes, that's **in a nutshell**.
  - 所以我們一定得調到另一個部門囉？　●嗯，簡單來說就是那樣。

▶ In a nutshell, we had to fire him.
總之，我們得解雇他。
Gary explained everything in a nutshell.
Gary 概括地解釋了所有事情。

to make a long story short

· to cut a long story short
簡單地說

長話短說，簡單地說　make 也可以換成 cut。

- Did you have a fight with Marsha?
- **To make a long story short**, yes.
  - 你和 Marsha 吵架了嗎？　●簡單地說，是的。

▶ To make a long story short, it was very nice.
用一句話來說的話，那真的很棒。
To make a long story short, I failed.
結論就是，我失敗了。

in other words

· namely
也就是
· as it were
可以說

換言之，換句話說　用不同的說法重新說明講過的話，好讓對方了解。

- My boss said he would promote me.
- **In other words**, you'll be making more money?
  - 我老闆說他會讓我升職。　●換句話說，你會賺更多錢囉？

▶ Some people were very kind, namely John and Vicky.
有些人，也就是 John 和 Vicky，他們非常親切。
This is the festival's last day, as it were.
今天可以說是慶典的最後一天。

1 職場・學校

2 電腦・網路

3 社交生活

4 日常生活

5 訊息・理解

6 想法・態度

7 情緒・狀況

8 行為舉止

9 時間地點・副詞片語

33 順道一提 by the way

9-33.mp3

by the way

順道一提，對了 話說到一半要改變話題的常用說法。

- **By the way**, someone called from your school.
- Oh, I should give them a call back.

 ●對了，有人從你學校打電話給你。　●噢，我應該回電話給他們。

▶ By the way, you still owe me twenty dollars.
  對了，你還欠我 20 美元。
  By the way, what time is it now?
  對了，現在是幾點？

as a matter of fact

· in fact
  事實上
· actually
  實際上

事實上 表示接下來要說的事實可能和對方想的不一樣。

- Have you ever been to Disneyland?
- No, **as a matter of fact**, I haven't.

 ●你去過迪士尼樂園嗎？　●沒有，事實上我從來沒去過。

▶ As a matter of fact I didn't go to bed last night.
  事實上，我昨晚沒睡覺。
  In fact, she looked forward to a quiet dinner alone.
  事實上，她希望能自己安靜地吃晚餐。

as I told you before

· like I said before
  就像我之前說的
· as you have already heard
  如同你已經聽說的

如同我先前跟你說過的 before 也可以換成 previously。

- Do you want to go to the concert?
- **As I told you before**, I have no time for that.

 ●你想去音樂會嗎？　●我之前跟你說過了，我沒有那個時間。

▶ As you've already heard, classes were cancelled.
  如同你已經聽說的，停課了。
  As I told you before, I am in a big trouble.
  如同我先前跟你說過的，我碰上了大麻煩。

701

now that you mention it

· speaking of...
  說到…
· speaking of which
  說到這個

經你這麼一說 由於對方的話而想起了某件事情。

● I'm sure we met somewhere before.
● **Now that you mention it**, you look familiar.

　●我確定我們之前在哪裡見過。　　●經你這麼一說，你看起來好眼熟。

▶ Now that you mention it, I remember that event.
　經你這麼一說，我想起那場活動了。
　Speaking of which, are you ready to go to lunch?
　說到這個，你準備好要去吃午餐了嗎？

generally speaking

· frankly speaking
  坦白說
· strictly speaking
  嚴格來說
· actually
  真的，確實，實際上

一般而言 frankly speaking 是「坦白說」，strictly speaking 是「嚴格來說」。

● Do you know what I mean?
● **Actually**, I have no idea what you are talking about.

　●你知道我的意思嗎？　　●實際上，我一點也不知道你在說什麼。

▶ Generally speaking, I don't like to fight.
　一般而言，我不喜歡打架。
　Really, sitting at that table would be fine.
　說真的，坐在那張桌子會很好。

---

34 | 有點，很多，至少 a bit of

9-34.mp3

quite a few

· quite a few times
  相當多次
· quite a lot
  相當多

相當多 a few 也可以換成 a bit 或 a lot。注意 quite 要放在 a 前面。

● Have you attended a soccer match before?
● Yes, I've been to **quite a few** soccer matches.

　●你去看過足球賽嗎？　　●嗯，我去過很多場足球賽。

▶ Someone knocked on the door quite a few times.
　有人敲門敲了很多次。
　They go to the movies quite a lot.
　他們很常去看電影。

a lot of

· plenty of errors
  很多錯誤
· plenty of time
  充足的時間

很多 可以接可數或不可數名詞，不像 many/much 有可數／不可數的區別。

● These boxes have **a lot of** paperwork in them.
● We'd better put them in the closet.
  ●這些箱子裡裝了很多文件。　●我們最好把它們放到壁櫥裡。

▶ There is plenty of food in the fridge.
  冰箱裡有很多食物。
  I found plenty of errors in the article.
  我在這篇文章裡找到很多錯誤。

a number of

· a number of + Ns
  + 複數動詞
  一些…
· the number of + Ns
  + 單數動詞
  …的數量

一些 後面接可數名詞複數形。the number of... 雖然也接名詞複數形，但它是表示「…的數量」，所以整體而言視為單數。

● There are **a number of** students outside.
● I think they are going to play some music.
  ●外面有一些學生。　●我想他們是要演奏音樂。

▶ A number of workers were hired at the company.
  有一些員工受到這間公司雇用。
  You need to buy a number of things for your apartment.
  你需要為你的公寓購買一些東西。

at least

· at (the) best
  頂多
· at the most
  最多

至少 除了表示數量和程度，也可以表示最低的要求或條件。

● I think it's going to rain today.
● **At least** the temperature is warm.
  ●我想今天會下雨。　●至少氣溫暖和。

▶ At best, he'll get a passing grade on the test.
  這次考試，他頂多能拿個低空飛過的成績。
  You will get third place, at the best.
  你最高會有第三名。

a bit of

· a bit of rain
  一點雨
· a bit of conscience
  一點良心

一點點 只說 a bit 的話則可以當副詞，用來修飾動詞。

● Can I have **a bit of** your chocolate bar?
● Sure. Here's a piece for you.
  ●我可以吃一點你的巧克力棒嗎？　●當然，這一塊給你。

▶ Tainan will get a bit of rain tomorrow.
  明天台南會下一點雨。
  Jack never shows a bit of conscience.
  Jack 從來沒展現過一點良心。

1 職場・學校
2 電腦・網路
3 社交生活
4 日常生活
5 訊息・理解
6 想法・態度
7 情緒・狀況
8 行為舉止
9 時間地點・副詞片語

a few + N

· a few of+N
　…中的一點

一點… 後面接可數名詞複數形。如果是不可數名詞，則用 a little。

- There are **a few** things I need to do.
- Well, let's meet up again later.

　●我有點事要做。　●嗯，那我們晚點再見面吧。

▶ Here are a few pictures from our trip.

　這邊有幾張我們旅行時的照片。

　Give me a few minutes to finish the work.

　給我幾分鐘做完工作。

a couple of

· a handful of
　一把，少數的

幾個 couple 本來是「一對」的意思，在口語中表示「幾個」。

- These shoes are killing my feet.
- It will take **a couple of** days to break them in.

　●這雙鞋把我的腳弄得快痛死了。　●要花幾天才能穿鬆。

▶ A couple of old women sat on the bench.

　有幾位老太太坐在長椅上。

　Jen grabbed a handful of nuts.

　Jen 抓了一把堅果。

kind of

· sort of
　有點…

有點… a kind of 的意思是「一種…」。這裡介紹的 kind of 是副詞，後面接形容詞或動詞，在非正式的情況下也會寫成 kinda。

- Would you like to join me for dinner?
- Well, I am **kind of** busy right now. How about tomorrow?

　●你想要跟我一起吃晚餐？　●嗯，我現在有點忙，明天怎麼樣？

▶ I'm kind of nervous about going on stage.

　我對上台有點緊張。

　I have sort of hard feelings for her.

　我對她有點不高興。

a piece of

· a piece of paper
　一張紙

· a piece of advice
　一個建議

一塊…，一張… 除了表示薄片狀的物品，也可以表示一塊或整體裡的一部分。

- Can I have **a piece of** your pie?
- It's right here. Help yourself.

　●我可以吃一塊你的派嗎？　●就在這邊，自己拿吧。

▶ I need a piece of paper.

　我需要一張紙。

　Mike gave me a piece of his gum.

　Mike 給了我一片他的口香糖。

1 職場・學校

2 電腦・網路

3 社交生活

4 日常生活

5 訊息・理解

6 想法・態度

7 情緒・狀況

8 行為舉止

9 時間地點・副詞片語

 a bit

bit 是名詞，意思是「一點點」、「少量」。a bit 則是副詞，表示「有點…」，在日常生活的口語中很常用，也可說 a little bit。所以「現在有點忙」可以說「I'm a little bit busy right now」。對方看起來有點醉，可以說「You seem to be a little bit drunk」。被感覺討厭的對象一直偷瞄的時候，就會「feel a little bit uncomfortable」了。a (little) bit of + N 則是表示「一點點的…」。

35 程度 as far as

9-35.mp3

more or less

· be more or less
  valueless/worthless
  可說沒有價值

或多或少，大約 「差不多是這樣」，somewhat 的意思。

● Do you have much work to do?
● No, I'm **more or less** finished.

　　●你有很多工作要做嗎？　　●沒有，我差不多做完了。

▶ These stocks are more or less worthless.
　　這些股票可以說沒有價值。
　　I can earn $100 a day, more or less.
　　我一天大約能賺 100 美元。

step by step

· little by little
  一點一點地

一步一步，逐步 「逐漸」的意思，也可以說 bit by bit 或 little by little。

● Our business hasn't done well this year.
● **Step by step**, your business will get bigger.

　　●我們的事業今年表現得不好。
　　●一步一步來，你們的事業版圖會擴張的。

▶ Step by step, I learned to speak Chinese.
　　我逐漸學會說中文。
　　Little by little we moved the giant piano.
　　我們一點一點地移動那台大鋼琴。

to a certain degree

· in some respects
  在某些方面，從某些角度
· to some degree
  在某種程度上

在某種程度上 degree 也可以換成 extent。

● How is your relationship with Hal?
● **To a certain degree**, it's pretty good.
  ●你跟 Hal 的關係怎麼樣？　●在某種程度上，還蠻好的。

▶ To some degree, this will help you and me.
  在某種程度上，這會對你我有幫助。
  In some respects, it was a very difficult week.
  在某些方面，這是很辛苦的一週。

as much as sth

· twice as much as sth
  程度是某事物的兩倍
· as many as 30
  passengers
  多達三十名的乘客

跟…差不多 much 能修飾動詞，many 不行。下面例句裡的 have as many as，many 不是修飾動詞，而是當代名詞，表示「很多的某個東西」。

● This TV weighs **as much as** an elephant.
● Come on, it doesn't weigh that much.
  ●這台電視的重量跟一隻大象差不多。　●拜託，哪有那麼重。

▶ You can have as many as you want.
  你想要多少，就可以拿多少。
  I hate this as much as you.
  我跟你一樣討厭這個東西。

as far as S+V

· as far as I know
  就我所知
· as far as I am
  concerned
  就我而言，對我來說
· as far as sb do
  盡某人…的限度
· as far as A goes
  就 A 範圍所及

到…的程度，盡…的限度 以 S+V 表示程度，或者表示盡 S+V 的限度。

● Did you break up with your boyfriend?
● Yeah. **As far as** me dating him, it's finished.
  ●妳跟妳男朋友分手了嗎？　●嗯，在跟他約會這方面是結束了。

▶ I will help you as far as I can.
  我會盡我所能幫助你。
  As far as his experience goes, he's second to none.
  就經驗來說，他是首屈一指的。

706

36 位置，場所
over there

9-36.mp3

1 職場・學校
2 電腦・網路
3 社交生活
4 日常生活
5 訊息・理解
6 想法・態度
7 情緒・狀況
8 行為舉止
9 時間地點・副詞片語

in front of

在…**前面** in the front of... 則是指「在…（本身）的前面部分」。

● Dan and his friends are playing video games.
● They are so stupid. They just sit **in front of** computers.
  ● Dan 和他的朋友們在打電動。　● 他們真傻，就只是坐在電腦前面。

▶ Helen got very nervous in front of the class.
  Helen 在全班面前變得很緊張。
  Our band played in front of a large crowd.
  我們樂團在一大群觀眾面前演奏。

next to
・beside+N
　在…旁邊

在…**旁邊** next to 和 beside 同義。但 besides 則是「此外」的意思，請區分清楚。

● Is it next to the stadium?
● No, it is across the street, **next to** the post office.
  ● 那在體育場旁邊嗎？　● 不是，是在對街的郵局旁邊。

▶ The prettiest girl in class sat next to me.
  班上最漂亮的女孩坐在我旁邊。
  The keys are next to my glasses.
  鑰匙在我的眼鏡旁邊。

inside of

在…**裡面** outside of 則是「在…外面」。

● Are Korean pop stars popular **outside of** Korea?
● Yes, especially in China.
  ● 韓國流行歌手在海外也很受歡迎嗎？　● 是的，特別是在中國。

▶ There were many plants inside of the greenhouse.
  溫室裡面有很多植物。
  You need to catch one of the shuttle buses outside of the airport.
  你得搭機場外面的其中一班接駁車。

over there

- over here
  在這裡
- far away
  遙遠的

在那裡 相對於現在位置的另一邊。

- The woman sitting **over there** is my teacher.
- You mean the one with brown hair?
  - ●坐在那裡的女士是我的老師。　●你説那位棕色頭髮的嗎？

▶ I've walked over there from here.
  我從這裡一路走到那裡。
  Is it far away from here?
  那離這邊遠嗎？

in the neighborhood

在近鄰，在周邊 neighborhood 是指「鄰近地區」。

- Where can I find the library?
- It's the largest building **in the neighborhood**.
  - ●我去哪裡才能找到圖書館？　●它是這附近最大的建築物。

▶ I'll stop by your apartment when I'm in the neighborhood.
  我到你那邊的時候，會順道拜訪你的公寓。
  There used to be a popular nightclub in my neighborhood. 我家附近曾經有一間很受歡迎的夜店。

---

37 | 條件，假設
if you like

9-37.mp3

if you like

- if you want to...
  你想…的話
- if you wish
  你想要／希望的話
- if possible
  可能的話

你喜歡／想要的話 用表示條件的說法徵詢對方的意願。

- I'm afraid to walk home alone.
- I'll walk with you, **if you like**.
  - ●我怕一個人走回家。　●如果你想要的話，我會陪你一起走。

▶ If you want to meet him, I can introduce you.
  如果你想見他的話，我可以幫你介紹。
  We can leave now, if you wish.
  你想要的話，我們可以現在離開。

in that case

- if that is the case
  如果是那樣的話
- in case S+V
  假使…，免得…
- in this case
  在這個情況下
- in any case
  無論如何

那樣的話 假設「如果是那種狀況的話」。

- Tony said that he'd pick up the tab.
- **In that case** I'll have dessert.
  - Tony 說他會買單。　●那樣的話，我要吃甜點。

▶ In that case I'll change the plans.
  那樣的話，我要改變計畫。
  I'm going to label them just in case they get lost.
  我要把它們貼上標籤，以免它們不見。

as long as

- as if
  似乎…
- as though
  似乎…

只要… 後面接 S+V。也有可能指時間長短，意思是「跟…一樣久」、「在…的時間範圍內」。

- It looks **as though** the country is on its way to recovery.
- I sure hope so. It's been a long and hard year.
  - 看來國家正在復甦的路上。
  - 我真的希望如此，這是個漫長又辛苦的一年。

▶ You can stay here as long as you like.
  你想在這邊待多久，就待多久。
  I haven't been here for as long as I remember.
  就我記憶所及，我從來沒來過這裡。

what if...

- otherwise
  否則

如果…怎麼辦／會怎麼樣 表示擔心，if 後面接假設的壞事。

- **What if** I said we had to work tomorrow?
- I'd pretend that I didn't hear you.
  - 如果我說明天我們要工作的話，你覺得怎麼樣？
  - 我會假裝沒聽到你的話。

▶ What if this ship began to sink?
  如果這艘船開始沉的話呢？
  What if the security guard doesn't show up?
  如果保全沒有出現的話呢？

let's say...

比如說…，大約… 表示估計，或者對未來的假設。

- **Let's say** the electricity stopped working.
- That would mean many people would have problems.
  - 比如說，停電的話。　●那樣的話，就會有很多人碰上問題。

▶ Let's say you and I had a date together.
  假設我們一起去約會好了。
  Let's say Kim can't come with us.
  假設 Kim 不能跟我們一起去好了。

1 職場・學校
2 電腦・網路
3 社交生活
4 日常生活
5 訊息・理解
6 想法・態度
7 情緒・狀況
8 行為舉止
9 時間地點・副詞片語

38 | 説到…
when it comes to

9-38.mp3

when it comes to...

説到… 這裡的 to 是介系詞，後面接名詞或動名詞（-ing）。
- When it comes to computer problems, I would ask Tina.
- Do you know where she is right now?
  - 説到電腦問題，我會問 Tina。　●你知道她現在在哪裡嗎？

▶ When it comes to winter, Ed likes skiing.
談到冬天，Ed 喜歡滑雪。
When it comes to love, I know nothing.
説到愛，我一竅不通。

as for/to

· as for me
  至於我
· as to the matter
  關於這個問題

至於…，説到… as for 後面接人或事物。as to 後面接事物。
- I really like to go on long trips.
- As for me, I like to stay at home.
  - 我真的很喜歡長途旅行。　●至於我，我喜歡待在家裡。

▶ As for Jen, she's ready to get started.
至於 Jen，她已經準備好要開始了。
As for him, he'll be at lunch for an hour.
至於他，他會去吃一小時的中餐。

concerning + N

關於… 用法像介系詞一樣，後面接名詞。
- I'd like to talk with you concerning tomorrow's meeting.
- What time would be good for you?
  - 我想跟你談關於明天會議的事。　●你什麼時候方便？

▶ These reports were written concerning pollution.
這些報告是關於汙染的。
I talked to three people concerning you.
我跟和你有關的三個人談過。

with regard to

· without regard to
不顧…

關於⋯ 比較正式的說法。也可以說 in regard to。

● **With regard to** a job, I am trying to find one.

● It's very difficult to get hired these days.

　● 說到工作的話，我現在正在試著找。　● 最近要找到工作很難。

▶ With regard to that car, it's been sold.
關於那台車，它被賣掉了。
With regard to the show, it's been canceled.
關於那場表演，它被取消了。

regarding + N

關於⋯ 和 with regard to N 的意思一樣。

● **Regarding** your flight, it will be delayed.

● I guess I will have to wait here.

　● 關於您的班機，將會延後起飛。　● 我想我得在這邊等了。

▶ Regarding the exam, I failed it.
關於那場考試，我沒及格。
He spoke to us regarding our future.
他跟我們談了關於未來的事。

1 職場・學校

2 電腦・網路

3 社交生活

4 日常生活

5 訊息・理解

6 想法・態度

7 情緒・狀況

8 行為舉止

9 時間地點・副詞片語

INDEX

索引

APPENDIX

be bonded together 222
be booked up 219
be bound to 196
be bound to 444
be broke 92
be burned out 29
be called 246
be calling to ask 145
be capable of 34
be careful of 466
be cautious about 468
be certain that S+V 444
be concerned about 499
be confident that 445
be confused 505
be connected with 260
be cool 561
be crazy about 252
be crazy/mad 524
be curious about 375
be cut off 153
be cut out for 656
be delayed for + 時間 202
be deprived of 623
be derived from 602
be designed to 203
be destined to 445
be devoted to 24
be different from 554
be difficult to 560
be disappointed in 511
be discharged from the army 647
be dissatisfied with 453
be doing okay 561
be done with the computer 118
be done with 39
be down 119
be drawn to sb 252
be due (tomorrow) 200
be due on 94
be due to 196
be easy to 559
be eligible for/to 656
be embarrassed 505
be engaged in 260
be engaged to 257
be enthusiastic about 24

be equal to 556
be excited about 491
be excused from 265
be exhausted 28
be expected to 196
be expected to 431
be expelled from school 105
be experienced in 559
be familiar with 368
be familiar with 558
be famous for 448
be fatigued with 29
be fed up with 517
be fine 531
be fined + 罰金 + for a traffic violation 170
be finished with 38
be fond of 508
be for sb/sth 464
be forced to 535
be forgiven 595
be frightened of 515
be full of 673
be full 315
be fun -ing 328
be funny 506
be getting late 201
be glad to 490
be going to 195
be good at 33
be grateful to... 503
be happy with 490
be hard on 619
be hard to 560
be harder than one thinks 543
be headed for 229
be hectic 26
be helpful 591
be hired as 55
be honest with 389
be honored for 581
be hung up on sth 574
be impatient with 459
be important 404
be impressed by 522
be in a good mood 492
be in a hurry 27
be in a meeting 73

be in a position 667
be in charge of 439
be in danger 642
be in good condition 539
be in need of 443
be in possession of 654
be in tears 285
be in the hospital 354
be in the mood to 476
be in the red 97
be in the same situation 539
be in the service 646
be in the subway 174
be in town on business 64
be in town 233
be in 450
be independent 32
be infected with a virus 123
be insane 525
be insured for + 錢 649
be intended to 202
be interested in 472
be into 473
be intrigued by 473
be just wondering (if S+V) 588
be knocked out 29
be known for 448
be late for 201
be leased in one's name 293
be liable for 441
be like 480
be likely to 469
be located in 177
be lost 177
be lucky 547
be mean to sb 455
be moved at/by 523
be nasty 456
be necessary for 443
be nervous 506
be next to 180
be nice to 491
be no surprise that... 661
be none of one's business 262
be not bad 561
be not in 148
be not one's cup of tea 478

715

get/be used to 558
get/find a job as + 業種 54
get/find a job 54
give (sb) a message 150
give (sb) a message 382
give (sb) one's word that... 598
give a break 553
give a discount 81
give a presentation on 76
give a reason for 396
give a ride 167
give a speech 75
give an excuse 394
give an explanation of 400
give back sth to sb 605
give birth to 258
give it a try 20
give it to sb straight 389
give one's best to 215
give one's opinion on 422
give permission to 579
give sb a call 144
give sb a chance 552
give sb a choice 564
give sb a hand 590
give sb a hard time 619
give sb a hug 253
give sb a task 70
give sb a warning to 585
give sb an answer 374
give sb full authority 667
give sb low grades 115
give sb one's email address 136
give sb some advice 584
give sb the impression that 481
give sth some thought 421
give sth to charity 608
give sth top priority 405
give support to 577
give up smoking 321
give up 633
give...a hard time 542
go + 動詞 231
go abroad 228
go ahead and 411
go all right 531
go along with 465

go as planned 193
go away (for + 時間) 322
go away 351
go back (to) 238
go back to school 106
go bad 536
go bald 275
go bankrupt 67
go behind one's back 629
go beyond 672
go by bus 173
go digital 657
go downtown 232
go easy on 37
go for + N 231
go for a drink 306
go for a drive 168
go for a walk 355
go for the day 57
go from bad to worse 537
go home 239
go in for 473
go -ing 231
go into business with 67
go into details 400
go on a business trip 63
go on a date 249
go on a diet 358
go on a hike 356
go on a trip to 325
go on a vacation 321
go on trial 648
go on with sth 21
go on with 562
go online 126
go out of business 67
go out on a blind date 249
go out to eat 303
go out with 249
go over there 237
go over 376
go pretty well 44
go south 2 blocks 179
go steady with 250
go straight 179
go study in America 108
go the right way 180

go this way 178
go through physical therapy 355
go through 611
go to + 地點 + on business 64
go to a doctor 353
go to a gym 356
go to a meeting 73
go to a movie 330
go to bed 268
go to college 102
go to lunch 303
go to one's junk file 140
go to someplace 228
go to the party 333
go to the rest room 277
go to work 57
go together (with) 236
go travel 324
go up to 230
go up to...degrees 300
go way back 222
go well with 280
go with 237
go with 565
go wrong 50
go/be against 461
good for nothing 471
good luck to... 548
goof up 51
grab a bite 305
graduate from 105
grill meat 319
groan with pain 288
grow out of 576
grow to be... 658
grumble about sth 453
guarantee that S+V 445
guess that S+V 430

prepare for one's presentation 76
prepare for 599
present the report 77
pretend to do 394
pretty soon 674
promise to 597
propose that S+V 410
propose to sb 257
protect sb from 578
pull into a parking lot 171
pull off 45
pull one's leg 618
pull over 163
pull through 37
pull up 163
punish sb for 631
purchase a new BMW 82
purchase US dollars with Korean won 101
push one's luck 549
put A before B 405
put A through to B 150
put forward sth 411
put gas in the car 166
put in + 時間名詞 186
put it 404
put money into... 87
put on one's brakes 163
put on some weight 359
put on 279
put one's heads together 227
put one's makeup on 276
put oneself in one's place 541
put pressure on 527
put sb in jail 648
put sb on a waiting list 213
put sb on the phone 151
put sth behind sb 417
put sth in 408
put together a report 75
put up with 459

Q

quit (attending) school 104
quit -ing 633
quit one's job 61
quite a few 702

R

rake in money 90
reach + 地點 235
reach a settlement 629
reach sb at 151
reach sb on one's cell phone 155
react to an Internet article 129
read on the subway 174
read one's email 139
read sth in the newspaper 383
realized that 369
rearrange one's schedule 199
receive a response 141
receive one's email 138
recently 681
recognize one's voice 154
recommend that S+V 584
reconsider 426
recover the data 122
reduce stress 527
reduce the cost 97
refresh one's memory 414
refund for sth 85
refuse to do 462
regard A as B 427
regarding + N 711
regardless of 263
register for 642
register sth 612
regret -ing 501
regret sth 500
relax 529
remain unchanged 567

remember sb -ing 413
remember that 413
remind A of B 414
remodel the house 298
rent a house 292
repair the house 298
replace A with B 568
report sth to sb 611
reserve a room at 219
resign from 62
resolve a conflict 615
resolve one's differences 628
respect sb for 519
respond to one's email 141
result in 576
resume one's studies 108
retire from 62
return to + 地點 239
ride a bicycle 167
ride with sb to 241
ring a bell 414
risk -ing 641
roast 318
rob A of B 622
ruin one's health 335
rumor has it that 379
run a business 65
run a check 376
run a risk 641
run an anti-virus program 124
run errands 71
run in the family 558
run in the marathon 357
run into 204
run it/that by 227
run low on 674
run out of gas 166
run out of 673
run the program 121
run two miles 357

最好用的第二外語學習課本！

本書利用大量的插圖、表格，讓你輕鬆學會法語的發音、句型、短句。並以有趣、幽默的圖畫解說法國文化，法語怎麼學都不無聊！

定價：350 元　附MP3

適用 0 基礎到 A2 程度學習者。字母、發音皆有音標，一次了解德語發音規則。學到對話、重點句型、單字、文法、慣用表達句等。

定價：499 元　附MP3

世界上第 2 大的溝通使用語言，全球超過 5 億人都在使用的西班牙語！本書利用大量的插圖、表格，讓你輕鬆學會西班牙語的發音、句型、短句。

定價：399 元　附MP3

適合初學、從零開始的俄語學習者。用最好懂的方法，征服俄文 33 個長相獨特的字母，文法規則講解條理分明連當地的俄羅斯人都會對你刮目相看！

定價：399 元　附MP3

用膩了傳統日語課本？本書帶給你不一樣的選擇！所有單字以圖片方式解說，還有 50 音輸入法的安裝及打字介紹，都是傳統課本所沒有的。

定價：350 元　附MP3

韓語學習書排行榜第一名！快速打好韓語基礎。適用完全初學、從零開始的韓文學習者！一次同時學會韓語的「發音、句型、文法、會話」。

定價：350 元　附MP3

從越南語字母、發音開始教起！大量表格、插圖輔助學習！史上第一本最適合國人，從零開始自學、教學兩用教材。

定價：399 元　附MP3

從泰語字母、發音開始講解，並有音檔輔助，從零開始也能學。利用課文、表格、插圖，輕鬆學會日常生活會話、文法。

定價：399 元　附MP3

本書編排清晰、條理分明，能循序漸進地學好印尼語基礎。極適合自學，亦極適合作為課用教材。不只是學印尼語、更學到印尼文化。

定價：399 元　附MP3

自學第二外語看完這本就能說！

自學法語看完這本就能說

定價／380元・附MP3＋字母發音示範影片DVD

本書從有系統的教學，循序漸進從「發音課、文法課、單字課、句型課到會話課」讓你輕而易舉開口說法語。

- -

自學德語看完這本就能說

定價／349元・附MP3＋字母發音示範影片DVD

「德語」是歐盟中最多人使用的語言！別讓自己的國際觀僅限制在英文而已！一本就學完初學者所需的字母、發音、單字、句型、文法、會話！

- -

自學西班牙語看完這本就能說

定價／380元・附MP3＋字母發音示範影片DVD

初學者需要的文法、單字、會話，這一本全收錄！7種基本時態介紹、21類主題單字、48個生活場景、超過1000句會話，本書讓你輕而易舉就能開口說西班牙語。

- -

自學韓語看完這本就能說

定價／350元・附MP3＋字母發音示範影片DVD

秒懂易學的韓語教材，全書除了標準羅馬拼音，同時加上漢字標音，好記好唸！結合聽、說、讀、寫 絕對超值的綜合自學課本。

- -

自學泰語看完這本就能說

定價／420元・附MP3＋字母發音示範影片DVD

書本＋MP3＋泰師影片教學，發音絕不搞錯！第一次寫泰語字母就純熟，清楚的筆順標示。還能從單字、短句、文法到會話，學會最道地的泰語。

重拾國高中英語，與老外對答如流！
輕鬆找回學過的英文，上班、旅行都好用！

把學過的英文找回來，文法真輕鬆！
不管幾歲、記憶力差也能再次學好英文文法

畢業後更想把英文學好！但對文法一個頭兩個大嗎？本書讓你快速把學過的英文文法找回來、學得更快更好！重建英文文法的基礎概念，圖像式解說根本不用背，立刻回復你的英文文法實力！

定價：299 元

10 倍速！把學過的英文找回來，單字真輕鬆！
首創蛛網式分類記憶，快速重拾最常用的 5500 單

運用字根字首＋各種生活面向與情境主題分類，讓所有單字互相關聯、永遠不忘！
從中學就學過的「核心單字」為中心，5500個單字重拾您的英文實力，工作、生活更得心應手！

定價：399 元 附 MP3

把學過的英文找回來，會話真輕鬆！
直接套用、自信開口、文法不會再用錯，10 年英文不白學

要搞懂會話句最原始的概念，並以此概念做延伸學習，「套用句型公式」＋「反覆搭配替換詞彙」，就能「零思考、零失誤、零秒開口說英語」！不管旅遊、聊天、交友都不再結巴了！

定價：380 元

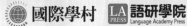 

台灣廣廈 國際出版集團
Taiwan Mansion International Group

國家圖書館出版品預行編目（CIP）資料

專賣在美國的華人！英文萬用短句5000 / Chris Suh著. -- 二版.
-- 新北市：國際學村, 2019.09
　面；　公分
ISBN 978-986-454-113-3(平裝附光碟片)
1. 英語 2. 慣用語

805.123　　　　　　　　　　　　　　　　108011859

🌐 國際學村

專賣在美國的華人 英文萬用短句5000

從求學到定居，從生活到職場！即學即用的簡單英文表達，單字、句子都超簡單、超好用

作　　　者／Chris Suh	編輯中心編輯長／伍峻宏・編輯／尹紹仲
	封面設計／張家綺・內頁排版／菩薩蠻數位文化有限公司
譯　　　者／Nina Wong	製版・印刷・裝訂／東豪・弼聖・紘億・秉成

行企研發中心總監／陳冠蒨　　　　線上學習中心總監／陳冠蒨
媒體公關組／陳柔彣　　　　　　　數位營運組／顏佑婷
綜合業務組／何欣穎　　　　　　　企製開發組／江季珊、張哲剛

發　行　人／江媛珍
法律顧問／第一國際法律事務所 余淑杏律師・北辰著作權事務所 蕭雄淋律師
出　　版／國際學村
發　　行／台灣廣廈有聲圖書有限公司
　　　　　地址：新北市235中和區中山路二段359巷7號2樓
　　　　　電話：（886）2-2225-5777・傳真：（886）2-2225-8052
讀者服務信箱／cs@booknews.com.tw

代理印務・全球總經銷／知遠文化事業有限公司
　　　　　地址：新北市222深坑區北深路三段155巷25號5樓
　　　　　電話：（886）2-2664-8800・傳真：（886）2-2664-8801
郵政劃撥／劃撥帳號：18836722
　　　　　劃撥戶名：知遠文化事業有限公司（※單次購書金額未達1000元，請另付70元郵資。）

■出版日期：2019年09月　　　　ISBN：978-986-454-113-3
　　　　　　2024年04月4刷　　　 版權所有，未經同意不得重製、轉載、翻印。